An Untold History

by Charles O. Wing

DORRANCE
PUBLISHING CO
EST. 1920
PITTSBURGH, PENNSYLVANIA 15238

Dorrance Publishing Co
585 Alpha Drive
Suite 103
Pittsburgh, PA 15238
Visit our website at *www.dorrancebookstore.com*

ISBN: 978-1-4809-2719-3
eISBN: 978-1-4809-2857-2

An Untold History

This is a story of mythology and what could have been. It is about one man's life and how he found a way to change and become a leader. It is also the story of how he built a city and learned to defend it. But it also has the religious topic of Celtic ways too. In the end, it leaves a mystery to be discussed long after you finish the story.

"Believe and it becomes real. Enjoy the journey."

Charles O. Wing

Chapters

- IN THE BEGINNING -

Long ago, before time took from us our memory of the world that was, the people of the world were one with nature. Spirit guides brought forth the best and the worst of humankind to trial on this earth. Among these early men were three brothers named Annwn, Bran, and Gwynvyd, who were fathered by Creatrix and born of mother Arianhod. They came forth out of the labyrinth of the Tree of Life, warriors born of enchantment, for their number was three.

Each of these men was raised by the creatures of the world: Annwn by the serpent, Bran by the horse, and Gwynvyd by the owl. Their presence in the world was to mark a pathway for all who followed. The trials of the warriors began in their three times three Spring. They were not men yet, that was to come.

The goddess Morrigan awoke in her Moon form from behind the cloud-draped mists in the highest mountains. The three brothers cast their eyes upward at her beauty, not knowing her other two forms.

She cast her spell of sleep upon them, and they entered into the realm of the other life. Their father stood beside them in the land of death and commanded of them, "Return to the earthly plain as mortals, and from your loins, spread the seeds of man. Forget not of my realm and use of the Earth as your own until I summon you again."

"Father?" asked Gwynvyd, in the wisdom taught by the owl. "What will we use for the receptacles of our seed?"

"Fear not, for I have created daughters that you are to have for wives. They await for your return, my sons."

The haze of sleep engulfed the three again, and they awoke beside the flowing waters of the Sacred Spring.

The creatures of the Earth called to welcome their return and moved about the three brothers, in the sheltered wood, to find of their father's words.

Out of the shadows of the night, amid the soft whispering from the dawn's early breeze, stepped the trio of beings that Creatrix called the receptacles of mankind's seed. They were, as were the brothers, without the coverings of modesty; that would come later, when they would lose the innocence of their youth. Each pair of three stood apart looking upon the other. They were reflections of each other — physically similar, yet different.

The pairing of the two groups came in the third time of the four Seasons. Their magic number was the twelfth rotation of the Earth about Creatrix — in his form as the "Giver of Light" — and changes took place in their bodies. They tried to hide their changes from the trio of brothers, which added to the strangeness of the process.

Creatrix looked down from the heavens and saw with concern the repression from the changes. He sent forth the beasts of the forest to demonstrate the need for intercourse through the joining of male and female.

Bran, as the most earthly of the trio of brothers, called the attention of the first people to the animal ways. "This must be the way of the seeding of mankind," he said. "Let us follow of Creatrix's commands and do as the beasts of the forest do."

Sarph, of the golden hair, stepped forward and took of Annwn's hand. "You I will join with, to do as Creatrix commands."

Aine, of the black hair, stepped forward and said of Bran, "And I will join of you."

Gwynvyd, in his wisdom, said, "Come forth, Brigantia, and join of me."

Brigantia held back. Her flaming red hair veiled the green of her eyes, which darted between the other two couples and then back to Gwynvyd. "I care not for this animal way. Choose of another, Gwynvyd!"

"There is no other, Brigantia, and it is of Creatrix's command."

"I care not! I will not join in this way."

Gwynvyd turned to look at the other two couples and went to ask of them what to do when Brigantia turned and ran into the forest.

Confused by her running away, he turned to his brothers and their mates again. He was met by the unexpected giggles of the females and smiles from his brothers. "What am I to do, brothers?"

"Follow her, Gwynvyd," called Annwn.

Again he turned and gazed after Brigantia's form; then he followed.

Creatrix looked down from the heavens and saw the action of Brigantia. He was not pleased with her refusal to do as he commanded. He called to Morrigan, goddess of the night sky, and bid her to deal with Brigantia that night.

With dusk and the setting of Creatrix in his "Giver of Light" form, the goddess Morrigan began her task. She called upon her demons of the Dark World and set them on the earthly plain amid a wild storm of her making.

Gwynvyd could see Brigantia in the distance in the failing light and the shadows caused by the storm approaching from the mountaintops. His eyes followed her form, helped in his sight by the training of the wise owl of his youth. He glanced again at the storm; it was strangely different than any other storm he had seen before. Hues of red and purple circled within its mass, and flashes of light, followed by echoing rumbles, warned of its danger. Gwynvyd sought shelter under a rock overhang from the first drops of rain and the following wind. Creatures of the forest, in their innocence, followed him out of the storm's path.

Closer came the danger of the goddess Morrigan. Her creatures of the Dark World followed within the storm front, ready to do as she commanded.

Brigantia climbed another hillside, unaware of the danger that followed her. Stopping to catch her breath, she turned and looked behind her. The red hair on her arms and neck stood in fright at the fear she felt from the sight of the storm's approach. Her head turned and looked for shelter. A fissure in the rocky hillside beckoned her to safety. She turned and ran for its entrance in the approaching darkness. Nettles scratched at her bare skin as she slipped into the narrow opening in the rock face. Fear became terror in the face of the unknown. She called out, "Creatrix, why do you do this to me?" Silence answered her plea.

Closer came Morrigan and her demons of the dark — shadows of the living, bringing death or worse to the mortals of the earthly plain. They called Brigantia's name, and it flew on the wind of the storm, eerily and softly.

Brigantia turned her head when she thought she heard her name called; then decided it was only the wind. The wind blew hot one minute, then cold the next. Brigantia could not shake the fear of the approaching storm and wondered of the reason. Again she called out to Creatrix, "Creatrix, why have you sent this storm? Why do you punish me so?"

Creatrix's voice answered in the echo of a thunder clap. "You, Brigantia, have failed to follow my command. For this you must answer!"

The laughing cackle of the goddess Morrigan's voice was shadowed with the voices of her demons calling Brigantia's name again.

Tears ran from Brigantia's eyes as she looked into the rolling clouds of the storm. Lightning flashed, and the sight vanished from Brigantia forever. The demons and Morrigan laughed at her plight.

Gwynvyd watched the storm pass and worried for Brigantia. With the rain falling, he left the shelter of the rock overhang and hurried after her on the path he had seen her take.

Brigantia squeezed from the fissure and stumbled in her darkness into the early night's cool air that followed the storm. She still shook in fear, as the nettles again clawed at her bare skin.

Gwynvyd was near but failed to see her in the total darkness of the moonless night.

He called her name. "Brigantia!" He waited and called again. "Brigantia!"

"Here, Gwynvyd!" she answered back while attempting to stand.

Blood trickled from the scratches where she had clawed at the burning nettle marks on her marble white skin. Then she turned and walked in the direction of his voice with outstretched arms. "Where are you, Gwynvyd? I see naught in this darkness."

He eased up beside her and took her hand in his. "All is well. I am with you now, Brigantia. Let us return to the others."

"Yes, Gwynvyd. But go slow, for I cannot see in this darkness."

He turned to gaze into her face, but the limited light failed to show her blindness. Together they walked slowly back to the others, arm in arm.

At the gathering spot by the Sacred Spring, they came upon the others. "Brothers, we return to your company," called Gwynvyd.

"Gwynvyd? Where is the light from the Sacred Crystal?" asked Brigantia.

"It stands before us. Do not you see it?"

"No! I stand in darkness. What is wrong?"

Gwynvyd turned to look upon her face again in the soft, green light of the crystal and was shocked by the sight of her eyes — white and glazed. The orbs of her eye sockets were red with the changes of the night's storm. He stood speechless before her.

The other brothers and their mates were likewise shocked by the sight of her and remained silent.

"Will someone tell me what is wrong? Why do you not answer me?"

Gwynvyd, with tears running from his eyes, answered. "Brigantia, you are without sight. Your eyes were burned from the storm of last night."

"No! It cannot be true. Creatrix would not do this to me!"

"It is so, Brigantia," Gwynvyd said, holding her hand tightly with both of his. "Come sit before the crystal and try to see of its light."

She allowed him to draw her to the Sacred Spring, where the crystal stood at its headwaters. "I still see naught, Gwynvyd."

"Have patience, Brigantia. Time is a cure for all things."

"I am without sight because I wished to have nothing to do with these animal ways. Was it so wrong, Gwynvyd?"

"Brigantia," he said, turning her toward himself, "Creatrix commanded of it. That makes it right." His right arm dropped from her shoulder, and his hand brushed across her breast and touched her nipple. She shivered at the strangeness of his touch and turned away from him again.

"Gwynvyd? Leave me to my thoughts, please."

"Very well. I shall be nearby if you need of me." He backed away from her and watched her form search for a place to sit and rest.

Hearing a noise behind him, he turned to look at his brother and his mate, Aine. They were holding each other, and Aine was moaning at his brother's touch. He wondered of this and continued to watch them. Bran's manhood became erect during this touching thing, and soon he rolled upon Aine, and they began to rock together — slowly at first, then with more intensity. Finally they rolled apart and held of each other, talking in low whispers. Gwynvyd was confused at their action and turned to look at Brigantia again.

He felt an emptiness in his stomach, and his concentration was centered only upon her needs. He picked up the stick for combing the hair and walked back over to her. "Brigantia? I wish to comb of your hair and help you with your meal."

"Gwynvyd, you are sweet to offer your help, and I am glad we are friends. You seem to know what I always need. Help me with a bath first, and then you can comb my hair."

He helped her stand and walked her over to the spring. They both entered into the water, which was warm to the skin, and Gwynvyd began to wash Brigantia's scarred and bruised flesh using a large leaf that had a milky sap that foamed in the water. He gently rubbed at her white skin.

"That feels good, Gwynvyd."

Gwynvyd felt a strange sensation and looked down at his own manhood, which had become erect, and backed away from Brigantia.

"What is wrong, Gwynvyd?"

"It is nothing. The animal ways are pulling at my soul."

"You know how I feel about that. Do not think of me in that way."

"I am trying, Brigantia. But something is pulling at my very being. I will leave you until it passes."

"No! Do not leave me alone. I need your help."

"I must. This animal thing is very strong. Here, see for yourself." He took her hand and placed it on his erection. She started to pull away and then stopped.

"It is a magical thing. I am beginning to feel of its power also," she said as her own nipples became hard and a strange feeling coursed through her body.

"I do not understand of this. I must leave, Brigantia."

"No. Stay here and help finish of my bath."

He nodded and began to wipe at her rough skin with the leaf again.

"No, here, Gwynvyd," she said and took his hand and placed it between her legs. "Rub slowly and softly."

She arched her back at his touch and tipped her head back while holding onto his shoulder with one hand and grasping his erection with the other. "That feels so good, Gwynvyd."

"Brigantia? I must leave. This thing is making my legs weak, and it begins to hurt."

"Not yet, Gwynvyd, please!" she said, as her body began to sway with the sensation of his touch.

"I must," he said, almost at the point of running from her. But her grasp upon his manhood was strong.

Suddenly she pulled herself toward him and lifted one leg. He felt her trying to thrust his manhood into her well of life. He could not help himself and thrust at her welcoming body and entered into her. She let out a gasp and slumped against him and then began to move her hips against him even faster than before.

Creatrix looked down from his position in the sky as the "Giver of Light" and smiled upon the pair. He waved his finger in the heavens, and the light entered into Brigantia's eyes again.

In the passion of the moment, Brigantia failed to notice the return of her sight. However, at the peak of their lovemaking, she opened her eyes wide and yelled out her discovery.

Gwynvyd pulled out of her at the shock in her voice and turned to look around for something threatening their safety.

Brigantia pulled him back to her. "All is well, Gwynvyd. I can see again. Perhaps better than before."

Later Gwynvyd slept from the exhaustion of the passion while Brigantia looked about her at the wonders of the world with her newly returned sight.

The creatures of Creatrix's garden who shared of that place with the trio of pairs watched their lovemaking with disinterest, but not so the gods.

Months passed, and the women became large with child. They passed through many mood changes, not unlike their bodily changes. The men became distant to protect their feelings from the sharp tongues of the women and felt confused by the changes.

Each of the men developed skills with their hands: Annwn worked with wood, carving intricate designs and shaping furniture of a simple design; Bran worked with the soil, raising and creating new plant forms (as a side hobby, he worked with the clay and made pots); Gwynvyd watched with interest of his brother's skills and chose the hard minerals of the Earth, casting metal in the fire to use as tools.

Brigantia, in one of her better moods, urged Gwynvyd to create jewelry for the women to wear from the metals of his forge. To this he added colorful stones that he had found.

They all changed over the few short months, understanding each other better and worse. Fights between the pairs and between each of the couples continued until Gwynvyd and Brigantia moved some distance from the others and built a round house of wood and straw.

This action upset the pair of brothers, and they plotted to seek revenge against their brother. One night in the late Fall, they came after dark and beat upon him with sticks and tore at his house until it was in ruins. They departed, casting words of hate upon their brother and his mate.

Gwynvyd swore to Brigantia that his brothers would never again have the chance to attack them as he picked at the ruins of his house. They moved deeper into the mountains, and he built a house of stone and worked at his forge creating the first weapons of metal.

With the first snow of Winter, a male child was born of Brigantia. The birthing was easy for her, and she was up and on her feet after a few hours. The process was not so easy for Gwynvyd, who felt unease at seeing his first child born.

Meanwhile the other pair of couples produced their children within days of the birth of Gwynvyd's and Brigantia's child. The child of Annwn's was a sickly female and those of Bran were a strong female and a loud male.

Annwn became bitter at the turn of events and blamed anyone who was near. He cursed his mate, Sarph, and walked into the woods and was gone many days. He lurked near Gwynvyd's house and blamed him for his sickly child. As time passed, he became bold and tried to attack Gwynvyd near his outbuilding.

Gwynvyd was prepared and brought forth his weapon of metal, to which Annwn retreated after being struck on the arm, which caused a deep wound.

Annwn's emotions were in a turmoil; his eyes filled with hate and became red like the serpent that raised him. He returned home and struck Sarph and then sought Bran's presence.

The two fought outside of Bran's house while their mates held their children and watched in horror. Gwynvyd appeared at the edge of the meadow that held the Sacred Spring and the houses of his brothers, Bran and Annwn. He held the glistening metal blade at his side and watched the fight between his brothers. Annwn pushed Bran down on the ground and reached for a broken branch that lay near the pair. He picked it up and raised it above his head with both hands. Death was near for Bran.

Gwynvyd screamed in rage and charged his deranged brother, the sword held before him.

It took ten steps before he reached Annwn, and with a lightning-quick movement of his wrist that was almost too fast to be seen, the metal blade removed Annwn's head from his shoulders.

Breathing heavily Gwynvyd stared down at his dead brother before glancing at Bran, who remained on the ground with his mouth open in shock at Gwynvyd's action. His eyes flicked between Gwynvyd and the still form of Annwn.

A high pitched scream from Sarph caused the two brothers to turn in the direction of the females.

The first blood had been drawn for mankind!

Gwynvyd dropped the blade, still dripping Annwn's blood, and helped his brother Bran to his feet. Together they walked over to the females.

Aine, Bran's mate, held Sarph while they each cradled their children. As Gwynvyd approached, the pair backed away in fear.

"Have no fear. I will not harm you," Gwynvyd said.

"Gwynvyd was only protecting me," Bran stated.

"Annwn is with our father, Creatrix. His trial on this Earth is done. Sarph, you will join Brigantia and myself in my home. Your place will be one of honor, and together we will follow the commands of Creatrix," stated Gwynvyd.

The confusion of the moment passed, and days became months, which turned into years.

They all sharpened their human skills and passed them down onto the many children who followed in the years after Annwn's death.

Generations followed, and the land reached its limited ability to support the children of the brothers. One by one, they moved away from the Sacred Spring.

The story of the trio of brothers was told and retold by all the children — who passed it down generation after generation — including the fight between Gwynvyd and Annwn. The brothers passed into history, and with their deaths, they returned to Creatrix's side as had been promised.

- SHADOWS AND STILL WATERS -

The children of Gwynvyd, only a few generations old, began their trek down out of the alpine heights. Nuada, the oldest generation of Gwynvyd, took a wife in his three times four year and became restless with the tribal ways. His hunting trips lasted longer than any of the other men-children, and he foraged farther and farther away than any of the others.

During the cold time of the year when the hunting and gathering had ended, Nuada felt confined by the others. He slept little and talked with the others less and less. His wife became concerned and talked with the mother of her husband about this problem.

"Crearwy, mother of my husband, I come to seek counsel for my soul and that of my mate."

"Ask child, that I may understand of your problem."

"Nuada sleeps little and keeps distance, even from myself."

"I see of your worries and will talk with my son of his ways."

In the cold light of the following day, shadows of storm clouds streamed past the hidden entrance of the tribe's shelter. Crearwy had little trouble in finding of her restless child, now a man.

"Nuada? What is of this worry that you bear upon yourself? Others wonder of your ways."

"Mother, I feel that there is more for me to do with my life than to feed of the others in our tribe. In my travels away from here, I have seen things that draw me farther away with each trip, and I find the world larger than we were told when we sat about the fire as children."

"I see, my son. Perhaps you should seek the counsel of Creatrix in a dream and find of your destiny."

Nuada nodded and departed of his mother's company and found a sleeping place away from the others.

Snow fell silently throughout the day as Nuada waited in the bleak, gray light. He fell asleep as the shadows of night crept into the gray afternoon.

Dreams invaded his sleep, but they began in the gray light of his world. Snow fell without sound, as he looked about his homeland, in the sleep of a man possessed by the restlessness of his soul. Slowly color entwined the drab gray in colors of red and green; soon splashed by all of the colors of the rainbow. A voice, mixed with the thunder from the mountaintops, called to Nuada in his sleep-troubled mind.

"Nuada! Awake of your dream sleep and hear of my wisdom."

"Who calls of me? What is it you want?"

"It is I, Creatrix — Father of our people and giver of wisdom in all things."

"Speak, that I know of your truth and what troubles my mind."

"Your troubles are of my making, Nuada. I call upon you to travel and spread of your tribe about the world. You will see many wonders and learn of many things."

"What is it that I am to do?"

"Leave of this mountain place and descend into the lower lands. You will encounter my life-giving warmth and the green of the land. Bring forth children to share of all that you learn and see."

"That is all?"

"That is all, my son."

Nuada slept in a deep and untroubled dream of what was to come and awoke to the cold grayness of the next dawn.

With the coming of the light, Nuada returned to the village of his birth and sought out his wife and mother.

"Wife, I have sought the wisdom of Creatrix and found of my ways. I am to travel into the lower lands and learn of the world and then share of it with our children."

"That is all that was troubling of you, husband?"

"That was all, wife."

It took two days to prepare for the journey from the mountains, and Nuada felt that it took two weeks. He hurried his family and felt confined by their slowness.

On the dawn of the third day, before the grayness of the light broke upon the mountain peaks, Nuada and his family left forever the mountain land that was their place of birth and childhood home.

They followed the great ice sheet that moved down between the peaks. In one week, they found of its ending and the lake of the river that flowed into the green lands below. The clouds parted, and the light from the creator, Creatrix, shone down upon them.

The evening of the second week, after departing their place of birth, they camped on the western shore of the great ice lake, near the river that flowed downward to the lower green valleys. Around them the thin scrub plant growth and rocky land hid the thick forests and plants yet to come on their journey.

"Nuada, the land grows warm, and I miss of the snow."

"I understand, wife. But Creatrix requires of me to follow this path. We will see many strange things and wonder of the reasons for the changes."

Silently the trio prepared its meal and watched the setting of Creatrix from the daytime sky. Stars began to fill the void of the nighttime blackness, and the goddess Morrigan rode into the heavens in her form as the moon. Both of the young lovers hung on each other and watched the changes in the night.

Throughout the night, thunder erupted from the ice sheet as massive plates of ice fell into the great lake, sending swells of cold water washing upon the shoreline. The action kept both young lovers from sleep and alert to fears of the unknown.

Sometime during the darkness, Crearwy, mother of Nuada, was swept from the lake shore and was not missed until the blackness was complete with the setting of Morrigan's moon form. Nuada and his mate searched and failed to find of Crearwy. With a heavy heart, they returned to their camp. The first colorful hues of light from Creatrix urged the pair to pack quickly and continue the downward trek.

"I am glad to be done with this place, Nuada."

"I too, wife."

They followed the steep, rocky path of the river and bypassed many waterfalls. Water tore downward and arched out of its channel in many places, washing the bare rock and the loose plant life along with it. The water glared in the sunlight, daring anything to stop it. The pair moved farther away from the water's dangers. After another week, they entered into the high mountain meadows, and their bareness was broken by a few weathered fir trees.

"Where is the green land you talked of, Nuada?"

"We will see of it soon, wife."

Two days later, they entered into the thick forests, and the warmth of Creatrix was lost in the shadows of the trees. New sounds from the forest brought new fears for the travelers.

"I do not understand of this land, Nuada. Why would Creatrix bring us into this place?"

"It is to be a place of learning for us. Fear not, for Creatrix would not bring of us into this land without protecting of us."

"I begin to distrust of his word, husband, not of you."

The man and his wife held onto each other, each with their own fears and hopes.

Noises grew loud from the shadows of the forest, and Nuada looked about for a place of protection. "Wife! We must climb into this tree or become food for some animal. Hurry!"

Together the pair moved upward into the branches until, short of breath, they stopped on a pair of larger, drooping branches. Both looked down as the forest parted and a large hairy beast came forth from the shadows. Nuada held his hand in front of his mate's mouth as she drew in a great breath of air. He looked deep into her eyes and shook his head and then looked down again.

Both of the young Celts sat quietly and shook from their fears, unsure of what would happen next. As the shadows of the night deepened, Nuada's mate fell asleep in his arms as he continued his watch of the forest and its unknown creatures.

The colors of dawn broke with Nuada shaking the sleep from his fogged mind, and they cautiously descended from their perch.

"Nuada, let us return to the snow and mountains of home. I fear greatly of this land."

"Nay, wife. We are on a quest of Creatrix and will never see of our old home again."

He turned on his heel and started down the slope of the forested mountain again; his wife watched and shook her head and then followed.

That day faded among the others that followed, and they moved deeper into the lower forested lands.

Four more weeks followed the incident of the hairy creature, and as the pair began to bed down for the night, Nuada felt fear of the unknown himself. "Wife, I think we should sleep among the treetops again."

"Husband, what bothers you?"

"I know not. Perhaps it is nothing, but do as I wish this night."

She nodded, and they found a tree nearby that was easy for them to enter into its branches.

After dark, when the shadows of dusk faded, a noise in the distance brought the pair to a standing position in the branches. "That is no animal, wife. It is men. Remain quiet, and we will watch while they pass."

Time passed slowly for the pair as the noise moved nearer. Suddenly the brush, yards from their tree, parted, and three men walked into view. They seemed unconcerned with the noise that they made and passed under the tree and continued on up the hill until their voices faded in the distance.

"What manner of men would make that much noise after dark?" Nuada said to himself.

"Husband?" Nuada's wife spoke in a whisper. "I fear that they would have heard my heart beating in my breast. Let us now return to the mountains."

"Nay, wife. We cannot. You know of the reason."

"Then call upon Creatrix in a dream again to reassure my fears."

Nuada nodded at her request, and they sat awake many hours before they found of the hard-fought sleep they needed.

Shadows folded in tones of gray and black within Nuada's dream, and he called out Creatrix's name many times. Slowly colors began to highlight the grays, and Creatrix answered him. "What need you, Nuada?"

"My wife and I fear the unknown. What is to be our fate?"

"As was told to you before, continue on and drink of the many wonders that greet you. Learn from them and teach of your children."

"But strange men lurk in this land. What of them?"

"They are beasts and are yours to do with as is required. Use of them and fear not. I shall watch over you."

The dream faded, and Nuada awoke with the light of dawn in his eyes.

He sat and rubbed the sleep from his eyes and thought of the quest dream. Suddenly, with conviction in his movement, he awoke his mate. "Wife! Creatrix has spoken with me. We are to continue and fear nothing. Our purpose is to learn and teach. Come arise and greet the light of Creatrix."

Nuada's mate said nothing and looked through him as if he were mad. Slowly she stood and started to prepare their morning meal.

"Wife, we need not of food, only what is before us. Hurry and pack."

"Husband, I fear for you and what pushes you forward. Take time to think of the results of what you do."

"All is well, wife. I know of what I do."

Time continued to pass for the Celtic pair until the form of Creatrix, in his form as the life-giving Sun, reached his peak, and the warmth of the Summer season touched Nuada and his mate. They had entered into the lower mountains, which had crisp, life-giving valleys. Game was plentiful, and wild herbs and berries filled the pair's lean bellies. They gave little thought to the coming of Winter and its harshness.

On a warm day when the wind blew softly, they came into another valley like many of the others that they had passed through. "Husband? This valley brings forth a warmth and holds out a welcome for us. Let us stay here for a while."

"Aye. We will linger for a while, wife."

While Nuada's wife prepared camp, Nuada explored the small valley. He foraged along the southern shore of the single lake and up along the broken ridge that protected the valley from that direction and found minerals that he could forge and a supply of running water. Moving down closer to the lake and along the eastern side, he found a plentiful supply of clay for pots and household tools. Finally returning to his mate, he felt secure with the valley and began to fish from the lakeshore.

His eyes wandered across the lake to the small island, with its abundance of trees and plant growth. "That could provide us with protection and feed us if strangers approach this valley," he thought. Again he looked about the valley and drew in its strengths. He could find no faults and put down his fishing staff and walked back to his wife.

"Wife, we will stay in this valley and make it our home. That island will become the playground of our children and the roof over our heads."

She smiled at Nuada and nodded her head. A glow abounded from her being, and silently she said thanks to Creatrix.

The days passed as they cleared the land and built a home upon the island. When that was complete, Nuada began to build a forge near the northern bluff when he was not out hunting for their Winter food.

Fall came and went, and Winter set upon the pair. Although it was the cold season, it seemed mild compared to their childhood home. Nuada's wife began to grow large with the pair's first child, and they talked of having many more during the shadows of Winter.

Other than the creatures of the forest, Nuada saw no sign of other men and felt secure on his island.

Winter came and went, and then Spring was marked by the birth of Nuada's first male child. The birth came with the Spring melt while Nuada was working at his forge during the midday. He heard the cry of the birth and then the calling of his mate to come home.

Crossing to the island, he turned and looked to the north for some strange reason. Smoke streamed upwards from another valley nearby. He thought it strange and then turned and walked home to his mate.

Later after washing the child and preparing a meal for his mate, Nuada returned to the island shore and watched the smoke filter the light of Creatrix in the afternoon haze.

"What would cause such smoke?" he thought. "I will search it out in the morning light and find of its cause."

Turning to view his island, he saw that the house was well hidden, and again he turned to view the bluff that held his forge and tools. "That might be a problem, if the smoke was caused by other men. I cannot hide of the forge's work. They will look for us, and I fear the island will not be enough protection," he pondered.

Nuada turned on his heel and returned to his mate; worries crossed his furrowed brow.

The full moon form of the goddess Morrigan was near setting when Nuada arose from his bed. He washed his face and slung his massive copper sword across his shoulder and departed his home without a word to his mate. With the worries of the night before still on his mind, he crossed the lake from his island and walked with purpose up the hillside on the east side of the valley.

Nearing the top of the hill, his pace slowed, and with caution, he peered over its zenith. A warrior band of twenty was camped in the next valley. A few guards patrolled the outer fringes of the encampment, and fires that were slowly dying marked the campsite.

Nuada looked up the bushy hillside and asked Creatrix for help from the invaders. Sleep crowded his mind, and Creatrix came into his dream. "Nuada! Fear not. I will help you in this matter. Stand before these warriors and make known my name and ask of them to turn from your valley. If they do not, my anger will descend upon them."

Nuada awoke from his sleep with the light of Creatrix in his eyes and looked down upon the warrior band. They were breaking camp and forming to march against Nuada's valley.

The pass into the valley was to Nuada's right, and he spied an outcropping of rock upon which to stand and challenge the warriors. He stood and walked with purpose to the outcropping rock.

Clouds began to form over Nuada's head before he reached the rock, and as he climbed up on the outcropping, the warrior party moved toward him. He waited with calm as they neared, and he could smell their foul odor before he could hear them. Death was with them. He shivered at the thought of them with his mate and the breath that they would take from him in his death. Still he waited with the conviction of Creatrix's words.

"Hold!" he shouted at the warrior band. "Come no nearer or death will be your reward from myself and Creatrix."

"Who is this Creatrix? I see none but you," called back the warrior leader.

"Creatrix is the creator, and I speak for him in this matter."

"I am the only god here, and you will be the one to die!"

Nuada drew his sword and held it before him. "Come to your death then. I am ready!"

The warrior band surged forward at Nuada's challenge. Nuada tipped the point of his great copper sword toward them and laughed at their insults.

Thunder erupted from the clouds overhead and shook the ground underfoot. The warrior band paused in their rush to get at Nuada and looked at the sky.

"Retreat now or die! I will ask of you no more," called Nuada again.

Again they began to move forward. Nuada stood his ground, and the sword tip gleamed in the darkening light.

A bolt of lightning flashed downward and struck Nuada between his shoulder blades. He began to glow in a white light, and the copper sword glowed red. Suddenly lightning shot from the tip of the sword and struck the invaders, burning their heads from their bodies. Their bodies stood without purpose and finally toppled. Nuada stood alone, and slowly the glow faded from his person. He sat and felt drained, wondering at the power of Creatrix to take their lives and spare his. Hours passed before he was able to return to his valley and family.

Nuada's mate noticed the change in him. "Nuada, what is wrong? What happened?"

"I fought a battle with Creatrix's help. It was a wonder! We are safe now, and I must sleep," he said and fell upon their sleeping place.

He was instantly asleep, and even the child's cry did not awaken him. Nuada's mate watched and worried for him.

At the setting of Creatrix, Nuada awoke and still felt drained of energy. Sitting on the edge of their sleeping place, he pulled his mate and child to him and told of the great battle. Nuada's mate said nothing and watched the expressions on his face as he told the story. The child did not cry but watched his father's movements.

After Nuada had finished the story of the battle, he stood and crossed the single room and raised up his sword by the hilt; the blade snapped and fell to the floor, where it shattered into many pieces.

Stunned Nuada turned to his mate and said nothing. She returned his smile and crossed the room with the child at her breast and put her arm around Nuada. "It is only a thing, husband. You can make a better one."

He nodded in agreement and kissed her. "I shall take a walk and return to eat later."

She nodded in agreement, and he walked with his head on his chest, thinking of what had happened.

Nearing the shore of the lake, Nuada turned his head to the evening sky and spoke. "Creatrix? Show of me the way. I am confused by the battle and these strange people. Is it always to be fighting?"

He received no answer from the silence of the setting sun and sat upon a broken tree, listening to the water lap at the muddy shore while insects buzzed about his head and birds called to each other.

Darkness settled about the island before Nuada returned to his house and mate. Still brooding about the battle and the sword, he ate in silence.

Time in Nuada's mind flew like the wind, and scenes shifted even faster.

Understanding became a part of his being, and the future was his. He awoke before the dawning of Creatrix; sweat adorned his body. Shifting in his bed, he awoke his mate, and she turned to look at him through sleep-fogged eyes that quickly cleared. "Nuada! Your hair! It has turned the color of your old blade."

"What mean you, wife?"

"Your hair is as red as the sunrise!"

Nuada jumped from his bed and found of the polished-metal looking glass that he had fashioned for his mate. Looking at himself, he staggered backwards, almost falling. "I do not understand of this."

Running his hand through his new red hair and remembering the light brown of yesterday, he turned to his wife and dropped the mirror. "I know not of what caused this, wife. Perhaps Creatrix has caused of it."

She nodded in understanding of the great God's ways and put her arm around Nuada. "Fear not of this. It is a crown for you. I like the color, husband."

Confused Nuada walked to the lakeshore and crossed the waters and made his way to his forge. Stopping before its rough building, he thought that he could do better with its design and began to gather stones and plan in his mind what he was going to do. The day passed into early evening, and still he worked at the building without food or rest. It was well into the dark hours, and the moon shone down bright on his labors when he looked around and was shocked by the lateness of the day. He hurried back across the lake to his mate and child and found them asleep. Sitting he ate of the cold meal left by his mate and thought of the passing day.

Sleep caught Nuada where he sat, and he dreamed the dreams of Creatrix again.

Nuada's mate awoke him when the sun was well above the hill ridge, and he jumped up with a start. "What happened? Why did you not awaken me before?"

"Rest, Nuada. You have all the time of your life before you."

"Nay, wife. Creatrix has many things for me to do. Follow me this day, and we will talk of the wonders he has shown of me."

Nuada's mate nodded and sat a cold plate before him to eat. An hour later, the small family again crossed the lake and walked to the forge.

Nuada worked at the new forge building and talked of the things that had been told to him in his dream talks with Creatrix. The midday came and went, and as the sun began to set low on the horizon, Nuada turned his head to the east side of the valley. "Make no noise, wife. We have company."

Nuada's mate turned her head in the direction that Nuada was looking and saw nothing. She picked up her child and entered the forge building while Nuada hurried off in the direction he had sensed the intruder.

At dusk Nuada returned with his captured foe. It was a small wolf cub, black and very alert to his surroundings. Its eyes, yellow and narrowed, watched Nuada's mate and child with interest.

"This cub was with its dying mother. She had been wounded by another animal, and this one would die without another to feed of it," Nuada told his mate.

She nodded and said, "Let us return to our home and have of our meal. This little one will need of food too."

Nuada nodded and gathered his family together, and they returned to the lake and crossed over to the island.

At the entrance to their home, Nuada's mate reached out and held him from moving forward. A question loomed in her eyes. "Nuada? Are we to always hide alone in this land? I miss the women talk of home, more so when you are away."

Nuada looked at her, understanding of her need, and said, "I too miss of the others. Tomorrow I will travel forth to where those raiders set fires and see if others are there."

Together they held each other with their worries and found sleep was a desolate longing of their souls. It was late when sleep finally found them.

- NEIGHBORS AND FRIENDS -

With the coming of Creatrix as the Giver of Light, Nuada set out to find the answers to his mate's questions.

At mid-morning Nuada found himself at his battleground of the dead barbarian band. He stopped and knelt upon the same rock outcropping where he had fought and surveyed the scene. He noticed their weapons first: stone axes, bone knives, and flame-hardened spears. He thought back at the wonder of Creatrix's hand and shook his head at the one-sided action of the battle. His eyes glanced down at the stone beneath his feet and thought, "This is an ore I am not familiar with." He scooped up some of the rock and put it into a pouch. Then his attention was drawn to the horizon again.

Some smoke still lingered in the distance. "Strange." he thought, "That smoke should have died out by now."

He set out again in that direction and focused on reaching it before dark.

Late in the day, he stopped again. He was near the smoke plumes; caution caused him to pause and study the land and its inhabitants from a distance. He found a tall tree near the clearing and climbed to watch.

Families stirred within the small village, which had many burnt houses. These buildings were simple structures made of wood but of a different design than he had ever seen before. High pointed roof lines seemed the norm, with cooking areas outside in the open air. He thought about moving into the village then but paused and thought better of it. "I should wait until the morning light of Creatrix is high. Not now."

The next morning, Nuada climbed down from his tree perch and slowly approached the village. People were milling about finishing their breakfast meal and preparing to begin their daily chores. A shout warned of Nuada's approach, and he paused until the people could see that he was alone and of no threat to them.

"Who are you?" called the man nearest him.

"My name is Nuada, and I am from a valley a day's walk south of here."

"What do you want of us?"

"The pleasure of small talk and a friendly drink."

"Come forward that I may see of you more closely and keep your weapons sheathed."

Nuada did as asked and waited until he was almost within arm's reach of the man before he again asked, "Do I appear to be of risk to you? I only require of some conversation."

"Come, sit by my fire, and we will talk, neighbor."

Walking to the fireside, Nuada's attention was drawn to the house structures again. "Why do you build your houses in this manner?"

The slope of the roofline reached to the ground, and yet the ends were squared. This puzzled Nuada.

"We build in this manner to allow snow to run off, and it gives us more room inside. Would you like to see inside?"

"Yes. Where I come from, we build in the round. A simple design, compact and warm." They walked to a house nearby, and the stranger pulled back a skin door cover and showed Nuada inside. It appeared huge to Nuada; inside there was a second floor above and a large fireplace stood across one end of the lower floor area. Tables and benches sat in front of the fireplace, where women worked at a midday meal.

"This is wonderful. My mate would be pleased with a house like this. What is on the upper level?"

"That is the sleeping area. The heat from the fire rises and keeps everyone warm throughout the night."

"I am in wonder at this house. I came to seek neighbors to move to my valley. My mate is lonely for company."

"Some talked of moving after a raid by warriors last week. Did they seek you out?"

"They approached my valley, but I challenged them."

"What happened?"

"They attacked me outside of the valley, and I killed of them."

"All of them? How?"

"I called upon the creator, Creatrix, and he, through me, removed their heads in one motion."

"I find that hard to believe friend."

"Still it is hard for me to understand. My valley is easy to defend, but I still need of neighbors."

"Very well. I will ask of the others to see if they are willing to move."

They returned outside to the fire and were brought a drink called beer. After more talk, the man turned to his friends and asked of Nuada's question about a move. Three families were willing, and they planned to walk to the valley the next morning. Nuada felt content and allowed the warm beer to calm his racing thoughts.

Nuada was asked to spend the night inside one of the strange houses but refused and slept near the outside fire.

With the morning light of Creatrix, the group set off toward Nuada's valley. They talked of growing plants for food and animals to be sheltered and fed through the Winter months. Nuada talked of the valley and his forge, and all parties were interested in what the other had to say.

By mid-afternoon they reached the battle scene, and Nuada again explained how Creatrix helped him defeat the warrior band. His new neighbors shook their heads in disbelief and yet wondered how one man could have done this alone. With a short break, all were ready to move on to the valley. Some were nervous, but others were laughing at the new outlook.

Nuada led them into the narrow entrance by the stream that emptied the lake overflow and from the valley. They stood high on another rock outcropping and surveyed the land below.

A new friend named Mor said, "This is a wonderful land. I am glad we came."

Nuada smiled to himself and nodded in agreement. "It is time we descend to the valley floor. My mate will be missing of me, I think."

Little sunlight remained of the day when they neared the lake shore. The new families began to set up camp for the night. Nuada crossed the lake and found his mate waiting for him.

"How is our child, wife, and the new cub?"

"Happy and full with their supper. Now I will feed of you and hear of your adventure."

They sat near the fire and held close of each other, and Nuada began the story. His mate fed him as he talked and asked many questions about the new people, their new neighbors. Nuada talked of the wonder of the strange houses and said that he would build one for them. His mate smiled at the tone of his voice and nodded her head in agreement.

Sleep came quickly for Nuada, and he awoke early, ready to begin the new life with neighbors. His mate stirred but remained sleeping. The wolf cub raised its head with ears cocked at Nuada's dressing. It crossed over from the fire and rubbed its head against his legs. Nuada reached down and scratched its head and then added more wood to the fire. "Little one, I cannot take you with me today. Remain behind and guard of the family."

The cub settled near the fire again, and Nuada departed his home, ready to meet with his new neighbors and begin the building of their homes.

Nuada found Mor awake and taking of his morning meal.

"Greetings, Mor. A wonderful day to begin a new life."

"That it is, Nuada."

They talked about how the new houses were to be built and where to build them. Nuada asked about the tools needed and was shown crude stone tools. "I can build you better tools, my friend."

Nuada pointed out an area on the west side of the valley, still near the lake, for home sites and then left them to walk to his forge. Thoughts on how to build better tools ran through his head.

Nuada fired his forge with help of his newly designed bellows and began to make new sand molds for the tools while the forge heated. He remembered the new strange ore he had found and thought about using it to make the copper stronger. By midday he was hard at work, and time slipped past without his noticing.

With dark and the setting of Creatrix, he felt satisfied with the results and was polishing the edges of the new tools when Mor found him.

"How goes the tool making, Nuada?"

"I have almost finished, Mor. Come and look at the results."

"This is wonderful, Nuada. I have never seen anything like this before. Are they to remain this sharp on the edges?"

"They will hold their edge but from time to time will require a new edge. How goes the tree cutting?"

"It is slow, but with these tools, it will pass much faster."

"I think that is enough work for today. My mate will miss of me, and I grow hungry."

Together they walked back to the lakeside and parted with talk of the day to come.

Nuada entered his home and found his mate busy feeding the child.

"Greetings, wife. I am home and tired."

"Nuada! Wash of yourself and I will feed of you."

He nodded and felt the effects of the day's work settle on him. A yawn was stifled as he sat at their table. "Today was a most memorable day, wife. I built new tools for which to build the new homes. The metal was made with a new ore that I found, and it appears much stronger. We will try them tomorrow."

Nuada's mate nodded as she placed his food before him. "Eat before you fall asleep at the table."

Nuada soon finished and walked to his sleeping area and was fast asleep, hearing not of anything.

Early the next morning, Nuada awoke before the sun arose. He dressed in silence and sat at his table to eat something before starting his day. Thoughts of the previous day's work ran through his head — had he forgotten anything that might help with the work ahead? He could not think of anything and was soon crossing the lake again to meet with the new neighbors.

Mor too was up and waiting for the others to rise. He greeted Nuada, and together they walked to the first of the new house sites with the new tools. "Let us try of the new axes and see how they work," said Mor.

Nuada nodded, and they each chose a blade. One of the preselected trees became their test. They each stood opposite of one another around the tree and began the cutting. Wood chips flew with their eagerness, and soon after they were joined by the other men, who also joined in the wood cutting.

By midday they had fallen five trees and had trimmed the branches from them. Nuada had stopped to inspect the wear on the blades and was satisfied with the results of his work.

"Is there anything else I can make for your use?" he asked of Mor and the other men.

"We need wedges for splitting the wood and maybe some chisels and hammers."

Nuada nodded and asked of the design that they would use. New thoughts raced again through his head. "Tomorrow I will return to my forge and make of these for you. If any problems arise, come for me."

A few hours later, Nuada left the work site and set off to the sites of his ore deposits. After many trips back to the forge, he was ready to begin on the new tools the following morning.

Tired and sweating, he returned to the lakeside and washed his sore body. He thanked Creatrix for making everything happen.

Nuada's mate was waiting for him near the lakeside as he poled his raft to the island. "How did your day go, husband?"

"Very well, wife. How is our child and the cub?"

"They are well and growing, as is expected. On the morrow, I would like to come and meet of the new neighbors."

"Please do, wife. After all, this was of your idea."

Together they walked arm in arm to their home and talked of the progress and the new people.

For the following two weeks, Nuada spread his waking hours between wood cutting and his forge. Progress was made in a short time, with hard work by all parties.

Mor approached Nuada one day and told him that he must return to his old village for supplies and help for the assembly of the first house. Nuada nodded and asked if he wanted him to travel with him. Mor said no, that it was not needed and that he should stay and work at his forge because he had some new ideas for Nuada to try. Nuada understood, and they parted with Nuada thinking of the challenges before him.

Three days later, Mor returned with many men and strange new animals. "What are these creatures, Mor?" he asked.

"The large ones are called horses. They will help us set the frames of the houses, and the small ones are sheep, for which to feed of us during the long Winter months."

"You surprise me, my friend. These are wonders I have not seen before. Come look at the works from my forge and share a drink with me."

Early the next day, before Creatrix was very far above the horizon, Nuada walked to the temporary camp of his neighbors. Already the men were at work, some still cutting trees, others moving the branch piles together, and still others using the horses to pull the cut logs into piles away from the building site of the first house. Nuada shook his head in wonderment and reflected that he had spent too much time at his forge lately and had missed much of the progress of the work. He told himself that would end and that he must be near to help and observe how they were to be built.

Nuada found Mor with another man, digging around one of the many stumps inside the site of the first house.

"Mor, what are you to do with these? Are they not in the way of the build?"

"Nuada, my friend, we will first dig around these and then try to pull of them out of the way. If we cannot pull of them, then we will burn them in place."

Nuada could see of their wisdom and began to help them with the digging. Many hours later, a team of the horses were hitched to a stump, and the effort to remove it began. The first two came out easily, but the following one remained rooted in stubbornness. Mor and some of the others began to bring the dried branches and pile them around the stump. A fire was lit, and they began to work at another stump.

This process was carried out for many days, and smoke began to fill the valley from their efforts.

Mor was found by Nuada one day, smiling at the work site. "What makes you so happy today, my friend?"

"With our efforts, we can begin soon to build the first home. Nuada, do you know of any place we can gather together rock for which to build of our foundations?"

Nuada thought for a minute and nodded. "There is a place of a great rock fall in the next valley, but you will need of your horses to bring of them here."

"Good. Tomorrow you will show of me this place, and we can start that phase of the work."

Nuada agreed, and they moved on to the work area and began another day of hard work.

Nuada's mate was not only looking after his needs but also learning of many new ways. She was finding out about how to raise plants and helped the other women develop the field to grow these things. They had chosen a field free of trees near the lake that flooded in the Winter and Spring but was dry the rest of the year. They turned the earth by hand and planted before the end of the Spring cycle. Also she learned how the fur from the sheep could be turned into cloth and worked at that too. Another skill was how to make rope from both the plants and the sheep; this would be needed for the building of the houses.

At the end of their days work, both were tired but excited about what they had learned and often talked into the late night hours about what they had learned.

Weeks passed quickly with the hard work, and Summer was upon them almost before they were ready for the hot time of the year. The foundations were laid, and the massive roof beams raised. The stone fireplaces were well near completed, and clay was being packed into them to make them smoke-free.

The men began to split trees that they had cut earlier in the year, and these were laid upon the tall roofs. Nuada watched how they overlapped the split wood to keep out the wet and found himself in awe of the thought that went into this building. Mor found Nuada watching and said, "We have done two years work in only six months, my friend, thanks to your new tools."

Nuada smiled deeply at this praise from his friend. "I had a skill that was needed and have learned many things from you."

"Come. Let us take part of our midday meal, my friend, and talk."

Together they walked to the temporary camp, talking about the work yet to do and how it was to be done. They settled at an outdoor table, as some of the women brought them food and drink; Nuada's wife was among them but did not disturb their talks.

Nuada looked up and said to Mor, "My mate is learning many new things, as well as I, and I am pleased that we both share of everyone's skills."

Mor looked up at Nuada's mate standing nearby. "We are all learning from each other, my friend."

They returned to work on the houses, and the day continued on without another word except what to do next.

Creatrix, in his form as the sun, was near setting when the men stopped work for the day, and again Nuada stopped at the lakeside to wash before crossing the lake to his home. The wolf cub greeted him with a wagging tail and bounding ahead toward the house.

Nuada thought, "I have been so busy that I have missed his growing and that of my child as well. I must make time to be with them more."

Nuada hugged his wife upon entering and told her of his thoughts before sitting down for his evening meal. She smiled at his concern and said, "There will be plenty of time this Winter for the young ones."

Sleep came hard for Nuada that night, and he spent much of it sitting at the family table in thought. In one of the few times that he slept, a vision from Creatrix came to him and calmed his worries.

Weeks passed, and the first chill of Fall was in the air. The first house was completed, along with an outbuilding for the animals and its fenced area. The second house was nearly done, but the third remained in only its framed form. The women had begun the harvesting of the plant crops, and everyone was in a warm and happy mood.

Still Nuada had pressing thoughts about the work yet to be completed, and he constantly fought back the urge to talk to Mor about these things. His only happy time was when he was at his forge or at home with his family.

Mor had seen the mood change in Nuada and found him one day at his forge alone and busy working at some new tool. "Nuada? What are you making now, my friend?"

Nuada looked up at Mor's question and answered, "These are arms that swing in and out of the great fireplaces to hold pots for cooking. I have also made a grate for meat that slides in and out."

"You are a wise and skilled man, my friend. These are things that will make life easier for all of us."

Nuada almost blushed at the compliment from his friend. "I do what is needed, that is all."

"Perhaps. But you find ways that no other thinks of, even those that receive the most good of your work. Perhaps you need of a helper, one that can learn of your skills and the way of which you think of these things. You take too much upon yourself."

"I could use the help and the company, my friend. I am willing to teach of my skills."

"I know of a child who is almost a man who would be willing."

"Bring him to me, and I will see if he is suitable and smart enough to learn."

Mor nodded and again looked through Nuada. "What else bothers you? I can see that you are troubled with your thoughts."

"I fear that we will not complete the house building this year and that the others will return to their old homes and leave us alone again."

"Fear not of that. They are in awe of you and respect of the things that you have done."

"I wish that I could do more. Perhaps it is the changing of the time of year that really bothers me."

"Come with me. We are removing the old encampment and moving into the new houses today. The women plan a great feast, and we wish you a part of it."

Together they left the forge building and walked to their new village area. Nuada stopped short of the new house and looked at its form. "Your design is slightly different from the ones I saw in your old village, Mor. You have included a roof extension over the door entrance that is also a platform from which you can stand on from the sleep floor."

"That was a simple change and much needed. But I know not what to do for the women when the time comes for the Summer cooking to begin. It will be too warm for them to cook inside."

Nuada looked around and said, "Why not build an outdoor fireplace and cover the ground with more of the flat stone upon which to place tables for eating?"

"Those are good ideas. Perhaps we could build a low stone wall to block the wind too."

Nuada smiled and nodded. Together they continued on and joined of the others.

Nuada found his wife with the other women and called her aside. "That Mor has a way about him. I have felt confused of late, but he found of answers that have settled me. I am grateful of his friendship."

"Perhaps you have been working too hard of late and need of some time alone and away from your problems. Why not do of some hunting, as you did before?"

"I find that tempting, but I am needed here; there is much yet to do."

"They can get along without you. Go and find of a place that you can relax. Why not search for new rocks that you can use or explore this land in other directions that you have not done before. Take a break, even a short one — it will help."

"Wife, you are wise, and I will listen to your words. But I must tell Mor of this thing."

They continued their small talk late into the night, even after returning to their island home. All of their neighbors had now settled into their new houses, and the feast had been enjoyed by all.

The next morning, Nuada found Mor and told him of his plan to get away for a while. Mor smiled and said it was a good idea.

Nuada returned to his home and told his wife of Mor's thoughts and began to pack of the things he would need. He asked his mate to stay with the others while he was gone for safety. Before midday Nuada was ready to begin his time away, and he took his family to the new village before stopping at his forge for last-minute items to take with him. He packed knives of the new metal, an axe, and a new sword. With a last look around, he set out. Before leaving the valley, he stood on an outcropping and looked back at his valley. It still looked much the same as when he first entered into it — only new smoke from the village marked the changes.

- HARDSHIP AND HEALING -

Nuada began his trip without a set direction of travel but soon settled upon a westward direction. Time slowed for him, and he gazed on an abundance of wildlife as the land began to level out. Trees were still in abundance, but the undergrowth became thicker and at times made the journey troublesome.

After the fourth day, he stopped and made camp below a small rise while the sun was still high and the warmth of Creatrix wrapped around him. A small stream nearby lulled his senses with its flow over the shallow rock bed. He thought to himself, "This is just what I have needed after all the work of this year."

He leaned back against his pack and started to close his eyes with the thought of just listening to the world around him. Bird songs filled the air, and insects buzzed with the hurry of the Fall weather ahead. Nuada dozed in the afternoon light without thought of any interruption.

Sleep came with dreams of his family and his new friends. They comforted him as he slept. He awoke later when the moon was high in the night sky and stars twinkled down upon the land around him. He stretched and found a more comfortable position and was soon back asleep again.

He finally awoke with the coming of the dawn, relaxed and ready for the new day. He relit his campfire and began to cook a meal after he had washed in the stream nearby.

After he had eaten, he again sat back without thought of doing any more traveling that day. Again he began to doze but was soon wide awake after a great noise stirred him from his slumber. Voices of a language he did not know came from the other side of the ridge, and the anger that they carried set him on edge.

He picked of his weapons from his pack: his sword, several knives, and two spears that he had tipped with metal. He started up the ridge and found a game trail that helped him find a path over the ridge. Staying low and moving with speed and stealth, he soon topped the ridge and started down to the voices. He slowed his approach and came upon a vantage point where he could see what was going on. Two men were kicking at an old man with a long, flowing, white beard, and they held heavy, wood clubs in a threatening manner above him. Another man was in the back of a large, wooden cart; it was unlike anything that Nuada had ever seen before. It had large, wooden, round wheels, almost as tall as the men themselves, and was drawn by an animal he had never seen before.

Nuada glanced back at the old man and saw that he was in deep pain from the blows. He thought to himself that this was not right and set himself to fight the men who caused such pain in another. He shifted his position slightly and took up one of his spears and aimed at the man doing the worst damage to the old man. He let it loose and grabbed for his second spear before he saw the results of the first throw. It had hit the man full on in the chest and pinned him to the cart. The second man turned to see where the spear had come from, and he too was hit in the chest and fell next to the old man. Blood poured from both men onto the old man, and he stirred and slipped away from the bodies. The third man jumped from the cart as Nuada ran at him with his sword drawn, and they fell upon each other. The man's club struck Nuada in the left arm with such force that he fell and dropped his sword. The man hovered over Nuada and was about to strike him with a deadly blow when Nuada recovered his senses and drew a knife from a sheath in his boot and struck backhanded at the man. It took him in the belly, and he dropped his club as Nuada recovered his feet and struck him again in the neck. The man dropped, and Nuada watched the light in his eyes go out forever.

Nuada stood catching his breath from the fight and held his arm and side in a protective manner. Slowly he picked up his sword and sheathed it before turning his attention to the old man. He cringed at Nuada's approach and again spoke in a language that Nuada did not know. Nuada held out his undamaged arm in a nonthreatening way and motioned that he did not know of the man's language.

Nuada glanced around again to make sure that they were alone and motioned to the old man that he was going to scout for any other attackers. Taking his time, he moved down the cart path and then circled back and found three horses that the men had brought with them. Pulling their harnesses, he brought them back to the cart and tied them to the back of it.

Together they settled upon the ground and took stock of their injuries. The old man appeared to have some broken ribs, and his breath came in short, painful bursts. Nuada checked his arm and found nothing broken, although he would be bruised and marked for many days.

Slowly they took stock of each other and began to find a common ground for language. They started out with their names: the old man was called Jan, and he indicated that he was from a land far to the southwest. Nuada found that after a few hours, his pain started to grow stronger in his side and arm. The old man dozed, and his breath still came in short and labored breaths. Nuada took stock of their surroundings and felt that it was time to move to another place before the sun set for the day. He stood and then helped the old man to his feet and motioned for them to begin to move away from the scene of the fight.

Jan took the reins of the great beast that pulled the cart while Nuada led the way along the ridge path. After a half hour, Nuada found a path that crossed the ridge and helped Jan to turn the beast up the hillside. They talked little during this time and guarded their injuries.

Once over the ridge, Nuada turned back toward his campsite. The animals of the forest fell quiet at their passage, and the sun was just above the hills and beginning to set when they reached his camp in its small meadow.

Nuada restarted the campfire and began to make a small meal for them. He helped the old man settle against one of the great wheels of the cart, where he would be comfortable. Again they tried to find a way to talk to each other, and it started with pointing at an object and its name. Soon Nuada stopped and brought the simple meal, and they ate in silence. A slight wind began to blow out of the north, and Nuada sensed a change in the weather — rain was coming.

Nuada took one of his knife blades and dug a shallow trench around the cart and then climbing into the cart, retrieved Jan's sleeping furs and spread them under the cart. He then went and retrieved his pack and pushed it under the cart before moving Jan under too.

That night with the rain falling, Nuada found he could not sleep with his arm in pain and watched the old man sleep in short naps, as he too was in much pain. Listening to the forest sounds did help Nuada to be distracted from their condition. He wondered of the men who had attacked Jan and where they had come from. He was on edge about being so close to the fight and knew that they had to move come daylight, regardless of the weather or their pain.

Hours later the predawn light of Creatrix stirred Nuada, and he awoke Jan and offered him a cold meal. The weather had passed, and together the two reloaded the cart and began to move from the campsite. Nuada had made up his mind to return to his home and knew that it would take longer to retrace his steps because of the cart and animals.

During the day, they had to make many stops while Nuada cleared a path through the brush, but they did make a decent headway. During the many stops, they worked on their language skills with each other, and a greater understanding grew between them.

With the coming of the setting of Creatrix, Nuada found a place for them to make camp for the night. He built a campfire and again started to warm a meal for them. They talked about their homes — such was the learning of languages coming so fast.

They rested and took naps throughout the day. At one point, Nuada fell into a deep slumber and joined of Creatrix in his heaven. Nuada told of his worries, and Creatrix reassured him that he would be in no danger from this point in time. Creatrix told Nuada of a bush that could be found nearby and that he was to cut of its root and boil it but cautioned of him that it was bitter and to add the leaves of the plant to the mix to make it easier to drink. Nuada nodded in understanding and was again folded into the mortal plain. He awoke and looked about, checking of the old man and then stirred himself to go and look for the plant that Creatrix had told him of.

Nuada found of the plant in short order and returned to camp with it. He set a pot near the fire with water from the stream and set himself to cutting the root away and cleaning of it. After cutting the root into small pieces, he ripped some of the leaves from the plant and put it all in the pot to steep. Nuada sat and looked around at the land and listened again for the sounds of the forest. All seemed normal, and he relaxed and turned his gaze to Jan. He seemed to be sleeping better, and his breathing was not as labored.

After about twenty minutes, Nuada poured two drinking horns of the mixture and went to arouse Jan. He handed him a horn and took of his, and together they drank of the mixture. Then they settled down again to doze through the rest of the day.

Later that night, long after Creatrix had set in his form as the sun, they were awoken by the calling of a lone wolf in the distance. Nuada checked on Jan and found him in much less pain and of himself. He was amazed at his own relief in his arm. "I must take of this plant back to the village," he thought.

Nuada awoke early the next morning, as was his custom, and set out in search of more of the plants that Creatrix had shown of him. Jan awoke later and had started to cook a morning meal for them both when Nuada returned. "I have need of something to place these plants in, my friend."

"There are some old buckets in the cart, Nuada," he responded. "But first come and eat of this food while it is still hot."

Nuada nodded and joined Jan at the campfire. While eating Nuada commented on his friend's recovery from his injuries.

"It is better after you gave of me that potion. I can breathe easier, and the pain does not hamper of my movements."

"It is much the same for myself, friend."

Jan then asked of Nuada's valley with many questions. Nuada responded and found himself thinking of his home and family. "We still have many days of travel ahead of us, Jan. Let us pack and begin the journey again."

They quickly broke camp, and Nuada again led them through the forest-covered hills. The birds of the forest called to them as they passed, moving further eastward.

Three more days passed before they were at the entrance to Nuada's valley. Their talks became easier with the passing of the days, and a much deeper friendship grew between them.

"1 shall go ahead and warn them of our coming. Keep to the right side of the valley and follow of the path from the forge building. I shall meet of you before you enter the village."

Jan nodded in understanding, and they parted ways with a wave of their hands. Nuada hurried over the entrance and followed his normal path home. Looking about he saw nothing out of place, and light smoke still showed from the new village: a good sign.

Always a cautious man, Nuada paused before he came in sight of the village and listened for the sounds of his friends. All appeared normal, so he continued forward.

Mor was the first to see of Nuada and called to him, "Welcome back, friend! We have missed of you and your skills."

"Mor, my friend. It is good to be home, and I have brought a friend."

Mor, looking past Nuada, sought out the stranger. "Where is he, friend?"

"You will hear of him before you see him, for he has a thing that will improve our way of life."

"Of this I must see for myself, Nuada."

"You will. Where is my mate, friend?"

"She is with the other women. Do you wish to see of her now?"

"No, I can wait. Come with me, and we will hurry our new friend to the village."

Together they walked back over the path to find Jan and his cart. They came across him just after he had passed the forge.

"Jan, this is Mor. We have come to bring you into the village."

Mor greeted Jan with friendship and then began to look over his strange cart, asking questions about its construction.

Nuada watched as they talked and finally said, "Come, let us enter the village. I am missing of my wife, friends."

The trio set off, and still they talked and asked questions of each other. Reaching the village, they headed straight for the animal shelter and pen so as to unhook the cart from the great beast and put the horses in with the others. After feeding the animals, they walked back to the first house they had built.

The others of the village were all together and greeted Nuada and his new friend without question. They were preparing a great feast to mark the end of their harvest and the beginning of Winter. Soon things in the village would slow, and it would become a time of rest before Spring.

Nuada found of his mate and held her close and whispered that he had missed of her and their child. The wolf cub circled around the three of them and wanted attention also. Nuada reached down and scratched the wolf's head while still keeping an arm around his wife.

Nuada looked in the direction of Jan and smiled at the attention he was receiving from the others. He thought, "It is a good thing that we were able to teach each other our languages."

Any thoughts of their recent injuries were fleeting, and before being questioned as to how they had met, Nuada called out that they were tired and needed of some food before answering any more questions.

Beer and the large meal added to the conversation around the large table until again Nuada and Jan were asked about how they had met. Jan took over and began to recall the events leading up to the point where Nuada charged out of the underbrush and fought the raiders. He recalled the injuries that both had received and how afterward they had moved to a safe camp with the horses of the attackers. Then he told of how after resting, Nuada cooked of a potion that eased their pain.

Nuada smiled at the attention he was receiving and said that he had brought back the plants that eased the pain. Then the conversation turned to Jan's great cart and the animal that pulled it.

Much later, after the meal had been cleared away and more beer had been drunk, the people of the village began to find their way to their sleeping places in the great house. Nuada wanted to return to his home on the island, but his mate said that the village people wanted them to stay here and share of the work he had put into the house. Nuada, greatly tired, gave into her wishes, and she showed him to their place in the loft. Jan made a place for himself near the fireplace on the main floor and was soon fast asleep.

Nuada awoke to the sound of the women preparing the morning meal and slowly stretched before removing his sleeping robes and found that the wolf cub had not stirred from its place next to him. "This is what home should be every day," he thought.

Then he stirred himself and climbed down to the main floor and found Jan and Mor waiting for him.

"It's about time that you awoke, Nuada," Mor said. "I have things to show you this day."

After eating the three walked down to the third house under construction.

"I cannot believe that you have done so much in such a short time, my friend." Nuada said.

"We have been busy since your travels into the lower lands, and the weather has been good to us. We have wanted to show our thanks for bringing us into your valley and the many tools that you have made for us. This is to be your home, my friend."

"But I cannot accept this; it is too much."

"Please do not disappoint us, Nuada. We all have agreed to this plan for you."

Nuada smiled and thumped Mor on the back. "Very well, my friend. I will accept it under one condition: that all of you will take part in a celebration to commemorate the building of our homes and our friendship."

"Done. We will begin the planning of this feast within the month, as the house will be completed by then."

Jan then said, "It looks like I have found the right place in my life for a change. I am pleased to be your friend, Nuada. Now that this is done, I wish to see of your forge that I have heard so much about."

The trio then began the walk to Nuada's forge building, pausing along the way by the first house. Mor showed them the start of the outdoor cooking area that Nuada had talked of.

"There have been so many changes in such a short time, and I am pleased at its coming together," Nuada said.

Later after the visit to the forge and down along the lakeside to the growing fields, they returned with a healthy appetite to the first house and joined of the others. More beer was shared with the meal, and little work was done that day. It was a day of good conversation and friendship.

- WINTER WINDS AND SNOW -

rue to his word, Mor was putting the finishing touches on Nuada's home. All of the people of the valley kept Nuada busy at his forge and out of the way of the work. The new home was to be a surprise with its finishing touches. A large stair was installed inside the entry door instead of the ladders that were in the other houses. A water cistern was placed near the fireplace, and a storage room was built for firewood. Winter snows would not take away the comfort of this house.

Even Nuada's mate kept quiet about the work being done, but he could see the pride in her face when he returned at night from the forge. He said nothing and carried the knowledge that this is what everyone wanted. Still he wanted to be part of the construction, and this, in a way, pulled at his being.

Finally with the weather beginning to change, they had some nighttime rains of late. Mor came to Nuada at his forge and urged him to see his new house. It had been four weeks when they told him that this house would be his, and now it was ready.

Walking back to the village, Nuada was looking toward the sky and mentioned to Mor that it looked like snow that night. Heavy gray clouds hung on the mountaintops and were lowering toward the valley, and wind out of the west blew lightly but had picked up in the last hour.

The people of the village were there to meet the pair, and they began to cheer at Nuada's presence. He felt nervous — more so than when he had battled foes in the past — and could not understand the feeling. Grinning at the response, he found of his mate and child, and as a group, they all walked to the house.

Outside the new house looked the same as all the others, but once inside, the differences stood out. Nuada felt his mouth hanging open in amazement and wanted to look at everything. People were talking, but he did not hear of their words. It was a lot to take in, and the details seemed to overtake him.

"This is too much, Mor. I cannot believe of this house."

"Then take it with pride. You have earned of it, my friend."

Later the feast began, and music filled the new home of Nuada and his mate. After a while, Nuada found Jan sitting alone and asked him to stay with them.

"It is an honor, my friend. I will accept of it and help you in any way I can."

Together they shared of the beer and the music and looked about the large room; both felt of the smallness of themselves among these giving people.

Late that night, the people of the village said their good nights and departed, leaving Nuada and his mate and Jan alone.

"This quietness seems wrong now, but I think it is what it should be," Nuada said to the others. "This is now our home."

Everyone awoke late that next morning and found that indeed the snow had come at last. It was a heavy, wet snow that came up to Nuada's knees, and Wolf enjoyed playing in it. More snow lingered in the air, and everyone kept close to their homes that day. Smoke from the fireplaces lingered low to the ground and swirled in and out of the trees that talked in the wind. Winter had arrived. To Nuada it reminded him of his childhood and how much he missed of the high mountains.

Returning inside to his family, he and Wolf curled up next to the fireplace, and Jan walked over and joined of them while Nuada's mate made up a small meal for them.

"Tell me more of the land where you come from, my friend," Nuada said.

"As I told of you, it is far to the southwest, amid many mountains that are dry most of the year. My people are called Basque. A day's walk away is the great sea of no end, and many of my people lived near its shore. It never gets as cold as this, and the rain does not last long. I began to wander while I was still a child and did so until I found of you this season. I have seen many things and the wonders of the people that lived there.

"However, I also saw of their meanness and distrust of others — not like you or your people. I will be glad to live out the rest of my days here, as I have found peace that I could not find elsewhere. Again I thank of you, my friend."

"Your thanks are not needed, Jan. I did what was needed of me at the moment, and I find pleasure in your company."

"Even so you have my thanks. I have been talking to Mor about the cart, and we think we can build small versions that would help with the crops and others that even you could use to gather the metal ores that you use. We now have enough horses to do the work of pulling them, and that will give of the men more time to do other work."

"This I like and will help you to work out the designs. Let me gather of some small skins and some of the charred sticks to make some drawings."

The two men worked at designs through half the afternoon until Wolf wanted to go back outside again and play in the snow. Gathering of himself, Nuada dressed warmly for the cold and stepped outside to find only a light, powdery snow falling around them. The wind had died to a light breeze, and the silence that followed such a storm held the valley in its beauty. Nuada breathed deeply and smiled at the freshness of the cold moistness of the air before calling Wolf to return inside again.

After removing his heavy outerwear, Nuada walked up behind his mate and put his arms around her while she worked. "Have I told of you lately how much I love you. We miss of our time together, and I was thinking that we need of it."

She turned to face him and said, "You are thinking of maybe making of another child, husband. I find I am too busy with one, and with you away most days, it worries of me."

Nuada smiled and shook his head. "The thought did not enter of my head, wife. But if you find it hard, only ask of me to help, and I will."

She raised her eyebrows in surprise at his response and pushed him away, laughing. "You to change of the young one's rags — that will be the day I will work for you in the forge building."

Nuada reached for her again, and she dodged his embrace, and they both began to laugh. Jan watched their antics and smiled, wishing he was young again himself, and then reached down to scratched at Wolf's head.

The day was near its end as they sat and ate of their evening meal, and Nuada realized that the village neighbors had left them to their own quiet time. Again he smiled inwardly to himself and thought of how good the changes had been for all of them.

After the meal was eaten, Jan walked to his corner and dug through his things until he found what he was looking for and returned to Nuada and smiled a large grin. "I have a gift for you, my friend."

Nuada, thinking it was a joke, laughed and pointed at the long stick and skinny bag of sticks. "What is this for? Fishing, Jan?"

Jan looked at him with a question on his lips and then said, "No. It is a true weapon of war that can also be used for hunting. Here, let me show it of you and how it works."

Putting the tip of the long stick on the outside of one foot and stepping across it with the other, Jan picked up the string and then with all of his strength bent the stick across his leg and fitted the string to the other end. "This is called a bow, Nuada."

Then he reached into the bag and drew of the sticks, a shaft with feathers on one end and a bone tip on the other.

"This is called an arrow or shaft. You place this here and draw of the string and shaft together. Then point at a target and release of it."

Nuada said, "Let me try of this thing, Jan." Nuada stood and took the bow and shaft from Jan. Then taking cues, he took a stance and pulled the bow-string back along his cheek. He aimed at a knot of wood on the far wall and released the shaft. It flew straight and missed the knot by inches.

"I like of this, Jan. Show me more of the construction of it so that I may understand of it."

They stood in conversation for almost an hour, talking about its workings and the things that Jan had seen in his travels.

Within a few days, the weather had cleared, and much of the snow had melted. Nuada took his new bow and went looking for deer to hunt. It did not take him long to bag a fine buck and return home. After gutting and hanging his hunt, Nuada went looking for Mor to show him his new tool.

Mor was with the animals at their shed and smiled at Nuada's approach. "What brings you forth this day, my friend?"

"I brought forth my new gift from Jan to show of you — something that you will find of interest and will wish to make more of."

After discussing the bow and the concept of how it worked, Mor was more than willing to attempt making more of them. "But these will have to wait. I found of some problems with the houses and wish to correct of them soon although some of it will have to wait for Spring."

Mor told Nuada about how some of the leather hinges for the doors had failed in the cold and asked his thoughts about making them of metal.

"It can be done, Mor. Let me think on the process, and I will attempt to make of them."

Nuada left Mor with his thoughts going over a design for the hinges and returned to his house. Jan was outside under the overhang and greeted Nuada on his return.

"I see you have made use of my gift, friend. How many shafts did you use?"

Nuada laughed, "Only one, Jan. It was more of a lucky shot than skill. But we will eat well this week. Tomorrow I am going to the forge. Do you wish to join of me? It will mean rising early."

"I am willing, Nuada. I am interested of your work and skill with metal."

"Good. Let us return inside and share of some of the beer."

The following morning, both men arose long before the sun and prepared a meal for themselves for midday. Then dressing warmly, they set off for the forge building. Small talk made the short walk seem even shorter, and upon reaching the building, Nuada set about lighting the fire under his forge.

"I had not planned for much Winter work, and I am in short supply of my ores. But I think I have enough for the few, simple projects that we are to do."

Nuada went to his sand-forming table and took some wood and a blade that he used for such work and began to carve the pattern for the hinges that Mor needed. While he worked, he mentioned to Jan that he had an idea for making metal tips for the arrow shafts. Jan thought it was a good idea and asked how he thought he could make them without them being too heavy.

"I will make them of the copper ore only, as it is much lighter."

Between checking on his forge fire and carving of the sand patterns, most of the morning passed quickly. Finally Nuada pressed his design into the sand, which had a thick texture, and then checked the bronze he had set to melt in the forge fire. The mold was of two pieces, with beeswax inserts for holes and the hinge-pin slots. Finally all was ready, and he took hold of the hot stone pot with the melted bronze. With a long pair of tongs that he had made long ago, he started to pour the molten metal into the sand mold. With that done, both men sat and ate of their midday meal.

Nuada's mind raced with the process of his work, and he only glanced at Jan when he said, "What is wrong, Nuada?"

"What? Oh, I was thinking about how to make of these better. But we shall see shortly if they will work."

"And if they work, how many do you make of these?"

"We will need twelve. But I will double that number for spares."

Jan nodded and both men fell silent with their thoughts. The afternoon wore on as they worked, and finally the needed hinges were complete. They choked the forge fire and cleaned up the work area for another day, then set off for the village. They stopped at Mor's house and presented him with their work. He was taken aback and startled that they had made them so soon.

Nuada showed how they worked and how to install them, and then the two men retreated to Nuada's house for their evening meal and some much needed rest.

After the evening meal, Nuada and Jan continued their small talk, and Nuada's mate kept busy with her womanly work. Wolf was curled up with the child, and all was peaceful within the household.

"Jan? I was thinking of visiting of my old house on the island tomorrow. Would you like to come along?"

"I would enjoy of the chance, Nuada. What time of the day would you like to go?"

"Midday should be fine. There is not much to see, but it is a thing to do."

The next day, after sleeping late, the two men set off for the island. They found of Nuada's old raft and poled across. Following the old path, they found the house much as Nuada had left it.

"See. It is not much, my friend. But it served its purpose during my first year."

"True. It is a simple design that I have seen before. But it had a purpose, and that makes it something to remember and be proud of."

"When I came to this valley, I was thinking of safety for my family and this island of its worth. See how it blends into the background and almost remains hidden?"

"It works in many ways, Nuada. Come, show of me the inside, and then we will walk of the island."

After about three hours, the two men returned to the village. They came upon Mor and two others cutting some firewood and stopped to talk.

"Mor, my friend. Do you need of help? We have just returned from my old house on the island and find of ourselves with too much time on our hands."

"That is why we are here, Nuada. Boredom is catching, and we found of something to do. Also it will make of our mates happy and get us out from underfoot."

Laughing, all the men stood and looked at each other.

"It is something we all have in common, Mor. Perhaps we should meet and plan for future things to do together."

They all agreed and decided to meet at Mor's house the following day. Nuada and Jan said their good-byes and left for home. At the house, Nuada walked in to find of his young child standing and called to his mate to show of her. She showed her surprise and picked up the boy.

"He is growing quickly, husband. Soon he will be wanting to go places with you instead of being with me."

"I think that time is still a long way off, wife. But we must plan on it." He placed his arms around them and smiled down at his son. "You are going to be trouble for me. I can see of it already, boy."

Mealtime was near, and Nuada and his family sat at the table. Nuada told of the trip to the island and their talk with Mor and the other men. Nuada's mate shook her head in understanding and said that it was a thing that they must do.

The next morning the air felt of more snow as Nuada and Jan walked to Mor's home.

"What are you planning to talk of, Nuada?" asked Jan.

"Our trip to the island brought back thoughts of our safety again, and I want of their thoughts about what to do."

"I agree. There are troubles in this land that we cannot understand. All we can do is prepare for what we think may happen, but there will be things that will happen that we cannot see."

Nuada nodded in agreement as they reached Mor's house. After knocking and being greeted by one of the other men, they all sat at the long table and began to discuss the future.

After about an hour of general discussion, Nuada brought up his thoughts about the safety of the village. It included fire provisions, threats from outside the valley, and a way to bring more people into the village society.

Finally the building of a water cistern near the houses in the Spring was agreed to for fire safety and possibly a wooden wall to surround the homes of the village. However, the men disagreed about the addition of more people into the village.

Nuada understood their feelings and thought that perhaps another time would be better for more discussion about the subject. Thoughts about the building of the work carts and other labor-saving devices filled out the rest of the morning before they broke up the meeting.

Returning home Nuada looked skyward again and noted the changing weather and how the wind had picked up. "We are into a big storm tonight, Jan."

"I can feel it in my bones, Nuada. What do we have to do before it comes?"

"We have plenty of food and firewood. I cannot think of anything else that we may need."

Entering the house, Wolf greeted them by running in circles and then he darted outside to do his business. Nuada's mate was working at food preparations as usual while his child slept nearby. Nuada took in the scene and waited for Wolf to return. Jan walked to his sleeping area and brought forth his stringed instrument, which he began to tune.

Wolf returned, and Nuada secured the doorway, then settled at the table and began to listen to the song as Jan began to sing and play his instrument. He thought, "I am comfortable with this way of life and my friends." The rest of the day passed without them thinking of the morning meeting or anything to do with the village. They enjoyed their own company and left it at that.

The weeks that followed were much the same, and outside the snow depth grew and held the valley in its grip of white silence. It was getting close to Winter solstice, the shortest day of the year, yet they hardly knew of its presence.

On one of these days, Nuada awoke early and dressed warmly. He felt the presence of cabin fever and a feeling to get out of the house for awhile. After stoking the fireplace and awaking his mate, he took down his tote and picked up his bow and bag of shafts. He stopped near the entry door and put on his snowshoes. Then he began to walk toward his forge. It was a good morning for the walk. The snow had stopped for the moment, and the wind was light. He could hear the snow underfoot crunch as he moved forward, and the glare was subdued by an overcast sky.

Reaching the forge building, he looked inside and found nothing had changed. After spending only a few short minutes, he stepped outside again and looked across the valley. Light smoke from the village homes drifted among the trees, and the lake appeared like a mirror alongside the snow. "This is so peaceful. We are one with the land," he thought.

Turning he walked toward the valley entrance. After a short time, he reached the high point and looked out toward the old village in the distance. Something caught his eye — there was no smoke from it.

"What could be the cause of this?" he thought. "I must seek help from the others and go to find of the cause."

Returning to his village, he sought out Mor and told of his concern. Mor agreed and sought out the other men of the village. They planned on a Winter trip the next day to find of the cause.

Nuada returned to his house and told Jan and his mate of the plan and the reason behind it. Nuada asked Jan to stay behind and watch over the women of the village while they were gone. He agreed but voiced his concern about leaving a trail if there was to be trouble.

"We will be careful, my friend. But if trouble finds us or you, make for the island and hide there until we return."

Early the next morning before even the predawn light of Creatrix began to show, all of the village men set off for the old village. They knew that it would take most of the day and only rested for short periods of time during their travel. The weather held for them, and they slowly entered the outer edges of the village before dark in two groups.

There were no footprints in the snow-covered ground, and the village was quiet. Mor called out, but there was no response. Carefully two of the men entered a house, and the others waited. After what seemed a long time, they came back outside.

"They are all dead! Rats and other animals have ravaged their remains, and we cannot see of the cause."

Quickly the other houses were checked, and the results were the same. Mor called the men together and said, "Let us leave of this place and make camp back along the trail before it becomes too dark."

A few miles away, they stopped to set camp. All were quiet while Nuada talked with Mor.

"Do you think it was disease or men that was the cause of these deaths?"

"I am thinking it was disease. We must be careful and wash of ourselves before entering our village again."

"I agree. We must protect of ourselves and our mates and children."

The next morning, they set off for their homes again but stopped to wash of themselves and their clothes in the stream that flowed from the valley. They felt of the cold and hurried to find the shelter of their houses.

Nuada entered into his house with a deep, tired feeling and slowly removed his damp clothes. Jan and Nuada's mate walked over to him and asked almost together, "What did you find?"

"They were all dead. Some kind of disease took of them. The animals had broken out of their shelters and had disappeared, and we left them as we found them."

Slowly Nuada found of his resting place in front of the fireplace and dozed in its warmth. His dream cycle took him to Creatrix, and he asked of him, "Are we safe from this pestilence that plagued our neighbors? I fear for my family and friends."

"You are safe, Nuada. I will look after all of you."

Nuada felt his return to life and awoke feeling better. Jan sat at the table looking at some of the drawings they had made earlier in the Fall and looked up as Nuada stirred from his sleep. "You have returned, my friend. I thought that you would sleep the whole day away."

"I could have, but I think my time was well used while I slept."

"How so? You have not moved from the position where you slept."

"I had visited with my creator, and he put my worries to rest about what I saw and worried about."

"Perhaps you will tell of me about him sometime. I am curious of your beliefs."

"Perhaps when the time is right, my friend."

Nuada stood and stretched and then smelled of the meal that his mate was preparing. He walked over to her and held of her and whispered into her ear. "I visited with Creatrix again. He told me not to fear of what happened to the other village people. We are safe."

She turned and kissed him and said, "I knew you would talk to him and keep us safe, husband."

"I am truly hungry. How soon before we eat, wife?"

"Sit and I will feed of you."

She placed a bowl of stew before her mate and a baked potato with cooked onions. He started to eat with great vigor as Jan joined him for his meal. While they were eating, a knock came to their door. Nuada's mate went to answer, followed by Wolf. It was Mor and the rest of the village people. Nuada stood and walked to greet the throng.

"Come, what is the problem, my friends?"

They all began to talk at once, and Mor held up his arms to quiet them. He then turned to Nuada and said, "We are worried that we may become sick as our other friends had. We want to know what to do and hope that you have an answer."

"I too had worries and had a waking dream of the creator and asked of him what to do. He reassured me that we are safe and that he would protect us."

Again they all began to talk at the same time, and Nuada shook his head trying to understand them. One called out, "We are to do nothing? That seems wrong. There must be ways for us to fight against this pestilence."

"I understand of your questions — only keep of your houses clean and all of your animals. The rest will be taken care of by the creator."

Most of them nodded their heads in understanding and trusted in the words of Nuada. Slowly the meeting broke up, and they returned to their houses. Nuada took his seat at the table after the last person left his place and sat staring at the far wall while Jan retook his seat and watched.

After awhile Jan spoke. "Nuada? These people fear for the unknown. You must not take their burden and let it draw you down with them. You are stronger than you know. I have seen of it."

Nuada turned to Jan. "They are filled with grief for their friends. I know that there is little I can do to relieve them of that burden. True, they fear the unknown, but is there anyone who could not feel of that also?"

"I can see that this draws deeply upon you. Perhaps only time will show everyone the way of the truth, and you will become stronger within the village."

Nuada nodded and then said, "Perhaps. For now I am tired and need of my rest, as this day has been long and draining upon my soul."

"Then rest, my friend. I shall watch over you and your family."

Nuada then stood and retired to his sleeping area as the shadows of the long day turned into night, and he slept a deep sleep.

The next morning he awoke to Wolf pawing at his arm, and he knew he had slept late. Rising he dressed and took Wolf for his morning run. Outside the wind blew lightly, and the sun shone brightly. It was mid-Winter, and they had only a light snowpack to show for it. Thoughts of yesterday came back, and he shook his head at the remembrance.

Returning to his house, he turned to look back at the village. Some smoke began to drift in the light breeze from the houses.

"They are awake and will want more answers, and I have none for them," he thought.

Inside Jan was awake and working at the table while his mate stirred at her cooking pots. Wolf ran to Jan and greeted him. Looking up Jan said, "Good morning, Nuada. Did your sleep help you in your quest for answers?"

"No. But I will take your advice and let time find a way. What are you working on now, my friend?"

"It is only a simple design of art. I had a thought about how things twist within each other, and this came to mind."

Nuada looked down upon the design and followed its pattern. He nodded in appreciation and said, "I can see of its meaning and how it flows like the things around us. Perhaps this was what I was looking for in our people. It is simple yet has a strong pull at the mind."

"Perhaps, Nuada, you can work the design into your house. It will take of your mind off the other problems."

"Yes! It will also make my mate happy too. What other designs do you have?"

They sat and discussed patterns and how to apply them to the house in ways that would be simple yet pleasing. Midday came and found the two men starting to work on a post that framed one side of the fireplace. Nuada used a ladder and began to carve at the top of the post while Jan drew his pattern below him for the carving that would follow. Time passed quickly for them, and finally Nuada's mate called them to eat of their supper. The one post was now covered by almost one-third of the design that Jan had developed.

"Time passes when you are busy, Nuada. I think you are pleased with what you have done."

Glancing up at the carving from his meal, Nuada nodded in answer to Jan's question. "I find it relaxing, and it pleases my mate too."

After retiring to sleep, Nuada kept dreaming of the pattern. Days followed as they continued to work at the carving until both posts that framed the fireplace were done.

Standing back both men studied the work and then looked around the house for other areas to continue the design. A knock at the door broke their trains of thought. Answering it Nuada was greeted by Mor, who entered and patted both men on their backs in greeting. Their work was hidden by the great stairway, and when Mor stepped around it and saw the new work that had been done, he exclaimed, "This is what has kept you from us this past week! I like it!"

He moved closer to study the intricate details of the carving and found it hard to take his eyes away from the pattern. Finally he said, "This is what the others need to see and do to their houses. It will take their minds off the worries of pestilence and other threats to our village."

"I agree," Nuada said. "It has done wonders for me. Come let us share some beer together and talk of how to get them to understand that time will take care of their worries."

That afternoon passed in friendship and good company, and laughter became frequent, something that had been lacking for some time. Nuada's mate smiled at their friendship and felt comforted by all the things that had come to pass.

The next day the other members of the village joined Mor at Nuada's house, and they all looked at the carvings in wonder, and loud conversation followed. Nuada served up more of his beer while Nuada's mate passed food around among all of the people.

Finally Nuada stood before the crowd and praised Jan for his design work and encouraged the village people to do this kind of work within their houses. Questions came from all of the people, directed toward Jan and his art work. Jan broke his silence and asked what other designs they would like to see. The most common design was with animals of the forest, mixed with plants.

Nuada himself thought through patterns that he would like to see in his house. Finally he cast his eyes toward Wolf and knew that he would have to do one based on him. He looked toward the door leading to the pantry and decided that was where his image belonged. Nuada walked to his mate and told her of his idea, and she agreed with him.

"He spends much of his time thinking about the next meal and that would fit his mind set."

Later after everyone had left the house, Nuada told Jan of his idea, and Jan sat down at the table immediately and began to draw Wolf. The animal knew he was the center of attention and posed in ways that were the appropriate stance of his kind.

Jan said to Nuada, "He is too smart for his own good. Look at him."

"I agree and why I put up with him."

Later after many drawings of Wolf, Nuada decided on one design and called Wolf over to inspect the image. Wolf sniffed at it and then returned to his place near Nuada's mate and the fireplace.

The next morning Jan was at work on drawings for the other village people while Nuada began the carving of Wolf on the pantry door. Before midday Jan left to deliver his designs as Nuada continued to carve. He would stop once in awhile to stand back and look at the progress and then go back to work on it again. No detail was too small for Nuada, and he pressed himself to do better with every chip of wood he removed. Nuada's mate called for him to stop and eat, and he reluctantly set his tools down and sat at the table looking across at his work. His mind was in constant motion and did not dwell on the meal before him. After a short while, Nuada stood, ignoring his meal, and returned to his work.

Late that same afternoon, Jan returned and paused at the table. He glanced at Nuada and then turned toward Nuada's mate, who shook her head at her husband and his work. Not wanting to disturb him, Jan sat and began to draw again. Every so often he would glance over at the work of Nuada to see if he was taking a break from his concentration on the Wolf carving. But no, Nuada continued with his mind set and was oblivious to anything else. Later that evening after Jan and Nuada's mate had eaten their evening meal, Nuada continued to work at his carving without a break. Finally Jan walked over to Nuada and said, "It is a fine carving, Nuada. Why not take a break and join us at the table?"

"Why? I am still seeing the details of him and find it hard to do anything else."

"You have been working all day, and night has settled upon the village. It is time to relax and talk of the others of the village."

"Perhaps you are right. My eyes are tired and my arms are heavy because of the work."

Setting his tools down, Nuada walked in a slow and measured step to the table. Only after he had sat down did he look at the carving again.

"Perhaps I am too intense with this work. I may need time away to gather of my thoughts."

"Possibly, my friend. But it has been good for you. I knew that you had it in you to do this work after seeing what you could do with your carving of the hinges you used for the molds. However, I had not thought that it would take over your every moment of the day. You need something for a diversion. Possibly go hunting or take Wolf for a run around the lake. Do something different."

"You are right. I will do something different tomorrow."

"Now as for the rest of the village people, they too have begun their own carvings, and their skills in wood have shown that they too are diverted from their fears of the pestilence. That is good, and I was happy to bring this change to them."

They said their good nights and found their sleeping places and all dreamed of a better day and diversions.

Nuada awoke early and dressed warmly and set out with Wolf for the forge. The Winter sky was overcast, with heavy snow clouds, and the wind blew fresh out of the west. Wolf romped in the shallow snow that still covered the ground in search of any game. Nuada watched every shadow for signs of an intruder and found none. Only game trails showed in the snow, and they were few in number. It took him longer to reach the forge than it normally would, and he found it undisturbed. He then set out for the valley entrance and the stream that flowed from its mouth. Moving upstream he crossed at a shallow and followed its course to the opposite side of the valley. He found the place where he had first entered into the valley and climbed up the rise that marked its entrance. Nothing had changed in that time, and he looked into the opposite valley where he had found the rock fall. No smoke marked any human trace, and he felt satisfied with his walk and called Wolf to him before turning back to the lakeshore and home.

Something called to Nuada's attention, and he again turned to the ridge that circled the back of the valley. Changing directions with Wolf following, he walked back toward the ridge and followed its path, his eyes looking for what he did not know. He had never taken this path before and paid more attention than he thought to the details of the land around him. After a short period of time, he found something that caught his eye: a cave hidden at the base of a rock fall. Moving cautiously he climbed the jumbled rock pile and peered into depths of the cave. Nothing moved nor could he hear any sounds that would warn him of any animals within. He paused, knowing that he would need light to enter, and slowly backed away from the entrance. He then continued his journey, still looking at the ridge. A little farther, he again spied another cave much higher up the rocky cliff and thought, "I must explore these when the weather warms." The wind had picked up, and he hurried toward home.

Jan greeted him outside of Nuada's home and asked of his walk.

"I found it an interesting walk. I found two caves not too distant and plan to investigate them when the weather warms. I might find of my ores that I will need for the forge."

"Then take me with you when you go, my friend."

"Agreed. But I think we will need of Mor also. Let me talk to him tomorrow."

"I think that you might have other ideas about this trip and the caves."

"Yes. It could provide a place of shelter if raiders return to the area. We will need to explore its possibility."

The next day Nuada talked to Mor about his discovery and his thoughts about it as a haven in an emergency. Then he returned to his work on the carving of Wolf. The weeks passed, as Winter soon ended and Spring approached. The village began to take on a new life with the warmer weather, and its inhabitants found time to do chores outside.

The work on the outdoor common kitchen was the first project to start and the gathering of stone the hardest part of it. Rain at least once a week slowed their project.

On one of the warmer days, Mor approached Nuada about the trip to the caves. "When do you want to start to explore your caves, Nuada?"

"Give me another week to complete some of my other projects, my friend."

"Then I shall be ready. This has been on my mind since you told me of them."

- SPRING AND RENEWAL -

Later in the week, Nuada was finishing the carving of acorns on the stair-railing posts when Mor came to see him again about the trip to the caves.

"That is fine work, Nuada. Did you finish the carving of Wolf?"

"Yes. Come see of it."

Mor followed Nuada to the pantry door and stood back to admire the details of the carving. "That is fine work. It looks real. How does Wolf like it?"

"He comes over to sniff at its tail from time to time, and I have heard him growl at it."

"What about the trip to the caves, my friend?"

Nuada looked about the room and at his mate. "I think tomorrow would be a good day to go exploring. How about you?"

"That would work for me also."

"Then it is done. Tomorrow we set out for some adventure."

Before the first light of Creatrix in the morning, Nuada arose and was packing for the trip to the caves when Jan awoke.

"You are an early riser, Nuada. Why the hurry?"

"It is not the hurry. It is being prepared for the unexpected. How long before you are ready?"

"Give me a few minutes and something to eat."

"I had forgotten all about food. We must pack for that also."

The two men sat and were eating when Mor knocked at the door.

"I see you are ready for this adventure. What are we missing?"

"We are only missing your company and the finishing of our meal," replied Nuada.

Mor joined the two men and picked at some bread and fruit that was at the table while he waited for his friends to finish. They passed some small talk about what was to come and what the other men of the village were going to miss.

Wolf had stirred and waited to be let out for his morning run. Nuada released him to run and waited for his return at the door while Jan and Mor checked each other's packs and supplies.

"Keep your weapons light and simple," called Nuada to the pair, and then he whistled for Wolf to return. After Wolf entered the house and settled by the fireplace, the trio set off for the caves.

They followed the ridgeline at the back of the valley for about twenty minutes before sighting the first of the caves.

"This is the second cave. See how high it sits on the ridge and overlooks the valley. The other sits low on the valley floor and has a rock fall at its base. I think that is the one I want to see first."

The others followed Nuada's lead and moved on to the other cave entrance. Jan lagged back and stopped once in awhile to pick the new wildflowers of Spring. Once in a while his head would turn at the birds singing in the warm weather.

"Jan! Keep up!" called Nuada.

Mor shook his head with a smile and said, "He is enjoying the new weather. Let him be."

Finally they arrived at the base cave and paused before it. Nuada stood looking up at the ridgeline above the cave entrance.

"The hillside appears solid. I cannot see any fresh rock falls."

Mor nodded in agreement, and they slowly climbed over the old rocks at the entrance base. When Jan caught up with the others, they unlimbered some prepared torches and started sparking a flame to one of them. Soon they had three torches burning and began their entrance into the cave.

Once the trio was inside the cave entrance, the temperature dropped over twenty degrees, and moisture dripped from the cave roof and walls as if they were at the bottom of a lake. Jan was the first to complain about the damp, and he visibly shuttered with its impact.

"How can you stand this cold, my friends?"

"We grew up in weather not much different from this, Jan. Where you come from, the heat would wear on us."

The entrance cavern was high and wide, with two smaller caves leading deeper into the hillside.

"Which way do we go now?" asked Mor.

Nuada thought for a moment and pointed left. "Let us try that one. It is slightly larger."

Nuada led with Jan in the middle and Mor following behind. After twenty feet, it switched left, back toward the mountains and the stream that fed the valley. It had a downward slope, and all three slid more than walked along its narrow path.

"This will slow our return, I am afraid," called Nuada back over his shoulder.

Jan answered, "As long as we can return, I will be happy."

Finally the slope leveled out, and the path remained straight. Water splashed at their feet as they walked until they entered another small cavern with a small lake at its center. They glanced about and could find no other caves leading out of the cavern.

"This is a dead end. We will have to return to the entrance cave and try the other cave."

It took them twice as long to follow their path back to where they started, and again Jan complained of the cold.

"You could remain outside until we return, Jan. That should keep you warm enough."

He nodded in agreement and stepped back outside into the warm Spring air.

This time Nuada and Mor took the right-hand cave and entered. This one had an upward slope and was drier than the other.

"This looks promising, Mor."

"Yes, although it is much narrower than the other."

After a short time, they again found another cavern — this one was roomier than the first and was dry. Nuada pointed to the back wall where someone had painted figures upon the rock face.

"It looks like we are not the first ones here. Let us look closer and see what we can find."

Mor was the first to find an old stone spear point, and it looked like that would be all they would find.

"My thoughts were correct. We could hide all the village people here if raiders were to return to the area."

"Nuada! Look over here." Mor was pointing at another small cave that led back into the hillside. "We must see where that one goes also."

The pair, upon reaching the cave mouth, felt a warm breeze blowing into the cavern.

"This is interesting. Let us see what it is all about," Nuada said.

Again they entered into the tight confines of the new cave. It climbed faster than the first path, and at points they had to crawl over obstructions. Still the breeze came fresh into their faces. Then with suddenness they were in the second cave's entrance, high on the ridge and overlooking the valley and its lake.

"This is better than I hoped. We have a place to defend those within and can use surprise against any attack." Mor's smile answered Nuada, and he nodded in agreement.

Mor said, "Let us see if there is a way down from here and find Jan."

Nuada nodded in agreement, and the pair stood on the small lip of the cave mouth and looked around. "Here. That looks like a way off this cliff, Mor."

Mor followed Nuada, and they began the tricky climb down. It took only a few minutes, and they were off for the first cave and Jan.

It took only a few minutes to return to the first cave where Jan sat outside on a rock, looking into the open mouth. Nuada motioned to Mor with a finger to his lips, and he moved forward upon the unsuspecting Jan. Steps away Nuada said, "Are you waiting for someone?"

Jan jumped at the unexpected question and turned to face Nuada. "Are you trying to scare an old man to death, my friend?"

"I was only having some fun. Are you all right?"

"I will be when my heart slows again."

The trio laughed, and they gathered all of their supplies for the return to the village. Mor then said to the pair, "I would like to walk all of the ridge around this valley and see what other surprises we could find."

Both Nuada and Jan nodded in agreement, and then Nuada said, "We will save it for another day. But it would be important for us to do so."

The trio set off in the direction of the village but turned toward the meadow where the crops were to be planted in the next few weeks. They stopped at the edge of the field and looked at the overgrown weeds from the Spring rains.

"Our old wooden plow will take weeks to make this ready for planting," complained Mor.

"Perhaps not," said Jan. "If Nuada could face the plow with his metals, my old ox could pull it and save much time in the process."

Both Nuada and Mor looked at Jan and then at each other. "I could do the metal work in a short time," Nuada said.

Then the trio all laughed together at the same time and turned on their steps to head back to the village.

Entering the village from the backside near the ridge, they stopped at the outbuilding for the animals as Jan wanted to check on his ox. Nuada and Mor looked in on the horses and were pleased with their condition.

"This Winter has been easy on all of us," Mor said, and Nuada agreed. After they collected Jan again, they set off for their homes.

Wolf was outside when the trio arrived at Nuada's house and came bounding for some attention. He jumped up on Nuada and began to wash at his face while his tail wagged in a random manner, which the others had to avoid.

"He is glad to see you today, Nuada."

"Yes. He is glad of the warmer weather and the ability to run at will now."

"Are you not afraid that he might run off now to seek a mate of his own?"

"If he does, I am sure he will return. However, if he does not, I am happy for his company and wish him well, as we share a common bond with the world and with the exploration of it."

Mor patted Nuada on the back and waved a farewell to the pair as he set out for his own house. Nuada and Jan entered after Mor disappeared from sight and found Nuada's mate sitting at the table with the child. Nuada looked at them with fondness and said to his mate, "I think it is time to name our child, wife. What think you?"

"I think it is time, husband. What name do you think would be in his favor?"

"How does Iolair sound to you?"

"The Eagle fits his manner. Perhaps it is an omen of his potential."

"Then he will be Iolair from this time forward. What think you, my son?"

The child looked up at his father and snuggled back to his mother. "I think he likes his name, husband."

Jan watched the conversation and smiled at the family. He missed the chance to have his own and felt empty inside. "You are both very lucky, and this boy will appreciate the love you have for him."

Nuada smiled and laughed at Jan's remark. "Now let us work on the design for the new plow, my friend."

They turned their attention to the appointments of the design while Nuada's mate prepared their evening meal. Hours later after eating and the design worked out on a skin parchment, they said good night and sought out their dreams in sleep.

Nuada again dreamed of Creatrix and visited him in his place in the sky. Creatrix said to Nuada, "I am pleased with you and your family. Your friends have also proved worthy. But understand that I must give you challenges that will move you forward to your potential. Be ready for what I send your way and do not be dismayed."

Nuada awoke early the next morning as was his custom and thought on the words of Creatrix. He was in deep thought when Jan arose and greeted him. "Why the serious look this morning, Nuada?"

"A dream only, my friend. I talked with the creator last night, and his words seem to be troubling to my mind."

"Anything that I can help with?"

"No. It is something that I must face and understand alone."

Jan nodded in understanding, but he did not. Nuada arose and took Wolf for his morning run. The wind had picked up overnight, and clouds scudded overhead, portending more rain.

Nuada thought, "I cannot go to the forge building today."

He had to find something to do to shake Creatrix's words from his mind. Calling Wolf he returned inside his house and again settled at the table. Jan still sat at the table working on another drawing.

Nuada said, "It looks like rain again, and I must postpone the work at the forge."

"Why not take the drawing of the new plow to Mor and see if he can begin the wood structure that will hold of your metal blade?"

"Perhaps, but that will only be a simple distraction. I need to do something that will take my mind from my worries."

"Then do some more carving. There are many things you have not started."

Nuada nodded and scratched at Wolf's head, then glanced again at his mate and child.

"What I do is for them. I only wish to protect them from the things I cannot see."

"Do not think of what you cannot understand. When the time comes, you will understand and overcome that which threatens at the moment. You are strong in that way."

Nuada again nodded and rose from the table. "I shall see Mor about the plow and return later."

His own thoughts were confused by Nuada's troubles.

Outside the rain began to fall lightly, and the wind had a chill in its gusts. Nuada made his way to Mor's house and knocked at the door. Mor greeted him, and they began to talk of the plow design, but Mor noticed Nuada's distraction and asked about his problems.

Nuada told of his dream with Creatrix and how it bothered him. He also told of Jan's thoughts on the matter. "Your creator has plans for you that you cannot begin to understand. Time will bring an understanding of his wishes and what he has in store for you. Let it go and do what you know best."

Somehow Nuada felt more comfort with Mor's words than with Jan's, and he began to relax. They talked of changes needed within the village.

Before midday Nuada returned home and set his mind to another carving. This time it was of an owl to be placed upon the table. He found and selected a piece of wood that had lines that pleased his eyes, and he set out to create and find distraction in his work.

He began to carve at the wood, and he glanced up at his family and then back at the wood. "I should do an eagle for my son instead of an owl," he thought and changed his mind set to do the eagle.

Jan looked up from his drawings and noted Nuada. He smiled and returned to his work. After a while, Jan stood and stretched. "I see you are taking my advice, my friend. What subject are you working on?"

"I was going to carve an owl, but I thought of my son and his naming, and I am going to create an eagle to honor him."

"What a wonderful idea. He will not remember this day, but that will be a reminder."

Nuada continued to work at the carving until his evening meal was set at the table. He put the work aside and noticed that his worries had disappeared with the attention he had placed in his carving. He smiled inwardly and felt much better with his life.

Dawn broke with the ringing of thunder, and Nuada awoke with the sound of the wind seeping under the eaves of his house. He dressed quickly and stoked the fireplace to warm the others. Wolf joined him and wanted out to do his business. Nuada walked to the doorway and was greeted with a strong gust of wind blowing ice pellets, which stung any exposed skin. The clouds scudded black and restless from the northwest, obscuring anything more than a hundred yards away. Wolf returned quickly and wanted back inside and away from the weather. Nuada stepped inside and had to use his shoulder to close the door against the strength of the wind. The commotion awoke Jan and Nuada's mate, and they hurried to his side and asked of the noise.

"This is a storm that I have never seen the strength of before," he said.

Jan changed the topic and asked again about the carving of the eagle.

Nuada replied, "I have nothing of my father to remind me of his ways. This will be for my son to remember of me."

"Why do you have nothing of your father, my friend?"

"He died when I was very young. They said that he fell into a split in the ice on the glacier near where we lived while hunting. But I have no memory of the happening."

"I am sorry that you did not know of your father or the things that he could have taught you. But you have turned out well for not knowing him."

"He was respected by the other members of our tribe, and they took me in and taught me of the things of life and the knowledge of Creatrix. I feel no loss at not knowing of him because of the others."

"Your son will never be in that position, Nuada. He will grow to understand of you and your love for him."

"I hope that will be the case, Jan. And I also hope he gets to know of you also."

Again an extremely close clap of thunder sounded nearby, and the pair became quiet and stared up at the roofline. Nuada's mate sat near the fireplace and held their child close. Worry lined her face as she too looked up as if seeing the weather outside. Wolf kept her and the child company as was his custom, but he was restless also.

Jan remarked, "Let us hope this storm passes quickly, so that we can get our work done."

Nuada nodded and again began to work at his carving, leaving Jan and his mate to do of their things.

Near midday Nuada stopped and took Wolf for another run. Outside, if anything the storm was stronger, and he did not linger in its grasp. The stinging ice had changed to solid rain, but the wind continued with its intent to do damage to things not prepared for it.

Jan ceased with his drawings and inquired of the weather, which Nuada told him of.

"We cannot stop of it. We can only wait and repair of its damage when it is done."

Four days passed before the storm began to blow itself out although the wind remained strong. The men of the village were finally able to go outside and check for damage and see if the animals were harmed in the storm. Things within the village area were found to be secure, including the stable and its animals. After feeding of the livestock, they began to venture about the valley to see if anything else had been damaged. The meadow for the crops was found to be flooded and unworkable. Some trees had blown down from the wind, but they could be used for building or firewood. Nuada himself set off for the forge to check upon it but stopped by the lakeshore to look at the island. The island appeared much smaller due to the massive amount of rain that had fallen. But he did not venture out to the island at this time. He continued on to his forge and found that one wall had collapsed under the wind, but again damage inside was not to be found. He then set off for the valley entrance near where he had fought the raiders, which seemed so long ago. The stream bed that allowed the water to exit the valley was a torrent of white water and debris that rose over the pathway that turned Nuada back to the village.

Stopping to talk with Mor, Nuada told of the damage to the forge building and asked of other repairs to be done. Mor said that nothing else had any damage although the planting of the crops would be a while because of the flooding. They talked a little more of the storm before Nuada said his farewells and returned to his house.

Inside his house, Nuada shed many layers of clothing and still felt warm because of the massive temperature drop outside compared to before the storm had struck. Jan sat huddled near the fireplace with a heavy fur draped around his shoulders. Nuada's mate stood nearby, with their child standing and clinging to his mother's leg.

"That boy grows bigger and stronger every day, wife. Before we know, he will bringing girls home for us to meet."

"It will be many years, my husband, before we are at that point, and you have much to teach him before it happens."

Jan looked up and said, "You two sound like you are older than your years. Perhaps it is time you thought of another child for him to keep company."

Nuada smiled, and his mate blushed at the comment from Jan. "It is something to consider, my friend."

Nuada sat at the table and considered returning to his work on the eagle carving, then shrugged his shoulders and made up his mind to let it be for another day or two.

"Jan?" Nuada called. "I may need help at the forge, as it needs repair before I can do more work on the village projects."

"If you need my help, only ask, and I shall be there."

The rest of the day was spent with more talk of the weather and the damage caused because of it. With the setting of Creatrix in his form as the sun, Nuada felt exhausted and fell asleep quickly. The others did the same.

Another week followed, much as the same before. Nuada returned to his carving, Jan to his drawings, and Nuada's mate with her household chores. The weather outside continued to improve and warm up. Things began to dry, and the men of the village again became restless. Work on the outdoor cooking area resumed, and some repairs to the houses were done.

Nuada finally finished his carving of the eagle and placed it on the table for everyone to admire — especially his son, who was still too young to appreciate the carving. Nuada's mind returned to his forge and the repairs that needed to be done. The metal work for the plow had to be completed soon, as were other projects that they had planned over the Winter.

Jan noticed the mind set of Nuada and asked about going to the forge. "Perhaps tomorrow we could start the repairs for your forge building and do some of the new expansion that you talked of."

Nuada smiled at Jan's inquiry and said, "I will talk to Mor today and find if he is able to help us. If he says yes, we will set out for the forge at daybreak."

Nuada left the house to seek out Mor and found him at the outdoor cooking area, setting stone for the patio walls. He told of his plans to seek help for the repairs to the forge, and Mor quickly agreed to help.

"I want to bring the young man I told you of, the one who could learn of you and your ways with metal."

Nuada agreed and asked for Mor to point out this young man.

Mor said, "Come, I will have you meet of him."

He led Nuada around to the backside of the wall where the young man was working at lifting a large stone to the back of the fireplace. "A'Chreag! Come meet of Nuada and your new teacher of the metals that he works with."

The two eyed each other up and said their hellos, each wary of the other. The young man was strongly built for one so young, and Nuada could see the possibilities for his strength. "I see that you are not afraid of hard work. Do you want to try your hand at working metal?"

"Yes, Nuada. I have seen what you can do, and I want a chance to try my skills with it also."

"Then it is done. Tomorrow we have repairs to do on the forge building, and when that is completed, I will begin to teach you." They clasped each other's forearm and laughed at the agreement.

Mor walked Nuada back to his house, talking of the young man, and they lingered outside talking about things to come in the next few weeks. Finally Mor departed for the work still going on at the cooking area, and Nuada stepped inside to tell Jan of the news about the young man.

They talked about the young man for awhile and then Jan showed Nuada some new drawings. Wolf came over to smell at the pelt drawings, snorted, and curled up at Nuada's feet. He reached down and scratched Wolf's head and said, "He is ready for warmer weather too. I think we will take him with us tomorrow."

The next morning dawned bright with a hint of warm temperatures. Nuada and Jan met up with Mor and A'Chreag at the outdoor cooking area, and the four set out for the forge. Upon arriving Nuada showed the damage to the building and how he wanted to modify it to increase its usefulness. They set to work moving stone and wood timbers that were damaged in the storm and plotted the increase in size of the structure. At midday they stopped to eat and began to talk about other things that the village required of them. A'Chreag showed his cautious side and was thoughtful about the ideas that they brought forth. He did render his thoughts, and they were not scoffed at by anyone. They treated him as an adult of the village, and Nuada studied how the young man thought and was pleased with him.

Nuada took Mor aside and asked if he thought that A'Chreag could build the new plow by use of the drawings that Jan had created. Mor said he could and that he was a talented artist with wood who could be trusted to render fine work that would last.

They began to pack for the trip back to the village when Nuada told A'Chreag that he wanted him to build the new, wooden structure of the plow and asked how long he thought it would take to build.

A'Chreag answered, "Give me three days, and it will be complete."

Nuada nodded and smiled at his brave answer. "Then start on it tomorrow, and I will continue to finish the work here." The men then began the walk back.

The next day only Nuada and Jan returned to the forge building. Mor stayed behind to do more work on the cooking patio, and A'Chreag started the work on the new plow. The roof was Nuada's first priority for the forge, and he and Jan worked at it throughout the day and had it completed before sunset.

"We have done much in a short time, Nuada. What is to be done tomorrow?"

"I need to complete the arrangement of the interior for my new tools and tables. You may stay at the house tomorrow, if you wish."

"No. I want to return with you and help if I can. The Winter has also made me restless, and the warmth helps to ease the pain in my bones."

"I understand. Your help will be appreciated."

They began the walk back to the village, with Wolf running ahead of them and catching a rabbit on the run.

"He too finds the warmth good, my friend." Nuada smiled and called Wolf back to them.

Soon they entered of the village and paused at the cooking area, where they had raised a sun shelter that day while the pair was gone.

"This is going to be most welcome to the women of the village," Jan commented to Nuada, to which he only nodded and was appreciative of the skill shown by the construction.

Mor saw the pair standing nearby and joined them. "What do you think of our work, Nuada?"

"It shows of your skills, my friend. How is A'Chreag coming with the plow?"

"The main frame is complete, and he is now working on the small wheels for it."

Jan nodded and said, "We will not need to change the harness for my ox, as that was part of the design. It should work well."

Nuada added, "It looks like all of our work is coming together. The forge building is nearing completion, and I will soon be back at work there."

Then Mor said, "Perhaps we should have a feast for the village here at our new cooking area."

Nuada nodded and said, "Yes. Something to mark the changing of the seasons and another year of good things to come."

It was agreed that in three days they would come together for the feast. That would give them time to complete the work on their projects. Nuada and Jan said their farewells and started for home. Wolf was waiting outside and greeted the pair in his usual manner.

The day of the feast dawned bright and warm; music was being played, and even the children knew that it was a special day. The new plow was used as a centerpiece, and much discussion was held about it. During the afternoon, Mor caught Nuada's attention, and they began talking about a new building to be used as a woodworking shop for year-round projects. Between them they thought that it should be placed across from the first house and that they should use stone in its construction. The paving of the roadway in front of the houses was also brought up. Mor made a statement that he would gather the other men and put these things before them. Nuada agreed with this approach, and then the pair rejoined the rest of the village people and began to lose themselves in the rite of their Spring party.

Late in the day after much beer had been consumed and the meal had filled their bellies, Mor began his rounds of the men of the village and tried to influence them to his and Nuada's thoughts about the new woodworking building and the paving of the road in front of the houses. Most came around to the new ideas, and then the discussion turned to the plowing of the meadow and the planting of the Summer crops. Nothing was said about the thoughts of Nuada from the Winter, where he expressed his concern about the village safety and increasing the people of the village. For the most part, it was a good day to set out the future plans for everyone.

At the setting of Creatrix in his form as the sun, everyone departed for their homes and a welcome sleep. Nuada entered his house with his mind still busy with things that the village would need in the future. He sat at the table — long after his family and Jan had gone to sleep — deep in thought. He could not get over the stubbornness of the men and how hard it was to get them to accept new ideas. Morning found Nuada asleep at the table, and Jan awoke him and asked of this strange thing.

"I was trying to understand of the men of the village and why they are so unwilling to see what the village needs to grow."

"They will come around to your way of seeing things, my friend. It will only take some time or an event to shake them out of their ways."

"I am afraid that an event will come too soon, and they will be too late to respond. Our way of life here is such that something like that may put an end to the village."

"Go to your forge and lose yourself in the things you know best. I will talk with Mor about your concerns, and we will see what we can do for you."

Nuada nodded and stood and stretched. His body ached from sleeping at the table, and he called for Wolf. Together they stepped outside. The late Spring air was warm, and a slight breeze greeted them. He was not hungry, and soon he and Wolf departed for the forge.

After Jan had eaten, he sought out Mor and told him of Nuada and his thoughts. While they were holding their conversation, A'Chreag appeared and asked of Nuada. Jan told him he was at the forge and that he should join him. He nodded and set out in that direction. The two men watched him leave, and Mor said, "He will be good for Nuada. They are both driven and skilled craftsmen."

A'Chreag found Nuada sitting and staring at the worktable in the forge building and asked if anything was wrong.

"No. I had a bad night of sleep, and worries that I had created in my mind bothered me."

"What can I do for you today? Are we going to build something new?"

"I do not have enough ore to start any new projects today. Let us do some rearranging of the work area, and tomorrow we will set out to find some new ore sources."

The sun was low on the mountains above the valley when Nuada and A'Chreag finished for the day and began their return to the village. They agreed to meet at the stable in the morning and parted ways in front of the first house. Jan was waiting for Nuada outside of his house and reported that Mor and himself had talked to the other men some more about the security. They had finally given in to the new ideas, and work on a palisade wall and gate would begin with the construction of the new woodworking building. Nuada would need to make new hinges for the gate and other hardware. Nuada smiled broadly and said that he and A'Chreag were going to look for ore in the morning, and then he would start on the needed hardware. Jan smiled inwardly and knew this was what Nuada needed and that it answered many of his problems. Inside the house, Nuada's son was standing, and when he saw his father, attempted to walk to him. Nuada picked him up and held him close. "Iolair, you are growing so fast, and I am missing much of your new adventures."

The rest of the evening was a family affair, and it was late when they all settled in for the night.

The next morning Nuada hurried to the stable, only to find A'Chreag already there. He had harnessed three horses and had mounted baskets along their flanks. Nuada was stunned by his early rising and the preparations of the horses. "You make me look like a laggard and you the master, A'Chreag."

"I am only trying to anticipate your needs, Nuada."

"Very well. We will start, and I will show you where I have found the ore for copper in the next valley. When we have finished with that, I will take you to the other site of the tin ore where I battled the raiders of your other village. Then tomorrow I will teach you of the metals and how to mix them."

Nuada led the way to the forge with A'Chreag following with the horses. They stopped at the forge only shortly to retrieve some picks and shovels for the work ahead, and then they pushed on to the stream and crossed to the other side before leaving their valley and entering into the next. Two hours later they were at the site of the copper ore.

"Tell me, A'Chreag, how do you find of copper ore deposits?"

"I do not know, Nuada. Tell me of this."

"Look for green water or the stain upon the other rocks around the ore site. Look about you and see of this."

A'Chreag did so and nodded at the ease of such a discovery. "I would not have thought to look in such a manner. The truth is in what you say."

"This is an easy one. Other ores are harder to find without knowing what you are looking for. Let us begin our work, and I will show you other wonders."

They climbed a short distance up the hillside where Nuada had claimed ore before, and they set to work with the picks to dislodge the copper. Hours later with the horses' baskets full, they started to return to the forge. "We will make one more trip today before we go home, A'Chreag."

Back at the forge building, they unloaded the ore next to the outside smelter that Nuada had created and stopped to eat a small meal. Nuada asked more questions about A'Chreag's earlier life and where he had learned so much in his short years. The answers were given without question by A'Chreag. Then they began their return to the next valley again.

As before they went to work, which seemed to go even faster than before, and again returned to the forge with the sun still high in the afternoon sky.

"You have made my work much easier, A'Chreag. Never before have I had this much ore at one time."

"It was not so much my work as the horses that did the carrying for us."

"Even so you were a big part of the result today. Thank you."

They began their return to the village but stopped at the lakeside to wash before entering the village.

"This water is still cold from the Winter," said Nuada, who shook the water from his hair.

"Yes, but it still feels good after the work of the day."

Laughing the pair set out again, and as they approached the village site, they found the men of the village digging a trench across the path into the village. Mor looked up from his position in the trench and called to Nuada. "This is the foundation for our new defensive wall."

"I had not thought that you would begin so soon. Why?"

"It was fresh in their minds, and I pushed to get it done before they could complain again. How went your day with A'Chreag and the finding of your ores?"

"It went very well. He is a hard worker and is quick to learn. Right now he is returning the horses to the stable for a good rubdown and feeding. Come by my house when you are through and share some beer with me."

"Gladly, my friend. What have you planned for tomorrow?"

"We have yet to bring in the tin ore to make the bronze and begin the smelting process."

"So, you have yet another full day of work at the forge."

"Yes. Unless you have need of me here."

"No. Do what you do best. In a few days, I could use of you and your skills."

"Very well. I shall see of you in a short while for that beer." Nuada took his leave and again started for his house.

Passing by the new cooking area, Nuada saw of his mate and Jan with others of the village women; the cooking fires were aglow, and they were working busily at preparing the evening meal for their men. Nuada diverted himself and sat at one of the new tables. Jan saw him and walked over to see how his day went.

"You are home early. Your day went well then?"

"Yes. One more day, and I can start working the forge again."

"Good. The women have been talking about the plowing and planting that is to start in a few days. Then everyone will be busy again. They are looking forward to it."

"Good. The Winter gives us a rest, but we need of the labors to bring life into the village."

"How true, my friend. Have you seen of the new wall trench the men are constructing?"

"Yes. I had not thought that it would begin so soon, but Mor is very persuasive."

"That he is. But he would not have of my help in that labor. Perhaps I am too old after all."

"He was only looking out for you, my friend."

"Possibly. But I need to work also and share of this village."

"Let me think on this matter and find something that fits your knowledge and skills."

Their conversation was interrupted by Nuada's mate and child. "Take this boy, husband. He is a handful today, and your strength is needed to teach of this."

"Iolair. What bothers you my son?" Nuada said as he picked up the boy and held him close.

"Da!" the child cried and hugged his father.

"He spoke!" Nuada turned and looked at his mate and then Jan. "When did this start?"

Nuada's mate said, "About a week ago. You have not noticed?"

"No. Other things have been on my mind. Perhaps I am a poor father after all."

"No. Your concern has been of the village, husband. It would have been easy to miss."

The look of concern on Nuada's face changed suddenly to a large grin, and he laughed loudly. The boy leaned back and touched his father's face and smiled with him.

"Watch of him, and I shall return soon to feed of you both. Jan, you can help of me."

"As you wish," Jan said and stood to go with her. "Nuada, you are a very lucky man."

After eating and spending some time with his family, Nuada soon remembered that he was to meet with Mor. "I have a meeting with Mor," he told his mate and Jan, then stood to go.

"Will you be long?" Nuada's mate asked.

"No. We will be at the house." Nuada waved as he left their company and decided to check where they were working on the trench first. A few short steps, and he found Mor still working where he had left him. "If you dig any deeper, I shall not be able to find of you, Mor."

"Nuada! Am I late? I had lost all track of the hour."

"No. I stopped and shared of my meal with my family."

"Then help me out of this hole, and we will talk and drink of your beer."

Nuada reached over the edge and pulled Mor up and out of the cut he was working on.

Mor tried to brush the earth from his clothes but was not very successful in his actions. Nuada laughed at his motions and said, "You will not remove of that without a wash, my friend."

"Then lead me to your beer. I have worked up a great thirst."

The two men set out for Nuada's house laughing. Their friendship was showing for all to see if they only looked.

Outside of the house, they sat upon a bench and talked of all that was going on before Nuada went inside to retrieve the promised beer. Many drinks later, Mor was on the verge of falling asleep from his labors and the fine beer, and Nuada walked him home. Upon returning to his house, he was greeted by Jan and his mate and child, who had just arrived from the cooking area. "How went your meeting with Mor?"

"It went well, although I fear I gave him too many beers for he was almost asleep when I walked him home."

"Then it was a very good day for him." Both men laughed at that thought.

It was an early night for all as they all had heavy work the next day.

Nuada arose early, as was his nature, dressed, and set out for the stable, where again A'Chreag was waiting with the horses harnessed.

"You do yourself proud, A'Chreag. I do not know how I am to be here before you unless I spend the night here."

"Then that is how it will have to be, Nuada." Both laughed at the inside joke and set out for the forge building.

Again they stopped only shortly to pick up the tools needed and started out for the tin ore site. They found the waters much lower than the day before in the stream that left the valley. They crossed out of the valley and within half an hour were at the ore site.

"Here, A'Chreag. See of the white mineral that shows above the earth on this rise. I found it by accident when I fought the raiders."

"Show of me the site of the battle. I have heard of the story, but being here brings out many questions of how it came to be."

"I stood over there and challenged them. When they began to rush at me, Creatrix, the creator, sent a bolt of lightning that struck of me in the back, and the flame of it rushed down my blade and took of their heads. That is where they were," he said, pointing below the rise.

"It is a wonder, Nuada. Were you hurt?"

"No. Although my hair changed color from brown to red after it had happened."

They began to mine the tin, and two hours later, the baskets of the horses were full. They returned to the trail for the forge. Nuada stopped short and sniffed of the air and then turned to look back in direction of the old village. "Look, A'Chreag! Smoke from the old village. I wonder if the raiders are returning again."

"What do we do, Nuada?"

"I will stay here and watch. You will stop at the forge and drop the ore, then return to the village to warn the others. Go to Mor. He will know what to do."

A'Chreag did as he was told, and he sought out Mor as he was instructed. He found him working in the trench, and after telling of what Nuada said, Mor gathered up the men of the village, and they set out to where the smoke was spotted by Nuada.

"Nuada! What have you found out about the smoke?"

"Nothing new. But I have a feeling that it is not good for us. We are not prepared to fight or defend the valley and our homes."

"I agree. What plan have you for this?"

"I think we should seek them out as far from our homes as possible. This would keep our women and children safe. Did you bring the weapons? What about the new bows and shafts?"

"I have it all."

"Then I shall scout out ahead of the others and find if danger awaits us."

Nuada gathered of the weapons he would need and set out toward the village and the smoke he had been watching. The others would follow after about fifteen minutes to allow him time to find if there was any danger. After an hour and a half, Nuada had seen nothing. He quickened his pace, and his mind became even sharper of any movement. Sounds of the quietest nature filled his ears as he moved forward. He became the hunter.

By late afternoon, he approached the old village. Nothing sounded out of the normal. He watched for movements within the village. Moving around by the old stable, he saw a small, smoky campfire. Still nothing moved. He sat on his haunches and waited. After awhile he became bored with waiting and started to move forward again. Something moved within the stable. He stopped and held his position. He drew his bow and followed the movement. Slowly Nuada lowered his bow and called out to them. "You in the stable! Who are you, and what do you want of this place?"

The four of them were startled by Nuada and his challenge and started to turn back. The man turned to answer Nuada.

"My name is Beag. I work in stone, and my family and I were only seeking shelter."

"My name is Nuada, and we were attacked by raiders here last year. I mean you and yours no harm. May I approach and talk of you?"

"Come and share of our small meal, and we will talk."

As Nuada approached, he studied the small family and noted the strength of the man. "I must warn of you that the men of our village are nearby. We were worried of who you were and chose to find of any intruders outside of our new village."

"I understand of your caution. That is the reason we are traveling; raiders from the north attacked of our village and destroyed our homes. We were seeking a new place to live in peace."

The conversation carried on for more than an hour before Mor and the other men of the village entered the old village. Nuada took Mor aside and told of the man and his family and thought it would be good to bring them into their village. "He has skills we could use and would be an extra hand in the new building projects. He only seeks shelter and safety."

Mor agreed, and they sought out the man and asked him to join of them.

Beag agreed almost instantly to join the village. "My children and mate have need of company and safety."

They helped gather the things of Beag and his family and began to move quickly away from the old village and its memories. With that they made camp at the same site where the original men of the old village had camped when they left before.

With the coming of Creatrix as the giver of light the next morning, they moved quickly again to their homes and the new village. Nuada paused at the forge building to leave his weapons that he had taken with him before moving on and following the rest of the group. He found everyone at the cooking site and joined in their conversation. Again Mor sought Nuada out, and the talk turned to where the new people would live. Mor said, "All of the houses are full now. Where will we put them?"

Nuada thought for a minute and then said, "We could put them up at my old house on the island or perhaps at the cave we explored."

"That's a good idea. Let us put it to them and see what they say."

The pair pulled Beag aside and told him of their thoughts and asked which he would prefer as temporary shelter until more houses could be built.

Beag responded by asking to see each of the sites, and the three men set out for the sites. The first stop was the island, and Beag was not too thrilled at its prospects, so they again set out for the caves. Stopping outside of the main cave, they looked up at its opening and the old rock fall outside of it. Beag said, "It will need of some work to enter, but let us look inside."

Inside they noted its cold temperature, and Beag shook his head. "It is much too cold for my family."

Nuada told him of the upper cavern and how much warmer it was and the fact that the lower cavern held water to drink and bathe with. Beag said, "Show it of me."

Nuada led the way into the lower cavern and its pool of water, and then they returned to the main cavern and onto the upper cavern. Beag was surprised at the size and warmth of this place. "Why is this room warmer than below, Nuada?"

"Come and I will show of you." Leading Beag to the back wall and the other cave portal, he said, "Feel of the warm air that comes in through here."

"Is this another entrance? Where does it lead?"

"There is another cave opening above, but it is too steep for entry. We thought of it as a place to defend the others in case of a raid."

"Show it of me."

They climbed through the narrow cave into the upper cave opening, where Beag said, "I can open the cave portals on both ends and make this a livable space. This will do for us."

Then Mor said, "Then it is yours until we can build more houses in the village."

Nuada nodded in agreement, and the three set out for the village again and their evening meal. They arrived back at the cooking area, where everyone had gathered and talked of the plowing of the meadow on the morrow. Jan had had too much of the beer and sat and giggled at the slightest joke, but the people of the village admired his skills and friendship, so they let him be. Mor poked Nuada in the ribs and said, "He will sleep good tonight, as will we all. Let us drink of this fine beer before we say good night."

Music and food, along with the beer, passed freely throughout the evening, and it was late when Nuada and his mate said good night and half carried Jan home.

The sun had been up almost two hours before Nuada stirred from his sleep. He felt rested and far calmer than in a long time. Jan stirred from his sleep when Nuada came down from his sleeping loft. Jan held his head and licked at his lips in thirst. "I think I took too much of the fine beer last night." Nuada nodded and smiled at his appearance.

"Come, wash of yourself and eat something. There is work to be done, and I think your great ox is already at work without you."

Jan did as he was told, and a half hour later, the pair set out for the meadow. Nuada had been right about the work being done and watched as Jan took over the reins of his ox. Looking about Nuada failed to see Mor or many of the men here and asked about them. He was told that they were working in the village on the wall. Nuada set out again for the village, and when he arrived, he found them working at the wall ditch with a fever he had not seen before in them. Finding Mor he asked of the hurry and was told that the scare at the old village motivated them to do more before it was too late.

Nuada nodded and thanked Creatrix for finding a way, and then his thoughts went to Beag and his family. "Where is Beag, Mor? I do not see of him today."

"He and his family went to work at the cave site. I will build him some furniture when he is ready for it."

"What can I do to help today? Do you want me to dig?"

"No. Go do your thing with the metal ores. We will have need of your skills soon enough."

"What of A'Chreag? Where is he?"

"He left for the forge about an hour ago. He said something about starting the furnace to melt the ores."

"Then that is where I shall be. If you need of me, come."

Nuada again set off for the forge building and to find A'Chreag. The boy was hard at work adding wood to the fire at the outside furnace when Nuada arrived.

"It appears that I am late today, and you have the jump on me again."

"Nuada? I thought you would have been here already and that I would be the one late."

"Not so, my friend." Nuada looked in on the fire and told A'Chreag to let the embers burn down. After another two hours, Nuada looked satisfied with the appearance of the embers. He put A'Chreag to work on the bellows to fan the flames hotter while he added the copper ore into a stone pot above the heat. It took time to melt the ore, and he relieved A'Chreag at the bellows and had him start work upon carving designs of wood, which they would use in the casting room for new tools.

Later Nuada removed the slag from the melted copper and then used a different pot to melt the tin ore. The process continued throughout the day, and at the end, Nuada added the tin to the copper in the right mix and showed A'Chreag how it was done.

"Tomorrow we will begin the casting, using the wood forms that you made today. Now let us clean up this place and return home. I am getting thin without food."

The pair entered the village and noted that the men were still digging the wall trench and stopped to talk with them. "Mor!" Nuada called out, "It is time to stop and eat before we all waste away from this work."

Mor looked up and smiled and said he was ready and reached for Nuada's outstretched arm. Climbing from the trench, he slapped Nuada on the back, and they both laughed. He then turned to the other men and called, "Enough for today. It is time to eat and share some beer."

All of the men were talking among themselves as they entered the cooking area, and the women looked up at them and called a greeting and also a warning to wash first before they would be allowed to eat. Again music began to flow from the gathering as food was set upon the long tables and stories told of the day's work from all. Even Beag and his family showed up to join in the meal.

After eating Nuada sought out Beag and asked of his day at the cave site.

"I have cut twenty feet of the lower cave to the upper one. It is slow going, but I have the need for it."

Nuada asked, "Is it possible to hang a security door in that part of the cave?"

"Yes. I thought of that already and have cut the stone to fit one too."

"Let me know if you have need of my hinges or other hardware that I make at my forge."

"I will have need of them but not for a few weeks. My family and I are camped outside of the cave entrance for now and will be so until I complete the work inside."

"Good. The stone cuttings will come in handy for the paving of the street through the village that we had planned. Has Mor talked to you about the woodworking building that is to be built?"

"A little. He said something about the walls to be built of stone also. Perhaps my skills will be of use."

"That they will be, my friend."

In the days that followed, the crops were planted, Nuada forged many new tools and parts that would be needed, the protection wall trench was completed, and wood poles were being placed upright and backfilled. Beag had finished the widening of the lower cave and had begun on the upper cave while his family moved into the middle cavern. The tailings of Beag's work were put to use on the street in front of the houses, and Summer was only about to begin.

One evening Nuada stopped to admire the changes of the village while he was returning from the forge. Mor saw him and walked over to him, thinking that something was wrong and that Nuada had paused to point out something.

"What is wrong, Nuada?"

"Nothing, Mor. I was thinking of all the changes in the village in the past year. Everyone had gone beyond the expected and poured their hearts into the work."

"It was your inspiration and what was needed."

"Possibly, but you had a lot to do with the inspiration of the people."

They both laughed at the moment and walked toward the cooking area for some beer together.

- SUMMER AND SWEAT -

The warmth of the day started early now that Summer had finally arrived to the valley. The protection wall was now complete, and work had started on the new woodworking building. Beag became the center of the work on the new building, as were Jan's drawings of the structure. In order to not expose the village within the valley, trees were cut in the next valley and hauled with help of the horses back to where they were needed. Nuada and A'Chreag continued to work at the forge building and hauling in new ore supplies when needed. A'Chreag proved a great help and a quick learner and was soon creating work of his own.

In addition to the work going on, the men of the village had also begun to build another house on the other side of Nuada's home. Beag was going to build a house of stone by his own design next to the woodworking building. The placement of the house added to the feeling of a more complete village.

Two new babies were expected within the month, adding to the family feel, as noted by Nuada. His own boy was now walking with more confidence, and he was talking and asking questions of anyone who was nearby. Jan took on the job as teacher to the young, which fit his skills and knowledge. The pace of everyone within the village continued at a hectic fever, knowing that the things they had planned must be done while the weather was good.

When the Summer heat pushed upward, the men of the village took time during the midday to rest and find shade where they could. But their determination did not lag for what had to be done. During this time, Nuada planned a trip of exploration again in the direction of which he had found Jan. A'Chreag was to travel with him, and together they would look for other ore sites and for people with whom to expand the village.

Mor had agreed to Nuada's plan and encouraged him to go, knowing his restless nature. Meanwhile Mor and Jan would have the men of the village practice with the bows and shafts to be prepared if trouble came their way. Nuada had made many new swords and knives for the men, along with his bronze-tipped spears. Some of the women had also shown interest in the weapons, so Nuada had created some that were lighter for them to use.

Meanwhile Beag had almost completed his house, and the woodworking building was done. The other new house was fully framed, and they had started work on the end fireplace and wall. The work on this house would be done when Nuada returned from his travels. The village was growing at a fast pace, and everyone seemed pleased with the results.

Finally after weeks of hard work, Nuada and A'Chreag were in the last stages of preparing for their travels. "Well, my friend, on the morrow we begin our exploration of new lands and the people who live there."

"What can we expect of these people, Nuada?"

"Anything, A'Chreag. Some will be friendly, others not so. Be prepared to fight or smile at the receptions we receive."

"I am not sure how to take that, but I am ready for these things."

The rest of that day was spent with family, as it might be weeks before they returned, if ever.

Nuada awoke very early this new day and packed his horse long before the sun even gave a hint of rising. With the first light of dawn, A'Chreag joined him, and they set out on the path by the forge and out of the valley. As they crossed by the stream that led from the valley, their weapons rattled from where they hung on the horses' backs, due to the rocky ground.

"We must quiet those things, A'Chreag. They could prove to be our downfall if heard by raiders or others like them."

A'Chreag only nodded and set out to secure the noisemakers. Shortly they made a left turn out and away from all they knew. They became alert to noises and visual changes.

Time passed quickly, and they moved with a sureness of the world around them. By nightfall they camped alongside a small meadow with a small stream where they could use of its water. They kept their campfire small and without smoke and ate in silence before bedding down for the first night. The horses were hobbled, fed, and unpacked for the night.

"I feel bad about taking of the horses from the valley," Nuada said to A'Chreag.

"They are not needed now, and we may have use of them," he replied.

They fell asleep with sounds of the forest around them. But Nuada found his sleep visited by Creatrix this night.

"Nuada, awaken and hear of my words."

Nuada awoke in the land of Creatrix and shook the sleep from his mind. "What is it you want this night?"

"Travel one more day in the direction you are traveling, then turn to your left again and follow it until you come to a big river. When you get there, turn right and follow of it."

"What am I to expect to find of this travel?"

"You will meet of some new people that you will embrace and take into your fold. They have need of you and will bring many new skills to your village."

"Am I to protect them of some other danger, or is there another reason of yours?"

"Both. You are my chosen one, and you are proving to have the skills of this."

"I do not feel of this special treatment, nor do the people of my village show of it."

"Trust of me in this matter. It is for you to show the way."

Nuada passed from the land of Creatrix into his own and awoke before the dawn light, the words of Creatrix still within his mind and trying to understand of its meaning. A'Chreag awoke shortly, and again the pair loaded of the horses, broke camp and set off without a word. By mid-morning A'Chreag noticed the troubled look upon Nuada's face and asked of him what it was all about.

"I had a visit with the creator last night, and he told of me what to expect of our travels."

"Will it be good or bad, Nuada?"

"For us it will be good, but we are to find of some new people, and how I deal with them affects of our village."

"I do not see of this."

"Nor do I, but this is what will be."

The pair settled on their path and followed the directions given to Nuada and finally reached the river.

"What now Nuada? I have never seen water this wide or fast-moving before. How do we cross of such a thing?"

"We do not. We are to follow of it, and then we will meet of the new people."

Two more days following the river and fighting the underbrush of the forest that was all around them finally brought them to the promised gathering of people. They were not in a village but more of a traveling encampment of tents. Cautious Nuada entered into the encampment and introduced himself and A'Chreag to the people. They seemed friendly enough and did not question him about why he was there.

But Nuada was of a questioning nature and asked of them, "Why do you travel in this manner? Do you not have a village of your own?"

"We did until raiders from the north took everything, including the seeds for the Spring planting, and then burned our homes to the ground. We have been on the move for the last two years looking for a place of safety."

"Perhaps I can solve that problem for you. Would you be interested in a valley that is secure and is fertile for crops of many kinds?"

"We would! What do you need of us for?"

"We have need of more people with skills that we lack. Although at this time of year, we would not have time to build more houses for you. But we do have a cave that is comfortable and would hold of all of you and protect of you throughout the Winter."

"That would be better than these tents in the Winter. When can we see of this place?"

"Soon. First I must meet of your people and see of their skills and the nature of their minds to make sure they would fit among us."

"Then let me introduce you to the others and hurry the questions."

Nuada looked around and noticed that A'Chreag was showing more interest in a girl of light hair who stood at the edge of the crowd. He walked over to him and pushed him on the shoulder. "You seem lost, and your mind is elsewhere. What do you look at so long?"

"At what age did you find of your mate, Nuada?"

"About your age. Why?"

"I think I have just found mine and do not know how to ask of her."

"Let me see if I can help." Nuada walked back to the man he had been talking to and asked of the girl.

"She is the daughter of our weaver and some think beyond the age to take of a mate because she is headstrong."

"My friend shows interest. What can we do to bring them together?"

"Leave that to me," he said with a smile. "He owes of me many favors."

They walked over to the weaver, and Nuada was introduced after some small talk about moving into Nuada's valley. Nuada pointed out A'Chreag to the man and asked of his daughter as a likely mate.

"I would be glad to be rid of her and her ways. She is beginning to drive me crazy."

"Then let us introduce them and be done with it."

Nuada called A'Chreag over, and the man did the same with his daughter. After talking to both of them, A'Chreag presented the weaver with a knife he had made, and the deal was done; the boy had his mate.

She did not blush as Nuada expected but took A'Chreag's hand, and together they walked away from the group of men to be by themselves.

"May the creator take pity on both of them and give of them a blessed joining," Nuada said.

"I think that is lost on both of them, but we will give of them time to grow together."

Nuada then went on to talk to other members of this clan and found of their skills and studied their nature. By the end of the day, Nuada was satisfied with all he met and told of them that on the rising of Creatrix in the morning, they would set off for his valley.

Dawn arose with a hint of the heat of the day, already testing the group's actions. It only took a short time to take down the tents and pack them on their horses, and they ate a cold meal to start the journey. With Nuada leading and A'Chreag at the rear of the group to hurry those who fell behind, they set out following the river on the same path that Nuada and A'Chreag used coming to them. Even the children knew that something important was happening.

Nuada continued to talk to the people of the clan and was interested in their history and trials. Among the group was a weaver, whom Nuada had met, a rock cutter, two who worked with wood, and two more who were the clan's hunters. The man Nuada met first was truly a farmer and worked with the crops and their seeds. All around they worked well together and had survived all challenges put before them.

By nightfall they turned from the river and stopped for the night in a meadow about a mile from the water. Nuada caught a glance of A'Chreag with his new mate while eating a hot meal before bedding down for the night. He had hopes that the distraction would not put the party in danger and then knew that even this was not of his nature and they would be safe.

The clan did not set up their tents but camped in the open, as it would speed up the leaving in the morning.

Day two began just as warm as the first day, and they set out knowing that it would only get hotter the farther they moved from the river. Following the trail that Nuada had cut from the low-laying brush, they moved steadily forward and made good time, considering the size of the group. The only thing that protected them from the heat of the day was the abundance of the trees over them.

Late in the afternoon a wind began to blow, light at first and stronger as the afternoon wore on. Nuada looked to the north and saw clouds begin to form and knew that a storm was forming. He had the group stop early to prepare for it and saw that they were willing to set up their tents and dig trenches around them, preparing for the rain that would come. Extra ropes were used to tie down the tents, and the animals were secured for the weather also.

The farmer joined Nuada in his watch of the weather and asked, "How many more days to your valley, Nuada?"

"I think we can make it in two more days, but the weather is the question now."

"I see. The people are willing, but children are the concern."

"I agree. We must pause and wait to protect of them."

With that said, a loud crack of thunder pealed in the distance, causing both men to turn toward the sound.

"It may be a long night with this storm."

Another rumble even closer caused both men to seek shelter before it began. The clouds darkened, and the wind grew with a fearfully strong howl that now blew toward the storm front. Before the rain began to fall, hail came down and covered the ground in a whiteness, looking like snow had fallen. Then came the rain, blowing sideways in a torrent of unhealthy wetness. None were caught outside, and they were thankful of their shelter.

Dawn of day three broke with a soft coolness in the air, and again the group broke camp and hurried to gain distance to their new home. The day remained cool throughout, and with evening they were all tired and ready to make camp again.

Nuada had seen little of A'Chreag in the last two days and sought him out before bedding down. He found him with his new mate; they were still holding hands and whispering together when he approached them.

"I see you are still together, and both of you are still alive. That is a good omen of things to come."

"Nuada! Do you have need of me?"

"No. I was just checking of you and how you two were faring."

"We are well and happy. I have been telling of her about the valley and what we do."

"Then I shall leave of you and let you return to your talk." Nuada walked back to the center of the encampment and sat near the fire and pulled a fur around his shoulders and then let his mind wander back to home and his family.

He had only been gone ten days, but it seemed longer. He thought about his family ties that only another married man might understand. He would be glad to see an end to this journey and was thoughtful that it would be his last extended one. He wanted to remain close to home from now on. Only Creatrix could see of that. With that thought, he pulled the fur even closer about him and waited for the sleep that he needed.

Dawn of day four broke cool but clear, and they hurried about preparing for another day of travel. Children's laughter filled the air, and small talk could be heard coming from the women of the camp. Nuada rose and stretched, preparing himself for another day of being the leader and sensing danger where none should exist. After washing of himself, the farmer joined Nuada, and they began the movement of the group.

Two hours later Nuada held the group, sensing smoke in the air coming from the direction into which they would be going. Moving ahead by himself, Nuada scouted the source of the smoke. The air became thick with smoke as Nuada moved even closer.

"This more than a campfire," he thought. Moving now with more caution, he found of the cause. The forest was on fire, and he thought back to the storm, knowing that it was the reason of this fire. He hurried back to the clan and told of the smoke and that it was now necessary to change directions and get as far as possible from its path.

The group turned to the right and away from the fire, still heading toward the valley. The ground began to rise slightly, and the hills could be seen in the distance.

"We are close now," Nuada said to the farmer. "Only another day, and you will see of the beauty of our land."

Again Nuada hurried ahead and climbed a small hilltop and watched for the fire behind them. He felt it would be safe to camp tonight, as the wind from the firestorm had changed direction. Returning to the group, he told them of another campsite ahead where they could camp for the night.

"It is a small meadow with a stream passing through it."

"Did you see of any game? We are beginning to run short of food."

"Yes. Send your hunters ahead and see if they can deliver of a stag."

Farmer did as he was told, and the hunters soon departed in the direction pointed out by Nuada. The rest of the day remained quiet for the group although the birds around them kept the forest filled with their song. Nuada's own thoughts were still filled with thoughts of his family and the changes he would see of the village when they returned. Every time he left the valley, he came back in wonderment of the changes that these people made in so short a time period.

Late afternoon came, and again the clan camped without setting up their tents. Nuada was questioned many times about the valley, with this being close to the last day before they would see it. He tried to describe all the things of the valley, including the lake and the island. He even told of the next valley and the things they had discovered about it. He had their attention all through the evening meal and up until the time that many wandered off to find sleep and dream of their new home.

Nuada awoke again before the dawning of Creatrix and found many others were also awake and eager to begin the last day of travel. Even A'Chreag was up and about with his new mate. They exchanged a few words before going about the business of preparing the clan to move.

Mid-afternoon found the group at the base of the steep ridge that followed the outside of the valleys. Turning left they followed the winding wall of rock and earth; at times the brush and trees blocked the very structure of the ridge from sight, but Nuada knew where it was and led them onward to the stream that marked the entrance into the valley.

The whole group now moved as fast as they could, eager to see of what they had been told. Passing by Nuada's forge building, they could still not see the village where it was hidden in the trees. Only when they were almost upon the outer protection wall did it come into view. Nuada hurried ahead to warn Mor and the other villagers of the group's approach and found them working on the last stages of the construction on the latest house. Everyone in the village came out to greet the newcomers as they approached the wall entrance of the village.

Nuada's mate joined him and gave him a hug, and the boy clung to his father's leg to keep him from leaving again. Nuada reached down and picked up his boy and walked out to the farmer and the others and welcomed them into the village.

This night the clan set camp beyond the last house under construction, and they joined in feasting at the cooking area with a stag brought down by the clan hunters. The next day would prove to be busy for all, and the merriment ended early.

The sun was well up when Nuada awoke, and Jan and his mate had already left the house; only wolf remained and followed him around until they went to join the others.

Outside Nuada stopped first at the site of the next house under construction and found Mor with Jan discussing the final work to be done.

"Nuada! We thought that you would sleep the entire day away," Mor said. "The new people have already been to the cave site and are now looking about the village for future housing sites. Everyone is getting along well, and the new stonecutter has joined up with Beag, and they were talking about how to build new houses that everyone seems to need in a hurry.

"Good. Have you seen my mate and child?"

"They are down at the meadow, working the crops and weeding the rows."

"I have some ideas how we can bring water to the field without carrying it. It would involve using a horse or two to run a wheel that would lift the water into a trough."

"Good. At the midday meal, let us discuss it more, and perhaps Jan can draw the design for us."

"Very well. I think I shall take a walk to the forge. Have you seen of A'Chreag?"

"He was with his new mate, and they were down at the meadow earlier."

"Then I will not bother him today. He will need of some time away from the work we have need of doing."

Nuada departed the pair and set off for his forge and thoughts of what it would need for tomorrow. Walking through the protection-wall portal gate, he saw the two stonecutters in deep discussion and waved as he passed. They returned his wave and returned to their discussions. Outside the gate, Nuada again paused and turned to look back at the village. "The changes are great for the time we have spent on the village. I hardly seem to remember what it was like before," he thought.

He then turned and followed the wall to the lake and the island that was his first home. He stopped and picked up a stick and stirred at the mud alongside the shore of the lake. "What lies ahead for us I wonder?" he again thought. With that thought in his mind, he again turned and moved on to the forge.

Nothing seemed to change at the forge building, and he wandered about it looking what he already knew was there. There was plenty of ore to work with, and his tools stood ready to begin another project. He paused to sweep at some unseen dust on one of his tables. Not really seeing anything, his thoughts remained within the valley and its people. He then turned and began to walk back to where his thoughts held him.

The village people were already gathering for the midday meal, and he sought out Mor and Jan. His mate had not yet returned from the meadow, and he watched for her and his child. He sat at a table, and Wolf curled up at his feet. He greeted all who passed by and passed the time making small talk. A'Chreag and his mate entered the cooking area and joined Nuada.

"I have need of you tomorrow, A'Chreag. But I do not want to take of your time together with your mate."

"I will be with you. What are we to do?"

"There is need of many more hinges and some parts for the new wagons. We have enough ore to do the work, and the smelter is not needed. It will be strictly a casting day."

"Then I will be there early to start the furnace and to prepare the casting forms."

Nuada looked up just as his mate and child entered the cooking area, and he called them over. "Wife, can you look after A'Chreag's mate on the morrow? We have much work to do."

Handing the boy to Nuada, she answered that she would like the company of A'Chreag's mate. Then she said she would go and prepare a meal for them before she had to leave the cooking area. Mor and Jan then approached the small group and sat down.

"What did you want to talk of Nuada?"

"The village is in need of more houses, and we now have the manpower to move ahead with that. Tomorrow I will be making more hinges for the houses and parts for the new wagons. We need of a wagon to haul the cut trees from the next valley, and I think that the stonecutters could remove stone from the path leading there to use in the construction of parts of the houses. This would serve two things and speed of the work."

"I see of your thoughts and will put them to work on these things."

"Give of me two days, and I will join of the tree cutting and help with the start of the houses."

"Good. Your leadership is needed, as well as your thoughts of the village."

"How soon do you think it will take to build of the wagon for the trees?"

"It will take four days and three men to do the work."

"Then set them at it as soon as possible. We must hurry if we are to beat the Winter weather and protect of the people. Another thing comes to mind: We must also enlarge the stable for all our new animals."

"We will find of the time, Nuada. Do not worry."

"That is all I do anymore, my friend." Nuada laughed at his words and was joined by the others.

Mor got up and began to talk to the parties that would be needed for the work and explained of the need for the rush. Nuada remained at his table and held his child close. Wolf rubbed against his leg and was rewarded with a stroking of his head by Nuada.

Farmer walked over to the table and said, "This valley and your people are all you said they would be. Thank you for bringing us here."

"The joining of our peoples was needed by all. But we have much work to do before the Winter closes in upon us. Urge your clan to help in any way that they can to complete the work."

"I will tell of them, and we will do as needed."

"What tools do your people need. I can make of them, and they will last for the work needed."

"I will ask of them for I do not know."

Other members of the village then sought out Nuada at his table, and a long discussion began. Nuada answered as best he could and asked questions of them as well. The midday meal lasted longer than was normal, but questions were answered to everyone's satisfaction. When at last everyone began to depart to finish of their chores for the day, only Nuada remained, more thoughts racing through his mind. He now had a long list of the tools needed and knew that his day tomorrow would be a long one.

At long last, he arose from the table and walked out to the new road in front of the houses; looking about he then started to walk home with Wolf following. After a few steps, he stopped again and looked to the sky and noticed of the warmth of the air and took in a long, deep breath. His ears listened to the noises around him, sounds filled with the hurried need of the village and the calls of the birds.

He thought, "I do not feel a part of here, but the cause of it." He then set out for his house again.

That night he slept deeply and could not remember of any dreams. Morning came early, and he arose with the coming of Creatrix in his form as the sun. He moved quickly and was at the forge building before A'Chreag. He set to work building the fire that would be needed for the casting work and began to carve new molds for some of the tools. Shortly after A'Chreag appeared, and the pair began their work in earnest. Within two hours, they began to pour the first of the castings. All day long they worked at what was needed, and with the shadows of evening beginning to approach, they halted their work and gathered what was completed to take back to the village.

Entering the gate portal, they stopped at the stonecutter's house first and left with him new hammers and chisels, along with a pair of pry bars. Next they entered the cooking area and handed out new axes to the wood cutters.

Finding Mor they gave to him the parts needed for the wagon to haul wood and a bag of new hinges for the houses. Mor said, "You two have been very busy today. These things were not expected until tomorrow or the next day."

"They were needed, and we have many more things yet to build," replied Nuada.

"Do not take on so much at once, my friend. We will complete all things as needed."

Nuada sat at a table and felt the weight of the needs for the village upon his shoulders.

"Mor, my friend, I try to set an example for the others only. But it wears upon me."

"Then slow down of yourself and let others carry the load."

"I cannot do that, you know. I am the one who brought everyone here, and I cannot fail these good people."

"I understand, but you will make of yourself sick and fail that way. Do as I tell of you, and all will be well."

Nuada nodded and placed his head in his hands, worry still on his mind. Mor departed looking back at Nuada, his own thoughts troubled by his friend's mind set.

After a while, Nuada arose and left for his house, hoping to find answers to his troubled thoughts. Sitting in his usual spot before the fireplace, Nuada dozed, and again Creatrix entered into his mind.

"Nuada! Awaken and hear of my words. All things will be as needed. Have no fear of this. I will make of those things that you cannot understand yet. Be the leader you are to be and only watch over those within your valley."

Nuada awoke later relaxed and comforted by the words of Creatrix. Shortly after awakening, his mate and child entered their house, followed by Jan.

Jan said, "I hear from Mor that you are troubled by the amount of work to be done before the weather changes again."

"I was. But again Creatrix settled of my thoughts and worries."

"That is good, Nuada. Now perhaps you can do the job you were brought here for — that is to led these people where they need to be."

"Jan, I will try although my heart is not there yet."

"These people believe in you. You have brought them from war and fear into peace. You are their leader, even if you cannot see of it yourself. It matters not. You are the one they believe in."

Nuada went to bed with these thoughts on his mind and slept comfortably.

The next morning Nuada and A'Chreag met at the front portal gate and returned to the forge and their work. No words passed between them during the walk although A'Chreag looked at him from time to time wondering of his thoughts. This day they continued the work of making new tools and parts that the village could use.

Meanwhile the people of the village went about the work to be done. Trees were being cut in the next valley, and the stonecutters set new stones as foundations for the houses to be built. The women returned to the meadow to care for the food being grown there, and the children, too young to help, remained with Jan to hear of his lessons learned during his travels. Three of the men worked at building the new wagon to haul the trees from the next valley. In all things, work was constant and moving forward.

With the coming of sunset, Nuada and A'Chreag returned to the village. Again at the gate portal, Nuada paused and looked around at the changes that were happening.

"Is something wrong, Nuada?" asked A'Chreag.

"No. Everything is beyond what was expected. Look about you at the changes everyone has made here."

"I see what you mean. We are growing at a fast pace, and we are in need of it."

"Tomorrow find of Mor and see what you can do here in the village. We will not go to the forge for a few days. Now go find of your new mate and relax."

"Thank you, Nuada. I will see of you tomorrow."

Nuada wandered about, looking at the changes and the work progress of the new projects. Everywhere he went, the people waved in greeting and called his name. Some stopped to talk about what they were doing and asked of any new thoughts about the village. Nearing the meadow of crops, one individual pointed out new trees that were found in the next valley.

"What kind are they?" asked Nuada.

"These are apple trees. We can bring them here to transplant where we want them."

"Good. Any extra food source will be well received by the others."

"That is not all. We found of a field of wild oats also."

"Food for the animals and us, that will also be of use."

Nuada continued on to the pass between the valleys, where men were cutting the rock path wide enough for the wagon to be used for the trees being brought into this valley.

"How goes the work, friends?"

"Well enough. We are taking the cuttings into the valley for the stonecutters and their work with the houses."

Nuada glanced at the stone and found no ores that he could use and again moved on. This time his direction changed back toward the caves and the ridge that protected the valley. Stopping outside of the first cave, Nuada found no one in sight and moved down the path to the second cave. Again he found himself alone and started toward the village itself. He had not gone far when he passed others returning from carrying stone into the village. Sweat dripped from their bodies, and the horses showed of the hard work being done. He started to say something and then thought better of it and let them pass.

The new house near Nuada's was now complete, and he paused to look at it. Mor was nearby and waved in greeting.

"What think you of our new house, Nuada?"

"It is a wonderful work of art, my friend. I was thinking that we will need of a cold storage place for the crops when they are harvested. Do you have any ideas about where to place it?"

"We could use part of the woodworking building this year. Then next year we could build a building just for that purpose."

"I can see of that plan. We have so much to do this year."

"Nuada, look across the path to the other side of your house. The stonecutters have already begun the foundations on three houses."

"Good. We are moving ahead doing what is necessary. I am not going to the forge building tomorrow. What can I do here to help?"

"You can help with the tree cutting in the next valley. There is not enough men for the job, and I will send A'Chreag with you."

"Would he not be of more use to the stonecutters?"

"I had not thought of that. Perhaps you are right about him."

"I think his strength and youth would work better there. Also I have a new tool for you. It is called a draw knife for shaping of wood timbers," said Nuada, reaching into his pack.

"Thank you, friend. What we have need of is a tool like a hoe to trim of the large pieces."

"When I return to the forge, I shall make it for you. Have you seen of my mate today?"

"A few hours ago she was at the cooking area. Where she is now, I do not know."

"Then I must leave of you and search her out."

Nuada departed the company of Mor and stopped first at his house, then walked to the cooking area where he found his mate working with some of the other women.

"Nuada! You are just in time to take the boy before he gets more in my way."

Nuada kissed her on the cheek and picked up his son. "What trouble have you been in, my son?"

The boy struggled in his father's arms and then hugged him. Sounds came from the boy that made no sense to Nuada, but it showed of the love between them. Nuada sat at a table and held tight to him, watching his mate work at the evening meal that all would share. A little later others of the village began to wander into the cooking area, and small talk filled the air. Two of the wood cutters joined Nuada and said that they had talked with Mor before entering the cooking area.

"You must show of me what to do tomorrow; it is not my skill."

"You will find of it easy compared to what you do, Nuada. We will leave with the rising of the sun in the morning."

Nuada nodded and turned in time to see the stonecutters enter the area with A'Chreag. He waved a welcome to them, and they sat across at another table talking in a deep conversation about their work. Soon the area was filled with people, and the meal began — beer flowed, and again music filled the air.

After about an hour, Nuada's mate joined him and sat with an exhausted expression upon her face. "What bothers you, wife?"

"The amount of people we now have has raised the amount of work to be done. I am only tired from the work."

"I understand. But we need of these people for friendship and protection. Soon the work load will ease, and we can rest. Tomorrow I will be working with the wood cutters. What of you?"

"They have found of a field of oats in the next valley, and they are ready to harvest. I shall be cutting or stacking of the stocks."

"Do not overwork yourself. Take many breaks and rest from time to time."

"I will try, but we have so much to do."

"I was thinking in the same way until Creatrix talked of me. He will see that all will come together in its own time."

"Come, let us go home and relax while we can."

Nuada nodded, and the family walked to their house and some time alone.

With the rising of the sun, the village came alive again with the work to be done. Everyone seemed to know what to do and where. Nuada still felt confused at his place in the work crews but knew that Mor had made sure the jobs fit everyone's skills. Nuada was given an axe, and he was to trim the trees of their branches. He was surprised at the number of trees already cut and waiting for him to trim. He set about the work and was soon stripped to the waist and sweating heavily from the work. The others followed suit as they too were sweating heavily. About every hour, they stopped to drink of water and talk between themselves. Nearing sunset they stopped and started to walk back to their valley, leaving their axes at the work site. Before leaving Nuada checked the edges for wear and to see if any needed to be sharpened. They were in good order, so he left too.

Nuada stopped at the stream leading into his valley and washed himself of the sweat and dirt from the work of the day. He paused after and listened to the work coming from both valleys. Soon his mate and other women from the valley came up the pathway from their work. Taking his water bladder that he had refilled, he joined her and offered a cold drink of the water.

"How went your day, wife?"

"Long and tiring, husband. And yours?"

"The same. We will sleep well tonight if the pain from the work will allow of it."

They turned and walked together back toward the village holding hands. Along the way, they were greeted by others from the village who also were returning after the work of the day.

"Do you now miss of the old village in the mountains, wife?"

"I have been so busy that it has not been in my thoughts. But I think not."

"We have made something here that will always make it our home. Our son will grow to accept of it also."

"I worry that he spends more time with Jan than us. But he has other children of his age with him too."

"With the coming of the colder weather, he will spend more time with us. And I am sure that he will understand as he grows older."

They found Iolair with Jan at the cooking area. Nuada picked him up and held him close.

"Jan? Has he been good today?"

"I worry that he talks little."

"He is learning. There will be time for conversation later in his life."

Nuada nodded and sat at his table with his son and let the talk around him fill his ears. The wagon for hauling the trees was complete, and tomorrow it would begin its task. The other workers were in need of the trees now, as the foundations for the new houses were complete, and the stonecutters were beginning to build the fireplaces on the end walls of each. One house was different from the others, as its fireplace would be in the center of the house. Mor shouted across the patio at Nuada and came over to talk about the work for tomorrow. They talked for almost an hour as the beer flowed freely. Nuada was glad when his meal came, for he was tired and ready for sleep, like his son already was. Nuada's mate joined him, and after waking the boy, they ate in silence before going home for the night.

Almost before Nuada realized it, the sun was up again for another day of hard work. The family walked to the cooking area and left Iolair with Jan and began the walk back to the other valley and the work to be done. The pair parted at the entrance to the second valley and went to their work sites. Nuada began his chore, and after about a half hour, the new wagon rolled to the work site with the big ox pulling it. The wood cutters had rigged a trio of poles to swing the large trees onto the wagon, and it only took a short time to load and send it on its way back to the other valley. The ox took the strain without complaining as it moved away from the cutting area. Nuada returned to his work of trimming the fallen trees and soon was bathed in sweat again. He stopped shortly to strip to the waist and drink some of the water that he had brought with him.

Just after midday, Mor found Nuada and asked of him to come back to the valley and help with the raising of the framing timbers. Nuada stopped and welcomed the relief of a different job. Picking up his clothes and water bladder, he walked back to the valley with Mor.

"I need to stop at the stream and wash of myself, my friend." Nuada said.

After Nuada washed, the great wagon and the ox passed them on another trip with a pair of trees.

"This has made of the work much easier. Too bad the idea came so late after the other houses," Mor commented.

"We learn, friend. We must think about what is needed and move on from there."

At the home sites, Nuada watched as the builders had again used a trio of poles to lift and set in place the trees where they were needed.

"I have not seen of this part before, Mor. I guess I was too busy at my forge."

"We have done it this way for many generations, and we do not even think of doing it any different."

"What do you want of me to do?"

"We need of your strength to hold lines as we swing them into place. A'Chreag is here too."

Nuada did as he was told to do, and throughout the afternoon, piece by piece, frame by frame, the work continued. Just when Nuada thought they would run out of trees, the ox would come rolling into the construction site and drop off more trees.

With the afternoon closing, people began to return to the valley, and many stopped to look at what had been done with the house before moving on to the cooking area and finding a place to relax. The construction crew was the last to stop for the day, and Nuada felt relief to be able to sit down again.

Day after day, the work continued. Sometimes Nuada was trimming the trees, others he was at the construction site. Time seemed to fly, but all could see the progress and were pleased. Slowly they began to feel the temperatures start to change, as the mornings were cooler and Fall was nearing.

The houses came near to completion, and the roadway in front of the homes was expanded further into the valley, almost reaching the second valley entrance and the meadow where the crops were raised. They had plans to make it reach into the second valley where much of the tree cutting had been done. They also thought to build another wall near that spot for more protection in the future. The people of the valley now talked about things that they thought the village could use, and plans were made to bring them together. Nuada was happy to see the change in their thinking and welcomed the ideas.

Harvest was beginning on the crops from the meadow, and the stonecutters had added an addition to the back of the woodworking building for storage of the grains and other crops that could be used throughout the coming Winter. The hunters had also been busy and had brought in three stags that they had cleaned and hung in the new addition.

Nuada had found some free time and had created a model of the waterwheel for the meadow. Talk was now about the need for a village well and where to place it.

Nuada had not been to the forge building in almost two months and made the walk to inspect the place. He expected to find spider webs everywhere and dust covering his work tables. However, it was not so. A'Chreag had found time to visit and keep everything clean and ready to work when Nuada was ready. Walking back to the village, Nuada sought out A'Chreag to thank him for his work at the forge.

He found A'Chreag at the cooking area with his mate and told of his surprise at the forge building.

"It was nothing, Nuada. When are we going to return to work there?"

"Will you be free tomorrow? We have some tools to make and other parts that are needed."

"I will make the time. I miss of the work there."

- FALL AND FORGIVENESS -

Weeks passed, and the work continued. Nuada kept busy at his forge and smelter preparing for the Winter months. New tools were developed, and other parts for the village were made to ease the people's labor. Within the village, all four of the new houses were completed. Two new wagons were built, and the addition to the stable was done. Trees were still being cut, and the branches were brought into the village to use as firewood. The harvest of the crops from the meadow were in and placed into storage. All things that seemed impossible only a few short months ago were now complete, and a feast was in the planning to celebrate the coming of Winter.

Nuada looked around the village and was pleased at the work done by his people. "We have come together to do the work necessary and have completed it," he thought to himself. Mor and the farmer were standing nearby and noticed the look upon Nuada's face and walked over to talk to him.

"What think you, Nuada?"

"Only that these people have done the impossible, and it makes me happy."

"It was through your inspiration and thinking that we came together."

"I may have been the inspiration but not the reason that they have done this. Both of you pointed the way for them."

"Then let us drink a beer together to have such good people around us."

The trio of men walked to the cooking area, where many of the people had gathered, and they poured a round of beer to mark the occasion. Music filtered through the area, and many joined in the music by singing.

"What plans have you for next year, Nuada?"

"I think we still have a need for at least three more houses, and the protection wall needs to be extended. A well needs to be dug, and other things still need a final touch."

"We agree with you on those things and will help to make it so."

"Another thing comes to mind: With so many people here now, there are bound to be disagreements, and we will have need of a law body to settle disputes."

The two men looked at each other, and Mor said, "We had thought of that also. But we do not know how to bring such a thing together."

"Put it before the people and let them choose."

"This we can do. Thank you for your thoughts on this matter."

Nuada's mate caught sight of the trio and came over and said, "What are you three up to now? Is it to be more work for these poor people?"

"Some work and a few changes in how we treat each other," replied Nuada.

"Here, take of your child, and I will find of some food for you."

The small talk continued long after dark, and still the people of the village remained at the cooking area as if something important was about to happen. People drifted over to Nuada's table and asked questions of him about how things had progressed and if he was happy. His answer to many was, "It is not about me but about you people and the things that were necessary for us to survive as a family."

After a while, Nuada noticed that many had broken into small groups in deep discussion. He wondered at their actions, then passed it off as if it was of no matter. Finally Mor and the farmer were seen with these groups, and Nuada, who had been busy with his son, was called to the front near the fireplace and put a question he could not answer right away: "Will you be the chieftain of our village?"

His only thought was, "Why me?"

Mor answered by saying, "This was your valley first, and you brought us into it without question and helped us develop into a family. We could not have become without you."

Nuada looked about the cluster of people and saw hope upon their faces, and he answered, "Then I will accept your offer although I do not feel of the honor."

Nuada's mate stood nearby and beamed a bright smile to his answer. She was proud of him as only a wife or mother could be. Nuada shook hands with many of the people and listened to their comments on his acceptance of the title. After a while, Nuada took his mate and child home and tried to understand of what had happened.

Early the next morning, Nuada awoke with the question still running through his mind. "Why do these people think of me in that way. I have done nothing to deserve of this."

Nuada dressed and walked to the cooking area, still in wonder of what had happened. Mor was there to greet him and said, "The people came together and made of myself, the farmer, and Beag, the stonecutter, the new lawgivers for them. We will try to do the best for everyone."

"Good. All of you are wise enough to judge of the problems these people face."

"We will need of your thoughts also, Nuada. Some things are not as clear as your way."

"Then you only need to ask of me."

"I was hoping you would see it that way. Now what say you to a walk around your village?"

They rose and walked out onto the paved street and began to look about them at what had been built and talked of where to place the new homes for next year. They were joined by the farmer and Beag, and the foursome talked of all the things related to the people of the village.

Decisions were made on the placement of the houses and the well for the village as they walked around. They also talked of the waterwheel that Nuada had designed for the meadow. Again as they walked, the question of where to place the second protective wall came up, and they continued across the valley to the entrance into the second valley. Climbing onto a place of high ground, they looked about and discussed the placement of the wall. Beag wanted to make it of stone instead of the wood timbers as in the first wall. They agreed with him on that matter and made up their minds on the placement of the wall.

They walked on into the second valley, down through the woodcutting area and beyond to the field of oats. They followed the ridge around both valleys, looking for new things or ideas that came up as they walked and talked. Nuada looked for new ore sites and was rewarded at finding another tin rock fall. Few had been beyond before, possibly only the hunters, but this group discovered more fruit trees and another field of wild wheat. As they circled the valley, the wild game showed themselves to be unafraid of their presence, having not seen men before. Finally they arrived at Nuada's copper ore site and followed the stream back to their own valley.

They passed the caves and entered into the village, having used most of the daylight hours and returned to the cooking area to talk some more. One idea was to run the flock of sheep in the next valley next year but not too near the fields of grain they had discovered. Farmer said that they should fence an area for them to protect the grains. But the others thought it would be easier to fence the fields themselves. A'Chreag joined the foursome to hear of what they had found as he was now settling into his new life with his mate after all of the Summer labor.

After the evening meal with the sun starting to set lower in the sky, a cool, evening breeze came up from the northwest, and many shivered for the first time from the coolness. Nuada said his good nights to the group and, with his mate, started for home.

Outside of the entrance to his house, Jan sat quietly by himself.

"Is something wrong, my friend?"

"In a way, Nuada. I feel that I am not doing my share of the labors. I know that I am getting older, but I am still useful."

"What would you like to do that can change of your thinking?"

"I do not know. I have been many places and seen many things. I have learned trades that others do not have here."

"Then let us talk of these things and see if we can find of your skills."

They began to talk of things that Jan had done before, and Nuada questioned him on how they would fit into the village. Jan was honest and still did not find of something they could use here.

"Jan, it is getting late, and I think we should sleep on the questions and perhaps find of an answer."

Nuada climbed the stairs to his sleeping area, worried of Jan's state of mind. "Perhaps, Creatrix will find of an answer for me this night," he thought.

Sleep came deeply for Nuada, and he dreamed of Creatrix in his slumber. "How can I help my friend," he asked in his dreams.

"Nuada, awaken and hear of my words. Jan's time was short when you found of him, and you took him in and gave him a purpose with children as teacher and caregiver. Do not think that he is as young as he talks of. I am thinking of calling him home. Honor him and remember of his help."

"But I still need of him. He is almost like my father to me."

"Then he has even more honor than is needed. Do not worry for him, for he will be with me and can talk to you when needed. All mortals are given only a small amount of time, and his time is up."

Nuada awoke with sweat running down his face and jumped from his bed and down the stairs to Jan. He lay with a smile upon his face but was not breathing; Creatrix had claimed him. Nuada straightened Jan's form and slowly covered his face, tears running down his face. He knew that he had lost a dear friend.

Nuada sat at the table near Jan's sleeping place and kept watch until the sun began to rise. He went upstairs and dressed and awoke his mate to tell her of the happening.

With the sun now fully up, Nuada set out to find of Mor and tell him of Jan. Things would need to be done soon, and help was needed to place him in a place of honor.

Nuada told Mor of Jan, and they set out for both of the stonecutters' homes. A crypt was needed to honor Jan in the fullest way they knew. After the meeting, the stonecutters set to work on a site that Nuada had picked outside of the wall but near the ridge of the valley. Trees sheltered the site and made it very comfortable.

Nuada returned home and washed Jan's remains in preparation for his entombment. Tears still clouded Nuada's red, swollen eyes, and soon members of the village began to drop by to view of Jan's body. Word had passed quickly, and even children knew of the event.

The sounds of the village people within Nuada's house drove him outside, where he sat near the site where they had talked last night. Mor found of him sitting and looking into the sky.

"We will all miss of him, Nuada. He gave without question and asked nothing in return."

Nuada nodded and returned to his inward thinking of his friend. Finally Mor wandered off and left him alone.

Late in the afternoon, the stonecutters stopped by to tell Nuada that the crypt was ready. He arose and walked to the cooking area to tell everyone that with the dawning tomorrow, Jan's body would be placed in his tomb. He did not linger but returned to his house to remain near his friend.

Sleep was far from Nuada's thoughts all that night as he sat and remembered all the things that had happened since they had first met. He had valued this man's company more than he had first realized, and now that he was gone, he would feel lost at times without his wisdom to guide him.

When dawn broke, Nuada was surprised by a knock at his door, and when he opened it, most of the village people were there to help bring Jan's body to the crypt. He welcomed them into his house, where he spoke a few words about his friend before they departed. Even the village children were here to say goodbye to their teacher and mentor. They walked slowly with Jan's body outside the protection wall gate and to his crypt; not a sound, except from the birds of the valley, broke the solemn parade. With the passing of the village elder, they placed him into the crypt, and the stonecutters set the final stones into place.

Nuada led the people back to the cooking area, and a solemn breakfast with beer was shared in his memory. Mor and the farmer joined Nuada with his family, and small talk was shared about the things that Jan had done for the village and its people.

Around midday the people began to wander off to their houses, and Nuada took his family home, his thoughts still surrounded by the special things about Jan. Finally Nuada dozed in the late afternoon. No dreams filled his sleeping mind.

He awoke in the middle of the night and could not get back to sleep. He arose and walked to Jan's sleeping area and slowly started to collect his friend's things. He picked up a bag, and its contents spilled onto the floor. Nuada kneeled and started to pick up the items. These were Jan's drawings, and Nuada took them to the table, where he started looking through them. To his surprise, some of the drawings were of Nuada and his family. He set the drawings down and shook his head in bewilderment. "Why did he draw of me?" he wondered. Slowly he again picked up the drawings and found the series that Jan had drawn of Wolf for the carving on the door. Beneath these were drawings of the village and its people. Nuada was in wonderment of his skill to capture the scenes of everyday life. "I did not know of this talent. Why did he not tell me of it?"

With the coming of the dawn, Nuada resolved to share the drawings with the village people. Nuada washed the sleep from his face and hair and then set off for the cooking area, carrying the bag of drawings.

Mor was with others preparing the work for the day and sending them out where needed.

"Mor, come see of these things of Jan's."

Nuada unrolled the drawings of the village scenes and spread them upon the table. "I had no idea of his skill with these types of drawings. Did you?"

Mor stood in wonderment, looking at the different drawings before he answered. "No. I had no idea that he had this skill. Look at how they seem so real. I remember this day here!"

Others began to gather around and look at the drawings. Many were silent, and others stood pointing at a scene caught by Jan's skill.

"We must find a place to show these — somewhere out of the weather and protected for the future, Mor."

Mor and the others all nodded in agreement. "Nuada, you must keep of them for now until we can make of a place for them."

At that moment, A'Chreag arrived and looked at the drawings with the others.

"A'Chreag! I wish to speak of you," Nuada called.

"What is it you wish to talk of, Nuada?"

"My house is much too big for just my family, and I would like you and your mate to move in and share of it. I know that you are crowded where you are now, and it would make of a better way when we have work at the forge."

A smile crossed A'Chreag's face, and he nodded in agreement. "I will tell of my mate right away. Thank you, my friend."

After a period of time, Nuada rose and picked up the drawings and walked back to his house. It seemed empty after the loss of Jan. Nuada walked back to Jan's sleeping area and looked down at the things left where he had placed them. After staring at the things for a few minutes, Nuada decided that he was not in the mood to pack them at that time and sat at the table again. Wolf came over and placed his head in Nuada's lap, hoping that it would result in a head scratch. Nuada looked down and knew that Wolf missed him too and rubbed his head.

He sat for almost an hour before he made up his mind to go for a walk and try to clear the sadness from his mind. Calling Wolf he set out for the second valley and the people working there. At the entrance to the second valley, Nuada paused and saw the stonecutters at work on the new protection wall for that end of the valley. It was massive — almost twice the height of a man wide — and he inquired about how high it would be when finished. When he was told that it would stand four times the height of a man, he whistled in wonderment.

He then continued on into the second valley to where the tree cutting was still going on. He stood and watched the men at work and wondered if he could help. When told he could help, Nuada stripped off his shirt and began to trim the branches from the fallen trees. Hours passed, and he did not notice the passage of time until one of the men told him they were stopping for the day. Nuada then picked up his shirt and stopped at the stream to wash before returning to the valley.

The work was good for his soul and took the problems and the loss of Jan from his mind. He knew that he must return to a regular pattern of work to keep these things off his mind.

Nuada entered the cooking area and sat at his regular table and looked around at the crowd of people filling the place. Someone started playing music, and others joined in with singing. This was a place of happiness, and Nuada was proud of their spirit.

Nuada's mate saw him enter and brought him his evening meal and their son to keep him company. "Wife, I am glad of your comfort and company this day. It has been hard for me."

"I know, husband. Find of your son's company and keep your mind clear."

Mor and Farmer joined Nuada at his table, and they talked of the things done that day. Nuada asked of what work he could do on the morrow. Mor replied that he could help with the new framing of a house they were starting tomorrow. Nuada readily agreed and said he would be there in the morning.

Another new day began with Nuada waking early before the sun, and after walking Wolf, he set out for the cooking area. A few of the early risers were there and greeted him as he rechecked his tool bag and waited for the work crew to arrive. He did not have to wait long as they were there within fifteen minutes. Some grabbed something to eat, and before long they were headed for the home site. As Nuada started to leave, Mor appeared, and they shared a few words about the village in whole before Nuada went on his way.

Three teams of horses were being used to bring the trees from the second valley, drawing their wagons without strain. Each team had only one man to help lead them, and as they approached the work site, the triple-pole lift was used to lift the timbers into place. Nuada was on one of the guide ropes, and the motion went smoothly as each was placed where needed.

All throughout the day, the framing continued, and late in the afternoon, the work was called to a halt. The stonecutters stopped by as they returned from working on the new protection wall and said they would be there in the morning to start the end wall and fireplace work.

Nuada walked back to the cooking area and was talking with Mor and A'Chreag about how fast the work was coming on the new house when he heard that someone new had wandered into the valley.

"Show them to me!" Nuada demanded of the person who had told him.

The man pointed out the newcomers and asked if he did something wrong.

"Anything like this must be reported to the village consul as soon as it happens — not hours later!"

The man apologized for his mistake and left Nuada to face the newcomers and ask questions of them. Nuada introduced himself as the village chief and began asking of them about where they had come from and why they were here. The family seemed safe enough, but the questions were necessary for everyone's protection. They had been driven out of their home by raiders, much as had everyone within the valley been. When asked if they had been followed, they said no. They had been careful and only escaped with their lives and few possessions. When asked about any animals, they said the raiders took them all.

"What skills have you to share with us?" Nuada asked.

"I am a worker of leather and make clothes." the man answered.

Nuada told them that they were welcome in the village, and as housing was limited at this time, they could camp near the new house construction until something was available for them. The man thanked Nuada and shook his hand very vigorously.

Nuada walked back to his table and sat with Mor again and told him of the situation with the newcomers.

"We are expanding faster than we can build, Nuada. What of the next family that shows? What are we to do then?"

Nuada thought for a minute and then said, "We will take all who have hardship, no matter what."

Thoughts of more people entering the valley bothered Nuada. They were near capacity now, and housing was very limited even for the people now living here. He turned to Mor and said, "Let us look at building smaller houses. They could be built in much shorter time periods, and then people would not have to share of them."

Mor thought for a minute and said, "I agree with you on this matter. Let us talk to the other village elders and plan on this approach."

"I agree. We could build another row of houses, starting behind the wood-working building, and follow the line of houses that face the paved street."

"A good idea, Nuada. Perhaps we could build a few work buildings there also for those of different trades."

"Yes! Then in the future we could use their extra products for trade with other villages."

"Now we are thinking like a city instead of just a village. We will grow, and it will be good for everyone here."

"True. But it will also bring some of the wrong types of people with it, including raiders that will want to take away what we have built."

"Then we will have need of a strong band to enforce our laws and protect of us."

The two men sat in silence and thought of all that they had just discussed and ways to make it happen in a positive way.

Just then, A'Chreag appeared and inquired of Nuada about where he was to live within the house.

"Just give me a few more minutes, and I will take you to the house and show you, my friend."

Nuada continued his discussion about the needs of the village and how to make the changes that were needed. He then said his farewells to Mor and, with A'Chreag in tow, walked to his house. Upon entering A'Chreag noticed the wood carvings of Nuada and asked of them.

"When I was feeling low, Jan inspired me to do these things to take my mind off my problems. I now feel lost without him."

"Then perhaps I can do the same if you are ever in need of such again."

"It is a good thought, my friend. However, I do not think I shall be that way again."

"Perhaps not, but I am there for you, Nuada."

They walked to the front of the house, where Jan had his sleeping area, and Nuada showed of the place.

"I do not think I would be comfortable taking of his place. Perhaps another area, for your house is large."

"My family and I sleep upstairs near the fireplace. So choose of where you like."

A'Chreag climbed the stair to look about and settled upon an area near the stair, upstairs. "This will do and I will not disturb of you here."

Together they walked back to the cooking area and joined up with their mates for the evening meal. Small talk surrounded them as everyone was enjoying the mild Fall weather that they knew would not last much longer.

With the coming of dusk, people returned to their houses, thinking of the work required for tomorrow. Nuada was no different in his thinking and slept well that night without any dreams.

With dawn showing the first light of the new day, Nuada arose and dressed and went downstairs to find Wolf to let him out for his morning run. A'Chreag heard him and quickly dressed and joined him.

"What work do you have planned for today, Nuada?"

"Today we are starting the siding for the new house while the stonecutters work upon the end wall and fireplace."

"Then we will be near one another, for I am to help the stonecutters."

"Then let us get something to eat and start of this day's work."

They walked to the cooking area, where the new weaver and his family had gathered.

"I feel lost. How can I help?" he asked of Nuada.

"Join of us, and if you do not know what to do, we will teach of you a new trade in the building of houses."

He nodded in agreement, and after eating, the trio walked to the new housing site, where others had gathered and began the day's work. Work crews were selected and given jobs, and within a half hour, noise from the work filled the village. All throughout that day, work consumed their every thought until the sun began to set. The men as a group all walked back to the cooking area and found tables to sit and talk about their day's progress. Mor and Beag joined Nuada and A'Chreag, and Mor discussed the building of the smaller houses that were needed. Nuada told him that two more days were needed on the house they were working upon and it would be ready for another family, and then they could start on the first of the smaller houses. Mor showed Nuada a drawing of the design for the houses, and after some thought, Nuada showed where changes were needed in the design. "Then we have an agreement about the needs of this work."

Over the next week, the first house was completed, and people moved in while the first of the smaller houses was started and well under way. The stone-cutters returned to work on the protection wall, and any rubble was brought into the village for another paving of a new street that faced the smaller houses. Nuada returned to his forge from time to time to make hinges and other useful parts needed. A'Chreag asked him one day if perhaps they should move the forge building into the village near the stable. Nuada thought it was a wonderful idea that would provide protection for them. "The present site is too exposed to raiders and shows of them that the valley is occupied."

The next morning they took a pair of horses and a wagon to the forge site and began to remove the tools and started to dismantle the building, as its materials could be used for the new forge building. Nuada, at the end of the day, looked around and said, "I shall miss of this place. Other than my first house, this was home to me."

"I understand your feelings, my friend," A'Chreag said. "But times have changed, and we must look ahead."

Within a few days, any sign of the old forge building had disappeared, and they began to build the new forge building at the hill outcropping next to the stable. Only Mor found time to visit their work and keep them up to date on the village construction. For Fall the weather continued mild, and everyone kept pace for the needs of the village.

After a few more days, the forge building was complete, and Nuada walked about the village looking at the changes. Two more of the smaller houses were under construction, as the first was complete, and a family had moved in. The last of the larger houses had the finishing touches done, and as Nuada walked on, he found himself nearing the new protection wall and was in wonderment at its size. It too was nearing completion. He found Beag and told him that he had outdone himself with this work. He crossed into the next valley and was amazed how much of the trees had been cut for the village. It had made a new meadow, where sheep were to graze in the Spring. He stood there looking about before returning to the village, while wonderment at the changes shook him at the progress of these people.

Taking his seat at his table in the cooking area, he was staring into space when Mor joined him and brought him away from his thoughts.

"Is something wrong, Nuada?"

"No. I am in wonderment of the changes that have come to the village."

"You are the cause of it, my friend."

"No, I am not. These people are the reason for everything. They have needs and are willing to do what is necessary."

"Perhaps, but you are their inspiration."

Nuada 's mate appeared with his evening meal and his son.

"Husband, take of your boy. Again he is underfoot and has begun to ask many questions, some I cannot answer."

Nuada smiled at his growing boy and held him upon his lap. Mor said, "I think he is beginning to look and act like you."

Nuada only nodded, and as the evening rolled on, music again filled the air around the people of the village.

Another week and a half passed. The next two houses were nearing completion, and the gate was installed on the new protection wall. The village hunters were out filling the larder, for the first breath of Winter now blew down from the northwest — colder and harder with each passing day.

Nuada and A'Chreag were out bringing ore back to the new forge building and getting ready for the Winter weather to come. Mor pushed the work crews to complete the housing so that everyone had shelter. The stonecutters continued to pave the second street and made a junction that joined the main street of the village.

That afternoon Nuada ended his day with a walk to the crypt of Jan and sat there for almost an hour without company. "My friend, I miss of your company and wisdom." With that thought, Nuada turned and walked to the cooking area and some real people with whom to talk to. Now most of the village people sat huddled close together because of the wind and its chill. Mor joined Nuada, and the talk turned to the weather and the coming of snow.

Mor said, "I think we are ready for the Winter now; only a few things need to be finished, and those can be done even if the snow comes."

Nuada replied, "Did you see of the ducks upon the lake today? I have never seen so many here before."

"They too are aware of the weather and will be moving south soon."

Two days later the first snow blew in hard and swift. All work was halted, and the men and women of the village spent the day together for the first time since last Winter. Nuada took Wolf for a run around midday, and the snow was at mid-calf on him. Wolf bounded from snow bank to snow bank, hunting for mice that had ventured out. The newest houses were now occupied, and everyone had shelter for the Winter.

Nuada did not venture away from the front of his house but looked at the sky and noticed how the smoke from the village fireplaces lay low and made it hard to see the sky above. He called Wolf back and went inside to the table, where A'Chreag and his mate sat talking about the weather.

"Nuada, is there any change in the weather?"

"None. I am afraid that this storm will last for many days. The snow is already up to my knees."

"What will we do to keep busy in this weather?"

"For myself I am going to draw up some designs for the Spring work projects."

"Can I help? I do not like this time on my hands."

"You can make models of the designs. That would help find of any flaws."

"Anything. When do we start of these things?"

"Let us talk of these things first and let it take us where it may. I might need of your ideas on them."

They talked for hours about the village in general and the second valley and how to develop it. Nuada suggested that a model of the village and both valleys would help future development. A'Chreag was enthused with the idea of that model and wanted to start right away, but Nuada told him to wait until tomorrow and let the work roll through his mind first.

Nuada fell silent as he let his mind wander across both valleys and the changes he saw coming. A'Chreag fell silent also as he saw the expression on Nuada's face and knew better than to interrupt his thoughts. Finally both men were brought back to the present by their mates with their evening meals.

Nuada's mind raced even while eating about the things he saw coming. His son pulled his leg and wanted to be held, which Nuada wanted too.

"These things are for you, son, and your children. Do not forget why they exist."

The boy looked at his father with the look of a child who does not understand the meaning of the words or the thoughts behind them. A'Chreag looked at Nuada with wonderment as he watched the exchange between father and son and knew his turn would come soon enough with a child of his own.

"Nuada, do you want to build the model here or at the woodworking building?"

"Here. The others will see of it soon enough."

"Then I will have to build a table for it. How big should it be?"

Nuada thought for a minute and then showed A'Chreag a rough size to get the details they would need.

"I shall start when the storm breaks. Is that all right?"

"It would be nice to start right away, but we have the time now to take it slow."

The snowstorm broke after four days and left almost two feet of wet snow that was hard to travel very far in. The men of the village banded together, and snow removal began — after the streets came the path to the lake for water. Nuada overheard talk again about a well within the village; it was needed. A'Chreag went to work at the woodworking building when he was free from the snow detail. When he was asked about the table he was building, he avoided what its real use would be. It took him only two days to complete, and he had some of his friends help to move it into Nuada's house. He brought some small pieces of wood to detail the model and even found a small evergreen bush to use for trees on it. A basket of dirt and another of small rocks completed the supplies.

After smoothing the surface of the table, Nuada started to draw the valleys from memory. This would be the pattern for the rest of the model. The hardest part was the making of the lake and its island and what to use for the water in the lake and stream. Nuada finally decided that he could use some of the copper deposits for the water on the model that could be ground into a fine sand. The work continued over the next few weeks, and it was found to be a hard taskmaster to get the details right.

Mor and Beag visited one day and found the model helpful for future development of the village and the next valley. Plans were made for the Spring work details and how to use the people to develop everything that they had worked so hard for. Now the people could see where they were going by use of the model.

Nuada suddenly felt tired of the project as it neared completion and sought another diversion for his mind. The weather had cleared enough for him to take another walk around the valley, and he visited the island where he first lived. It seemed so long ago to him that he had to think about the short time frame that it really was. He found that his old house on the island had collapsed in on itself and that many things did not look or feel the same to him. This depressed him, and he left the island and walked to his old forge site near the entrance to the valley. Again he felt that things were changing too quickly for him, and he found himself doubting himself regarding the changes he had pushed for. He pushed himself to return to the site of the fight with raiders that brought the first of the villagers to the valley. He felt crowded by their company and sought time to be alone. Perhaps Creatrix felt differently about his thoughts, and he told himself that he would seek his wisdom in a dream that night.

Nuada turned and started the walk back to his home, still not understanding the cause of his feelings. Looking back across the valley from here, it still looked the same. He could not see of the village or any signs that the valley was occupied. That made him feel more comfortable and safe.

Entering through the village gate, he stopped again and looked toward Jan's crypt. "Why, my old friend, did you leave me so soon?"

Receiving no answer, he turned and walked toward the cooking area, knowing that it too would be empty. Hearing noise from the woodworking building, he entered to find of the cause. Many of the men were discussing the weather and how it was holding them back from their work. Many of the men greeted Nuada and invited him to join in the discussion, which he declined. Finding no answers to his mind set here, he left and continued home.

Outside of the house, Wolf greeted him by running in circles around him and jumping up and down. "Why are you so full of energy today, my friend?" Then opening his door and entering, he found Mor and Beag waiting for him near the model of the valleys.

"We see that the model is almost complete, Nuada. What remains to do with it?"

"Only the changes for the Spring work, my friends."

"Do you want to go over it now?"

"No. I am having trouble thinking on what the future holds for us."

"What do you mean?"

"All the changes that we have made within the valley bother me, and I do not understand why. These are the changes I had hoped for, but it still troubles my mind."

"Perhaps we are moving ahead too quickly and need to slow down."

"Perhaps. I miss of the wisdom of Jan. He would point the way for us."

"Then we will leave of you while you think on these matters."

The pair departed, and Nuada settled in front of the fireplace and stared hard into the flames, hoping for a vision from Creatrix or Jan. Slowly his eyes began to droop, and sleep found him.

When Nuada awoke in his dream state, something was different than the many times before when he had a vision. The site was filled with a fog, and nothing was clear to his mind.

"Creatrix? What is different, and why do you hide from me?"

"I am not Creatrix, Nuada. This is Jan. Did you not want to see of me?"

"Yes. But where are you?"

"I was all around you a minute ago. Let me find of another way for you to see of me."

"I can see of a shape forming before me. Is that you?"

"Yes. Are you not afraid?"

"No. Creatrix would not fool of me in this way. I have worries that need of an answer."

"Then ask of me, and I shall answer in the best way I can."

"I fear that the village has grown too fast and we are only asking of trouble from the outside. I know that the reason for the growth was of my doing. But I worry that it may cause of us to fail and all of us will be homeless again."

"When I was alive, I too had of these worries. But this is of Creatrix's plan for you and the test to come."

"What test? Am I to cause of the failure of these kind and hardworking people?"

"What the test is, I cannot tell of you. But Creatrix has shown of me many visions of what will come. It is you who will determine which course of action will be reality."

"Now I am afraid. Does Creatrix wish of this?"

"He does. It will determine of your place here when your time comes."

"I had hoped to find a resting of my mind with this visit. But now I find it makes of me more worrisome."‘

"Relax, Nuada, and remember that you have always found a way. Now return to your home and family."

Slowly the fog disappeared from Nuada's mind, and he awoke sitting in his chair in front of the fireplace. He was still alone and thinking of what was said to him when his mate came down from their sleeping area and gave him a hug.

"Husband, you have been sleeping the day away. Why?"

"I sought a vision with Creatrix and talked with Jan instead. He told of me some future event that will happen, but it is I who will determine of the result. I am still troubled by the answer."

"You will find of the way. You always have, husband."

The evening meal was shared with A'Chreag and his mate although Nuada did not tell him of the vision. Nuada's sleep that night was restless and broken many times by his dreams of what would come.

Day followed day, and now Winter was upon the valley and its people. Contact was limited, and only a few ventured out into the rain or snow. The wind seemed to howl with a strength not seen in the valley before. Even Wolf balked at going outside.

- WINTER AND WORRIES -

The morning light was dark, and haze filtered through heavily overcast clouds. The wind was lighter, and Nuada ventured out into the village. This was the kind of weather he remembered from his youth. It seemed so long ago to him, and he had to think hard on the memories of the time and place. Stopping near the village gate, he looked about with a critical eye at everything within.

"If we are attacked, how do we warn everyone?" he thought. "We need of a warning system, something that everyone would hear and understand."

Ducking his head in thought, he walked toward the forge building near the stable. Standing outside he looked about again. He bent over and picked up a rock and threw it toward the side of the building. It hit something metal leaning there and gave off a ringing sound. Curious Nuada walked toward the sound. An old piece of metal that he had discarded stood leaning against the building. Picking up another piece of metal, he struck the other piece, and again the ringing sound pealed in protest.

"This is the answer I was looking for," he said out loud, entering the forge building.

He looked around at his scrap-metal pile and found many pieces of sheet metal that he had formed long ago and discarded. Picking several pieces, he set them on a work table and began to roll them into drum shapes. On one end he fashioned a cover with an attachment to hang the drum. With this done, he found a place to hang the bell device. After raising it up, he hit it with a wooden club he used for forming other metal products. It rang loud and clear and brought A'Chreag and others from the village to the forge building.

"Nuada, what are you doing? That noise woke the whole village," Mor said.

"I have just made a warning system for the village. If we make a code for the number of rings it makes, we can use it for raiders or fires or any other things that need of us in a hurry."

"I can see of the need of it, and it was loud enough that we heard of it inside of our houses."

"I have made five of them, all of different sizes and sounds, so that we can tell of where the problem is."

"Have you thought of where to place them?"

"I have thought about it. But I think we need of everybody to bring their thoughts on this matter."

"Then I will call for a meeting tomorrow at the woodworking building, so we may discuss of this."

"It is important. It must be answered as soon as possible."

Those there saw of the need to get it resolved as soon as possible, and they left Nuada and A'Chreag alone at the forge.

"Nuada, why did you not call of me? I would have liked to have helped in this thing."

"I would have, my friend. But the inspiration came on me all of a sudden, and I just fell into working on it."

"Is there anything else that needs of my hand today?"

"There is. We need to make of some fire-hardened clubs to ring of them."

"How many do we need?"

"There are five bells. I think we will need of at least two each for a total of ten."

"Then let us get to work."

By the end of the day, the clubs were made and loaded with the bells onto a wagon that was parked near the forge.

"After the thing tomorrow, we will take them to where they want to place them. We will need to build of a small building for each. Are you ready for this next task?"

"I am, Nuada. Just show of me what you want done, and we will make it so."

Early the next morning the meeting was held, and the placement of the bells was decided upon. The first bell would be near the entrance to the valley, close to the old forge site, and another near the stone wall by the entrance into the second valley. The third bell would be near the crop meadow and the fourth inside the village, near the protection wall. The fifth bell was for the other valley, but its site was still open to discussion for the Spring.

The weather held for the village people, and Nuada, with A'Chreag and three other men, set out on the task to build the bell towers. They started with the first near the valley entrance and within two hours had it completed. The next site was near the stone wall by the second valley. Again it was completed quickly before they ran out of daylight.

The following day the other two bells were installed into their towers, and only the fifth bell remained on the wagon. This bell was taken back to the forge building and put into a storage area until they could decide where it was to be placed. A'Chreag then asked Nuada, "What is next on your mind list?"

"We will need of more tips for our bow shafts and spears. I see of a need for a great many."

"Are you expecting trouble?"

"Times are dangerous, and I want us to be prepared."

"Anything else?"

"I think we will need of some ladders to be placed against the cliff behind the village so that we may have an advantage of height over any attackers."

"How many do we need of them?"

"I think four. No, make that six."

"Then I will work on them in my spare time."

"Good. This day is done, so let us return home, and tomorrow we will start on the weapons we will need of."

The following day Nuada and A'Chreag left the house before the sun had risen and the forge fires were started. The pair worked at the sand table creating molds for the arrow and spear tips. Just after mid-morning, they poured the first of the tips and worked at this project throughout the day. When they finally stopped, they walked back along the protection wall and stopped at the woodworking building. Inside a small group spoke of the different things. A'Chreag told of the need for some ladders and the reason for them, which they agreed to work on. After sharing of some of the beer, they continued on home to their mates and a well-earned supper.

Sleep came easily for Nuada that night and without the dreams that had troubled his mind of recent times. For A'Chreag his sleep was troubled now with the worry of an attack before they were prepared.

The next morning the pair returned to the forge and continued to make more of the tips for the weapons. More knives and swords were also made and set aside until they could be sharpened and the handles made. They were back at full production in the forge throughout the week, each of them driven by the needs of the village for protection.

The men at the woodworking building had completed the ladders and then went to work on making shafts for both the spears and the arrows. They did not know what was driving all of them to work so hurriedly in this fashion, only that Nuada said it was needed and quickly. Others within the village had heard of the projects and joined in the work, not knowing why. One day Mor, Beag, and Farmer called Nuada aside and asked of him why this was needed. He told them of his dream vision with Jan and the worry that followed. This was the reason for the work and preparations. They agreed with his reasons and felt that it was time for them to train the village people in the art of war.

In the weeks that followed, weapons of war were created, and the men of the village began to practice for war and the defense of the village. Nuada had pointed the way for them — now it was up to them to learn and act when it became necessary.

Nuada continued his walks around both valleys, looking for improvements to their defense. This lasted until the snow began to fall in earnest, and again the people of the village huddled within their homes.

A'Chreag asked of Nuada when he expected an attack one day.

"Not in this weather, but when the weather warms, we can expect of anything from Spring to early Winter. The most likely time will be in the Fall after our harvest."

"I agree. Then should we not post guards at the valley entrance during this time?"

"Yes. Some kind of guard tower that can see out and away from the valley would be the best choice. That would give us time to prepare for an attack."

"What else do we need of?"

"The protection wall here of wood needs a walkway to stand and fight from. The stone wall on the other end of the valley is wide enough for that purpose. Then there is the lake. I cannot see of any way to stop an attack from across the water."

"Can we not build a wall along the stream that would protect of us?"

"We could, but it would take another year of work to build of it, and I do not think we will have time for it."

"Let me talk to the others and see of their minds about this matter."

"Do not forget that we must build more houses next year and our well for water. I do not think we can do it all."

Nuada let his mind drift off on the memory of what Jan had told him and the words of Creatrix before that. He thought, "This is a test of me. Why threaten the village people?"

Later that night while Nuada slept, he was drawn into another vision sleep by Creatrix.

"Nuada! Awaken and hear of me. You are doing well with your preparations, and the test will come for you in mid-Summer. Do not lose sight of the things you have done to prepare for this test."

"But we are not ready yet. Will you protect of these people when the time comes, or are we alone in this matter?"

"You are never alone, Nuada. Do not forget of this."

Nuada drifted back into his sleep and awoke after the sun was well up. Nuada dressed quickly and sought out A'Chreag and found him at the woodworking building. Calling him aside, he told of the vision last night and that they were to expect an attack by mid -Summer.

"Then there will not be time to build that wall along the stream."

"No. But I have given it some thought and think that we could build a short one near the valley entrance. This way we could bottle up any large force in a narrow area. What think of you?"

"I agree," A'Chreag said while his mind drifted back in memory of the area. "It is so limited that any more than ten could trip over each other."

"That is what I thought. What are you working on now?"

"More arrow shafts. Nothing too difficult to make."

"True, but something that we will need of in large numbers. It gives us a distance advantage, where we can bring down a large number without danger to our people."

After a few more words, Nuada left the building and walked along the wood wall to his forge. Thinking that it was too late in the day to begin any work, he walked over to the stable and checked on the livestock. Finding no one there, he set out for home. His walk took him through the outdoor cooking area, and again it was empty of people. "Perhaps I should look at the model of the valleys and make wall models where I think we should place of them," he thought. Then he quickened his pace and returned home.

Inside his mate was busy cooking a meal at the fireplace, and his son was sound asleep at Jan's old sleeping area. He stopped without a word and started to model a wall for the valley entrance. It took him only a couple of hours to make the wall model, and he was pleased with the result. Standing back he took in the overall view of both valleys. "This was the best idea ever. It gives of us an overlook of everything."

After cleaning up after himself where he had done the model work, he sat at the meal table and waited. Wolf, who had been asleep with Nuada's son, awoke and came over and rubbed against Nuada. Reaching down Nuada rubbed his ears and let his mind wander to other things still needed.

"Why are you smiling while staring into nothingness?" his mate asked, which broke his train of thought.

"I was lost in the future, wife. Things are beginning to look up for the village and its people."

"As was I. Your supper will be along shortly. Go wash of yourself."

Nuada did as he was told and then awoke his son to prepare him for his meal. While Nuada ate of a venison stew, A'Chreag returned, and Nuada told him to look at the new changes to the valley model.

"Yes! This is what we need. Have you thought of anything else?"

"No, not yet. I am afraid to plan on too much for there is not enough time."

"What about a battle plan for our defense. How can we make the most of what little we have?"

"You think like Jan used too. I had not given it much thought."

"Then let it be our next project: how to organize our people to the best advantage."

They finished the evening quietly going over the resources that they had and how to best use them.

"Tomorrow, I must meet with Mor, Beag, and Farmer and show of them these plans. It will be best if they came here, so they could see on the model how things would happen."

Both men slept well that night, but their dreams were filled with all that they had talked of the evening before.

In the morning, Nuada and A'Chreag together went looking for the trio of village leaders. Surprisingly they found them all together within the woodworking building.

"Mor, A'Chreag and I have been discussing the need of a defense battle plan and think that we have come up with something that would work to our advantage."

"What have you two come up with?"

"Come to our house and look upon the valley model, and we will explain."

Back at Nuada's house, the pair began to explain how things would come to pass.

"I can see of the need for the new wall, and your ideas about how to fight are good, but we do not expect of an attack before Fall."

"You are wrong. Creatrix came to me in a vision and said that it would happen in mid-Summer."

The men knew not to question Nuada's visions, and the plan was approved. As soon as the weather would break in the Spring, they would start the new wall before anything else.

Tension and worry seemed to melt from Nuada's shoulders. He and A'Chreag returned to work again at the forge, making more tools of war. The village men worked at the tools needed also within the woodworking building. The women were not without their projects too.

The first full moon of the new year passed unnoticed by Nuada's village. The weather seemed mild for this time of year although from time to time heavy snow did fall with blustery winds out of the northwest. Nuada's child was growing faster every day. He could put whole sentences together now, and he seemed to run everywhere he went, causing his mother to worry with his activity. Wolf was just as bad, as he followed everything that Iolair did.

With the coming of the second month, the weather again began to clear, and the Sun peeked out from behind the clouds now. This seemed good, but the cold that was a part of it could shake anyone to the bone. Nuada knew of this type of weather, and he limited his time at the forge. On these days he spent it teaching his son and watched him change into a young man-child.

The village people too began to back off from the urgency of preparing for war. More time was spent in domestic things.

Nuada joined the monthly meeting at the woodworking building with Mor, Beag, and Farmer. They went over the preparations and discussed other things to be done within the village. A code for the bells was worked out, and Mor said he would make sure that everyone understood it.

Returning home Nuada had the thought that he had not had a vision from Creatrix or Jan since early Winter and wondered of it. "Perhaps I need of them now. I shall try to join of them this night and see of their thoughts."

Entering the house, he walked to the pantry door, where he had carved the image of Wolf, and ran his hands over the work. "Jan was right about the need of this work then. What about now?" he wondered.

After his evening meal, Nuada settled in front of his fireplace and let his mind clear of the day's thoughts and waited for the vision into Creatrix's world of light. He did not have to wait long, as the shadow world found him and carried him to Creatrix.

"Nuada, awaken into my world and hear of my words. I would have called for you sooner, but you were busy with your worldly duties. I am pleased with your progress and have watched you grow, as was necessary for your test."

"Am I to remain in the dark regarding this test, or will you tell of me about it?"

"You already know of it and have prepared well."

"Where is Jan? I miss of his wisdom."

"He has other duties and will help you when the time nears."

Nuada looked about this shadow world and wondered of it. He could not see beyond the light that surrounded him and Creatrix.

"I see you are curious of my world, Nuada. Do not be. It will come soon enough to you and all of the others, for this is the real world."

With those words, Nuada awoke in his own house again and shook the fog from his mind, then reflected on the words told to him. He stood and knew that he had only been away for only a short period of time. He walked back toward the valley model and looked down upon it for a long period of time, not really seeing it.

Hearing a noise, he turned to see his mate cleaning up after their meal and preparing for sleep. "Nuada, it is time for bed. Help me finish this, and we will climb up to our sleep area."

Nuada slept well again that night and awoke refreshed before the light of Creatrix crawled over the valley ridge. He let Wolf run and felt the freshness of the morning air with his first deep breath. He could not tell if it would be overcast today, as the darkness held that from him. He exhaled again, and a small cloud of moisture floated across his face. He looked for Wolf and saw him running back toward the stables. He called for him and waited. Wolf came running and dropped a small rabbit at Nuada's feet. "That is yours. You have earned it." Turning they went back into the house and settled before the fire. Nuada watched Wolf roll on the dead rabbit before starting to eat it.

After a short period of time, Nuada rose and walked down to his forge building. He stoked his fire for the forge and turned to his sand table and began to tinker with some of the molds. His thoughts returned to the last vision, and he wondered of all the hidden meanings. Shaking the doubts from his mind, he returned to the molds and began to create something new: a ring for his mate.

A'Chreag showed up about an hour and a half later and asked after any projects.

Nuada told him that he was just tinkering and that nothing was pressing that day.

"Then I shall go to the woodworking building and do some of the work I have there."

Nuada nodded and watched A'Chreag leave.

Nuada listened to the wind whisper through the roof eaves and stepped outside to look at the sky again. Heavy clouds rolled across the valley, showing signs of snow again. Stepping back inside, he worked the bellows at the forge fire and watched the molten metal become a crisp golden orange. Using his tongs, he lifted the molten mixture and walked back to the sand table and poured it into the new mold. Setting the hot pot aside, he waited for the mold to cool. Again he walked outside and looked at the weather. It was beginning to snow now, and he wondered how heavy it would be.

Returning to the table and the mold, he cracked it open and looked at the results of his work. Picking up a small pelt, he began to polish the ring he had made. Near midday he stopped and banked the fire under the forge. Then he slowly wrapped the ring in another pelt and put it into his pocket and set out for home.

Entering the house, he found his mate at her usual spot, cooking at the great fireplace. Sitting at the table, he watched her work and slowly set the pelt on the table and waited. She turned and looked at him and asked if he wanted anything. At first he said no. Then he asked for a mug of beer. She brought it to him and started to turn back to her work when he reached out and took her by the hand.

"Is there something else you need, husband?"

"Only your company for a minute," he said, pushing the pelt across to her.

"What is this?"

"Look and see for yourself."

She opened the pelt and the glow from the ring sparkled in the firelight. She lifted it and then looked at him with questions in her eyes.

"It is for all the times you supported me and never questioned."

"This is too good for me. I cannot wear it."

"You will and proudly, wife."

Nuada took the ring from her and placed it on her finger and then looked up at her and smiled.

"It fits you perfectly. It glows like you do."

"Nuada? I…"

"Do not say another word. That is my thanks to you for all you have done for me."

She only nodded and then turned to her pots and served up a meal for Nuada. He remained silent, and then his thoughts returned to the village and its people. This did not last long, as his son came to him for attention. Seeing this, Wolf joined the pair for his share of attention too. It was a family evening.

The next morning Nuada walked to the woodworking building to meet with the other village men and find of their thoughts. Now that the weapons were complete, they turned their attention to things that the village needed and projects expected to be built for Spring. He found that they had started the construction of his waterwheel, and he inspected it closely to see if anything needed to be changed. Finding nothing out of order, he looked next at the ladders that were now finished and wondered of the craftsmanship, which was well done. At that moment, Mor entered the building and saw Nuada. He asked after any problems, and Nuada told him no. They sat and talked of many things, which lasted well into the morning. Among the things talked of was the need to cut down many of the trees in front of the wood protection wall to give them a field of fire for their bows. The wood would be brought into the village to use on new houses, which would save them time bringing them from the other valley. The trees near the lake would remain as cover for the village hunters should raiders breach the new stone wall at the valley entrance. This, plus the bowmen on the ridge, would cover the entire meadow with fire and should stop any attack. Nuada wanted to make sure that none survived so as to not bring more raiders at a future date.

Finishing the talk, Nuada stepped outside and looked at the weather. It was clearing, and it felt mild to him. He walked through the portal gate and continued to the site of Jan's crypt. He paused before it and thought again of his lost friend. "I still miss of you, my friend," he thought. Then he turned and started for home.

Almost reaching his house, he thought of the boredom of just sitting there and changed his direction toward the lake. He reached the shore and looked across at the island.

"How can I use of this?" was the thought that ran though his mind. He found no answer because he knew that there were not enough men to go around in the defense of the valley. He then set out for the stone wall at the other valley's entrance. Along the way, he saw rabbits scurry about searching for food. They stopped and peered back at him before turning and disappearing into the underbrush. He reached the wall and knew that none were there to talk to. He then changed his mind about going into the next valley and began to follow the ridgeline back to the village. Again he stopped outside of the first cave and marveled at the way the stonecutters had hidden the entrance. He started to climb up to the entry but stopped and set his direction for home again.

Entering his house, he found it empty. His wife and child were somewhere else, and even Wolf was gone. He looked long and hard at the valley model, then settled in front of the fireplace to wait for his family to return.

After a while, he grew bored and went outside again. The wind had shifted and was growing stronger. The clouds billowed and rolled upon themselves. Every once in a while, Nuada could hear thunder in the distance, and it was growing louder by the minute. He stepped back under his porch and watched the sky show. Again he looked into the distance and could see the first flash of light from a distant lightning strike. He began to worry about his family but knew that they would seek the nearest shelter. The time passed quickly, and the storm settled down on the valley — rain at first, then snow. The wind began to bite with its icy touch, and Nuada retreated inside his house.

Only a few minutes passed, and A'Chreag entered with Nuada's mate and child in tow; they had been at the woodworking building. They were shaking from the storm's chill and stood close to the fireplace to warm.

"It will be a nasty night, Nuada," A'Chreag said.

Nuada nodded in agreement, and all of them sat at the table waiting for the full brunt of the storm. After an hour, Nuada, followed by A'Chreag, stepped out onto the porch to look at the sky again.

"Look, A'Chreag. The sky has become green, and it is hard to see where the sky and the ground separate."

"Let us go back inside. Our evening meal should be ready now."

They went back inside and ate of their meal and then settled down for the night. Tomorrow would show them of any damage in the morning light.

Winter had settled again on the valley, and it was many weeks before the sun broke thru the clouds. Few had ventured outside during this time, including Nuada. With the coming of the sunshine, everyone seemed to want to venture outside. Even though it remained cold, some projects began to be started. First was the stone wall at the valley entrance. All of the men helped in some way during this building, and it went up quickly. It would be taller and wider than the other stone wall, with a protection barrier for the men who were to fight from it.

Nuada was right in the middle of all the construction and directed those who were not familiar with the design. Even Beag and the other stonemasons consulted with him about details. With the work nearing its completion, Nuada went to work at the forge and made hinges for the gate; these were larger and stronger than any other that he had made. Strips of metal were placed upon the gates themselves in order to prevent fire or use of a battering ram.

Finally the wall was done, and all who saw it were impressed with the massive structure.

"Now we can move on to other things that need to be done," Mor said to Nuada.

"Yes, the clearing of the meadow in front of the wood wall needs the trees removed, and we can start building more houses."

"That and the digging of the well for the village."

Although the wall marked the beginning of another Spring, it was the cutting of the trees and the house building that really set the tone for the village people. Meanwhile the weather too changed for the good. The first birds of Spring filled the air with their songs, and some of the insects joined in the musical aspect, setting a tone for everyone. The village people now gathered in the outdoor cooking area at the end of each day for their meals, and their own music filled the valley. This was a happy time for all.

One afternoon while Nuada was sitting and holding his son, his mate brought him his evening meal and told him that she was with child again. This caught him by surprise, but he smiled at the thought of his growing family. When Nuada told Mor and A'Chreag about another child, they both said he was not alone; many of the women of the village were with child.

"I guess the Winter was just long enough," he replied.

- SPRING AND
HURRIED CONSTRUCTION -

The short days of Winter were over, and each day grew longer. The things needed to be done were marked with the completion of each project. None slowed or held back their pace. Things were done without complaint, and then they moved on. The village women began the preparation of the crop meadow with weeding and the plowing that was needed. Soon it would be time to sow the seeds and then watch over the young plants. Everyone in the village now kept their weapons of war near them wherever they went.

Another plan was put forward at the monthly meeting as to the safety of the pregnant women and the small children. In the event of an attack, they would stay within the cave on the valley rim. This was agreed to although some of the women resented being hidden away.

Nuada spent his days working on the new houses, the forge, and going down by the lake to build the frame for the waterwheel. The edge of the lake had to be trenched for the waterwheel to work, and it was a tedious job moving the clay bottom out of the way. The lake level was high, as was to be expected from the Spring runoff, and they knew that it would drop during the Summer months to come.

In the village, work progressed on three new houses, and they also began to dig the well for the village. The wood wall had men building a fighting step along the side of the village. The sheep were moved into the second valley for grazing, and the horses were used everywhere that heavy work was being done. Even the ox was hard at work hauling things. The ladders built during the Winter were placed into position against the valley rim where they could be used and certain areas of the top of the rim cleared for field of fire.

Even with all the preparations, no one had devised a plan for an attack from across the lake or how to defend there. This still worried Nuada, and he thought long and hard about it. But he could not see a way with the limited manpower he had. The only answer was to pull men from the wooden wall and move them into the trees that bordered the lake, but that would not work if the raiders split their forces. The villagers could not be in two places at the same time.

Nuada told Mor of his worries about the lake and asked for his thoughts on the matter. The next day Mor told him that his only thought was to retreat into the second valley if they were pushed that hard by raiders.

"But we have not defense there or any hidden places from which to fight," Nuada said. "Only the trees to mask our movements."

"It is better than being trapped here," was Mor's answer.

Nuada shook his head, and it made him worry even more. "I will not give up this village after all the hard work that was done."

"Then we must stop them here and hope for the best."

Nuada had hoped for more visions about his test, but none had come. This brought on more worries. "Am I alone in this matter?" he thought from time to time.

Nuada even sought input from A'Chreag about the way to protect the village. He suggested that Nuada seek out more people for the village who could help defend the valley. Nuada was surprised at the thought and took his own consul and waited a few more weeks to think about that.

By mid-Spring, three more of the smaller houses were complete, the well dug, and the stonemasons finished it off with stone work of much beauty. Now the tree cutting again moved back into the second valley, and work was begun on three more houses. The waterwheel and its wooden flume to supply water for the crops was finished. The design used horses to turn the wheel when it was needed. The woodworking building was expanded because it was needed, and the stable that everyone thought was large already had to be added onto also.

Nuada continued to walk around both valleys to check on everything being done, and his energy showed for all to see. But his mate began to worry about his health and told him he was spread too thin looking after the smallest details of the work.

"Go forth on another of your quests and see of other things. It will take your mind off your worries."

Nuada thought back to the words of A'Chreag and decided to leave the valley and seek out more people. He only took two days to prepare for the journey and felt that his absence would not take too long.

On the day of his departure, Mor found him starting for the wooden wall gate and asked of him the reason for this trip. "I am going forth to seek out more people for the village and the help we need to defend the valley. I cannot see of any other way for us to be successful in a battle."

"Then I wish you success in your quest and understand of the need for it."

Nuada turned and headed out of the portal gate toward the valley entrance and the new stone wall there. He passed his old forge site and paused for a minute before continuing on to the gate in the stone wall. Passing through he headed toward the site of his battle with the raiders long ago and walked on past without pause. He was trying to decide on a direction as he walked and then felt that his fate would lead him to where he was supposed to go. This time it was in a north direction, and he moved on without thought.

At the end of the first day, he arrived outside of the old village of Mor's. It had not changed much, which said a lot about the sturdiness of the housing design, although the forest around it had started to reclaim it, and weeds grew tall covering the old pathways. Nuada camped on the far side of the old village and slept well and without fear of the unknown. No visions came that night, and he awoke with the coming of the first light of the new day.

Eating a light and cold meal, he set out again and let the path show itself without thought. He relied on his instincts as a hunter and kept caution near the farther he traveled. No signs of people were about although game trails were everywhere he looked. He did not stop at midday but kept moving forward and away from his own village and valley. Once he thought of his family but knew that he had to find more people to protect them. Late in the second day, he saw some smoke in the distance and moved in that direction. "Are they friendly or raiders?" he thought. He kept moving, only now a little faster than before.

Late in the afternoon, he came up to the area from which the smoke originated from, and he cautiously watched from a safe distance. He found it was not a village but a camp of about thirty people with children. He watched until the sun began to set, and he settled down for the night again, eating a cold meal. He knew that he would seek them out in the morning light and ask them to join the village.

Before dawn he heard loud noises coming from the camp and made his way to a better advantage point where he could watch. The camp was being attacked, but the raiders were small in number — about ten men. Nuada did not hesitate but charged in, weapons at the ready. He killed three with his bow before drawing his great sword and cutting down the other six. The people of the camp could not believe their eyes at his actions and thronged around him when the fight was over.

A man called Cam pushed his way toward Nuada and introduced himself. "These are my people, and we thank you for your help."

Nuada asked about their village and was told that it had been burned to the ground in a fight the week before. Nuada nodded and said, "Would you like a place of safety and peace? I can offer this to you."

They said yes and asked many questions of him and his valley. He answered to the best of his knowledge everything about the valley and his need for more people. Within the hour, they broke camp and followed Nuada back toward the valley and his home village.

Two days later they entered the valley and were greeted at the stone wall built that Spring. The coded bell marked their sighting and warned the village of their coming. Making their way through the gate portal, they moved deeper into the valley and neared the wooden wall and its gate. Men lined the protection wall and watched as Nuada led the newcomers into the village. Taking them first to the outdoor cooking area to rest and meet with the people of the village, he then took them to an area on the other side of his house and told them to make camp there until housing was to be built for them. Again the village grew at Nuada's hand, and he knew now they could protect it.

While the new people settled in, Nuada sought out his family. He did not see them at first but found them at the cooking area. Nuada's mate pushed through the crowd around Nuada. The crowd was asking questions about the new people and how he had found them. "Nuada! I and our child have missed of you. Wolf was worried as much as I."

"And I have missed of you. Can you get me something to eat? I have only had cold meals since I departed, and I am lean between the ribs."

She quickly returned to the cooking hearth and made up a meal for him. Wolf pushed his way to Nuada and kept the others at a distance with his presence. Nuada called out that he would answer all questions later and sought some quiet time at his table. Even the village consul of elders did not bother him then. He was left with his thoughts and given time to relax. Nuada's mind was filled with the memories of each group he had brought into the valley and how they had made everything change for the better. He loved them all for each and every talent they had brought with them. Later after returning home with his family, Nuada fell asleep quickly. Exhaustion had caught up with him.

Early the next morning, Nuada joined Cam at his camp site and asked him to meet with the village counsel. Mor, Beag, and Farmer greeted Cam warmly and asked him many questions about his group. Later they took Cam on a tour of the village and throughout the valley. When they came to the stone wall near the second valley, they told him of its resources and how they used them. Although they did not enter the second valley, he asked about its protection. When he was told that they had no plan for it, his mind began to work through the problem. Nuada then suggested that they return to his house and look at the model of the valleys. Everyone thought it was a good idea and turned back to the village.

While showing the changes to the valleys on the model, Nuada explained the worries he had about defending for an attack from across the lake. Cam looked at the layout and said why not build an extension of the wood wall around the village to stop such an attack. The idea was so simple that they were all shocked that they had not thought of it before.

"We will need of your help to build that wall," Nuada said, and Cam agreed quickly. "Can you have your people help us starting tomorrow?"

"Yes. The sooner we start, the better protected we all will be."

Then they talked of where to build the wall and how to make it fit the village plan. By the time they finished talking, it was late, and they all gathered at the outdoor cooking area. Again music filled the air, and danger seemed far away.

Early the next morning, work crews were assigned details, and work continued on the new houses. Another crew began the trench for the new wood wall around the village, and others were sent to cut trees for all the projects. Nuada and A'Chreag returned to the forge and made more hinges and other items needed for the houses. Mor oversaw all the construction in the village and sent men where needed the most at the time. The women worked at the meadow of crops and gossiped between themselves about family and the newcomers, who they welcomed with cheer and goodwill. The young boys of the village tended the horses, which pulled the wagons hauling the trees from the second valley, although some of the trees were being cut where the new wood wall was going up.

Two weeks later the next three houses were nearing completion, and the new wood wall extension was almost three hundred feet finished and nearing the corner turn to wrap around the village to the ridge of the valley. Spring was nearly over and Summer about to begin. Everyone knew that time was running short to finish everything needed for the protection of the village. The newcomers were trained in the use of the bows and assigned defense positions throughout the valley. Everyone pushed to get things done, and rest was now a catch-on-the-fly thing because the work never seemed to end. Many worked throughout the nights to finish things needed.

Nuada still had no visions to guide him, and when he had time to think of it, it worried him. He had talked to his mate about this, and she tried to comfort him as best she could. "When the time comes, you will know of Creatrix's wisdom in this matter."

One day a freak late Spring rainstorm slowed the work of the village people, and Nuada and Mor pushed them to work in the rain. The wind tore at their clothing as they worked, and the rain blew sideways at times. Still they worked on without pausing. At the end of the day, the village consul met and praised all who braved the storm. Nuada himself was out in the weather and appraised the work done. He found himself satisfied with everything done but noted what had yet to be finished. Another trio of houses were started, but the men working on them were pulled off onto other things needed for the defense of the valley, mainly the finishing of the wood wall around the village.

After another week the wall and its new gates were finished. The people of the village held a feast to mark the end of that job. Hopes were high, and beer flowed throughout the evening to wash down the meal. Mor came over to Nuada's table and said, "Now that the wall is done, we must build more houses for everyone."

"I agree. We are as prepared as we can be now. The needs of all of the new people must come next."

The back street, behind the woodworking building, was now lined with new houses, and the plan now called for more across from Nuada's house, down the original roadway that led past the caves and into the second valley. The idea was to build four more houses in this area, as it would take care of everyone.

The next morning Mor did his usual thing and sent work crews to cut more wood and others to start the beginning framing for the new houses. None complained as this was a needed job for everyone. Nuada and A'Chreag returned to work at the forge, making more hinges and other detail parts for the houses. They now had enough of the weapons of war, and they felt that any more would be an overkill of the village's needs.

During the day, Nuada and A'Chreag took the last of the bells and hung it on the new wood-wall extension in a place where the workers could see and warn the village of an attack from across the lake. The noise from all of the construction carried across the valley and drowned out the sound of nature. Wagons filled the street hauling trees, and the horses straining from their loads whinnied in protest. The young children who controlled the paths of the horses called to each other as they passed on the street. This was the sound of progress and a growing village.

Late in the afternoon at the outdoor cooking area, the people talked happily and joined in the songs backed by the musical instruments. Children ran with shrieks and screams of happiness around the tables. It was controlled chaos, and nobody complained.

Nuada awoke early the next morning, as was his usual pattern, and strolled to the cooking area to see Mor. "Mor, my friend. A'Chreag and I are finished with our work and would like to lend a hand at whatever you need done."

"We now have enough help for everything, but perhaps you need to take a walk outside of the valley and check for problems. If the raiders are near. you could tell of us before trouble starts."

"I can do that, but I expect to have a vision again before they come.".

"You have never let us down with your visions before, so I will leave it to your thoughts on the matter."

At that moment, A'Chreag showed up, and Nuada told him to gather of his weapons as they would be going for a walk outside of the valley.

"Are you expecting trouble, Nuada?"

"No, but we need to check anyway."

Within a half hour, the pair departed for the entrance to the valley. They traveled lightly and moved quickly. Outside of the valley, they split up and went in different directions. They thought they could cover more ground that way and agreed to meet before the sun set that afternoon. Nuada went north, and A'Chreag turned to the west.

Before midday Nuada was almost at the old village of Mor's. He stopped, looking for anything out of place. But even the animals of the forest showed no signs of alarm, so he turned back to the valley, taking a different path than the one he had traveled on earlier. This took him a little further to the west, and he kept his caution and was alert to anything.

Meanwhile A'Chreag found nothing, and he too turned and followed a different path back to the valley. He knew that anything could happen and was prepared for it. He listened to the sounds of the forest and knew that they would warn him before he could sense any danger.

Late in the afternoon, the pair rejoined each other and told how they both had found nothing.

"I did not even see of any trace of humans — only the creatures of the forest," reported A'Chreag.

"The same here. Let us follow the lakeshore after we enter the new gate. I want to see how the ambush sites look."

Walking up to the stone wall at the valley entrance, Nuada waved at the guards there, and the pair passed through and turned for the lakeshore. They walked on in silence, looking carefully at the protection from the tree line and thinking about how a fight would develop here.

"I think the hit-and-run fight would be the best in this situation. Whoever is here can run and dodge the raiders' weapons, then hide in the brush or climb a tree. The idea is to trap the raiders so none survive. We can hit them from three sides."

"But what if they circle and come at us from the second valley entrance wall?"

"Then it will be the new wood wall and the ridgeline at the back of the valley."

"I can see the wisdom of the plan. I hope it works well as we think it will."

They continued on and entered the village and stopped at the outdoor cooking area for a much needed meal and some beer. Mor was there and sought out Nuada and asked if he had any luck finding raiders.

"We found nothing human or a threat to the village. But it was a nice day for such a walk."

Nuada sat back, full from his meal and the fullness he felt from the beer. He had not felt so relaxed in months. His mate had brought his son to keep him company, and Nuada watched the boy play with other children of his age. All thoughts of the village vanished from his mind as he continued to keep an eye on the boy. No one bothered him in this time of family. A few hours later, they made their way home and to the quiet solitude that they deserved.

The next day Nuada helped with the housing construction and felt that this was finally a place of peace and security. Everyone was friendly with each other and worked in harmony. Only the noise from the construction disturbed the tranquility of the valley. The only noted change was the need for men to be on watch at the stone walls all the time.

Over the next few weeks, the housing came to a finish, and Cam's camp was reduced in size as each house was completed. Those with time on their hands cut brush and weeds within the village, and this gave a pleasant appearance to the village. All thoughts of an attack were far from everyone mind's as the village settled into what everyone thought was the way it was supposed to be. Even Nuada felt at peace, although at the back of his mind he knew it could not last. Summer was about to begin and that meant that his test was near.

One warm, late Spring day, Nuada took a walk to the lakeshore and stared across at the island that had been his first home in the valley and thought of the memories that started all of the changes in the valley. Every step was recounted in his mind, as was each of the people who had influenced him. He remembered with affection how he and Jan had met and how they had talked about so many things. Then there was Mor and his strength of mind about how things should be done. Beag came to mind and his attention to details and his talent working with stone. And there was the Farmer, who became responsible for the good crops that fed the people. Nuada shook his head and felt that he had played only a small part in the development of the village. He then thought, "If Creatrix takes of me tomorrow, I shall be satisfied although I shall miss of my mate and child."

He did not feel the weight of leadership as he turned and walked back to the village. Passing through the new wood wall around the village, he waved to the guards and was greeted in return by their friendly voices. He passed the new houses and paused in the stone-rubble street and looked around at the changes of the village. He thought about new growth as only a successful village can have and then moved on to the cooking area and his friends.

- SUMMER AND NUADA'S TEST -

Creatrix, in his form as the sun, broke the early-morning sky, carrying the promise of another warm and clear day. Nuada awoke early, as was his nature, and took Wolf for his morning run. Nuada wandered toward the forge building but stopped and turned to the outside cooking area and his friends who also awoke early. As usual Mor and Beag were talking about the village and things that needed to be done that day.

"Morning, you two. What are you planning for this fine day?" greeted Nuada.

"Welcome, Nuada. Just the usual building problems and how to fix them," replied Mor.

"Anything that I need to be aware of?"

"No. The guards last night saw and heard nothing either. I know it is getting close to the time for the raiders, but the villagers are getting tired of all the practice and with the plan to defend the valley."

"They will understand soon enough. Keep them at it."

"We will. Just let us know of any new visions. It will help."

After some more small talk, Nuada departed their company and walked to the wall at the valley entrance. Arriving there he climbed the ladder and stood looking out toward the north, where he expected the attack to come from. Time passed without his knowing it, and soon he climbed back down and went outside to search the area away from the valley. Birds called to each other as he walked, and deer turned and looked at him as he passed. His only thoughts were on where his enemy would be and from which direction they would come. Slowly he circled the whole area and found nothing. Finally he turned toward home and the village again.

His thoughts were so filled with different ways of battle that he walked right past the entrance wall and continued along the stream to the second valley wall. It startled him when he looked up finally and realized where he was. He paused, taking a deep breath, and then entered into the second valley. "Why did I come this way?" he thought. On he walked, knowing not the direction he was going or why. His steps followed the stream, and soon he was deep into the second valley and nearing the backside of that fertile ground where they found the oats last year. He looked long and hard at the ridgeline there, wondering if it was possible for anyone to breach it and enter that way into his valley. On he walked, studying the landscape and trying to find an answer to his restless questions. He knew it was impossible to scale the ridge from the second valley into his, but still he looked and wondered.

It was late afternoon when he finally finished his walk around the second valley, and he found nothing that would change his mind about the direction of a raid. It could only come from the entrance into the first valley. He picked up his pace and hurried back to the cooking area and his friends.

Stopping by the crop meadow, he talked to his mate for a few minutes and told her of his walk and his thoughts on the matter of the direction of the raid. She gave him a kiss and a few words of encouragement before he went on his way. Entering into the village, he continued his walk to the woodworking building and had a word with A'Chreag. Again Nuada told him of his walk around both valleys and his thoughts about the direction of a raid. A'Chreag told Nuada that a practice defense was planned for a little later in the day and asked him to observe how the villagers did. Nuada agreed to watch, and then he set out for the cooking area.

When he got there, he saw Mor talking to some of the village men, who had their bows with them. Walking over to the group, Nuada said, "I see that the preparations for the practice are coming along. Are there any problems?"

"They were just talking about how to judge the distance from the wood wall and how it would be for the best effect against raiders."

"I am going to watch, and if I see a problem, we will find an answer."

Nuada and Mor continued to talk until the time came for the practice, and the pair followed the others out to where they could observe the results. The village men lined the wall and waited for the order to fire a volley from their bows. Mor and Nuada stood outside and near the wall to watch the results. Beag was the one giving the practice, and when he thought all was ready, he gave an order for a volley shot at great distance. Nuada watched the fall of arrows and their effectiveness. He called up to the wall for a hold on firing of the arrows, and he and Mor walked out onto the field where the arrows had landed. Most of the shafts landed about one hundred yards from the wall and some as much as two hundred.

"They are fairly even on distance, although some did reach further," Mor said.

"True, but we need for them to be able to judge distance as well. What if we put some kind of markers out here for them to be able to do that as well?"

"What think you of some kind of stakes with colored cloth on them?"

"That might work. Let us try."

They returned to the wall and called up to Beag about their thoughts, and he sent some of the younger men to the woodworking building to get such items and some rope.

When they returned, Mor stayed at the wall while Nuada took one end of the rope and walked back out onto the field. He counted his paces at average distance for the long shots, then set a pole into the ground and called for Mor to move down the wall so that the distance could remain constant all along the wall. After setting out five more stakes, Nuada cut the distance in half and repeated the placement of more stakes. When he and Mor finished, they called up to Beag to again have the men fire a volley and stood by to watch the results. All of the arrows from the initial round had been retrieved while Mor and Nuada were placing the stakes, so a clear answer would be seen from this round.

Nuada and Mor did not have to wait long before Beag called out for another volley toward the farthest markers. The sky over their heads was filled with the shafts as the men let fly from their bows. This time the shafts found their distance, and both Mor and Nuada were happy with the results. They waited for another round at half the distance and were soon watching them fly overhead and toward the shorter target line. Again the results were good, and they went back through the gate portal and waited for Beag to come down to them.

When Beag joined them, Mor said, "It looks like all they needed was the markers to find their distance. Tomorrow I will put out more of the markers at distances in between the others. This will give us the results that we need to protect the village."

Mor and Nuada returned to the cooking area as it was almost time for the evening meals. They sat at Nuada's table and talked about what they had observed and thought about ways to improve the results. Finding nothing that they could improve upon, they waited for their supper.

Nuada's mate had returned from the field and dropped their son off to Nuada. Nuada looked down at the boy and smiled as only a parent could. The boy was growing every day and talking a mile a minute. It seemed that every other sentence was a question, but Nuada was patient and answered them as best he could. Mor watched the interplay between them and kept silent, but he smiled to himself.

The villagers filed in to eat and talk between themselves. Soon music filled the air, and they became relaxed and comforted in their own company. Only those on watch worried.

That night Nuada relaxed and played with his child before sleep called him to bed. Again no dreams followed. The next morning he did his usual walk to the cooking area but found it empty. Wondering why sent him toward the woodworking building, but he stopped when he found the answer as to why the cooking area was empty. The village men were up early and had lined the wall again. Practice was in full swing, and this time it was Mor directing them.

Nuada climbed the ladder up the wall and watched, this time alone. It seemed to him that the accuracy was on the mark. He felt safe in knowing that the men of the village were here to protect what everyone had worked so hard to create. After spending a half hour there, he climbed back down the ladder and went back to the cooking area, knowing that the others would soon follow.

Some of the women were there, preparing a small meal for their men before they returned to their regular work assignments. Nuada waited and smiled inwardly to himself with the results of what he saw earlier. It was not long before the men began to come into the cooking area. Nuada watched, and when Mor finally showed, he waved to him. Mor came over and sat.

"The practice went well today. I saw you there and waited to talk with you, but when I looked again, you were gone."

I saw no reason to interrupt, and I knew you would return here. Have you picked the men for the entrance wall, the ones who will retreat into the woods near the lake?"

"Yes. The hunters are the best for that job. They know how to hide and how to strike when it is right."

"Good choice. What about the ridgeline on the left of the meadow?"

"A'Chreag — and he has picked four others to fight from that side."

"Again, good choice. I think we are ready now. We have only to wait."

"All this practice has slowed the work on the houses, but I think they will be ready in another two weeks, and then everyone will have a house of their own."

"I think it is time for a feast to mark all that has been done in such a short time."

"Everyone will agree to that. Because we both know that war costs lives, it may be the last time for some of them."

"Yes. We must keep their minds off that aspect of all of this."

"I agree. They must think that no one will be hurt except the raiders."

"Do you need help today with the houses? It will keep my mind off that too."

Mor arose and went from table to table talking to other men of the village, assigning jobs for the day. Nuada watched and waited for his return. Soon he did so, and the pair, who were followed by others, walked down to the houses under construction. Nuada spent the rest of the day working where he was needed.

Three days later the great feast was held, and it was a joyous occasion. New music and some favorite tunes filled the air. Dancing wore many out before the evening was half over; the beer they consumed did the rest. However, this time they continued to stay late into the early-morning hours; even Nuada did not feel sleepy. However, he did have concerns over the lateness of the hour did. "This would be the perfect time for an attack," he thought. It made him leave the party and wander out to the entrance wall. He found he was not alone in his thinking. Mor and A'Chreag were already there.

"What think you about the possibility of an attack this morning, Nuada?" asked Mor.

"It is a strong possibility. That is why we are here, right?"

"Perhaps I should scout out the area in front of the valley," said A'Chreag.

"Yes, and I will go with you. We will use the same plan as before and split up our search," responded Nuada.

The pair climbed down from the wall and walked through the gate portal. They followed their same paths as before, cautious because of the darkness. They both returned about the same time, just as the sun began to rise.

"Nothing new on my side. How about yours?"

"Nothing. That worries me."

The pair returned to the wall, where Mor was still waiting.

"Nothing to report, but we will send out others later. I have a bad feeling about this."

Nuada walked to the streambed and washed his face and waited at the wall while the other two returned to the village. Two hours later they returned with a pair of hunters who looked like they had not gotten any sleep either. Mor told them what he wanted and sent them out to search again. Nuada sat against the cold stone wall and dozed while he waited for their return. A'Chreag kept watch on the wall with the regular guards as he too waited.

Before noon Nuada awoke and returned to the stream to wash his face again. His mind filled with the dangers out there that awaited anyone who was not prepared. As he stood there, A'Chreag came to wash his face also.

"I worry for those two. They had little sleep and could become lax in their search," commented A'Chreag.

"I too worry. If they are not back within the hour, we will go out again."

Fifteen minutes later, one of the hunters returned.

"Anything?" asked Nuada.

"Nothing. Has Mathas returned?"

"No. What direction did he travel?"

"North, toward the old village."

"Then A'Chreag and myself will go in search of him. Get some sleep until we return."

This time Nuada was worried, and he set a fast pace with A'Chreag in the direction that the other hunter had taken. After two hours, they still had seen no trace of him, and the pair became more cautious the farther they traveled. Nuada kept watch for signs of smoke or any other signs. Even the animals of the forest kept silent as they moved forward.

They paused at one point, and A'Chreag said, "I like this not. We should have heard or seen something."

Nuada agreed, and then they pressed onward. As they neared the old village around midday, they split up and circled the village site. On the far side where they again joined up, they found tracks of a great many men and horses.

"Do we follow?" asked A'Chreag.

"Yes. We must find of the hunter and why the tracks are here and where they came from."

They tracked the passage of the strangers for another hour and found of the hunter. He was watching them from a distance and kept silent as he pointed out the group to Nuada. About twenty-five men on horseback had captives of about another ten men and women with their children.

"Do we interfere or only watch?" asked A'Chreag.

"I would like to help them , but it would bring them down on us and the valley. There are too many for us to handle by ourselves."

"Then what do we do?"

"We wait and watch. Perhaps an opportunity will present itself for us to help."

As the day started to find sunset, the large group made camp, and the trio that was following separated to watch their movements from different angles. The group of captives were kept in the center where they were easy to watch, and they did not appear to give any opposition to their foes. Nuada watched as two of the male captives were beaten for no reason. Laughter from the raiders echoed in Nuada's ears as he was unable to do anything about it. As the darkness of the night surrounded the campsite, shadows from their fires flickered off the trees. They had posted only two guards, one at the horses and one to watch the captives. Nuada sought out A'Chreag and the hunter with a plan. If they could remove the one guard at the horses and then spook the horses to run, it would cause a loud commotion among the raiders and perhaps a chance to help the captives.

They waited until it was deep into the night before trying the plan. The hunter would take out the guard and free the horses to run, possibly through the campsite. The hunter came very close to the guard and sent an arrow into the man's head. He dropped without a sound, and the hunter spooked the horses after untying them and directing them into the campsite. A'Chreag and Nuada watched the action, and during the unexpected stampede, sent volleys of arrows into the unexpected raiders, who awoke within the campsite.

Within minutes most of the raiders were killed and others wounded. Surprise had worked in the favor of Nuada and his men. The captives stood in shock and did not know what to do. The trio entered into the campsite and took two of the wounded raiders captive and dispatched the others without mercy. Nuada then took up a conversation with the captives' leader who had been beaten that early evening. He asked about the raiders first, then about the people whom he had saved. It was the same old story, how they had attacked and burned their village and had enslaved the people, although this time the raiders had a large group of warriors. This group was only a small part of it. When asked where they were, the man did not know.

Nuada told him of the valley and offered them its safety, and they readily agreed to come back with the trio. Meanwhile A'Chreag and the hunter questioned the captive raiders. After some forceful attention to their wounds, they told everything about the large group of raiders and where they were going. They then dispatched the pair of raiders and rejoined Nuada. Some of the horses were nearby and easy to catch while the others had taken off for parts unknown. The group, led by Nuada, then moved out on the path back toward the valley and safety.

The hunter scouted to the west of the group watching for the raiders. Meanwhile A'Chreag followed at the rear, protecting them from a surprise attack from there. They traveled without stopping to rest, and as the day wore on, they made good distance from the site where Nuada's group had dispatched the first party of raiders. Nearing sundown they were about a mile from the valley entrance when Nuada sent A'Chreag ahead to warn the guards of their approach. After A'Chreag told them what to expect, they sent a runner to find Mor and Beag. A'Chreag then returned to the group to assist Nuada. Just as they reached the gateway, the hunter returned to the group and said he had found no sign of any more raiders.

Mor and Beag had the gateway portal wide open and had brought a large party of the village people to welcome the newcomers. The newcomers were tired and looked it from the forced march; the children fared the worst, and the village people helped them carry their baggage to the outdoor cooking area, where they could rest for awhile. The village women brought food and drink to them, and small talk followed with the warmth of the valley's welcome. Soon music filled the air again while Nuada and the other village leaders met to talk about the large raider party that was still outside their valley.

"This is what we have been practicing so hard for , but I would like to put some guards on the cliffside above the village now, at a place where they can look out to the west. I think this is where they will come from." Nuada said.

Mor replied, "But they still have to come to the valley entrance, and they may miss of the valley altogether."

"They may, but any warning we have is for our protection."

"When was the last time you had any sleep, Nuada?"

"Two, no, it was three days ago. I feel of the need , but the situation will not allow of it."

"Get some sleep. We will need of you when the time comes, and you must have all of your energy to lead us in this battle."

Nuada only nodded in response and arose to walk home. His mate was nearby and waiting for him to help him to their door and his awaiting bed. His feet had only left the floor when he drifted off to sleep still dressed. His mate sat and watched over him all that night without sleep herself.

During his sleep, Creatrix came to him in a vision and told him that today was the day of his test and that he would watch over the village people, along with Jan. "Expect the unknown, Nuada," were his final words.

Nuada awoke with a start and sat up in bed, which awoke his mate, who had been dozing at the table. "Nuada! Is something wrong?"

"Only a vision from Creatrix again. Go back to sleep."

"I am awake now. Tell me of your vision."

Nuada explained the vision and the strange words from Creatrix. Then he got up from the place where he had been sleeping and collected his weapons. "I must warn the others of the village," he told her and then departed to find of the others.

It was still long before the first light of dawn when he walked into the cooking area where the new people found a place to sleep where they could, not having time to make camp. The area was lit with small lanterns, and he could see their sleeping forms. Looking about he sought out Mor or Beag. They were not here, so he went to the village wood wall and asked of the guards there. They had not seen of them since the evening before and thought that they were probably at their houses. Nuada made haste to Mor's house and pounded on his door. After a few minutes, Mor came to the door and, seeing the look on Nuada's face, made him step back. He asked, "What is wrong, Nuada?"

"I had my vision from Creatrix. Today is the day for the fight. We must awaken everyone and prepare."

Mor said that he would get everyone to their battle defenses and then asked Nuada where he would be.

"I shall be at the valley entrance wall. Make sure that A'Chreag and his men are on the ridge and watching for the raiders."

As Nuada walked toward the wall, the first hint of dawn began to light up the shadows at its base. He looked around, back toward the village and then out at his island in the lake. "Things have changed, and now is the time of my test," he thought.

He climbed the ladder to the top and talked with the guards before he settled against the stone wall. His eyes scanned the open area before him and strained to see over the horizon before him. The sounds of the rushing water from the stream hid outside noises, and birds began their morning calls, which added to Nuada's anguished mind.

With the dawn now above the hill line, the shadows disappeared, and the waiting began in earnest. Soon a runner from the village came to tell them that the raiders had been spotted from the ridge. He warned the guards that they were not to ring the bell until the enemy was within sight. Baskets of the arrows were all along the wall top, and spears were bunched together about every twenty feet. Nuada climbed down from the wall and went outside the gate portal to find if the raiders were going to bypass the valley entrance or turn toward them.

Quickly Nuada went to the site where he had fought raiders before and hid in the brush. He found he was holding his breath and forced himself to breath normally. He waited and watched.

Slowly the raiders approached the valley entrance, and Nuada watched as the number of them increased. He thought at first that they would pass by, but the recent tracks from himself and the new people showed the way to the valley. They turned and followed the path. Nuada eased himself from his hiding place and hurried back to the wall.

Crossing through the gate portal, he stopped and pushed the gate closed and then set the braces behind the gate to stop them from battering through. Quickly he climbed the wall and warned the guards. They drew the arrows shafts from the baskets and prepared themselves. Nuada took up a position nearest the valley entrance and the end of the stone wall. He thought to himself again, "It is good that it is so narrow here. There are so many of them that they cannot all come at once.'"

He was wrong. The raiders marched in formations and made their way over the top of the valley entrance. After they saw the wall, they paused, and their leader sent a large formation forward. Nuada was more afraid than he had ever been before in his life, and he knew that the others on the wall felt the same. Some of them began to talk in an excited nature out of fear. He hushed them, and they waited.

Nuada waited until they were within seventy yards of the wall and gave the signal to fire their bows at the intruders. He had one of the men begin to ring the bell as a warning to the village. A cloud of arrow shafts filled the air and began to rain down upon the enemy. Quickly they fired again and again. The formation stopped in its tracks, and many of them fell before being able to fight. The leader of the raiders sent two more formations forward, and the men on the wall began to tire of the endless pulling on their bows. Slowly the enemy made up ground toward the wall, and now spears began to be thrown down on them. This battle went on for almost an hour before Nuada called for the retreat back into the valley and the trap set there. Nuada felt that they had killed almost fifty, but there were many more of the enemy to come. He was the last man off the wall, and he stopped only long enough to kick the braces from the gate portal and run back to the village. The hunters split from the wall defenders and edged into the forest along the lakeside; this was their natural skill and the ground that they knew well.

Nuada did not have to hurry the wall defenders as they ran. As they approached the wood wall, they called out to the other defenders. Mor answered back, and the gate swung wide to allow them to enter. Nuada quickly climbed the ladder that was nearest the gate, as the gate portal was closed and secured. Mor was waiting for him and asked, "How many of them are there?"

"Many! I think they have about three hundred. We killed about fifty."

"That is more then we planned for. How can we defend against that many?"

"We must! Keep everyone calm and stick to the plan."

The pair looked out onto the meadow and waited again as the enemy approached.

Drums filled the air as the enemy formation regrouped in front of the wood wall. Their lines spilled across the meadow and looked endless to the defenders. The bell rang out in defiance from the base of the wall, and the village men lined it, ready to defend their homes.

Suddenly the bell from the entrance to the second valley began to ring its warning. Nuada and Mor's heads spun in its direction.

"They have split their force. What do we do now?" asked Mor.

"We fight. We have no other options."

Slowly the raiders closed the distance to the wall. The villagers peered over the wall, waiting for the word from Mor to fire their bows. The raiders shifted their positions, and men with shields moved to the front of their lines. A horn blast sent them forward marching in step and massed from behind. The other warriors waited to see what would happen. Closer they came to the markers on the open meadow. It wasn't until they had passed the distant marker that Mor called for a volley of arrows to fly. Again the sky was filled with a cloud of shafts, and they hailed down with uncanny accuracy upon the field of warriors; their shields did little to protect them. The defenders now formed two rows to keep up the rate of fire on the raiders. Shaft after shaft filled the air, and the numbers of the intruders were reduced quickly. Within fifteen minutes, half of the raiders had fallen from the ferocity of the defense. Arrows continued to reduce the intruders' numbers. Shafts from the ridgeline and from the lakeside forest hit them from the backside of their massed position. Nuada knew that it was only a matter of time before they would have to meet them in the field and fight them hand to hand. Before that happened though, the raider leader called for a full retreat, and they began to fall back to the stone wall at the entrance to the valley.

The raiders that had attacked the wall at the entrance to the second valley retreated too. They were followed by the defenders from that wall, who kept a hail of arrows firing at them as they ran. At the entrance wall, the second group of invaders entered through the gate portal, expecting to join up with the larger group. They found them in full retreat and stopped short. The defenders from the second valley wall quickly closed the gate from outside, and using a large wood beam, they locked the invaders inside the valley. They had nowhere to go. The trap was complete.

The village defenders moved from the wood wall out onto the meadow and followed the raiders. Nuada was in the lead and soon put his bow away and drew upon his great sword. The other defenders did the same, and the distance closed quickly. Some spears were thrown by both groups , but the intruders also added rocks thrown from slings at the defenders. Those were quickly targeted by the ridgeline defenders and those from the lakeside woods. The air smelled of death for all who took the time to notice. Cries of pain echoed around the valley, almost all from the attackers. Only a few of the defenders had been wounded in the battle.

The distance from each group was now down to a few yards, and then they closed ranks and fought hand to hand. Nuada did not have to seek out the raider leader; he found Nuada. It was sword against battle axe. Each warrior fought with a strength that they did not know they possessed. Nuada got in the first cut and drew blood from the leader's arm. His balance on the battle axe shifted, and he fought back as if nothing had happened.

Nuada again had to fight the man's strength, and the blades rang with determination as they made contact time after time. Nuada's determination did not waver, and he fought on. At last the man's defenses faltered, and Nuada struck him in the neck so hard that it seemed that his foe's head would fall from his shoulders. He toppled sideways and fell to the dirt. Nuada's attention was still on the leader when he was hit by a spear in the left side. He spun, looking for the attacker, who was killed by one of the villagers. Nuada knelt and pulled the spear from his side. Pain seared his mind , but he knew that the fight was not over, and he rallied and found another opponent to fight. Blood ran from his wound , but he failed to notice it in the heat of the battle. Soon all of the invaders were dead or badly wounded. Nuada called for the wounded to be killed, so as to prevent them bringing more warriors back to the valley. He leaned on his sword, and his vision began to blur. He felt weakness in his arms and legs, then toppled to the ground. Mor saw him fall and ran to his side, but Nuada was unconscious. Mor held pressure to the wound and called for help to send his friend back to the village for treatment.

Nuada awoke not back in the village but before Creatrix. He was in the vision-quest state again, or so he thought.

"Nuada. Awaken and hear of me," called Creatrix. Your wound is great, and now I have a decision to make regarding your future. Will you return to your family or stay here with me?"

Nuada pleaded, "Return me to the village. My work there is not done yet, and I have many things to do for them."

"We will see. For now you will remain here with me."

Jan appeared before Nuada, and he had a sad look in his eyes.

"You are so young, my friend, but you have done many wondrous things in that short life of yours. Many pass through their life cycle without accomplishing anything. Not so you."

"Then speak for me with Creatrix. You know that I am needed by the village people."

"That I cannot do. my friend. That decision is his alone."

Shadows filled Nuada's eyes as he drifted into the void. Time would reveal the answer from Creatrix.

In the village, Nuada was taken into the woodworking building and placed with only a few of the wounded from the battle. He was treated, and Mor stayed nearby to watch over him. Others gathered outside to wait on word of his condition. Nuada's mate hurried to the building after learning of his wound. Wolf was at her heels and found Nuada first. He laid down and waited like everyone else. Nuada's mate began to wash the blood from Nuada and called for clean clothes for him. There was nothing else to do for him at that time.

A'Chreag and Beag organized the villagers and the horses and wagons to pick up the dead invaders and transport them outside of the valley to where the first battle had happened. Their bodies were piled together as wagonload after wagonload went to and fro from the battle scene. During one of the trips, it was found that the raiders had six wagons of their own that were found alongside the ridgeline outside of the valley. They were filled with the booty and grains that they had taken on their foray across the land. A'Chreag himself brought the wagons into the village and helped to transfer the loads into the new warehouse behind the woodworking building.

Three days later, with no change in Nuada's condition, village life was starting to return to normal. Construction of four more houses were begun, and the women returned to working the crops in the meadow near the lake. Horses turned the wheel that powered the waterwheel for irrigation of the crops. Nuada was moved from the woodworking building to his house, where his mate watched over him. The villagers still continued to inquire about him, and many spent hours outside of his house waiting for a change in his condition.

The woodcutters spent the days in the second valley cutting the trees needed for the new construction, and during all of this, Mor and A'Chreag traveled about checking on the needs of the villagers. Beag and the other stone-cutter worked at building end walls and fireplaces needed for the new houses. Rubble from the stone work was used for extending the streets, and a second water well was starting to be built. This was a busy time for the village and its people. What was lacking was Nuada's presence.

On the fourth day, Creatrix called on Nuada.

"Nuada, awaken and listen to my words."

Nuada stirred from his fog shrouded sleep and answered his call.

"I am going to send you back to your people and family. You have passed the first part of your test but prepare yourself for what follows. It will not be easy."

Nuada stirred, and his eyes fluttered open to find the presence of his mate hovering nearby within the house. He tried to speak but found no words. Wolf was the first to notice the change in Nuada and came over to him and licked at his hand. Nuada's mate turned and saw that Nuada was awake and hurried to his side. Tears began to flow from her eyes in relief of his return.

Slowly a single word passed from his lips: "Food." His mate quickly brought a soup to him and helped him sit up enough for him to take of it. He felt the pain of his wound for the first time, but the smell of the soup and the comfort of her presence kept him calm and under control of the discomfort.

After eating a small amount, he looked down at his wound and found that it had been bound but showed a large stain. He settled back and fell asleep again. Time was what he needed now for him to heal.

Word passed quickly through the village that Nuada was awake after four days. Mor came to visit that evening and told Nuada of all the things that the people of the village were accomplishing. Nuada asked questions, and the answers pleased him. When he asked how the new people were settling into the village, Mor told him that it was as if they had been here a long time and they helped to define the purpose of the village.

After about a half hour, Nuada began to get sleepy, and Mor left him, feeling better about his recovery. Outside Mor passed on information about Nuada's condition and asked them to leave him alone until he could greet them himself. Nuada slept through until the next morning, and after he awoke, he spoke with A'Chreag about the forge and the parts needed for the new houses. A'Chreag reassured him that all would be taken care of without his help. This was the first morning when Nuada sat up at the bedside, and he could not believe how it tired him. He tried to stand for a minute but found the effort too much to continue. Nuada's mate brought him a potion made from the plants he had recovered when he first found Jan. This eased the pain in his side and relaxed him enough to fall asleep again. He did not awaken until almost sundown and found his son curled up asleep next to him; Wolf lay next to his bed but watching everything. Nuada found he was extremely hungry and waited for his mate to bring him something solid to eat. She served him a thick slice of venison liver, telling him it would restore the blood he lost in the battle. After eating he fell asleep again and did not awaken until the early sun of the next day stirred him.

Sitting on the edge of his bed, he was determined to stand that day and waited for his mate to feed him. After eating Mor arrived and handed Nuada a staff that was capped with a bronze head made by A'Chreag. Nuada looked closely at the intricate design on the head and then asked Mor to help him stand. Mor was not too sure if it was a good idea, but Nuada was determined to do so. With the help of the staff, Nuada found success in standing. He took a few short steps, and then he became dizzy and had to sit again.

"I am getting better," he told Mor. "But I will need time to heal and gain my feet under me."

Mor nodded in agreement and then reported the work planned for the day by the others. After a short talk, Mor departed, and Nuada settled back onto his bed again. His inner strength kept him from falling asleep again, and his mind raced with all of the things that needed to be done.

Later that week Nuada was up and moving throughout his house with the help of the staff, although climbing the stairs still eluded him. He did not think that the wound would impose such a limit on his mobility, and he fought to change that. He finally decided to go outside and see what the village was doing. He made it to his front deck and heard all the noise of a busy village at work. His views were limited, so he stepped down and out into the street. He looked up and down and saw no one in sight and decided to venture further, following the noise of the construction. He crossed to the second street and still saw nothing. Going further he found a third street had been built, and down it the new houses were quickly going up. He walked toward the work, and the thought of his wound for the first time slipped from his mind. He paused in the street, eyeing the work and the craft of the workers. Mor was there and saw him. Giving a wave, he joined Nuada and asked after his wound.

"It is better. Although I still feel of its tightness."

"It is good to see you out in the sunshine. The fresh air will do more good for you than any potion."

"I agree. What is next on the construction list?"

They continued to talk as they walked around the site, and then Mor asked if he had seen the new well for the village. Nuada said no, so Mor walked him to its site, which was near Nuada's house. After about an hour, Nuada began to feel the weakness returning to him. He said his farewell to Mor and returned home to sit outside in the sunshine. A gentle breeze began to blow. Its coolness was welcomed, and Nuada slept in its comfort.

Late in the afternoon Nuada's mate returned from the crop meadow and awoke him for his evening meal. He told her of his walk around the village, and she said that it was too early for such things. He heard her but made no comment.

Another week passed, and Nuada's mobility increased, but he was still too weak to do anything. He was finally able to walk to the wall at the second valley and return, but he had not returned to the killing field in front of the village. One day he paused at the gate portal leading into the field and found himself shaking as if from fear. He steadied his nerve and pushed himself out onto the ground. After going only a short distance, he turned and walked to Jan's crypt. Standing before it, he asked, "Jan, what is wrong with me? I have nothing to fear our here, but I am reluctant to travel into it again."

He received no answer and returned to the village. He stopped at the out-door cooking area and sat for a long time, looking into the thin air wondering.

"Nuada, it is good to see you up and about," called Beag. "We have missed of you in the village meetings."

"My strength is returning, although it is taking more time than I thought it would."

"Then it is a good time for it, as things have been quiet."

"Not that quiet. The noise of all the construction roused me from my bed last week."

"But that is a good thing. The village continues to grow, and we are happy and healthy."

"You are right. It made me want to find out of all the changes going on here, which has made me stronger."

They talked for awhile longer before Beag had to leave. Then Nuada walked back to the wood wall portal and gazed out onto the meadow again. He steeled his nerve and walked out onto the battlefield and kept going this time. As he neared his old forge site, he paused and looked around. "What was here to fear?" he thought. Looking up he saw the stone wall and some of the guards still keeping watch. Then he looked around again and sought out the site where he fought the raider leader. Slowly he knelt down and touched the earth and felt the tightness of his side. "I was caught unaware. That will not happen again." Then he stood and turned for the village again.

The staff he carried had become a part of him in the last weeks, and he knew that it would remain a part of him for the rest of his life. Passing through the gate portal, he turned to the new housing construction to view the work of the villagers. As he passed the woodworking building, Mor stepped out and greeted him.

"Nuada, you are looking better today and seem to be moving without difficulty now."

"I am still stiff, and I know that the injury will remain a constant reminder throughout my life, but I can live with that."

The pair walked to the housing construction discussing the work there and the timeline for finishing it.

"The village is still growing, and I think we should plan on more houses to be built. I don't want to limit our size or the number of people who will join us here," Nuada said.

"I think you are right. We should plan on our growth and expect that more people will want to join us."

"In that case, we should plan on another field for our crops in the second valley and build another waterwheel to irrigate it from the stream. We will need to feed our growth."

"What if we add another stable and a house for someone to watch over it in the second valley?"

"I think that would be a wise idea. Maybe another wall at the entrance into the valley?"

"I will put these ideas before the consul at our next meeting."

Nuada walked around the construction while Mor sought out some of the men working high up in the rafters of one house. Soon he became distracted and started to walk down to the crop meadow. Taking his time and leaning on the staff for support, he stopped under a tree that looked out on the meadow. He could see his mate and many of the other women, who were now beginning to show their pregnancy. He did not see his son and wondered where he was. "I should be spending more time with him now," he thought. Then he turned back to the village, slowly taking his faltering steps carefully. He was beginning to become weary from his journeys today.

Instead of going to his house, he went to the outdoor cooking area and sat at his table. The area was empty, and slowly he began to fall asleep at his table. It wasn't until the late afternoon, when the people began to gather for their evening meal, that he awoke and looked around to see if anyone had noticed his sleeping. None let on that he had been sleeping, and he stretched to help clear his mind of the sleep fog. A'Chreag saw his movements and walked over to him.

"Nuada, it is good to see you up and about."

"I took an extended walk around the valley today, and it wore me out I am afraid. It may take me longer to heal than I thought."

"After your injuries in the battle, it is a wonder that you survived at all. Everyone appreciated your leadership and the way you fought even after being wounded."

"I only did what was needed."

"Well the people noticed. The forge is in good shape, and when you feel up to it, it is waiting for you."

"It will be a long time before I return there, so I leave it in your hands to do what is needed."

At that moment, Nuada's mate waddled into the area and came over to him. Sweat crowned her brow, and she reached down to kiss him.

"I will fix you something to eat shortly, husband."

"No. Sit and rest first, wife. You have been working too hard, and I think you should take time to realize it."

"But the people think I must do so as your mate."

"I think you must protect of yourself and the child that you carry."

"Very well. I am tired."

She sat next to Nuada and said that she had to collect their son from A'Chreag's mate soon. Nuada told her that he would pick up their child on his way home. Then they became quiet, each immersed in their own thoughts. The evening wore on, the people happy in their own ways. Before sunset Nuada and his mate walked home hand in hand.

Another week passed as Nuada continued to take his walks and build his strength. The distance lengthened with each walk. He now spent a few hours a day at the forge building just tinkering with small projects he created. A'Chreag kept him company, and they talked about many things. Nuada was glad of his company and felt that he was now contributing to the village life.

Slowly the Summer was coming to a close, and preparations began for the Fall harvest and the stockpiling of food for the Winter time. Another feast was in the planning stages, and the new group of people added a lot to the coming party. Nuada found time to talk with many of the new people and found them very talented in both their work skills and their music abilities.

The new houses were within a week now of being completed, and framing on two more was started. The village's second well was dug, and the stonecutters had built another impressive work around it. The village was growing fast, and more stone rubble was spread for another new street for the planned housing expansion. Mor kept Nuada informed of the new changes, and at times they walked around the work being done. The stonecutters had found time to make an oven at the cooking area, and the fresh breads filled the air with their smells, which added to the friendship of the area.

Now that Iolair was nearing his fourth birthday, he began to follow Nuada everywhere and asked many new questions. He was smart for his age and learned fast. Nuada's pride in him overflowed, and he tried to teach him everything that he showed interest in. Nuada crafted him some tools to improve his hand skills, which he used to make toys for the other children.

One day the sky began to fill with clouds, and a noticeable change in the temperature filled the valley. The wind began to gust out of the northwest, and many could feel the moisture in the air before the storm. Fall was upon the valley.

- FALL AND VILLAGE LIFE -

Rain and more rain followed, with wind enough to take your breath away. The harvest was in, so nothing was hurt by it. Temperatures dropped by almost thirty degrees over one weekend. The dramatic change caused the village people to stay indoors and find shelter from the weather. The last of the houses to be built was finished on the outside, so work continued inside. The last of the new people were waiting to move in when they were complete. They had found shelter within the cave and were more than ready to move.

Nuada continued to improve from his wound, and his mate grew large with the new child expected within weeks. Iolair was growing fast, and if it had not been for Wolf, he would have been underfoot more. The two of them shared every moment together and were bonded deeply. Nuada returned to his carving, and his art was found throughout the house. From time to time, Mor or Beag stopped in to talk with him, sharing ideas about the village growth and defenses.

A'Chreag and his mate were happy with the expectation of their new child and still shared the house with Nuada and his mate, but come Spring they wanted to move to one of the new houses planned earlier. Families were growing quickly, and none saw an end of it.

Nuada looked at the model of the valleys almost daily and thought of different ways to make life easier for everyone, yet let the village grow. The village heads had planned for another eight houses come Spring, and there was talk of a third water well in the village. Plans were also put forward to replace the wall around the village with one of stone , but it was to be expanded further away from the houses.

Nuada now joined in the village consul meetings as the head chief of the village, and he continued to lead the others with their changes to the valley. At one such meeting, he was called back to his house for the birth of his second son, and he beamed at the child's entry into his family.

Two weeks later A'Chreag's mate produced a girl, and the crying of the pair almost made sleep impossible for everyone in the house.

Snow falling became the normal weather now, and everyone knew that Winter was near. The village needed a wet Winter to offset the dry one of last year, and so none complained. The village men kept the streets clear so that people could travel between houses or to work that was going on.

Two of the infants and one of the mothers had died in childbirth, and crypts near Jan's were constructed. They were laid to rest with the whole village attending. This was the second time since the battle that Nuada had visited the crypt of Jan's. He paused after the rest of the people had returned to the village. "Jan, my friend, watch over these we have entombed near you. The village will miss of them greatly I fear." With that said, he returned home.

Nuada paused at the portal gate and looked skyward. The clouds still rolled and were full of moisture although the wind had abated to a moderate breeze. Turning to the west, he scanned the horizon for any change. Nothing new there either. Pulling his cloak tighter about his shoulders, Nuada made for the woodworking building and some small talk with his friends.

Entering he found most of the village men drinking beer and talking about the entombments. At the far end of the hall, the husband of the woman who had died had a gathering about him. Nuada knew enough to avoid that topic of conversation and found Mor, Beag, and A'Chreag. They were discussing the new waterwheel, which was under construction on a table nearby. Beag was telling them that he could fit a stone wheel to it, and they could have ground flour from the grains it crushed.

"Show me what we need to change for it to work," A'Chreag said.

Beag sat down and began to draw the design he had in mind while the others watched. It took him only moments to complete the drawing, and Nuada complimented him on the design. Farmer showed up and asked what was going on, and when he was shown the drawing, he too said he liked the concept.

"Can we adapt it to the wheel we now have?" asked Mor.

"Possibly, but it will take some time to change over."

"Then we had better wait and get this one going first."

The talk returned to other subjects the village had plans for, and no consensus was agreed upon at that time. After several beers, Nuada knew it was time to return home and have his evening meal. His family needed him now, and that was the important thing.

The following morning, Nuada returned to the woodworking building to meet with Beag again about the grain-stone design.

"Nuada, I will need of your help with the stone. I will need to build it in four parts so as to make it easy to move. I will need of you to make a band of your metal to bind the pieces together."

"Tell me what you need and the size of it."

Beag showed Nuada the layout of the stone wheel, and they did some measuring for the band.

"What of the center slot?" asked Nuada.

"It could use your metal also, but it is not necessary. Other wheels I have built did well without it."

After some discussion, the pair agreed to try to make a sleeve for the center of the stone wheel. Their thoughts on the wheel were broken when Mor arrived, and the talks turned to other needs about the village.

It was about midday when the discussion broke off, and Nuada went outside to find the weather had turned nasty. Snow fell heavily, and the wind was so strong that it went right through his clothes with a heavy chill. Looking around Nuada peered up at the tree line and found none to be seen. The clouds had lowered to the point where anything more than a hundred feet disappeared from sight. Nuada hurried home to his mate and children.

Throughout the next three days, the storm continued to batter the valley. The people of the village hid within their homes, and none ventured outside while the weather battered the valley. Sounds of the storm could be heard within the houses, and many feared the howling winds.

On the morning of the fourth day, Nuada and Wolf stepped outside to find sunshine had pushed the weather away. The snow was waist deep and the drifts as high as a man. Mor had organized teams to remove the snow buildup from the streets, and by the afternoon, they had pathways cut to where people could walk from place to place, but it would take many more days to clear away the snow and the damage from the winds. Many trees had fallen, and branches littered the area.

On the morning of the fourth day, Nuada and A'Chreag ventured to the forge building to check on damage there. They found it intact and, except for some tree branches that littered the ground around it, without damage. They returned to the woodworking building and the warmth within. Beag was at work on the new stone grain wheel and was making progress on his design. Nuada asked questions about it while he worked before turning his attention to Mor and the other men within the building, who were talking about the storm.

"Some damage to the stable , but nothing that can't wait for a few more days," Nuada overheard.

"Mor? What of the protection walls? Were any damaged'?" asked Nuada.

"Ah, Nuada. No reports of any damage to the walls. Why?"

"Just curious. Anything else hurt?"

"Not that we know of yet."

The conversation continued on for another hour, and Mor reported that two children had been born during the storm. No one had been hurt, and that was a wonder. Soon Nuada and A'Chreag returned to the house to check on their mates and children. They spent the rest of the day and night at home, quietly talking about the storm themselves.

Another week passed while cleanup continued. Nuada remained close to home and ventured to the woodworking building only when boredom consumed him. His wood carving continued to fill in the empty hours and fill the house with his work.

One morning while he sat at the table thinking about what to do that day, he looked over at the map table of the valley and then stood and walked over to it and stared at the projections for the Spring work. "We have so much to do next year. I hope we can complete it," he thought.

A'Chreag was coming down the stairs and saw Nuada and asked what he was doing.

"Just thinking about next year's work," Nuada replied.

"Anything we need to change or add to the design?"

"No. I was just wondering if we can complete everything. It is a lot to do."

"The people of the village understand its importance and will get it done."

"I know. They have a strong heart for the valley."

"It is not just that. They believe in you, and what you think matters to them. You have brought all of them here and given them protection and hope for the future."

"I only did what was needed for them. They have made this work for all of us."

"You are rare. They see that in you. You could have ignored them and kept the valley to yourself, but you did not. What they do, they do for you because of your insight."

"It was Creatrix who taught me to look after them, not something deep within me."

"Whatever. They think it was you and you alone."

Nuada smiled outwardly, but inside he felt worried about the perception the village people had of him. He was never one to push his beliefs on anyone else. Perhaps it was time to change. "I shall try to find of Creatrix if this is the right thing to do," he thought.

Iolair came running up and jumped for Nuada, with Wolf following.

"What is with you two this morning, son?" Nuada asked with a smile on his face.

The boy snuggled close to his father and looked deeply into his eyes. A'Chreag could see the love between them and quietly moved away. Nuada returned to the table holding his boy and sat down. Wolf curled up at his feet and closed his eyes.

Nuada's mate, who had been breast-feeding their new child, laid the child down on its bundle of furs and came over to the table to be with Nuada and their oldest boy.

"Husband? Is there something that you need?"

"Only answers to things that I do not understand."

"What are you going to do about it?"

"I shall seek the wisdom of Creatrix in a dream again. Perhaps tonight."

Nuada's mate took Iolair, who was now fast asleep, and placed him with his baby brother on the furs. "Go for a walk and talk with Mor or Beag. Perhaps they can help."

Nuada nodded and dressed warmly for the walk to the woodworking building and the advice from his friends. Wolf stayed with the children, as that was his job now as he saw it. Outside it was cold and clear with only a few clouds high in the morning sky.

Inside Nuada saw the usual crowd of men working or talking. Mor stood at the fireplace at one end of the building, giving instructions as usual. Nuada pulled a beer and sat down at a table near the conversation. He just sat and listened. Occasionally someone would stop and share a few words, but for the most part, he was left alone. Finally Mor spotted him and came over and sat with Nuada.

"What brings you out today, my friend?"

"Only some good company, Mor."

"I can see by the look on your face that something is bothering you. What is it?"

"I am still bothered by how the village people view me. Is it wrong to question myself in this way?"

"No. I ask myself the same questions. Then I smile at my foolishness. They have no idea what we go through to do what is necessary for them."

Nuada laughed at his comment and then settled back and took a long pull on his beer.

"You always seem to have the right answer. Thank you, my friend."

The talk between the pair lasted several hours, and Nuada felt better the longer they talked. The subjects changed by the minute, and many things were discussed. Finally Nuada said his farewells and returned home.

Inside the children were asleep, and his mate was preparing supper. She said, "Did you enjoy yourself today husband?"

"Yes. Mor and I had a long talk, and it made me feel better about how the village people see me."

"Then you learned something. Do not doubt yourself. I don't doubt you."

With that said, she leaned over and kissed him.

"You are my rock, and I depend on you, wife. Thank you."

"Remember when we first came to this valley, and I was so scared to go on. You understood, and we built our first home together here. I learned quickly that you were a natural leader then. Don't look back, only ahead. You have something to give to everyone. That is why they follow you."

Nuada only smiled at her words and felt even more secure with his place in the village.

That night Nuada slept deep and without dreams. Creatrix did not bother to add to the conversation about Nuada's place in the village.

Many more weeks passed, and the full measure of Winter was coming. Nuada continued to help where needed, and nothing more was said of his doubts.

Slowly the weather changed, and snow started to become the normal thing, although the wind remained light. You could see the moisture within the clouds if you looked up in the sky.

- WINTER AGAIN -

Nuada awoke to the howling of the winds and quickly dressed and peered outside. Snow was drifting against the side of his house, and he knew that they were in for another strong storm. He quickly returned inside and stoked the fireplace. Soon the fire raged, and he felt secure against the storm. Soon A'Chreag came down the stairs and stretched to his full height with a large yawn.

"Nuada? How is the weather? I hear the wind blowing hard."

"This is a nasty storm. It may last for several days again. You may as well make yourself comfortable and ride it out with me."

Nuada had brought out his carving tools and was sitting at the table working on a figurine of several village workers clustered about one of the village wells. A'Chreag admired the workmanship and picked up a piece of wood himself and began to carve. The pair continued to work at their projects until the women joined them and set about their preparations for a morning meal. Nuada and A'Chreag cleaned up their individual messes and then moved away from the table and sat near the fireplace. The quietness of the morning was interrupted by Wolf barking and telling the adults that the children were awake. The two women hurried upstairs to bring down the children after cleaning them. The pair of men were grateful that it was not their job to rear the babies.

After the women had finished feeding the babies, it was the men's turn to eat, and Nuada was joined by Iolair. The boy sat in Nuada's lap, and when they finished eating, the boy noticed the carving on the table and slowly reached for it. Nuada reached over his head and picked it up. Showing the work to the boy, he asked if he knew who it was he was carving. The boy said, "Mor, Beag, and Farmer."

A'Chreag was stunned at the boy's answer. "How did he know that?"

"He is smart for his age, and he knows them well."

The rest of the day continued much as it started. The men sat and worked at their carvings, and the storm raged outside.

Several days later the storm finally blew itself out, and the village men were soon out and clearing the drifts of snow again. It was hard work that took many shifts to do. Nuada and A'Chreag joined in the labor, and they felt it in their muscles at the end of every shift of work. Nuada, who had almost forgotten the wound in his side, now complained of the soreness of it. His mate prepared a compress of hot cloths to the old injury, and Nuada moaned at the discomfort but relished the warmth. A'Chreag, although much younger, felt the strain of the work on his muscles and stayed near the fireplace for warmth.

Nuada's mate said, "You both know it is going to snow again. Why work so hard at it?"

"Because it is needed for the village to function. People must be able to meet and talk and to do certain jobs."

It took four days to clear the village streets, and then the weather again began to close over them.

"I hope this storm is not as strong as the last one," commented A'Chreag.

Nuada nodded in agreement and then said, "Let us go to the woodworking building and get some more wood for carving, in case it is a bad one again.'"

Inside the topic of conversation was all about the weather. For many there had been no rest after the street cleanup. Beag saw Nuada and motioned him over to the great grain stone wheel he was working on. The outline of the wheel was complete, and Beag had cut a groove in the outer edge for the band that would tie the four main pieces together. He was now cutting grooves to allow the flour to run out from beneath and into a trough that would round the outside of it. Nuada understood the design and marveled at the precision of Beag's work.

"I hope my metal is up to the detail of your work, my friend."

"You have never failed us yet, Nuada."

Mor saw the pair talking and joined them. "What are you two up to? I thought you would be taking it easy after that storm."

"I was just looking at the fine detail of Beag's work on the grain wheel. Have you ever seen anyone who could find the craftsmanship that he can?"

"No. His talent is exceptional. Nuada? Have you given anymore thought on how we are going to use this waterwheel and grindstone?"

"Yes. At the back of the second valley, where the water cascades down from the mountain. If we build a wall and dam with a building that contains the waterwheel, we will have a constant source of water to run it. We will not have to depend on horses to turn it. Not only that, we could use the power of the water to run a saw also."

Mor and Beag looked at each other and nodded in agreement with Nuada's ideas.

"Nuada? Can you make a drawing of what you have in mind for more details?" asked Beag.

"Of course I can, and I will add it to the model map of the valleys."

They continued to talk for many more hours, and the day hurried past unnoticed. When Nuada finally returned home, the house was quiet, and the children were sleeping. Nuada's mate was also fast asleep at the table while Wolf lay nearby with his eyes open and watching over everyone. Nuada retrieved some wood and began to carve the new ideas for the model table map. He knew the details of the location by heart and size. It was well into the dark hours before he stopped and stirred his mate awake.

"What have you for me to eat, wife?"

She got up and went to the fireplace and stirred a pot over the embers.

"I can feed you some soup soon," she told him.

That night ended after they had eaten. Sleep found them quickly, and they stayed that way all night — even the children slept well.

The next morning Nuada looked outside and found the weather again had closed down on the village. He let Wolf run for awhile before returning back inside. Sitting at the table alone, he began to carve again and didn't think of awaking any of the others. After two hours, he sat the carving down and then began to draw the design of the waterwheel house and its dam and wall. Well into mid-morning the rest of the house came to life, and he set the drawings aside and waited for them to settle down again before he could draw more of the details. He had no such luck. The children had gotten too much sleep the night before, and they filled the house with their noise and crying. Even Wolf tried to cover his ears and finally came over to Nuada to be let outside for a run.

Nuada stood and waited for Wolf's return. He looked about at the light snow on the ground and noticed that the wind was also light. "This storm is good," he thought.

The next morning Nuada again rose early to have time to himself. He pulled the drawings he had been working on and studied the work. He made a few changes and then continued to add other details. After an hour, he set the drawings aside and called Wolf for his morning run. Outside the snow had stopped, and the wind was only a light breeze. The sunlight was only beginning to emerge from behind the mountain behind the village, but he could make out details of the village as it began to awaken. Smoke drifted down from the chimney stacks and hovered low to the ground. The smell brought comfort to Nuada as he waited for Wolf's return. He knew that he would find the other men and Beag at the woodworking building later. When he returned inside, he packed the drawings in a skin bag and waited for the sun to rise higher before he went to the building. To pass the time, he started to carve again and became lost in the details of it. It wasn't until A'Chreag came down the stairs that he noticed that he had spent almost another two hours on the carving.

After greeting A'Chreag, he put on a warm coat and his cloak and left for the woodworking building. He stopped outside and looked up and down the street; it remained empty. He then turned and entered the building. It was almost empty too. He went to one of the fireplaces and added wood to the fire that burned dimly before him. Then he sat at one of the tables and waited for his friends. He did not have to wait long. Beag entered and was talking with Mor in a loud voice.

"If that is what you want, I will see that it is done," Mor replied to Beag's questions.

They both saw Nuada at the same time and shouted a greeting to him. After they settled at the table, Nuada pushed the drawings across to Beag.

"I think you will have need of these," he said.

Beag pulled the drawings from the bag and spread them out for the trio to view them.

"Nuada, these are extremely detailed. I did not expect this. It will make the work go faster and easier."

"Later when you have time, come to my house and view the model of the valleys. It helps to explain the need of this design. It also shows the saw building and a place for someone to live and watch over everything."

Mor commented, "As long as we don't have to wage any wars, we can get these done this year. Last Summer slowed us down a lot."

Nuada nodded in agreement and leaned back and smiled at the pair.

"We won't have any more wars in the near future. We only need to grow and protect what we build."

"Are you going in search of more people this Spring, Nuada?" asked Beag.

"I had not thought about it. Perhaps it is time to think about bringing more people into the valley again. How many houses will we build this year, Mor?"

"We have the three new houses that were to remain empty for growth that we can complete in late Spring, but if you are going to bring in more people, we could build as many as six houses by Fall. That will give us nine houses this year."

"Could we do that with all the major projects we have planned?"

"It will be tight , but I think we could do it. We could delay the stone-wall replacement if time is short."

"All right, but talk it over with Farmer and meet with me at my house later."

Nuada got up and said his farewells to the pair and went outside where the chill of the Winter air bit at his exposed skin. Pulling his cloak tighter about him, Nuada set off for his house and family. He would have liked to wander about the village to look at its coat of white from the morning frost, but he continued home.

Entering he was greeted by Wolf, who jumped up and walked backwards into the house with Nuada. Laughing Nuada pushed him down and then rubbed his ears. Iolair came running and grabbed Nuada around his legs and didn't let go.

"Wife, help me. I am under attack by my own family."

"It serves you right, husband. Find a way to deal with it and then come and eat something."

Nuada reached down and picked up his son, and with Wolf circling them, he walked to the table and kissed his mate.

"We will have some company later. The consul is coming over to view changes for the valley next year on the valley map."

"Am I to feed them too?"

"No, it will be a short meeting, and only a few beers are needed before I send them on their way."

Later that afternoon, the trio of the consul arrived at Nuada's door and were shown the changes on the valley model map. Nuada explained the reason for the placement of the mill and its walls and how everything would work. Beag had a question about how they could disengage the stone mill wheel when it was not in use, and again Nuada showed them the process by which it could be done and how the stone wheel could be lifted for repairs or cleaning. Then their attention was turned to the new saw mill building and how it worked. After two full hours and a few beers, everyone was satisfied with the design and its operation. Nuada knew that it would be accepted as is but felt relief at their sanction of its design.

After they had left his house, Nuada again sat at his table and found himself lost in thought about other things the people of the valley might need. His thoughts were broken by his mate, who had come over and begun to braid his red hair.

"Husband, I love the color of your hair that Creatrix has given you."

"I have not given it much thought since that battle, but that was the start of everything done within the valley."

"Yes, and it seems so long ago now. I am glad that everything has worked out for us."

"It does seem long ago, but the truth is that it was only a little over three years ago that it all started."

They were interrupted by A'Chreag, his mate, and child coming down from upstairs and preparing for their evening meal. A'Chreag greeted Nuada and his mate before sitting at the table and asking about the meeting today with the consul. Nuada told him about the meeting and their agreement to the plans. After that their talk turned to the children for awhile before their meals came to the table. Tonight it was a lamb stew with thick portions of potatoes and onions. After eating and filling themselves, they all felt sleepy and retired to their sleeping areas. Another day had passed, and things were accomplished.

A few weeks later the grip of Winter began to loosen, and the snows began to change to rain, although the chill of the wind didn't reflect this. One morning Nuada took a walk outside and down to his forge building, which had sat quiet now for many months. He was ready to return to what he knew best and had many projects to do. Although he did not start anything that day, he made sure that he had enough materials and that the equipment was ready to work. Returning back to the main street, he stopped at the woodworking building and found A'Chreag there working on some of the wood parts for the new mill.

"I was just down at the forge building, and it is ready to begin making the new parts we will need. When will you be ready to start there again?"

"I will need two more days here on this work, then I shall be ready to work the forge again."

"Good. I am more than ready. It has been too long for me."

Mor came up behind Nuada and placed his arm around his shoulders.

"You need to find of something to do, my friend. Here, come and talk to these men and explain all about the design for the waterwheel and mill house."

"Mor, my friend, I was just inquiring about A'Chreag's ability to come back to work at the forge again. It is time we began to make the parts necessary for our Spring projects."

"I understand of that, but today talk with these men. The design was all yours, and they will be building it."

Nuada agreed and for the next three hours explained the design and how the whole thing would work. When he was done, he felt worn out and asked to sit for awhile and relax. He knew that the Winter had been too long and that his lack of exercise would show for many weeks while he readjusted to the work he needed to do.

Beag came over to his table and sat down before speaking.

"Nuada, you look worn out. Perhaps I can lift your spirit with something I have made for you."

"What is it, Beag?"

"Come and I will show you."

Nuada slowly arose and followed Beag to his work area. "What is it that cannot wait, my friend?"

Beag drew back a cover from his work table and two large rollers presented themselves.

"What are they?" asked Nuada.

"These are for you to make sheets of your metals instead of you hammering all day long. Here, look at this model and see how it would work. The gear and cog design is now made of wood, but you could replace them with your metal. As the hot metal is poured into the spout, you can control the width of it. Then with the adjustment on the rollers, you can vary the thickness of your sheets. The sheets are then laid out on the flow table to cool."

Nuada looked closely at the model and could find no flaws with the idea behind it. He walked around the model and peered at each moving part as he went. He forgot how tired he was, and his mind raced with the concept.

"You have made another masterpiece, Beag. I will find many uses for this."

"Then you can repay me with some new tools when you find the time, Nuada."

"Done. Give me a list of what you need, and I will provide them for you."

Later that day the sky had turned liquid. Rain poured heavily, and the south wind gusted to such an extreme that when Nuada left the building, he had to walk backwards to keep the blowing debris out of his eyes. At his house, he huddled on its porch and waited for a gust to pass before entering. Leaning against the door to close it, he caught his breath and waited for some sense of normalcy to return.

His mate called to him. "Nuada, what is with this storm? Are we to be blown away?"

"No, wife. It is just a strong Spring rain storm. It will pass."

Later that afternoon the temperature dropped quickly, and the rain began to freeze as it fell. Again the village became quiet, and everyone huddled indoors.

All throughout the night, the freezing rain came down, and only at daybreak did it pause. When Nuada stuck his head outside that morning, everything was coated in a layer of ice that shimmered in the dim light.

"This is going to be a day when everyone will remain indoors," he thought as he returned inside, sitting at the table where he had already set out his carving tools and a project he had started a few days before. A'Chreag joined Nuada, and they worked in silence.

It was almost midday when he got up to stretch and again looked outside. The sky had cleared to a soft blue , but the temperature still remained extremely cold. Winter still had its grip on the valley.

"A'Chreag? It looks like it will be days before we can return to the forge again, so let me know when you have finished your work at the woodworking building."

It took four more days for the temperature to rise again to a reasonable level and the sky remained clear. Slowly the village came to life again. A'Chreag returned to his project at the woodworking building, and Nuada became bored with waiting on the weather. Most of the ice had melted, and to combat his boredom, Nuada took a walk to the lake. Here the ice remained around the shoreline, and Nuada did not linger long. He looked across at the island that used to be his home and then wandered back to the village. He took the path by the crop meadow and then to the last section of the wood wall that had been built before the battle. He entered through the gate portal there and followed the new street by the new houses, some of which had yet to be completed. Finally he entered the woodworking building and sat at a table inside to watch the activities of the other men. He remained alone.

After an hour, Mor and Beag entered the building, followed by Farmer. They joined Nuada, and small talk followed. They were all waiting for the break in the Spring weather pattern.

Two days later both Nuada and A'Chreag returned to the forge and began all their projects for the village. Nuada created the parts necessary for the new sheet-roller system designed by Beag, and then he began to assemble it three days later. A'Chreag was busy with making molds for the waterwheel and the mill stone project's metal parts. Between these jobs, they made hinges and latches for the new houses. Time now passed quickly, and warmer weather found the valley and its people.

- SPRING AND HARD WORK -

At long last Spring was here, and the people of the valley returned to their normal enthusiasm and work for the valley. They began with the taking down of the last section of the wood protection wall, whose wood would be used in the construction of the new houses. Beag had a crew already working the quarry in the second valley for his stone work that would replace it. The horses of the village began their task of moving things from place to place, which was slow to begin with after the long Winter.

Although the Winter had been a hard one, there were no deaths this year. At the lake the water remained high, and the birds and waterfowl returned early. The wild grasses were tall, and the livestock fed off it early this year. The stream roared in loud protest to the amount of water it had to move, which delayed the start on the construction of the new mill house and dam in the second valley. This allowed the work on the new houses to go ahead without interruption. The three houses started in the Fall were completed in short order and the next three started. A'Chreag and his family moved into the first of the new houses, which left Nuada and his family alone in the large house by themselves. At first Nuada accepted this, but he missed the company of them.

Iolair now followed his father almost everywhere, and Nuada could not have been more proud of him. Of course Wolf remained with the pair and was greeted by almost everyone within the village. Nuada now spent more time at his forge and was busy with the creation of many new things for the village. The parts for the new mill complex were now finished and awaited the stream to calm down. Behind the first houses built, Beag had started another street for workshops for those who wanted a place to make their products. The buildings there would come later in the Summer. These workshops would be in front of the stable and Nuada's forge building. The village was becoming more complete with this aspect of building.

Early one morning while Nuada sat at his usual table with his son in the cooking area, Mor and Beag joined him, and small talk about the village began as usual.

"Nuada. A good morning to you. Do you have any new thoughts about the village?" asked Mor.

Nuada looked down at his son and thoughtfully said, "We have a need for a school and a teacher for the young. Ever since Jan's death, we have been without one to fill the job."

"I too see the need for this. Is there anyone within the village who could do this job?"

"I do not know of anyone. Perhaps we have a need to look outside of the valley again."

"Will you go in search of more people?"

"No, not this year. Perhaps someone younger this time is needed for the search."

"Let me think on this, and I will let you know who I can send who would have the vision to bring the right people back with them."

Shortly the meeting broke up, and everyone went to their projects. Nuada and his son returned to the forge , but thoughts about what was said earlier remained on Nuada's mind. He wanted to travel again, but his responsibilities within the village would keep him here. His family was growing quickly, and he needed to share that time with them. He pondered who to send on this quest, and the only person who kept coming to mind was A'Chreag. He had been with Nuada before and knew how to approach newcomers.

Nuada took his son and went to seek out Mor with his thoughts. He found him at the new housing construction.

"Mor, a minute of your time. I have been thinking about who to send in search of new people, and the only answer I can come up with is A'Chreag. He knows how I seek them out and the questions to ask."

"I agree with you, but is he willing to leave his new family?"

"Let us put it before him and find out."

They went in search of A'Chreag, who was working on the newest house, and asked him if he was willing to travel in search of new people for the village.

"It would be an honor to do this for our people," he replied.

"But it would mean leaving your mate and child for about a week or longer. Are you sure?"

"Yes. We have needs for the village, and that comes first."

"Very well, but we have a need of a teacher for the young this time. Do what you can to find of someone for that job. It is important."

"I understand. How many families are we looking for this time?"

"We will have eight houses at the end of this season. Try to limit it to that number if you can."

After some more small talk, A'Chreag returned to his work, and Mor and Nuada wandered about the construction site.

"When can you let him start this quest, Mor?"

"Let me keep him for another three weeks. Then he can begin his search."

Nuada nodded, and his thoughts returned to other things. He almost forgot about his son, who was at his side all the time. It wasn't until Iolair reached for his father's hand that Nuada broke from his thoughts. They continued their walk toward the new stone wall and found Beag hard at work shaping the stones for use on the wall. They stood back and watched his skill and craftsmanship on many pieces before they approached him. Many piles of stone chips lay about, and these were being loaded onto a wagon for transfer onto the streets. Beag's crew worked smoothly, and as Nuada watched, he could see how quickly things were taking shape.

"You are making good time, my friend. Any problems?"

"Nothing we cannot handle. Have you seen the changes at the old wood wall?"

"Not yet, but I am going that way next. Why?"

"Nothing, but everything changes so quickly around here that it is hard to keep up with them."

"Yes. I am always in wonderment at the changes myself. I do have the new hinges that you need at my forge. When would you like me to bring them to you?"

"Sometime in the next two or three days will be fine. I have a lot of other work to do before I can fit them."

Nuada nodded in understanding and departed Beag's company with his boy in tow, headed for the old wood-wall work. When they got within viewing distance, Nuada was surprised at the amount of removal that that crew had accomplished. Tall piles of the timbers were stacked all around the area, more than enough to build many more houses than had been planned. Then Nuada remembered that they would also be building the workshops too. He wondered why they had not been moved to the construction sites, but he realized that most of the horses and wagons were being used for the stonework projects. He wondered to himself how Mor could organize everything so well when he himself had a hard time just to watch the things being done.

Nuada picked up Iolair and placed him on his shoulders, then turned back toward the cooking area and the company of his mate. Wolf, who had also been following the pair, fell in step with them as they walked back. Nuada noticed the fragrance of the grasses around the village, and the birds were in full song. The insects kept up their part by joining into the background noise. In all it was a very pleasant day.

As Nuada walked through the village on its newly paved streets, his eyes scanned everything. People of the village stopped what they were doing and waved as he passed, which he returned with a cheerful smile on his face. Iolair waved at everyone and laughed out loud and hard.

When the pair entered the cooking area, Nuada's mate called a greeting, and she was with a small group of new mothers who were gathered about the fireplace preparing the evening meal already. Nuada did not approach them but sat at his table and waited. Iolair climbed down and went to play with some of the other children, followed by Wolf.

Nuada was enjoying the role of a parent as he watched his son; he could not hide the smile on his face. After about an hour, some of the village men began to arrive, and the evening routine began again for everyone. One of the things Nuada enjoyed most was the music that seemed to spring up almost immediately. He got up from his table and went to retrieve a beer before his meal. While he was there, some of the men began to inquire about projects that were coming up in the future. Nuada put them off by telling them to ask Mor; he was not about to lose the warm, family feeling tonight with their questions.

Later after eating his meal and sharing some small talk with his mate, he took his family home. As he laid down to sleep, he could never remember a more pleasant day before in his life.

Four days later Nuada arose early and went to wait for A'Chreag to remind him of the purpose of his quest out of the valley again. He felt that it was wrong for him to remain behind but knew that it was time for him to change his way of thinking. This was the right thing to do.

Nuada did not have to wait long. A'Chreag and one of the hunters were packed and ready to move out of the wood-wall portal gate when he caught up with them.

"Have you decided on your direction of travel?"

"I think we will go west again this time. The chances are good we will come across more people who have been run out of their homes by the raiders again."

"Good thought, although if you move south, you may find of the teacher we seek."

"Then I shall do both, Nuada."

"A safe and good trip to you both. Be ready for anything."

The pair passed through the gate and moved across the meadow of the battle from last year. Nuada climbed the wood wall and watched until they passed from view. He felt lost because he did not go with them and slowly climbed down and wandered back to the construction area again.

Nuada stood back and watched the men work at setting new frames on one of the houses. His gaze drifted toward the saw pit, where planks were being cut, and then over at another group splitting timbers. He thought, "When the new sawmill is built, it will make this work easier and faster."

Nuada was startled from his thoughts when Mor came up behind him and clapped him on the shoulder.

"Nuada, what are you doing now?"

"I was just watching the men working. It took my mind from the quest that A'Chreag is on. He only just left, but already I worry."

'Do not worry. He will find of what we need, and he has proved resourceful in the past."

"I know, but still things can go wrong."

"Leave those thoughts alone. Let us take a walk to the new mill sites and find of a diversion from worry."

The pair set off for the second valley and passed the new stone-wall work. Already it was about half done, and they were building the opening for the new gate portal. Beag was there pointing out some detail to his crew when they paused to talk with him.

Mor called to Beag, "This is the first time I have not seen you in the thick of the work, my friend."

"It is only a short break. I find I spend half my time teaching these men of my art."

"Nuada and I are going to the new mill sites. Do you have time to go also?"

Beag looked around and then said, "I can spare two hours. I want a closer look at the footings of the site anyway." With that said, he called to one of the men and told him what he wanted done and that he would be gone for two hours.

Quickly they passed the caves and then on past the stone wall outside of the second valley. They followed the stream, which was beginning to slow from the Spring runoff. Soon they stood on the site where the new mills would be built. Nuada walked to the back of the area and looked at the streambed, and his mind raced with how the area would look after the dam and mill run were built. His eyes scanned the small waterfall at the back of the ridge, and he knew that it would disappear when the dam was constructed. He then rejoined his friends and listened in on Beag's thoughts on when they could start the work.

"Another week and I can begin the work needed here," he said to Mor.

"But what about the other work being done now? Will that not be held up while you are here?"

"Not really. I have a good crew, and they will be able to continue that work. This is what will be important for everyone."

The discussion continued while the trio walked back to the village. Nuada told Mor that he would need a wagon and two men in the morning to transport the mill parts to the mill site. Mor agreed and then said that he would also provide enough men to start bringing stone to the site from the quarry. He asked Nuada to supervise that part of the crew and to set up the rigging for the work of placement of the stones. Nuada agreed, and by the time they had set up the program for the next day, they found themselves back at the stone wall under construction. Beag left them and went to study what was done while he was gone with the other two.

Mor and Nuada continued back to the housing site and stopped to talk about that work.

"I expect A'Chreag to bring back more people soon, and I hope we are far enough along for them to move into the new houses."

"We should have five empty houses by the end of next week, Nuada. Beyond that it will probably be another month for the next two."

"Good. By that time we should be able to start on the shop buildings. When those are done, we can again start to build more houses."

"I agree. Houses are important , but the shops are needed too."

Nuada left Mor and went to the cooking area to watch over his son, who would be waiting for him. As he entered, his mate saw him and brought Iolair to him.

"Good. You are free now. Take your son and let me get some work done today."

Nuada smiled at her comment and picked up his son. The boy laughed, and together they walked back out into the village again. Nuada went to the woodworking building to look at the millstone that Beag had made, and he studied the craftsmanship of it. The picture of the completed mill filled his mind. After seeing what had to be done, they again walked out into the warm, sun-filled afternoon. Instead of going home or back to the construction area, they walked out to the crypt of Jan's.

Pausing before it, Nuada set his son down and then let the memories of his friend roll through his mind. It was a quiet time for Nuada. Soon they returned to the cooking area and waited for the work crews to arrive and receive their evening meals. Nuada loved the music that was part of every evening, and it added to the friendliness of the village.

The smell of fresh-baked bread began to fill the area, and other smells made him hunger for his supper. Soon the workers began to fill the tables in the area, and they filled the air with their greetings for their mates and children. Laughter soon followed, and then the music began. Nuada was happy to be there.

As the days passed, Nuada kept busy between the forge and the new houses. He tried to keep his mind from the quest of A'Chreag by staying hard at work on the projects. His only free time was at the evening meals in the cooking area, and here he spent most of it with his son Iolair. The boy was growing fast and learning many things daily. His questions filled Nuada with pride, and at times he found he could not answer many of them. The boy abounded with energy and was the leader of the other children in his age group.

Nuada's second boy was now eating solid foods and had begun to sit on his own. As a father, Nuada was quick to show to others how quickly his children learned things that other children could not grasp. Both boys had inherited the red hair that Creatrix had given Nuada.

Almost before Nuada realized it, a week had passed, and they still had no word of A'Chreag or his quest. Nuada was beginning to fear the worst had happened and was tempted to go in search of his friend. Mor told him to wait a little longer and see what happens. Reluctantly Nuada agreed, but worry still plagued him. Every afternoon Nuada would walk to the stone wall at the entrance to the valley and watch for A'Chreag before his evening meal. He even posted watchers on the ridge behind the village.

Four more days passed — nothing.

Nuada finally went to Mor and asked for two other men to go with him in search of A'Chreag. Mor silently agreed, and the next morning they were to leave in search of him. Nuada packed the things he would need the night before and was restless all night long. Before the dawning of Creatrix, Nuada went to the cooking area to wait for the other men. Just as the sun began to come over the crest of the mountain, the warning bell at the entrance to the valley began to ring. Nuada grabbed his weapons and hurried to the wall. When he got there, the watcher told him it was A'Chreag returning to the valley.

Nuada hurried out of the gate portal and down the path to where his friend was coming from. A'Chreag was leading a group of about twenty families, and Nuada went up to him and swung his arms about the young man.

"Where have you been? I have worried and was about to go in search of you."

"Some of these people were injured, and they slowed us down, but there were no signs of any raiders this time."

"Did you find of a teacher for the children?"

"Yes. And he is a healer also."

"When we get to the cooking area, introduce him to me. It is good to have you back, my friend."

The group slowly moved into the village, and many of the village workers stopped their work and came to greet the newcomers. At the cooking area, beer was passed around between the adults of the group, and food was prepared for everyone. Music soon followed, and the conversation seemed nonstop. Those of the new group who were injured were the first to be placed in the new houses, but many more houses would now need to be built — and soon.

The new teacher and healer was brought to Nuada, and they talked for more than three hours. Nuada explained the needs of the village and asked if he was up to the challenge. The man said yes, and from that time forward, Nuada was impressed with the man's knowledge of many things. He was from a land far to the south, where thinking was the goal of everyone of his land. Nuada studied the man's features as they talked and was surprised that he was clean shaven and wore his hair short. He had a deep, dark tan that marked him as being outdoors a lot. Nuada invited him to share his house until one could be built for him, and the teacher agreed.

It wasn't until late in the evening that everyone settled down and turned in for the night. Nuada showed the teacher where he was to live within the house, and the man settled in right away. It wasn't until in the middle of the night that Nuada realized that he had forgotten to ask his name — that would wait until morning.

With the coming of dawn, Nuada waited downstairs for the teacher. It wasn't until almost mid-morning that he descended the stairs and was surprised that Nuada was waiting for him. "Come and wash of yourself, then I will give you a tour of the valley. By the way, I did not ask of your name last night. What is it?"

"My name is Pytheas, and long ago I came from a city-state called Athens. Your valley reminds me of there."

"Come here and look at this model of our valleys."

Nuada pointed out the new construction and how it served the community with its location. After some discussion, they set out for the housing construction area. When they arrived, Mor was with a group giving directions as usual.

"Mor, you will wear yourself out with all those directions, my friend."

"Nuada! Do not worry about that. Someone will always be asking, and I will be there to show them the way."

"Mor, this is Pytheas. He is to be the teacher of our young."

Mor shook his hand, and then Nuada said, "Pytheas, Mor organizes all of our construction and is a member of our village consul."

The pair nodded at each other, and then Mor had to leave as someone else needed help.

"Come let us walk into the next valley. That is where our next big construction project will start."

The pair entered into the next valley and continued on down to the site of the new mills to be built. Huge piles of cut stone were stacked all about the area, and men labored with the horse teams moving even more to the site. When are you going to start this work, Nuada?"

"Soon, possibly within a few days. We have been waiting for the stream to settle."

"Show me more. I have a lot to learn here."

They continued the tour around the second valley, and Nuada pointed out the field of wild grains and the quarry for all the stonework projects. On they moved until they had fully circled the second valley. As they passed the field of tree stumps, Nuada said that this was where they had harvested the trees for the building of the village. They then returned to the first valley, and as they walked, they talked about more of Pytheas's travels.

Nuada began to understand the man, and they settled into a stronger friendship. They passed the crop meadow and most of the village women at work there. Nuada waved to his mate as they passed, and she returned his wave. As they neared the village, they came to the stone wall under construction, which was almost done at this time. Beag was standing atop the wall setting stones and yelling at some of the men nearby. Nuada did not bother him as he was busy but told Pytheas of his skills and that he too was a member of the village consul.

On they moved until they came back to the houses under construction, and Pytheas asked about a site for the school.

"We have not built a school yet. Other things have gotten in the way of that thought. Let us look for a building site that you can use."

Nuada led him to the street in front of the stables and forge building and told him of the plan to build shops for the men of skilled trades. "Perhaps we can use one of these buildings for your school."

Pytheas looked around and told Nuada that the area was good for him although the smell from the stable might be a little too strong for the young to study well.

"Then we will only use it for the first year and build you a new school building next year on the other side of the village."

Pytheas agreed to that idea, and then he asked about the forge building. Nuada showed him the building with pride and explained how it worked.

"This is my skill, and I make all things of metal for the village."

"I thought by the wood carvings in your house that you would be a wood worker."

"No. But it is required for me to make my molds that I have that skill."

They walked back through the cooking area and then on over to the woodworking building.

"During the Winter months, the men gather here to do projects and socialize."

"This is a large building. What else is it used for?"

"Behind is the grain storage and a meat locker. Everyone shares of it. There is also an extra storage area that holds wood and stone for our projects."

"Do you need of all this space?"

"No. A lot of it is wasted and could be better used."

"Then why not use it for your school?"

Nuada turned and looked about the space and then nodded, "It would be better used for that purpose, my friend. If we build the small shop buildings, then it will be empty most of the time."

They then walked back to the cooking area, and the children that were there where watched over by some of the mothers. Iolair came running when he saw his father and asked who the stranger was.

"Iolair, this is your new teacher. He is called Pytheas."

Boldly Iolair looked at the stranger and said, "Teach me about the world and the history of it."

"That I can do. Anything else that you would like to learn of? What about numbers and languages?"

"That would be alright. What are numbers?"

"Numbers are what make things happen and the reason they happen. When you can understand numbers, there is nothing that you cannot do."

"Show me, please."

Pytheas laughed and turned to Nuada. "He is your boy — anyone could see of that."

Nuada smiled and then turned Iolair. "He will teach you when we begin the school soon. Do not be too hard on him, my boy. Now go and tell the other children of him."

Iolair ran off to join the other children, and Nuada followed him with his eyes all aglow with pride.

"Nuada, if your boy is a sample of those I have to teach, it will be hard on me and easy at the same time."

The two continued to talk for another two hours, and soon the men and women of the village began to gather again for the evening meals. Mor, Beag, and Farmer all came in together and joined Nuada and the new teacher at their table.

"I am sorry that I was too busy to talk earlier. I am in a hurry to settle the new people in the houses," said Mor.

Nuada then told the trio that it had been decided to place the school in the woodworking building and that when the new shop buildings were completed, the men would have to meet there during the Winter months. They all agreed to the idea, and Mor told Nuada and Pytheas that they should be built by the end of the Summer season. A'Chreag showed up and brought beer for the group. They settled down, and small talk followed.

Beag had finished the new section of the stone protection wall and was ready to start on the dam complex in the second valley. They had a few small rain showers over the last couple of days that did little to slow the work at all the work sites. There was still a lot of the timbers from the old protection wall, and it was not necessary to cut more trees at this time. Nuada had completed all of his metal projects and was ready to help Beag at the mill sites. The village women had built a fence around the crop meadow, and some had begun to build fences in the second valley around the grain fields to keep out the sheep and deer that now grazed there.

Early one morning they could feel the heat of the day beginning early, and Nuada joined Beag at the dam site. Loose rock and other debris was being removed from the side of the stream away from the valley, and Beag then began to build the first section of the dam wall. It was to include a spillway for overflow on the side by the mountain. Nuada toiled in the heat as it rose, and soon he had to stop and find shade from the sun. Others joined him, and they bathed in a tree-covered section below the work site. Beag broke up the work crews to work in shifts so as to keep the project going. Every hour they changed workers, and they moved ahead slowly but with determination. Nuada pulled Beag aside and said, "If this is any indication of the Summer ahead of us, we will be behind with what we have to do."

"I agree, but we must finish of this work so as to return to the other work needed in the village."

The heat held for almost another week before some relief came in the form of rain and light breezes. Beag was nearing the completion of the dam wall on the east side of the stream and had only a small section of the spillway to finish. It would then be time to move to the west side of the stream and begin the double wall for the mill raceway. The raceway would become the new stream bed while they finished the face of the dam over the original stream bed.

Mor had decided to move from his large house to one of the smaller one's under construction. This would give room for three or four families to live in his old house and put him closer to the construction area.

Spring was drawing to a close, and Summer was about to begin. The people of the village knew time was pushing hard on all the work that had to be done that year.

- SUMMER AND FORCED LABOR -

Summer was here, and the heat continued from the Spring, which slowed some of the work in both valleys. Nuada awoke early, as was his custom, and dressed lightly for the weather. He wore a light pair of trousers and that was about it. He carried a shirt, a work apron, gloves, and a hat; of course he always carried his weapons with him. He had been working with Beag on the raceway at the mill sites from the start of that project and had learned many new things about stonework.

He left his house and made his way down through the housing construction, and as he passed, he waved at Mor, who was already there with a large crew that was ready to start their day. These three houses were being completed quickly, and he was almost ready to start another three. The street in front of these houses was not yet paved with the stone rubble, as it was being used for fill in the walls at the mill sites.

On he walked, again passing the crop meadow and then on past the caves. As he neared the stone protection wall at the entrance into the second valley, he caught up with other workers heading to the mill sites and others who were moving on to an area where they would be cutting more trees for the construction of the shop buildings.

They had a lot of help now that the new group began to help with all the construction within the valleys. Pytheas stayed with the children now, and they spent their days at the outdoor cooking area. New walls had been built within the old woodworking building, and it began to take on the appearance of a school at last. The men of the village still had room for Winter work projects within that building, but they knew that they must limit their time in the structure now and keep the noise level down.

Nuada arrived at the mill sites and greeted Beag as soon as he saw him. He asked about the work to be done that day and then went on to the area assigned to him. The raceway was nearing completion, and tomorrow the new waterwheel was to be installed. Although many weeks of work remained to complete the dam, the site was beginning to take on the appearance of a solid structure. Once the dam was completed, buildings for the grain wheel and the sawmill were to be built. Now it looked like they would be able to finish everything needed before Fall.

Nuada, now dressed in his apron and gloves, worked at setting stone on the end of the raceway. It did not take long before sweat began to run from his muscled body, and those around him still stared at his old wound site, which seemed to shine in the sunlight. He had forgotten of the injury until asked by some of the new people how it had happened. He was almost embarrassed to mention how it had come to be, but he was glad to tell the story anyway, giving most of the credit to the other village men instead for the success at the battle.

At mid-morning Nuada took a break from his labors and found shade under a tree nearby. He drank long on his water bladder before looking about at the others working here. Beag saw him and came over to get out of the sun himself.

"These are good men, Nuada. I hope I do not work them too hard before we can get near the end of the project."

"They understand the need. That is enough."

Beag nodded in understanding, and that was all that passed between the pair before they went back to work again. The other workers followed Nuada's lead, and they pressed on with what had to be done.

When the sun neared the end of the day, Nuada took his usual wash in the stream before returning to the village. A'Chreag joined him, and they passed small talk about the work progress and what tomorrow would bring.

Instead of taking his usual path through the stone protection wall and down by the crop meadow, Nuada followed the stream out to the valley entrance and to the rock outcropping, where he had fought his first battle with Creatrix's help. He stood looking into the distance and cleared his mind of the day's work. "I miss of the adventure of travel," he thought. Then he shook his head and turned back to the valley.

He again stopped at the crypt of Jan's and focused on the memory of his friend. After about ten minutes, he turned, and with his head lowered, he continued on to the cooking area. His son was waiting for him and came running to grab on to his hand and tell his father about his day. This brightened

Nuada's mood, and he picked up his son and held him high above his head. Laughing Nuada set his son down on the table that they shared and asked about the boy's day. Iolair told him about the world of numbers that Nuada did not understand but acted like he did.

A'Chreag and his mate were fussing over their child and soon joined Nuada and his mate at their table.

"This weather makes the children restless," A'Chreag told Nuada.

"The adults too," Nuada replied.

"What mean you, Nuada?"

"I myself feel restless and miss of the adventure of exploring new lands and meeting new people."

"Not I. I would soon miss of my family, and the quest of this Spring is still strong in my mind. I would not want to do it again anytime soon."

"I understand of that too. But still there is always that pull to go and seek new things."

"Then be happy with the challenges of the building that we have been doing. This is what counts."

Nuada nodded, and still his mind could not think of anything else but another adventure. Perhaps he was just tired and that was the cause of wanting change.

Soon their attention was diverted by music that filled the cooking area and some of the people that danced with the happy sounds. Soon the smells of the cooking also filled the air and wrapped everyone with its comfort. Night came quickly, and sleep followed shortly after.

Day followed day. Projects were completed, and still others started by the village people. Nuada went from job to job, sometimes learning new things, and with others giving of his knowledge and skills. Both mill houses were now under construction, as was the final part of the dam. The fields of wild grains were finally fenced, and the new houses were nearing their final stages. Mor was going to start three more houses soon but asked Nuada if he should start the shop buildings first. Nuada replied that he thought that the houses should come first, although they could probably start both together. Mor agreed to that, and plans were set in motion for both projects to begin the following week.

Nuada knew that he would be needed at the mill sites soon to place the bands of metal on the grain millstone and to design new parts for the sawmill. His well-muscled body did not feel of the work like early in the Spring, and he forged ahead with many things that would have weakened others.

Although Creatrix had always been a part of Nuada's thoughts every day and night, he was now so busy that many days would pass before he thought of him and how all things were by his will. He was sure that Creatrix would understand of him and allow the lapses in his devotion.

A week later Nuada had placed the bands on the stone millstone and inserted the core sleeve. The roof on the mill building was still to be completed, as it was necessary to lift many of the parts into the building that way. The last of the dam was nearly done, and water was beginning to fill the new pond behind it. The new sawmill was slower to be finished as it had the lower order of need. The house for the watchman was nearing completion and would soon be occupied. This fell to one of the people new to the village. Nuada had also built another warning bell for the mill site, and it sat outside near the dam.

The weather had reached its peak for heat in the valleys that same week, and everyone looked forward to the cooler weather ahead. The week ended with a thunderstorm that shook the ground throughout both valleys and poured rain upon the dry ground. It was a needed respite and gave everyone a little time to rest.

Nuada met with Pytheas at the new school and looked at the changes that were done. New walls divided the large building into small sections, which provided ample space for the workshop area and the school too. Between the school room and the work area, a storage area was made to shield the sounds from the children of where the men would be working. This made Pytheas happy, as it had worried him that it would be too distracting for the young ones to learn.

Wolf had always kept the children close, and with the school near, Nuada wondered of his reaction to the change. Perhaps it would be necessary for Wolf to now be kept near Nuada while he worked. He asked of his mate her thoughts on the subject, and she said she saw no reason he could not still stay with the children at the school. Nuada said he would ask of Pytheas his thoughts on the matter.

The following week the crops from the meadow began to be harvested, and it seemed that the year had passed too quickly for everyone. Nuada was helping with the last of the work to be done at the new mill sites, and already the pond behind the new dam seemed to be filled close to its capacity. The waterfall behind the pond was now swallowed by the manmade lake. The raceway had its diversion boards raised to make the new waterwheel turn for the first time, and it showed the thought that went into the design. The roofs on both mill buildings were now finished, and the new watchman had moved into his house. Nuada met with Beag and did a last walk around the project.

"This was a long and hard build, Nuada. I am proud of what we did here. It is something the village will use for a long time."

"Yes. It will stand long after we are gone, my friend. The people will use it and prosper from its design."

"Agreed. Let us share of some beer to mark its completion."

"I am more than ready for that. Let us return to the village and find of the others."

The completion of the mill sites was marked by a feast by the whole village. Even as tired as most of them were, it lasted well into the late night hours. Ten men volunteered to work the new sawmill , but Mor would only allow six, as there was other work yet to be completed. There was still a month of Summer weather and houses and shops to build. Beag was going to hold off the next section of the replacement wall until Spring. The harvesting of the meadow crops was almost completed by the village women, and after that they would move on to the grain fields in the second valley.

Slowly the morning temperatures began to drop, telling everyone that Fall was soon to arrive. The village men now switched gears and pushed on with the building of the shops and finishing the last of the houses for this year. Beag was now in demand to build fireplaces and some of the surrounding walls for the houses and shops; this was an easy job for his skills, and he enjoyed the change of pace.

Nuada returned to his forge, as hinges and latches were now needed for the new buildings. At first he felt isolated from the rest of the village , but that soon passed as he worked at his skill. Iolair was taking his schooling to heart, and Nuada missed his company. A'Chreag was working between the houses and shops and rarely was at the forge building.

One morning the weaver and the man who made clothes stopped by the forge and presented Nuada with some new clothing.

"Nuada, you have need of these, and we want you to wear them with pride before the village people."

"Am I looking that ragged? I have not given it any thought as to how I was dressed except for the weather."

"You are the village chief and must look the part. We only do this out of respect for you."

"Then I shall wear them proudly. Thank you for thinking of me."

That afternoon when Nuada had completed his work at the forge, he traveled down to the lakeside and washed of himself and dressed in the new clothes before returning to the cooking area and the others. The clothes fit comfortably, and he walked with his head held high into the area, a large smile upon his face. His mate saw him from across the area and beamed at his appearance and hurried over to him.

"Who are you, stranger? I do not think you belong here among us lowly peasants."

Then she laughed and kissed of him before the whole gathering. Whistles and yells of encouragement came from everyone there. Mor strode over and looked Nuada up and down and then clasped him across his back.

"You look all the better because of your clothes , but I think the real man is still underneath them."

"I am and never forget that, my friend."

The next few weeks passed as had the whole Summer season — construction everywhere within the village. The grain crops were now harvested, and the village was ready to settle in for another Fall season. The first of the grains were put through the new millstone house with much success, and flour started to fill the storehouse. Newly sawed planks from the new sawmill drew much praise for their trueness, and some were to be used in the new shop buildings. The last of the houses to be built this year were coming close to completion, and the children of the village were now in school on a regular basis. Nuada now had time to look about the village again, and pride showed in the way things had turned out.

Although Creatrix had promised Nuada that there would be not attacks this year, men still patrolled the outside of the valleys and manned the protection walls. The village hunters used this excuse to hunt for the village and were very successful. The sheep that were now kept in the second valley had their own stable, and this made everyone happy that their smell was not part of the village anymore.

Any thoughts that Nuada had earlier in the Summer about traveling were now the furthest thing from his thoughts. Daily he took walks all over the valleys and smiled inwardly to himself with the progress of these people. They had accomplished a hard task this year. Maybe next year would give them some respite from their labors.

At the monthly meeting of the village consul, Nuada stood to one side of the meeting table and listened into the talk about the state of the construction sites. After that discussion, Mor asked if anyone had given any thought to projects for next year. Beag said he would be involved with the new stone protection wall replacement for most of the year and any new projects would slow that again. Farmer said all of the animal projects had been completed this year and nothing was planned for next year. Nuada only shook his head when he was asked if he had any thoughts. Mor said he wanted to build at least six more houses in case new people were found in the Spring.

Nuada then said, "It looks like we have found a way to live as common people, without the pressure of trying to catch up with things we were not prepared for."

The other three members nodded in agreement to that statement.

"Let us find a way to relax next year, my friends."

The meeting broke up, and the foursome left for the cooking area and some beer to wash down the agreement. At the cooking area, A'Chreag found Nuada and took him aside.

"I have a problem. Two of the men I was working with today are not happy with the living arrangements. They are talking of leaving the valley."

"Bring them to me, and I will see if I can find a way to settle of their problems."

A'Chreag hurried across the area and soon returned with the two, who appeared sheepishly before Nuada.

"What is the problem? Can I find of a way to settle the problem?"

The largest of the pair stood forward and said, "These houses are too small for my family. If I cannot find of more room, then I must leave of the village."

"How many children do you have?"

"Seven."

"Then I understand. Let me see if I can find a larger house for you. And you, do you have the same problem?"

"Yes."

"Then I have much work to do to find of houses for both of you. Give me a week to find of the answers."

Mor noticed Nuada talking to the two men and came over to see what it was all about. "Is there something I can help with, Nuada?"

"The new houses are too small for the families of these men. Do you know of a solution to their problem?"

"Yes. The families that had moved into my old house are now moving into the new houses. If they are willing, we can put both into my old house, and they will have the space they need of."

"Then let us put it before them and see if it will work for their families."

Both Nuada and Mor got up and walked over to the pair and their families and put the question to them. They instantly agreed, and the problem was solved , but Nuada told them in the future to seek him if any other problems arose. With that said, they drank of their beers and settled down to enjoy the evening music and entertainment.

Nuada walked back to his table and was soon joined by his family, with Iolair sitting in his lap and telling of his day at school. After about a half hour, Iolair asked Nuada if he could come by the school tomorrow and tell of their family history. Nuada agreed to his son's request and said he would walk with his son to school and tell of their history.

The next morning Nuada and his son walked to the old woodworking building and waited for the others to come. The first to arrive was Pytheas, and he greeted Nuada warmly and showed him where to sit until it was time for his story of their family. Soon the children of the village began to arrive, and the room was filled with noisy voices until Pytheas called for some order to the discord. After some early questions from some of the students, Pytheas called both Nuada and Iolair to the front of the room and asked them to begin the story of their family. Nuada only talked for about fifteen minutes and then said he was sorry that he did not know more about his family, which was probably because his father had died when he was so young. There were some questions, and finally Nuada was allowed to leave the building. He felt pride in his family and was happy with the telling of his story.

The experience of telling his family history made Nuada pause and wonder if in the future people would remember of him. His mind thought back to the beginning of the leaving of his family home and the trip down out of the mountains and snow. The loss of his mother came to mind and how he searched in the early-morning light unable to find her. The worries of his mate as they moved closer to the valley that they now lived in also came to his thoughts, and he wondered what life would be like if he had stayed in the mountains. Then came the finding of all the people that now lived within the valleys and how it was his charge to care for them and make them safe. Slowly he pondered all the questions as he walked to the cooking area.

As Nuada found his table in the cooking area, Mor came looking for more men to work at the construction area. Mor shouted a greeting to Nuada and walked over to him.

"Nuada, it is good to see you this morning. Do you have any projects to do today? I am in need of some more help on the houses."

"No, I am free now. I just left the school and told of my family history that I know of. On the way back here, I was wondering if anyone would remember of me in the future."

"Fear not. These people will be talking of you for many years and what you did to help them. Your place in the history of this valley will last long after your bones turn to dust."

"I am glad of that thought, my friend. Me to dust, really?"

"Come help of me with the houses, and we will talk of it more later."

Nuada got up and followed Mor back to the housing construction area and the work that would take his mind off questions in his mind.

That evening after work at the housing sites, Nuada's mind went back to the questions that had flooded his mind that morning. Iolair did not distract his father from the questions as they ate their evening meal in silence. Nuada's mate saw the mind set he was in and did not ask what was bothering him; she knew he would ask of her when he was ready.

That night while Nuada slept, Creatrix called to him again; this was the first time in many months.

"Nuada, awaken and hear of my wisdom."

Nuada's mind's eye opened in the white fog of the land of Creatrix.

"I know what bothers you, and you need not fear of the answers. You will be remembered long after you leave of the mortal plain, and the things that you have done will also be remembered. Your children and their children will mark of the things that you have done and are still to do. Ease of your fears and enjoy of the life you have made."

Nuada awoke in the morning relaxed and ready to fill out his day with happy pleasures and memories. As he dressed, he hummed a tune that he had heard one evening at the cooking area. His mate awoke to the happy music coming from him and asked of the reason. "I had a vision with Creatrix last night, and it has filled me with pleasure."

After eating a light morning meal with his family, Nuada walked Iolair to school and then walked slowly, still humming the tune in his mind, to the cooking area. The cool morning seemed to stimulate the senses this morning, and Nuada looked up at a flock of the waterfowl flying south for the Winter months. He took a deep breath and smiled broadly to the world around him. A'Chreag was already in the cooking area and came over to talk with Nuada.

"You seem in an especially good mood this morning."

"I am at that, A'Chreag. The world is alive with many pleasures this morning."

"I wish I could say that. My child kept me awake most of the night."

"Then you will appreciate it all the more when you are older."

"What do you mean?"

"You are building memories that will remain with you your whole life, my friend."

"I still do not understand."

"You will"

Nuada then departed the cooking area and walked to the housing construction area to watch the work under way. Mor was giving directions again and pointing out something that was overlooked by a pair of workers. A few men were adding to the street paving with rubble and getting it level with the help of a pair of horses pulling a large sled across the work site. Noise filled the air, and it pleased Nuada. It was the sound of progress.

Nuada did not stop to talk to Mor but instead walked on out through the new stone wall portal gate and down to the lakeside. He stood there and watched the waterfowl on the lake, then across to the island of his original home site. He wondered if the house that he had built there was now completely taken over by nature. He did not want to cross to find out but instead turned and walked back to the second valley and the new mill sites. As he approached, he could see that the new sawmill was working full time cutting lumber to be used throughout the village. Again he watched for awhile and then turned and made his way back along the stream toward the village.

He took the path that went by the caves and followed the cliff on down to the shops being built. Here he stopped and admired the work going into the shops and passed some small talk with a few of the workers. Then he went to his forge building and looked inside. He thought, "I have no work to do at this time. Why am I here?" Turning he walked alongside the original wood protection wall to the entry gate and climbed the wall to look out onto the meadow in front of the village. He cast his gaze over the large area and then turned his head toward Jan's crypt. He still missed his friend, and then he shook his head. "This is to be a happy day. Enough thoughts about what has happened and time to look to the future," he thought.

Nuada heard laughter from the school room and turned his head in that direction; the children were outside playing some game that was unfamiliar to him. He climbed down the ladder from the wall and walked over to see more of the game. Pytheas was watching the children and encouraged them when he could.

"What game is this, Pytheas?" asked Nuada.

"It is a simple game of my childhood, and the children seem to enjoy it."

Nuada watched as Iolair became the center focus of the game and the other children began to chase him.

"Your boy always seems to become the main attraction, whether in games or with his studies."

"He is a natural leader and is very smart."

Pytheas nodded and called the children back into the school. Nuada waved and moved on down the street to the cooking area. Mor had come back from the housing construction sites and was sitting at a table by himself. Nuada called a greeting and went and sat with his friend. They talked about the village again, and then Nuada asked, "I know little about where you came from, my friend. Tell me of it."

"I have been thinking of my family history and now wish to find out more about everyone else."

"I was asked to tell of my family at the school in two days. Can you wait?"

"Yes, my friend. I will be there to listen to your story. Is anyone else to tell of their family story that you know of?"

"Yes. Beag is to speak tomorrow."

"I must give Pytheas credit. He is teaching the children things that they need to know."

"Again it is because of your direction. You have always shown us our way."

"You give me too much credit, Mor."

"Not so. You think of these things before anyone else. That is what makes you our leader."

Nuada felt embarrassed by the topic but said nothing. Soon others began to arrive for the evening meal, and greetings were passed by all who entered. Before long music again filled the area, and people talked in happy tones. Nuada looked around with pride in the people of his village. His foot was tapping to the music, and then his boy joined him, and they talked about his day at school. The boy kept talking about his father's story and how others took to it.

"What else has your teacher been teaching you, Iolair?"

"We have been learning his language and how to count numbers."

"You mean speaking his language?"

"That and how to make marks that can be understood on skin or paper, which he is also showing us how to make."

"What is paper?"

"It is something made from wood , but you can see through it if you hold it up to the light."

"I must see of this. Where is Pytheas?"

"He went home, I think."

"Then I will ask of him on the morrow."

Nuada's mate brought their meals and kissed him on the forehead. "How is my youngest son, wife?"

"Like the rest of my men: stubborn and headstrong."

By the time they had finished their meals, the wind began to blow with a chill out of the east, and they soon departed for home.

As usual Nuada awoke early and waited for his son to rise and join him. He took Wolf for his early-morning run and noticed that some of the trees were starting to turn color. Looking around he saw the golden shades of the grasses were dying off, announcing that Fall was here. Nuada returned inside. Iolair was up and having his early meal before school. Nuada kissed his mate on the cheek and said, "It will not be long before we begin to take our meals in the house again."

"I am looking forward to the day, husband."

"But you will soon miss of the village gossip from your friends."

"We will find a way, as do you."

Iolair was soon ready and looking forward to school and his friends. Outside of the house, they walked slowly, and Nuada asked more of this paper making from his son. "Pytheas is the one to ask, father."

Nuada nodded and they crossed the street and moved on down to the school. Pytheas was waiting outside and greeted every child as they entered. Nuada stood aside and waited for an opportunity to speak with Pytheas. Soon the last child entered the school and as Pytheas was about to follow, Nuada asked about the papermaking thing that his son had told him of.

"It is a simple thing, and I will show of you, Nuada."

Nuada followed Pytheas inside as Beag arrived to tell of his family history. Beag's story lasted almost an hour, and Nuada was extremely interested in it. Nuada shared a few words with Beag and thanked him for the story of his family. Pytheas soon had the children working on making marks on some paper that had been made in the classroom. Nuada looked closer at the material and was amazed at it. It was simple and effective for the needed work of making marks. Also they were using some dark, liquid material to make the marks on the paper. This was applied with the use of tail feathers from some of the valley birds. Nuada had to try it and was soon sitting and drawing a design on it at a table with his son. Pytheas said nothing but watched Nuada work at his design.

Hours later Nuada set his design aside and looked about him, just as Pytheas sent the children outside to play for awhile.

"Come Nuada, let us get some fresh air."

Nuada stood and was surprised at the stiffness in his back. The pair walked outside and watched the children play while they talked of the paper process and the making of the ink. After awhile when Nuada had a grasp of the making of the items, Nuada asked about the writing of the language his son had told him of.

"It is the written language of my youth, and it has lasted through many generations to understand of our past."

"Can you have the children write of our families as the stories are told to them?"

"Yes. It would make a good project for them and help them to refine their writing skills."

Nuada and the teacher talked awhile longer before Nuada set out for the construction site and Mor to tell him of the things he had learned today. Nuada thought as he walked that these things would not be wasted on the adults of the village either. Then he thought, "We will need more teachers in the future."

Nuada found Mor, Beag, and Farmer all talking together, and he walked up to them, listening in on the conversation.

"The children really seemed interested in my family history," Beag was saying.

"As was I," Nuada interrupted.

"Ah, Nuada. So you were in school today too."

"Yes, and I learned many things."

"Such as?"

"I learned how to make paper and ink. The children are learning to make marks of a language on this paper. They will soon begin to write the history of us all. Then that can be passed down from generation to generation for all to remember of us."

"Then that is the answer to your worries of late."

"It is. The answer always seems to come if I wait long enough."

"We were just talking of the weather again. Do you think it will hold a little longer, Nuada?"

Nuada looked at the sky and knew that it was only a matter of time before the changes would come. "We have maybe another week before the first snows begin. Why?"

"We were wondering if there is time to begin another house, but if you say that the snows are that close, we will hold off on it."

"Yes. Finish what you have on the shops and these houses. Winter will be here before you know it."

The group nodded together as one and started to walk off to do their projects. Nuada, knowing that the day was short, turned and began to walk to the cooking area. After a few steps, he stopped and turned toward the lakeside for a look at the island again. Reaching the shore, he paused and reflected on his time in the valley again. He let his thoughts wander until he was stirred from those memories by a flock of geese taking wing. Then he turned and made his way back to the cooking area to wait for his son to arrive from school.

He did not have to wait long, as his son rushed into the area and joined his father.

"Father. We have begun to write of the family histories of the people of the valley. It is fun!"

Nuada smiled and thought, "He is much smarter than I, and he learns so quickly."

Iolair pulled out a piece of the paper the school was using and showed his father the marks on it. Nuada looked down at it and knew that it stood for something , but he could not understand of it. Pytheas came into the cooking area and saw Nuada and his son sitting together and walked over to them.

"Good evening, Nuada. Your son is the best of his class, and I see that he is showing you some of his talent."

"Yes, but I need to talk to you about the adults of the village and their education. I have already thought that we will need more teachers next year. Your load to teach will soon become too much, even for you."

"It will. The teaching of the adults of the village will require at least one more teacher that must work around the tasks of them."

"I see the wisdom of that, Pytheas. How can I help?"

"It is too late in the season to go looking for another teacher, but when you go in search, I would like to go with you."

"Done. You would have to question them to make sure that we get the right people."

Pytheas smiled at Nuada's answer and went to get himself something to eat. Nuada turned to his son and said, "Your teacher is very wise and brave. Never forget that, my boy."

The last days of Summer were upon the valley, and the people knew it. The days were short, and the temperature was dropping quickly now with the setting of Creatrix in his form as the sun. The village hunters were now out in search of deer that could fill the locker in the old woodworking building. Hurried finishing touches were made on the new shops and houses. The livestock were kept within the stable area now, except for the sheep, which were to remain this year in the second valley at their stable. The millstone building was going full strength making flour for the villagers, and it was being stored in the school building. Although little rain had fallen so far this time of year, everyone knew it was only a matter of time and did what they could before the change.

Nuada returned to his forge building to prepare it for the expected weather change. A'Chreag helped as he could; he was still working on the shop buildings and helping Beag with stonework.

- A WET FALL AND A LONG WINTER -

Rain blew in from the east in a strong Fall storm; lightning flashed all around the valleys, and the rumble of them shook the very structures of the people living there.

Wolf lay near the fireplace with his ears laid back during the height of the storm. His yellow eyes never closed but kept watch of the second child of Nuada and his mate. Nuada sat at the table and carved a small figure of Jan from his memory. His mate sat nearby and watched as he worked at the carving. No one from the village was going to venture out this day, and it pleased Nuada to have some time to himself.

Hours later Nuada drew on his cloak and stepped outside to check on the weather and to stretch the stiffness from his form. Wolf peered out the doorway and returned to the fireplace, not wanting to venture into the storm raging outside. Nuada soon returned himself and shook the rain from his hair. "Wife, it has not let up. We may be in for many days of this weather."

She looked up from mending some of Nuada's work clothing and only nodded at his words. Nuada slowly walked toward the table in front of the fireplace but stopped and looked down at the map table. After looking at it for some time, he gave up trying to find some new project for the valleys. He returned to his carving and let the afternoon wear itself out. Three days later the storm finally broke, and people began to venture outside again.

Nuada walked to his forge to find out if it had suffered any damage. Along the way, he looked at the wood protection wall and saw no damage there. His eyes followed the street completed this year to the new shop buildings, and things still looked undamaged from the storm. Looking across to the stable, he still saw nothing out of order and then entered into the forge building. Moisture seemed to cover everything, and he set about trying to dry things that might become damaged from the wet. After awhile he stopped and set out for the school and hopefully a conversation with Pytheas.

Nuada found Pytheas inside cleaning the room, and no children were present at this time. "Pytheas? You never seem to stop and look about at the world in wonder."

"Ah, Nuada. I can find no time to do so now. The children are very demanding in their search for answers to their many questions."

"But you seem to enjoy the quest for their answers."

"Yes. It fills my day, and I feel that I have accomplished something."

"Where did you learn of this?"

"From my teachers in the great library in Egypt."

"Where is this Egypt, and how did you learn of it?"

"In my homeland, we quest for education and search for answers where we can. The land of Egypt has been known for as long as my country has existed. It can be found across the great inland sea."

"Would it not be wise to seek the teachers we need there?"

Pytheas thought for a minute and then answered, "It would, but it would take many months to travel there and return. There are things there that we could use to make this village grow and prosper."

They continued to talk for many hours and finally settled on a course of action for the Spring months. They were to travel to this Egypt land and seek the teachers the valley needed.

Finally Nuada departed and made his way to the construction site of the new houses and sought out Mor or Beag to tell them of his decision for the trip in the Spring. Both men were not at the houses, but Nuada was told that they were at the shop buildings. He set out in search of them with excitement in his breast and hurried his pace. At the third shop building, he found them and quickly told them of his conversation with Pytheas.

"But Nuada, can you spend that much time away from the valley?" asked Beag.

"It is something that I must do for the children. They are our future, and what we have done must be preserved."

"Then we will do our part and protect of the valleys and the people of them," said Mor.

"Mor, you have shown the leadership the people need, and you will take my place."

They all agreed, and the conversation moved on to other domestic problems of the valleys. Soon, Nuada retraced his steps to the school and told Pytheas of the conversation with the consul.

"Then we have about seven months to prepare for our journey."

"I think we will need of it all, my friend."

Iolair came in looking for his father at that moment and told him to hurry home for his meal.

"Iolair, can you find of the other children and tell of them that tomorrow we will hold school again?"

The boy nodded and ran out the door in search of the other children.

"Pytheas, I must leave now, but I wish to talk more about what to expect of this journey."

"We will, Nuada. Go in peace and think not of the future now. We have other things to consider for the people."

Nuada nodded and departed for home and his mate.

Nuada did not discuss the planned travel with his mate but would postpone it until later when the time drew close for his leaving. After their evening meal, they settled in for a good night's sleep, but Nuada was too excited by the prospect of the journey and lay awake into the middle hours. Finally he fell asleep, and during that time, Creatrix called him home to speak with him. Nuada awoke in the white fog of Creatrix's place and called out to him, "Creatrix! It is I, Nuada. Why have you sent for me?"

Slowly Creatrix's shadowed form stood before Nuada, and he said, "You are right to take on this travel. It will be your second trial, and I have a gift for you."

"A gift? What will it be?"

"You will have the gift of languages, both written and spoken. You will need of it to survive in the lands that you will travel into."

"I understand, and then I do not. Will I be successful of this journey?"

"That will be for you to determine."

The fog closed in around Nuada, and he slept deeply until the morning light of Creatrix awoke him.

Nuada got out of bed slowly, trying to remember of the words of Creatrix and what he was supposed to do. Finally the words of the gift came to mind, and he dressed to seek out Pytheas. Iolair was downstairs getting ready for school, having already eaten his morning meal.

"I see you are ready for another day of school, my son. I will be ready shortly and walk with you."

"This school thing is a wonder. It gives him purpose, husband," Nuada's mate said.

"It does, and he will need of it as he grows older, wife."

Nuada and Iolair were followed by Wolf to the school, where he played with the other children while waiting for Pytheas to open the school building. Soon Pytheas opened the school door and stood aside as the children entered. Nuada suddenly greeted Pytheas in his native language, and the man looked at him in shock.

"Where did you learn of my language, Nuada?"

"It was a gift last night from the creator. He said I would need of it in the future and during our travels."

"Yes, I have heard of your ability to talk with him, but I had no idea of this."

"He told me that I would have the ability to both speak and write of the many languages we would encounter. Shall we see if it is true?"

Pytheas nodded in excitement at the words and hurried Nuada inside to the school room.

Pytheas sat down and talked to Nuada in the languages of the Phoenicians, Egyptians, and several other peoples. Nuada understood and replied in the appropriate language, and then Pytheas had him write of the languages on some of the school paper. Nuada did so as if he had done it all of his life and without pause.

"This is amazing, Nuada. I have never known anyone to do of this."

"As I have told you, it was a gift from the creator."

"I must work with the children now, but I wish to see more of your gift later."

Nuada nodded in understanding and departed the school to seek out his friends. Walking down to the new shop buildings, Nuada again glanced upward at the sky to measure the weather for the day. It was clear with some clouds and a cool temperature. "A perfect Fall day," he thought. Turning onto the street of the shops, Nuada still looked about at different things as if to measure them for the first time. Mor and Beag were inside the third shop doing some finishing touches for the maker of clothes.

"This is what he wanted, a place to hang and display his clothes." Beag said.

"It will make selecting them easier for anyone coming inside the shop," replied Mor.

"Good morning, you two. What are you crafting now?" called Nuada.

"Nuada. I see you are in good spirits today," answered Mor.

"Very good spirits, my friends."

"We need to finish early today and share of some beer for a change."

"I agree. What say we meet in about three hours and do so?"

"Done."

"Have you seen of A'Chreag today?"

"I saw him early, but he was going to take a walk to the new sawmill and bring back some of the cut lumber from there. I do not know if he has come back, but we can wait for him."

"Then I shall be at the forge. If he returns, send him to me."

"We will do so, Nuada."

Nuada departed the shop and made his way to the forge and began looking around the building for some of the metals he had used to make jewelry before. Shortly he found it and then set about setting up a casting table for some of the metal. He began carving a design to be used as a mold from some wood he had and waited for A'Chreag.

After an hour, A'Chreag appeared and asked of Nuada, "You wanted to see of me?"

"Yes. I plan on making some more of our jewelry and thought that you might want to help."

"I found of the old metals we used before, but I do not know how much of it we have. Could you see while I work at this mold?"

"This yellow metal is too soft for anything but making of jewelry. Why did you bring of it into the forge?"

"It looked good to the eye, but as you said, it is too soft for anything else."

"What are we to make of it?"

"Some rings and perhaps a bracelet or two. It gives me something to do and makes the days pass quickly."

Nuada worked at the jewelry for the rest of the early afternoon and only stopped when he remembered of the promise of beer with his friends. He found his way to the third shop building and his friends and asked of their need to stop for a beer. They jumped at the chance to get away from their project, and the three men set out for the cooking area and the warmth of its fireplace.

There was no more talk of Nuada's adventure in the Spring but only of the things going on within the village. The trio was soon joined by Farmer and several other men, and they continued their talks of the valleys and what they had done this year. Pride was in their voices, and this made Nuada happy. Soon it was time for everyone to depart for their houses and their evening meals and family. Nuada walked to the school building and waited for Iolair to walk him home. He found Wolf waiting there, and when he arrived, he sat down beside him and rubbed his head. Soon the children of the valley started leaving the school, and as usual Iolair was the last to leave. Pytheas walked him out and greeted Nuada in a different language this time, which Nuada responded to without hesitation. Iolair asked about the language, and Nuada told him it was a gift from Creatrix, to which the boy only nodded.

Pytheas said, "The boy seems to understand better than I about your gift, Nuada."

"He does. I expect him to soon talk with the creator himself."

"Why do you say that?"

"Because he is my son, and the men of my family have always been able to do so."

"I wish that I had the strength of your belief. It would be a wonder."

"Perhaps one day it will come to you."

Nuada and Iolair, followed by Wolf, made their way home and a welcome meal.

Early the next morning Nuada again walked Iolair to school and then returned to the forge and his project of making jewelry. After firing the forge, he continued to make molds and prepare for the first pour of the yellow metal. At mid-morning A'Chreag stopped to check on Nuada and his project, just as Nuada was pouring the first of his castings.

"Nuada, do you need of me today?"

"No. This is just something for me to do today."

"I shall be at the third shop building doing some finishing work if you need of me."

A'Chreag soon departed and left Nuada to work at his project. Late in the afternoon, while Nuada was doing the finishing polish on the jewelry, he looked up in surprise at the lateness of the hour and quickly banked the forge fire and pocketed some of the jewelry to finish at home and then made his way to the school.

Pytheas was standing outside with Iolair, and they were talking in the native language of the Greeks. Nuada greeted Pytheas in his tongue and asked of his day.

"These children learn quickly but not as fast as your son."

"He makes me proud of him with his skills. I must assume it is a gift from Creatrix also."

"I am unsure how to answer of that, Nuada. I have never been touched by the gods."

"Perhaps it will come someday. Until then trust in yourself. I have something for you." Nuada reached into his cloak and produced a ring that he had made that day and handed it to Pytheas.

Pytheas took it and looked at it closely. "How did you come of this, Nuada?"

"I made it today, and I thought it would suit you."

"It is gold. Where did you find it?"

"It is found in the second valley, and I only use it to make of these trinkets."

"Where we are going it has value and is not taken lightly."

"I had no idea that it had any value. It is too soft for anything useful for us in the valleys, other than this jewelry."

"Do you have more of it?"

"Yes, there is a hillside filled of it. Why?"

"We will need of it for our trip. I had not thought of the cost to us to travel; it will help ease the way."

"Then we will have more of it. In what form do you think it would be best for our adventure?"

"Make small bricks of it. It has weight, and we can carry it easier that way."

"Then I will do so."

Nuada and Iolair departed for home with a wave from Pytheas. Pytheas now felt better about the adventure of traveling to Egypt.

Morning broke with the wind blowing hard out of the east again. Nuada studied the sky and decided that the rain would hold off today. After dropping Iolair at the school, he made his way back to the forge building. He fired the forge and set out making the forms for the small bricks that would be needed for the adventure in the Spring. He remained alone throughout the day as he worked steadily at the yellow-metal castings. He knew that he would have to venture to the quarry site in the second valley soon, as the ore supply was low. Late in the afternoon he sought out Mor to ask for help at the quarry if the weather held for the next two days. He then went to the stable to arrange for two wagons and the horses to pull them for tomorrow. As he was leaving the stable, he ran into A'Chreag, and they talked about the retrieval of the ore of yellow metal, and A'Chreag said he would help tomorrow. Nuada then had to hurry to the school to pickup Iolair and tell Pytheas of the work ahead.

Nuada had time to show Pytheas the samples of his day's work with the yellow metal before hurrying home to his evening meal and time with his mate and youngest child. During the meal, Nuada showed his mate the small bricks of the yellow metal and asked her for her opinion of them. When she asked him what they were for, he paused and said they were to be used in the Spring for a quest for teachers. He did not tell her that it would be himself going on the quest. She looked at him but did not say any more.

The next day after taking Iolair to school, he set out for the stables and then to the forge to acquire some tools to dig out the ore. A'Chreag wandered in just as Nuada was finishing the preparations to move onto the second valley.

"Good. You can help with the second wagon. We need to pick up the two men Mor has picked to help us with the dig. They will be at the outdoor cooking area."

A'Chreag nodded, and the wagons began to move off.

Slowly the wagons followed the street out of the village and down to the second valley's protection wall and its gate. Once through they turned to the right and followed the cliff edge until they arrived at the quarry on the far side of the valley. It was located between the two fenced grain fields and near the sheep stable.

The four men worked at extracting the ore until mid-afternoon and then set out for the forge building to unload the day's work. They had filled almost both wagons, and Nuada seemed satisfied with the amount of work done. As they passed under the second valley's portal gate, the guards there waved as they passed and shouted encouragement to the four men. Down through the village's streets they passed and onto the forge for unloading. Nuada knew that it would be a repeat tomorrow as he stretched his tired muscles after jumping down from the wagon he drove. He offered some beer to the pair of workers who had helped them today, and they gladly accepted it. When the wagons were unloaded, A'Chreag took the horses to the stable for a rubdown and a feeding. Nuada went to the school again to pickup Iolair and to see if Pytheas had any more comments for preparations for the adventure.

The second day of ore extraction went the same as the day before, and Nuada could really feel the soreness in his muscles this time. He was glad when the day was done and the ore stockpiled at the forge building. The process of removing the metal from the basic rock took time, and he knew that it would be another two days before he could again start casting the ore into the bricks.

As Nuada departed the forge building, he happened to look skyward again, and he knew that it was more than soreness in his muscles that hurt; the weather was about to change again. The old wound in his side began to ache as he headed to the school and his son. On his arrival, Pytheas was still inside, and Nuada entered to have a word with him. He found him bent over the shoulder of Iolair, talking as the boy was writing.

"Pytheas? A word with you?"

"Ah, Nuada. We were just working on the story of your family. Do you have time to read of it?"

"Not right now, but if Iolair would bring it home, I will read of it tonight."

"Very well. What is it that you wish to speak of?"

"I was wondering of the yellow metal. Should we make some smaller pieces?"

"A good idea. Do so that we may barter with it."

"Also do you have maps of the quest? It will make planning easier."

"No, I do not. However, I will make of them for you so that you will understand of the time it will take for us to travel there."

Iolair did not understand of the conversation and kept working at his writing until they had finished talking, then picked up his papers and rolled them to carry under his arm. "I am ready Father to go home."

Nuada nodded in response and said good night to Pytheas and took his son home for supper.

The weeks passed quickly for Nuada as he kept up his work at the forge making the small gold bars they would need. The weather began to follow its normal pattern, and it became cold and windy, day by day. Finally the snow began to fall in greater strength; Winter was near.

At the last monthly meeting for the village consul, Mor again asked for any new plans for the Spring. Beag thought that he should move the new wall out into the meadow where they had fought the raiders.

"How far out?" asked Mor.

"Four or five hundred yards should do it. That way we will have more room to expand the village."

The plan was agreed to, and they settled the thought with a round of beer before they broke up the meeting. During this time, Nuada asked about the building plan for more houses. Mor said that he had thought that only four or five more houses would be needed next year. Nuada shook his head in disagreement and said, "Build ten or more. We will have the new teachers, and possibly another group will be found that need of our safety and protection."

Mor agreed to Nuada's request and said he would plan on the building of that many houses.

"What about more shops for the men of trades that we will need for growth?" Mor said.

"Build what we need and then add one more for the future," replied Nuada.

"Then we will have a full year of construction again. The men are starting to grow weary of all the work."

"Then explain to them the need for it again and do so as my request."

Mor agreed, and Beag only smiled at Mor's discomfort and knew the work would be done as Nuada wanted. When the meeting broke up, they walked out into a heavy snowstorm and each hurried to their houses, knowing that tomorrow would be a dreary day for all.

Nuada awoke in the middle of the night with the sounds of a feverish wind blowing at his roof. He got out of bed and made his way to the front door and slowly opened it to peer outside. The cold wind pushed at the door, and Nuada fought to hold it closed. Snow wrapped around his ankles as he latched the door and then made his way to the fireplace to add more wood to the light embers still burning there. Soon flames warmed him, and he sat at the table near the fire and shook the cold from his body. He could not go back to sleep now, and he waited for the first light of Creatrix in the morning. Wolf came down the stairs to see what Nuada was doing and then curled up at his feet and enjoyed the heat of the fire.

Nuada was asleep at the table in the morning when his mate came down the stairs to begin a light meal for her family. She set a fur cloak around his shoulders, trying not to awaken him, but it did stir him. Quietly she worked at her pots and then returned upstairs to retrieve the boys. Something within Nuada told him to awaken, and with stiff muscles complaining, he sat upright and rubbed at his eyes. The smells coming from the fireplace told him that his mate was awake, and he looked about to see where she was. Soon she came down the stairs again with the two boys and saw Nuada awake.

"You must have been up most of the night, husband."

"I was. The wind awoke me, and I could not return to sleep."

"When are you going to tell of me about the adventure you have planned for the Spring?" she asked offhandedly.

"You knew? I did not wish to disturb you with the thought of it until we were to go."

"I know you, and you should understand that from me. Now tell of me what it is all about."

Nuada explained the need for more teachers and his discussions with Pytheas. Then he told of his vision with Creatrix and the gift given to him for the quest. She then asked when he was to leave and how long it would take. He told her the start date was still up in the air and that Pytheas had said it would take months to find and return with the teachers needed.

She came over and wrapped her arms around Nuada and then kissed him deeply before saying, "In the future, tell me of something before everyone else knows."

Nuada nodded and returned her kiss before he went to the door to check on the weather again. Wolf followed him but soon returned to the fire and watched his family with sleepy eyes.

Nuada returned and told his family that there was to be no traveling today and that school would not be for Iolair today. After eating Nuada sat and worked at a new carving while Iolair worked at his writing skills of the family history.

The day passed slowly, but the comfort of the family together seemed soothing for all. From time to time, Nuada had to stand and work the stiffness from his body. He thought it was only the weather causing the ache and thought little of the discomfort. Midday came and went with little thought, and soon it was time for the evening meal. Nuada looked down on the carving he had been working on and then set it aside for another day. He then spent the rest of the evening holding his youngest child while his mate did other chores. Soon it was time for them to sleep — or at least try to sleep if the storm would let them.

Four days later Nuada slid open the front door to check on the storm and found that the light of Creatrix spilled across his snow-covered entry. Wolf bounded out into the snow and was soon out of sight. Nuada returned inside and wrapped himself in his warm clothes and returned outside to wait for Wolf. His breath cast a foggy cloud in front of his face, and he shook from the chill that greeted him. Soon Wolf returned and threw the light snow from his back all over Nuada and then ran inside to the fire that awaited him. Nuada slowly closed the door and then walked to his family standing near the front table.

"The storm has broken although it is very cold today. Iolair, you should stay home again today, and maybe tomorrow you can return to school."

The boy began to complain and then finally agreed to his father's request.

Nuada, instead of returning to his carving, took time to read the writing of his son about the family history. He offered added details and then told him that he was doing a very good job of the history. "In a few years, you again will write of the family, but you will use another language."

By the afternoon, Nuada began to feel the walls of his house closing about him, and he returned to his entry to check on the weather again. Although it had warmed up, he knew it was still too cold for anything other than what he had been doing. He then noticed that the leaves that had been so colorful only a few days before were now gone with the passing of the strong winds of the storm. Smoke from the village houses still clung close to the ground, and the smell from them was pungent with the wood odor of the fires. No one was seen, so he finally returned inside. The day would end much as it had begun.

The following morning Nuada heard the noise of the village men outside before he had dressed and went downstairs. Quickly he called Wolf, and together they stepped out onto the entry and looked at the activity of the village.

Men were everywhere removing the snow from the streets and loading it onto wagons for transportation out of the village. Some of the snow went to the lakeside or wagons took it out onto the meadow in front of the wood protection wall, where it could melt in the full sun of Creatrix and run down to the lake.

Nuada left his entry and went to seek Mor. After asking of some of the men, he found him at the first shop building.

"Mor, do you need of my help?"

"Your help is always welcome, Nuada."

"Where do you need of me?"

"You can join the second shift at the school in another half hour."

Nuada made his way to the school and found some warmth inside with Pytheas while he waited.

"Nuada! Good to see you after this storm. What think you of this weather?"

"This is normal for here. Just wait for next month — it will last many more days at a time."

"How is Iolair? I hope he is working on his writing skills."

"He is, and the family story is coming along well. He hardly takes a break from it."

"Good. I do not know what to do without the children here. Do you think they will be returning soon?"

"Yes. Plan on them for tomorrow. They look forward to being here."

Soon their conversation was broken by the men gathering to replace the men removing the snow from the streets. Mor came and then assigned men to different parts of the village, and they soon moved off to continue the work; Nuada was with them.

When it was nearing the end of the hour-long shift, Nuada again felt the old pain in his side and began to slow because of it. The relief men soon showed, and Nuada made his way back to the school and the warmth of the fire inside. "Nuada! You look ill. Sit and relax until it passes," said Pytheas.

"I do not understand why this old wound still pains of me. What think you?"

Pytheas lifted the shirt of Nuada and looked at his old wound site. After probing around the wound, he asked many questions about it and then sat back in deep thought.

"Nuada, have you used any of the root that you used when you hurt your arm long ago?"

"No. I have not thought of it. This pain comes and goes, and I was unsure of the cause."

"Try the root and see if it removes of the pain. I cannot find of the cause other than you may have overused of the muscles there."

Nuada said he would try the root and asked Pytheas to tell Mor that he would not return to work today. Doing so Nuada departed for his house and the comfort of the root that he would drink.

Nuada's mate prepared the root drink and helped Nuada drink of it after he had settled in a comfortable position in front of the fireplace. Sleep soon found Nuada, and there was relief from the pain of his old wound.

Winter settled over the valleys of the people who lived there. Nuada, from time to time, would work at his forge preparing the yellow metal for the quest in the Spring. The weather brought a wet and badly-needed storm once a week, which limited the outdoor activities of the people there. The school was open on a limited basis from the weather , but Pytheas managed to still inspire the children to learn on their own at home.

One morning Nuada went outside and found the valley wrapped in a dense fog. The chill from it felt colder than the many snowstorms that had covered the valley this Winter. Nuada dressed himself warmly and took a walk to the school and a conversation with Pytheas.

"I have been looking at the maps that you drew for me and still have many questions about the land and the people we will meet there."

They talked for many hours before deciding to seek out some of the other men of the village at one of the shop buildings. Pytheas found that Nuada's curiosity drove him harder every time that they talked and admired him for it. At the second shop building, they found many of the village men sitting about and drinking beer while others were playing music and adding to the comfort of the room they were in. Nuada and Pytheas settled at a table near the door and listened to the sounds of the room without saying anything to each other. The door to the room opened, and Mor and Beag entered talking to each other. Nuada called them over to the table, where he sat and waited for them to get comfortable.

"What are you two up to now?"

"We were just discussing the order for the work to be done in the Spring," Beag said.

"Is there a problem?"

"Well Mar wants to tear down the wooden protection wall for the new houses, and I have been trying to get him to wait until I have built more of the new stone wall in the meadow. That way we will still have a place for defense until the new wall is done."

"I can understand the needs of both of you. However, we still have the stone wall at the entrance to the valley and that should be enough until the new second wall is done. I believe that Mor can tear down the wooden wall and we will have enough protection."

"See, I told you that it would be enough," Mor said.

Beer was set before both men ,and then they settled down to relax with their friends. After awhile Nuada said, "We need of this shop for this purpose all the time. It is a place for all to gather and put their worries behind."

Mor looked about and quickly agreed of its need. "I will make it so and add more tables to the room."

Soon the beat of the music picked up, and they found their feet were tapping to the beat of the sounds. All thoughts of what was going on around them disappeared, and happiness seemed to fill the air. Many men began to sing, and it added to the atmosphere of the place.

Nuada lost all track of the time, and soon his stomach began to growl from hunger. He said good-bye to his friends and hurried home to his evening meal and family. Darkness had already begun to cover the valley floor as he found his entry at his house.

"Husband, you are late tonight. Sit and eat of your meal before it grows cold," Nuada's mate said. "Did you learn anything new today?"

"I did, and I settled a dispute about the new construction for the Spring."

She did not question him any further but knew that he would tell her of it when he was ready. The two boys were already asleep near the fireplace with Wolf watching over them.

"It seems that my family has had a busy day too." He smiled at his children's forms and ate of his meal.

As the weeks passed, the weather began to improve, and the sun added warmth to the people of the village. They knew that Spring was now near and that the new work projects would soon take over their daily lives. The weekly snowstorms now turned to rain, and it quickly melted the snow that had began to rot along the streets of the village.

Nuada was ready for a change but had a healthy fear of the quest ahead of him. When he began to doubt himself, Nuada would talk with Pytheas about it, and soon the fear was replaced with a yearning to begin the adventure.

That time would come soon enough, and he spent more time with his family now. Iolair was growing quickly and had a mind to match. Nuada's youngest child was now beginning to stand and mouth some words. Each child was quickly changing, and Nuada knew that he would miss of the many things coming from them this Summer. As for his mate, she did not complain as to his leaving as she knew it was a needed thing for the village.

- SPRING AND THE QUEST -

Spring was here at last. The weeds and wildflowers were abundant, due to the wet Spring weather and the heavy snows of the Winter. Trees were beginning to leaf out, and the temperatures were warming to comfortable afternoons although the mornings were still cool.

Nuada dressed for the weather and was out early. He took a walk around the village and briefly talked with some of the people who were up and about. He came across Beag just leaving his house, and together they decided to take a walk to the dam and mill houses. Beag felt it was time to inspect the dam, and he and Nuada hurried to the site. The caretakers of the mills, who lived nearby, greeted them, and as a group they checked the dam and retaining walls of the mill pond. They found no major problems, as the spillway and design of the dam itself took care of any major water runoff from upstream. There was some seepage between some of the stonework, but it presented no problem for Beag. He was happy with the way it handled the water and said so to Nuada. After the inspection, Beag asked Nuada to go with him to the site of the new stone protection wall in front of the village. Nuada agreed and wanted to see where it was to be built. They took their time walking to the site and talked about some of the other things to be done this year. Nuada said he would like to see more of the houses built from stone this year instead of wood, and Beag jumped at the chance to do it. "Just clear it with Mor, please," he asked of Nuada.

Nuada said he would. They arrived at the new construction site for the wall, and Beag pointed out the placement of it and why it would help in the growth of the village. Nuada nodded in the understanding of the design and said he agreed with the concept of it. He left Beag and made his way back into the village in hopes of finding Mor and talking with him about the things that he and Beag had discussed.

He found Mor with a small crew working at tearing down the old wood protection wall and preparing to transport the timbers back to the sawmill for proper cutting. Some of the men had already taken off their shirts, and sweat glistened off their backs as they worked. Nuada stood and watched as they worked before talking with Mor.

"Mor, a word with you, please," Nuada called.

Mor joined Nuada, and they sat on one of the timbers already taken down and talked about the discussion with Beag that morning. Nuada told him of wanting Beag to build more of the houses in stone this year, and Mor slowly agreed to the concept but wanted to see the designs first on some of the new paper. Nuada said he would have Beag prepare them for him. Then the talks turned to the quest that Nuada and Pytheas were to go on.

"I plan to leave in another week and will be gone for most of the Summer months. Are you ready to lead the village people while I am gone?"

Mor said he was, and they left it at that. Soon Nuada made his way to the forge building and checked on the supply of gold bars that he had been working on all Winter long. Most of the bars had been packed into leather bags to make the trip, and each of those weighed in at about seventy pounds. He counted twelve bags and nodded at the amount on hand. Soon he turned and made his way to the school and the needed talk with Pytheas.

The children were outside in the sunshine playing at a new game, and Pytheas was standing at the school entrance.

"Ah, Nuada. Good to see of you today."

"Pytheas. I am getting ready for our quest. We have twelve bags of gold now. How many do we need to take with us?"

"What do they weigh?"

"About seventy pounds each. Why?"

"Then we will only need of about five of those. We must conserve our weight for the travels. That will give of us more than we will ever need to pay our way and eat."

"What about clothes? What am I to take with me?"

"Take only two changes. We will purchase new clothes as we go — for the weather and the attitude of the people we meet."

"What mean you, attitude?"

"The people you will meet will judge of you on how you are dressed. Different peoples are influenced by their religions and history. You must blend in with them."

"I understand of this. Anything else that I must know of?"

"Not now. We will change with the need of the lands we enter into although I would suggest that you trim of your beard close. If it is too long, they will think of you as a barbarian."

Nuada stroked his beard as if to say, "I understand" and only nodded at Pytheas's request.

"What of the children? Have you told of them that you are going on this quest?"

"I have. They will understand, but for now I have picked a helper to carry on with the school, and she has been here the past week helping with the children."

"Then you will be ready in a week to begin the quest?"

"I will be ready, and I am looking forward to it."

"Come to my house later and share of my food and drink. My mate may have questions for you."

"I will, and I can answer her questions, so she will be without fear of our trip."

Nuada departed Pytheas's company and made his way back to the work on the wooden wall. Mar saw him standing and watching the work and joined him.

"I take it that your preparations are in order now?"

"Yes. But I regret having to depart the valley and the things needed here."

"All will be done. Think only of what you need on this quest."

"My mind has been torn by the thoughts of it. The things that I will see and do add to my fears, and yet I look forward to them."

"Then relax and let the future find of you."

Nuada nodded and turned to return home and find of his mate. Entering his house, he stepped around the stairs and saw her bent over the fireplace cleaning it.

"Wife, I will need of your help soon. Finish what you are doing, and I will wait on you."

She stood and pushed back a lock of hair that had fallen across her eyes. "What is it that you need, husband?"

"Pytheas said that I should trim of my beard. He said it should be short. What think you?"

She looked at him with a girlish gleam in her eyes and smiled at his question. "It would do no harm to your good looks, and it might even make the red of your hair stand out more.

"Wife, do not make fun of me. I am serious about the trim, and the only thing I have for what is needed for this quest is what Pytheas tells of me."

"Sit and I shall see what I can do with that mess you call a beard."

Nuada did as he was told and waited for her to finish the fireplace. Soon she turned, and after washing her hands, she began to comb his beard and then took to cutting at it. About a half hour later, she said, "Get up and brush of yourself. I can do no more with it."

Nuada went to look in the polished-metal looking glass that he had made for her so long ago and was taken aback by the reflection of himself in its surface. "I look much the same as I did when we first joined, wife."

She turned her head from side to side and then said, "You are the same but different. Your wisdom is beginning to show through with your age."

Thinking that she was teasing him, Nuada frowned at her remark. "I shall see what Pytheas has to say about it now," he said as he got up to leave.

She stopped him and said, "I was only having fun with you. It is a marked change over before." Then she kissed him deeply and sent him on his way.

The school day was nearing its close, and Nuada waited outside for Iolair and Pytheas to show themselves. He watched as more of the wooden protection wall came down but did not approach the work site. Soon school classes finished, and the children came running out of the building. Laughter and loud noises accompanied their exit, and Nuada held his hands over his ears as they passed. Soon Iolair and Pytheas appeared and were talking of the lands where the quest was headed.

"It is a land filled with sands and little else except a lush river that feeds the people there."

"Then why do they stay there?"

"Because it is the only home they have ever known."

"That is a good answer, Pytheas," Nuada interrupted.

"It is the only answer," he replied.

"We are lucky in that we have seen other lands and understand of the need to find out about the outside world."

"That is a truth in itself, Nuada. You look different somehow. You trimmed your beard!"

"Is this what you wanted? My wife made fun of me for it."

"It is perfect. That is the look you will need on our travels."

"Then the only thing we need now is the start date. It will not take me long to pack, and I have chosen three good horses to travel with us."

"I ask for five more days, then we can go."

"I will be ready. Iolair, are you ready to go home?"

"Yes, Father. I wish I could go with you and see of the things you will see."

"You will have the rest of your life for such things, my boy. Have patience and learn of the world before you now."

"Your father speaks the truth in this matter, Iolair. Grow and learn of your valley first, then travel as you may."

The words did nothing to take the glimmer from his eyes, and Nuada turned him toward home and the evening meal. Nuada called back over his shoulder to Pytheas, "When will you come for a meal and some of my beer?"

"Before we leave. I promise."

Nuada waved back a response and kept on walking home. Nuada's mate was waiting on the entry with their youngest child and asked about Pytheas's response to the beard trim. "He approves of it. He thinks we will travel easier among the different peoples."

The rest of the evening went past with family time, and a quietness settled on the house.

For two more days, Nuada slowly packed things he thought he would need on the quest and with his free time walked about both valleys, just taking in everything, as if it would only be a memory in the future.

On day three, after Nuada went to the school to pick up Iolair, Pytheas said he would like to join Nuada's family for their evening meal, which Nuada quickly agreed to. The trio walked on to Nuada's house talking about the upcoming quest. Iolair asked many questions about the countries that they would be traveling into. Pytheas tried to answer them as best he could but told him that the only way to appreciate them was to go there himself. Iolair wanted to go with his father in the worst way but knew that it would have to wait until he was older.

Entering the house Nuada called to his mate and told her that they would have company for their evening meal. Pytheas paused at the map table and looked closely at the details that it held. "I see that you have updated the new construction plans onto the model."

"Yes. The placement of the new stone wall will double the village area and still give us the protection that we need. The new houses that Beag wants to build of stone will fill in that area eventually."

"For a valley that only four years ago that was virgin, you have created a city that you can be proud of."

"I am. The people have made it so, and they can see of the changes in the short amount of time involved. Come, let us have some of that beer I promised you before we eat."

The two men sat and talked until the meal was ready and even during the meal continued to discuss the upcoming travel. Nuada's mate said nothing but listened carefully to every word. Much later Pytheas said his good nights and departed for his house and his own preparations for the quest.

After the children had gone to bed, Nuada and his mate sat before the fireplace and held each other close without words. Finally she could not hold her tongue any longer and asked if it was really necessary for Nuada to go.

"You know it is needed. I will not be any longer than what it takes to find of the teachers, wife. Know that I love of you and I will return."

The day of the departure Nuada awoke before dawn and hurried to the stable to gather the horses and then stopped at the forge to pack the gold that he was taking with him. Moving back through the streets to his house and his things that he would be taking, he looked about again at the changes in the village. The first light of the new day was breaking with no hint of bad weather, and the first birds of the morning were calling to each other. Although the temperature was still cool in the mornings, he knew it would become warm soon. Entering into his house he gathered his pack and weapons and sat before his fireplace for the last time for many months. Iolair came running and hugged his father.

"I wish I was going with you, Father."

"Your time will come. Be patient and help of your mother until I return."

Nuada's mate came forward slowly and reached out and held him tightly. A single kiss passed between them, and then Nuada said he had to go and gather of Pytheas and depart.

The family stepped out onto the house entry, and Nuada was surprised, as most of the village had come to wish him well on his departure. Pytheas was there waiting, and it was Mor who stepped forward from the crowd and shook Nuada's hand first. Soon many others came forward, and Nuada was overwhelmed by the village response to his leaving on the quest; he felt that he had to say something.

"I am overwhelmed by your coming. I and Pytheas are leaving because of the need for more teachers. We will return as soon as possible. I thank you for coming, but now I must go and search out the things needed."

While Nuada was talking to the crowd, Pytheas loaded his pack onto the horse being used for that purpose, and soon both men mounted their respective horses and made for the valley entrance.

As they passed through the valley entrance portal gate near the stream, Nuada held his horse and turned to look back onto the valley and everything it held for him. "I shall miss of this place, Pytheas," was all he said, and then they continued on around to the left and away from the valley.

Day after day they moved south, farther away from home with every step of the horses. They moved through valleys that seemed to have no end to them. They seemed to channel both riders onward. The hills became steeper as they moved south, to which Nuada noted the climb in elevation.

"When do these hills end, Pytheas?"

"Only when we reach the great inland sea, Nuada."

Three weeks passed, and still there seemed to be no end to the hills and mountains around them. Few people were seen, and villages were nonexistent. More days passed when Pytheas said, "We are now entering the land of the Etruscans. You will see more people , but they keep to themselves."

"How much longer until we reach the great sea you talk of?"

"We should be there within the week, Nuada. We will need to buy some clothes for our trip across the water."

"You never told me that part of the quest. How will we cross the water?"

"There is a seafaring people who cross the waters all the time for trade. They are called Phoenician. We can use of the gold to buy passage across to Alexandria and the Great Library located there."

"How many times have you been there, Pytheas?"

"Only once, but it was for many years as a student."

"What about the city and the people we will meet there?"

"The city is a country unto itself and is mostly Greek or of the Egyptian people who live in that area. When Alexander the Great of Greece entered into Egypt in 331 B.C., he built the city of Alexandria with its two great harbors and then built the library in the following year. The lighthouse of Pharos was built in 279 B.C. and served the city well. You will find that many different peoples visit or study there. Learn of the way the law is given in the city, and you will understand of the needs for your own village."

"I think I understand of its nature. I want you to know that I wish for you to stay in the village with us and undertake the position of leader of the new teachers."

"It has always been my nature to travel and see of the world , but now that I am older, I would like to stay and grow with your village."

"You had me worried, my friend. I understand the willingness to visit new places and learn of them myself. I am pleased that you will stay with us and help us grow."

No more was talked of about the possibility of Pytheas moving on after the new teachers arrived in the village.

From time to time, as had been the nature of Nuada's travels, he checked the maps drawn by Pytheas and made daily notes about the things he had seen and where they were in relation to the port city that they were headed for. He found that the gift of Creatrix for languages helped him to understand more of what was going on around him. He liked the nature of the written word and worked at it when he could.

Pytheas watched him when he did this and only smiled at Nuada's response to the writing.

"You will be a true scholar of the world when we are done with this quest, Nuada."

"It has opened my eyes to the whole world, and I see things now that I never understood before."

Nuada had been so taken by this trip that he had little thought of home or his family.

One day during the mid-morning, they crested a rise and looked out across a city below them. Beyond it was a vast sea of water that Nuada had never seen before, and he was in shock at its size. "That is the great inland sea you talked of, is it not?"

"It is. It is the lifeblood of many nations that live around it. All trade passes across it, and wars are caused because of it."

"I have never been on any waters that I could not see across to the other side of. What of the dangers of crossing it?"

"There is always danger. Storms come up quickly, and then there are the nations who try to control the trade lanes."

"Is there no other way across?"

"We could go by land around it, but it would take years to do so."

"Then we cross the water. I trust of you and what we will find on the other side."

They continued on down to the city and a place to stay until they could find passage on a ship going to Alexandria. Nuada was alert to the strangers of this city and felt danger at every cross street. After finding a place to lodge and a stable for the horses, they sought out a place to eat and another to buy new clothes that would not stand out in the city. While trying out new clothes, Pytheas was very selective about the clothes that Nuada was to wear.

"You are to go as a man of royal blood and must dress the part, Nuada."

"But these clothes are so thin that I feel as though I am wearing nothing, and the colors feel out of place."

"Trust of me. I know what is needed."

Later after the purchase of the clothes, they returned to the room that they had found and talked about the finding of the right ship and men to carry them across the sea.

"What of the horses?" Nuada asked.

"We can sell of them, or we can board them at the stable until we return in about a month."

"They are good horses. I would prefer to keep them."

"Then tomorrow after we find of a ship, we will find a stable to keep of them until we return."

After both had changed their clothes, they went to seek their evening meal and relax before tomorrow. A tavern of sorts provided the food they needed, and it had music that Nuada enjoyed. Pytheas ordered food and a new drink that Nuada had never tried before; it was called wine. The taste of it pleased Nuada, and he had several before Pytheas held him back from more.

Several hours later they returned to their room, and Nuada went to sleep quickly while Pytheas sat and watched out over the city, thinking about tomorrow. It was late before he found sleep.

Pytheas awoke to the sound of Nuada sitting at the side of his bed, holding his head and groaning.

"My head feels as though it has many hammers hitting inside of it."

"That is only the wine from last night. Now you understand of me holding more of it from you."

"It is powerful. I will take care from now on."

After dressing they made their way to the same tavern and had a light meal with a single glass of the wine before walking down to the ship-filled dock.

"Nuada, let me do the talking, and I want you to stand back and act disinterested as to the whole thing."

Pytheas talked with four different people on the dock and finally settled on one ship and its master. Nuada stood back and acted bored with the whole thing until Pytheas walked back over to him.

"All the other ships are headed west. This one has a stop in Crete at Salamis, then he is headed to Alexandria. I arranged a deal that will cost us two of our large gold bricks. It will give us privacy and all our meals."

"When do we leave?"

"Tomorrow at first light. The tides will be right then."

"And when do we board the ship?"

"Tonight. We must be here at dark."

The pair walked back into the city and their lodging. Along the way, Nuada asked about the buildings and the way they were built.

"Some are of stone, as you can see. Others are of wood that has a plaster covering on them. They do not get much rain here, so it lasts. Most houses are painted white to reflect the heat of the sun, but others add a colorful appearance of different colors. Inside they usually have an open courtyard to cool the houses with plants of many different types."

"That would not work in our village, but I can see of the useful nature of it here."

It was just after midday, so they stopped again at the tavern and had a light meal with more of the wine. Afterward they went to the stable to make arrangements for the horses and then back to the room and out of the heat of the day.

Nuada was restless and paced within the room, waiting for the cool of the evening and the chance to board the ship. Pytheas took a nap and seemed too relaxed for what lay ahead to Nuada. He wanted to ask more questions but decided to let Pytheas sleep.

The sun was near setting when they came downstairs and asked about help to transport their packs to the ship. The innkeeper called into the back room and two men appeared. After settling their bill with the inn, they set out for the dock and a new adventure for Nuada.

When they arrived at the dock, the shipmaster was busy, and he had another show Nuada and Pytheas to their sleeping area. After their packs were put aboard, Pytheas paid the two men and then settled back to wait for the morning sailing.

Nuada awoke in the morning to the sounds of men rushing about and shouts being directed to the men before sailing. He was surprised that he had slept so well, it being a different place with many different smells. Pytheas was already up and was outside their sleeping area watching the preparations. Nuada soon joined him, and they watched together as lines were castoff and men used long oars to shove the ship from the dock and out into the channel. Orders were shouted, and long lines of oars appeared through the side of the ship and began to propel it out of the harbor and to the waiting sea. Seabirds circled around the ship and screamed at their departure. The winds were light but out of the east in a favorable direction.

Nuada watched in fascination at the fluid movements of the ship and crew. Soon a drum began to beat time for the men working the oars while the master stood at the back of the ship and called orders where needed. Then with a shout, men began to climb the single, tall mast and made preparations for setting the main sail. While the water within the harbor was smooth when they cleared the headland, the waves began to roll and toss the ship about. Nuada grabbed the rail nearby and held on as his world began to move about him.

Pytheas stood nearby with his legs apart, and his body swayed with the motion of the ship.

"Nuada, you will soon get your sea legs, and it will seem that the land moves when we get to Alexandria. Relax and enjoy the motion now."

Nuada nodded, and then the thoughts of getting something to eat passed through his mind, which he quickly passed on. His stomach was in motion with the ship, and he felt dizzy with the new feeling.

Looking up the main sail bellowed in the early-morning light and was soon trimmed. The oars were drawn back into the ship, and they settled on a course with the ship leaning slightly to the left.

The air was filled with the freshness of its moisture, and it had a salt tang that even pleased Nuada's senses. He continued to watch as the land slowly passed from view and only the sea remained.

By day's end, Nuada finally had an appetite, and he felt that his stomach could handle it, now that he was becoming accustomed to the ship's motion. Pytheas did not laugh at Nuada's condition, as he himself had gone through the same thing on his first travel by ship. They both ate lightly inside their sleeping place and settled down for the night.

Day after day passed, and Nuada wondered if they would ever see land again. He took walks about the ship and watched as the men went about their daily chores. The air was warm despite being on the water, and the winds remained light. Often he went about bare chested, and the sun turned his skin a dark bronze. Some of the sailors noticed his wound scar, and any comments about it were kept to themselves. Nuada overheard the comments and ignored them. He thought that it added mystery to him, and he wanted it that way.

Pytheas was looking forward to the docking in Crete, as it was part of Greece at that time. Possibly he would hear news of his home city-state or of old friends that he had not seen in many years. He told Nuada about some of the mythology of the island and also the history he knew. Nuada was interested in the story of the Minoans and their worship of bulls. He could understand that people could relate to stories of monsters and that their fears drove them to tell stories of them. Pytheas warned Nuada that the land would shake hard from time to time. He said it was the same in his homeland of Greece.

On their fifth day at sea, the waters became rougher, and clouds filled the sky. Nuada watched with interest at how the shipmaster changed course to avoid the storm at sea, but it would be in vain. By nightfall rain poured down on the ship, and the sail was taken in, and the men of the ship began to row it again. Lightning flashed throughout the sky, and Nuada and Pytheas took shelter in their room.

By dawn the rain had stopped, and the sail was reset. Nuada cautiously stepped onto the deck of the ship and looked about at how fast the weather had changed. He was ready for land again. The sea remained rough , but by midday the island of Crete became a distant shadow on the horizon.

All that afternoon Nuada watched as the island became larger, and he wondered if they would make it by dark. The noise of the ship, as it pushed forward, became part of the everyday background, and Nuada hardly noticed it now. Pytheas had joined Nuada, and the pair watched the island grow until it filled their view.

"Do you think we will land tonight, Pytheas?"

"I think not. It is too dangerous after dark because of the rocks that surround the island."

The pair continued to watch until they went to their sleeping place to have their evening meal. The sun began to set behind them, and the ship stayed well out to sea off the island. Finally Nuada and Pytheas settled down for the night, but Pytheas warned Nuada that it might be wise for Nuada to stay aboard the ship tomorrow.

"But I was looking forward to having land under my feet again."

"Let me find of the local ways first. As I have said, this island has seen many wars, and I wish to find of the safety first."

Nuada agreed, and the pair found sleep hard to come by that night with the land so close.

Nuada awoke to the sound of the drumbeat for the oarsmen and dressed quickly before going up on deck. Pytheas was close behind, and they watched as the ship drew into the harbor at Curium. Colorful ships lined the docks, and the houses above them matched their brightness. The smell of the land had a pungent odor about it that intrigued Nuada, but he did not ask about it.

The pair remained on deck and watched as the ship found its docking space. The oars were drawn in, and the ship settled against the stonework of the jetty before being tied to its massive form. Pytheas quickly went below and added some of the small gold bars to his purse before returning to Nuada's side. He told him he would not be long ashore.

Nuada continued to watch the routine of the ship's crew as some of the men from shore began unloading items onto the jetty. Soon wagons arrived, and the items were then loaded and hauled away. About two hours later, wagons returned with items to be loaded aboard, but Nuada watched for some sign of the return of Pytheas. The shipmaster joined Nuada and told him that they would sail again with the coming of the afternoon tide. Nuada wondered at the haste of their departure and then dismissed it.

Just before midday, Pytheas returned. Nuada called down to him on the jetty and told him to hurry aboard. When he finally stood on the deck, Nuada told him that the shipmaster had said they would sail soon.

"That is good. The land is in turmoil again, and there is talk of an invasion from the east."

They went down to their sleeping area, and Pytheas told Nuada of the changes in the people and the land there. "But Alexandria is safe. We should arrive there in about two more days."

Soon the noises of the ship and its crew filled the air as they began to get under way. The background noises of seabirds and work crews on the jetty soon disappeared as the first waves began to lap at the ship's bow. After about an hour, Pytheas and Nuada appeared on deck again to observe the changes of leaving the harbor.

Time began to pass slowly for the pair until the sun began to set, and it cast a red hue on the sea itself. Nuada was amazed at the colors, as he had never seen anything like it before. He stood and watched until the darkness began to enfold him. Pytheas urged him to come to the cabin and eat, which Nuada did reluctantly.

Two more days passed, and the pair were ready for life on land again. Near midday the first signs of the distant land began to show. Land birds, along with the seabirds that seemed to follow them everywhere, began to arrive in droves, screaming for food handouts. Nuada stood and pointed at different types of birds to Pytheas, who just smiled and nodded his head at everything pointed at.

"Do you think we will stay at sea again like before or dock with the setting of the sun?"

"The lighthouse here will provide for us, and we will land even if it is dark. Do you wish to stay on board the ship tonight or sleep ashore?"

"Which is safer, Pytheas?"

"I think we should remain on board and then find of a suitable house in the morning before going to the Great Library."

The ship docked with the setting of the sun, and Pytheas talked with the shipmaster about staying aboard until morning. He agreed, and Pytheas returned to Nuada's side and told him of the answer. Nuada still played the noble and let his friend do the running and the asking of all questions.

New sounds filled Nuada's ears in this city, and he listened to it as best he could. Soon he became sleepy and found his berth and any dreams that passed his way.

The morning dawned warm and dry, and Nuada was up and about, dressing for the city. Pytheas wanted him to still dress like the noble and had him decked out in crisp white linens, with a rich purple cape that had a silver inlay around the edge, and all of his weapons. "You look like a warrior king, Nuada, but that is what you are."

Nuada laughed at the comment and hurried Pytheas with his dressing. On deck Nuada stood near the ship rail and watched children running up and down the jetty laughing. It brought back memories of his children, and he wished that this would end soon so he could return home. Pytheas went ashore and sought help with the packs and information about suitable housing. He soon returned and, with Nuada, went and thanked the ship's master for the good voyage. They then left the ship and the memories that went with it and made their way along the jetty with two men following with their packs. Children gathered about them begging for any handouts they could get.

"Is it always this way here, Pytheas?"

"Yes. This is a poor land, and many go hungry."

They made their way to a house near the library and found the rooms they rented spacious. After settling in, they walked to the library and inquired of some old friends of Pytheas and then found a place to wait for some of the library heads to meet with them.

After more than two hours, Nuada found himself pacing the smooth stones of the courtyard where they waited. "What is taking so long, Pytheas?"

"Nuada, in here time stands still, and nobody is in a hurry."

Nuada continued to pace until finally a man of many years appeared and spoke with Pytheas. After a long conversation with Pytheas telling of the needs of Nuada, the man departed and said nothing to Nuada himself. Nuada was becoming bored with the whole thing and said so to Pytheas.

"I know what you need is to sit and study of the old ways of machines. Follow me, and you will learn something for yourself about this place."

Pytheas led Nuada to a branch of the large building and pulled some scrolls down from a shelf and laid them on a table for Nuada to read.

"Stay here until I return. I think these will keep your restless mind busy until then. If you need to make notes, there is paper over there and ink with a quill."

Pytheas hurried away as he knew the building well, and Nuada sat and stared at the scrolls in front of him without unrolling one. Finally he reached over and opened one of them and was instantly enthralled by the information held within. He got up and retrieved paper and the ink to make notes. Hours passed and Nuada had notes piled all around him, and still he read and read without letup. Nuada finally looked up from his study and found Pytheas sitting across from him, smiling.

"I did not hear of you coming back," Nuada said sheepishly.

"It matters not. I seemed to have found something in you that takes all your concentration."

"I would not have believed that all this was written here. There are things here that I could not have dreamed of in my entire life. I must return tomorrow and read more."

"We will. For now we will leave and get something to eat. We are to meet with several men from here at an eating place nearby. Again let me do all the questioning."

Nuada agreed, and they left the building and made their way down the street to a tavern.

"They seem much different than the other people of the city we have seen," Nuada said.

"This is a gathering place for the students and teachers of the library. No local people come here, which is good for us."

"Why do you say that? Is there something wrong with the local people?"

"No. They are just poor and that usually leads to crime of a sort."

Nuada had taken his great sword from his shoulder and placed it on top of the large pile of notes and drawings that he had made that day and let his mind wander back to the library itself. The building would have filled most of his valley, and the ceilings were higher than any he had ever seen before. Huge stone columns supported the high ceilings, and art was displayed everywhere. Men dressed in white wandered about and were seen in deep discussion with each other. Again he had never seen anything like it before.

Soon six men entered the tavern and walked over to Pytheas and greeted him in the Greek language. Pytheas talked with them and soon asked them to join them for their evening meal. The men agreed and sat at the table, only glancing at Nuada and not asking about him from Pytheas. Nuada played the noble and acted like one — what they were saying did not matter to him, but he did listen closely and only glanced at Pytheas from time to time.

After an hour, one of the men happened to look at Nuada's pile of notes and asked about them. "Does he speak our tongue?"

Pytheas smiled and said, "He speaks every language of the known world and can write it as well. Gentlemen, this is King Nuada. He seeks three who will become teachers in his land."

The six turned in unison with questions on their lips, but Nuada spoke first.

"I have kept my tongue to find out more about you. If you have questions, ask now."

They all began to speak at once, and Nuada held up his hand and pointed to one of them. "You may speak first."

"Why do you seek teachers?"

"Let me tell of you the history of my land, and then I will explain the need for teachers."

Nuada began to give the history of the valley and the people who now lived there and how it came to be. In the end, he said that he found a need to educate everyone, including the adults of the valley.

Another of the six asked, "What will we receive in return for teaching if we return to your land?"

Nuada replied, "All of your housing, food, and clothes."

Another of the six said, "No gold?"

"There is no need for it in my land. We share of everything."

Nuada watched their faces closely, looking for signs of greed or other things that could be seen as a weakness of spirit. Pytheas was also watching the men and had his mind made up as to who would be good for the village people. The meeting started to break up, and the six men said they would give their answers in the morning. Nuada stood and towered over the men. He looked each in the eye and gave a departing question to each of them; it was to be answered in the morning.

After the six had left, Pytheas began to talk about his observations of the men. Nuada listened carefully and added his thoughts to the discussion. Before they departed the tavern for their living area, they had made up their minds as to who would return to the valley with them.

Although their search for teachers was almost complete, Nuada felt that he needed to stay longer at the library to research more about the machines of history. Pytheas had needs too, and they planned to remain here for at least three more weeks.

When the dawn brought its welcome light back to the city, Nuada and Pytheas returned to the tavern for their morning meal and to wait for the six men to join them. They did not have to wait long, and as the men entered and joined the pair, Nuada again asked the single question he had asked the evening before of them. Each answered in turn, and when it was over, Nuada waited to hear of their answers about returning with them to the valley. Five said they would be willing to go and teach; the single one remaining said it was not enough in return for his skills. Nuada nodded and asked him to leave, which he did.

Both Pytheas and Nuada stood and then told them who their choice was for the return, and of them, the two not chosen were again asked to leave but thanked for their time.

Of the three remaining, two were Greek and the other was Egyptian.

Nuada spoke, "I am glad of you three, to chose to return with us. We will be remaining here in Alexandria for another three weeks before joining a ship for the return. I wish that we continue to meet and learn of each other until the sailing."

Pytheas added, "Prepare for the trip and say your good-byes to your friends and teachers. We will advise you as to when we will depart."

The five men then left the tavern and made their ways to the library and a day of study. Nuada returned to his research while Pytheas went in search of other things he needed.

Late in the afternoon Pytheas found Nuada still doing his research and asked him to join him and have some time for relaxation at the local bathhouse. Nuada had not heard of any such thing before and was curious about it. He again gathered his notes, and the pair walked to the bathhouse.

As they entered the bathhouse, Nuada looked about and found nothing about the building different than other buildings. Pytheas led the way, and they entered into an inner court with a large pool of water, which steamed from its heat, and people bathing in the nude — young, old, and children were all together in the water or standing on the edge of the pool. Nuada felt uncomfortable in the situation but continued to follow Pytheas as he undressed and entered into the water.

"Ah, this is the life. What think you, Nuada?"

"I feel uncomfortable with this. Is this normal for these people?"

"All people of the nobility or of a certain class bathe in this way around this part of the world. Now forget all your worries and enjoy of the warm waters about you."

Nuada slowly felt the tension of his muscles relax and began to enjoy the water. He looked about him and saw that the people only seemed interested in those with them. He cautiously began to accept the nature of these baths.

After an hour, Pytheas said it was time to leave for their evening meal. Getting out of the water, the pair toweled off and dressed. They again walked the short distance to the tavern and began to discuss the trio of men they had chosen to return as teachers.

The weeks passed quickly, and Nuada's knowledge of the past increased with every day of study. Finally Pytheas said that it was time to collect the others and find passage back home. Nuada hated to leave all this knowledge behind but knew it was time to return to his family and friends.

While Nuada collected his notes and drawings, Pytheas went to find the others and have them meet at the tavern in the morning for the return trip to Nuada's lands.

After doing so, Pytheas returned to Nuada, and the pair again went to the tavern for a final evening meal and to share of the fine wines there.

Later they returned to their house and packed before turning in early for the busy day ahead of them. Sleep came easily for the pair, and before they knew it, it was dawn again.

Pytheas was up before Nuada and had gone and paid for the house and for porters to carry their packs to the docks. On his return, Nuada had dressed in his finest clothes, and with his weapons close, they walked to the tavern to wait on the three teachers.

Two of them were already there, and they had only a short wait for the third man. They all talked of the journey ahead and after eating set out for the docks and their new future.

When they found a suitable site to watch the ships at dock, Pytheas left them and went in search of a ship to return them to the land of the Etruscans. He found three such ships and, after talking with their masters, found a suitable one and paid for the voyage. Meanwhile Nuada had located the porters and collected their packs. They then waited for Pytheas's return.

"I found a ship for us. It is small but has lateen sails on two masts that can sail against the wind. This will cut our time returning to our home. The master is from the city of Carthage and wants a swift voyage, so he can return home to his family. I arranged a price that will work for us, and we can board as soon as possible."

Nuada was distracted by the sight of strange animals being loaded on another ship along the jetty.

"Pytheas, what are those?"

"They are animals native to this land although they are from deep within this continent. There are lions, elephants, crocodiles, and many others too numerous to mention."

"But why are they loading them onto ships?"

"Men of power use them to impress others of power by their collections of such things."

"That makes no sense to me, but they are welcome to them."

The five men hurriedly collected their packs and bags and walked quickly for the ship that Pytheas had found for them. The master greeted them at the gangway and showed them to their quarters. Shortly they could hear men shouting at each other, as lines to the dock were cast off, and preparations for sailing got under way. Soon the tiny ship began to roll and dip with the wave motion as it headed out of the harbor.

Soon the sails were set, and the little ship began to bound over the waves outside of the harbor. Nuada and the four others were on deck to watch the city of Alexandria slip over the horizon behind them as they made their way west. Nuada marveled at the design of this ship; it was so different from the one that had brought them here in the first place.

"Nuada? Have you noticed that we are well into the Summer now?" asked Pytheas.

"Summer? Already? It seems that we have just arrived, and each day was the same as the one before it. No Summer storms, little wind, except to cool the afternoons."

"Believe me, it will be almost Fall when we enter into your valley again."

"I wonder at the changes they have made while we were gone."

"You made the plans for the changes. All of your people will work hard to make them so."

"I know. They will probably go beyond the plans, and that makes me excited about the return. I can hardly wait to see of the changes."

"Your children will have grown too. That is your real challenge, to understand of them."

"You are right. I have not had the time to think of them while here."

The small talk continued until the late afternoon as they watched the sun slowly begin to set on the deep, blue sea and turn it a burnt-reddish color. Going below deck, they gathered to eat a small meal and really began to know each other. The first of the teachers was Andocides, a Greek who was a poet; the second was Dionysins, also a Greek who loved his music; and the third was Amasis, an Egyptian who wrote plays of all types. Although they were all good teachers, none were outstanding in mathematics. But they knew enough to teach its basics. Nuada thought that if the need arose again for more teachers, he would make sure that he would find one of that nature.

After four days, the horizon beckoned with the first hint of land again. Birds followed them as they approached their landfall: Tarentum of the Etruscan's homeland. It was the same port city from which Nuada and Pytheas had sailed from to Alexandria.

"That was a fast passage, Pytheas," Nuada commented.

"We were lucky. It normally takes a week in good weather. This ship was fast, probably due to its sail design."

"I am looking forward to the landing and the return to my home."

"We will need more horses this time. Probably as many as five, in addition to the three we already have."

"The stable had horses in abundance. Maybe we can make a deal for them."

Thoughts were on the landing, and again they gathered at the rail to watch the city come into view. Nuada had another thought while watching the city: What of the need for weapons for these new teachers? He would make sure that Pytheas sought out some as it would be a dangerous return trip without them.

This time the ship docked with the jetty just after midday. Pytheas paid an additional fee for the fast passage, and the five set out for the inn where they had lodged the last time there.

They secured lodging, and then Pytheas went to the stable to inquire about the additional horses and to check on their other three. Nuada took the teachers to the local tavern, and they sat, talked, and ate while waiting on Pytheas. Soon he was at the door to the tavern and was just beginning to look about for his companions when a large detachment of soldiers marched by outside. Pytheas went to the tavern keeper and inquired as to the nature of them being here and why. He was told that they were on their way to fight in the east and that it was no concern if they did not return.

Pytheas quickly sat and told of the warriors outside passing by and the reason.

Nuada said, "We may find more danger in our travels than we had hoped. We need to find a way to avoid the main roads going north."

"I agree. I have secured the horses that we need and some additional weapons. All will be ready in the early morning, and I think we should leave of this city as soon as possible."

Nuada turned to the three teachers and said, "Have you had any military training?"

The two Greeks responded that they had both seen service , but the Egyptian said no. They soon left the inn and went to the house to try and get some sleep before the morning light. Nuada was restless and spent most of the night outside on a balcony overlooking the city.

The first hint of the dawn came, and Nuada went and awoke the others. They hurried down to the stable without stopping to eat and were soon on their way out of the city of Tarentum heading north. Even as they passed out of the city, groups of military men could be seen gathering and moving toward the harbor.

"It looks like we are departing here just in time," Pytheas said. Nuada nodded at his comment and said nothing more.

They rode their horses over many hillcrests as they moved into the center of the Rasenna peninsula, hoping to avoid any military groups. They finally settled on a valley that appeared empty of any population and steadily moved north.

A week later they were far to the north, where the mountaintops had lost all of their snow from the Sumer heat and sun. Some of the grasses near the streams that flowed continually remained green, but for the most part, everything was now the golden brown of late Summer. Slowly the ground began to rise as they neared the pass onto the main part of the European continent.

Nuada, as was his habit, scouted ahead of the teachers, and on this day he found an army encampment at the pass site. Returning to his group, he told them of the gathering and asked Pytheas what he thought about going around them.

"There are some goat paths , but they are steep and dangerous."

"Then we could wait and see what happens, or we could confront them and see if we can bluff our way past them."

The four teachers looked at each other, and finally Pytheas said, "I think we should wait and see what happens."

Nuada nodded and said that they should seek shelter in the trees as near to the army detachment as possible so as to watch their movements. Cautiously they walked their horses into a bushy, tree-lined fold in the rocky ground below the encampment. After they hobbled their horses and removed their packs, Nuada climbed up to where he could observe the movements within the pass encampment.

Hours passed, and Nuada hated the delay. He wanted to return home as soon as possible , but this blockade by armed troops stopped him. He watched and noted their patterns of guard changes and where they were looking and for what. He saw one group approach the army only to be turned back to where they had come from, but he noted that they seemed more bored with the situation than aggressive about it. Perhaps it would allow a gap in their attention, and they could slip through.

The day began to fade, and Nuada became more intense with his watching of guards. Pytheas had joined him in the watch and pointed out things that seemed lax of their attention. Nuada nodded as he watched and told Pytheas to have the others repack the horses and prepare to move at a moment's notice. After another fifteen minutes, Nuada came sliding down into the hiding place and told them to follow him but to be quiet. They circled around the guards and kept to the high ground. The horses seemed to sense the need for quiet and gave no problems. The darkness now enveloped them, and shadows became their friends. Slowly they crossed through the pass and away from the encampment of soldiers. After an hour and a half, they themselves camped for the night. The tension of getting through the pass had tired them all, and rest was needed.

In the morning, they quickly packed again and moved north, steadily away from the army and into far more friendly land. Now the ground sloped downward, and mountains in the distance peaked above the hills they passed through. They saw no others, and time passed quickly.

Now time passed as weeks rolled by. To Nuada it could not pass quickly enough; he missed his family and friends. One day Nuada noticed a familiar landmark and knew he was close to home. He quickly pointed it out to the others, and their pace became more hurried.

"One more day, and we shall be in the valley and home," he said.

The others began to talk loudly between themselves. Some of their questions were aimed at Pytheas, others at Nuada. They answered all that they could, hoping to end the questioning.

The next day Nuada knew where he was and hurried his teachers as best he could. With luck they would be home by late afternoon. At midday they began to follow the ridgeline outside of the valleys. Nuada observed no changes there and was relieved by that. Three hours more, and they began the slight climb into the valley entrance. Nuada rode ahead to the first protection wall and called out to the guards there.

"I have returned with our teachers. Let us pass."

Quickly the portal gate was opened, and the five entered into Nuada's valley and were only a short distance from the village.

The first thing Nuada noticed was the new stone protection wall and that the road was now paved with stone. He could not see any workers along the wall and wondered why. They passed through its portal gate, and Nuada was amazed by the sight that greeted him. New stone houses lined the roadway, and men were working hard on the details of their completion. He saw Mor outside of one of the houses and called to him as they approached.

"Mor! I have returned. Did you miss of me?"

"Nuada! Good to have you home. The whole village was wondering when you would arrive. Your wife and children are at the outdoor cooking area now."

Nuada raised his head and tried to look ahead into the village, as if to see his family, and then looked down at Mor and said, "I must go. We will talk later."

The five continued to ride into the village, and Nuada again noticed that all of the old wooden protection wall was now gone. He glanced over to Jan's crypt as they passed and said a silent prayer to him. They turned down the street toward the stable, and again the changes caught Nuada's eye. More shop buildings had been added, and even his forge building had an addition to it. When they stopped in front of the stable, some of the older village children took the horses, and Nuada led the way to the outdoor cooking area for the others.

Entering Nuada saw his mate near the fireplace and ran to her. He picked her up and kissed her in front of everyone. Loud shouts of welcome and laughter filled the area. Nuada whispered to his mate that he had missed and loved her very much. She responded in the same manner, and they turned while holding hands and waved to the people gathered there. Turning back to her, he said, "Where are my children?"

"They are sitting at your table, husband. Do you not recognize them?"

"It seems like it was only yesterday, but we all know it was much longer."

"Yes, the valley and village had changed much in the time I was gone. What of its people? Have they changed too?"

"Only in that they have worked hard to give of this to you. It was your vision of what was to be that made them work so hard while you were gone."

They walked to Nuada's table, where Nuada hugged his children and talked with Iolair about his schooling. He was talking so fast that it was hard for Nuada to follow his thoughts. Soon music filled the air, and the village people gathered to honor Nuada's return. Pytheas and the other teachers held back and watched everything until Nuada called them over and began to introduce them to everyone. Questions came fast, and stories filled the conversation around them. Nuada had the largest smile on his face and welcomed the friendliness of his people. All of Nuada's friends asked of the quest, and he tried to answer them as best he could at the time. He knew that certain memories would be slow to return about events that had happened.

Mor did manage to tell Nuada that tomorrow he would show him the changes to the village. A'Chreag was there and asked if he noticed the change to the forge building, which Nuada responded that he did see the change and wanted to know more about it. A'Chreag said he would show it to him tomorrow and that he would be pleased with the change. Beag said that the work was almost done on the new houses, and the wall was now complete. Nuada asked if any of the houses could be used for the new teachers, which Beag said yes. He told Nuada that he would see that they were settled tonight in them. Nuada responded that he was pleased with everything. After many hours, Nuada led his family home to the needed rest after the return.

Nuada awoke early, as was his nature, and dressed in the clothes that he had used in Alexandria. After fitting his cloak of purple with the silver trim, he set out for the shop buildings and his meeting with Mor and Beag. The streets were empty of people, and he thought of the lateness of the homecoming last night, knowing that it was the cause. The village seemed so open now that the wooden protection wall was gone, and Nuada turned and looked across what was the large, open meadow in front of it. The new houses of stone broke up the empty feeling. Continuing down the street, he looked at the changed forge building and wanted to go look closer at it but remembered that A'Chreag was to show it to him later. He thought, "It can wait." He found the shop building now used for meetings and waited outside for someone to arrive.

He heard voices coming down the street and knew it was his friends. They both stopped in mid-conversation and looked at Nuada in his fancy clothes.

"Who are you, stranger?" called Mor.

Nuada began to laugh and went and warmly greeted his friends. "I never know what to expect of you two," he said.

Beag circled around Nuada and looked over his clothes. "You cannot work in those, my friend."

"I felt as though it would help of you to understand what I had to do to get our new teachers. I have also brought something new for you both. I researched the machines of the past and have brought you drawings that will help build things and provide for the village's protection."

Mor grew excited about this information and wanted to see them right away.

"Not now. I want you to show of me the changes you have made."

The trio walked back toward the new houses of stone and talked about the design of them. Standing in front of them, Nuada looked closely at the great detail that had been put into the work.

"Beag, you have outdone yourself again. This is great workmanship."

They continued out to the new stone protection wall, and Beag pointed out the new towers that framed the portal gate through it. Then Nuada noticed that he had also built stone steps to the fighting ledge near the top of the wall. "That is better than the ladders we used before. What else is new?"

"Come. The other new houses are on the other side of the village," Mor said.

They retraced their steps through the village and turned onto the street near Nuada's house. In the distance, Nuada could see that the portion of the wooden wall near the lake had been removed, and in its place stood another stone protection wall.

"You changed that wall too?"

"Yes. It was needed," replied Beag.

"How did you find the time?"

"We made the time for it and some other projects that were needed."

Finally they turned onto a new street that Nuada had not seen before, and along it were new houses of wood that numbered ten. Nuada stopped with his mouth open and stared at the changes.

"How could you do this much? It was impossible in the time you had."

"We did it, but there is one more project for you to see."

They followed the street to its end and turned back into the core of the village. At the point where the old wooden wall used to stand, a large, single-story building stood that was near completion.

"What is this?"

Mor and Beag turned to one another and smiled. Mor spoke, "We knew you would be successful in your quest for teachers, and we built a new school for them."

"Pytheas and the others must see of this! Is it done?"

"Almost. We have some small details to finish yet, but it will soon be completed."

Nuada shook his head in wonderment at his friends and clapped both men on their backs. "I am in wonderment at you two and the people of the village. How can I show my appreciation for the work done?"

"The smile on your face is enough. We are glad that you are happy."

The trio returned to the open-air cooking area, and inside the people of the village filled the area. As Nuada entered, they began to cheer, and Nuada became sheepish at all the attention from them. He held up his arms and spoke, "I have no words to express my happiness at all of your hard work while I was gone. Let us eat and enjoy of each other's company."

Pytheas appeared with the company of the other teachers. Nuada waved them over to his side and told them of the new school. They wanted to leave and see it, but Nuada told them that it could wait until after eating of something.

Andocides, the oldest of the teachers, told Nuada that the village was beyond the description that they had been told of. They were very pleased that they had come with Nuada and Pytheas. Their new houses were very comfortable and beautiful.

Nuada was happy with their response and told them to begin to prepare for their Winter teaching. He also told them that Pytheas was to be their supervisor in all things with regards to that teaching program. They could tell of myths and other stories of the past, but he wanted them to limit their religious convictions. Nuada felt that these stories would enhance why the great civilizations grew like they did.

Slowly the people of the village began to leave and return to their work projects for the day. Before Mor departed, he told Nuada that a feast was planned for that afternoon, and the teachers and Nuada were to be honored by the people of the village. When Nuada began to protest, Mor told him it was what the people wanted, and Nuada reluctantly agreed.

Nuada and the teachers soon left the cooking area and walked to the new school to see of it. Outside of the school, the four teachers looked at the amount of work being done and they held an animated conversation while Nuada stood by with pride in his chest at what his people had done. "Let us go inside and see what they have done for us," Nuada said.

The men followed Nuada inside where workmen were still cutting and placing wood within the rooms. They slowly walked around and counted six classrooms and an office at the back. In the back of the school, a playground had been constructed for the children.

"Nuada, this is beyond anything I had envisioned for our school here. It is much better than the old school room I was teaching from," Pytheas said.

"It looks like there is room for expansion too," Nuada commented.

After an hour of looking things over, the group returned to the cooking area and waited for the others to return.

After settling at Nuada's table, A'Chreag soon appeared and asked Nuada if he was ready to see his new forge building. Nuada nodded and told the others to wait as he would return soon. A'Chreag had a great smile on his face as he took Nuada to the forge.

"These are the last things you told to me before you left about the forge and the changes you wished to see."

"I have forgotten. What changes were they to be?"

"You will see for yourself."

As they entered the structure, Nuada noticed that the building had almost doubled in size with an addition on the right. Nuada's eyes followed that section of the building, noticing that many things had been moved. The forge itself remained in the same place, but it now had two large bellows to increase its heat factor. The sand tables were no longer nearby but moved into the new section along with the stone rollers that Beag had fashioned for making sheet metal. A large cooling table stood nearby with a water trough beneath. An overhead roller track went from the forge to this area for transportation of the hot metals. A new table stood against a wall for the making of new molds with their tools hung above for easy use. And there was room for building other things as they allowed for growth of the metal designs. Nuada was shocked and happy at the same time.

"You have done a great job of thinking ahead, A'Chreag. Now we can grow as needed."

"I have heard that you brought back designs for old machines. When can I see of them?"

"Soon, but we will need time to redevelop them to fit our needs."

"I look forward to that time, Nuada."

"If you would, there are some things that I left at the stable. Among them is the yellow metal I took with me. Could you bring them in here for now and store them? There is no rush, but I would like to move them soon."

"I will see to it. Anything else that you need done?"

"No. That will be enough."

They soon departed the forge with Nuada looking back over his shoulder at the structure. He was ready to leave the politics behind and return to the simple life of a metal worker.

They entered into the cooking area amid a large crowd of the people. Music was playing, and many people were dancing to the sounds. Nuada looked to his table and saw that the teachers were still there waiting for his return. Mor, Beag, and Farmer were also at the table and waved him over. Nuada joined them and was asked by Mor to introduce the teachers to the people of the village. Nuada hesitated; he did not expect this. A'Chreag brought him a beer, which Nuada promptly emptied as he looked about at the people. Finally he nodded and asked the teachers to follow him to the front of the cooking area and the band stage.

Nuada had the band hold their music while he prepared himself for the introductions. The people returned to their tables and became quiet while waiting for Nuada to speak. Nuada drew upon his inner strength and turned to the people.

"Thank you all for the wonderful work you have accomplished this year. I wish I had been with you while it was being done , but I had another diversion. I had to seek out the teachers we badly needed. I now present them to you. First, it could not have been done without the help of Pytheas. Please step forward. We together found you the best, and I will start with Andocides. He is a teacher and a poet of Greek heritage. Second is Dionysins — also a teacher and a man of music from all of the known world. Third is Amasis — a fine teacher and a playwright who I hope will create some fine entertainment in the future. He is Egyptian. Together all of them will teach everyone within the valleys, young and old, how to read, write, and use numbers. History of all lands will be brought to your attention, and you will learn of it for us to grow and be better than those who have gone before us. Now let us return to the music and our friends. Begin the feast, friends."

Nuada and the teachers walked back through the crowd of people with much backslapping and laughter and rejoined the others at the table. Nuada's mate and children stood as he approached. She said that she was proud of him before handing him his youngest child and going to prepare his meal. Iolair took his father's hand and looked at him with adoring eyes. Mor smiled and said, "You look and act the noblest of all gathered here today. Everyone is proud of you."

"This is something I am not used to. I prefer to be the common man and do of my work with the forge."

"You are both, and it fits you well."

Nuada sat back and watched his people while they danced and laughed with each other. It was good to be home with his friends. Conversation filled the air, and the smells from the feast brought comfort to all. Hours passed, and slowly the people began to drift away from the cooking area. Nuada felt tired and soon gathered his family and went home.

The next morning arrived with the warmth of another late Summer day. Nuada dressed in his leather clothes, and taking Wolf with him, he started a walk around the village, taking in all of the changes. He avoided the areas where work crews were laboring and kept to himself, thinking hard about the future. His steps took him into the second valley, and he wandered down by the mill sites but kept out of sight of the men there. The sounds of the forest called out as he passed. He just allowed his steps to go where they may, not thinking of any particular place to go. He found that he had circled the entire second valley and was back at its entrance. Again he let his feet take him where they wanted to go. He passed down by the field of crops near the lake and then onto the new stone wall and its towers. He stood and admired Beag's work before moving back into the village and toward the forge.

He entered into the forge building and made for his pack that A'Chreag had brought from the stable. Inside he pulled out the drawings and notes he had made in Alexandria and spread them on a table. He looked at them without really seeing them. Then he rolled them again and carried them as he walked back to the cooking area.

He found the area empty, and he sat at his table in the warmth of the Sun. His mind wandered from project to project, and he wished that someone would come and talk with him, but he knew that all were busy with the work being done.

Wolf stayed close and watched his master with his yellow eyes. Nuada happened to look down at him and called him close. Nuada scratched his head and talked with him, as no other was near. "I have missed of your company, friend," he told Wolf.

As the morning wore on, Nuada became bored and gathered up his notes and drawings, then set off for the school where he knew he would find Mor and Beag.

Outside of the school, A'Chreag saw him first.

"What have you, Nuada?"

"These are the notes and drawings I made while away of the old machines."

"May I see of them?"

"When we find of Mor and Beag, I will share of them then."

The pair entered into the school and in the second room found Mor.

"Where is Beag, Mor? I have brought my notes and drawings of the old machines."

"He is down the hall."

The three went in search of Beag and located him finishing a fireplace in a classroom. Mor called him over and told him of the paperwork that Nuada had brought. The four then went to the new office space at the end of the hall, and Nuada spread the papers out on the table there. One page at a time, Nuada explained each of the machines and how they worked. The others asked questions as they looked at the notes, and time passed quickly for the four.

After several hours, Pytheas arrived and asked what they were doing. Nuada told him about the notes, and this caught Pytheas's attention. He too stood and looked over the machines of the past — many he had never heard of before. "You have a good eye for things mechanical, Nuada."

Mor said he could build some of them, but others he had no idea for what they could be used for. Nuada tried to explain as he understood of them, and slowly the others began to understand. Beag was more interested in the lifting machines for his stonework, and Mor was interested in all the others. All were drawn into the world of Nuada's mind with his notes.

Nuada finally said that he would keep the notes at his house but that they were all welcome to come and study them at any time. The day was into its late afternoon, and Nuada departed for the cooking area again so as to let the men return to work.

Before he stopped at the cooking area, Nuada stopped at his house and stored his notes and drawings. As he left the house, Pytheas and the other teachers were walking down the street talking to each other. Nuada called a greeting and joined them.

"What think you of our village?" he asked.

Dionysins answered first and said that he liked every aspect of it. He was pleased that the people were so friendly, and he loved the music that they played. Amasis said that he could understand the love the people shared here, and he would write a poem to express it. Andocides answered that he would help with the poem but wanted to see more of the valleys first. Nuada responded that he would be glad to give them a tour and point out the things that had changed from the beginning. Pytheas said that he missed the fine wines that they had shared of in Alexandria. Nuada asked if it was possible to grow the grapes needed for wine here. Pytheas thought for a moment and said it was possible, but they would need the vines to begin it.

Nuada said that in the Spring he would go in search of the vines and see what would come of it. The five went to the cooking area and settled at Nuada's table. "Tell me, have you begun to think of the things you are going to teach?" asked Nuada.

All of them nodded in reply, and Pytheas said it would be his job to teach the older people of the village. Amasis would teach the youngest, while the other two would teach the older children.

Nuada said, "I talked with Mor this morning, and the school will be ready within the week. Will you?" They all responded that they would be ready.

Andocides then asked Nuada if it was possible to add some glass into their houses as they were so dark. Nuada responded that they did not have any glass and did not know how to make it. "We know how," answered Amasis. "Let us teach you."

Nuada was immediately drawn to something new and said he would be glad to learn. "We will need of the whitest sand you can find and a place to heat it."

Nuada answered that they could use his forge building and that it was equipped to make such things.

"When you find time, I will show it to you."

A group of the village women entered into the cooking area to begin the evening meal, and the men became quiet.

"It seems that you are in need of mates. My mate knows of many who would suit you."

All of the teachers looked at each other and laughed at the prospects of having a mate. Nuada shook his head and laughed with them. The idea had not crossed their minds until then of having a mate. Nuada waited until the laughter settled down and said, "It will make your life simpler and more intense at the same time, but it will make you a real part of the village."

The small talk continued throughout the rest of the afternoon, and many of the village people dropped by Nuada's table to talk with the new teachers. Soon the evening crowd filled the cooking area, and music again filled the air. Mor dropped by too and asked Nuada if he had made the new changes to his valley-map table. Nuada responded that he had forgotten about the table and said he would fix it soon. That made Nuada consider all the new things done this year, and he smiled at his own inner thoughts about what these people needed. "They are beginning to think for themselves," he thought.

A'Chreag came to the table and told Nuada that they were running short of hinges and latches for the new houses. Could he help with making more to-morrow?

Nuada responded that he would like to return to making things at the forge building again. It had been too long for him. A'Chreag said he would see him in the morning about the time the sun began to rise, as it was their normal pattern. Then he left to join his own mate at another table.

Soon Nuada's mate and children joined them, and they sat in silence and took of their evening meal. Iolair surprised the new teachers by talking to them in the Greek tongue. Pytheas laughed at their confused looks at the boy.

"Nuada's son is the smartest of all of my students. Do not be surprised by anything that he has to say."

That day ended, and time passed quickly over the next week. School was to start the next morning, and the projects were winding down throughout the village. The crops were soon to be harvested and preparations for Winter about to begin. Nuada had completed the forge projects with A'Chreag, and then they finished the new upgrades to the model map at Nuada's house. The teachers had been busy getting ready for the school and had not found time to show Nuada about the glassmaking although he knew that they would when they found the time to do so.

The village monthly meeting of the consul was to be that afternoon, and Nuada was looking forward to seeing what they had to talk about this time. It would be his first meeting since he had gone away.

Nuada had plenty of time before the meeting and took a walk out to Jan's crypt. He stood before it and said that it had been too long since they had spoken. Nuada hoped that he could seek new wisdom through a dream state with either Creatrix or Jan. Then he departed the site after laying his hand on the cool stone of the crypt and made his way to the meeting.

The first shop building was now the village meeting hall, and all of the consul was there when Nuada arrived. They stood talking between themselves and greeted Nuada as he entered.

"Nuada, we were just talking about the new school and the teachers that you brought back to us," said Mor.

"Is something wrong?" questioned Nuada.

"No. We were just thinking about all the things you said about them teaching all of the people of the village. That is a big order for us to take all at once."

"They will teach us all with any free time you have, that is all. Do not be afraid of the teaching. It will make all of us wiser and able to understand of the world around us. Then there is the thing with numbers. It will mean making things easier because we can measure and design things that are needed."

"We can understand of the need , but the common man here may not understand of it."

"Then talk with them to try to point out the need."

They then sat and reviewed the work projects completed over the Summer and talked about the things for the next Spring. About an hour later, they finished the meeting and went to the cooking area for a mug of beer and some companionship.

Nuada finally wandered away from the group, his thoughts guiding his footsteps. He wondered about their reluctance to his plan about the teaching of everyone, and it weighed heavily on his shoulders. When he happened to look up, he was surprised to find that he had wandered up to the valley entrance wall. He glanced up at the guards and waved a greeting but did not bother talking with them. He passed through the portal gate and on out onto the far rock outcropping, where he had fought his first battle for the valley. He stood looking out into the distance but did not really see it.

The afternoon had worn on, and Nuada did not notice the time. He could still not understand of these people and finally turned and made his way back toward the village. After he passed through the portal gate again, he turned and followed the path to the lakeshore and looked across at the island and the site of his first home. He thought about crossing over but soon changed his mind. He made for the village school and a talk with Pytheas.

He found Pytheas in the new office at the rear of the school building.

"Pytheas, a word with you if you have the time."

"What is it, Nuada?"

"I have come from a meeting with the village consul and have learned of some reluctance to the teaching of the adults of the village. What can you do to change their minds to this?"

"I can see why you want them to learn, but I can also see why they are reluctant to this notion. Let me talk with the other teachers and see if we can find a way to show them why it is important."

Nuada nodded and hoped that he could find a way to convince them for the need to be taught. Nuada left the school and walked to the cooking area and hoped for some relief from the thoughts that plagued him. Before he entered the area, he could hear new music that he was not familiar with. He found Dionysins playing a flute, the source of the music. Andocides was playing a drum, keeping the rhythm going for his fellow teacher. Nuada waited until they had finished the tune and clapped at the composition that had been played. Although the area was still almost empty, those there came over to thank them for the music that they had played and commented that they had never heard anything like it before.

Nuada had a sudden thought that this could be a way for them to teach the adults of the village. He would ask of Pytheas later about this thought.

Nuada rose again and said, "Wait here. I should have an answer soon."

Nuada walked across the patio and stood before Pytheas and placed his idea before him. The other teachers joined in the response, and from the distance all seemed positive to Nuada's idea. Nuada then turned and returned to his table and friends. "They will try this approach and see what happens. I hope it works."

The rest of the day was uneventful, and when all had drifted home, some were thinking of the new day that would begin with the opening of the school.

- FALL AND THE SCHOOLING BEGINS -

Nuada awoke to coolness in the air and quickly dressed and went downstairs. He was followed shortly by his son, and they fell into a conversation about what to expect in school today. Iolair was hoping to find out more about other countries that he had heard about over the Summer months and from the time his father had returned to the village with the new teachers. Nuada's mate joined them with their youngest son, who was now beginning to walk and talk. She quickly fixed a meal for them and asked what they were expecting today. Nuada responded that he was going to observe the new teachers at work and see how successful they were going to be. Iolair said that he wanted to learn everything he could.

Father and son soon left the house and made their way to the new school. Iolair joined his fellow students and began to play some games while he waited for his classes. Nuada stood at the entrance to the school and waited for the teachers to arrive. He could see his breath in the cool morning air and knew that this was going to be a rough Winter again.

Pytheas was the first of the teachers to arrive and greeted Nuada warmly. Nuada responded that he was going to observe the teaching methods that the teachers were using. Pytheas responded that he was welcome to do so and that he himself would be doing the same.

Soon the other teachers arrived, and they broke the children down into groups by age for their classrooms. They then led them into the building and, when all were settled, started the day with the programs that they had planned. Nuada and Pytheas sat in the office at the back of the school and waited.

The youngest children were settled into the first room near the entrance while the older children that Pytheas had taught last year were in the third room near the office at the back of the school.

After about an hour, Pytheas and Nuada walked into the large hall and stood near the open doors of each classroom, listening to what was going on inside. The children were quite well-behaved and remained silent, listening to their teachers. Inside the first room, Amasis taught the younger children and was holding up a large piece of paper with Greek letters on it. He was giving them the basics of the alphabet and having them recite it over and over before adding a new letter. In the second classroom, Dionysins was discussing the countries around the great inland sea and holding a large map showing where they were located. Nuada watched in silence until the lecture was nearing its end, when Iolair asked a question about where the village was located on the map. Dionysins paused for a minute to think and said he was not sure, but it would be located somewhere about here, as he pointed at the map. This brought some excitement to the children, who pointed at the map and talked between themselves. Dionysins then gave them copies of the map and sent them out to play for awhile.

Nuada and Pytheas entered into the classroom after the children had departed, and then Pytheas and Dionysins began talking about the subject matter while Nuada stood in front of the map and studied it. Dionysins then asked Nuada if the village had a name. Nuada said that it never come up before and that he would ask of the village consul for a name. "Then we can mark it on the map and give the children something to be proud of," was his response.

Shortly Nuada and Pytheas went down the hall to the first classroom while Dionysins retrieved the children for more teaching. Amasis was still working with the alphabet and noticed the pair at the door. Shortly he too gave the young children a break and sent them out onto the playground. Again Nuada and Pytheas entered the classroom after the children had departed, and the trio talked about the lesson. Amasis asked Nuada about the written language of his people and was told that they had none, but Nuada said he would work on creating one. Soon Nuada and Pytheas left and went outdoors to get some fresh air and talk about the teachers and their lessons.

Both men were happy with the results so far, and Nuada then told Pytheas that he would return later in the day when some of the adults of the village would come for their classes. Nuada had not said anything , but he had noticed that a few of the mothers had sat in back of the classrooms during the lessons and were also taking notes. It gave him hope that the men would come around to taking the classes.

Nuada wandered back through the village, noticing that the air had warmed to a comfortable temperature. Birds were singing in the sunshine, many preparing to fly south again. Nuada's eyes were drawn into the trees of the village as he watched them call to each other. He really wasn't paying attention to where he was going, just enjoying the moment. A few of the trees had begun to change colors, adding to the changing of the season. His footsteps brought him down to his forge, and he entered and found nothing had changed from his last visit. He turned and stood outside. The shop buildings across from him showed no signs of life, so he started to walk to the cooking area to see if anyone was there.

"Nuada, where have you been? We have been looking for you," Mor said.

"I was at the school, and then I took a walk around the village. Which reminds me, the teachers want us to name the village so they can add it to their maps."

"A good idea. Any thoughts about a name?"

"No. I will leave that to you and the other of the consul."

"You know, we could name it after you, do not you know?"

"Do not do that. Think of the place we live and find of a name that way."

"As you wish. Do you have time to show of us more of the drawings and notes that you brought back from Alexandria?"

"I was wondering when you would ask. How about later this afternoon? I need to return to the school and see if any of the village men are going to attend classes."

"We can do that. Would you like our company at the school?"

"If you would like to see the results of my quest, you can come."

The foursome stood and walked back to the school. They arrived in time for the midday break, and the children were outside playing in the playground. The four teachers were standing and watching them when the village elders arrived. Mor was the first to speak.

"How do you find the school building?"

Andocides spoke up. "It is comfortable but dark. We need to add windows of glass."

Nuada nodded and said, "Amasis is to teach me how to make the glass, and when he does, I will have Mor install them."

"What is this glass?"

"It is a transparent wall that lets in the light from outside."

"Now you have my interest. I would like to see how it is made also."

They talked for awhile before returning inside, and Pytheas led them down to the office, where they sat and talked about the classes and how the students were doing. Nuada made a comment about how some of the mothers were sitting in and learning alongside their children. This caught the attention of the consul members, and they asked about it from the teachers.

"They too have a thirst for learning and wish to help their children with their studies."

"This might make the difference in getting the men to attend the classes."

"We can only hope," replied Nuada.

They heard the children returning to the classrooms and waited until things settled down before entering into the hall again and standing outside to watch the teachers at work.

In the first class, Amasis was now showing them numbers and how they could be used. In the second classroom, Dionysins was now teaching history of some of the oldest countries that were known. This caught the interest of the consul members, and they stood quietly and listened deeply to the stories. Nuada left them and returned with Pytheas to the office.

"I have given some thought to the making of our native language. The gift I was given has given me an insight into how words can be made and strung together."

"Use your gift well, Nuada. Then you can teach some classes too."

"Me? But I thought that was the teacher's job."

"You will be the expert in this matter. Do not doubt that you can do it."

Nuada nodded in understanding when he realized that was to be his lot in this.

"I can see of your wisdom in this, but it shocks me that I will become a teacher too."

"Perhaps it was always to be. You have been the leader here, and this is only an extension of that."

By midday only six of the men had come for the teaching. This made Nuada wonder at his hopes for the village. He thought, "I cannot fail in this. There has to be something I can do to make them see of the need."

Nuada left the school deep in thought, and then he realized that perhaps time was all they needed. "I will wait and see if they come," he thought.

He walked to the cooking area, where his friends waited for him to see the notes and drawings he had brought back.

"Nuada, we found the school interesting and see that you did do a good job of selecting the teachers. Now can we see those notes and drawings you brought back?" asked Mor.

Nuada answered that they could and led the way to his house. Inside he brought out the papers and spread them on the table in front of the fireplace.

Beag was looking at the drawings of the heavy-lift machines and asked some questions about them when Mor asked about another machine for war and how it worked. Nuada took his time and explained each machine as he knew them. After an hour, Nuada said that he had found some interesting notes from a civilization long lost in history. He sorted through the notes and began to read to the others. It described machines that flew through the air and machines that could cut stone with water or light. Also it talked of moving things large and heavy with sound. Then Nuada said he tried to find more about these things , but all other notes about them had disappeared.

"That would be a marvel to be able to cut stone in that manner and then to move them without effort," said Beag.

"I think that we were not to know of this knowledge," replied Nuada.

Mor was thinking about the ability to soar in the sky with the help of a machine when Nuada asked them to return to the cooking area and have some of the beer and talk more about these wonders. They all agreed and set out for that area.

Nuada took along some paper and an inkwell with its quill for writing. He wanted to start making notes about how he was going to create a language for his people. Those thoughts were now never far from his mind. They settled at Nuada's table, and Farmer went to get the beer for them. Beag had asked for copies of the new machines for lifting, and Nuada said he would provide them to him. Mor sat back and crossed his arms across his large belly and watched Nuada begin to make marks on the paper in front of him.

"What is that, Nuada?"

"A start for a language of our own. We will need of it in the future."

"But we already have a language. Why the marks?"

"This will be the written language of our people. It will last through history and let those who come after us understand the things we have gone through. It will be much the same as the words on paper that I have brought back."

"I think I understand. That is why you have pushed for the people to go to school, is it not?"

"It is."

Nuada continued to make his marks and then looked up at the sky. It was getting late in the afternoon, and he wanted to return to the school and see how the adults were doing in the class. He quickly gathered his notes and told the others where he was going and why. Then he hurried to the school.

Nuada found Pytheas in the hall outside of the room for the adults of the village. Nuada quickly asked how things were going. Pytheas put his finger to his lips and motioned for Nuada to follow him to the office. Once there Pytheas said he was surprised that they were accepting the teaching.

"Amasis is doing a wonderful job of inspiring them with his ways of teaching. I had doubts, but it is working."

"I hope word gets around about him, and we have more show up to learn," Nuada responded.

Pytheas nodded and then went back out into the hall to watch. After a half hour, Nuada went and collected his son and made for the cooking area again. Nuada found that his friends still remained at his table and greeted them warmly. He set his notes on the table but did not return to making any more notes. Soon the area began to fill with the people of the village as they knew that the days were numbered for them to remain and eat together before the weather closed in around them for the Winter.

Nuada remained at home for the next three days working on his language writing. He had added Greek letters to the front of the ones he had made for his people so that everyone would understand of it. Then he began to develop words and slowly began to string them together for whole thoughts on the paper.

On the morning of the fourth day, he awoke stiff and knew that he needed a break. He waited for his son, and then they walked to the school. Pytheas, as usual, was standing at the entrance waiting on the students.

"Good morning, Pytheas. Any problems?"

Pytheas smiled and said, "Maybe."

"What do you mean?"

"We were worried about the adults of the village coming to learn, remember? Well that is not a problem now. I have been teaching in a second room for them. We are full, and still more arrive every day to learn."

Nuada's smile beamed so bright at the notion that his face began to hurt. "How did this happen?"

"The first ones we had for classes told the others, and it just came to be."

"I have something to show you." Nuada reached into a shoulder bag and drew out his notes about his language. He handed it to Pytheas and waited for a response.

Pytheas turned page after page and was amazed at the amount of work and detail that Nuada had put into making this language work.

"I had no idea that you would find of the necessary skills to do this, Nuada. It is beyond the nature of most men to do something like this. And you have even added the necessary crossovers to other languages to help in its understanding."

"I used the gift I was given and then put in the time."

"I think I was right about you becoming the next teacher of languages for the school."

"But I do not think I am ready for such a thing."

"This proves otherwise. Do not be afraid of this."

Nuada slowly replaced the notes into its bag and then after some small talk about the other students, departed for the lakeside and some time alone. He wandered without aim, and he passed the women working the crops, then moved onto the second valley where he sat just inside its entrance. He looked across the valley toward the mill sites without seeing it, and finally his gaze centered on the small forest of trees within the center of the valley. "We need to leave these for the future," he thought. His mind raced from idea to idea, and time passed quickly. At long last he arose and returned to the village. He passed the cave site and only glanced up at them before continuing into the village itself.

His footsteps started to pass the school, but he paused and then entered the building. He stopped at each classroom and watched the teachers at work until at the end of the hall, he stood watching Pytheas with the adults of the village. He was teaching them how to work with numbers, which included addition and subtraction. He waited awhile and then walked to the office to wait on Pytheas.

Another hour passed before Pytheas returned to the office and found Nuada working on his language papers.

"I see that your mind never rests, Nuada."

Nuada looked up, and the thoughts on his mind slowly cleared before he responded. "I have never thought of it in those terms, my friend. But no, my mind never rests."

"Nuada, now with all the teaching that I do, we will run short of paper in the classrooms within a few days. We have need of someone who can spend the time making the paper that is required. Do you know of anyone who can do the job?"

"I am sure that Mor can find of that person, but it will require someone to teach that art to them."

"Then ask of him, and I will make the time to teach how it is done."

After some more small talk, Nuada gathered his papers again and set off for the cooking area to find Mor. Entering the area he found Mor and Beag talking and sharing a beer together. He told Mor of Pytheas's concern about the making of the required paper and wanting to find someone to teach that skill to. Mor thought for a minute and then said he might have the right person for the job. Nuada was relieved by his response and sat with his friends and joined them with a beer himself.

The afternoon was growing late, and a few people began to gather for their evening meals. The area slowly came to life, and soon it was filled with the usual music and laughter. Nuada listened to the village people starting to talk about the classes that they were going to and what they enjoyed about the lessons. He heard nothing bad and considered that it was going to be a successful venture for them. Mor broke his thoughts with a question regarding the paper making.

"Where will this paper making be done, Nuada?"

"Pytheas has been using the old classroom in the woodworking building. I think it can still serve that purpose."

Mor nodded, and at that moment, Nuada's family joined them. Iolair wanted to tell his father about the school today, but Nuada's mate held him back with words of her own.

"Nuada, the crops are almost ready to harvest. We will need additional help with that. Can the school be stopped for a short time for the harvest?"

"How long will you need?"

"Two weeks, I think."

"Mor, that would give us the time to teach the new papermaker and get a small supply on hand for the school."

Mor nodded in agreement, and Nuada said he would speak with Pytheas and the other teachers about a break for the students. At that moment, the teachers entered the cooking area, and Nuada got up to go talk with them. Nuada told them of the need for the people to go to the harvest and that a break was needed in the teaching. He also told of Mor's help in finding a person to make the paper needed and that this break could give them time to stockpile a supply. The teachers in whole responded that they could do this and would need two more days to prepare their students.

Nuada returned to his table with a smile on his face and told them that everything had been arranged.

Two days later the harvest began on the grains of the second valley. These were transferred to the mill house and turned into flour after drying. Half of the village people were used at this harvest. Beag brought a young man to Nuada for training as a glassmaker, and Amasis started to work with him after Nuada showed them the forge building operations. Five of the village men were used to bring in sand from outside of the valley, where it was cleaned and piled for the glass process. Mor directed the operations throughout the valleys. Pytheas and the other two teachers worked with two young men and made the necessary paper for the school. Nuada himself worked with everyone where it was necessary.

The weather held fair for the village and, outside of some light winds, was very pleasant. But this was a very busy time for the village people, and they worked hard to make sure that all of the tasks were finished before the weather changed.

At the end of the first week, some of the people were brought down to the crop field near the lake and began to harvest the root plants there. Even the children worked at the harvest to make sure that no one would go without food this Winter.

There were some problems with the glassmaking. They found that sometimes the glass was too brittle and snapped when taken from the molds. Amasis thought it was the regulation of the temperature caused by the bellows, which made it too hot or too cold during the final process of the melting. Nuada had more experience with the forge and found that he had to tell them when to pour the melted glass into the molds, but they did manage to make many sheets of small panes of the glass to set into frames for the school and then began to make more for some of the houses.

As they neared the end of the second week, most of the crops were now harvested, and the grain mill was working as fast as it could turning it into flour. The root crops were now in the cold storage room in the old woodworking building, and a few of the village hunters were out hunting for deer to add to the locker supply. Planning was underway for the Fall feast, which was to be held the next day before the school was to reopen. Everyone was tired but happy and ready for the feast.

Nuada had been so busy that he had almost forgotten about the written language he had been working on for his people, but it was still there in the back of his mind. At midday before the feast, he took a walk around both valleys to clear his thoughts. He stopped at the mill sites and watched the grinding of the flour and then went into the sawmill to observe the cutting of the trees into lumber. He wandered over to the mill pond and just watched the water flow through the raceway and under the massive waterwheel. He finally turned and made his way back to the village and stopped at the school for a talk with Pytheas. He found him stacking paper in one of the unused classrooms.

"Pytheas, are you ready for the school to begin again?"

"Yes, Nuada. We now have enough paper for the rest of the year, and Mor was here to install the new windows in the classrooms that we use yesterday."

"Show it to me. Then I will understand of it more clearly."

Pytheas led Nuada across the hall to one of the rooms that held the older children. Light flooded the room, and Nuada could see the results immediately. "I now understand why it was needed."

He walked over to the window and tried to look out through it, but the images from outside were distorted. But it was the light that was needed, not what was outside.

"It is too bad that we cannot clear up the images from outside, but that would probably be a distraction for the students."

"Yes, it probably would be," responded Pytheas. "Have you had time to work on your written language anymore?"

"No. Time has gotten away from me with the harvest and the other things going on, but I will return to it soon."

After a little more talk about the school, Nuada returned to the cooking area and the preparations for the feast. He found Mor, Beag, and Farmer going over things that were to be discussed at the monthly meeting of the village consul. Nuada drew a beer before he joined them and listened into their talks. He was tired and added little to their talks; even his thoughts were disjointed, and he felt sleepy.

Iolair came running into the area, followed by Wolf, and woke Nuada from his dazed thoughts. Nuada smiled at the interaction between the pair and watched them play. He thought, "He is growing so fast and is so smart for his age. It seemed like only yesterday that I held him in my arms." Nuada wondered if this was the result of feeling guilty for being gone this Summer. Then he shook that thought from his mind and knew that the time away had been necessary for the village.

The sun had begun to settle for the afternoon, and soon music began to fill the area again. The smells from the food wafted throughout, and soon the women began to serve everyone. The feast was under way. Nuada left his friends and joined his family at his table; he felt their comfort around him.

- WINTER AND ENLIGHTENMENT -

During the weeks that followed the feast, Nuada continued to work at his written language. During breaks from his challenge to create, he took walks to the forge building to watch more of the glassmaking. It helped to clear his mind and added another outlook upon the skills being used there. He spent less and less time at the school, where things seemed to run very smoothly. Mor and Beag were installing the new glass windows into the village houses as fast as they were made, and Nuada saw little of them. He missed their company and the talks about the old machines that they were going to reproduce in the future.

Nuada's youngest child was now running around the house and getting into everything he could. He added a distraction to Nuada and kept him focused on his work while Iolair was at school. Nuada's mate had now settled into her Winter routine and was doing all of their cooking at home. She watched Nuada as he made his marks on the papers and wanted to know more about it. He showed her how it worked and helped her to understand the written words. Soon she too was taking classes at the school, and this left Nuada alone for most of the days.

On one of the days when Nuada was going to take a break from his work, the weather changed dramatically with a wind storm followed by heavy rain. He stood on the entry to his house and paused as lightning flashed throughout both valleys. He could feel the temperature fall in just the few minutes of being outside. He turned and reluctantly went back inside and added more wood to the fire there. Then he sat at his table wondering what to do. He was nearing the burnout stage with his writing and needed a distraction. The warmth of the room seemed to wrap around him, and soon he was dozing where he sat.

Many hours later he awoke to the silence of the house. He looked around for his mate and found her gone. He stood and stretched before returning to the entrance door of his house. He peered out and noted that the weather had passed as quickly as it had arrived.

He set out for the shop building that was now used as a meeting hall for the men of the village. Entering he found it full of the village men, who were sharing many beers and talking between each other. The room fell into a sudden silence as he entered, and he wondered of the reason. Mor, Beag, and Farmer sat near the front of the room near the fireplace and watched as he walked toward them. Mor called a greeting and waited for Nuada to settle at the table before talking.

"We have put the naming of the village before all those present and have come up with a name. Borg Jan. What think you of it?"

"Jan's fortress. I like it. How did you come to name it this way?"

"When you said that you did not want it named after you, we thought of Jan and how much he was appreciated by you and what he did for the people of the village."

"Then I shall tell Pytheas of the naming and have him put it on his maps."

"Then it is settled."

After some more small talk and discussion about the village, Nuada departed the meeting hall and made his way to the school. At the school, it was quiet, and Nuada entered and sought out Pytheas to tell him of the naming of the village. He found him in the office with the other teachers going over the teaching plans for the next week.

Nuada waited until they were done and the other teachers had left the office. Pytheas had noticed Nuada as soon as he had arrived but waited until the other things were settled with the teachers.

"What need do you have of me, Nuada?"

"The village people have named the village, and they want it to be Borg Jan. Can you add it to the maps of yours for the teaching of the children?"

"Yes, but I thought they might name it after you."

"It is something that I did not want."

"But why? It has been all about you and your plans for the valleys that have made it what it is."

"That I do not want credit for. It was the people who have made the valleys what they are, not me."

"But you provided the direction for them."

"I had a small part in that, but I will not take that credit."

Pytheas knew that it would be useless to argue with Nuada any further on the subject and let it drop.

Nuada looked around and asked about the children. Pytheas said that the morning storm was so strong that they sent them home for the day. Then Nuada asked if the adults would be there today. He responded that he did not know. "But I shall be ready if they come."

As Nuada exited the school, he thought that he still was not ready to return to the language work. His footsteps carried him back to the meeting hall and his friends. Before he entered the building, he could hear the happy music coming from within. As he stepped through the doorway, the heat from the fireplace and the many gathered hit him. He paused and looked about in the dim light and found that his friends were still sitting near the fireplace at the front of the room. He joined them, and they began to talk of the old machines to be built in the near future. Beag was the one pushing for the lift machines to be built first, and he gave many reasons why. Finally the others agreed with him, and the matter was settled. Time passed quickly, and Nuada was enjoying the moments with his friends. At last the crowd began to thin, and Nuada said his farewells and went home; it was late, and the sun had already set for the day.

Nuada found himself whistling as he walked, and he looked into the heavens at the many stars that adorned the night sky. He stopped outside of his door and continued to look at the stars. Then he entered to find of his family. Nuada's mate heard him come in and told him to sit and eat of his meal before it got cold. He did as he was told, and after he asked his mate, "When was the last time you just stopped and looked at the nighttime stars?"

She looked at him like it was a crazy question and then, after thinking about it, responded that it had been when they were traveling down from the mountains and had slept in the trees. He nodded and said that was what he thought. "Tonight I happened to look upwards and found of them again myself. I have forgotten how beautiful they could be."

His response, for some reason, made her uncomfortable, but she said nothing more on the subject. Soon they went upstairs to their sleep area and found comfort in each other's arms before sleep took them.

The next morning Nuada dressed and went downstairs to wait for Iolair. After he rekindled the embers, he watched the fire spring to life again. He felt comforted in the warmth of his life — his house, children, and mate. The village had changed again for the better, and now that Winter was upon them, they all had time on their hands. He looked around at all the wood carving that he had done in the past and wondered if he had anything to add to the work. Nothing came to mind, and he let the thought pass. Wolf came downstairs and wanted to go outside and run. Nuada walked him to the door and opened it for him and then took a deep breath of the cool, morning air. A fog of his breath drifted out into the freshness, and he could tell that snow was not far away. Soon Wolf returned, and they reentered the house to find that Nuada's mate and children had awoken and were now coming downstairs.

"Good morning, wife," Nuada called out as he stepped from around the great stairway.

"You are cheerful this morning. You must have slept well."

"I did, at that."

"Then I have something to tell you. We are to have another child."

"How? When?"

"It must have been from your return from your quest. You had a passion that night, remember?"

"I remember it well, wife. Still it is a surprise for me this morning."

Nuada felt pride in himself and wanted to tell his friends but knew that this was a time for family now. After their morning meal, Nuada walked Iolair to school and found some small talk with Pytheas that morning. He questioned Nuada about the written language for the village, and Nuada responded that he thought it was now complete.

"Good. When do you want to start teaching it?"

The thought of teaching was still foreign to his thoughts and caught him without anything to say. He just stood there, and Pytheas said nothing. Finally he shook his head and said, "I do not think I am the one to do the teaching of this."

"There is no one else, Nuada. It is your work, and it must be you who will do the teaching of it."

"Let me think on it, my friend."

Shortly Nuada left the school and walked to the meeting hall. His mind was racing with what Pytheas had said, and he needed to talk with others before making a decision about the teaching. Entering the hall he found Mor and Beag sitting up front near the fireplace again. He joined them and told of the good news about the expected child. Then after some small talk about the village, he asked them about what they thought about him being a teacher of the new written language.

Both Mor and Beag said that they did not understand of the written words , but it was something that in the past Nuada had shown a passion for, and it would be wise of him to continue his path with it.

Nuada could see the reasons that they had pointed out for him, but still he felt unsettled about it. His thoughts drifted back to the many times that Creatrix had told him of his path, and it too showed that he was to teach of it to the people. Nuada reached a decision and stood to return to the school and to tell Pytheas that he would do the teaching of the written language.

A light snow had begun to fall before he reached the school, and he paused to look around again at the changes of the village. Wisps of smoke drifted with the snowflakes as he let his eyes move from building to building. "We have a place of beauty and safety now," he thought. "I need not be afraid of these people who I have brought here."

He stepped up to the entrance to the school and entered. As he walked down the hall, his attention was drawn to the classrooms as he passed, and he listened in to the discussions going on inside of them. Pytheas watched him from the office door and waited for him to speak first. Nuada saw him and said as he approached, "Pytheas, I will do the teaching, but I wish a week to prepare."

Pytheas smiled and slapped Nuada on the back, then welcomed him into the office for some discussion about the format of the teaching. Nuada listened closely, as this would be something new for him, and he welcomed the thoughts of his friend about it.

When Nuada started to teach, it would be to the older children, who had a grasp of the Greek language. The others would come later. His class would only be for an hour a day, and this took some of the pressure from Nuada's mind.

Nuada went home with the thoughts of the coming work and stopped by the old woodworking building to collect a large pile of the new paper and some ink for them. He did not linger after getting what he needed and went directly home and set everything on the table in front of the fireplace and began to make copies of the new alphabet with its crossover of Greek letters. He was still working on the copies when his mate returned from the cooking area, where she had a meeting with her women friends. She did not disturb him as he worked but waited until he stopped for a break. His second child was already asleep and added to the silence of the house.

After many hours, Nuada stopped and stood to stretch.

"I see that you will become the new teacher after all, Nuada," she said.

Nuada turned, not even realizing that she had come home, and replied, "Yes. It was the right decision after all. Partly because of Creatrix's gift of languages to me."

"When will you start?"

"I told Pytheas that I needed a week to prepare, but he told me that I would only be teaching an hour a day. That has taken much of the worry away about the teaching."

"Well it is a start. I know you will be good at it, like everything else that you do."

She gave him a kiss and then started to prepare his evening meal. Nuada cleared the table of his copies and placed them in the pantry away from the children and Wolf.

Nuada walked outside to the entry porch and stood drinking in the fresh air before his meal. The sun was starting to set, and it had been an eventful day for Nuada. He felt the tiredness in his shoulders and back from the many hours of writing. Slowly he turned and returned inside for the company of his family.

The next morning Nuada took a walk to the meeting hall and the company of his friends. He hurried from his house to the hall because of a light mist of rain that made everything feel damp in the village. He found his friends at their usual spot near the fireplace making small talk.

"Do you ever spend time at your own houses?" Nuada quipped.

Mor replied, "What, and be underfoot of our mates? It would not happen in our lifetimes, friend."

Nuada laughed at Mor's response and took a mug of beer handed to him by A'Chreag.

"The company of our fellow men is all that is required, Nuada," he said. Everyone responded by nodding their heads and laughing.

"A'Chreag, you are beginning to sound like an old married man now. How long has it been? A year?"

"And a half again," he responded with a great smile on his face.

"Wait for more children, and you will forget the time that has passed."

A cheer went up from the men at the table at Nuada's reply. "See. They know of the meaning."

More beer was passed around, and they settled into a relaxed morning of friendship. It was near midday when Nuada asked if any of them were taking the classes at the school. All of them responded that they were and finding it enjoyable and interesting. Nuada felt happy inside and left the discussion standing where it was. Shortly he made excuses to leave and took the walk to the school to find out how Pytheas was viewing the adult classes.

Nuada found Pytheas in the hall, watching the classes going on, and waited for him to notice him standing there. Slowly Pytheas turned and put his finger to his lips and motioned for Nuada to follow him to the office.

"You need something, Nuada?"

"I was at the meeting hall with many of the village men, and they were talking about the classes that they were taking. How do you find of them?"

"After we finally got them to come, they are responding well to the teaching. I have no complaints about their speed of understanding."

"Good. I was worried about them losing interest in what was taught."

"We change it up when we feel that they are becoming bored with the lessons."

"I will not have that option with it being only one topic."

"Do not worry, you will find a way."

After some more discussion, Nuada left Pytheas and took a walk around the village. The snow became heavier, and the wind began to gust out of the north. He did not linger outside and made his way back home to the comfort of his family.

Inside Nuada soon became bored and went and retrieved his papers from the pantry. Sitting at the table, he began to work on a program for turning the letters into words and then into phrases. Nuada's mate watched him work and said nothing. His meal would be late tonight, as she did not wish to bother him at his work.

Several days passed, with Nuada continuing to work on his lessons. From time to time, Iolair would ask about the language, and Nuada began to teach him without realizing it. Sometimes they would talk in their native tongue and other times in the Greek language. This was lost on Nuada's mate, who had no understanding of it.

At last the day had come for Nuada to begin to teach, and this time he felt no fear of the prospect. He arrived long before his class and stopped to talk again with Pytheas, who was busy working on his own teaching lessons. Nuada did not disturb him but sat and watched how he prepared for his own classes with the adults. The other teachers had also arrived early, and Nuada took up a conversation in the hall with them. As always the topic was the students and their lessons. Soon the children began to arrive, and the teachers drifted off to direct them into the classrooms and begin their day's lessons. Nuada waited patiently for the time for his teaching. He was alone with his thoughts for most of the morning as everyone else was busy.

Nuada was to begin his teaching the hour before midday break, and at long last it was time. He entered the classroom, and the older children waited quietly for him to begin. The first thing Nuada did was to pass out the alphabet, and then he waited for the children to settle down again, and he began to explain how it worked. At the end of the first hour, they seemed to have a grasp of it, and Nuada called for a halt in the first lesson and sent them out to play. Nuada was gathering his papers when he looked up and glanced out into the hall. Pytheas and Dionysins had been listening in on the lesson from the hall.

"What think you of my first class, friends?"

"You are a natural teacher, Nuada. We could not have done better."

Nuada beamed with pride in their comments and asked them to join him after school to share a beer. They agreed, and Nuada departed the school and made his way to the meeting hall. Inside he found his old friends doing their usual discussions about the village. They saw him as he entered and called him over to join them.

"How went the teaching, Nuada?" asked Mor.

"Very smooth, but they were expecting it and kind of knew what it was about."

Beag then said, "I have a question to put before you about what we were discussing."

"What is it?"

"We can expect trade to start in the future, and I was wondering about new shops and where to place them. I think we should place them near the new stone wall to give some protection to the village."

Nuada thought for a minute before he answered. "That would be a wise choice. I suppose you wish to build them of stone also."

"That was the idea. It would make everything look more substantial and lasting."

"I agree. How many shops are you talking about?"

"Ten. I now have the time to build that many."

"Mor, what about you? Are you going to build more houses next year?"

"I too will have more time and plan on building about fifteen houses."

"Will those be around the school, as were the others?"

"Yes, that is the plan."

"Then you two have everything in hand. Why did you ask of me about them?"

"It is still your valley, and you are our chief. That is the reason we asked."

Nuada laughed at that remark and shook his head in wonderment. "Please get me a beer and do not forget that I am only a man who works in metal."

"You are much more than that, Nuada. You lead, and you teach, and when times are troubled, you fight like no other. You always know what the village needs and inspire all others to build for that reason," said Mor.

Nuada drank long on his beer and looked at each of his friends and still shook his head at their ways. The conversation then turned to other things while the music began to be played. After awhile some of the men began to drift off, and Nuada asked where they were going.

"It is time for their classes. Soon you will begin to teach them too."

Nuada watched as most of the men departed and made for the school. It became quiet, and he made up his mind to follow them and see their learning. After a farewell to his friends, he walked back to the school.

He took the long way around the village by the site of the old wooden wall and looked out toward where the new shops were to be built. It was a long walk out there, but it gave some safety to the village. He had to give his friends credit for thinking of that placement for the buildings, and yet he knew that the village would grow to the new shops within a few years.

Turning he made for the school again. Before he got there, he could hear the children playing outside and knew that their day of learning was done. Pytheas and Andocides would begin the classes with the adults of the village while Amasis and Dionysins would be in the office planning on tomorrow's classes for the children. Nuada paused outside and almost turned and went home instead, but he wanted to observe the adult classes too.

Going inside he made for the office and greeted Amasis in his native Egyptian language. Amasis responded and then looked at Nuada with a strange look on his face.

"What is wrong, Amasis?"

"That is the first I have heard of my language since leaving Alexandria. It makes me homesick."

"I am sorry that I have disturbed you with its use."

"No. I wish to hear more of it again, Nuada. Will you speak it to me when we are together? It will make me feel more comfortable."

"As you wish, my friend."

Nuada talked with both men for a short time and then went to stand in the hall and listen to the teachings of the other teachers. Pytheas was teaching the history of many other countries, and Dionysins was teaching the Greek language to the others in another classroom. Time passed quickly, and soon the men of the village began to leave. Pytheas was the first to notice Nuada standing in the hall and walked over to him.

"Do you not get enough time here, Nuada?"

"Although I am now teaching, I am still learning too, but my interest is in how the people react to the teaching. That is the important point to this."

"I see of no problem with them. They are eager to learn."

Nuada nodded and said his farewells to Pytheas and Dionysins. He again made his way back toward the meeting hall before going home for the day. As he turned the corner onto the street to the hall, he looked across to the forge building and noticed activity within. Curious he made his way there and looked inside. A'Chreag was there with two young men, and they were making large sheets of copper sheeting.

"A'Chreag? What are you working on now?"

"Ah, Nuada. I talked with Beag about new work projects for the Spring, and he told me of the new shops to be built near the new stone wall across the meadow. We talked about the roofing needs of them and then decided to make the covering of copper sheets. I have some new help, and they are eager to learn the process, so we began to make the needed sheets today. Is there a problem with this?"

"No. I feel that I have not enough time to return to the forge, and you have the necessary skills to carry on with the needs of the village here. I am glad that you have found some needed help. Do not forget that they will need hinges and latches."

"I have planned for that need, Nuada. If there is no problem, I shall carry on with the work."

"Do so with my blessing, my friend."

Nuada looked at the results of the work so far and then turned and made his way to the meeting hall. He found the hall was filling up quickly, and he only had a quick word with Mor and Beag before he went home for the day and a welcomed meal with his family.

From time to time, Nuada would drop in at the forge to see how A'Chreag was doing, but every time he found his work without reproach. Nuada had no time to be bored now, and the progress of his students showed his intensity for the new language teaching. He found time to converse with Amasis in his Egyptian tongue, which made Amasis happy, and they bonded with a closer relationship because of it.

Andocides, who shared the children of the older age with Nuada, was now teaching them the different types of measurement of all the countries that had been part of his classes. Nuada listened closely to this as he knew that there would be a need within the village soon. He thought, "If we are going to expand and include trade with others, we must have a way of measuring things and some form of money, as gold was in many countries. It has weight, and there must be a way of telling how much of it was to be used for an item of worth."

When Nuada found time to visit his friends at the meeting hall, he brought up the subject of measurement and how it would affect trade and the exchange of goods. They thought that Nuada had made a good point and would discuss it at their next meeting and give an answer to his thoughts. Beag found time to render drawings of some of the lift machines he was starting to build and took pride in showing them to Nuada.

Although Mor did some drawings of the war machines, he was not as compelled to go further with their building. He thought it was a time to build, not tear down, and so the machines were set aside for the future.

Winter was now nearing its final blows, and Spring was now close. All the new projects would take time away from the school and its students. No one had given any thoughts to seeking new people for the village this year, and if anyone was found, they too would be welcomed into the village.

Nuada's mate was now beginning to show the presence of their third child and had asked Nuada to now name their second son. This time he took his time finding the right name for him. After many weeks of thought, he decided to name him Uilleam. When he told his mate of the name, she approved of its noble nature and said that it fit him well.

Then the weather began to change in earnest. Snow came no more; it was now the rainy season, and the temperature continued to climb. Many were now ready for the change in seasons.

- SPRING AND NEW WAYS -

One morning Nuada decided to take a walk around the valleys as the rain held off for the time being. He went down through the new houses and then by the caves, heading for the entrance to the second valley. He had not thought about where he was going, only that he needed the walk. He paused at the entrance to the valley and then continued on toward the mill sites. Once he was there, he looked at the massive mill pond and the dam. The water runoff was mild compared to last year, and he stood mesmerized by the turning of the waterwheel. Slowly he shook his head to clear it and then set off again, following the ridgeline across the back of the valley. He came to his copper ore site and noted that it was almost time to look for another site, as this one was nearly done. He then walked on to the site of the quarry, where almost all of the stone for the village had come from. It too was time to move to another site, as it would soon cause it to be a liability for the safety of the valleys.

Nuada moved on, looking for something else to note, and his footsteps took him by the grain fields and their new fences. On he walked. He passed the stable here for the sheep and saw many new lambs in the pasture. He did not linger but followed the ridge on around the valley. As he neared the cleared field where many of the trees had been cut for the village, he again looked toward the ridge that separated the two valleys and thought that they could cut a road through it and add the stone from it to the building of the village. It would provide a quick path to the mill sites and the sheep stables but not hurt the security of either of the valleys. Nuada knew he had to bring it up to Mor and Beag before the new work was to begin.

He quickened his footsteps back to the village, hoping to find his friends at the meeting hall, but he knew that they could be anywhere in the village.

They were not at the hall or near the new houses of Mor's. Nuada continued his search for them and finally made his way out to the stone protection wall and the site for the new shops. They were there measuring for the placement of the shops and discussing the materials needed. Nuada called to them as he approached. "Beag, a word with you."

"What is it, Nuada?"

"I have just returned from a walk into the second valley and need to talk to you about moving the quarry site."

"I had given it thought too, but did not know what to do about it."

"If we cut a roadway between the two valleys, it would provide the needed stone for your work and give us a quicker route into the other valley."

"Yes, and it would make the journey shorter for the stone to the sites, where it is needed."

"That was my thoughts too. You need to select where to make the cut, and then we will need a crew for the clearing of the ridgeline there."

"I am done here for now. I will take a walk there and see what needs to be done. Mor? Will you come with me?"

"Yes. I have time right now for this."

After some small talk and a promise to meet for a few beers later, the pair set out for the ridgeline at the back of the village. Nuada then set out for the forge building and to talk with A'Chreag about finding a new site for the copper ore.

Nuada found A'Chreag casting hinges for the new houses and helping shape the new sheets of copper for the roofs.

"I see that you are keeping busy, A'Chreag."

"Nuada! It is good to see you. Is there anything I can do for you?"

"I took a walk around the valleys today and saw that the copper ore site is almost gone. I would like you to seek another site, as we will have need of it soon."

"I too noticed the need. Do you have any thoughts as to where I should look?"

"We both know that there is not another site inside of our valleys. You should seek it outside and close to the mountains on the east side of the stream."

"That would have been my choice too. I shall seek it when we complete this work — perhaps in two days."

"Good. Have you anything for me to do here?"

"No. We have everything under control. It just takes time, as you know."

Nuada continued to linger, as he had no class to teach today. The portion of the forge building that was used for glassmaking was empty, and finally Nuada departed for the old woodworking building to pick up more paper, which he would need soon. After retrieving the paper, he walked home to his empty house and deposited the paper in the pantry. He did not remain long at the house, as he knew that boredom would soon find him, so he set out for the meeting hall and some friendship. Inside Mor and Beag had just returned and were talking about the ridgeline, where they would soon start to cut the needed stones for the valley and the new roadway into the second valley.

"Well my friends. Did you find a site to make the cut into the other valley?"

"We did, Nuada, although we were wondering if we would find of any more caves or underground lakes there. We will take a chance that we will not uncover that aspect of the ridge."

"I see of your concern, but it is a needed thing, and we will find of a way to deal with it if we should uncover such."

They then talked of other things concerning the village, among them the need for a well in the second valley for the sheep and grain crops. It was late when Nuada finally left his friends and made his way home to his family.

Two days later Nuada awoke to a heavy rainstorm and the wind blowing it sideways. He settled in to spend some time with his growing family and the needed work on a form of dictionary for their new written language. Iolair wanted to help his father, and Nuada welcomed his support. Together the time passed as they made headway on the words. Nuada's mate watched them together and was happy with them sharing the time and work. She now had some understanding of what he was doing and knew how important it was for everyone.

Before midday the weather broke, but the dampness still lingered across both valleys. Clouds scudded low overhead with the wind pushing them. Wisps of smoke from the village chimneys drifted down the streets in a low, random pattern, adding its smell to the budding plants of the new Spring. Nuada knew that it would hamper the needed work of the village, but it was to be expected this time of year. He did not take any walks that day as the dampness had also settled into his old wound again, and he felt its stiffness. After the many hours of work at the table, he settled into his sitting area near the fireplace and dozed throughout the afternoon.

The next day was clear and warmer, but Nuada still felt the stiffness in his side. He knew that he had to take a walk to ease the discomfort, and he set out for the meeting hall first. Inside he found it almost empty, and he again knew that Mor had sent out crews to begin the needed work of the village. He crossed over to the forge building, and it too was empty. He thought, "A'Chreag must have gone in search of the needed copper ore deposits." He then headed out to the site of the new shop buildings. Beag was there placing string lines and marker stakes for the beginning of the foundations for the buildings. He had only a small crew, and when Nuada asked of Mor, he was told that he was at the site on the ridge, clearing it of brush and small trees so that the quarry work could begin.

Nuada nodded and watched Beag work for awhile, then turned and made his way back through the village and on through the portal gate of the new stone wall on that side of the village. He could hear the men working the ridge before he saw them. Shouts between them and the falling of the small trees echoed off the side of the ridge. As Nuada neared the site, he could partially see the bare rock standing out from the rest of the ridgeline. On he walked until everything came into view. He was amazed at how quickly the men had cleared so much of the hillside. He stopped and watched them work for almost a half hour before he sought out Mor.

He caught sight of Mor hanging from a rope, halfway up the slope, calling out orders. Nuada called to him, "Do you not have younger men to hang about like that, Mor?"

"Nuada! Hold on. I will be right down."

Mor swung down the slope like a man half his age and quickly untied the rope from around himself. Brushing himself Mor strode over to Nuada and shook his hand before saying, "Things are moving quickly. We should be done with this today, and tomorrow Beag can begin the stonework we all need."

Nuada grinned and then pointed to Mor's great paunch of a belly and said, "You are not even breathing heavily."

"Oh, that is only from the fine beer that we shared over the Winter. It will soon be gone with all the work to be done."

"I agree. I myself have felt the lack of exercise from the Winter."

They continued to talk about the hillside and the work being done there and then turned the conversation to the start of the houses and shop buildings. Mor did not ask about the school, and Nuada did not say anything either. Both now knew that it could wait for the Fall season to start again.

It was late in the afternoon when Nuada returned to the village, and he took a walk through the streets looking at the new house construction area. Their village was fast becoming a city, and it showed.

The next morning dawned bright and warm. Nuada was up early and made his way to the meeting hall, hoping to find Mor and Beag there. As he entered, he caught sight of them at their table going over the day's work schedule and the men needed for the projects. He joined them, not saying anything, until they were done. Beag had a drawing in front of him that showed the design of the new shop buildings. Nuada looked at the drawing and then commented that they would be beautiful addition to the village. Beag beamed at the comment and was quick to point out certain aspects of the design. Nuada thought for a moment and then said, "When I was in Alexandria, all of the streets had walkways made of stone. What would it take to add such to our streets?"

"Were they raised above the street level?"

"Yes. It defined the street from the walkway."

Beag thought for a few moments before he answered. "I could do it, but it would take time away from some other project."

"I think it would make our village stand out for any visitors or people of trade."

Mor added his thoughts to such an idea. "We could just start with this site and then work back to the others when we had time."

Beag agreed to the idea and said he would add it to the project of the shop buildings. Nuada was happy that he had thought of the idea and followed the two men out to the site. Already men had gathered, and Mor sent twenty with Beag to the new quarry site to begin the stonecutting that was needed. Six more men were sent to the sawmill for five wagonloads of the new cut lumber so he could begin the new houses near the school. Another ten men were to wait at the housing site and wait for the first of the lumber to arrive. Ten more men were to start cutting trees just outside of the valley and then move the trees to the sawmill for cutting.

Nuada knew that within the hour the noise from the new construction would fill the valleys with the sounds of progress. He walked back into the village and wandered toward the school. He stopped outside of the building and saw that his fellow teachers were just inside talking together. Nuada entered and greeted them warmly. He asked if they had anything that was needed of him today, and they responded that nothing was pressing with everyone now working at other things. Even the children had other things to do.

Pytheas asked how Nuada was coming with his dictionary of words and phrases. Nuada responded, "That is a work that will take many years to finish, if ever, because words come and go so quickly."

Pytheas nodded in understanding and said no more about it. Amasis said that he was going to be at the forge building later to make more of the needed glass for the shops and houses and wondered if Nuada would join him there when he had time. Nuada said he would take the time to drop by later as he was curious about the work.

Nuada said a farewell to the teachers and began to walk toward the new quarry. Along the way he again paused at the new housing sites and saw that the men had already begun to start the framing for the first house. Noise from the first wagonloads of lumber shattered the morning quiet, and then Nuada moved on to the quarry. Standing below where the hillside had been cleared of its covering, Nuada watched men on ropes working with hammers and levers prying stone that tumbled down to the base of the ridge. Almost as soon as it hit bottom, other men gathered the stone and moved it away for the dressing of the stonework. Here he found Beag at work cutting the stone into workable shapes. Nuada did not disturb any of the men working but only watched them. To one side of the dressing area, one of the new lifting machines began to load the cut stone onto a wagon for transport to the shop site. Nuada watched mesmerized for almost two hours before he shook himself free and walked back into the village.

Nuada paused again at the housing site and stood dumbfounded at the sight of two houses almost completely framed already. "If I blink, I would miss everything being done," he thought. Moving on he made his way to the outdoor cooking area and had just started to sit down when he heard another wagon coming through the village streets. Curious he waited to see who it was and where they were going. It was A'Chreag with two wagonloads of copper ore, and he was headed for the forge building with it. Nuada watched them pass and then started to walk to the forge to talk with A'Chreag. He caught up with them just as A'Chreag and his help were climbing down from the wagons.

"You look tired, my friend," called Nuada.

"Nuada! Good to see you today," he answered.

"I see you were successful in finding a new ore deposit. Did you have to travel far?"

"No. We found a small valley about three hours out, and it had a rich deposit of the copper ore and also a tin deposit too."

Nuada reached into one of the wagons and pulled out a sample of the ore. He studied it closely and then nodded in appreciation at the quality of it.

"You did well, A'Chreag. After you unload it, we will have to meet for a few beers. Oh by the way, Amasis is going to be making glass here later so the two of you will not be in each other's way."

A'Chreag nodded and then said that he would join Nuada for the beer but wanted to return to his house soon and see of his mate and child. Nuada nodded in understanding and then let them get to work unloading the ore from the wagons. Nuada walked back to the cooking area and settled at his table and became lost in thought about the village and the new changes.

A few hours later Nuada stood and walked back out to the new shop site, and when it became apparent that none of the construction was going to start today, he set out for the housing site. When he got there, the men were taking a break for a midday meal, and as Nuada looked around, he saw a third and fourth house were being framed already. Mor was sitting on a pile of the new cut lumber, eating a haunch of meat and a piece of bread. He did not see Nuada but was lost in thought about the houses. Nuada circled around the work site and saw it too had one of the new lifting machines. He walked closer to look over the design and see if there was anything he could do to make it better. Nuada was surprised to see that inside the main frame all of the many gears were made of his bronze metal. A'Chreag had been busy, he thought. I did not even realize it. Finding nothing that he would change, he followed his footsteps to the new quarry again.

There too the men were taking a break, and Nuada did not even stop but turned to return to the village and his meeting with A'Chreag. This time Nuada did not walk through the village but followed the ridgeline to the stable and then to the meeting hall. The door was open to let in the fresh air and empty it of the stale odors from the Winter. Nuada paused at the entrance and turned to look around at the forge building. He could hear voices from within and knew it was Amasis by the sound of his voice there. Nuada went into the meeting hall and saw A'Chreag and his two helpers sharing a beer together. He went and joined them and listened to their stories about the new ore site and the valley they found it in. After their second beer, they began to get up to leave. Nuada stood and told A'Chreag that he had a chance to look over one of the new lifting machines and praised him for the gear design and workmanship of them. A'Chreag thanked Nuada for the kind words about the work and then said he had to get home to his family. Nuada nodded in understanding and followed them out before he went to the forge building to see Amasis.

Inside he stood to one side and watched the glassmaking process. Before he knew it, the whole day was nearing an end, and after saying good-bye to Amasis, he went to the outdoor cooking area to find his family. The workmen had just finished their day and were entering the area, and soon music filled the area, along with the smells of the evening meal for them. Iolair was sitting at Nuada's table watching over Uilleam. Wolf was nearby and watched them both, as was his nature. Nuada hugged his two boys and patted Wolf on his head before he sat down to wait on his mate to join them. Iolair asked about his father's day, and Nuada told him what he had seen and heard that day. Nuada then asked about the boys' days, and they said that they did nothing important. Following their meal, the family went home for the night, and thoughts about tomorrow filled the heads of everyone.

Over the next two weeks, Nuada remained close to home and his family. He worked on his dictionary and played games with the boys and Wolf. When he eventually became curious about the construction work, he took a walk again around the village.

He first went to the housing site and was surprised that all fifteen houses had been framed. When he got there, they were preparing the lifting machine to be moved to the site for the new shops. This was not Mor's usual work, as he would build two or four houses and then start the framing on the next set of houses. The first two houses were a busy place as the men worked to finish them. Mor was there, and Nuada went to ask him about the change in his work program.

"I changed the work here, as I knew we would need the lift machine at the other site. Other than that, nothing is any different in the building."

"But everything went up so quickly. I am amazed at the work you have done here."

"It was the machine that made it possible, Nuada. I wish that we had had it earlier."

"I am just now going out to the other site. Will I see the changes as fast there too?"

"I think so, but that is up to Beag and his crew."

After a few more words, Nuada made his way out through the village to the shop construction site. As he walked across the meadow, he could see both of the lift machines at work, and the walls of stone were climbing quickly with them. The workmen were everywhere, setting stone at a furious pace. Beag himself stood out as he pointed to some part of the latest wall of stone. Nuada stood outside of the work area and watched them work their art. Dust rose and fell as each section was finished. Scaffolds went up and then down at a furious pace.

Nuada found a place on the stone protection wall to sit and watch the work below him. He spent the entire day just watching. When at last the work began to slow, he climbed down and went to talk with Beag. Beag was taking a long drink of water from a bag hanging from his shoulder as Nuada approached him.

"I think you need something a little stronger than that, my friend."

"I do at that, Nuada, but my body says water is the thing to use right now."

Nuada laughed, and then Beag joined him. Both men slapped each other on their backs and wandered throughout the construction site. Beag pointed out details that he had cut into the stones and asked Nuada about his thoughts on the work.

"I like the details. I see that you are making time with your work too. Mor surprised me with the speed he made on the houses."

"It is these new machines. They cut the time and save the backs of everyone with the placement of the stones. I want to thank you for bring the design back with you."

"I see that you have also started the placement of the new walkways too."

"Yes, it fits in with the design that you wanted. Also if you notice, we have spaced the shops away from the wall too. This still gives us a place to stage the people if we are attacked again."

"I like the idea. You were thinking ahead on that."

Nuada let Beag get back to work and stood and watched some more before heading back into the village. His footsteps took him back toward the school, which was now empty, and then out to the crop meadow. The plowing had already been done and planting of the crops begun. The village women worked hard at providing the necessary labor for the village, and Nuada thought that they needed to be thanked in some way for it.

Nuada knew that the day was late and did a quick circle back by the quarry and the new houses before he made his way to the cooking area again. His four teachers were already there and in deep conversation at their table. Nuada did not bother them and sat at his table and waited for his family to arrive. Noise from the construction still drowned out the sounds of nature in the village, but this did not bother Nuada or his outlook on the work being done; he was happy with the progress.

Another week passed, and the valley was green from the Spring rains. Work was nonstop as the village continued to expand. Nuada was thinking of taking a trip outside of the valley to check on the security against another raid and possibly to find more people to bring back to the village.

He continued to become restless as his role in the village had changed with him becoming a teacher and village leader. He brought up the subject of a trip outside of the valley with his friends one warm morning. They thought it would be good for Nuada to seek others again and to see if any of the raiders were nearby. Nuada told his mate of his thoughts, and she encouraged him to go. She knew her husband well enough that to say otherwise would only depress him.

Nuada took the next two days preparing for his trip, and when the morning of his departure arrived, he kissed his mate and children and set out for the stable. He stopped at the meeting hall to check on his friends before he departed. Everyone greeted Nuada warmly and told him to bring back more people to help with the building. Nuada laughed and said he would if he found anyone out there in need of their help. Soon he had packed his horse and weapons and started for the protection wall portal gate and the adventure awaiting outside of the valley.

This time Nuada traveled in a northwest direction away from the village. He was enjoying the time away although he was cautious in this new territory. The weather favored his travel, and the animals and birds were not afraid as he passed by.

At the end of his third day out, Nuada made camp and was thinking that it was time to change direction before returning to the village. He dozed in the late afternoon sun and listened to the insects and birds about him. Then sounds not of nature caught his attention. He sat up and peered in the direction that the sounds had come from. He saw no one, and that made him more alert to the things he could not see. He picked his weapons and walked into the underbrush toward the sounds. He had his bow in hand as he moved closer to the noise. He found an encampment of tents and wagons in the next meadow. It was a large group, and he stayed hidden and watched them. After determining that they were not a party of raiders but more people on the move away from trouble, Nuada walked down into the meadow to talk with them.

Before he got to the outer edge of the encampment, he was surrounded by ten armed men. They took his weapons and brought him before the leader of the group. Nuada remained relaxed and calm, and this settled the nerves of those there. When he was asked who he was and why he was there, Nuada explained about his valley and the village. He then asked about them and why they were on the move. It was the same old story about raiders and the damage they had done to their village. Nuada invited them to come and share his valley and protection. The leader said he wanted to talk to his people first before committing an answer to Nuada. Nuada told him he understood and waited while they held a meeting in the center of the encampment. Meanwhile Nuada's weapons were returned to him, and he sat and enjoyed the moment in peace.

After about an hour, the leader returned and said that they would follow him to his valley. Nuada said he had to return to his camp and retrieve his horse and supplies and would join them in the morning. He asked them to be ready to travel with the coming of first light.

Nuada returned to his camp and knew that his trip had been successful. He slept light and long before the sun began to rise, and he was on his way back to the encampment. They were ready to move, and this encouraged Nuada to find a more direct way back to the valley.

They followed the path of least resistance along a wide stream. The group consisted of about seventy people and their children. Nuada knew that his people did not have enough houses for them, but it was early in the year, and maybe they could, with these people's help, build more houses this year.

The next day they continued to move quickly, and Nuada began to recognize the land around him. The stream that they had been following was possibly the same one that emptied from his valley. Just after midday, scouts from the group found a trio of men and their wagons. Nuada went forward to talk with them. They were traders in search of someone to trade with. Nuada asked of their goods and if they had seen any raiders. They gladly showed Nuada what they had to trade and in answer to the raiders said that they had seen none. Nuada invited them to follow the group to the valley and some well-needed trade. They agreed and fell in at the rear of the group as they continued on.

Nearing dusk they came to the entrance into Nuada's valley, and Nuada rode ahead to warn the guards of their approach. Runners were sent into the village and told of Nuada's return and his success at finding more people. Slowly the group passed through the portal gate and on past the new shops being built.

Nuada had the group leader make their encampment that night outside of the village in the meadow across from the teacher's houses. He promised that the next morning they would have a chance to see everything about the village for themselves. This did not prevent the people of the village from coming out and greeting all of them before the sun was fully set.

Nuada took his horse back to the stable and unpacked, then went home feeling tired and satisfied with what he had done again. His mate was waiting and took his pack from him as he sat at the table and almost went to sleep there before his meal was ready.

Nuada slept deeply and in the morning was up early again and out the door on his way to the encampment. He had almost forgotten about the traders and sought them out first. At the encampment site, Nuada found Mor talking with their leader and asked him to come with him to meet the traders and see what they had for the village. Mor and Nuada found the traders just sitting and looking bored with all those around them. Nuada called a greeting and then asked to see the items that they had brought with them. They were gladly shown many items, few that they could use. However, they did have bolts of cloth and a new type of metal in long bars. Nuada asked what they wanted in trade, and when asked if they had any gold, Nuada said yes. They then haggled over how much gold was required for the cloth and the new metal. Finally they settled on an amount, and the deal was settled with a handshake. Nuada asked them to follow with their wagons to the forge building to complete the deal. Once at the forge building, they began to unload, and Nuada noticed some casks at the front of one of the wagons.

"What do you have in the casks?" he asked.

"Those are wine from our land called Iberia. Are you interested?"

"Yes. I have some Greeks here who miss of the grapes. You do not have any of the vines with you, do you?"

"Yes, but I thought that they would not suit you of this land."

"You were wrong. Let us agree on a price and move forward with our deal."

This time Nuada did not argue the price but paid what the trader wanted. As a bonus, the trader gave Nuada two bags of salt that he had. Nuada went into the forge building and returned with the agreed amount of gold and had them unload the wine casks at the outdoor cooking area. These where set on the low wall that surrounded the area. Nuada then asked if they would return next year, and the trader said he would make a special trip just for Nuada, as the trade was very successful for him. Nuada then asked them if they were going to remain in the valley another day, to which the trader said no, they had to return home.

After the trader's departure, Nuada went to seek out his fellow teachers and present them with his surprise gift of the wine.

Nuada made his way back out to the meadow and found Pytheas with Mor and the leader of the new group. Pytheas was making a list of the names, skills, and needs of the new group. Nuada joined them and asked questions that the other two did not think of. The empty houses of the village were to go to those who had the greatest needs first — those with the youngest children and the old or injured.

The leader of the group was to have the last of the stone houses near the teachers, and when Mor asked for the needed help to finish the houses under construction, he was told he could have all the help he needed. It was then noted that those houses could be finished within the month and that they would need to build another ten to give everyone shelter before Fall.

Mor turned to Nuada and told him that by the end of the month he would have to take back one of the lifting machines from Beag to build the other houses. Nuada said he would speak to Beag and that he could see no problem there.

Nuada then asked Pytheas to gather the teachers at the cooking area later, as he had a surprise for them. Pytheas was curious but said he would have them there. Mor and the new group leader then began to gather the new people and show them where they would live. Sounds of the people filled the meadow and almost drowned out the sounds of all the construction going on.

Nuada made his way out to the new shop buildings and found Beag at work setting stone and hurrying his crew at their jobs. Dust flew everywhere, and the lifting machines never seemed to stop as they moved great amounts of the stone into place. Nuada watched for a while before talking to Beag about Mor's need for one of the machines at the end of the month.

Beag said he would have most of the work done by then, and Mor was welcome to take one of the machines then. Nuada felt relief at his answer and asked him to join him after work for some beer. Beag grinned and said he would not miss it. Nuada also said that they needed to talk about the new people and their needs and the skills that they would add to the village.

Nuada then turned and made his way back to the meadow, where the new people were beginning to move in groups into the village. Nuada followed them until he caught up with Mor and the new group leader. Nuada told of his talks with Beag to Mor and that everything was set for the end of the month to return one of the lifting machines to the housing site. Everyone was happy now, and things settled into controlled chaos as the sorting out of the people continued throughout the day.

By midday Nuada was becoming tired and decided to take a walk away from everyone and settle his mind with all the things going on. He returned to the cooking area, which was empty of people, and settled at his table to relax. The warmth of the sun settled on his shoulders, and he began to doze in it's comfort.

He awoke an hour later and looked about to see if anyone had seen him sleeping. He found no one was here, and he stood and stretched before taking a walk to the forge building to seek A'Chreag and have a talk with him concerning the new metal he had traded for.

Before reaching the forge, he looked in the meeting hall to see if anyone else was there. As it happened, A'Chreag was there. Nuada walked over to him and asked if he had seen the new metal that the traders had brought. He said no, and the pair departed the hall and went directly to the forge building to look over their new find. Nuada pulled one of the bars from under a cover and handed it to A'Chreag.

"This is very heavy," was his first remark. "What other properties does it have, Nuada?"

"I do not know. It came from the Iberian lands, and the trader called it iron. I have a sample of the ore it comes from, so if it has any worth for us, we will search it out in our lands."

"I would like to work some of this to see what we can do with it."

"Do so. I am curious about it too."

After some discussion about what to make, the pair returned to the cooking area and the crowd of people soon to gather there. Nuada and A'Chreag sat at Nuada's table and looked around at all of the new faces of the people starting to gather.

"There are so many, I wonder how long it will take me to put face to name this time," Nuada said.

A'Chreag nodded in agreement, and they continued to look at the new people. Soon Mor arrived with the leader of the new group and brought him over to Nuada. The leader said, "How can I thank you for all your people are doing for us?"

"Help where you can and do not fight between each other. That is all I ask for now. Oh did Mor show you the school?"

"Yes. I understand that you want everyone to learn of the skills from the teachers."

"Yes. I am also one of the teachers. My skill is languages."

"Then I will have my people learn of all of your skills."

"They are not now your people anymore but our people. You will have a say at the monthly meetings of the village consul because of your former leadership."

The man started to object but then thought of all that was offered in exchange for them staying in the village and found no fault in the words of Nuada. He nodded in agreement and held out his hand to that end.

Mor laughed and got up to retrieve some beers for them all. Soon more people entered the area, and music filled the air as women began to prepare the evening meals. Nuada's family soon arrived, and Iolair sat next to his father and started to ask the new man about where he had come from and why they were there in the valley now. He answered the best he could to the many questions the boy asked and finally turned to Nuada and said, "He must be your son. He questions every point."

Nuada smiled at the remark and decided not to answer it now. The man suddenly realized that they were not alone as he looked down into Wolf's yellow eyes, which did not waver from him.

"What is this, Nuada?"

Nuada looked down and patted Wolf on the head and said, "This is Wolf. He is my family's best friend and protector. Be nice to him and my children."

The man swallowed hard and nodded to Nuada's answer.

Soon the teachers entered the cooking area and started to turn and leave after seeing all the people gathered there. Nuada got up and called to them to wait, and he brought them back to his table and had them sit while he got them the gift he had told Pytheas about earlier. Nuada returned with four full tankards of a liquid for them.

"What is this, Nuada?" asked Dionysins.

"Taste and see," was Nuada's response.

"Wine! Good wine too! How did you come by it?"

"The trader who followed us into the village had it. They also had the vines for which to grow the grapes. I leave that part to you to take care of."

"We can do that! But we will need of the making of a press for the grapes when they are ready."

"Draw a design and give it to A'Chreag. He will see that it is made for you."

All of the teachers were now happy, and it made Nuada feel good about the gift for them.

After the evening meal, everyone went home early because tomorrow would not be easy for them, and rest was needed.

From that next morning and for the rest of the month, construction went on at a frantic pace. House after house was finished, and families moved in as fast as they became available. Nuada was the only one of the village leaders who had the time to move from work site to work site and oversee everything going on. This was Mor's usual job, but he was busy with the houses that were needed. After some slowdown at the sawmill, Nuada went to see what the problem was and found that even though they were working as fast as they could, the single saw was not able to keep up with the workload. He looked around for a solution to the problem and thought that the only answer was to add another saw. They could not do it this year, so it was a project for next year. While he was there, he walked to the raceway for the waterwheel and looked hard at the design; they could add another wheel to add to the uses of the water power they controlled.

Returning to the village, Nuada stopped at the school and found some paper and set to work making notes and drawing a design for the added waterwheel. He also set to work redesigning the sawmill itself. After making some basic notes, he returned to both work sites and became involved in the building again. At the housing site, he told Mor of the problem at the sawmill and how he planned to change it when they had time. Mor wanted to hear more, but the work cut into the discussion. Nuada told him he would explain more later and hurried off to the shop construction area and Beag.

Beag had the same problem as Mor: He needed more lumber to build forms. When Nuada told him of the problem with the sawmill and how it could be fixed in the future, Beag wanted to hear more also, but problems with the stone workers came up, and he had to hurry off to set things right.

About an hour later, Beag returned and told Nuada that until they could get more wood, he was going to shut down the stonework and shift his crews back to the quarry. Nuada agreed and asked for some of the men to help at the housing construction site. Beag agreed, and soon the work ceased, and men moved back into the village and other jobs. Nuada walked around the shop site and looked at all of the changes before heading back to the housing site and Mor's company.

When Nuada arrived, he sent a runner to the sawmill and told them to divert all of the lumber loads to the housing site. Soon the wagons began to deliver all the new cut lumber, and the pace again picked up, and they moved ahead with the building. Nuada was now able to concentrate all of his time there and not have to worry about being in two places at the same time although he still took the short walk to the quarry site from time to time to escape all of the questions being asked of him at the housing site.

Late in the day he departed the work site and made his way to the forge building. A'Chreag was there with his help and a new man who Nuada did not know. He asked A'Chreag about him and was told that he was from the new group and had worked with metals before. Nuada talked with the man and found his knowledge about working with metals good. Nuada also asked if he had worked with iron before, and the man said yes. Nuada questioned him further and was surprised at his knowledge of it. He told Nuada how it held up better and lasted longer than bronze, and he had made many different things with it before. He also told Nuada of different ways to form the metals that Nuada had never tried before. Nuada invited him to share a beer after work, and the man agreed quickly to the offer.

Nuada soon left the forge for the cooking area and a meeting with Beag and Mor. They had to talk about the problems with the sawmill and Nuada's plan to correct it. Entering the cooking area, Nuada found the teachers sharing more of the wine and stopped to talk with them before the others arrived.

They told Nuada that they would be returning to the forge themselves to make more of the needed glass tomorrow. Nuada told them to be sure and check with A'Chreag first to make sure they did not conflict with each other.

When Nuada looked up, he saw that Mor and Beag had arrived and were in deep discussion with each other. They were followed by the new group leader, and Nuada went to join them. Nuada asked how things were sorting out for his people, and when he said that everything was working well, Nuada again asked his name as Nuada had forgotten it already.

"My name is Aonghas, Nuada. I hope that you will remember it next time we meet."

Nuada said he would, it was just that he had been so busy that it had slipped his mind at the moment. Men and women began to fill the area, and their footsteps showed how tired they were from the work going on in the village. This evening there was no music as they did not have the energy to make any although their conversations were full of happiness, and they seemed to sense the needs of each other now. After Nuada talked with his friends about the sawmill, he retired to his table and his family. The evening ended early, and the village became quiet.

Weeks passed, and Summer was close now. Temperatures rose, and the sky remained clear. Birds and insects, who called out over the din of the construction, were ignored by the people of the village; they had too much to do in the short term.

Beag and his crew returned to the shop building site and were making headway with the work there. Nuada continued to oversee all of the work being done, and he walked many miles every day going from place to place where he was needed.

The teachers had found time to plant their grape vines on the island and told Nuada about it. He was glad that someone had found a use for the island and gave them his blessing for thinking of using it. Amasis had worked hard to make sure that he had enough glass for all the new houses, and Mor made sure it was installed for the new people.

The weaver had made use of the new cloth that Nuada had acquired and had been busy making new clothes for as many people as he could. The material was lighter and good for Summer wear.

A feast was planned to mark the end of Spring and to mark the coming of the new people into the village, but they had almost outgrown the outdoor cooking area, and it was time to expand it. Plans were made to include two more fireplaces for cooking and another oven for bread making. The short wall around the area had to come down to allow for the laying of more stone floor and add to the capacity of the area. Beag was busy with the shop buildings, but he had a good crew that knew what to do, and they began to move ahead with the rebuild. Nuada now found that it was impossible to relax in the cooking area, and he spent his extra hours at the meeting hall even though it was much warmer than he would have liked.

Still Nuada continued his supervision of the construction and from time to time checked in at the forge building to see what was going on there. He was impressed by the amount of copper sheets that were produced by A'Chreag and his crew of two with the help of the new man. Many of the new houses had the new, copper roofs, and it added to the beauty of the design. Soon they would begin to add them to the new shop buildings too.

Several weeks passed, and Beag finished the new shop buildings, but they still needed the finishing touches of lumber on the insides and the new glass windows installed. Beag shifted his crew to the cooking area and to the addition of some new streets with the rubble from the quarry. Other crew members finished the fireplaces on the new houses, and at last the people could see the changes made by all on the projects.

The biggest downfall of the construction was all of the dust found throughout the village. The women worked hard at trying to keep the village clean, but for the most part, it was a losing battle. They needed for it to rain and for the wind to blow a little harder to get ahead.

- SUMMER AND ADDED GROWTH -

Seasons changed, and the feast was held with much success. The changes to the cooking area were completed in a very short time. Beag was thinking that he had too much time on his hands and asked Nuada what he wanted him to do now that the other projects were done. Nuada told him that he could start another protective wall at the entrance to the second valley that would span the creek and add much needed protection. Beag jumped at the thought of more building and said he would look at the site and come up with a plan for it. Nuada also reminded him of the expansion of the sawmill building for more saws. Again he said he would look at the site and come up with a plan for it.

Mor still had several weeks of work at the housing site and then he had to go finish the shop buildings. Nuada did not press him for a finish date and let him work at his own pace. Even with all of the added help from the new people, things were a little behind in Nuada's mind. He knew they could do better and encouraged them where he could.

Raiders were still in the back of Nuada's mind, and he kept patrols out in search of any signs of them.

Nuada's mate was now very large with the new child, and she cut back her workload. Nuada's two sons were growing fast, and he took pride in the way they attempted to help every chance they got. Wolf followed the boys everywhere and stood guard over them.

One day Nuada dropped by the forge and had a chance to talk with the new man there. He presented Nuada with a new sword made of the iron metal. Nuada took it and felt the balance of the blade and then asked of the process of its construction. The man told him it was something that made it stronger. He folded the metal many times and hammered it into the blade now held by

Nuada. Nuada asked if it would make the blade too brittle, and he answered that no, it made it stronger. Nuada thanked the man and asked if he had plans to make more of them. He answered yes and that he would go in search of the ore for it when he had the time. Nuada said he would like to explore with him, and they agreed to meet in the future for such a quest.

After leaving the forge, Nuada made his way to the building site and a chance to talk with Mor again. Nuada found him inside one of the last four houses being built doing finishing work.

"You never stop, do you, my friend."

"Nuada! No, I have too much to do. What is on your mind today?"

"The same as always: how to make the village better."

"When you do that, it always adds to my work load," he said with a laugh.

"Yes. It must seem that way," he said and chuckled.

Mor looked around and then stretched. "We have done a lot in a short time again, but the work goes on."

"I think you need to take a break before you start the work at the new shop buildings, my friend."

"That would be nice, but I do not think I have the time to do so, Nuada."

"Take the time. You have earned it."

He nodded in response and went back to work again. Nuada left him to his details and walked to the quarry. Beag's work crews were still cutting the stone from the ridgeline, and now it was half as high as when they started. He watched them work and noted that they had not found any of the obstructions that they had been worried about when they had started the cut. Nuada thought that by the Fall they would have the roadway through the ridge done, what with the stone required for the new work Beag was starting.

Nuada then made his way to the entrance to the second valley and a look at the possible site of the protection wall there. He looked around and saw three possible sites for where it could be built, but that was up to Beag. He had a feel for the needed base for such a project.

Nuada followed the stream back to the protection wall at the entrance to the first valley and paused outside of it. He had no idea why he had come this way, and he looked about and wondered of the reason. He decided to continue on outside of the valley and see if there was a reason why he had come this way.

He stopped at the site of his battle long ago and looked out to where they were cutting the trees for the sawmill. A wagonload of cut trees passed close by, and he said nothing but just watched them go. Nuada looked skyward and thought that he had not talked with Creatrix in a long time. He needed to do so soon. Nuada turned and walked back into the village, as the day was now starting to grow short.

At the cooking area, Beag joined Nuada, and they talked about the new protection wall into the second valley. He had found a suitable site and would begin building the next day. Beag also asked if Nuada or A'Chreag could make a moveable wall of metal where it crossed over the stream, something that could be raised or lowered. Nuada said he would talk with A'Chreag and come up with something that would work. At that moment, Mor came in wiping sweat from his face and sat heavily at the table.

"I think I will take your suggestion, Nuada, and take a break before starting another project. I have not felt this tired in a long time."

Beag said, "You look it, my friend."

"I think the men feel the same way. A break will do everyone good."

"Beag, what about your men? Do they need a break also?" asked Nuada.

He thought for a minute before answering, "It would not hurt, and I could use the time to sharpen the tools again."

"Then let us call a halt to the work for now and give everyone a chance to rest."

Both men nodded in agreement, and they shared some beer together. Word was passed quickly, and Nuada could already feel the energy return to the men of the village as music again filled the air in the cooking area.

The village took a week's break to rest, and Nuada filled his time working on his dictionary. He had also talked with A'Chreag about the metal wall that Beag wanted, and after A'Chreag talked with Beag about the size and design, he came up with a plan to make it.

The new man at the forge had also made some tools for Beag out of the iron metal. Beag was happy to receive them and thanked the man many times over the following week, as they were superior to the other tools he had.

Noise from the quarry filled the village again as men cut the rock and moved it to the new wall. The energy of the men was high, and the break they had showed in the amount of work they accomplished. It did not take long for Beag to have the base for the new wall laid, and soon the stones began to climb upwards.

Mor also returned to finish the shop buildings, and he made sure that he had enough lumber on hand before Beag started his work as it might stop the flow from the second valley and the sawmill.

Nuada returned to supervise both projects, and his footsteps covered many miles a day again. He had not seen the other teachers in a week and wondered if they had any problems preparing for the coming school year. He made a mental note to check in on them soon. A'Chreag and the other workers of metal were making the gate required by Beag, and Nuada saw little of them too.

One day while Nuada was checking the work at the new shop buildings, he took time to look around at what had been done and was surprised that the weaver and the man who worked in leather had joined their trades to come into the first shop completed. Inside the first shop, they had set up a display of their goods of clothes and shoes made of leather. Bags made of leather also filled the shelves that they had put together; this was truly a store that outsiders would visit when they came. Nuada asked questions of them and then had to return to his job of supervisor of the village projects. As he walked away, he wondered what the other shops might hold in the future. Perhaps A'Chreag could provide tools in the same manner in another shop. Then there were the teachers — they could provide their paper and ink in a similar manner, along with carvings provided from the village people over their long Winter. "We can make a go of this if we work it right," Nuada thought.

All of the new people now had shelter for the coming Winter, and everyone began to relax and not push as hard trying to get things done. But Nuada was worried that it was possible that some other group might need shelter and protection soon too. They had no more houses if that happened.

He shared his thoughts with Mor and Beag and asked them their thoughts on that problem. Mor said the only thing to do was build more houses, and Beag agreed, but they had to finish the projects they were working on before that could happen. Nuada asked if there would be a problem with getting the villagers to do the extra work. The other two said they did not think so once it was explained why the building was necessary. Nuada then suggested that they put off the sawmill expansion until the next Spring and work on more houses instead. This was agreed to, and the plan moved forward to build the houses instead. They decided to add another eight houses for shelter in case more people arrived in the village.

The Summer heat was now at its peak, and the village men took many breaks out of the hot sun. It really did not slow any of the work being done and actually helped the morale of them. Down where they were working on the new wall, many of the men played in the cool waters. It was a good diversion for them.

One day while Nuada was walking between the two projects, he happened to see the teachers on the island and wanted to cross over to see how they were coming with their grapevines. He knew that they looked forward to sharing their wine, as it reminded them of their former homes. He then thought that he would talk with them later in the day and ask them about their vines. He moved on to the new wall to see what, if anything, was needed there. This project was ambitious on the part of Beag. He had not only built a portal gate, but the span over the creek held two tall towers that would support the new metal gate for it. It would allow water to flow freely at all times but would stop any raiders who approached it. Nuada liked the design and the beauty of it. The wall was nearing its completion, and he knew that it would only be a short time before they returned to the housing problem. Mor had finished the shops and was waiting on Beag before they started that work.

The crews at both the sawmill and the tree-cutting sites were still working as fast as they could. The piles of lumber that were finished were stacked alongside the sawmill and waiting for transport to the new sites. Mor kept a close eye on the amount of lumber being readied, and when he thought it was time, he would have the lumber wagons bring it to the new sites. Time was beginning to run short if they were to finish the new houses before the first snowfall.

Nuada was not worried now that Mor had returned to take over as supervisor of the construction site. He would see that they finished on time and as fast as they could.

Nuada was now thinking of the coming schoolwork for him, and he sought out the other teachers for advice on how to present the new studies. They shared many horns of the wine while talking, and Nuada turned the talk one day to how the new vines were coming.

"We will not have a true harvest this year, as the vines need to mature more," Amasis said.

"But they are doing well, and we expect our own wine for next year," piped in Dionysins.

"Perhaps the trader will return early in the Spring, and I can get you more wine until your vines are mature."

Nuada also brought up the shops and got their ideas about trading paper and ink there. They said that they would try it and asked about his thoughts on other things that would also make it a good trading shop.

"Do not limit what you can trade, as anything can be used for barter," Nuada said.

Nuada departed his fellow teachers with a light heart at their responses and walked to the forge to see what was going on there. A'Chreag and his crew were still making sheets of copper for roofs, and they thought they had little time for anything else. A'Chreag himself was making castings for more hinges and latches and between pours talked with Nuada.

"Mor's need for the houses has kept me busy, Nuada. Is there anything I can do for you?"

"No, but I have been thinking about the needs for the new shops, and I was wondering if you had given it any thought. Perhaps over the Winter you could make tools for trade or even jewelry?"

A'Chreag paused and thought for a moment. "I could do those things. Even these house parts have value for trade."

Nuada nodded and thought that even he had not thought of these simple items as trade goods. "If you can think of anything else for the shops, please tell me. We will have a great need for ideas if we are to expand the village."

Nuada watched the work for awhile before returning to the cooking area. As he entered the area, he found that it was almost empty again, and he walked on to the housing site. Mor had four of the new houses framed now, and men swarmed over them getting ready to sheath the outsides. Piles of the cut lumber surrounded each of the houses, and as needed men hauled it to each house. Nuada did not see Mor but knew he was nearby and pushing the men to complete each step needed. He again watched for awhile before moving on to the quarry and the needed cut through the ridgeline.

At the quarry, dust still floated about the whole area, and it took awhile for Nuada's eyes to adjust, so he could actually see the cut of the ridgeline. Here too men worked a feverish pace, and stone moved from where it was ripped from the ridge, down to the bottom, and then to the cutting site. Wagons were loaded with the rubble and hauled out into the village for more street paving. They were now moving that rubble out in front of the village by the stone houses that Beag had built for the teachers. They had a plan as to how the village would expand in that direction, and the street plan was a big part of it.

Nuada saw that some of the cut stone was moving by wagons to the protection wall that Beag was in the finishing stages of. He followed and wanted to see how close Beag was to finishing that project. Nuada was surprised the wagon did not stop at the wall but continued into the second valley. Nuada paused and watched as another wagon of rubble passed, and it too went into the second valley. "What is going on?" he wondered.

Instead of seeking out Beag, Nuada followed the wagons and was taken aback when he found them splitting just inside of the valley. The cut-stone wagon went on to the mill sites, and the other turned and followed the ridgeline to where the cut was being made. Again Nuada paused, undecided as to which wagon to follow. He made up his mind to follow the rubble wagon and see what was going on with it.

Just past the cut line, they were forming a new street that would follow the ridgeline around to where the sheep stable was located. The dust that had partially blocked his view on the other side of the ridge was absent here, and he could see that it would not be long before the cut would be finished. It would be wide enough for one wagon to pass when it was opened for traffic, but he knew that Beag would continue to cut stone from here until it was wide enough for two wagons.

Nuada then turned and walked down to the mill sites to find out what was going on there. Near the sawmill, piles of cut stone sat waiting for the new construction. Nuada looked around but did not see Beag or any of his crew although one of the lift machines sat nearby.

Nuada turned and walked back to the new protection wall. He found Beag working on a set of steps along the backside of the wall.

"I see you are not waiting for Spring to begin work at the sawmill," Nuada called as he approached.

"Nuada! No, I am only moving in the supplies for the Spring work there."

"I see. I have also just come from the quarry cut between the valleys and see a lot of progress there too."

"Yes. We are close to opening it to traffic soon although I will continue to remove the stone needed for our other projects and make it wider."

"I thought as much, my friend."

"I should finish this wall in another two days, and then I will get to rest and drink of our fine beer again," he said with a laugh.

Nuada smiled and then laughed out loud with his friend. They continued to talk as Beag worked, and finally Nuada said he had to return to the village.

As Nuada walked away, he noticed that the temperature had started to drop with the late afternoon sun. "Fall is near," he thought. He followed the stream out to the first valley entrance wall and turned into and through the portal gate and on to the secondary wall and shops there. Just past the shops, the rubble wagons were unloading, forming new streets in the meadow. He slowed his pace and watched as he moved slowly back toward the village. As he neared the village and the new stone houses, his eyes turned toward the crypt of Jan. He stopped and then made his way across to the crypt. Stopping before it, he brushed some dirt from the stones and thought of his friend. "I still miss of you old friend." He stood there for about a half hour and then made his way to the cooking area and the evening meal.

The next morning Nuada lingered at home and spent some time with his family. Iolair was growing quickly, and if Nuada blinked, he would miss the changes happening to the boy. Uilleam now followed Iolair everywhere and was into the ask-questions stage about everything. Nuada's mate was near with their third child, and her moods changed by the hour. Nuada made some of the changes to the valley model map to update the things now complete. He was thinking of moving it to one of the unused shop buildings near the forge and stable. As he sat at the table, he remembered the drawings of Jan's and thought he could move them there too. Slowly he looked around his house that was now filled with many memories and wondered at all of the things that had happened here. Nuada stood and walked to the pantry door that held the image of Wolf and ran his hand across the carving. Wolf saw him do so and came over and rubbed against Nuada's leg. Nuada reached down and scratched his head and then looked over at his children sitting near the fireplace. Iolair was reading to Uilleam a story that he had gotten from Pytheas.

Pleasure filled Nuada's heart, and he reluctantly started for the door and a return to the village needs. Nuada paused on his porch, trying to decide on where to go first. He then set out up the street toward the teachers' houses and the new streets being built in the meadow. As he passed the site where the old wood wall once stood, he saw three wagons with cut stones now unloading across the street from the teachers' houses. Out in the meadow, more of the wagons loaded with rubble were unloading, forming a new street there. "Beag is making more work for himself," he thought. As an empty wagon passed heading back through the village, Nuada fell into step and followed it. It pulled to a stop at the quarry, and Nuada saw that Beag was there now. "He must have finished with the new stone protection wall," Nuada again thought. Nuada walked up to Beag and asked about the wall and then about the stones being hauled to the meadow.

"I am just getting ready for the Spring work so as not to have any delays. Besides we need to finish this cut this year because we will need of it with the new protection wall in place."

Nuada nodded and then looked at the cut through the ridgeline. He could now see into the other valley, and the view stunned him. They were almost ready to finish the roadway through the cut now. However, men still worked high up on the sides of the cut removing rock and making it wider.

Beag looked at the expression on Nuada's face and asked, "Is something wrong, Nuada?"

"No. It is just the completion of an idea of mine, and I am surprised of the result."

Beag stood and stretched. Then he slapped Nuada on the back and said, "You now owe me many beers, my friend." Both men laughed and felt a deep bond between themselves.

Nuada then asked about Mor and if Beag had seen him that morning. Beag said yes, he was still building the houses that Nuada had pushed for. Nuada then said he had to go and see him and left Beag's company.

At the housing site, men were busy starting to set frames for the next four houses. Nuada wandered through the site until he found Mor.

"The days are getting shorter, Mor. Do you think you will finish before the first snows?"

"It will not snow before I finish, Nuada. It would not dare."

Nuada laughed at his response and then said, "Is not the monthly meeting tonight for the consul?"

"Yes. Although I do not know what we will talk of tonight."

"I do. I will praise you for all of the work you have done this year."

Mor looked at Nuada like he was joking and just shook his head. "It is all of these people. It is just like you used to say all the time."

"I know. We must make the feast this year something special for them."

"Nuada? I have been thinking that we should shut down the sawmill for awhile to remove the sawdust and then move the unusable cut wood into the village for firewood."

"A good idea. If we haul the sawdust outside of the valleys, we could also bring back the trimmed limbs from the trees that have been cut outside of the valleys and use them for firewood too."

"I agree. We will have only four or five more weeks to prepare for the coming Winter weather."

"True, and the harvest should start within two weeks also."

Nuada departed Mor's company and returned to the sawmill to tell them to shut down and to start to prepare for the removal of the sawdust. He said that he would arrange for wagons to come and load tomorrow. Nuada returned to the village and made his way to the stable and told them of the work for tomorrow and the need for wagons and horse teams to remove the sawdust and the need to bring in firewood for the houses of the village.

Nuada then returned to the quarry and sought out Beag again. He explained to Beag about the need to slow the quarry work so that the wagons could be used for the removal of the sawdust and the retrieval of the firewood for the village. He agreed, and again after some small talk, Nuada turned and walked back into the village.

Nuada stopped by his house to check in on his mate and children before he again went out into the village. He stopped at the old woodworking building and talked with Amasis about how much sawdust he required for the paper-making process for the Winter. It was finally agreed that two wagonloads would be enough, and then Nuada made his way out onto the meadow in front of the village again.

Already the sun was low in the afternoon sky, and as he watched the new streets being built, he knew that time was running out for all of their projects. Overhead waterfowl called to each other as they passed Nuada; they were starting to fly south again.

A cool breeze wrapped itself around Nuada, and he turned back for the cooking area and the wait for the consul meeting.

He sat at his table and looked about at the nearly empty area. They had been so busy that even daily chores had taken a break for the need to finish everything.

Slowly the women were the first to begin entering the cooking area. Nuada waited and watched until the men began to filter into the area, and the sound of exhausted conversation started to fill the air.

Nuada knew that his family would not be there tonight, and he waited for his friends to enter, and they would share a few beers together. Soon Beag, Mor, Farmer, and the new man, Anoghas, joined Nuada at his table. Everyone was tired, and Nuada decided that their meeting could be held right now so that they could call an early night of it.

It did not take long to go over the points for the meeting, and agreements were completed about the needs of the village. Nuada was going to discuss the new waterwheel for the sawmill but decided that it could wait for another day. The meeting broke up, and Nuada started to walk home to his family just as the sun began to set.

As he approached his house, he saw several of the village women, who were friends of his mate, outside on the porch. As he stepped up on the porch, one of them said that the baby was coming and that he had better hurry inside. Nuada stepped through the door and around the stairs to see that his children were still sitting in front of the fireplace. He made his way upstairs and sought out his mate. She was in their sleeping place and looked in much pain. He talked with her for a few minutes, and then the women told him to leave and return to his other children. He had been through this before and knew that he would sleep little tonight. He gathered the boys' meal and sat them at the table to eat and then began the long wait for his new child.

Sometime in the middle hours of the night, Nuada awoke from a short nap at the table and heard the sound of a crying baby. He looked across at the boys and saw that they were fast asleep along with Wolf. He then turned his attention to the sound from upstairs. He stood and made his way to his sleeping area to check on his mate and new child. The village women who had stayed were just cleaning his mate and new child when they saw him. One of them put her finger to her lips and motioned for him to stay away. He stopped and waited for some information from them. Then one of the women pulled him aside and told him that his mate had a hard time with this child but was doing well. He was told the new baby was a girl and that he could see both in the morning. Nuada reluctantly returned downstairs and fed the fireplace again and waited for the morning light.

- FALL AND A QUIET TIME -

The next week was a busy time at home for Nuada. He never got outside to even check the weather. Finally his mate began to feel better and had started to move about the house. The new baby girl was surprisingly quiet, and the two boys were well-behaved. Nuada continued to do the cooking and kept the house clean.

One day Mor dropped by to see how things were going after he had heard of the new arrival. He told Nuada that the harvest had begun and that the houses were almost finished. He did not see any problems within the village and said that Nuada should continue to remain at home. Nuada's heart sank, as he needed some excuse to get out of the house. He was becoming restless with doing the family rearing; it was not his nature to do this. He had hopes that he would be needed at the school or at some building project. Mor dashed that hope.

After another two days, Nuada's mate noticed his restless nature and sent him out to get away from the house and family. Nuada felt guilty about his needs to get out but gladly did as he was told.

The first place Nuada visited was the school and his friends, the teachers. Pytheas was in the office sorting papers for the first classes.

"Nuada! Good to see you. Are you ready to teach again?"

"More than ready," he replied.

"This year I need you to teach your language to the same children as last year and the first class of the older adults, who now have an understanding of the Greek language. This will help you to teach them your written language. Also the younger children who began last year will be ready for you to teach them too."

"Then I will have three different classes to teach?"

"Yes. Your work will continue to grow every year from now on."

"I had not thought of that happening, but I am ready."

They continued their talks until Dionysins needed to talk with Pytheas. Nuada said his farewells and walked down by the new houses to look at them. His eyes followed every change within the village as he walked. Slowly he circled the site and then down by the quarry site and the new cut through the ridgeline. He walked through the cut and stood just on the other side looking about the second valley. He drew in a deep breath of the cool Fall air before turning again and heading back to the cooking area. He followed the ridgeline and came up by the stable, forge, and shop buildings. He stopped and looked in the last shop building that was still empty, remembering that he wanted to move the model map of the valleys here, along with Jan's drawings. He moved on after seeing what he wanted too. Then he stopped at the meeting hall to see if any of the others were there.

It was truly Fall now, and there were his friends sitting at their table, sharing mugs of beer.

"Is this all you two do now?" Nuada said as he sat down with them.

"It is too cold to sit at the outdoor cooking area now, Nuada. Besides the beer is the perfect temperature now for us to share," replied Beag.

"How is your family, Nuada?" asked Mor.

"Healthy and underfoot already," replied Nuada.

"Then share some of our beer before you have to return to them."

Nuada nodded and then asked about the village and if everything was getting done. Mor replied that he had everything under control and that the harvest would be done soon. They had planned a feast in about four more days to mark the harvest and an end to the Summer work. Nuada said he would be there with his family, as they too needed to get out of the house. Too soon Nuada had to say his farewells and return to the house again.

Nuada returned to his preparations for the classes at the school. He made many copies of his written language alphabet and a simple glossary of common words. When he began to run short of paper, he took the time to go to the old woodworking building to retrieve more, along with the required ink. All of his thoughts were on how to make it easier for his students to grasp the concept of the written language. Nuada's mate was always nearby to help him when he became stuck on a phrase or word. Her strength was returning, and she took up the chore again of the children, trying to keep them from bothering Nuada.

The new man who was working with A'Chreag had ventured out of the valleys to search for the iron-ore rock and had found a suitable deposit. With A'Chreag's help, they had brought enough back to the forge building to start processing it and had already formed many bars to work with in the future. Nuada had wanted to go with him when he went searching , but the schoolwork prevented him from doing so. Although Nuada had never felt that he was giving up one trade for another, it was somewhere in the back of his mind. He missed the simple life of the work at the forge , but Creatrix had other things for him to do.

The day for the feast came, and late that afternoon Nuada gathered his family, and they went to the cooking area to see friends that they had not talked to in many days. As they entered, people of the village stood and cheered them. Nuada looked around and did not understand the reason for this welcome. They waved to the gathering and found their table and sat while music filled the area. All of the consul members came by and talked with the family. Mor sat next to Nuada and asked him what he thought of his village now.

Nuada replied, "It is the same as always, my friend. I never know what to expect from them. They go the extra measure and always surprise me."

"You know that they expect you to speak today and tell them what to expect next year."

"I am not prepared to say anything. What do I tell them?"

"What you always tell me: Be prepared for the unexpected — more people, more building, and the adventure of just living here."

Nuada nodded and said that he thought that Mor should give the speech, as he knew what they wanted to hear better than himself. Mor said no, they wanted Nuada to tell them their future.

Finally Nuada agreed and ran thoughts of what to say through his mind. His mate encouraged him and said that it was his place to give the speech. Even young Iolair supported this notion and pushed his father to talk with the people.

Then just before the meal was to start, Nuada stood, and his red hair stood out as he walked to the front of the crowd to where the band usually played. He was dressed in the fine clothes that he had worn in Alexandria. He turned and faced the gathering, then held up his hands to quiet the throng. He waited for them before starting to speak. It did not take long for silence to enter into the area. They all respected him and what he stood for.

"Welcome, my friends! What a great way to end another season of growth. You have all reached down deep within yourselves to make this another prosperous year. We have been lucky to have our health and no injuries with what you have done. Look around you at the changes you have accomplished this year. You have built more houses than in any previous year; new shops line our inner protection wall that will be used for trade next year, and another protection wall guards the second valley. Streets cover all avenues throughout the village, and more were formed both in the second valley and in the meadow in front of the village. You made the ridge cut into the next valley, which makes it easier for us all to go between the valleys. Next year we will build more houses and do an expansion of the sawmill site, which will include a new waterwheel to power it. We are growing at a fast rate, and it is all because of what you have done when the need arose. Now enough of this speech, and let us return to the music and our meat. Thank you for everything you have done this year."

Much hand clapping and table thumping, along with wild cheers, filled the cooking area as Nuada walked through the throng and back to his table. As Nuada approached his table, his fellow consul members stood and slapped him on the back, and their faces were filled with smiles and praises of well-wishes. Slowly the area settled down, and the meal was served. Nuada's eyes wandered over the crowd of his people, and from time to time he would see a face he knew, and he nodded to them. As the afternoon wore on, people would drop by his table and pass small talk with him. He was open and friendly to them all. Then as the sun began to set, Nuada rose and, with his family, returned home to some well-earned peace.

After the children had gone to bed, Nuada's mate snuggled close to him and told him how proud of him she was. Shortly they too retired to their sleeping area.

The next morning Nuada awoke late and lay under his sleeping covers and let his mind wander back to the afternoon before. Finally he got up and dressed and then made his way downstairs to his table. He started to return to working on his teaching materials but stopped and thought he had better take another walk around the village first. He told his mate that he was going for a walk and then set out for the streets and another look around.

Although the weather remained mild, Nuada knew it would not last much longer. He set out for the new shops and the inner protection wall. As he followed the street out, he passed the stone houses that Beag had built and admired their appearance. Across the street from them, piles of cut stone awaited the coming Spring to build more of these houses. He glanced out into the meadow, and his eyes followed the new streets where more houses would follow. He continued on until he arrived at the new shops, and again he looked up their street, admiring the paved walkways that bordered the street and shops. He glanced up at the protection wall and saw that it was empty of guards and wondered of the reason. He moved on to the first protection wall. Here three guards still watched out over the entrance into the first valley. Nuada waved to them and then crossed through the portal gate and turned right, back toward the second valley. He followed the stream that flowed through both valleys and looked out at the lake and his old island home. "I wonder how the new vines are doing out there?" he said out loud. On he walked until he found himself at the new protection wall into the second valley. He paused again, looking up at the massive towers that Beag had built on the wall to hoist the metal gate that A'Chreag and his crew had made for the stream portal. Then without pause, he made his way through and on down to the sawmill site and its companion the grain mill. Nuada was again looking at piles of cut stone that would be used for the sawmill expansion in the Spring. He climbed up on the raceway wall and watched the waterwheel turning slowly in the water that flowed below. Then he turned and made his way back and turned toward the new ridgeline cut and its road between the two valleys. Even here more cut stone greeted him, and he did not pause but made his way on to the houses. There he paused again. He studied the area and knew that ten more houses would fill the last of the sites here. He listened to the village sounds and knew that many were helping in the last stages of the harvest. They would have enough food again this year but would have to expand the crop fields next year if any more people arrived. His footsteps then moved on to the school, and he entered to see his fellow teachers. All four were in the office at the rear of the school, sitting and talking with each other. They held cups of the wine that Nuada had gotten for them from the trader this year. As Nuada entered the office, they offered Nuada a cup, and he sat and joined them and their discussions. They had planned to reopen the school in another week and a half, and now it looked like it would. When asked if he was ready, Nuada said he was. They continued to talk for about two more hours, and then Nuada said he had to leave, as he had other things to do. After leaving the teachers, Nuada crossed through the cooking area, where he found it empty, and made his way to the meeting hall. Inside Mor, Beag, Farmer, and Anoghas were sitting together drinking their beer. Nuada joined them, and as he sat, they asked if he would like a beer. He said no, as he had been drinking wine with the teachers and it did not mix well together. Nuada asked if they were enjoying their time away from construction work, and they all just laughed at him. Nuada responded that he found the time well-used getting ready for teaching. Mor said he was sorry that Nuada could not find the time to relax himself. Nuada responded that he did and that just this morning he had walked around both valleys and looked at everything that had been done again. It filled his heart with joy, just seeing everything. After another two hours, Nuada felt his stomach growl and knew he had to return home to his family. He said his farewells and went home.

Home life was returning to normal for Nuada's family. Nuada remained close to home over the following week, preparing for the return to school. It must have rubbed off on Iolair, as he too returned to his studies even before the school reopened.

The weather remained crisp, and they had a few rain showers during the nighttime hours. The village hunters had been out hunting and had good success; dressed deer now hung in the storage area of the old woodworking building. All of the fruit trees had a good bounty this year, and it had been harvested and stored too. The grain mill was now working nonstop making flour for the village. The sawmill was also back cutting lumber while the weather held good, but the rest of the village people were now taking a long needed rest from all of the work they had done.

Nuada had arranged with A'Chreag's help to move the model map and Jan's drawings to the empty shop building near the stable. Nuada had asked A'Chreag to build him two chests for the storage of the pelts and paper items he was also going to be moving there. The chests were to be made of bronze and lined with cedar to protect the items. Nuada then cleaned his house of his unnecessary items and stored them with the other things in that shop building too. In the few remaining days before the school was to restart, Nuada found he had time on his hands and looked for something else to do.

Nuada's mate watched her husband start to become bored with the free time and sent him off to the meeting hall and his friends, as she knew that soon he would not have any free time.

At the meeting hall, Nuada sat with his friends, and slowly ideas began to form in his mind again about what the village would need soon. They talked about the need for some kind of garbage service and where to dispose of it. Sanitation was another topic and how to remove it from the village. Fire was a dreaded thing, and they looked through Nuada's notes from Alexandria about firefighting machines that would help the village. The subject of some kind of building to be used as a hospital was another thing they talked about but decided it could wait until the village grew some more. Then there were the lift machines that they needed more of, and finally it was decided to build two more. A lot of beer was gone through during the discussions, but it had little effect on how they thought.

It was late when Nuada returned home that night, and he sat at the table making written notes about the discussions long after the rest of his family had gone to sleep. His mind raced with what the village needed, and at long last, he fell asleep at the table.

Nuada's mind awoke in the land of Creatrix. The white fog surrounded his vision, and through it came the voice of Creatrix.

"Nuada! Awaken and listen to my voice. You have gone beyond all that was expected of you. Your people have pleased me, and I watch to see what they will do for you next. I sent you into this land to learn and to teach; you have done both. Now you work to improve what you have made. I had thought to bring you into my world , but you will stay where you are and grow some more. I will be watching. Now return and continue sleeping."

It was still the middle hours of the night, and he could not go back to sleep. He glanced down at his notes and then let his mind wander back to the words of Creatrix. After a while, he began to feel the chill of the house and added wood to the fireplace. Soon the warmth began to wrap around him again, and his thoughts again returned to the words of his creator.

With the early morning light, Nuada stood and stretched. He then changed his clothes and prepared for another day. The school would reopen tomorrow, but he was now ready and anxious to begin. Wolf came down the stairs and wanted to be let out. Nuada opened the door and walked out onto the porch. Wolf ran off to do his business, and Nuada took in a deep breath of the cool, morning air to clear his mind of the fog of sleep. He looked about at his village and was pleased with what he saw. His mind raced around the village and everything that he knew about it. Then he reflected back to what had been there before. "I have seen the changes, and I have a hard time to accept what we have made of it," he thought. He shook his head and called Wolf back to the house, and they entered and again sat at the table.

About an hour later, his family came down to join him, and they ate a comfortable meal before Nuada had thoughts of going for a walk again. Soon Nuada walked to the school and the company of Pytheas. Nuada found him again in the office, and he sat, and they talked about the school and students. Nuada did not mention his waking dream with Creatrix to Pytheas. He would share that dream with Mor only, as he understood Nuada's connection with the creator. Two hours later Nuada made his way to the forge building to talk with A'Chreag before he sought out Mor's company.

As usual A'Chreag was preparing to do some casting again; this time it was tools and some parts for the housing projects of the next Spring. Nuada asked if he needed some help, and he said no, it was just a make work thing today. They talked as he worked, and soon it was close to midday. Nuada said his farewells and made for the meeting hall and his other friends.

Nuada joined his usual friends, and small talk followed. During the conversation, Mor got up to get another beer, and Nuada followed him.

"Mor, my friend. Last night I had a talk with Creatrix. He was very pleased with our development and wants us to continue as we have been."

"It has been a long time since you last talked with him, has it not?"

"Yes. Too long. But our results have made it so."

"Then I am pleased too. Did he say what we are to do now?"

"No. Just that we are to continue as we have been."

Mor pulled Nuada a beer and handed it to him. "Then that is what we will do."

They returned to the table, and no more mention of Creatrix was said. Later in the afternoon, Nuada went home to his family and continued to prepare for school the next morning.

Nuada awoke early and took Wolf for his morning run. He noticed that the sky was overcast today and wondered if the weather was going to change. The wind was light but held no smell of moisture. Nuada shook his head and called Wolf back, and he went in to wait for his morning meal and his son to get ready for his classes.

When it was time, Nuada and Iolair walked to the school. Wolf remained behind to watch over Uilleam and keep Nuada's mate and daughter company. At the school, Pytheas was standing outside, as was his routine when the school was open. He greeted each and every child as they entered. The other three teachers were already in their classrooms waiting for their students and another year of study to begin.

Nuada greeted Pytheas, and they talked for a short time before the classes were to begin. Nuada had one early class with the older children and another later in the morning with some of the adults of the village. His last class was just after the midday with the youngest of the children from last year. Nuada's classroom was near the entry door this year, and he waited there for his students to finish coming in and sitting down before he began. He made a list of their names as they sat and then handed out his alphabet and glossary to the students. Then he began to explain how the language was made and its uses.

Throughout the day, his classes were much the same, and he added humor to the lessons to make them stick in the minds of the students. After his last class, Nuada felt drained of all of his energy but was upbeat about the results. His first day this year was well accepted by all.

After saying good-bye to Pytheas, Nuada walked slowly to the meeting hall. Iolair had already departed for home, and Nuada felt he needed some time to relax before returning home to his family.

Nuada walked into the hall and sat heavily and then set his stack of papers on the table. He only glanced at all of the papers and then got up to retrieve a beer. Beag was the only member of the consul here now, and he saw how tired Nuada looked and left him alone with his thoughts.

After his second beer, Nuada began to feel better, and he retrieved his papers and departed for home and his family. Beag watched him go and never said a word to him.

The weeks passed quickly now for Nuada, and he became familiar with his new routine. For the people of the village who took his classes, understanding came easily. Soon Nuada's written language would become an everyday thing for them, just as the numbers being taught by the other teachers had found use with the people of the village. The world history also helped them to understand where they belonged in the world and where their future would take them.

At long last Winter began to rear its head, and the weather changed with the season. The temperatures dropped dramatically, and light snow was now an everyday occurrence.

Nuada watched as Iolair's mind expanded, and he took in everything that the teachers could teach him. Pride filled Nuada's heart with the growth of Iolair. "Someday, he will lead these people," he thought. Then he realized that what the future held for Iolair may not be in this village.

- WINTER AND PEACE -

Winter had arrived. Mor had started the construction of the new water-wheel in the old woodworking building, and A'Chreag was making the center hub and race bearings for it. Farmer had started a new project for the Spring by planting apple trees and storing them inside of the same building; he spent many hours in watering and caring for the trees that would be planted around the village. Beag spent most of his hours at the meeting hall tasting the beer. Nuada found little time for anything except the teaching of his students. As for the rest of the village people, they had hunkered down for the Winter weather and rarely went out in the snowy weather. Occasionally crews were sent to clear the streets of the snow, but it was only a make-work thing for them.

At the monthly meeting of the consul while they were talking about the coming work at the sawmill expansion, it came up that they would need a drying shed for all the cut lumber, and it was to be included in the expansion. Mor said that he would build four more houses near the sawmill for the men and their families who were working at that site. Nuada had brought his notes from earlier in the Fall, and they went over them about the needs of the village that needed to be addressed. Still nothing was finalized on those items. Nothing new was planned except for the things that they had talked about in the Fall. The meeting broke up early, and after a few beers, everyone went home.

Early the next morning while Nuada was dressing, he could hear the wind blowing through the eaves. Going downstairs he looked out through the new window and could tell that a new storm was blowing into the valleys. Wolf stirred from his sleeping place and nudged Nuada to let him out. Opening the door Nuada could smell the moisture in the air and waited for Wolf's return.

The early light showed that the clouds had started to fold upon each other and cast an even darker shadow on the mountainside that protected the eastern side of the valleys. Wolf came running back and wanted inside even as Nuada wanted to return inside. He could feel the old wound start to tighten in his side and wondered if this was a warning as to how severe this storm would be.

As Nuada rounded the stairs, his family was waiting at the table, and he told them that a heavy storm was coming today. "Iolair, you will remain home today. I will make sure that the school will remain closed and that all are safe. I like not the feel of this weather."

After eating a light meal, Nuada set out for the school. He took his walking staff that he had used after his battle wound and hurried toward the school. The pain in his side continued to grow more severe. Before he reached the school, sleet started to blow in sideways. It pelted his face and caused him to turn his face to the side as it continued to increase in intensity. The wind now howled out of the north and was increasing in strength too.

At the school all four teachers stood huddled inside the front door. As Nuada entered, he told them that there would be no school today or possibly for several days with this storm coming. He told them to return to their houses and wait for him to tell them when it would be safe for them to return to the school. They quickly gathered their papers and other items that they would need and departed the school. Nuada took a deep breath and again stepped out into the quickly changing weather.

He now faced directly into the storm front and raised his hand to protect his eyes from the sleet that blew directly at him. He was almost home when he thought to check the meeting hall to make sure that no one was there and would be caught in the storm.

He struggled against the wind and finally made it to the meeting hall. Inside it was almost empty, but there sat Beag at his table.

"You must return home, my friend. The storm is upon us now and will only get worse," Nuada said.

Beag nodded and then said, "Perhaps I shall have one more beer first."

Nuada shook his head and said, "There is no time, Beag. You will be trapped here with no food for many days if you do not leave now. I will walk with you to your house."

Beag agreed with Nuada, and the pair set out for Beag's house. They struggled against the wind and blowing snow that had settled on the village. At times they could not see the next house in front of them. Beag began to shiver from the cold blasts, as he was not prepared for this kind of storm. At last they made it to Beag's door, and Nuada said his farewells quickly and turned toward his own house. The wind pushed him along the street as he struggled to keep upright.

Nuada's limp grew in intensity as he made his way home. He was glad he had thought to bring his walking staff with him. Although he was dressed for this kind of weather, the cold from the storm still cut through to his skin. As he reached his own porch, it was all he could do to step up on the riser and make his way inside.

Inside he pushed with his back to close the door, as the wind was now that strong. He crossed around from behind the stairs and began to slowly peel the layers of clothes that he had on. He kept the staff to help him walk, and he at last made it to the fireplace, where he sought out the heat to ease the pain in his side.

Nuada's mate showed concern for her husband and asked if he wanted some of the potion to ease the pain he felt. Nuada said not yet, as he needed the heat first. Slowly the pain began to recede, but he still felt the stiffness of the old wound. "I must be getting old," he thought. At last he felt better and sat at the table, then he turned to look at his sons. Both had gone back to sleep in front of the fireplace with Wolf watching over them.

Nuada's mate sat down at the table holding their daughter and asked if there was anything she could do for him. Worry still showed on her face at Nuada's reaction to the weather. He shook his head and said that it would only take time to ease the pain.

Several hours later Nuada got up to stretch and again walked to the window. As he looked through it, it seemed that the day had turned to night already. He could barely see across the street, and his view was interrupted by the snow that blew across his sight.

Needing something to do, he went to the pantry and retrieved his dictionary. He sat at the table and began to add words to the long list. Hours passed, and his concentration on it took the thought of the pain away. After midday his children began to stir, and he set aside the work and spent time with them.

Uilleam was now in the question-everything phase, and Nuada tried to answer all of his questions. Iolair helped when he could, and Nuada's mate smiled at her children and their interaction with each other. She was glad that Nuada had taken it upon himself to become a teacher, as it helped him become a stronger parent. Late in the day they shared their evening meal and went to bed early.

Sometime during the middle of the night, the stiffness returned to Nuada, and he got up and went downstairs. He added wood to the fireplace and sat at the table hoping that the stiffness would pass. Too soon the boredom entered his mind, and he got up to find something to do. He found his old woodworking tools, retrieved a piece of wood, and began to carve.

Outside the weather had not changed. Snow banked up against houses and filled the streets. Drifts as high as a man formed and then blew with the wind in all directions.

With the coming of morning, Nuada's mate came downstairs and found him asleep at the table. In front of him was a carving of a buck deer of much detail. She picked it up carefully to look at it closer, and Nuada began to stir from his sleep. Quickly she set it down again and picked up a skin robe and placed it across his shoulders. "I had fears that you would not sleep well, last night," she said to him.

Nuada rubbed the sleep from his eyes and then turned to stand. His left leg felt asleep, and he found he could not stand without help. He reached for his staff, and it tumbled to the floor. He tried to reach it but fell from his seat and lay on the floor.

"Nuada! Are you hurt?" his mate called out.

"The old wound burns! Make me some of the potion."

Nuada dragged himself into a sitting position on the floor and waited for the pain to pass. Nuada's mate quickly set her pot on the fireplace swing arm and then attempted to help Nuada back to a more comfortable position.

"It is no use. I cannot move," he said with tears in his eyes.

She then brought him some pillows to support his back and went back to the pantry for the root and its leaves to place in the pot. Nuada drew deep breaths with every spasm in his side. The pain was not going away.

About twenty minutes later, the potion came to a boil, and Nuada's mate poured it into a mug for him. He could smell the brew and waited for it to cool a little before he attempted to drink it. Slowly he sipped at the potion until finally it was empty. He waited for the next spasm to hit, and he noticed that it was not as severe. A half hour later he was able to return to the table and his seat there. He was still not able to stand without the help of his staff.

"Wife, I do not understand of this. Why do I feel of the old wound like this?"

"Perhaps it is another test from Creatrix."

"No. He would not do it this way."

The rest of the morning Nuada remained at the table. His body remained stiff and sore until he made up his mind to stand and walk about the room. Using his staff, he took faltering steps with a heavy limp in his left leg. Slowly his feet began to allow him to walk to the window at the front of the house, where he looked at the weather again. The sky remained dark, and snow continued to blow across his vision.

His mind, which had been fogged by the pain, started to function again. He was worried about his people and how they were faring in this weather. His thoughts raced with all their problems, but he was unable to help them the way he was. "I cannot even help myself. I must wait and see what will happen," he thought. He returned to the table and the warmth of the fire. That night Nuada slept downstairs by himself, and no dreams came.

The next morning Nuada awoke without any pain, but the stiffness continued. He slowly dressed with the help of the staff. Then he again walked to the front window to look out at the storm. It was still there. Wind continued to blow the snow sideways, and what Nuada could see looked deeper than ever. He wondered, "How many days will this keep up?"

Returning to the rear of the house, he added more wood to the fireplace and sat heavily at the table. He looked around the empty room and waited for the other members of the family to awake. Iolair was the first to come downstairs, followed by Wolf.

"Father, has the storm stopped?" he asked.

"No, son. It is still as strong as ever. You will have no school again today."

"Are you feeling better, Father?"

"A little. I have no pain like yesterday, but the stiffness continues."

"Can I help you in anyway?"

"No, but continue your studies. You will need of them in the future."

Iolair did as he was told and settled at the table with many papers from the school classes. Soon Nuada's mate and other two children joined them, and she made a warming meal for them that morning.

After eating Nuada felt a warmth inside him from the fine meal she had prepared. He began to doze over the new dictionary and fought to stay awake, but the exhaustion from yesterday's exertions caught up with him, and he slept. At midday he awoke and looked around, not knowing where he was. When he was fully awake, he stood and found only a mild stiffness in his side. That leg gave him no problem, but he still took his staff and walked to the window again.

The wind had dropped to a light breeze, but the snow still came down. He tried to look up the street and failed at the attempt. Around the glass window ice had formed into many patterns, and he wondered of the cause. He then turned and made his way back to his family and their comfort.

Iolair had some questions about the many countries that his teacher had told him of. Nuada was at a loss to answer these questions but told his son to write them down for his teacher. He respected his father and did as he was told. Nuada could only smile at the things that must be going on inside his son's head. Late in the afternoon their talk turned to languages. Iolair wanted to know about other languages that these people spoke and wrote about from their countries. Nuada tried to explain that he knew nothing about the people, only that he could speak and write their languages. Then Iolair said, "Tell me the words that I might understand of them."

Nuada did try to teach him two more languages, and they talked about them until the evening meal came. After eating Nuada returned to the window for a last look before bed. Nothing had changed since midday. That night he slept upstairs with his mate.

Three more days of bad weather blanketed the valleys, but with each day Nuada began to feel better about himself. Nuada's mate watched over him, and while he worked on his dictionary, she began to sew a couple of sheep pelts together. He did ask her about it, and she said it was a surprise.

On the morning that the weather broke, Nuada knew that he was still not ready to venture outside. He stood at the window and wondered about his people and if any damage had been done to the village. Nuada placed his hand on the frosted glass and quickly drew it away. The cold still lingered although the wind had dropped to nothing. He returned to his papers and waited for something to happen.

Around midday Nuada could hear the men of the village out clearing the streets. Horses complained about having to pull the wagons that were used to haul away the snow. Nuada returned to the window, still using his staff to help him walk, to watch and see if anyone would come to his house. He continued to watch for about an hour and then returned to the table.

"Nuada? I have something for you," his mate said.

"What is it?"

"It is a warming support for your old wound," she said as she held it out to him.

The sheep pelts that she had been sewing together greeted Nuada, and he looked at it and nodded at its usefulness. "This will help me although I do not know of the cause for my pain from the old wound."

"Creatrix will provide you with the answer when he is ready."

Nuada saw the wisdom of her answer and did not comment further. Suddenly a knock at their door echoed through the house. Nuada started to rise to go answer it, but his mate told him she would see who it was.

She opened the door and saw Mor and Beag standing there. She ushered them inside and out of the cold. They quickly made for the fireplace and the heat that filled the house.

"Nuada, we have been cleaning the streets and wondered of you. Can you help?" asked Mor.

"No, my friends. I have been ill from my old wound, and I do not think it would be wise to venture outside yet."

"How? I thought it was only a scar now," asked Beag.

"I know not of the reason, but it caused me to fall and have great pain. I had to use my walking staff just to get around the house for two days."

Both men looked at each other, and then Mor said, "Can we do anything for you, Nuada?"

"If you see Pytheas, I would like to ask of him to check of it for me."

Mor said he would tell Pytheas about Nuada's request, and the pair of men returned to the work on the streets after Nuada said he would like their company and to share a few beers at the end of the day. They both agreed and smiled at their friend before leaving.

Nuada felt more relaxed now that he had talked with his friends. The rest of the afternoon was filled with his sons and teaching them words and phrases of their language. Even Uilleam at his age was picking up the words and how to use them.

Before the sun set, Beag and Mor returned and had a long talk with Nuada while they shared many beers. They had cleared all of the main streets in the village, but the new cut through the ridge was blocked with high snow drifts. Beag also said that the new protection wall gate portal was also blocked and that they had no way to check on those living in the second valley. Many trees had also fallen, and it would take many days to correct the damage that they had found. Mor said that he had talked with Pytheas, and he said he would come by tomorrow.

It was dark when the pair decided to leave even though Nuada's mate had invited them to stay for the evening meal. They declined and wished Nuada well. He walked them to the door with the help of his walking staff and in his mind wished that they had stayed for their meal and talked more. He missed their company.

The next morning Nuada was up and about at his usual time and was standing on the porch after letting Wolf go for his morning run when Pytheas came by.

"I see you are bored with this weather also, my friend," Nuada said.

"Yes. I am more than ready to return to teaching. What is this I hear about you and some problem with your old wound?"

Nuada called Wolf, and they retuned inside to the warmth of the fire. Then Nuada recalled the story of how he was out in the storm after he had them go home from the school.

"From the time I returned home, the old wound began to tighten in my side, and during the night it awoke me from my sleep. I came downstairs and began to carve at the table until I fell asleep there. The next morning my left leg was asleep, and the pain was as if I had just been wounded that day. When I tried to stand, my leg would not support me, and I fell, unable to move. I remained in pain for two days even after taking the potion to relieve the pain. Slowly I was able to walk again with the help of my walking staff. Do you know of any reason why my old wound would return in this manner?"

Pytheas asked to examine the wound site and afterwards could not find any reason why it reacted in the manner it did. "Perhaps it was just a reaction to the cold. You should take care when the weather turns cold like this."

Nuada said he would, but he had to help the people of the village too. There would be times when he could not just stay inside and avoid the weather.

"Then find of a way to protect your old wound and keep heat on it when you can," he replied.

Nuada showed Pytheas the wrap of sheep pelts that his mate had made for him and asked if he thought it would do any good.

"It should work but use caution in the future, Nuada. Avoid the weather when you can and keep warm."

The conversation then turned to the school and its reopening. Pytheas said he had talked with Mor, and he thought that the streets should be clear in about two more days. Pytheas then planned to reopen the school. Nuada said he would be there, and soon Pytheas departed for his own house.

After Pytheas had left, Nuada stood looking out the window, watching wagonload after wagonload pass by his house with heavy loads of snow from the village. "I wish I could help them," he thought.

Finally he returned to the table and wondered what to do with himself. His family left him to his thoughts and kept quiet. Then he decided to return to his carving and retrieved another piece of wood and started to carve again. Just before his evening meal, he cleaned up the table and put his tools and the form he had been working on away. When his mate asked about the subject of the new carving, Nuada said it was Pytheas.

"And why do you honor him in this way?" she asked.

"Because he is my friend," was Nuada's answer.

The evening wore on, and they finally went to bed. It ended another day, and Nuada looked forward to the next.

In the early-morning light, clouds still blanketed the valleys although it was slightly warmer. Nuada wrapped his cloak tightly around his shoulders as he again looked out through the window of his house. The wind had died totally, and now Nuada could look up and down the street without obstruction. Some of the early work crews were up and about cleaning the streets again.

Nuada returned to his table and sat heavily as he thought about all of the things that had gone wrong during the storm. "How can we make the second valley such that we can get to them in an emergency?" he wondered. The more he thought about it, the solution seemed further away.

It was not until later in the morning that he seemed to hit upon an answer. "If we tunnel through from the safety cave on the ridge, we will have access to them." It was the best solution to the problem he could come up with.

He had returned to the carving of Pytheas, and now it was nearing completion. With that project that he had used to take his mind off the stiffness in his side almost finished, he cleaned up the table and waited for some of his friends to return and talk to him again. It was not until late in the afternoon that Mor and Beag dropped by to see how Nuada was feeling and to give him an update on the snow removal and damage report.

Nuada greeted them at the door, and when they had settled at the table with a beer in hand, Nuada told of his thoughts about making a tunnel through to the other valley from the safety cave on the ridge. Beag quickly agreed, but Mor had doubts about it being blocked too by the snow. Nuada told them that he could see no other solution to the problem.

Mor then told Nuada that they had finally cleared the cut into the second valley, but it would take another day to clear the road to the mill site. As for the new protection wall, it remained blocked, and they had only gotten to it by snowshoes and had raised the new gate over the stream to prevent ice from causing a dam effect there.

"I hope that the men at the mill site had enough sense to block the raceway and allow the ice to run over the spillway there. Otherwise we will have to repair the mill wheel too."

Nuada nodded at Mor's comment and then asked about damages to the village houses.

"We have found nothing yet although a tree missed a house by only a few feet."

Beag added that two babies had been born during the storm, and everyone was doing fine. They talked on for about two more hours and then departed for their evening meal. Nuada sat and reflected on everything going on and then settled back after eating and watched his boys read to each other. Wolf was nearby as always to watch them, and slowly his eyes closed. Nuada felt the tiredness drop over him too, and soon the family went to bed.

Three more days passed until Pytheas dropped by to tell Nuada that the school would reopen the next day. Nuada said he was ready to return, as he was getting cabin fever staying at home. After midday Nuada took a walk to the meeting hall; this was his first venture outside since the storm had come upon the valleys. The building was almost empty, and Nuada sat and waited for his friends to arrive, as he knew that they would. Late in the afternoon Beag and Mor, along with Farmer and Anoghas, came through the door and saw Nuada sitting there. They all pulled some beers and sat with him.

"It is good to see you out of your house, Nuada," said Mor.

"How is your old wound today? I see you still use your walking staff."

"It is still there. I feel of its stiffness, and the staff helps."

The village people had pulled together and removed the snow from all the streets, including from the new protection wall into the second valley. The people who lived within the second valley were safe, and they had pulled together to protect the mills and the dam. No damage was found, and life began to return to normal.

Nuada returned to his teaching when the school reopened. Surprisingly it seemed that more people now came to the school to learn. All of the teachers commented on how busy they were, but they were happy with the results.

The storm that had hit the valleys was the heaviest of the Winter season, and from then on until the Spring, the snows were light and manageable. Nuada never returned to his full strength again, and he never understood why.

Spring was again drawing close, and the village people were more than ready for the season change. At the last consul meeting before the Winter ended, last-minute changes to projects were settled, and now all they needed was for the weather to follow its normal course and allow the village people to move forward. Nuada looked forward to the changes coming to the valleys, and for himself he knew that the school year was fast approaching its end. He would have to find something to do, and the thought of his long walks gave him pleasure. The coming warmth of the season was an added bonus for Nuada, as he felt it would end all of the discomfort from his old wound.

Nuada now was able to return to his old forge and the company of A'Chreag again, but Nuada never tried his hand at forming metals there, as it was now A'Chreag's forge. They talked for many hours about the needs of the village and what projects were going forward with new metal items. A'Chreag had cast the new center hub for the new waterwheel, and the bearing races were almost ready to cast. Many new hinges and latches were made over the Winter getting ready for the construction to come. A'Chreag had also found time to make some jewelry for the new shop in front of the village, along with some tools and weapons to barter with. A new plow was built for the additional crop fields that the village would need this year.

- SPRING AND CONSTRUCTION -

One morning as Nuada was going to the school, he noticed that the village men had gathered at the outdoor cooking area. Mor was standing at the front of the crowd giving orders, as was his normal thing. Construction was about to start, and the men were sent to where they would be needed. Beag was already at the piles of cut stone across from the teachers' houses and awaited a crew to begin the work there. Nuada continued on to the school and found it beginning to fill with the young students. Pytheas was at his usual place near the entry and greeted Nuada.

"Pytheas, it looks like we are to lose our older students today and probably for the rest of the year. They are starting the new construction today."

"It was expected. We have maybe another week with the young ones before they help with the planting of the crops."

Nuada nodded and entered his classroom. He felt distracted by the thought of the work beginning outside today, but he settled down and began the classes for the children.

After Nuada's last class just after midday, he walked out to the site where Beag was building the new stone houses across from the teachers' houses. Beag was not there. Nuada was told that he had gone to the sawmill site to prepare it for the new work. Nuada looked around and saw that some of the foundations for the houses were started. Nuada turned and walked back into the village and made for the housing site, where Mor would be working. He took his time, as he was still using the walking staff. His eyes roamed around the village, and he could still see some of the Winter damage from the falling trees. On he walked until he rounded the last of the houses built last year and came to the site where the new houses were starting to be framed.

Nuada sat upon a pile of lumber and crossed his hands atop the brass head of his walking staff. He watched as the men worked and felt left out of everything now being done. Mor came around one of the framed forms and saw Nuada sitting and called a greeting to him. Nuada waved and called back. Mor came over, and they had a simple talk about the things being done there at that site. Finally Mor had to return to the work, and Nuada stood and walked toward the cut between the valleys. He noticed that snow still lay in the shadows and wondered when it would melt.

At the quarry site, a few men worked at removing stone from the high banks of the cut. Nuada paused and then walked on through to the second valley. He stopped short of entering the valley and let his gaze wander around to the changes he could see. The sheep stable was blocked from the view there, and he turned his head toward the mill sites. The massive dam was the backdrop for the mills , but again Nuada could see little of what was going on there. He thought about going on down to the mills but then thought better of it; he was not ready yet to venture that far. He turned and went back toward the village.

He passed the school again and turned toward home. Walking up the street, his eyes followed a wagon now making its way toward the new stone houses. He thought about following it, but again he did not feel up to making the short walk and turned toward his house.

He stepped up onto the porch and sat in the sunshine. He was tired and had no energy to do anything else. The cool Spring air soon drove him inside, and he sat before the fireplace and waited for his family to come home. He reached down and rubbed at his old wound and still wondered at his condition. "I need to speak with Creatrix about this, as no one else seems to know anything about it," he thought.

Needing something to do, Nuada looked through his papers and made notes about changes that he would make soon. But his mind was not in it, and he let his mind wander about the village and the things being done.

Soon Iolair and Uilleam came home, and sounds filled the empty house. Nuada watched them and noticed how tall Iolair was getting. "Soon, he will be as tall as me," Nuada thought.

Shortly Nuada's mate entered the house and began preparing the evening meal. She asked about his day and how he was feeling between steps for the meal. Nuada told her of the lack of energy and said that he had started a walk about the valleys but stopped short when he began to feel worn out. She reassured him that it would take time to find the needed rest that his body needed and that only by moving about would it come. Nuada nodded, but in the back of his mind, he was not so sure.

That night Nuada again revisited with Creatrix. He awoke in the white fog of Creatrix's domain and called out to him.

"Creatrix, I have concerns of myself. Talk to me about it."

"Nuada. It is I, Jan. What questions do you have?"

"Jan! I have no energy, and the old wound in my side still bothers me. Is it of Creatrix's making?"

"It is. It is time for you to let others do what you have done for them. When they learn of this lesson, then you will be returned to as before. Not until then will it happen."

Nuada awoke in a cold sweat; his fears were doubled by his doubts. It was near dawn, so he dressed and went downstairs. He prodded the fire and was soon comfortable with the response of the heat from it. He sat at the table and waited for the other members of his family to come down and join him. His mind wandered back to the words of Jan, and he knew he could do nothing until Creatrix was ready to release him from the grip of his old wound.

The next afternoon Nuada fought his fears and the tightness in his side and walked to the mill sites. The weather was pleasant today, and Nuada was enjoying himself as he reached the site. New stone walls, chest high, greeted him, and as he looked around, Beag came around a corner and greeted Nuada.

"What think you, my friend?"

"You and your crew work so fast that if I blink, it appears from nothing."

Beag looked around and said, "Then we have done well. How are you feeling?"

"I have not changed. The tightness remains, and I have no energy to do but what is needed."

"Is there nothing that can be done for it?"

"Nothing. I sought help from the creator last night and was told that he was the cause of it. I have to wait until he thinks I am ready for a change."

Beag nodded and then asked if Nuada would like him to drop by this evening and share of some beer. Nuada said yes, he would enjoy his company. Nuada waited until Beag returned to work and then walked back to the village.

This time Nuada walked toward the second valley protection wall and through the portal gate. He stopped and turned to look at the portal through which the stream ran. The waters were almost whitecapped as they tore downstream. Broken branches flowed in the turbulence, catching on anything nearby. Ice still reamed the shoreline and showed that Spring was still not in its full measure.

Nuada continued on toward the village. As he went past the caves, he could see the crop meadow — and beyond the island in the lake. Some waterfowl flew overhead and called as they prepared to land in the lake. Nuada paused to watch as they made their final turn before landing.

After watching the landing, Nuada continued on to the new housing sites and wondered how much Mor had done today. Passing the quarry site and the cut through the ridgeline, Nuada slowly made his way to the houses. Although the walk was simple, his side still remained tight , but it seemed to be getting better. He did not depend on the walking staff as much for support now but kept it with him always.

Nuada found Mor sorting lumber at one of the piles and called to him as he approached.

"Mor, I see you are playing with your sticks today."

"You seem in better spirits today, my friend."

"Much better. I have just come from the mill sites and Beag's company. The walk helped me to stretch the tightness from my side."

Nuada looked about the site and saw many changes had happened since yesterday. "You have made a lot of headway again, but why the rush now?"

"I will have to shift my crew to the new stone houses soon, and there is still the new waterwheel to complete for the sawmill. Anything I can do here will help later in the Spring."

Nuada nodded in understanding, and then their conversation tuned to other projects coming soon. The sun was beginning to get low on the horizon, and Nuada said he would talk with Mor at the cooking area later. Nuada set off for the new stone houses in the front meadow and made his way through the village. Teams of horses pulling wagons filled the streets, and Nuada had to be careful as he walked. Loads of lumber and stone, along with rubble for the streets, continued to pass while he made his way to the stone houses.

As he approached the site, he could see all of the teachers standing in front of Pytheas's house. He called a greeting and walked up onto the porch to join them. They were watching one of the lift machines swing stone blocks into place on one of the houses. Nuada turned to watch himself before making a comment about the work to them.

"Another season of building and growth for the village. What do you think of all of this?"

Amasis was the first to respond to Nuada. "If we continue to grow this fast, soon we will need more teachers and a bigger school."

The others agreed with Amasis, and Pytheas added, "Perhaps one of us should return to Alexandria to seek more teachers this year, Nuada."

"I cannot go this year, but if one of you thinks it is necessary, then make a plan for it, and I will put it to the consul."

They said that they would talk more of this matter and come to a decision for Nuada. Nuada left them and circled around the work site before making his way to the cooking area and his family.

Nuada took the long way around and passed the forge building. Inside he could hear them working metal and wondered what they were making now. He crossed the street and entered the building. A'Chreag and the other three were hard at work forming sheets of copper roofing material. Nuada stood by the door and watched without bothering them. A'Chreag glanced up and saw Nuada. He walked over, rubbing at his apron, and asked, "Is there something I can do for you, Nuada?"

Nuada shook his head and said, "I heard you working the metal and just stopped in to see what you were doing."

"Mor needed more of the copper sheets for his roofs, and we are trying to stay ahead of the need."

"I understand." Nuada paused and then said, "I have just come from the teachers, and they are talking about traveling to Alexandria this year to find more teachers. Do you know of anyone who would travel with them to keep them safe?"

"I thought you would want to go with them."

"No. My health is not good enough. Besides my family needs of me here."

"I see. I shall see if I can find of one who is worthy of this trip."

"Thank you, my friend."

Nuada then departed again for the cooking area and felt it would have been wrong for him to ask A'Chreag to take on this quest; he too had a family to look after now.

As Nuada entered the cooking area, he noticed that many of the village women were already there. Only a few of the men were seated around the tables, and he wondered of the cause. Nuada sat at his table and waited for his family to arrive. Soon more of the men began to fill into the area. Nuada's gaze wandered about the tables, and shortly Mor and the other members of the consul arrived. They waved in greeting as they passed his table, and then Nuada's mate and children came in and joined Nuada.

Although the weather was still cool, the village people seemed to enjoy being together. Winter had lasted just long enough for them, and they were ready to work and party together again. Soon music filled the air, along with laughter and conversation.

Although Nuada was happy, he felt that he did not belong with them. He felt left out of their lifestyle and wanted to be more like them. They were not strangers, but it felt that way to him. He shook his head to clear that thought from his mind and waited for more from them. Then he thought, "Is this because I cannot work with them anymore?"

He became more determined to change that. "Tomorrow I shall walk around both valleys and increase my strength. I will not let this stiffness in my side stop me."

After the evening meal, Nuada and his family returned home, and he wanted tomorrow to hurry and arrive so he could begin his rebuilding of his soul and body.

He slept little that night and during the middle hours went downstairs to sit at the table. His thoughts shifted to his time in Alexandria, and he pulled out his notes from the trip and looked at them. He focused on the machines of the past, wondering if there was anything else that they could use here in the valleys. With the coming of dawn, he awoke with a start — he had been asleep at the table. His papers were spread before him, and he glanced down at them before gathering them to put them away again.

He washed quickly and then dressed. He still had his classes to teach that morning before he could take his walk. He felt full of energy and looked forward to seeing everything again. The new changes were fully focused in his mind, and he wanted them done so he could admire the craftsmanship of the work, but he still wanted to be part of that creation.

Nuada waited for his family, and soon they joined him for the morning meal. Iolair still wanted the school to remain open during the Summer so he could learn more. His mind took in all that they could teach him. Nuada looked at his son and thought, "He is in his seventh season, and still he surprises me every day with his thirst of knowledge."

At the school, Iolair went and joined his classmates while Nuada talked with Pytheas about the need for more teachers.

"I am looking for someone to make this quest who will protect the one sent in the search. I have enough gold to make the trip easy for them."

Pytheas said that he had talked with the other teachers, and they thought that Amasis would be the one to return and find of the teachers for the valleys. Nuada thought about it for a few minutes and said that he was a good choice.

"Have you given any thought about the expansion of the school? How much bigger do we need to make it?" Nuada asked.

Pytheas said that they had talked about that too and thought it should be doubled in size.

"Then I will talk to Mor about it and see if he can start on it this year. How many teachers are we planning on getting?"

"I think three or four are still needed, but if more people come into the valleys this year, we may need six."

The rest of the morning seemed to drag for Nuada, who wanted badly to get out and walk his valleys. At last his final class was over, and Nuada quickly departed the school and made for the new stone-house construction site. Beag was not here but at the sawmill site. Nuada appraised the work done already and saw that they were beginning to start the foundations for four more houses already. They had laid the stone curbing around the houses, and out in the field the work continued, making streets of the stone rubble.

Nuada walked on to the stone shops built last year and the new inner protection wall. He passed through the portal gate and continued on to the outer wall and its guards. He waved as he passed and, once through its gate, turned right and walked along the stream. His eyes took in everything as he walked. The sounds of the insects and birds filled the bright Spring day. Soon he was just outside of the new protection wall for the second valley with its high towers over the stream. He looked at the stream and noted that it had settled down from only yesterday. He passed on into the second valley, and where the new street joined from the cut between the valleys, three wagons passed back toward the village, loaded with new lumber. Nuada waved at the drivers and continued on to the mill sites. Before he got there, he could see the lift machine moving huge stone blocks onto the site. This made Nuada hurry his pace, and soon he was standing just below the mill. He had forgotten about using his walking staff and had it tucked up under one arm. Beag saw Nuada and waved from on top of the new stone wall of the sawmill expansion. Nuada waved back with a large grin on his face. Nuada moved around the site looking at every detail; this building would be more than double the size it was before. But Nuada realized that it would have two more saws in it. The new foundation under it held places for wagons to back in to remove the sawdust from underneath. A short distance away the foundation for the drying shed was laid out, and men had started to use wood frames for its construction. Nuada's attention was drawn back to the street, where two wagons loaded with more cut stone arrived. Beag came down from the wall to supervise where they were to unload and called Nuada over.

"You look better today, my friend. I could use your help , but I will not put you to that test yet."

"I wish someone would. I think that is what I need — work to take my mind off this stiffness."

"Do not push it yet, Nuada. There is lots of time for you to return to the work."

Nuada nodded in answer and then asked questions about the work going on there. Beag led him around the site, pointing out things that Nuada had not noticed.

About an hour later Nuada said good-bye and started the walk back to the village. Wagons still moved, loaded and empty, between the two valleys. When Nuada arrived at the quarry cut into the village, he stopped to gaze up at the men still cutting stone from above. He watched them tumble large blocks down to where they were moved to the cutting area. He moved cautiously through and made his way to the house building site. Mor was moving a small crew from one house to another when he noticed Nuada watching the action.

"Are you checking up on me, Nuada?"

Laughing at the remark, Nuada said he was just watching.

"Be careful, Nuada, or I will put you to work."

"I wish someone would."

Nuada asked a few questions about the timeline there, and when Mor answered the questions, Nuada then asked about the other houses in the second valley that were to be built near the mill sites.

"Those I will start in about a month. There is no rush for them right now, but they will be done before Fall."

Nuada nodded and said his farewells and started to walk toward the cooking area. Just before turning into the area, he looked toward the old woodworking building and noticed that the third lift machine was in the assembly stage outside of the building. He walked over to it to look at its design and was surprised that the gears were not yet installed. "I must ask A'Chreag about this," he thought.

Looking up he saw that the first two houses of stone had their stonework done and were waiting for the finishing wood and roofs. Nuada had time to return to the forge building and did so. Inside A'Chreag was removing the castings from the gears for the lift machine. Nuada watched as he worked and then saw that they had a new machine in the back of the shop. Nuada walked over to it and wondered of its use. The other three men were still working at forming copper sheets for the roofs. Unable to understand the new machine,

Nuada asked about it. The new man who worked with the iron said, "It is for forming ridges along the sides of the copper sheets to make them water tight."

"What do you call this machine?" asked Nuada.

"We call it a brake," was the answer. "It has many uses."

A'Chreag had finished his work and joined Nuada near the new machine. "What think you of our machine, Nuada?"

"I would like to see it in action and see how it forms these ridges."

"Perhaps tomorrow you can come by and watch us use it."

"I would like that. Is there anything else new?"

"Not yet, but we have some ideas that would help us to improve the quality of those things we make."

Nuada felt that he had missed much of what was going on in the forge and had some regrets that his health had kept him from being there. After watching them work for about a half hour, Nuada made for the cooking area.

During the next week, Nuada extended his walks and became stronger. He was tempted to leave his staff at home but thought better of it. During the nighttime, some rain showers fell but not enough to slow any of the work projects. Two more of the stone houses were finished, except for the finishing woodwork and roofs. At the wood housing site, two houses were complete, and four more were fully framed now. At the sawmill site, the new lift machines helped with the walls of the mill, and they were almost up to the point that the roofing frames could be installed within days. Some of Mor's crew were framing up the drying shed now, and the more Nuada watched the speed of the people working at these projects, the more pride he had in their workmanship.

Two of the wagons hauling rock had broken their axles and had to be repaired but that did not slow any of the work. At the school, it was business as usual although it now seemed empty because the adults of the village were at work throughout the valleys. It seemed strange because they began to speak in both their native language and that of the Greek tongue that they had learned in the school. Even Mor carried a wooden board that had paper attached to it to make notes about the construction. They had created a standard of measure for all the projects, and things became more uniform.

At the old woodworking building, a fourth lift machine was in the finishing stages and would soon be put to use. Other buildings in the village were filled with projects, such as candle making, glassmaking, and crafts to sell at the shops, and paper production was almost full time now. Down at the crop meadow, the plowing had begun and would double or more the amount of food grown there. The second plow had proved its worth, and they moved on quickly, getting ready for the planting.

Tomorrow there were plans to install the new waterwheel that would drive all of the sawmills saws. It seemed that the only thing they were short of was more manpower in the carpenter areas of the construction. They were spread thin across both valleys.

The days kept getting warmer, and the air was filled with the smells of the wild flowers and weeds that grew in abundance in the valleys. Dust was not yet a problem because of the rains, but they knew that would change.

Nuada now spent some of his time at the forge building to learn about the new machines that they had built, and he asked about the designs of others that they were thinking of making. Nuada jumped at the chance to be part of the designs and spent many hours making drawings of these machines. One such machine was a rotary lathe, turned by wind power from a cloth windmill above the forge building. The cutting blade was of the iron metal, which had proven its worth on other things. Another machine was a punch press driven by the same wind power. Nuada was happy to be of use again, and it showed with everything he did.

One afternoon he came into the cooking area whistling, and he surprised many people with his attitude of happiness. He had been so dour because of his old wound that it was a complete change in him. People were now not afraid to talk with him; he was his old self again.

The following week they closed the school for the Summer season, as the children were needed to help with the planting now. Nuada had met with the teachers again about the new quest for more teachers, and they made a plan for it. One of the new men from that last group had wanted to go on the trip to Alexandria, as he had never been that far before and wanted to see more of the world. He was a skilled outdoorsman and would protect them. Amasis had also picked another from one of his classes who had picked up the Greek language quickly. They were to leave the next week, and Nuada provided the necessary gold for their trip. Before they were to leave, a Spring feast was to be held at the cooking area. Everyone was looking forward to this feast as a reward for all of their Spring work.

One day Nuada walked again to the sawmill site to see how it was coming. The building was now complete and roofed over. The new saws were installed, and it was ready to begin working. The drying shed was complete too. The area around the site was cleaned, and the extra stone blocks and lumber shifted across the street for the building of the new houses there. Beag had returned to the new stone houses at the front of the village and was pushing his men there now. At the quarry site of the cut between the valleys, the roadway there was now wide enough for two wagons at a time, and still they continued to remove rock from the site.

The man who made the leather for the village was busy making replacement gloves and aprons for all of the work crews. Nuada watched as things seemed to flow so smoothly from one thing to the next. Where people saw a need, they stepped up and filled the needs through hard work. They were thinking ahead now, and that is what made it work.

With the school now closed, Nuada had more time on his hands and had begun to help with the woodworking of the new houses of Beag. Mor noticed that Nuada seemed happier now that he was able to do some of the work, but Mor was also cautious of Nuada's health and kept the workloads light for him. Nuada did not notice that from his friend.

Days passed quickly around the village, as everyone was so busy with the Spring projects. Soon it was time for the Spring feast, and on that day, the work projects ended early and everyone gathered in the cooking area. Music filled the air, and laugher fought for its place in the gathering. Nuada and his family were also enjoying the gathering and went from table to table talking with everyone there. Mor and Beag joined with Nuada, and they went through many beers before the food was served.

The teachers, who still felt apart from the village people, sat alone at their table and talked between themselves. Nuada noticed and sat with them and told them that they should join the gathering. Soon Andocides and Dionysins took their musical instruments up onto the stage area and began to play for the crowd. Loud cheers went up from the village people at their music and humor as they played.

Amasis went to join the two men who would accompany him on the new quest, and they talked, leaving Pytheas alone at the table. Nuada went back and asked him to join his family at his table, which he did, glad to have company to talk with.

"You seem worried, Pytheas."

"I worry for Amasis. As you know, it is a dangerous trip that we send him on. He is able to find of the teachers that we need, of that I have no doubts. He will return with them if they remain free of the troubles in those lands."

Nuada thought of the dangers that they had faced before and knew what Pytheas was talking of.

"If you are that worried, I will talk with the creator about his safety."

"Do so, Nuada. We have become strong friends over the last year."

Nuada did not know if he was talking about being a friend with Amasis or himself; it did not matter. Pytheas was worried, and that mattered to Nuada. Nuada turned the talk toward the grapevines on the island to divert the problems his friend was having.

Andocides and Dionysins rejoined them shortly after turning the stage back to another group of musicians and singers. It was getting harder to talk between themselves as the night grew on. The people were really enjoying themselves tonight. Finally Nuada's mate asked for them to return home so the children could sleep. Nuada looked at his children, who were already asleep, and agreed. He carried both of his boys while she carried their girl.

The next morning Nuada hurried and dressed and then made his way to the stable where Amasis and the two men who were to accompany him were getting their last-minute things together for the start of their quest. All were well-armed with the new weapons of iron and their bows. Nuada wished them a safe journey and watched as they departed the stable and headed for the protective walls around the village. Somehow he felt he should be going with them but knew that he was needed here now.

Nuada followed as far as the new stone houses and stopped. Across the street, Pytheas was up early and watched them go by. Nuada walked over to him and said, "You are feeling much the same as I: We should be going with them."

"Yes, but they will find their own way as we did."

Nuada nodded, and they both turned their heads to watch as they passed through the portal gate. Soon work crews returned to the work site across from the teachers' houses. Progress began again.

Nuada left Pytheas and walked to the houses that Mor was working on near the cut. He found Mor, and he assigned him to one of the crews working on a house nearly done that day. At midday they finished that house, the sixth of this Spring. Two more awaited their finishing touches, and Mor had framed four more at this site. There was room for only two more houses here, and Nuada wondered if he was going to do them this year, as he still had four to build near the mill site. Part of his crew was still out at the stone houses doing the finishing touches there. Nuada looked about and realized that they had already done a lot this year, and Summer was still weeks away.

The lift machines that had been used at the sawmill site were now out in the meadow working on the stone houses. The newest lift machine was at the wood house site with Mor. Nuada knew that these machines had helped to make the work go that much quicker. What would they do now since what they had planned was almost done. Then he remembered that the school needed to be expanded too.

Nuada left the wood house site and walked to the school building to look at what possibilities were there for an expansion. As he walked around the building, he knew that he did not want to take anything away from the playground — if anything he wanted to add some more to it. There was space to add to the building toward the shop building sites along the backside toward the ridge. Nuada paced out the size of the building and looked closely to see if it would hamper other work needed in the area. He could find no problems if it was done that way. Satisfied that he had enough land around the school, Nuada went inside of the school and into his classroom. He wanted a building that would last many years, and he settled on the thought that it should be made of stone. He began to draw the whole school area and then did some simple drawings of what he had in mind. It would be a two-story building that looked almost fortress like. He knew that Beag's skills could make it happen, and he worked at the design for many hours before he was finished with the layout. He sat back and studied his work with a critical eye. "This will work," he thought and then went to seek out Beag.

Nuada returned to the stone housing site to find Beag. He found him setting stone at one of the new houses and called him down from a wall to show him the drawings. Beag became instantly drawn to Nuada's concept and wanted to know when he wanted him to start on the school. Nuada looked around at the houses of stone and then said, "Finish your work here first, and during that time, have your stonecutters start to bring in the stone for the school expansion."

"We will need to tell the other members of the consul about this too," Beag said.

"I know, but I can see no problems coming from them about this project."

"You are right. It is something that the village will need, and now is a good time to do this."

"I will go and show Mor my drawings and have him convince the other members of the need."

The afternoon was getting late, and Nuada knew that it would only be a short time before everyone would be at the cooking area. He walked there to wait for Mor to arrive.

While he was sitting at his table, Pytheas came into the area and joined Nuada at his table. Nuada showed Pytheas the drawings that he had made and asked for his opinion on the concept. Pytheas was excited about the expansion idea and went over all of the design with Nuada. Shortly Mor arrived with many of his work crew. They were discussing the work for tomorrow, and Nuada did not interrupt his thoughts yet.

When Mor finally became free and had drawn a beer to relax with, Nuada then approached him to show him the drawings.

"Mor, my friend, I have some drawings to show you for the school. I talked with Beag about them, and he thinks we could begin on this soon. What think you?"

Mor studied the drawings and turned page after page of Nuada's concept of the school. At last he turned to Nuada. "We should build this, and I agree with Beag. It is needed."

"But we will need of the consul's agreement for it. Will you help convince them that it is really needed?"

"Yes. You are now thinking ahead again, like the days of old, and I will help in any way I can."

Nuada smiled at his friend and returned to his table to await his evening meal and the arrival of his family. Soon Nuada noticed that Mor was talking to Farmer and Anoghas and telling them of the school-expansion project. Their heads were nodding in agreement to what he was telling them, and Nuada felt pride in knowing that his friends were doing everything in their power to make this concept come true.

Another week passed, and Summer was close at hand. Nuada had continued to help Mor at his building site and was growing even stronger with each passing day. He did not think of his old wound anymore and had begun to leave his walking staff at home. Six of the new houses here were now complete, and only two remained for their finishing wood work. Nuada had noticed that Mor had not framed the last two remaining house sites. When Nuada had asked him why, Mor said that he was moving his work crews to the second valley to build the four houses needed there.

Later in the morning Nuada walked to the stone houses in front of the village to see what was going on there, as he had not been out there for many days. As Nuada walked through the village streets, he passed the school and saw the new piles of cut stone being stacked near the old school building. Piles of lumber were also nearby, and more wagons were waiting to unload. Nuada's thoughts went to Amasis and his quest for more teachers. He knew that they should be crossing the great inland sea now and hoped that everything was without problems.

Nuada turned and went on to the stone houses. Here he found that Beag had stopped building anymore houses and was in the finishing stages of his stonework on the last of them. His work crews had still continued to lay more of the curbs and sidewalks on out to the new stone shops by the protection wall. Nuada walked on to the new shops to see if any more of the shops had been occupied and what they had been stocked with.

The third shop building contained the work of A'Chreag and his men. In it Nuada found tools and weapons of much beauty. Parts that had been common in their housing construction, such as hinges and latches, were also on display. Jewelry was inside a counter that had been built for that purpose and showed great thought in its design.

Next door in another shop, the village women had blankets and clothing that they had made over the Winter. The shop also contained wood carvings made by the village men too. Some drawings were framed and held up on the walls for all to see. Nuada was pleased that the people had come together to make this happen. Now all they needed was for outsiders to come and begin to trade with them.

Nuada departed the shop area and returned to the stone houses and Beag. Beag was not here, and Nuada asked of one of his crew where he would find him. Nuada was told that he had gone to the school and that he would find him there. Nuada walked back into the village and made his way to the school. He found Beag going over the drawings that Nuada had made and was making notes about the needed supplies of stone.

"You are not going to start today are you, Beag?"

"No, but it will not be long before I do. I will need all of my crew for this project."

Both Nuada and Beag looked up as both of the lift machines from the stone-house project were rolled onto the property being pulled by teams of horses. Beag ran over to the team drivers and told them where to place the machines. Nuada watched and admired the mind of Beag and how he was going to make them work. Shortly a third machine from the wood houses came into view, as it would be needed too.

Pytheas, who had been inside of the school, joined Nuada, and they watched as the third machine was placed where it was needed. Pytheas turned to Nuada with a smile on his face and said, "Soon we will have a school that anyone would be proud of."

Beag returned to them and returned to his study of the drawings that Nuada had made. From time to time, he asked Nuada a question about some detail and was given an answer.

Before Nuada departed the site, he told Beag that he thought that the village people needed a break before starting the school project and that it would be a good time as Mor's crew were almost finished with their houses here in the village too. Nuada said that he would talk with Mor about it and that the village women needed to be notified so as to prepare for it.

Nuada left his two friends and went in search of Mor. He was still working at the wood housing site, and Nuada told him about the need for a break for the village people.

"We should mark it as an ending to the Spring and have a feast," was Mor's comment.

Nuada agreed and said the women needed to be told of the plan. Mor said he would take care of it. They parted, and Nuada strolled to the cooking area and a break himself.

After sitting awhile alone in the cooking area, Nuada's thoughts went back to the shop buildings near the stone wall. A'Chreag's items stuck in his mind, and he thought he should praise him for the items he had made. He started to get up but changed his mind and thought to wait until A'Chreag came there.

It was not long before people began to filter into the area, and soon it was filled again. The evening meal was not long in coming, and Nuada shared his time with his family.

When Mor came in, he made his way around the tables, talking to the people about the coming break and the need for another feast. You could tell from the sounds of their voices that it was well-received, and music highlighted the evening. Before the gathering broke up that night, the feast was planned for three days away and a needed break that would last for one week.

Over the next three days, everyone worked that much harder preparing for the coming construction phases and the ending of the others. The piles of needed supplies for the school continued to grow, and at last a halt was called for. The wood houses in the village were finished, as were the stone houses in the meadow, along with the curbs and sidewalks.

The afternoon of the feast it seemed that everyone had dressed in their best clothes and came early for the gathering. Nuada and his family were also early, and Nuada's mate gave Nuada his daughter to hold while she went to help with preparing the meal. Many people stopped by the table to talk with Nuada and praised him for the needed break. He shook it off and talked with them about things like the need for traders to enter the valley for trade. Iolair kept Uilleam under a close eye, and Wolf watched them both. The feast grew louder as the evening went on, and finally Nuada took his family home to its peace and quiet.

Early the next morning while the village was quiet, Nuada took a walk again with Wolf at his side. He walked to the school and looked around at the piles of materials there. The sun warned of a hot day, and soon Nuada went back home and sat on his porch waiting for someone to come by.

- SUMMER AND A NEW SCHOOL -

The week after the feast went slowly for Nuada, and he was ready for the work to begin again. Both Mor and Beag had dropped by, and they were feeling the same way. A'Chreag had brought his family by, and while their mates talked, Nuada asked about any new designs for machines in the forge building. He said there were none, but there was always something that needed improvement. Nuada agreed with him on that thought and asked about the items he had made for the shop building. Soon he and his family departed, and Nuada was feeling alone again. He knew that it would not last, as they were all returning to work tomorrow.

The sun brought promise of more warmth today as Nuada dressed and made ready to begin work on the school. He knew that everyone would feel the same, as the weeklong break was over. Stepping outside Nuada drew in a deep breath of the morning air. Birds filled the air with their calls, and insects buzzed in the tall grasses around the village.

Nuada set out for the school and found that he hurried his footsteps the closer that he got to the site. Already there was a large crowd of the village men gathered around Beag. He was assigning jobs and preparing for the foundation work to begin. He had already set out stakes to mark where the first stones were to be laid. A table next to him held Nuada's drawings of the school. Nuada walked up to Beag and asked where he would be working, and Beag told him that he would be with him today to supervise the other crews. Nuada at first felt let down — he wanted to be part of the construction of the school — but he knew that Beag had better use of him. After Beag finished the assignments for the crews, he went over the drawings with Nuada.

Shortly all three of the lift machines began to swing into motion; blocks of stone began to move with purpose to their place in the foundation. Some of the men were setting up scaffolding, and others were clearing the ground where the stones would go. Nuada looked up and saw Mor pass down the street with his work crew from the cooking area. They were headed to the second valley to begin the framing of the four houses there by the mills. Nuada's eyes continued to scan the area when he noticed that Pytheas had pulled a chair out of the old school and was watching the progress. Nuada waved to him and got a response in turn.

Soon teams of wagons added to the structured clamor of the construction site. More stones and lumber filled in around the site, and men moved about finding places to set them so as to not block the work going on. Beag seemed to be everywhere, and Nuada followed him as best he could, watching as the foundation took on shape.

At midday the foundation was complete, and they had to move the scaffolds into place and begin to move upward with the stone placement. The lift machines were in constant motion, swinging back and forth across the entire project. The men looked like ants preparing for Winter. During a break in the mid-afternoon, Nuada had time to talk with Pytheas.

"What think you of our progress, Pytheas?"

"It grows quickly. I still worry that Amasis will never see of it."

"He will. He is in good hands, and he knows what is at stake."

Worry still reflected in Pytheas's face, and Nuada knew that it did not matter what he said; it would take Amasis being there to erase that worry.

Nuada then said, "After our work is done for the day, we will share of the wine that is left. Soon I expect that the trader will return, and we will have a good supply on hand."

That comment made Pytheas smile, and he said he would be glad to share the wine with Nuada. Soon Nuada had to return to the work site, and he found that he was carrying the drawings about with him because details always seemed to come up that needed answers.

Late in the day just before Beag called a halt to the work, Nuada could begin to see the school finished in his mind. Already the entry steps into the school were complete, and now the first stones were as high as a man over the foundation. At each corner of the building were the towers that would give the building a personality. Although they were far from complete, it added to the bulk of the building that Nuada had designed.

When Beag finally called a halt to the day's work, Nuada also noticed that many of the village women were watching the building grow into its concept.

Soon they joined with their mates, and all headed for the outdoor cooking area for their evening meal. Nuada held back and walked around the building before he too went in search of his family.

Over the next week, huge beams of wood were in place on the first floor, awaiting the lumber to cover them. The outer walls continued to grow, and soon they were at the level for the second story of the building. Again beams were starting to be placed there before they moved higher with the walls.

One afternoon Nuada took the time to walk to the second valley to see how the work was going with the four new houses that Mor was building near the mill site. Nuada was surprised that Mor had again changed his design, and the new houses were elegant in their concept. Nuada walked around each of the houses and finally found Mor inside of one.

"You have changed your house design again, my friend. Why?"

"I grew bored with the other design and wanted to see what I could do with this layout."

"I like it. It adds to the beauty of its purpose."

"Thank you, Nuada. I had a few problems to solve, but it has worked out."

Nuada walked around with Mor awhile before he started to return to the school. He paused to watch the men working at the new sawmill and then went back to the school.

When Nuada arrived back at the school, he saw that the last of the second-floor beams were being placed and already men were back to placing stones even higher on the outer walls. He watched as the lift machines continued their non-stop swinging of lumber and stones into the building. Beag, still carrying his board with his notes, moved from place to place giving orders and making sure that everything was level and clean. The outer walls were still very thick even here on the second floor. Nuada had designed it so that it would support the loads when it was finished. Wind or snow would not bring it down, and that was what Nuada wanted. This was a building that would last into the future.

Time continued to move on for the people of the village. One day, Nuada heard the ringing of the warning bell from the front protection wall and hurried with many of the workmen with their weapons, to see what was happening. Most of the men gathered on the inside protection wall while Nuada went forward to see what it was all about. He topped the wall and asked the guards there what was going on; they pointed out the wagons coming toward the valley. Nuada waited to see what it was all about. Soon the wagons, numbering four, pulled to a halt before the wall. The leader called out and asked for entry into the village. Nuada answered back that he wanted to know who they were.

"I am a trader who came here last year. I have with me two families who are seeking shelter too."

Nuada hurried down from the wall and went to open the portal gate. He cautiously walked to the group leader and instantly knew him.

"It is good to see you again. I hope you brought more of that fine wine you had last year. Now tell me of these people you brought with you."

"It is the same old story. Their village was burned, and they fled those who would have killed them or turned them into slaves. I see much of that in my travels."

"Come inside the wall, and we will talk of trade. They can camp there until I decide what to do with them."

The wagon teams moved forward, and the portal gate was closed behind them. Nuada went to each of the families and told them where to camp, then returned to the trader. Before he began the talks of trade, Nuada called up to the men ringing the inside wall and sent them back to their work on the school.

"Now what have you brought for us to use this year?"

"Much as last year and some new things as well."

"Show me."

The trader took Nuada to both of his wagons and displayed the items he had with him. Many of the items the people of the village could use, and Nuada also noticed that he had brought two more casks of the wine with him. When they were through looking at everything, Nuada led him inside of the wall to the trade shops that the village had built last year after he had departed. He went through each of the shops, and they struck a deal on most of the things that were there. They then haggled of the remaining items on the wagons and the amount of gold the trader wanted in exchange of them.

After they had made a final bargain, Nuada asked him more about the people he had brought with him. Then they talked about bringing more traders to the valley, as they would have food crops to trade next year. Nuada also asked that he send anyone of need to them. The trader was helpful and said he would do all that Nuada had asked of him.

"Now I must go talk with these people that you have brought to me," Nuada said and excused himself and walked to the wagons of the new people.

Nuada introduced himself as the chief of the village and asked many questions of them about their past and why he should give them the protection of the valleys. When he was satisfied with their answers, he invited them into the village to find a house to their likings. They left their wagons between the walls and followed Nuada on foot into the village. The first stop was at the cooking area, where Nuada had the women wait while he took the men around the village. He showed them the woodworking building and told them it was used for paper making and the storage of the village foods. Then they moved to the school next. Nuada explained that everyone in the village, adults and children, went here to learn of the world, language, and mathematics. They were in awe of the building going on with the new school. Then they continued on down the street to the new empty houses.

"You may chose of the house you want," Nuada told them and waited while they made up their minds. "Tomorrow I will take you to the second valley and all that it contains. After that you will be expected to work alongside everyone else of the village."

They then returned to the outdoor cooking area and their families. Nuada watched as they talked about everything they had seen. Some of the village women went and talked with them, and soon the men began to return from their day of work and filled the area.

When Mor and Beag arrived, Nuada took them over to introduce them to the new people. Both of them asked about any trade skills and found that they were simple farmers and herdsmen. Mor then said, "We will teach you of different skills." Before they departed the new people, Nuada said he would meet with them in the early morning here at the cooking area. Then he warned them, "Do not be late."

Beag brought the men some beer, and then the village women brought food for the new people. After awhile the village people did their usual thing, and music filled the area again. It was a way to relax from the day's work.

The next morning Nuada was up at his usual hour and walked to the cooking area to see if they took his words of warning to heart. To his surprise, both of the men were waiting for him.

"Good. You are here. Have you eaten yet?"

Both men said no. Nuada nodded and said there would be time for that later. He had them follow him to the back of the village to the forge building and showed them around it. The next stop was the stable, and here men and boys were getting the horses ready for another day of work. Some were already hooked to wagons and preparing to move to where they were needed. The noise of construction was already beginning to start, and Nuada and the men moved on. He showed them the meeting hall and the other shops there before following the ridgeline onto the new houses of Mor's work. They could see the work on the school beginning from there as they moved onto the quarry and the cut through into the second valley. Just through the cut, Nuada paused and pointed to the right. "That road leads to the stable for the sheep and the grain fields." Then he continued on to the left toward the mills and the dam. Before they could see the mill site, they passed the protective wall into the second valley and where the stream ran through it. Again they were speechless of the size of the wall. Nuada paused and then hurried them on to the mills. As the dam came into sight, they were talking and pointing at the massive structure. Soon he took them into the sawmill, as it was working at full capacity, and soon the noise of it stopped all speech between them. Nuada motioned them to follow him, and they moved on to the grain mill. Nuada showed them how it worked, and then they crossed to the new houses, almost finished, across the street. From here they walked around the valley to the sheep stable and the grain fields. The tour was now complete, and they walked slowly back to the village.

Nuada said, "As you can see, we are very industrious here and work to make it better for everyone. If you think you cannot do as much as everyone else, then it is time for you to say so."

Both men said they would try, and Nuada nodded in response. "That is the right answer. Now I must do my work and return to the building of the school. You are free to walk around as much as you like today. Tomorrow you will meet at the cooking area and be assigned a place to work."

Nuada rejoined Beag and Mor at the school. Beag had started his detail work on the outside of the building while Mor was inside doing floors. The outside structure was almost complete and would be within a week. Now all four of the lift machines were here at the school, and they kept up a steady flow of building materials. Men swarmed everywhere around the structure.

Pytheas still watched the construction from his chair outside of the old school building while Andocides and Dionysins worked their grapevines on the island. The trader had brought more vines to plant, along with the casks of wine.

The Summer heat was now approaching its highest point, and the grasses around the valleys had turned a golden brown. If Amasis had any luck, then they should be returning soon from Alexandria with the new teachers. The longer that the Summer went on, the more worried Pytheas became. Nuada kept reassuring him that all would be well and that Amasis would be all right and return soon.

Another week passed, and the school now looked complete from the outside although there was still much to do on the inside. The internal walls were going up, and doors still had to be hung. Most of the glass windows were now installed, and they were nearing the last installation of the copper roof panels. A'Chreag had a new device for the roofs that he called a vent. It was made of copper too and would provide air circulation year-round in the structure. Eight such vents were to go on the roof of the school.

Nuada worked with Mor on many of the details going into the school while Beag had now returned to his stone houses in the front meadow. All of the extra stones were moved out there to begin building some more houses. Crews of men worked at cleaning around the new school, and the wood scraps were taken to the outdoor cooking area for fuel.

The new families had become part of the village now and worked as hard as anyone there. Nuada's pride in the people was reflected in the evening gatherings at the cooking area. He talked with everyone and encouraged them when it was necessary.

Summer time marched on, and now Nuada was becoming worried about Amasis; he should have returned by now. Nuada sent the village hunters out to seek them on one late Summer day. He could only wait and see what was discovered of them.

The new school was now complete, and the large piles of paper and ink supplies from the old woodworking building were moved into the new school. One day Nuada stood outside of the school. He was happy about the completed concept that he had designed. Pytheas saw him standing there and walked over to talk with him.

"They have built a fine school for us, Nuada. The new teachers should be impressed with it."

"Yes, if they ever get here, Pytheas."

"Then we have no word about them yet?"

"Nothing yet. The hunters are still out looking for them."

They talked for awhile about the coming school year, and finally Nuada departed his company and walked out to the outer protection wall. Nuada greeted the guards on the wall and stood looking into the distance. An hour passed before Nuada turned and walked back to the village. He stopped to talk with Beag on the site of one of his houses, and Nuada expressed his concern over the lack of word about Amasis.

"He will return, Nuada. Something must have slowed his travels. That is all it is."

Nuada nodded and then walked to the forge building to take his mind off the delay. He found A'Chreag and all of his crew relaxing just outside of the building.

"You have time now to just sit back and talk?"

"Yes. The building had slowed enough for us to sit and talk of new designs for the forge."

"Tell me of them."

They spent several hours discussing new machines and how they could be of use before it was time for the evening meal. It was good for Nuada, as it took his mind off the worries about Amasis. They all walked to the outdoor cooking area together and joined of their mates and families. Just after sitting at their tables, the warning bell from the front protection wall sounded. Nuada hurried with many of the village men to the wall.

"What is it?" Nuada asked of the guards.

They pointed to a large dust cloud that could only come from a large group coming their way. Nuada sent a runner back to the village to gather more men for the protection walls. Then they waited to see what was the cause of the dust.

It took almost another hour before the guards pointed to the dust, and out of it came one of the village hunters. He hurried forward to the wall and called up to them that it was the teachers returning and with them was another group of people who were searching for protection from raiders.

"How many people seek of our shelter?" questioned Nuada.

"There are twenty-five families and all of their livestock."

"Bring them into the inner field between the walls."

He quickly returned to the group, and Nuada waited to hear their story. Soon Amasis and another group with him turned through the portal gate. Nuada came down off the wall and called to Amasis, "My friend, it is good to have you back. Take our new teachers to the cooking area, and I will join you there soon."

Amasis looked tired and those with him the same. Nuada watched them pass without counting how many he had with him. They had many pack horses also.

Minutes later the first of the wagons with those seeking shelter started to come through the portal gate, and some of the men from the wall showed them where to camp within the field. Nuada studied each face as they passed and noticed how tired they all were. "They have had a hard time," he thought.

It took almost a full hour for all of the newcomers to enter through the portal gate. Finally the gate was closed and locked for the night. Nuada climbed the wall and told the guards to keep a sharp eye out for anyone who might be following the group. Then he went down to the new group and sought out the group leader. After another fifteen minutes, he found him. Nuada only spoke to him for a short while and then hurried to the cooking area. The new people would wait until tomorrow to be sorted out.

At the cooking area, Amasis was being hugged by Pytheas, and some laughter came from the new group of teachers. They had settled at the teachers table and were sharing some wine together. Nuada walked up to them and was handed a mug of wine too. Shortly Amasis began to introduce the new teachers to Nuada and Pytheas. He brought seven teachers from Alexandria and many books for the village. Nuada said that all of the new teachers were to have the new stone houses in front of the village. Pytheas said he would show them where they were and explained to the group that they were the finest houses in the village.

Soon food was being passed around, and Nuada went and settled at his table with his family. Tomorrow would be a busy day for Nuada, and he decided that he and his family would retire early tonight. As they started to leave the cooking area, Nuada had a final word with Amasis and told him that tomorrow he would meet with the teachers at the school about mid-morning.

Before dawn of the next day, Nuada was up and dressed early in his clothes from Alexandria. He wanted to impress the new teachers and not have them think of him as a barbarian, but first he had to meet with the new group who sought shelter from raiders. He walked out to the field between the walls and found the group leader. The man knew him by his red hair and not the way Nuada was dressed this day. The man was huge. He stood a full head higher than Nuada and had shoulders to match. They sat in front of a fire in the early light and began to talk. Nuada told him of the village rules and how everyone was to have an education. Work was expected of them, and then Nuada told them that they would have houses soon. Nuada would return after midday to give them a tour of the village. Then he made his way to the school.

Nuada found all of the teachers standing outside of the new school building. Amasis was the first to ask Nuada about it.

"It has sixteen rooms on two floors and should provide us with enough room for many years now," Nuada said. "Come, let me show you around the building."

After the tour of the new school, Nuada was introduced to all of the teachers and what their specialty was. Two were teachers of mathematics, two world history, and the others general teachers. They were told of Nuada's skills with languages, and one of them tried to find out how extensive Nuada's skills were by talking to him in the language of the Hittites. Nuada responded quickly and shocked the man with his knowledge. They talked about how they were going to divide the students this year, and soon a solution was found. Then he told them that he had to settle the new group of people into houses and give them a tour of the valleys. He did not want to leave this group of teachers, but he had responsibilities to the village as a whole and needed to get the new people under shelter as soon as possible. They did agree to meet later at the cooking area and talk some more.

Nuada started to walk back to the field between the walls and on the way stopped to talk with Beag. He was working on one of the stone houses and stopped to talk with Nuada when he was called off a wall.

"What is it you need, Nuada?"

"After the teachers are settled in their houses, how many more houses do you have left empty?"

"I now have five, and we should have these four done soon."

"Do you know how many Mor has empty?"

"He has eight in the village and the four by the mill site."

"That is not enough. We will need three more for these new people."

"I can build six more before Fall here."

"Good. If you see Mor before I do, ask of him how many he can build."

"I will do so."

Nuada continued on to the field of waiting people and the expected problems of housing them. He found the group leader waiting, and Nuada could not remember asking of his name.

"What do they call you, my friend?"

"My name is Millert."

"My name is Nuada. What skills do your people bring with them, that I may find work to their liking?"

"Come, I will take you around and introduce you to each of them, and you can ask of that yourself."

"Good. But first I have told you of some of the village rules and that we have a consul to decide what work is to be done and settle all problems of the village people. As you have brought in such a large group, you are extended the office as a member of the consul too."

The man was taken aback by the offer and did not know what to say, but he was a proud man and then took up the offer and took Nuada around the gathering of people. After Nuada questioned each of them, he had the men follow him into the village and began to assign houses to them. As they went about the village, Nuada showed them the different buildings and where the cooking area was. When they came to the school, the mass stopped them short, and they were speechless at the sheer size of the building. Nuada smiled at their reaction and told them that it was nothing compared to the dam and mill sites in the second valley. He also said that he did not have time today to show them the second valley but tomorrow would do so. When Nuada finished assigning the houses that they had, Nuada told the others that they could camp where they were until the other houses were built for them. He told the whole group that they were expected to help in the building, and that the day after tomorrow they would be assigned to a work crew and told where to work.

Nuada returned to the school and found Mor still doing some finishing work inside. He told him of the need for more houses and asked how many he could build. Mor thought about it and said that he could do two more at his housing site, and he had been thinking about adding four more by the sheep-stable area for expansion there. Nuada nodded and asked if he could do four more by the mill site as well. He thought again about the needed supplies and said that if he had more help, he could. Nuada then told him that he could have all of the new men and that should make his work crew complete. Mor agreed and said that he would assign them to his crews tomorrow and begin the building in the second valley.

Nuada then went to the old school building and found the teachers had gathered inside one of the classrooms, as the office was not now big enough for all of them. They were having a general discussion about the coming Fall classes and the topics that were to be covered. Nuada sat and listened to the plans before he again had to leave and seek out Beag at the stone house site.

It had been a long and busy day for Nuada, and as he exited the school, he saw a small crew of Beag's starting to lay new curbs and sidewalks in front of both school buildings. He paused to watch them at work before he turned and walked back to the stone houses. At the stone house site, Nuada found Beag already starting to mark out the foundations for four new houses.

"Beag? I talked with Mor already about more houses, and he agreed to build more in the second valley."

"Good. I will start the new ones here tomorrow and should be able to move quickly with them."

Nuada nodded in answer and then said, "I have assigned the new men to Mor's crews, as he has a greater need for them now."

"That is all right with me, as I do not have the time to teach them myself."

The afternoon was growing late when Nuada departed Beag's company, and he walked back to the cooking area. The place was filled with women and children when Nuada entered. Most of the new women and those of the village were beginning the evening meals. Nuada watched the interaction between all of them as he sat at his table. The village children were getting along well with the new ones, and they played well together.

Soon men from the village work crews and the new men began to enter into the area. Nuada was thinking of all of the growth in the village this year and started to wonder about next year's expansion. His thoughts were interrupted by the coming of the teachers to the cooking area. They stopped at Nuada's table and asked if he would like to share of some wine with them. Nuada declined and told them that he had to seek out his family right now. They understood and left him to his thoughts.

Shortly Iolair and Uilleam came to the table, all excited about the new children they had met that day. Nuada calmly listened to their stories and the adventures that they had shared with the children. Nuada suddenly felt very old in their company and wished that he could share of their childhood thoughts. Nuada's mate appeared then and handed him their daughter before she went to help with the evening meal. Noise filled the whole area, and soon music added to the din coming from there, but it was a happy noise and that did not bother Nuada and his thoughts.

When the members of the consul arrived, Nuada sought them out and told them that he had added the new group leader to the consul. They all wanted to meet him. Nuada looked around and found him near the front of the area by the music stage. Nuada told the others to wait and he would bring him to them. He stood and walked to where Millert was sitting.

"Millert, my friend, the other members of the consul wish to meet you. Do you have time now?"

"I do, Nuada. This music makes me feel young again. I do not remember the last time I could just sit and listen to such."

"I understand you. It was much the same for everyone here at one time."

Millert rose and walked with Nuada back to the group of consul members and then left them to talk between themselves, as he had to return to his children.

The evening wore on, and soon the village people began to go home. Nuada and his family were much the same as everyone else: tired and happy.

The next morning Nuada dressed in his work clothes and made his way to the cooking area and the sorting of the work crews. Mor was already with Millert, and they talked between each other before their crews moved out to the second valley. Beag was already out at the stone house site with his crew, and Nuada walked out there to see if Beag needed his help today.

Beag's crews were already at work on the foundations for the four new houses. Of course Beag was in the thick of the work and did not notice Nuada standing there. They had a lot to do before the sun wore them down during the afternoon. Nuada turned and walked back into the village, thinking that it was probably better for him to work with Mor's group and the new people.

As Nuada passed the school building, he saw that some of Beag's men were still at work on the sidewalks and curbs there. He continued on to the quarry site and the cut between the valleys. Here they were busy too. Rock was removed from the walls of the ridge and moved to the cutting area before being hauled by wagon to the front housing site. As Nuada crossed to the junction of the road on the other side of the cut, he wondered which way to go: left or right? Both were going to a housing site , but which one would Mor be at now?

There were no wagons to indicate which site was the busiest construction site, as the sawmill could supply both from the road at the back ridgeline of the valley. Nuada decided to follow the road to the right and down to the sheep stables. Already the heat of the day began to make Nuada sweat, and he hurried his footsteps to the stable area.

At the new house sites at the stable area, about twenty-five men were making the foundations for the houses before starting the framing of them. Nuada looked around and did not see Mor. He then continued on to the mill site of the new houses. It was a little cooler here as he neared the dam and its man-made lake. Nuada was surprised that the new houses here were back along the ridgeline and not out near the other houses that Mor had built for the sawmill crews. Again it was much the same as he had seen at the stable site. A crew was building the foundations for the houses, but this time wagons of lumber were being unloaded here first. Nuada looked around and finally found Mor with his board of notes, giving orders to different crews standing nearby.

Nuada waited until Mor was free and walked up to him.

"Do you have need of me today, Mor?"

"Nuada, no. It seems that we have everything under control for now. Have you talked with Beag?"

"No. I was at his housing site but felt I would be in his way today."

"Well until tomorrow, I have everything under control. I could use your help then."

Nuada nodded and slowly walked toward the mill sites. He had not been prepared for the rejection of his help today, but he held his head high and continued on to see what other things he could do. Maybe A'Chreag could use him at the forge.

Nuada paused at the sawmill and watched as a line of wagons were waiting to be loaded with the cut lumber from there. He stood and watched for almost an hour before the noise of the saws made him continue back to the village. He followed the road by the stream and stopped once to drink from its cool waters. When he got to the protection wall into the valley, he started to continue on back to the cut, but something made him go through the portal gate and onto the road on the other side of the ridge back by the caves.

His mind wandered back to the day when he had taken Jan there to explore the caves. So much had changed in the few short years since then. Even the caves were different now. The work that Beag had done when he first arrived had changed their appearance. Somewhere in the back of his mind, he regretted the changes but knew that it had all been of his doing. "I cannot go back but only remember what was," he thought. He looked across to the island and fondly remembered his early days there. "That island is one of the few things that is still as it was," he reflected. Taking a deep breath to clear the thoughts that plagued him, Nuada moved on to the village.

He followed the road around the back of the village by the ridgeline to the forge building. Inside the crew of A'Chreag was back at making copper sheets and casting more hinges and latches for the newest houses. Nuada watched them work, and during a break at the casting table, A'Chreag asked Nuada what he thought of all of the new people.

"They are hard working people, just as everyone else who has come into the village."

"Just as I thought also. By the way, Nuada, we have been thinking of moving the forge to the second valley near the mill sites to use of the water power there. The stable here needs of an expansion also because of all the new horses and could use of this property."

Nuada glanced around and knew what he was saying was the truth , but it hurt deep within him to think of moving the forge again. But it was now A'Chreag's forge, and he would help him improve it if it was needed.

"I will talk with the consul members about it for you at the next meeting."

A'Chreag thanked Nuada before he had to return to the casting table again. Nuada stepped outside and looked around at the building and then over at the stable and knew that A'Chreag was right about everything he said.

Slowly Nuada walked away from the forge with his head down, and his footsteps took him back toward the old woodworking building. He looked at that building too and decided that soon they would need of another building just to make paper and the ink. He turned his head and realized that they also needed a building for the making of glass too. "What other changes do we need to make for the village?" he wondered.

He continued walking on out to the inner protection wall and the shops there. His mind raced with projects that could make things in the village easier. He climbed the wall and looked down onto the field between the walls and then glanced back toward the village and stone houses that were going to be part of the field in front of him. "We could build a building to house new people before their houses are built and also use it for traders to stay in while they are here," Nuada thought. These were all projects for next year, and they were needed. Nuada made up his mind to put them forward to the consul at the next meeting.

Nuada climbed back down off the wall and went to see if Beag needed of him. If not then he would go home and write down his thoughts while they were still fresh in his mind.

Nuada found Beag still setting stones on the new houses, and Beag told him that he was not needed today but tomorrow if he was free. Nuada expected that answer and made his way home to make his notes about things that the village needed.

It only took about an hour for Nuada to put his thoughts on paper, and then he went in search of the teachers again. He found them sitting at the cooking area still talking and sharing wine together. The new teachers were sharing their stories about the return from Alexandria, and Nuada was interested in why it took them so long to return. Their return from across the great inland sea was simple enough , but they did have one storm on the way. It was not until they arrived in the former land of the Etruscans that trouble began. The Etruscans had lost badly in their war to the east, and then the native people of their land had revolted and took power over all seaports and major cities. The native people had also proved to be fearless warriors and dominated everything there. They were also builders and had started creating new buildings and machines of war too. The teachers had only slipped through all the troubles by cunning and being watchful of the things going on around themselves. After finally crossing out of that land, they had run into the group of people seeking safety from raiders. It took several days to get them to follow the teachers back to the valley, and that was a slow march. Nuada did ask some details about the troubles but for the most part listened to the story. When the story was complete, Nuada asked about the books that they had brought with them. Most were history books, and a few were about mathematics, but Amasis had also sought out books about machines for Nuada. He would give them to him when Nuada had time to look them over. They continued their talks until the village people began to find their way into the cooking area for the evening meal. In the days that followed, house after house was built, and they moved forward with more. The Summer weather held, and the village people pushed themselves hard. Nuada had not had time to talk with his fellow consul members about the things that he thought that the village needed, but the monthly consul meeting was drawing close, and Nuada was going to make a point about the needs for next year's building.

Millert and his group had proved a worthy addition to the village and worked as hard as anyone else. They had many skills and in some ways were superior to many in the village. As the houses were finished, families moved in, and the village began to settle down in preparation for the Fall weather. They were ready for an end to the Summer of work.

One morning they awoke to a heavy rain that stopped all of the work in the valleys. Nuada decided that it was time for the monthly consul meeting, and he had them gather in the meeting hall across from the forge building. After many beers had been drunk, he called the meeting together, and they talked about everything that had been accomplished that year. When they had covered all aspects of that which had been done, Nuada brought forth his ideas for the changes for next year, including the moving of the forge building. No one debated his ideas — even the building for travelers and traders near the new shop buildings was agreed to. Nuada sat back and listened to some thoughts that they had for next year, and these were also agreed on. Then it was time for more beer and the sharing of their friendships.

A couple of days later Nuada walked to the school and paused outside of both buildings. They were beautiful to the eye, more so now with the completion of the curbs and sidewalks in front of them. They were framed with some of the natural trees left on the sites, and this added to a welcoming feeling around them. Pytheas was at the old school building and saw Nuada outside and went to join him.

"It feels like a place of learning now, does it not, Nuada?"

"It does, my friend. I am ready to begin the teaching again."

"As we all are."

They talked for awhile before Nuada had to leave for the second valley again. Nuada made his way through the cut and turned left to the mill sites and the new houses there.

Mor had built all of the houses he was asked to build and had started four more against the back ridge wall. Some of Beag's crew had dug a new well nearby and were doing the finishing touches around it. All of this work caught Nuada by surprise, and he sought out Mor to ask why it was being done now.

Mor saw him first, and before Nuada could ask him questions about it, Mor told him that they had the weather and just moved forward with the work. Nuada nodded in understanding and then asked about Beag.

"He is still out in front of the village doing his thing too," was Mor's answer.

Nuada wondered what that meant and, after a short talk, made his way back to the village to seek out Beag. As Nuada approached the second valley's protection wall, he could see more construction going on behind the sawmill site and walked over to see what this was going to be. He found A'Chreag and his crew and many of Beag's crewmen building a foundation near the creek.

"A'Chreag, is this to be the site of the new forge building?"

"It is, Nuada. What think you?"

The site was close enough to the dam raceway for power yet far enough away from the sawmill so as to not present a fire danger to it from the forge itself.

"You have chosen well your site, but what about the Winter weather problems for travel to it?"

"Myself and my crew will be moving into houses over here when Mor has finished with building them."

Nuada understood the need to be near the site and did not question A'Chreag further about it. After walking around the site, Nuada continued on to the front of the village. Again Nuada was surprised when he arrived at the stone house site and found Beag building yet four more houses next to the teacher houses. The whole area was taking on a new look, and it filled in the surrounding streets with the business of construction. Nuada did not see Beag and continued on out to the shops near the inner protection wall.

Before Nuada got there, he could see two of the lift machines working on the right side of the portal gate. "What now?" wondered Nuada. He hurried his footsteps and saw Beag working on a foundation wall under the machines. Nuada waited until he was free and sought him out to ask about the work.

"What is this, Beag?"

"It is your idea for travelers and traders to stay in while here."

"But that was for next year. Why now?"

"Because there is a need, and we have the weather to do so now."

Nuada could see the reasons and felt any other questions would only hamper the results. Beag showed him the plans he had for the design, and then he had to return to his work, leaving Nuada alone to watch the construction.

Nuada had not pushed to build more this year, and it left him wondering why these men who were tired would continue to push themselves.

After a couple of hours at the site, Nuada turned back to the village and the company of the teachers there. He found them all at the old school building sitting outside and drinking of their wine. He could hear their laughter before he got close and wondered of the reason.

One of the new teachers was being questioned by Nuada's oldest son, Iolair.

"What is this all about?" asked Nuada as he approached.

Pytheas, still laughing, said, "Our new teacher here has just met your son for the first time. When he was questioned in the tongue of the Phoenicians by one so young, he choked on his wine."

"Then my teaching skills have paid off with him," said a smiling Nuada.

"Indeed, Nuada. He still scares me when he does something like this."

"I feel the same at times myself. He has a mind that does not quit when it comes to finding knowledge."

They all raised their mugs of wine in salute to Iolair, and Nuada sat and joined them. They continued to talk about the skills of Iolair even after he had left them. Nuada was proud of his son, and to have the teachers talk of him made him feel more so. Nuada began to think that it was time to teach the boy about the skills of war too. Someday he will lead people; if not in the valleys, then somewhere else, and he will have need of them. Nuada's mind wandered over the possibilities that his son would have in the future. It was late when he departed the company of the teachers, and Nuada returned to the cooking area for his evening meal.

As the late days of Summer dwindled, work continued on in both valleys. Nuada still went from work site to work site watching as more things filled him with wonder about these people he had brought into the valleys. The forge building that was going up near the mill sites was a thing close to Nuada's heart, and he watched it develop from an idea into something real. It was twice as big as the present site and would have many new tools and possibilities within it.

Mor was near to finishing the new houses now and was starting to shift some of his people out to the stone houses to finish them. The village had grown this year, and every change made it seem even bigger. Nuada no longer knew everyone by name, and this bothered him at times. They all knew him and what he stood for.

Out at the inner protection wall where Beag had started the new building for travelers, Nuada continued to watch here too, and as the walls went up, he had to hold his breath for the sheer size of the design. Beag had outdone himself when it came to the beauty and practicality of design. Again it was a two-story building, but his attention to detail made it stand out above all other buildings in the village except the new school building. It was almost ready to have its roof installed, and then it would be up to Mor to finish the inside details of this structure. That could be done even if the weather changed quickly. Nuada was pleased that they had pushed on and made all of the things possible.

The days pushed on as the construction had, and Summer was in its last days of warmth. The harvest was now near, and plans were made for the feast that would follow. Everyone was looking forward to the end of the season and a time to relax with family again. Nuada was looking happily at returning to his teaching, as were the other teachers.

Mor had one of his craftsmen carve both Greek and native alphabets onto long boards that were hung in each of the classrooms in both the new and old schools. He had easels built too for the teachers that would help them display thoughts and images on paper for the students.

Beag has finished all of his stone work and now had time to enjoy his beer. Two of the lift machines were now in storage for the Winter at the stable building, and the other two were at the sawmill site. Mor's crews still had their hands full with finish work on the stone houses and the new building near the inner protection wall.

While the hunters had now been out hunting for deer, they reported that there was no sign of any raiders in the area. A'Chreag and his team had brought in more copper and tin ores for Winter projects and were ready to close down the forge near the stable in the village. The new forge building had most of its work done now, and all of the new ores were stockpiled there. Nuada did have a chance to look around the new building and noted that it now contained two massive forges for the melting of the metals and many new areas that he could only use his imagination to think what they would be used for. The new machines from the old forge building were already transferred into the new building and sat waiting to be placed where they would be used best. Nuada could see the thoughts behind all of this work and would praise A'Chreag and his crew when he could.

Then one day they began to harvest the grain crop and transfer them to the grist mill to make the needed flour for the Winter months. The women and the children of the valleys worked hard and quickly, as they knew that the other crops would soon need their attention too.

Summer was now over, and the village settled into its hurried preparations before the weather changed.

Nuada now worked at preparations for his teaching. He spent many long hours making copies of his language program. It was tiring work, but Nuada knew of the rewards that it held for him and his students.

- FALL AND THE STATUE -

It had been a long time coming, but now the crops were in, and the planning for the feast moved ahead quickly. At the final meeting for the Summer of the consul members, they decided to build a pair of buildings in the Spring for candle making and glassmaking near where the forge building was built. Two new water wells were to be built in the second valley and two more out by the stone houses in front of the village. Beag had planned to build eight more houses of stone there too. A discussion was held about adding to the stone shops near the inner protection wall, but that was put on hold for now. Mor would also add eight more houses in the second valley. Also an expansion of the stable for the horses would be done after the old forge building came down. They had another full work year ahead of them, but they did not mind the work.

At the school, Pytheas had set up a schedule and assigned classrooms to all the teachers, including Nuada. They had now planned to reopen the school in about three weeks. This was something that Nuada really looked forward to; he wanted to teach again and get away from the politics of the village.

One morning Nuada was up and about walking around the village, taking in all of the changes again. Memories filled his thoughts about what was before and what would come later. The cool, morning air that had greeted him when he first set out had now warmed to a comfortable temperature. He had walked out in the meadow in front of the village and had stopped at Jan's crypt; for some reason it had always comforted him in the past. After a short time there, Nuada continued on to the stone shop buildings to see if any of them had been restocked. Looking inside them, he saw that some items were replaced, and in others they were still empty. His footsteps then took him out through the gates of both protection walls, and he turned left and on past the ridge that hid the village. He stopped near the spot where he had fought the raiders long ago by himself and with Creatrix's help. He looked down to where they had been cutting the trees for this year's construction; it looked bare. Crews had already been there to gather the branches for firewood and had burned the rest of the debris. Nuada then looked across the stream toward the old village of Mor's, and more memories came back of that adventure. He stood there, not knowing how long he had been out of the village, before he again turned and walked back following the stream. He continued on and, on a whim, looked out to the island. "I miss the simple days when I first came here," he thought.

He moved on and passed through the second valley's protection wall without really seeing it. He came to the junction in the road and again paused. "Which way now?" he wondered. He finally turned to the right and back toward the cut between the valleys. Looking out to his left, he could see the last place in the valleys where they had cut trees. New scrub growth had started to fill in the area again. He nodded and knew that this is what was normal. "In a few years, you would not know that we had removed any trees from here," he thought.

He passed through the cut, still marveling at how they had done so much in such a short period of time there. On he walked, slowing his steps as he walked through the new houses that Mor had built. The curbs and sidewalks added a sense of lasting to the atmosphere of this latest project. Nuada was pleased by the comfort it brought.

He now moved toward the stable area and the empty forge building. He knew that he would find no one about here at this time of day, and then he paused outside of the meeting hall. "Would anyone be here?" he wondered. Then he stepped up on the porch and entered. It was dark inside after being outside all day, and when his eyes became adjusted to the dark, he could see that at his usual table sat Beag with a beer in his hand.

"Nuada, draw a beer and join me," he called.

Nuada got his beer and sat across from Beag and took a long drink. "I have just had my morning walk, and it brought back many memories. Some were good and some were bad, but I have no regrets."

"That is how it is supposed to be, my friend."

"What about you? Do you ever think back to your old home and wonder if things had been different?"

"Of course I think about it, but my fate brought me here, and I am glad of it."

"Why? You could have done the same anywhere else."

"I think not. Because of you — you inspired me to be more than I was. I have pushed myself to dream about what could be and not just settle."

"It was not me. You had a chance to change this valley, and you have done so through your own hard work."

"But it was your ideas and inspiration that made me do so."

"Do you think the future children of these people will ever remember of us?"

"Yes. We have made what is for them to see for a long time. Never doubt that we will be a part of the history of these valleys for many generations of our children."

They continued to talk of the valleys and their place in them for many hours, and finally Mor dropped by to join in the conversation. The beer was good, and the talk continued long after the evening meals. When Nuada departed the meeting hall, he was surprised by the lateness of the hour and hurried home.

On the morning of the feast, Nuada slept in, and when he finally arose to greet the day, Wolf was staring him in the face as he stretched and had a large yawn. Nuada reached over and scratched him on the head and said, "I know. I am becoming lazy, my friend. Let us go downstairs and see of our family."

Nuada's family had already departed the house and had gone to the outdoor cooking area. Nuada looked around the empty house and then quickly dressed. He let Wolf run, as was his usual routine. When he was done, the pair walked to the cooking area and the company of others.

When they arrived, it seemed like the whole village was already there. Pytheas and the other teachers waved and called to Nuada as he walked into the area. Nuada walked to their table first and greeted them. Soon they would have the company of each other for most of the Winter months. After some casual talk, Nuada went to find his mate and retrieve his daughter, as he knew that his mate would be busy preparing the feast.

Nuada's mate saw him first and hurried to meet him. "It is about time you got out of your bed, husband."

"Did I miss something, wife?"

She laughed and handed him their daughter. "Only your family. Take care of them and keep them from underfoot."

Nuada walked back to his table and sat holding his daughter. Soon his two boys came running up to the table out of breath.

"Father, I was just questioning the new teachers again, and they told me to ask of you my questions."

"They wish to be left alone for now, Iolair. Save your questions for the school. That is when it will mean something."

"I do not understand, Father. I thought that it was always good to question."

"It is, but there are times when the asking and the answers must come later."

Iolair nodded, not really understanding but willing to take his father's words for truth. The boys joined their father and watched the people of the village and tried to listen in on their conversations. Most of the talk was about all of the things that had changed in the valleys. Nuada was interested in what they thought of the changes and kept his thoughts to himself.

Millert dropped by Nuada's table and thanked him again for allowing his group into the valleys. "You have given us a purpose and protection. We wish that we could do more to honor you for it."

"You have done that already, my friend. Through your hard work you have helped us add to the village and what it means."

"But what are we to do now that most of the building has finished?"

"Possibly the hardest part is yet to come. The school will open soon, and the learning will seem impossible for many of them, but they will learn. Then there are the storms of Winter ahead. Work crews will be required to keep the streets clear and repair any damage from the storms. Do not be fooled by this short break."

"Whatever is required, we will be ready to help."

Nuada nodded in reply, and then they were interrupted by Mor returning to Nuada's table to ask a question of him. It was about the need for furniture for the new building for the traders and others who would come to the village. "I see no hurry for that now, Mor. We will have all Winter to make what is needed," Nuada said.

After more discussion about the details of the building, Mor returned to his table and family. Throughout the rest of the morning, Nuada had village people stopping by to ask more questions of him about different things, and at last Nuada felt that he had to get away from them for awhile. He took his daughter back to his mate and told her that he must get away for awhile. She understood, as she had been watching all of the people coming and going from their table.

Nuada felt he needed something to do to clear his mind of all of the questions. He walked home and went to the pantry to retrieve the notes that Amasis had brought back from Alexandria. He had not had time to even look at the papers about machines of the old worlds. Nuada spent almost three hours going over the notes and was surprised at the amount of details about these machines. Many would benefit the village. His attention was broken by the music coming from the cooking area, and he could hear the loud laughter too.

He started to return to the area, but he was torn by the thought that it would only bring more questions from those gathered there. He changed his path and walked to the lakeshore and looked across to the island again. It had now been many years since he had last stood over there. He thought of crossing over but changed his mind at the last moment and again turned to go back to the cooking area.

Nuada walked into the area and got himself a beer before he sat down again. He felt detached from everything going on and just looked around at everyone there. He really did not even hear their talk and felt that he was outside of everything going on. The area was filled now with the odors from the cooking. Wild pig and venison smells wafted by Nuada's nose, and he could detect other smells that were mixed in with them. He was starting to feel hungry. His stomach growled to add to this feeling. He took another long pull from his beer and got up to retrieve another. As he passed Pytheas, who was getting another mug of wine, Pytheas said, "I am beginning to grow exhausted of all this company. What of you, Nuada?"

"Yes, but I need of the food first, my friend."

"Oh no! Andocides and Dionysins are about to play their music now. I do think I shall leave. Talk with me tomorrow."

Two of the other new teachers joined the others and began to play their music. Nuada turned to watch as they started and then returned to his table. As he sat, Pytheas hurried away from the area.

The music was different than anything Nuada had heard before, and at times it hurt his ears. He too was beginning to wonder if it was time to leave. His mate settled the argument by bringing his meal to him.

"I wish you had done this a little quicker, wife. Then I would not have to sit and hear of this while I try to eat."

"It is not so bad, husband. It makes the people laugh."

About the time Nuada finished his meal, they stopped playing. He got up to get another beer and watched them return to their table. "I hope they are better teachers than those who played of their music tonight."

Beag saw him and raised his mug to salute him, and then he returned to his conversation with others at his table.

The night continued long after Nuada had returned home with his family, and he found peace there in its quietness. Tomorrow was another day, and he waited for the needed sleep to come.

The next morning Nuada went to the school and inside sat in the assigned classroom by himself. He had brought his dictionary with him, and he settled down to add some new words to the long text. About an hour later, Pytheas stuck his head into the room and asked, "Are you in need of a break, Nuada?"

Nuada set his quill down and turned to face Pytheas. "I could do with a short walk to ease the stiffness from my bones, friend."

Together they stepped outside and walked slowly around the new school building. They talked of the classes and how they would need to find a way to promote the students from one age class to another. That way, they would not be repeating things taught earlier for the benefit of new students. They set upon the idea of a test at the end of a season, so those could move forward with the learning of other things.

"Have the new teachers come by today, Pytheas?"

"No, I think last night was a little much for them."

After they had circled the school three times, Nuada returned to working on his dictionary. Just after midday he decided to walk to the front of the village again and look into the new building, where he thought Mor still might be working.

As he passed the teachers' houses, he noticed that they were very quiet. He hurried his footsteps past, as he did not feel like talking to them today. As he reached a junction onto a new street that as yet did not have any new houses on it, Nuada turned and followed it out into the open meadow. As he reached another junction, he paused and turned to look back. "Next year there will be more houses here and more changes," he thought.

He looked up at the sky and wondered when the weather would change. Only a few soft, white clouds filled the distant horizon. Then he turned to make his way on to the inner protection wall and the shops and new building nearby.

He entered the shop-lined street from the ridgeline and walked slowly toward the new building, but something made him turn and look back at the ridge. He turned around and walked back. At the end of the line of shops, Nuada began to mentally make a design of a new building there. It could be used for storage or as a hospital when a battle returned to the village again. He knew that it was possible for raiders to find them again, and he never let the thought go far from his thoughts.

When he was satisfied with the size of the building in his mind, he made his way to the new building. As he stepped in the building, he could hear men working upstairs. He followed the noise and found Mor in one of the rooms doing finishing work on the walls. Mor saw him, and they stepped out into the hallway to talk.

"What did you think of the feast last night, Nuada?"

"The food was good, as was the company of the people, but the noise did drive me away for awhile."

"I can understand of that."

"Mor, while I was walking out here, I had a thought for a project for next year. Perhaps we could build another building at the end of the shops here. We could use it for storage or as a hospital if the raiders ever return. What think you?"

Mor walked over to the window that looked down the street and then turned and said, "We should do that. Do you want me to talk to Beag about it?"

"No. I will ask of him."

They continued their small talk as Mor took him around the building and showed him what he had in mind for the rooms. After about a half hour, Mor had to return to his work, and Nuada headed back to the village. Again as he passed the teachers' houses, it was still quiet, and he hurried his footsteps past them. Nuada turned onto the street that would take him to the meeting hall and hopefully his finding of Beag.

When Nuada entered the hall, he found that it was almost empty, and there was no sign of Beag. When he asked of him, he was told that he had gone to the quarry. This made Nuada curious, and he departed the hall following the ridgeline to the quarry.

When Nuada got to the quarry, he saw Beag up on the cut with some of his crew, and they were cutting a large block of stone from the side of the ridge. Nuada waited until they began to move it down from the cut. He called out to Beag and was answered in return. Beag hurried down off the side of the cut and hurried to Nuada's side.

"What can I do for you, Nuada?"

"I was talking to Mor out at the new building about another building for next year. I came to talk to you about it but found that you had come here. I thought that you had finished with your stonework for this year?"

"I am finished. This is for the Winter. I plan to do some sculpting, and this was a good time to retrieve the stone I need. Now what of this new building?"

Nuada explained the concept of the building design he had in mind and its uses. He also said that Mor thought it was a good idea too. Beag then said he would look at the site and give his thoughts on it later in the day.

Nuada left Beag to his stonework and walked back to the outdoor cooking area and a chance to sit in the sun while the weather was still mild. Here too it was still almost empty, and he sat at his table. He thought that the feast last night must have been a success, as the village people had almost all slept in today. Nuada listened for the sound of the village and the wildlife that lived within the valley and found it lacking. Nuada felt comforted by the lack of sound and slowly closed his eyes and felt the warmth of the sun on his cheeks. Nuada awoke about an hour later to the sounds of the village coming to life again. He stood and decided to return to the school and the work on his dictionary.

While walking back to the school, a wagon hauling the stone that Beag had cut from the ridge trundled past on its way to the woodworking building. Nuada only paused for a minute and then continued on. Nuada returned to his classroom and began to work on his book. It was not until late in the afternoon that he stopped and walked back to the meeting hall.

As soon as Nuada walked through the door, Beag and Mor called to him. He waved back and went and drew a beer before he joined them.

"We have been talking about that building you mentioned. I think the site is large enough for what you had in mind, and the ground there is solid enough to hold it," Beag said.

"I think we are limiting ourselves because we were thinking about the crews required to build all of the other things we had planned. With this new group, we have all of the skilled labor we need to push ahead now," Nuada responded.

The others nodded in reply, and they sat back to enjoy their beer and the company of each other. They talked for another two hours before Nuada said he had to return home for his evening meal with his family.

At last the day arrived for the reopening of the school. Nuada arrived early and as usual found Pytheas waiting to greet the students. Some of the children were already out on the playground, and Iolair, along with his younger brother, went to join them after having walked to school with their father.

"I see that your boys are ready to learn, Nuada."

"They did not stop over the Summer, my friend. Every day was a question from them both."

Pytheas smiled at Nuada's response, as he had seen them question the teachers many times during the year. This year Nuada had six classes to teach, and it would involve most of the day now. Nuada had prepared himself for the challenge and looked forward to the teaching. After talking for a short time, Nuada went to his classroom and set up the needed supplies and had his dictionary with him. Soon his students started to file into the room, and the teaching began.

At the end of the first day, Nuada felt tired, but he looked forward to the next day already. He had taught their native language, along with Greek and

Egyptian, to his different classes of children and adults. Iolair was disappointed that the teaching did not include the Phoenician language. Nuada told him that he would continue to teach him at home and that right now it was not needed by the people of the valleys.

Because the weather was still mild, the village people continued to join together at the outdoor cooking area. Nuada walked with his two boys there and sat at their table to wait for their evening meal. Nuada's mate brought him his daughter to hold while she prepared the meal.

The other teachers arrived shortly after Nuada and sat and talked between themselves at their table. Nuada wanted to hear what they thought of the school and their students, but his family came first.

The boys talked about their different classes, and Nuada listened in on what they had to say. Iolair was almost as good a teacher as any in the village and helped his younger brother to understand many points of the teachings. Nuada himself was learning from the boy about history and mathematics although Iolair was unaware of it happening.

After eating Pytheas dropped by their table to talk with Nuada.

"The teachers that Amasis brought back are doing well and are a little surprised that the people are so willing to learn," he commented.

"We all learn from each other. That is the main lesson to be learned, Pytheas."

"There is a lot of truth in that thought, Nuada."

Over the next week the weather began to change, and rain and wind followed day after day. Nuada was so busy with the school that he did not notice the changing weather. It was only in the evenings when he was with his family that it did enter his thoughts. He missed the companionship of his friends and the people of the village. One day he went to the meeting hall and found Beag at his usual spot near the fireplace enjoying his beer.

"Beag, my friend. What is new with you?"

"Ah, Nuada. I had a talk with A'Chreag the other day, and he wanted me to think about adding to the raceway so he could add another waterwheel for the forge building. What think you?"

"With all of his new machines, I think it is a needed thing."

"Then it will be another thing for my work list in the Spring."

"It will not be too much for you?"

"I think not. I have the trained help now, and if nothing else is added to the list, I can make it happen."

"Good. That will make A'Chreag happy. Have you seen Mor today? I have been so busy that I have missed of his company."

"Not yet, but he should be along any time."

They sat and enjoyed their beer together until Mor arrived. While they were waiting for Mor, Nuada glanced around the room and found some new things hanging on the walls. Above the fireplace was a rack of antlers mounted on a plaque of wood, and on the wall across from him was a tapestry with a fine pattern showing a hunting scene.

Nuada admired the added touches to the room and felt that it made it more comfortable.

Shortly Mor pushed his way through the door of the hall. He shook the rain from his cloak and walked to the table to join his friends.

"It is beginning to rain harder, and the wind is picking up, friends."

"What delayed you, Mor?"

"I was with A'Chreag at the woodworking building, and he wanted my advice on the new waterwheel."

Beag laughed, "So he cornered you too. He wants me to extend the raceway at the mill site come Spring."

Nuada laughed at his friends. "Well he did not ask of me for anything. Of that I am not surprised. He has completely taken over the forge building and made it such that I do not understand of all of the new machines anymore."

After a couple hours of friendship and the sharing of many beers, Nuada said his good nights and went home to his family. Outside the rain began to blow sideways, and Nuada pulled his cloak tighter around his shoulders. Rain ran into his eyes, and he fought to stand against the wind. "This will be a bad night," he thought.

With the coming of dawn, the darkness remained in the valleys. Thunder crashed against the mountainsides, and everyone remained hidden in their homes. That day the school remained closed, and Nuada taught his boys in the comfort of their house. It was not until midday that the storm began to pass, but the dampness remained. With the passing of the storm, the temperature dropped quickly, and Nuada knew that snow was close at hand.

Nuada remembered the pain of last Winter and had begun to wear the lamb belt under his clothes again to prevent the stiffness from returning. Within two days, the valley returned to its normal Fall weather although it still remained cold. The school was open again, and Nuada returned to his teaching of languages.

One afternoon Amasis stuck his head into Nuada's classroom, which was empty at the moment, and asked of him, "Would you like to taste of our new wine, Nuada?"

"Is it ready?"

"Yes. It is from the first vines that we planted on your island."

Nuada followed Amasis back to the office in the old school building and joined the other teachers already gathered there. A small cask sat on a shelf at the back of the room, and Andocides was pouring mugs for all gathered in the office.

"Has anyone tasted of it yet?" asked Nuada.

Pytheas laughed. "They plan on poisoning all of us together."

This brought a round of laughter from all of the other teachers, and they stood and saluted the small cask with their mugs.

"To a good death," said Andocides. Then they drank of the wine.

Nuada took a small sip and then smelled of the wine. It was different than the wine that the trader had brought but very pleasing to the taste. He drank some more trying to find of the difference and then just enjoyed it for what it was. They all spent the afternoon talking about the wine and some of their classes, but it was mainly about the wine and the process of its making.

When Nuada thought it was time to go home, he stood and felt the effects of the wine. He had not felt like this since he had first tasted wine long ago. He slowly walked home, knowing that the effects would last many hours.

The next morning Nuada awoke with a massive headache and slowly dressed as he thought of the afternoon before. He went downstairs and stoked the fireplace to warm the house. "I must not share of that wine again," he said, holding his head. At that moment, his two boys came down the stairs loudly. This made him feel worse, and he asked them to hold the noise down. Nuada's mate and daughter joined the rest of the family shortly, and she looked at the expression on Nuada's face and shook her head. "You look worse from this side than you must think from the inside."

"I shared of the new wine from the island with the teachers yesterday, and I feel of it now."

"Go and wash of your face while I prepare some food for us."

Nuada did as he was told and felt slightly better. When he returned to the table and the food was placed before him, he suddenly felt as if he had already taken of it, and it sat in his throat. He pushed it away and sat back holding his stomach.

"I think the fresh air will do me more good, wife."

He stood and went outside to stand on the porch. He took deep breaths of the cool, morning air and felt dizzy.

A while later his two sons came out to join him and asked if he was going to the school today.

"Yes, although I do not feel of it," Nuada said.

They gathered their papers for school, and the three set off. Nuada started to feel slightly better, but when he got to the school, Pytheas was not to be seen. This was unusual for him, and Nuada wondered if the wine had the same effect on him. Nuada went into the old school house and looked around to see if any of the other teachers were there. Only three of the new teachers were in the building. Nuada asked after Pytheas and was told that he would be along, but he did not feel well today.

Although Nuada's throat felt dry, he did not drink anything to soothe it. He made his way to his classroom and began to prepare for the day's teachings. It would be a long day for him.

That afternoon when his classes were done, Nuada gathered his papers and hurriedly made his way to the meeting hall and some beer to ease the discomfort of his body. He was not even thinking of his friends as he arrived there, but after pouring a beer and tasting of it, he began to feel better and looked around the room for them. Mor, Farmer, and Anoghas were sitting at their usual table talking among themselves. Beag was not seen, and when Nuada joined them, he asked after him. Mor said, "Beag is doing some sculpting today at the old woodworking building and will be along shortly."

When Nuada was drinking his third beer, Beag arrived and joined the others. He was still dressed in his leather apron and work clothes, which were covered with small, stone chips and dust. When Beag had finished his second beer, Nuada asked how his sculpting was coming along and what the subject was. Beag glanced across at Mor and said, "I have made a start, but I know not the subject yet." Nothing more was said, and they settled into discussion about the village. Again it was late when Nuada went home to his family.

The following week a light snow began to fall on the valleys. At the school, things remained the same, and classes followed classes for the teachers and students alike. In Nuada's spare time, he studied mathematics from the papers that Iolair had brought home with him. Also of interest to Nuada were the papers that Amasis had brought back from Alexandria about the machines of the past. As his understanding of mathematics increased, the machines became clearer within his mind, and he had a greater understanding of their design.

Nuada now avoided the wine of the teachers and spent less time with his friends at the meeting hall. He made his own learning a prime objective, and it involved being with his family more.

One afternoon when Nuada had finished his last class of the day, A'Chreag appeared at the school. He had with him some drawings of machines for the forge and wanted Nuada's opinion on them.

"This machine is called a drill. Amasis told me of the design from his homeland and thought it could be of use here."

Nuada looked over the design and then at the bits that were powered by the drill.

"These will be tricky to make and keep sharp. Do you have a plan for that too?"

"Not yet, but it will come."

Nuada told him of some of the machine designs that Amasis had also brought back. They continued to talk about how these machines could benefit the village, and then A'Chreag had to leave.

With his departure, Nuada continued to think about the machine designs, and in the back of his mind, he missed working at the forge, but he knew that Creatrix had him teaching for a reason.

Nuada picked up his papers and started to walk home but decided that it was time to talk with his friends again. He made his way to the meeting hall and found all of them except Beag sitting at their table. He drew a beer and sat down. He listened into their conversation, which was subdued, as they had all become one with the weather now.

Just as Nuada was preparing to leave and go home for his evening meal, Beag entered the hall dressed in his work clothes again. Nuada wanted to hear what he had to say, so he drew another beer and waited for him to tell of his day. Beag remained quiet about his sculpting, and they talked about the village again. Nuada, after finishing his beer, went home, as nothing else was said.

Time for Nuada passed quickly over the next four weeks. School occupied his time and mind. His students were doing well, and outside of some small talk with the other teachers, Nuada kept to himself. His old wound had not bothered him so far this year, and Winter was fast approaching the valleys.

Outside of his walks to the school and home, Nuada had not ventured out into the valleys. He depended on his friends to tell him if anything had changed. A few new babies had been born and were doing well. Other than that news, the village life remained quiet.

One afternoon when Nuada had finished his last class of the day, Mor and Beag dropped by to talk. Both of them seemed a little excited to Nuada, and he wondered of the reason. Beag asked if he was done for the day, and when he said yes, they asked him to follow them to the old woodworking building. Nuada was still wondering of the reason but followed them.

At the building, they went inside to the storage area, where Beag had been doing his sculpting. The stone he had been working on was covered with a large piece of cloth, and Beag asked him to stand in front of it. Beag went around to the side of it and slowly drew the cloth aside. Underneath a statue of Nuada appeared. Nuada did not know what to say but looked closely at the results.

"What is this, Beag? I do not understand why you did this of me?"

"You were always wondering if anyone would remember of you in the future. This way our children's children will remember of you and what you have done for the village. Your outstretched arms show that you welcomed all into the village."

Nuada was at a loss for words and shook his head at Beag's words. Finally he said, "I do not deserve of this. Both of you have had a great part in making the village what it is. If anything you need to be recognized for that effort on your part."

Mor then replied, "We will come later. This is about you now. We plan to set the statue on the inner wall above the portal gate. It will be seen by all who come to the village."

Nuada felt pride in being recognized by his friends and said nothing more about it except to thank them both. Nuada walked home dazed by the recognition and told his mate of the statue.

"They understand the value that you have been to the village and wanted to honor you this way. It is time that you yourself understand of that too."

Nuada still felt confused by the statue and needed time to understand of it.

Another week passed, and Winter was now on their doorstep. Nuada continued with his teaching as if nothing had happened and waited for the season to change.

- WINTER AND CONTENTMENT -

Nuada awoke as on any other day and dressed for school, but this was not just another day. Today he was giving his first test under the new system that Pytheas had devised. It would be used to measure the learning curve of the students. But it was more than that. It would also rate how well the teachers were doing with their communication skills.

Iolair and Uilleam had both been studying for this day, and they felt prepared. As for Nuada, he was not sure how he really felt about the test. Tomorrow would answer any questions.

Nuada and his boys stepped out into a snowy morning , but the wind was absent. They walked to school and were greeted by Pytheas, who was standing just inside the entry door to the new school.

"Good morning, Pytheas. Where are the other teachers this morning?"

"They are all in their classrooms. They worry that the test is more about them than the students."

"Well in a way it is. They must change their teaching to fit the students, and this will measure that difference."

"What about you. Are you prepared to change too?"

"I am always prepared for that, be it for something for the village or in my teaching; it will also improve me too."

"Well said, my friend. I will talk with you later."

Nuada went to his classroom and set out the tests he had prepared for his classes. He covered the carved alphabets on the wall and waited for his students to arrive. Soon they filled in, and the tests began.

At the end of the day, Nuada felt drained, and after walking his boys home, he went to the meeting hall. He knew he could not stay long but had to return and grade the tests at home. As usual his group of friends welcomed his arrival, and they talked about the village again. Nothing was new there, and finally Nuada returned home to his tests and the long night ahead of him.

Long after his evening meal and after his family went to bed, Nuada continued to work on the tests. He found few errors, which showed a great interest by the students. He was pleased with the results. However, the sheer number of tests to be checked kept him up late, and he was surprised to awaken in the early morning still at the table with the tests covering the table. He quickly finished the last of the tests before his family awoke and started to come downstairs for their morning meal. He was just placing the tests into his bag when Iolair and Uilleam came down.

Iolair asked first about the tests, and Nuada told him he had to wait along with the other students for the results. Soon it was time to walk to school, and the boys hurried ahead of Nuada. Pytheas was in the office waiting for the results of the tests when Nuada appeared and handed him the scores.

"They did exceptionally well on the tests. I see no need on my part to change any of my teaching."

Pytheas nodded and said, "Some of the new teachers had some problems, but I think it was because of the language difference. You may have to tutor them some."

"If they are willing, I will do my part, Pytheas."

"Good. We will talk later when I have had a chance to talk with them."

Nuada returned to his classroom and began his day with the returning of the tests and going over the answers. Some questions followed, and then they moved on to new studies.

At the end of the school day, Nuada returned to the office and met with the new teachers who Pytheas felt needed more instruction in the native language by Nuada. He began by asking questions of each of them and then setting a time to meet with each of them in turn. They were eager to learn themselves and accepted Nuada's words. Finally they agreed to meet after classes tomorrow, and this pleased Nuada, as he was exhausted from the work late last night.

Nuada left the school and walked to the meeting hall again. It was not really for the company of his friends but to find some time to relax. He did not linger, as he had only one beer and then went home for his evening meal and some needed sleep.

For a period of two weeks, Nuada taught the new teachers. At the end, he thought that they could now learn the fine points of his language by themselves.

He would still be open to questions from them at any time and felt it was better this way. Pytheas agreed to Nuada's plan, and they all moved ahead with their teaching.

One morning Nuada awoke to bright sunshine and, after dressing warmly, went for a walk before returning to school. They had a light Winter so far, and this was a surprise after the Winter before when Nuada's old wound had acted up on him. He still carried his walking staff in this weather as a precaution, but he was ready for the warmth of the Spring. The darkness of the continuous snowy weather was depressing, but he was glad to be teaching instead of sitting at home doing carving.

At the school, the conversation between the teachers was about the weather and when it would break. Nuada smiled at their worries and said nothing. Spring would come when it was ready.

Later that day A'Chreag stopped by and asked Nuada to come by the woodworking building and look at his new waterwheel that he had built for the forge. They talked a little about items that he had made for the shops for the Spring traders when Nuada asked him to make a sword for Iolair. He explained that it was time to teach him a little about warfare. A'Chreag agreed, and they parted company shortly after.

As Nuada was leaving the school and heading for the woodworking building, Mor was passing in the street. Nuada called out to him and asked him to make a bow for Iolair. Again he explained that it was to teach him about warfare. Mor quickly agreed, and they then said they would meet later at the meeting hall.

Nuada entered the building to meet a A'Chreag and wandered into the back storage room where he saw the massive wheel. He was looking over the design when A'Chreag walked in from the back.

"What think you, Nuada?"

"It is massive enough to drive anything you could possibly want to make."

"It is, and now that we have a true building built for the work, it was the only way to make it."

"Let me know when you are going to install it. I want to be there."

"I will."

Nuada soon departed and made his way to the meeting hall and a few beers. He joined his fellow consul members, and they chatted about the coming Spring work. Mor asked Nuada if he was coming to the next meeting, as they had missed him at the last two. When Nuada asked when it would be held, he was told tomorrow night. He promised to try and make it, but the school came first, and if there was a problem, he would be absent.

Soon Nuada again departed early, as he had work to do at home for the school. After his evening meal, Nuada settled down and went over the day's work and began to prepare for tomorrow. Nuada's mate watched him working over his papers and finally said, "Husband, you are working too hard. You need a break from this studying that you do all of the time now."

Nuada looked up at her and realized that it had indeed taken over his life.

"Wife, I will ask Pytheas for a day off tomorrow, as I also have ignored my friends too. They asked me if I was coming to the consul meeting, and they said that I had missed the last two meetings. Perhaps it is time for me to look around at everything again."

"Indeed. They need of you to advise them, and you cannot do that sitting in the school or being here doing the same."

The next morning Nuada talked with Pytheas about some time off from his teaching and the need to be closer to the village people again. Pytheas reluctantly agreed and asked when he needed to go. Nuada told him it needed to start today, which shocked Pytheas, but in the end, Nuada got his wish, and Pytheas would take over his classes. Nuada explained what was going on in his classes now and where they needed to go.

About a half hour later, Nuada walked out of the school, and suddenly he felt free again. As he was dressed warmly, he set out for the second valley and anything going on there. He passed through the cut between the valleys and turned toward the mill sites. When he got to the junction road going toward the protection wall and then to the mills, he paused to look over the new sites, where soon they would start to build the buildings for the candle shop and the glassmaking. There was still room for two more buildings, and Nuada began to wonder what they could be used for.

He continued on to the forge building and walked inside. No one was around, and Nuada looked at the new machines, which he had no idea what they were used for, and he thought that he would ask A'Chreag for a demonstration of their uses. He walked around and thought again that he had been away too long. He next went to the sawmill, which was now quiet for the Winter. This he understood better, as he was the one who designed it. As he stepped outside, he looked across at the new houses and then toward the ridgeline, where more of the new houses sat. All were now occupied, and as Nuada glanced toward the flour mill, his eyes looked up at the massive dam. He thought, "Beag did well with this project, and it has brought prosperity to the valleys."

Nuada turned and walked back to the protection wall for the second valley and then through the portal gate before turning left and back toward the village. He slowed his footsteps as he passed the caves and looked out toward the island again. Then he hurried on to the village and around to the meeting hall. It was still early, and he stopped before going into the hall. He could look across the meadow and see the new stone houses and the shops in the distance. "Should I go there?" he pondered. Then he made up his mind to do so and set out at a brisk pace. He had to follow the street, as there was still snow on the ground that had not been removed in the meadow. He turned onto the street that held the shops and walked into each one to look at the items waiting to be traded in the Spring. In one shop, two of the village women were stocking a shelf with blankets that had been made by some of the women recently. Nuada did not disturb them but turned and walked back to the new building. Inside he went from room to room, seeing that Mor had also been busy making furniture for them. Some rooms were empty, but Nuada knew that Mor would see that they would all be furnished before Spring. Nuada then returned to the meeting hall to wait for his friends.

He did not have to wait, as they were already here. Nuada went and pulled a beer and then joined his friends. After Nuada had a long drink of his beer, he told them of his walk around both valleys. Then he praised Mor for his work on the furniture for the new building. He was asked why he was not teaching today, and he told them that he needed time to himself for awhile.

A little later they began their meeting of the consul and discussed the building program again. As Mor would have the most time to do extra building programs, they wanted him to go ahead and build four more houses in the second valley near the sheep stable. Beag had the largest work projects to do, which included the new warehouse and more of the stone houses in the front of the village; he also had to build the two new shops near the mill sites. Then there was the adding to the water raceway for A'Chreag. About half of his crew would be required to do the quarry work. All of the building would last until mid-Summer, and then if nothing else was required, they would continue to build more houses.

Mor had been working on rebuilding some of the wagons that had been hard-used from last season, and he inspected the lift machines for wear, which looked good to him.

Farmer said that he expected to add to the fencing in the second valley this year and that the sheep were doing well. They would not add to the crop meadow this year, as they had enough ground for what was needed and enough food to trade too.

Millert and Anoghas reported that their people were in good spirits and knew what was expected of them in the coming work.

Nuada reported on the school and told them of the new tests and that the results of the tests were encouraging. He thanked them for the hard work in building the new school and said that they had found no problems with the building.

They broke up the meeting with more beer and settled in for an evening of companionship together. While Nuada was drinking of his beer, he again looked around the room and now noticed that A'Chreag had also added to the displays above the fireplace. He had added two crossed swords, which were mounted on a large, wood plaque.

When Nuada departed the company of his friends, he noticed another change in the weather. It was warmer, and the scent of rain was in the air. He hurried home for his evening meal and the company of his family.

Two more weeks passed, and outside of the expected Spring rains, there were no surprises from the weather. It was growing warmer day by day, and everyone knew that soon the work would begin again.

- SPRING AND MORE WORK -

The weather broke quickly that year, and almost all of the Winter snows had disappeared from the warm Spring rains. The stream remained low enough for the raceway work to begin. The two lift machines that were stored near the mill sites were quickly put to work, and one of the other machines from the horse stable in the village was moved to the sheep-stable area in the second valley for the building of Mor's houses. The fourth machine was moved out to the area where more of the first stone houses were going to be built this year. But most of the work began at the quarry site. Soon wagons were moving the cut stone throughout the valleys.

Nuada had just returned to his teaching, but his mind was on the building going on, and he wished that he could become more of a part of it. He knew that soon, probably within three or four weeks, the school season would end, and then he could return to the work outside again.

One afternoon after school, Nuada walked out to the front meadow to look at the work going on out there. The four new houses were going up quickly. These were behind the houses across from the teachers' houses on one of the new streets there. The new curbing and sidewalks were already done, and Nuada walked around admiring the workmanship. He wanted to go to the second valley and see how the new raceway addition was coming but knew that he did not have enough daylight to go today. That did not stop him from walking to the quarry site, where he was amazed at the amount of the ridgeline disappearing from the cut between the valleys. The roadway between the valleys was now wide enough for five wagons at a time. He watched as men cut the stone from the hillside and then lowered it down to be moved to the cutting area. Beag was nowhere to be seen, and Nuada knew he was busy at the raceway project.

Darkness began to settle around Nuada before he walked to the meeting hall to await his friends. Mor was the first to arrive, and they talked about the new construction until Beag arrived. Mor said that tomorrow he would begin to shift some of his crew to the new houses in front of the village. Nuada was just preparing to leave when Beag entered the hall. After a few short words, Nuada went home for his evening meal.

For the next two days, Nuada was working on a new test for his students, the last of the year. It was hard for him to concentrate on the tests, as his mind was on the work outside. Pytheas noticed Nuada's distraction and had also noticed it in many of the other students as well. Soon the planting and other work would force the school to close, and Pytheas knew that these were the cause of the distractions.

The following week the tests were given, and again Nuada's students did well. The other teachers had improved, and it showed in the results of their tests as well. By the end of that week, Pytheas knew that he could not keep the school open any longer and told the teachers, including Nuada, that he was closing the school until the Fall.

Nuada could not have been happier, and when the school finished about halfway through the last day, Nuada hurried home and put away his school notes and then walked over to the second valley.

His hurried footsteps took him quickly to the raceway project that he had yet to see. It had only been three weeks since they had begun the work, but already the outside wall near the creek was already done, and they were making headway on the inner wall behind the forge building. The water into the raceway was dammed off, and that had stopped the sawmill from working, and Mor was in need of more lumber. Piles of newly cut trees were piled around the sawmill, waiting for it to begin working again.

A'Chreag had already moved his new waterwheel to the front of the forge building and was waiting for the raceway to be finished. Nuada stopped to talk with A'Chreag, but he was busy making more hinges and latches for the houses. His crew was making more of the copper sheets for roofing, and the noise inside made Nuada hurry and leave. He followed the ridgeline across the back of the valley until he arrived at Mor's houses. Here too the work was almost done on the four houses, and again he saw no sign of Mor.

Nuada continued on around the valley, following the ridgeline until he returned to the cut between the valleys. After passing through the cut, he followed a wagon on to the front of the village. The wagon did not stop at the houses, and Nuada followed it to the shops at the inner protection wall and the site where the new large building was to be built. Nuada climbed the steps to the top of the wall where he could look down on the whole meadow. He sat where he could watch, and soon more wagons pulled up and began unloading their stone. Beag had already placed stakes in the ground where the foundation was to be placed. Some men were digging down to the base rock for that work. Nuada was lost in thought and did not notice how quickly the afternoon had passed. When he did look around again, he realized that he soon had to go home for his evening meal. He climbed down reluctantly and began his walk back. Tomorrow he wanted to become part of the crews doing the work.

The next morning Nuada awoke early and dressed in his work clothes. He then quickly walked to the outdoor cooking area and a chance to work on the projects. When he got there, Mor and Beag were quickly sorting out crews and sending them where they were needed. As he waited, Nuada could hear the wagons and their horse teams moving to where they were needed first. At last Mor and Beag saw Nuada and called him over to them.

"Are you ready to work today, Nuada?" asked Beag.

Nuada nodded and asked where he could be of use.

"Go with the team to the front of the village and help move the lift machine out to the new building site near the inner protection wall," Beag said. "I will be along shortly after I check on the raceway again."

Nuada hurried out to the housing site and waited until the horse team arrived. He told the lead man there that Beag had sent him to help with the moving of the lift machine. The man nodded and showed Nuada where he needed to be and what to do. After the team was hooked to the machine, they began to move slowly toward the new building site. It took about a half hour to arrive and then be setup where it was needed.

Soon it began to lift the cut stone into the foundation trench, and then it became a repeated motion as stone after stone was moved. Soon Nuada became bored with the work and looked for something else to do, as he really was not needed for this work. Beag arrived and was quickly in demand by others on the crew. Soon he was down in the trench checking the placement of the stones, and Nuada knew that he would not get a chance to talk with him.

Nuada then left shortly after and went in search of Mor in the second valley. Mor put him to work on the roof trusses on the houses he was building. By tomorrow these houses would be done except for the interior finishing touches. Then most of the crew would be moved to the new stone houses in the front meadow, but the lumber supplies were now very short. Until the raceway was done, Mor's crews would have to wait.

At the end of the day, Nuada walked home by way of the mill sites to see how the raceway was coming. It looked to Nuada by how much had been done that it would probably take another three days before the raceway would fill with water again. Then he remembered that the waterwheel had to be installed too — add another two days for that project. He continued on home and the end of a satisfied day of work.

Over the next week, Nuada continued to work with Mor's crews doing finishing work at both housing sites. He did not get a chance to look again at the new building going up near the protection wall, but it was far from being on his mind at the moment. On the last day at the houses near the stable in the second valley, Nuada again walked down to the mill site to look at the raceway project. It was done and the waterwheel installed. Already water was flowing through the raceway, and the mill wheels were turning again.

Nuada just stood there and watched them go around and around. Finally something told him it was time to go home. He did stop at the quarry site and found Beag giving some direction for certain cuts of stone blocks. When Beag was free, Nuada asked about the new building near the wall.

"Come by tomorrow and see for yourself, Nuada," Beag said. "It is going up fast now that I have two of the lift machines."

Nuada said he would, and they parted company, as Nuada had to get home for his evening meal.

The next morning Nuada made his way out to the new building as Mor's crews were still waiting on the sawmill to provide enough lumber for more construction. As he passed the teachers' houses, Nuada looked across at the stone houses and saw that some of Beag's crews were laying out new foundations for yet more houses. He continued on out to the new shops and turned left down the street toward the new building going up there. Already the lift machines were moving stone up onto the walls, which were now almost as high as the protection wall.

Nuada paused halfway down the street and watched as the machines continued nonstop, hoisting the blocks ever higher. Some of the wagons bringing in more stone partially blocked his view, and so he turned and climbed the protection wall for a better view. Noise filled the air as men shouted to each other and the horses complained under the loads they had to pull. Standing along the back wall of the building, Nuada saw Beag directing his crew with the placement of the stones. Nuada could see into the building from his vantage point that massive wood beams were already in place to support the second floor of the building.

Time passed, and Nuada did not bother Beag but continued to watch as the building grew higher. The heat of the day pushed ever higher as the morning wore on. Soon the men began to strip off their shirts, and sweat mixed with dust from the stone adorned their bodies.

Just after midday Nuada came down off the wall and started to return to the village. But all at once, Beag called for a halt to the work so the men could get something to eat and drink. Nuada stopped and turned toward Beag, who was going over the drawings next to the construction site. Beag looked up in surprise at Nuada.

"My friend, what think you of the building?"

"It is bigger than I thought it would be, Beag. Do you have any problems with the design?"

"None. It has gone smoothly, as we had the practice from the last large building down the street."

"You are moving fast. When do you expect to finish with it?"

Beag turned and looked at the building and then said, "It should be done in about two weeks. Then we can begin the shop buildings near the mill site."

Nuada told Beag that he had to return to the village and find Mor, as he had to find out if the lumber for the other crew was starting to arrive in the village. Beag told Nuada that Mor had told him that morning that they were going to start tearing down the old forge building this morning and that he could probably find him there. Nuada hurried his footsteps to the forge building.

Just before Nuada got there, he could see that one of the lift machines had been brought from the second valley. Wagons with loads of lumber were lined up waiting to be unloaded. The forge building was gone, and part of the stable wall on that side was also torn down. Men were still clearing the area when Nuada saw Mor.

Nuada caught up with Mor and told him that he had been out at the new building site with Beag. Nuada asked where he would be working and was assigned a place on the crew, cleaning up the site for the stable expansion.

After an hour they began to build the new stable. Nuada worked as hard as anyone, and soon the framing was close to complete. Already it was beginning to get dark when Mor called a halt to the day's work. Almost every one of the men made their way to the outdoor cooking area and were lined up to draw beer. Nuada was in the line too, as he was very thirsty.

The smell of the sweat from their bodies and the loud voices filled the air. The women soon joined the men, and another day began to draw to a close.

Nuada was on his third beer when his mate and children joined him at their table. He found he had a large appetite that had been enhanced by the beer and after eating found himself very sleepy. The family made their way home shortly after, and sleep found Nuada very quickly.

For the next week Nuada continued to work at the stable building, and they were nearing the finishing stages when Nuada wanted to return to the site of the new building near the protection wall.

Mor walked out there with Nuada, as he had to start soon the finishing touches on the building. Some of Mor's crew were already at work laying the floors for the building, and soon the interior walls would start going up too. They walked around the inside and climbed a ladder to the second floor. Mor was going over his notes and doing some measuring. Nuada had noticed that already the two lift machines had been moved back to the second valley. Nuada was curious about the new shop buildings that were going to be built there, so he told Mor that he would see him later and walked back toward the second valley.

Nuada's path took him out through the outer protection wall, where he followed the stream back to the wall outside of the second valley. He passed through the portal gate and could already see the lift machines in the distance. They were again moving stone blocks and swinging them into place at the site. The foundations for both of these buildings were already in place, and the walls on one of them was going up. Nuada stood in the street next to the wagons, again waiting to unload the stone blocks.

Other wagons hauling lumber passed going out to the building at the front of the village. Then some passed going to the sawmill with fresh cut trees from outside of both valleys. Nuada watched the steady movement all around him, trying not to get in the way. He at last walked to the forge building to see what A'Chreag was doing.

Inside it was much the same as when he was last here. A'Chreag was making hinges and latches while his crew was making copper roof sheets. A'Chreag looked up from his latest pour and asked of Nuada if there was anything he could do for him. Nuada said no, as he was just looking at everything going on. A'Chreag nodded and then asked him to follow him toward the back of the building. A'Chreag reached under a blanket on a table and handed Nuada a new sword and scabbard. Nuada looked at it and was amazed at the workmanship of it. The hilt alone was a thing of beauty, and Nuada drew it and examined the fine blade.

"You wanted a sword for Iolair. This is it, my friend. Also the two chests that you wanted for the things of Jan's are done. I will take them to the map table shop for you soon."

Nuada was speechless, but the smile on his face said everything. A'Chreag slapped him on the back and said that he had to return to his work. Nuada nodded and followed him back to the front of the building.

Nuada walked slowly back along the work site, holding his son's sword in his hand. The traffic from the wagons going in both directions held back Nuada's pace as he began to return to the village. He decided that taking the road along the inside of the ridgeline by the caves would find the least amount of wagon traffic. He passed through the portal gate of the second valley and turned left to the village. As he passed the caves, he looked down on the crop meadow, where some of the village women were hoeing the crops. Some of the children were there too, but Nuada did not see of his children.

As Nuada went by the school, he could see some of the village children there and thought that maybe he would find Iolair here. He went into the old school first and found it empty. Then he went to the new school building and inside found Iolair talking with Pytheas.

Nuada waited patiently until they had finished talking, but he held the sword behind him and out of sight. Pytheas spoke first.

"Nuada, do you need of something?"

"Only a word with my son."

"What is it, Father?"

"I have a gift for you," he said as he held out the sword.

Iolair drew the blade and held it before him. "This is a fine sword, Father, but why?"

"Because it is time that you also learned of the ways of warfare too."

Before Iolair could reply, Pytheas said, "It is time that you learn of the outside world's dark ways too."

Iolair only nodded at the response from both men. Then he replaced the blade in its scabbard. Nuada put his arm around his son's shoulder, and they walked out into the sunlight. They went home without a word between them, and Iolair placed it near his sleeping area. Afterwards they walked to the outdoor cooking area and waited for their evening meal.

The action of giving his son the sword made Nuada again think of raiders coming to the village. He thought, "We have many new, untrained men now, and that must change too."

It was getting close to the monthly meeting of the consul again, and Nuada knew that he must bring up the training of the new people with the bows and swords. Iolair would become part of that group too, as would some of the children of the village who were now of that age.

These thoughts were still running through Nuada's mind all through the evening meal, and it continued into his dreams that night.

He awoke in the morning and returned to work out at the new building near the inner protection wall. He did ask Mor about the monthly consul meeting and was told that it was still a week away. They were framing the inner walls of the building, and Nuada could see more and more of the finished structure in his mind. At the end of that day, Nuada took a walk over to the new stone houses in the meadow and circled around the ones under construction by some of Beag's crew. These four were nearing completion, and they had already begun four more foundations across the street from them. He was tired and did not linger but made for the cooking area and a beer before his evening meal.

Pytheas and the other teachers were already in the area, and Nuada stopped to talk for a minute before sitting at his table.

"Nuada? I was thinking about the other day when you gave your son his new sword, and I know that many of the new people do not understand of your need for defense of the valleys. Would you like us to train them, as most of the men have been working so hard on the buildings, they do not have the time."

Nuada thought for a moment and answered that he was going to bring it up at the monthly consul meeting, but if they were willing, then it was all right with him.

Nuada sat at his table and felt much better about the training, as the Greeks were known to be fierce warriors in the past. Soon his family joined him, and he did not say anything about the training to come.

The next week passed quickly with the work being done. One day Mor told him that this evening they would hold the consul meeting. Nuada was ready to explain the need for the warfare training and that the teachers had the time to teach this art to those that needed it.

Nuada left the work site at midday and made his way to the new shop buildings in the second valley. Although the wagons were still going to and fro from the sawmill, the other wagons that hauled the stone blocks had stopped running to the buildings here. The last of the stone walls were within hours of being finished, and soon Mor would need to transfer some of his men there to do the finishing woodwork required. Most of Beag's crew were now out in the meadow in front of the village working on more houses.

Spring was drawing to a close, and Summer was near. They had finished almost all of the planned projects from last Winter. Nuada wondered what was to come next.

After the evening meal at the outdoor cooking area, the consul members walked together to the meeting hall. Although all of them were tired, each of them told of the accomplishments that were now done. Nuada praised them each and then mentioned the training by the teachers for the defense of the valleys. They all agreed that the teachers were the perfect choice. In other business Mor was going to continue building more houses again near the sheep-stable area. Then Nuada asked about the possible building of two more shop buildings in the area of the mill sites. Beag felt that the houses should be done first because of the history of people coming into the village later in the Summer season. If it proved otherwise, he would consider the shop buildings for late in the Summer. Nuada proposed a feast and a break in the construction for next week. This was agreed to, and then they finished the meeting with more beer and small talk about other things going on in the village. When Nuada got home, he found his family already asleep, and he soon joined them.

The next day Nuada was back at work doing finishing touches on the new, large storage building near the protection wall. Late in the afternoon he walked back to the stone house project site to see what had been done there. Of the four new foundations, two already had their walls up and completed. Next to these houses four more foundations were in the beginning stages. Beag was pushing ahead on the houses, and it amazed Nuada that his crews could work so fast. The meadow was almost half filled with new houses now. By next year they would not have room to build anymore here. Nuada wondered if expansion outside of the valleys was possible. It would mean building another protection wall if they did.

The week quickly passed, then it was the day of the planned feast. No one worked that day, and all projects were put on hold for a week. The new, large building was now finished, and some of the stone houses were also complete. Beag had moved the third lift machine to the meadow, and it added to the fury of construction there.

Nuada arrived at the outdoor cooking area early and noticed the happiness of the village people who had also gathered early. Music filled the air, along with the smells of the food being prepared. Children ran through the area laughing while parents tried to quiet them. The teachers were also early, and Nuada had a chance to talk with them. They were ready to begin the teaching of the arts of warfare, and they would use the area between the two protection walls at the front of the village. But today they were here to enjoy the company of the people and share wine between themselves.

Beag and Mor arrived a little later and helped themselves to the beer and a little conversation with Nuada. Nuada told Beag about his thoughts of expanding the village next year outside of the valleys and the need for another protection wall if they did do it. Mor said that they still had room for building in the second valley and did not see a need to build outside of the valleys so soon. Then Beag added that he would need another quarry site, as he only had enough stone to finish the stone houses now and maybe the two shop buildings at the mill site. Nuada knew he was outnumbered on this idea and asked them to think about it for the future.

Shortly after this discussion, A'Chreag arrived with his family, and they sat across from Nuada's table. His daughter had grown since Nuada had last seen her; now she was taller than Uilleam. Nuada reflected on how fast time had been passing. Nuada then casually asked how the new waterwheel was working out for A'Chreag. He told Nuada that it had been a wonder and that now they could move ahead with other new machines that the village needed.

Many other of the village people stopped to talk throughout the rest of the day. Nuada felt comfortable with them now and laughed at their jokes and at times sang along with the music.

Late in the evening Nuada's mate asked to go home, as she was tired and the children were too. Nuada hated to leave but knew it was time. Nuada took his sleeping daughter, and they walked home, the end of a perfect day.

A couple of days later Nuada took a walk out to the front of the valleys to look at the land out there. He was surprised by the amount of trees that had been cut and used for lumber in the valleys. The cleared land was expansive. He had a hard time trying to remember what it looked like before. Even the site where he had fought the raiders for the first time looked different. He slowly turned and returned to the shop sites by the inner wall.

He sat on the lower steps going up the inner protection wall and wondered of the changes to the valleys. His eyes looked across at the shops and then toward the new storage building. No one was around, and it made everything seem so dead to him; there was no life here. He felt alone and got up to return to the cooking area and the companionship of his friends.

He walked through the stone housing site to look at the changes there and paused where more foundations were already started. "Beag is being very ambitious this year," he thought. Ten houses were now complete, and six more were awaiting to be built. He then continued onto the cooking area.

As he passed the teachers' houses, he looked over at the site where Jan's crypt was almost hidden near the ridgeline. Nuada wondered if Jan could have foreseen all of the changes that had happened to the valleys. He shook his head and continued on.

There were a few of the village people there, but Nuada still felt lonely. As he started to turn away, he saw Beag drinking his beer alone near the front of the area. Nuada walked over and said, "Are you hiding or just enjoying your time away from the work, my friend?"

"Nuada, sit and have a beer with me."

Nuada did sit but did not have any of the beer.

"The village seems so quiet now that the work has stopped, Beag. I took a walk out to the front of the walls this morning, and it felt so lonely that I returned to find someone to talk with."

"Then you have good company. I myself took a walk and quickly returned. It felt like there was death in the air out there."

"I wonder if it is because of the work stoppage, or is there something else that bothers us. Do you think that maybe the raiders might return?"

"Anything is possible. Have the teachers begun their training of the new people yet?"

"They were going to start today, but I have yet to see of anyone."

"Perhaps we should send out the hunters to scout for trouble."

"It would be wise of us to do so."

While Beag was finishing his beer, Mor arrived, and they talked to him about sending the hunters out as scouts to look for signs of raiders. Mor said he would go and talk to them and send them to look.

While they were talking, a large group walked up the street from the school, led by Pytheas. The trio turned to watch as the group headed out toward the inner protection wall.

"They must be going out for the training of their weapons," Nuada said.

The others just nodded in answer, and then Mor said, "I was wondering about the two new shop buildings by the mill site. I know we had planned that they were to be used for candle making and the making of glass, but I think that they would be better used for the tanning of hides and as a new woodworking building. We need of more wagons, and I can see of the need to build some large, wood projects too."

"I agree with that, as I was thinking of that when I proposed to build two more buildings over there," said Nuada.

Beag looked at the two of them and then said, "I can see what you are thinking. Perhaps I spoke to soon before. I will then build two more buildings there, but they will have to be built across the street from the others."

This was agreed to, and the three of them settled back and shared of some of Beag's beer. It was close to midday when they went back out together to the front of the village to watch the training of the new people and the village children that were old enough now.

Two of the teachers were teaching sword play with wooden swords to one group while the rest were working at practicing with their bows toward the ridgeline. The trio of consul members watched from the top of the inner protection wall. Soon they became bored watching and decided to walk to the second valley to look over the building sites for the two new shop buildings.

They walked along the wall around the village until they came to the cut between the valleys and then descended. Beag was looking up at the wall of the cut, thinking about the amount of stone he had left to work with. Nuada glanced up but did not disturb his thoughts. They carried on to the site where the buildings would be built and paused to look around.

They would have to cut some more of the trees here, but the ground was level enough to build on. Nuada shared his thoughts that these buildings would not have to be as big as the other two, as the nature of the products was much smaller. Mor and Beag agreed and made some notes on some paper that they had brought with them.

While they were discussing the buildings, Nuada saw A'Chreag walking toward the forge building and decided that he needed to talk with him too. He hurried over to him before he went inside and said, "A'Chreag? We need to talk about some of the machines that we may need in the new building next to you."

"But I thought that it was to be used for the making of glass. What need would they have of my machines?"

"We have changed our minds about its use. It will now be the new woodworking building, and I can see of the need for your drill and perhaps some of your other machines."

"Yes. I can see the need for many different types of saws too. It will need of the drives from the waterwheel too."

"Good. Think of the needs and begin it when you can. I will be back to talk more of this later. Now I must return with Beag and Mor to the village."

Nuada returned to the others, and they walked toward the cut again. Along the way Nuada told them of his talk with A'Chreag and the needs of the woodworking building. All the other two would say was that they would be glad to return to work soon. Nuada agreed.

They made their way back to the cooking area and shared of some more beer, only thinking of the boredom of the week away from work.

The following morning Nuada returned to the mill sites to talk with A'Chreag again about the needs of the new woodworking building. They walked around the inside of the building, and A'Chreag pointed out where he would set up some of his machines. Nuada also told him that it must have room to work on the wagons for the village too. Finally they had a plan in mind, and Nuada started to return to the village.

The heat of the sun arrived early that morning, and Nuada slowly made his way to the portal gate into the second valley. He had thought of going back by way of the caves again but continued to follow the stream bed back to the front of the valley. It seemed cooler walking by the stream, and he listened to the wildlife that still lived along this area. Then before he knew it, he was at the outer protection wall of the valley. He stopped and looked around. A few of the village guards stood on top of the wall, and he waved to them before passing through the portal gate and across the inner field where the teachers were training the new people. He really was not thinking of anything when the people there began to clap and whistle and then call his name as he passed. He stopped and turned to see what it was all about. The crowd as one began to move toward him. He saw Pytheas and called to him to ask what was going on.

"Today they honor you, Nuada."

"What? Why? I have done nothing to be treated this way."

"You are wrong, my friend. Turn and look back at the portal gate and understand of it."

There on the wall above the portal gate was the statue that Beag had carved over the Winter months. Beag was standing there and waved down to Nuada, and then he started to make his way down to the field and the company of his friend.

Nuada stood with his mouth open and was at a loss for words. Nuada's eyes glanced from the statue to the crowd around him and back again. He felt trapped by the crush of the village people. At last Beag joined him and said, "I told you that I would do this, Nuada. You were always wondering if the future people would remember of you. Now you know the answer."

"But why? I have done nothing to be honored in this way."

"The people feel otherwise. You have given them hope, protection, and a future here."

"This is wrong, Beag. I do not feel as if I deserve of this."

"Give it time, my friend. Now let us return to the cooking area and share of some beer together."

Nuada followed Beag, and as he walked, he talked with the people who had gathered around him. Below the portal gate, Mor stood watching with a smile on his face.

"Mor, did you have a hand in this too?"

"Always, my friend. We have been planning this for a long time. Enjoy the moment."

Nuada felt his stomach muscles tighten as he again looked up at the statue. He could only shake his head at what his friends had done for him. They moved together to the cooking area and the sharing of some beer and companionship. Nuada's mate and children were already sitting at their table when Nuada and the group walked in. When Nuada finally had a chance to sit down, he asked his mate if she knew of this thing that they had done. She smiled and nodded in reply.

That evening the celebration continued for the whole village. Nuada gave a speech and thanked the people of the village for the honors, but everyone knew that soon the work would begin again.

- SUMMER AND BECOMING A CITY -

Too soon the village came to life again as the work on the stone houses began in earnest. At the quarry site, rock was again being removed from the cut and moved down to the stonecutting area. Wagons moved through the village at a faster rate now, as there was something in the air that said to hurry. A'Chreag and his crew worked at providing the necessary equipment for the new woodworking building and still made hinges and latches for the houses. Sheets of copper roofing material also were made at a record pace. Back in the village, the teachers made the glass that was needed for the houses and still found time to teach the skills of war. Nuada continued to work with Mor's skilled woodcrafters and did the interior finishing touches needed. Beag worked his skills and crews hard, as they also laid out ten new foundations for houses in the meadow. All of the lift machines were now at use in the building of the houses.

Mor took part of his crew, and they had begun to build four new houses near the sheep-stable area too. The village was growing quickly, and at times Nuada wondered if they would have enough people to fill all of the new houses. Three new wells for water were dug: two out in the meadow with the stone houses and one near the sheep-stable area.

Mor had arranged for the village hunters to scout outside of the valleys to see if any raiders were near also. All of their reports showed nothing in the area, which made all of the consul members breathe easier. They did not need to have the problem of raiders now.

The Summer heat also continued to rise, and this caused the village people to take breaks out of the sun when they could. They welcomed the light breezes that came up in the afternoon, and it made life more bearable for everyone. Nuada's son Iolair was now grown enough that he joined in with Mor's crews and worked alongside of Nuada. The bond between the two was stronger than ever.

One evening after the work for the day was halted, Nuada walked around the stone houses and looked as the last of the meadow began to disappear with new houses. Curbs and sidewalks were a part of the ongoing construction here too. It gave a finished look to everything. Nuada was pleased, but he also knew that many of the streets in the village still lacked the curbs and sidewalks too. Perhaps next year they could correct that.

When he got to the outdoor cooking area, he found Mor and Beag in conversation about the day's work, and he sat and listened to what they had to say. Mor told Beag that he had almost finished the four new houses in the second valley and that he would begin four more soon. It had been almost a month since Nuada had been to the second valley, and he wondered of the changes there. He would need to take a break and look at everything again.

Early in the morning Nuada set out for the second valley while it was still cool. He paused shortly at the quarry site and was surprised at the amount of rock that had disappeared from the cut. The passage between the two valleys was now almost ten wagon widths, and still more of the cut was expanding daily. He turned right to go down by the sheep-stable area and followed the street around the ridgeline. Soon he came to where Mor's crews were building the latest houses. Again Mor had changed the designs of the houses, and they were very pleasing to the eye. They were slightly larger than the other houses, and Nuada wondered of the reason. Nuada did not see Mor, so he continued on following the ridgeline. The meadow for the grain crops had also been enlarged, and new fencing encircled them. Farmer had been busy too.

Soon Nuada was near the mill site area. As the first of the houses there came into view, he slowed his pace and looked at everything here. He passed the grain mill and the sawmill but looked closely at the raceway behind them. Its size still amazed him. He could see the top of the mill wheels turning, and the large belts that powered the sawmill and forge were in constant motion. The noise coming from the sawmill drowned out all other things there. Piles of new cut trees lined the outside of the mill, and at the back lumber was being loaded onto wagons for the trip out to the stone houses.

At the forge building, it too was full of noise, and Nuada thought for a moment about stopping but continued on to the new woodworking building to look inside. A'Chreag had done his magic with his machines and the pulleys that were to power the shop. He wandered around looking at everything and finally moved on.

He crossed the street to where the new buildings were to be built. Here too the ground had been cleared, and it was ready for the start of the foundations. Nuada turned and looked around the whole area, and where things were yet to be built, he filled in the view with his imagination.

Back across the street, the foursome of men who worked with leather had also moved into their new building. One of them waved to Nuada, and he waved back before moving on to the protection wall for the second valley and its passage back along the stream.

He paused there to wait for two wagons of new cut trees to come through the portal gate. It was getting close to midday, and he moved on to look at the area outside of the valleys where they were still cutting trees.

He passed the outer protection wall and moved on through the narrow opening out of the valley. He stood on the rocky outcropping where he had fought the raiders so long ago and looked down to where they were doing the tree cutting. Again the whole area was expanded, and fewer of the trees marked the outer boundary of the valleys. He could see the tree cutters in the distance and thought about going down to them but changed his mind again.

He turned and walked back to the protection wall and entered through the portal gate onto the practice field there. A small group was practicing with its bows, but Nuada did not stop. He glanced up at his statue as he crossed through the inner protection wall and made his way back to the stone house construction site.

Dust floated through the air, and the sounds of men busy at their work added to the atmosphere of change. Nuada looked for Beag or Mor and found that he did not see either of them. He wondered where they were. Iolair came out of one of the houses and waved to his father. Nuada walked over to him and asked if he had seen Mor or Beag. He responded that both had gone to the meeting hall to retrieve some drawings for the houses. Nuada quickened his pace to find them and see what they were up to now.

Nuada found them at their table in the front of the hall going over some papers on the table; each had a mug of beer in his hands.

"Are you two working or taking an early day off?"

Mor looked up and said, "Working. What else?"

"It looks like you are taking the day off, what with the beer in your hands."

Beag laughed. "We were dry too."

Mor said, "Where have you been? I could have used you earlier."

"I made my way around both valleys to check up on you two. What did you think I was doing?" Nuada said and laughed.

The three men broke out in laughter, sharing the joke that they all knew too well. Nuada then asked about the papers on the table.

"These are the drawings and material lists for the new shop buildings near the mill site," said Beag.

"I thought those were on hold until Fall?"

"We might start early. The houses are coming along, and we could begin the shops soon."

"I was at the sites earlier and saw that the land had already been cleared. Show me what you have in mind."

The three poured over the drawings and talked about what they were going to do and when.

Soon the three walked back to the stone houses to check on the work the crews were doing. The last of the ten houses were nearing completion, and four more foundations were under way already. Beag said he could leave a small crew there to work on those houses while he shifted the rest to the shop sites. He would take two of the lift machines with him and leave the other two there. As they walked around, Nuada glanced toward the crypt of Jan's and the other graves located there.

He asked Beag, "Could we build a stone wall around the grave sites?"

"I can do that, Nuada. It will not take much to do."

"I would like that very much, Beag. We must not forget those that came and worked here too."

They spent the rest of the afternoon going from house to house and directing some of the men on things that needed to be done. Then they called it a day and returned to the outdoor cooking area for their evening meal and families.

Nuada awoke in the middle of the night with an uneasy feeling. He got up and dressed and went downstairs and sat at the table. Something was not right, he felt. When the sun began to filter light over the ridge, he took Wolf and made his way to the front of the village and out to the outer protection wall. He checked with the guards there, and they reported that it was quiet. He still felt uneasy and waited for the sun to fully rise.

Soon some of the woodcutters began to come from the village to start another day of cutting trees for the sawmill. Nuada stopped them at the portal gate and asked them to wait. He sent a runner back to the village for two of the village hunters, and when they arrived, he asked them to scout the area outside of the valley. Soon it was a waiting game until they could report.

At midmorning one of the scouts returned and told Nuada that he had seen dust rising to the southwest , but it was too far away to tell if it was headed their way. The hunter returned to the direction he had seen the dust and searched again. Nuada still held the woodcutters and had also sent word back to Mor and Beag that something was happening outside of the valleys.

The men of the valleys stopped work for the day and took up posts on the protection walls around the valleys. All were well-armed and knew that possibly a battle would take place today. Mor and Beag had joined Nuada on the outer protection wall and waited with him.

Mor asked, "Could it be the trader returning?"

Nuada replied, "It could be, but I have had an uneasy feeling since the middle of the night."

Soon Pytheas and some of the other teachers arrived. They asked questions, and when Nuada could not give them an answer, Pytheas said that he had an idea about a new way to fight if it was the raiders coming back. He explained to Nuada how the Greeks had fought long ago, and it involved a small group with shields and spears to form as one and force its enemy where it wanted them to go. Pytheas said that they had been training the new people in this manner of warfare and that he would like to lead them in this manner. When Nuada asked where they would form up at, he was told that they would stay hidden in the trees outside of the valleys and, when it was time, attack from the rear and force them against the wall.

Nuada could see the wisdom of this kind of battle plan and sent Pytheas to gather his group. Then he continued to wait for word from the scouts.

Soon Pytheas returned with twenty men, and they made their way out into the woods beyond the tree-cutting area. The sun was high in the midday sky when again one of the scouts returned to the wall.

Nuada called down to the scout, "What have you seen?"

"It is the trader with about ten or more families, but they are being followed by raiders too. I think they number about fifty."

Nuada nodded and turned to Beag and Mor. "We will send the trader and the families into the second valley and wait for the raiders."

Mor said, "We can put ten men on horseback to circle around them and, with Pytheas's men, cut them off from retreat."

Beag and Nuada agreed, and the word was sent back to send out the riders. Soon the men on horseback passed through the portal gate and headed north away from the dust cloud. An hour later the group led by the trader was below the valley entrance and was hurriedly making for the protection of the outer wall. Some of the village men directed them on to the second valley, and still the village men waited for the raiders to show.

Soon they appeared outside of the valley in the area that had been cut of its trees. They paused and looked toward the valley entrance. They were well organized and formed into a battle formation. Slowly they moved forward sensing a trap but determined to catch their prey. As they moved forward, the entrance narrowed, and they had to reform. Nuada watched and kept his men hidden behind the wall. A silence from the village men followed, and the only noise was from the raiders as they continued to move forward.

They could now see the outer protection wall and wondered of it, but it did not stop the movement. When the first of the raiders had passed within easy killing distance of the bows, Nuada still waited for his attack. When they had almost reached the portal gate, Nuada gave the signal for the bows to be released, followed by spears of those close enough.

Arrow after arrow flew through the air and cut down over half of the raiders. They began a retreat and fought back as best they could. Slowly they made their way back outside of the valley entrance. Then Pytheas and his men moved forward and engaged them from the rear. They turned to fight at the same time that Nuada and a large group of the village men swarmed out through the portal gate. They were trapped between the two forces. The raiders fought back hard and soon began to force Pytheas and the men there back. Then the men on horseback charged down on them from the path that they had used to come to the valleys. The battle was almost over before it began. Again the village men made sure that none of the raiders survived. In under an hour, the village had destroyed all of the raiders. Now it was time to clean up the mess.

From behind the inner protection wall, wagons began to roll out to remove the bodies and move them away from the valleys. Nuada and the other two consul members went to the second valley to talk with the trader and ask questions about the raiders and the people he had brought with him.

The wagons and the new people they had brought with them were lined up on the street from the second valley's protection wall to the cut between the valleys. The trio found the trader near the cut and asked him about the people he had brought with him. He shrugged his shoulders and said it was the same old story again, but this time they were followed. He asked about the raiders and was told that they had been taken care of. Nuada asked to talk with the leader of the new group, and the trader took him to the man.

When they approached the man, he was shaking with fear, and Nuada told him that all was well now — the raiders were no threat. The man's family was close around him, and Nuada waited until he could talk with the man alone. Beag took the trader with him to move his wagon out near the inner wall. Nuada and Mor finally had the leader alone for a moment and asked him about his people and their skills. When Nuada was satisfied with the answers, they walked back along the wagons to talk to each man. Two of the families were skilled with sheep, so Mor had them follow him down to the new houses near the sheep-stable area. The others were skilled with wood, and one had his own forge in the village that was raided. Two more of the men were skilled with stone, and this only added to the workforce of the village. But one was a real doctor, and this made Nuada feel better — the village lacked a real doctor. Another was the village teacher, and Nuada smiled at this surprise.

When Mor returned, he and Nuada led the caravan of wagons through the cut and into the village. They moved on to the new stone houses and began to assign houses for each family. The doctor was given a house across from Pytheas, as was the teacher. The others were to have the other houses going up the street of completed houses. In all there were fourteen families in this group. Each family was told to meet in the morning near the protection wall, except for the teacher and the doctor. Nuada would personally take care to show them around in the morning.

Nuada carefully counted the number of houses that were still vacant. Of the stone houses there, there were six completed houses and four under construction. He also knew that there were still six more in the second valley. He thought that it was good that both Mor and Beag had pushed to complete as many of the houses as they had.

Nuada and Mor finally were able to return to the cooking area and found Beag already there with a beer in his hand.

"What? You could not wait for us?" Mor said.

"This tastes too good to have waited, my friend."

The trio all laughed together, and when they all had a beer, Nuada spoke.

"Both of you have done well today, and it is good that you both pushed to build so many houses this year."

Beag said, "We had a few reports of minor injuries from our people but no dead. This battle was very one-sided for us."

"Because we were prepared for this. All of the training paid off."

Then Mor said, "We will not be able to return to work until the day after tomorrow, but our men needed a break anyway."

Soon others began to filter into the cooking area, and they began to celebrate with their music and many beers. The evening meal was still hours away.

When Pytheas arrived with the other teachers, Nuada went to talk with him and told him of a teacher with the new group. Then he mentioned the doctor. Pytheas wanted to meet him, but Nuada said that they needed their rest tonight and would do so tomorrow. A few of the new group heard the music and followed the sound to the cooking area and were welcomed. Soon the women arrived and began the meal for everyone. Nuada could not have been happier.

But when Iolair arrived, he had a bandage on his right forearm. Nuada immediately asked him about it.

"I was with Pytheas's group outside of the wall and got a scratch from a battle axe, Father."

Nuada nodded at his answer and then said, "What did you learn of this battle?"

"I do not like of the death, but I found it necessary."

"Then you have learned a great lesson. Protect those you care about but avoid the fight when you can."

Nuada put his arm around Iolair's shoulders, and they returned to their table. Nuada was proud of his son, and it showed in the way he looked at him throughout the rest of the afternoon. After the evening meal, the village became very quiet as it reflected on the day's happening.

The next morning Mor and Beag sorted out the new people at the meeting near the inner protection wall. Nuada joined with Pytheas and the new doctor and teacher. First, to avoid the crowd at the wall, they walked to the school. Pytheas was talking with the doctor while Nuada and the teacher walked through the halls and some of the classrooms. Nuada did find that the teacher had also spent time in Alexandria and was well versed in mathematics. Nuada explained that it was a notion of his to teach everyone in the village and that Nuada's skills were with languages that crossed all barriers. When they rejoined the others, they walked out to the new hospital and storage building near the stone shops.

Nuada saw the trader peering into the shops and left the others to talk with him.

"Did you find the new quarters comfortable last night?" asked Nuada.

"It was a pleasure that I find hard to come by out here on the road."

"Good. What did you bring us this year?"

"Many new things although I did not bring wine this year. I have also noticed that your village has grown over the last year too."

"Yes. Every day we find new things to build. Perhaps you might be interested in some of our inventions."

"Show me, and perhaps we can find a way to trade."

They went from shop to shop with Nuada showing the crafts that the village people had made over the Winter, but when he got to A'Chreag's display of machines that he had made, the trader was in awe of the designs. Although the room was filled with jewelry and tools, it was the machines that caught the trader's eye.

Later they went out to look at the things that the trader had brought with him on this trip, and then the haggling began in earnest. It was not until the following day that they settled the trader talks and shared some beer together.

The people of the village returned to the building of more houses, and the construction of the new shops in the second valley resumed. Small talk of the battle was one topic that lasted for many weeks that followed. The trader spent a full week in the village before he departed for another city to the south. The new doctor spent some time with Mor and Nuada and requested some small changes for the hospital, but he was happy with the building, and that made the pair feel proud of their work on it.

Mor also began to build two more houses behind the school — the last spaces left in this area. The stone houses under construction quickly came together, and four more foundations were started. The new people from the latest group settled in quickly and helped with the building. Nuada did not have time now to return to doing the finishing work in the houses, as he went from place to place checking on the needs of the people and his friends.

The new shop buildings in the second valley went up quickly, and soon it was time to add more of Mor's crews for the finishing touches to them. Beag moved his lift machines back out to the front of the village near the stone houses. Just as quickly he began to build even more houses there.

The peak of Summer was already on the people of the valleys, and preparations for the coming of Fall began too. About the only problem that occurred was that the cooking area was now filled to its capacity, and they needed more room, but that would be a problem to be solved next year. Beag had found time to build the wall around the grave-site area, and it made it more complete. Nuada was pleased that he had done so.

Pytheas and the other teachers were now preparing for the coming school year, and Nuada had a hard time trying to fit it into his busy schedule. They also worked at making sure that there was enough paper for the coming year too. This was on top of all of the glassmaking for the houses.

Pytheas continued to teach the warfare arts out between the protection walls. Scouts were still out looking for any more trouble for the village too, but the valleys were secure now, and thoughts of any more battles were out of everyone's minds except Iolair. He began to have nightmares of the battle and could not shake the images.

Because Nuada had to be in so many places in both valleys now, he began to ride a horse around the sites. He chose an all-black stallion that still had a lot of spirit, and you could see him give the horse its head as it raced from site to site. Nuada enjoyed the air flowing against his body on these hot Summer days. However, the Summer was beginning to wane, and Nuada knew it would not last.

The building went on, and more houses were finished and others started. The new shop buildings were complete, and the candle makers and glassmakers moved in to complete that project. Mor began four houses again near the sheep-stable area, and Beag was Beag. He worked hard during the day, and when he was done, he settled in for many beers in the evening.

The new doctor soon grew bored with nothing to do, so he helped with the glassmaking alongside the teachers.

One day Nuada did have a problem with one of the new men. Nuada saw him beating his son with a leather strap across his back. Nuada dismounted his horse and stopped the man. He asked what the problem was and was told that the boy had talked back to the father. Nuada told him that was no reason to whip the boy, and the man then told Nuada to mind his own business. Nuada was not the kind to be talked to in this way and stood between the man and his son to prevent any more beating. The man pushed Nuada and then was in the motion of using the leather strap on Nuada. Nuada reached out and caught the man's wrist and twisted underneath his arm. The motion was so quick that the man was caught off guard, and the twisting was so quick that the man's arm snapped. He swore at Nuada as Nuada stood over him and reached out to help the man back on his feet. Again the man tried to use his other arm, and Nuada blocked his blow. Nuada turned and took the boy away from the scene. Later Nuada asked to see the boy's back, as he looked in much pain. Many raw welts crossed the boy's back, and Nuada was in shock of the damage. He took the boy to the doctor to see if anything needed care. The doctor was surprised at the damage and said that it was going to take time to heal. Then Nuada told the doctor about the man and how his arm had broken.

"When he comes to me, I will set it, but I will do little other than that."

Nuada nodded and went to seek out Mor to tell him of the event. Mor could not believe the man was so stupid and asked Nuada if maybe they should send him out of the village. Nuada thought for a few moments before he said, "I will give him one more chance. If he continues in this manner, then he must go."

Mor nodded and went in search of the man. He did not need Nuada to be there, as he had a few words for the man himself.

Later in the afternoon Nuada was checking on the supply needs of the men working on the houses near the sheep-stable site when Mor happened to be there too.

"I talked with the man who whipped the boy, Nuada. I think it will not happen again, and I also believe that he did not know who you were at the time."

"I think he will remember me now," was all Nuada said.

As usual the day ended with the gathering at the cooking area. At Nuada's table, he had his boys close, and they talked about their day. Nuada's thoughts were on the young boy who had been whipped, and he thanked Creatrix that it would never happen with his boys.

A few days later the village weaver and the man who made clothes approached Nuada and asked if it were possible to have a building built for them to make their goods. Nuada told them it would not be possible this year, but now that the old woodworking building was vacant, they could use it until one could be built.

Nuada was still making his rounds of the building sites, and one morning he was out at the stone-house construction area making notes about the amount of lumber needed there. After getting the information needed, he had a chance to look around again and made his way to the rear of the site near the ridgeline. He counted only twenty more sites that could be built on. "Where do we go next?" he wondered.

He then mounted his horse and made his way toward the sawmill, but at the quarry site, he paused and looked at the amount of stone left to be removed. The site was now limited, and he knew that a new quarry would be needed for next year too. He continued on to the mill and left the order to be filled for the stone houses and then followed the back ridgeline to the sheep-stable area.

The grain fields took up a large portion of this area, and beyond that the area needed for the sheep to graze took up the rest. In the center of the second valley, trees still left unbothered filled it with its natural state. Nuada did not want to change that section of the valley if it was possible. Nuada knew that the land behind the ridge was an option for more building, but it lacked the natural protection within the valleys. "I will need to talk with the others at the consul meeting soon about what we do next," he thought.

Throughout the valleys, it still buzzed with activity — wagons and their horse teams were in constant motion. Houses were built with amazing speed, and it seemed nonstop. Over at the mill sites, noise from the sawmill drowned out all other things in the area. The pounding from the forge building seemed in a battle with the sawmill as to which could make the most noise. Nuada was glad that he did not live near either of them.

As the days drew near for the end of Summer, Nuada did ride his horse outside of the valleys and down to the tree-cutting area. They had created a large meadow out of the forest there. Nuada rode on past and followed the mountainside across the stream to where A'Chreag had his ore quarry in a blind valley. He did not go into the valley but climbed up the mountain to get a better view of the surrounding area. In the distance, he could barely see where the old village north of the valleys once was. His gaze took in the tree-cutting area and the forested land beyond. Men looked like ants to him from this height — and the wagons that hauled the trees not much better. Looking back toward the village, he could only see a part of the outer protection wall there. Coming back down, he followed the mountainside and found an area that could be used for a quarry in the future, but it was well outside of the valleys and had no protection there. Thoughts of how to keep the valleys growing still crossed his mind as he rode.

He returned to the village, not knowing what the future held for growth. Deep inside he wondered if this was as large as the village would get. He hoped that the monthly consul meeting would be held soon; he needed answers.

That evening he pushed Mor and Beag to hold the meeting soon, but they were still busy with all the building going on and wanted to wait a little longer, as they still had good weather to work with.

Already crews began to bring in small pieces of tree limbs and unusable wood for the fireplaces. It was getting close to harvest time for the crops, and the women of the village began to prepare for it. The teachers were no different, as they too began to prepare for the opening of the school and held regular meetings. Nuada missed a lot of these meetings , but it could not be helped with all of the other things going on.

The days were getting shorter, but still no signs of any rain. Dust filled the air in the valleys, and they could do with some rain to settle it.

Nuada's worries would not go away as he continued to ride his horse daily out to the front of the valleys. Ideas came and went about what to do for expansion of the village. He could see no other way but to move forward with an expansion outside of the valleys. He just had to convince his fellow consul members to listen to what he had to say.

- FALL AND NEW IDEAS -

The harvest began with a light rain shower that quickly dropped the temperature. Luckily the wind was light and did no damage. No new houses were started, and everyone worked to complete the ones under construction. There was a lot of cleanup to do in both valleys after all the construction. At last the consul meeting was scheduled for the end of the week, and Nuada needed answers. Also in two weeks the school was going to reopen, putting more pressure on Nuada.

Nuada did not let up on his work, and the pressure of it showed. He was tired, but so was everyone else. They were running out of time. Every day Nuada made at least four trips between the two valleys making sure that things were organized. The grain crops were the first to be harvested, and the separating of the grain from the chaff was hard work. Then it had to be transported to the mill for grinding into flour. At the sawmill, the sawdust was removed and transported outside of the valleys as before, but they needed part of it for the papermaking.

They were still bringing in wood for the fireplaces of the homes for Winter, and it took away some of the village manpower. It was Nuada's job to balance the manpower available into crews where they were needed the most. Mor did not have the time now to do it, so it fell to Nuada.

At the end of the week, Nuada was glad that the consul meeting was that night, and he was looking forward to the sharing of many beers with his friends and getting the answers he needed too.

Coming back from the mill sites late in the afternoon, Nuada stopped at the school for a quick talk with Pytheas about the class schedule. Nuada's classes would remain the same this year with six classes, which took some of the load off him, and he felt it was a good balance.

Nuada went to the stable and put up his horse before crossing the street to the meeting hall. Inside he found Beag doing his usual — enjoying his beer.

"Beag, I see that you are enjoying the Fall weather now."

"That I am, friend."

"We had a good year. If not for those raiders, it would have been perfect."

"I agree. We built more houses this year than we have ever done before. Then there were the shop buildings too."

"True. The crops are good also, and the sheep flock has grown. We did well with the trader too."

"I think this calls for another beer, Nuada."

They sat back and drank their beer and waited for the other consul members to arrive. Shortly the others drifted into the hall, and soon they began the meeting. The open discussion covered all of their accomplishments this year, and after Mor asked if anyone had more to add, Nuada again brought up the need for more space for growth next year. He covered how they had used just about all of the land in both valleys, and still people continued to be added. If they were to grow, they would need to expand their village outside of the valleys. That would mean building another protection wall, but they were reluctant to discuss it now. Nuada pointed out that he had found another site for a quarry, but it lacked protection, as it was outside of the current protection walls. Then he also pointed out that he had counted the number of building sites, and there were only twenty sites left to build on. If they did build another protection wall, they could do it over two years without stopping other projects for next year. Then he said if they did not do it, they would have to limit the new people admitted into the valleys.

The other consul members were for building the new protection wall, but still Mor was holding back. Beag sat quietly and did not say anything for a while. He listened to the others argue about the need for growth, and finally he said, "As this new wall will be up to me to build, I think I can do it without holding back any other projects."

Mor gave into the pressure from the others and finally agreed to the new wall. Nuada was pleased. Shortly they closed the meeting and sat back to enjoy the evening together.

Over the following days, the crops from the meadow by the lake were harvested, and they moved ahead with the planning of another Fall feast for the village. This was to be held the day before school was to start, and it marked the beginning of a time of rest for the village people.

Nuada took Beag out to the site for the new quarry, and then they took a rough outline for the new protection wall. Beag thought that it should be higher and wider than the others and have several towers on it, but it would only have two portal gates. Nuada agreed to the ideas he pointed out, and a plan was put on paper. The new wall would cover over a mile and a half in distance and encircle the open area that was made by the tree cutters. A bridge would have to be built too to cross the stream for the loads from the new quarry. Nuada pointed out that it would also serve the ore deposit site of A'Chreag's valley.

On the way back, Nuada remembered that the weaver and the maker of clothes wanted a shop building too for next year. He told Beag about it, and he said that it could be built near the other shop buildings. Beag said that he would build it when he found the time, but it would have to wait until some of the other projects were done first.

As they passed through the outer protection wall, they found Pytheas with a group using the inner area for more bow practice. Beag went on ahead, and Nuada stopped to talk with Pytheas. Iolair was there also, honing his skills with the bow, and stopped to talk with his father. Every time Nuada saw his son, he was amazed at how much he had grown. He was now as tall as Nuada but still lacked the fill out of his muscles to mark him as an adult of the village. But what he lacked in muscle, he made up for in his smarts. They talked for awhile about the school opening and how the other teachers were doing in their preparations for it. Finally Nuada said he had to return to the village and departed for the stable area to put up his horse.

As he passed the teachers' houses, something told him to continue on toward the second valley. He rode on at a casual pace and looked over the village as he went.

He knew that there were still some streets that lacked the curbs and sidewalks that the others had, and he wondered when they would find time to correct that. He glanced over at the school as he passed, and then he moved on to the cut between the valleys. The site of the quarry and the cutting area had been cleaned up and showed little signs of what had been going on there. He turned toward the mill sites, and still his eyes took in everything.

He passed the two new shop buildings and then moved on to the forge and sawmill buildings. Both buildings still hummed with noise as they continued to make needed things for the village. The area just outside of the sawmill now only had a small pile of cut trees piled there waiting to be cut into lumber, and then it would shut down for the Winter months. The drying shed was almost filled with cut lumber, and Nuada knew that it would only last for a short time when they began to build again.

Nuada considered going into the forge building, but he did not wish to disturb A'Chreag while he was working. As Nuada was turning his horse to return to the village, A'Chreag appeared outside of the forge building. He waved, so Nuada dismounted and walked over to talk. He told him about his ride with Beag outside of the valleys to look at a possible building site of a new protection wall. He told him about Beag's idea to build a bridge over the stream that would also serve his ore site too. A'Chreag was surprised, but he had thought about that happening a year ago. After some more small talk, Nuada had to leave, and mounting his horse, he waved a good-bye to his friend.

Nuada made for the stable this time and noticed the weather was turning colder. After he passed through the cut between the valleys, he looked to the north and saw a small bank of clouds building in the distance. He hoped that it would not stop the Fall feast that was planned.

After tending to his horse, Nuada made for the meeting hall across the street. Inside Beag was already on his fourth beer, and Nuada poured himself one and joined his friend. Beag raised his mug in greeting and asked where he had been.

"I rode over the to the mill sites to talk with A'Chreag and told him of our plans for the wall and the bridge. He said that he had thought of that about a year ago."

"That does not surprise me. If anyone had bothered to look around, they would have seen the need."

"Then why did Mor hesitate on the idea?"

"Because he is tired. It has been a long year for all of us."

Nuada nodded, and he felt the weight of the year on himself too. The pair sat back and drank of their beer and reflected on all of the work that had been done. Soon Mor wandered in, and they enjoyed the company of each other until it was time for the evening meal.

Before morning a light dusting of snow covered the village, but it melted quickly and caused no harm. The clouds continued to blanket the valleys for the rest of that day, and it brought a quietness to the village. Although people continued to walk about the streets doing little chores, there was a slowness to their pace. It felt like Fall now.

Nuada returned to working on his dictionary, but his mind was not ready with doing the work on it. Finally he gave up on it and pulled out the notes and drawings that Amasis had brought back from Alexandria. He spent many hours with the machines and found some useful for the village, and he set those aside to return to later.

Time passed slowly for the rest of the week. Nuada still continued his trips around the valleys and checked up on those still finishing the work around the village. The weather began to warm again, although slowly. The afternoon of the feast, Nuada found he had time on his hands and went to the meeting hall.

The building was almost full with the village men, who wanted to stay away from their women, who were preparing the feast for that afternoon. Loud voices drowned out even the simplest conversation, and the din from the music inside made many want to leave. Nuada joined his friends, and they shared many beers together. Flames from the fireplace cast a dancing shadow around the walls, but nobody noticed.

Beag said that he had finished the drawings for the new protection wall and passed them across to Nuada. They were a thing of beauty. The first rough drawings showed the size of the wall in comparison to the ridgeline outside of the first valley. It had five towers that broke the wall line and the two portal gates that they had talked of, along with a grated passage for the stream, like the one going into the second valley. It circled around the open area in front of the valleys and went from the valley of A'Chreag's ore deposit to about the site where the ridgeline between the two valleys joined. Nuada was impressed with its size and told Beag so as he pushed the drawings back across the table.

Then Nuada said, "Can you build it in two years as we talked of?"

"I must if we are to grow as you have pointed out, Nuada," replied Beag.

"How do you plan to go ahead with it? How many men will you need?"

"The first year will be the foundation, and I will need all of my men, but I will leave enough to build houses on the sites we have left. But the second year will require all of the village men that we can put together and no other projects to build."

"What about the lift machines? You will need all of them for this project, will you not?"

"Yes. I will need all of them. I see no other way to do the work in the time we have planned."

Nuada turned to Mor and said, "Could we build one more lift machine?"

Mor thought for a moment, then said, "Yes. I could build one over the Winter at the new shop building. Let me talk with A'Chreag about it, but I think we could do it with little problem."

"Good. We will need it at the houses and then in the second year move it out to help with the wall."

Nuada felt better about the building of the wall now that they had a solid plan for the work. Later on they left the meeting hall and made for the cooking area. It was almost time for the feast to begin. Mor saw A'Chreag with his family there and went to talk with him about the lift machine. Nuada joined his family, and they waited and listened to the music. Nuada looked across at his daughter and realized that they had yet to name her. It was time, he thought. She had grown a lot this year too. Then his gaze turned to Uilleam. He too had grown, but it was his son Iolair who had grown the most of his family this year. He was almost a man now, and Nuada's pride in him was there for anyone to see.

Nuada felt very relaxed but also very old now that he had looked at his children. It seemed to him that just the other day he had been holding Iolair in his arms and the valleys had been a wild land with no other people. He was pulled from his thoughts when Mor returned to his table to tell him that A'Chreag would help with the building of the new lift machine. Nuada thanked him for the asking of A'Chreag and then again turned his attention back to the music.

He found himself laughing when the teachers got up on the stage and performed some of their odd music for everyone. They knew how to make the crowd laugh, and it helped smooth out the thoughts in Nuada's mind.

Wonderful smells began to fill the area from the cooking, and it made everyone hungry.

Soon the feast was on, and everyone was enjoying the fine meal. Nuada's mate joined her family, and Nuada asked after her day. She told him and then asked about his day. He told of the agreement about the wall and then mentioned that they should name their daughter soon. She said she had already picked a name for her and then told Nuada that it was Sine. Nuada liked the way it rolled off his tongue and agreed to the name.

After eating they stayed a little longer, but Nuada and the boys had school tomorrow, and they had to get some sleep before their classes. It was early to bed that night and some needed rest.

Nuada awoke before the first light of dawn. After stoking the fireplace, he took Wolf for his morning run and looked at the sky to determine what kind of day it would be weather-wise. The light of the morning sun was just coming over the mountainside, and it showed no clouds. Although the air was crisp and bit through Nuada's clothes, he knew that it would be a nice day. Some light smoke was in the air, and he knew that others were also up early preparing for the day. After calling Wolf back, he returned inside and started to gather his papers for his first day of class this season. His boys soon appeared, and together they all ate a light meal and started off for school.

At the school, Nuada was surprised that he did not see Pytheas outside greeting the students, as was his usual thing. Nuada went inside to his classroom and set out his supplies for the morning class. He could hear voices coming from the other rooms and decided to find out where everyone was before his class.

Nuada walked up the hall on the first floor and found Pytheas with the new teacher from the last group that had come into the village, talking about his class with the new children. He did not wish to interrupt, so he continued to wander the hall and saw many of the other teachers within their classrooms. Andocides and Dionysins were together, and he waved as he passed that room. They waved back, and he moved on. He decided not to go up onto the second floor but returned to his classroom. His language class would start within minutes, so he settled down and passed out some papers on the tables of the room. He drew a deep breath and waited for his students. Another school year was about to begin.

At midday Nuada had a break between classes and went to seek out Pytheas again. All of his morning classes had gone smoothly, and he looked forward to the last class in about an hour. Nuada found Pytheas standing outside of the old school building and called to him as soon as he stepped from the new building.

"Pytheas. I had a good morning. How are the others doing?"

"The usual start-up jitters, but I think they are doing well."

"What about the new teacher? I saw you talking with him early this morning."

"He is an excellent teacher. He knows more about mathematics than any of the other teachers and has a way about him that the students respond to quickly."

"What about you? Did your classes go well today?"

"As well as I expected them to. I had only minor problems, but I think that I can correct them."

After some more talk about the school, Nuada returned for his last class of the day, and he was looking forward to spending some time with his friends at the meeting hall afterwards.

When Nuada finished his class, he stepped outside and found Wolf waiting for his boys. He patted him on the head and told him that they would not be long and to wait. After readjusting his pack of school papers and notes, Nuada set out for the meeting hall and a beer with his friends.

Inside Beag was at the table as usual, but Mor was not to be seen. After Nuada poured himself a beer, he asked about Mor.

Beag said, "Mor went to the woodworking shop early this morning, and I have not seen him since."

"What would he be working on now? I thought he would be taking it easy."

"He probably went to repair some of the wagons, but he should be along shortly and tell us what he has been up to."

Both men sat and enjoyed the comfort of the hall while they waited. About an hour later, Mor came through the door and went and poured a beer before he joined Nuada and Beag.

"Mor, tell us what you have been up to today," said Beag.

"I started another wagon this morning and then began to build the new lift machine. I had time on my hands, so I thought to start it."

"But I thought you would be taking it easy now that the construction season is done," said Nuada.

"I cannot just shut myself down, and I enjoyed the challenge of the work."

"I know what you mean, my friend."

They sat and talked about Nuada's school work and a few things about the village but mostly it was about being together. Time passed, and the building began to fill up with other men from the village, and Nuada knew that he had to return home for his evening meal. Nuada arose and told his friends that he would talk with them tomorrow and departed for his home and family.

The following weeks passed quickly as the days grew shorter and the weather colder. Soon it began to snow every other day, but it was light and no problem for the valleys. Few people visited the outdoor cooking area now, and the sounds within the village remained quiet.

In the second valley, the shop buildings remained busy. The leather shop was busy making new aprons and gloves for the coming season. Harnesses for the horses had to be repaired, and there were other minor things that were needed. The glassmaking was halted, but the weaver and the man who made clothes never stopped year-round. Some of the women were still making candles in their shop, but the forge was another story. Noise continued to pound from deep within the building. A'Chreag, who had started the new gears for the lift machine, was also stockpiling hinges and latches for the houses for next year already. His crew continued to make the copper sheets for roofing too, but they also were making new swords and other weapons on the side. Parts for the valleys' wagons were also needed, and they pushed ahead to make these too. The sawmill was done for the season, and the lumber was stacked in the drying shed next door. At the flour mill, it was still turning out flour, but that was almost done now too.

The village hunters had a good season too. The cool room in the old wood-working building was full with fresh deer being hung and waiting to be cut up. A few wild pigs were also in the room. The village would eat good this year.

The teachers had harvested their grapes for their wine and were in the process of making their wine too. It was also a good crop, and they had few problems on the island although the birds felt it still belonged to them.

Winter was drawing close, and every day the village slowed just that much more in anticipation of the season's change. The village people only ventured out if it as necessary or for school. Every day it seemed to grow colder, and this was made worse when the wind blew out of the north. Nuada had returned to wearing the sheep belt that his mate had made for him when he had that reoccurring tightness in his side from the old wound. Although the pain never returned, he was always aware that it could.

- WINTER AND WAITING -

Nuada awoke to an extreme silence around him. He lay in bed and listened for any sounds. Nothing. He got up and dressed and went downstairs to investigate why. He went to the front window first and looked outside. A dense fog shrouded everything. Moisture dripped across the glass in front of him. He turned and went to the fireplace to stoke the fire and await his family. Wolf came down first and went directly to the fireplace and curled up by its heat, He was not interested in going outside at all. Nuada wondered at the change in the weather and thought that it was unusual for this time of year.

Soon his family started to stir, and they came downstairs. While his mate prepared their morning meal, Nuada returned to the front window again. Nuada rubbed at the glass, which had fogged on the inside from the fireplace heat, and peered out into the gloom. He could not see across the street, let alone the houses across the street. Nuada returned to the table and began to gather his papers for the school day. The depth of the gloom outside carried into his thoughts. He really did not feel like going to the school today.

After dressing warmly, Nuada and his boys walked to the school. Nuada went directly to his classroom and added wood to the fireplace in the room. He again set out his papers for the day and was preparing for the midseason test of his students. That test would be tomorrow, and he was not looking forward to spending the time to grade the results.

Before his first class, Nuada walked out into the hall and looked around. He saw Iolair talking with the new doctor. He walked over and found them conversing in Phoenician. The doctor was telling of his travels when he was much younger, and Nuada was surprised by the depth of his knowledge. The doctor looked up at Nuada as he put his arm around the shoulders of his son.

"Your son has a thirst for knowledge, I see," he said.

"He does, but I am surprised by your knowledge of the world too."

"It was the way I was raised by my father. I think that you have done much the same with your son."

"I only wished that he prepared for the world around him, but things change so fast that any knowledge is out of date by the time we get it."

"Not all of it. You have done a wonderful job of inspiring him, and I think he can handle the world, changed or not."

They talked a little longer before Nuada had to return to his class and begin his teaching. The conversation had taken away the feeling of the gloomy weather outside, and Nuada now felt inspired to do his teaching.

At the end of the day, the weather had changed little; fog still shrouded the valleys, and little movement by the people of the village followed the weather. Nuada did go to the meeting hall, but he could not linger, as he had those tests tomorrow.

Nuada soon returned home and set to work on the tests. Later after his evening meal, he talked with his son again about the doctor and the places he had been. They talked late into the evening and finally went to bed.

In the morning, the weather remained much the same as the day before. Thoughts of the doctor's travels raced through Nuada's mind, and he wanted to talk more with him, but those tests had to come first. All day long he could not shake the thoughts of all of those strange lands that haunted Nuada. After his last class, Nuada went to talk with Pytheas and ask him about the doctor. Pytheas said that he had little knowledge of the doctor other than he was well-versed in the different lands around the world. He had asked him to teach about them, but the doctor had turned him down. This surprised Nuada, and he wanted to ask the doctor why. Nuada asked Pytheas if he had seen the doctor today, but he said no.

Shortly Nuada left the school and thought about going to the meeting hall but knew that he had to return home to correct the tests he had given that day. When he arrived home, he set to work and started going through the tests. Much as before, his students had learned their lessons well. Nuada had thought that perhaps he was not pushing them hard enough and that the tests were too easy, but he knew better and set that thought aside. He did not finish the work until later that night and was so tired that he thought of sleeping downstairs, but he forced himself to climb the stairs and find his bed and mate.

It was not until many weeks later that Nuada had a chance to talk with the doctor again. It was after the school classes had finished for the day and he had gone to the meeting hall to find some relaxation. The doctor was sitting with Amasis, enjoying some wine, and they were talking of Alexandria. Nuada stopped by their table after drawing some beer and said hello. Amasis invited Nuada to join them, but Nuada would have felt out of place had he done so. He told them that he had a meeting with some of the consul members and would do so after he had talked with them.

Nuada reluctantly joined his fellow consul members at their table and listened in on their conversation for awhile. He did ask Beag if there would be a chance to finish any of the curbs and sidewalks in the village next year. Beag said he did not think so but would try if the chance came up. When Nuada finished his beer, he returned to the table of Amasis and the doctor. Nuada did ask why the doctor had turned down the chance to teach about the lands he had visited. The doctor replied that he felt that his knowledge was limited by only his experiences, but Nuada persisted and told him that any knowledge was helpful. The doctor said he would think on it, and they left the idea where it was. They continued to talk about many other things, and finally Nuada said that he had to return home. He left the hall with a resolve to have the doctor become a teacher.

Again the weather did a changeup and returned to heavy snow. They had been lucky this year, and it had not stopped the school from being open until now. The valleys were blanketed with wet, heavy snow one morning, and Pytheas sent everyone home for the day. Nuada was at a loss about what to do with his free time and returned to the drawings and notes of Amasis. Soon he became bored with the papers and started to pace back and forth in the house. Nuada's mate watched him and told him to go to the meeting hall; she needed him out from underfoot.

Stepping outside Nuada pulled his cloak tight around his shoulders and turned toward the meeting hall. The icy wetness of the falling snow brushed against his cheeks, and he hurried his steps to the hall. As he stepped on the entry porch, his feet slipped, and he had to catch himself from falling. He pushed through the door and saw heads turn in his direction. Quickly he closed the door from the draft outside. He shook the snow from his shoulders and feet as Beag called to him from his table. Nuada moved quickly to the fireplace to warm his hands before going for a beer and the company of his friends.

Time passed quickly that day, and the conversation and music kept him in a good mood. "I miss the days when I had time to enjoy life like this," he thought.

He did have one fleeting thought that maybe he could get Iolair to talk the doctor into becoming a teacher. They had become friends over the last month. It seemed that every day Iolair would come home with more stories about the world around them.

Late in the afternoon Beag told Nuada that he had another idea for the protection wall. He would build wall extensions out from where the portal gates were to be built, giving them a killing hole for raiders. Nuada disliked the thought of it being used for murder, but if it protected the village, then it was worth it. Nuada told him to go ahead and add it to the design, and then they would bring it up at the next meeting of the consul members.

Just when Nuada was thinking of going home, Mor returned from the new woodworking building. He had just finished the new lift machine, and only the final assembly was needed in the Spring.

"How is the weather outside now?" asked Nuada.

"The snow has stopped, but it remains cold," he replied.

"Then I must go home for my evening meal," he told them.

Nuada struggled against the wet snow that was now over his knees as he made his way home. He was breathing hard before he had gone twenty steps, and still he forced himself on. At last he reached his door and hurried inside to the warmth of his fireplace.

The following morning work crews were out removing the snow from the streets, and the village returned to a familiar place. Nuada walked to the school although it remained closed for one more day. He went first to the office in the old building and, finding no one around, went to the new building. It too was empty. He stopped for a minute in his classroom and then returned to the street to make his way over to the meeting hall again.

Nuada did not get very far. As he started to pass the old woodworking building, he saw Pytheas coming toward him on his way to the school.

"Greetings, my friend," Pytheas called.

"Greetings, Pytheas. I have just come from the school, and no one was around."

"I expected as much. The weather keeps everyone inside, except those that have to be out."

"I was on my way to the meeting hall for a beer. Will you join me?"

He thought for a moment and agreed to come. They made their way around the bend in the street to the hall and entered. Inside Beag was there but few others.

"Do you not ever go home, Beag?" Nuada said with a laugh.

"If you knew my family, you would find any excuse to get away."

"Where is Mor? Did he go to the new woodshop again?"

"Yes. He left about a half hour ago. He said something about building a new wagon."

"He does have a love for wood. I wonder what this wagon will used for?"

"I do not know. He is very tight-lipped about it."

"I think he will tell us when he is ready."

Their conversation carried on for the rest of the morning until Pytheas said he had to go to the school to check on something. Nuada thought about leaving too, but he remained with Beag. He had nothing to do for the rest of the day, and he enjoyed Beag's company. Slowly other men of the village began to drift into the hall, and soon it was almost full.

Nuada watched the men around him and noted that they seemed happy. It was a good sign, and he felt pleased that everyone was comfortable with the situation. The weather had slowed the village life, but it could not stop it.

Later in the afternoon Mor had still not returned from the woodworking building, and Nuada knew that he had to go home soon. After a few more words with Beag, Nuada started for the door and made his way home.

Outside the clouds hid the sun and drifted across the valleys under a light breeze. "If it clears, it will be cold in the morning," he thought. He reached down and touched his old wound, but it was still not giving him any problems.

He entered his house and found his two boys working on schoolwork at the table. He peered over their shoulders to see what subject they were working on as he removed his Winter wear. Nuada's mate was preparing their evening meal and had their daughter clinging to her skirt. Nuada kissed her on the cheek and then reached for his daughter. She quickly grabbed for him, and he lifted her high over his head. She screamed with delight, and he held her close. His two boys turned to watch, and smiles filled their faces.

"You are in a good mood, husband," his mate said.

"I had a very relaxing day."

Soon they settled down and ate of their meal. Nuada asked his boys what kind of day they had. Iolair said that he went to talk with the doctor again, and he told Iolair about a land called the Hittite empire. It was far to the east, which had mountains and deserts too. It was a very old land that had lots of stories about it. The story lasted about an hour, and it kept Nuada's interest.

The next day school made the family rise early, and they soon made the trip for another day of learning. There was really nothing that day that was new for Nuada, and after school he went directly home with his boys.

In the weeks that followed, everything seemed to remain constant with no surprises. One day the snows stopped, and it began to change to rain instead. Some days it was foggy, on others it was just rain. The village was hoping that the sun would break through, but it remained gloomy.

One afternoon Nuada decided to walk out to the shop buildings by the inner protection wall to see what the village people had produced over the Winter months. Most of the shops were still nearly empty, as the weather had not allowed them to bring anything out there yet. Nuada wandered about not thinking of anything else and finally made his way back toward the village. He took the back streets by the new stone houses that would take him by the graveyard and Jan's crypt. He stopped, as he had not been there for a long time again. Memories took him back to a time when they had first learned to talk with each other. Nuada lingered and finally went to the meeting hall.

Nuada's thoughts were still in the past as he settled at a table. Thoughts of how the village had grown and the people with it crossed his mind. He did not hear the voices of the others around him, and visions flashed in his memories. He finally shook the thoughts from his mind and looked around the room. Mor and Beag were in a conversation near the fireplace, and Nuada stood to join them. He went and poured himself a beer and walked to their table. He said nothing but listened in on their talk.

"This weather must break soon. We need to begin on the work," Mor said.

"It will break when it is time, not before, Mor."

"You have become lazy over the Winter, Beag. We need to start soon!"

"If you had bothered to take a walk outside the valley, you would have seen that I have started."

"What do you mean?"

"I have had my crew clear the site of the new quarry. When the weather does break, I will be ready to build again, not before."

Nuada laughed out loud at the two of them. "You sound like you two are married."

Beag turned with a smile, and Mor had a frown, which made Nuada laugh all the louder. He raised his glass and said, "To Spring and the work ahead."

Two more weeks passed, and the rains stopped. The weather began to grow warmer and the days longer. Soon the village came to life again, and the work began in earnest.

- SPRING AND THE FOUNDATION -

With the change in the weather, Nuada took a walk after school to the site of the new quarry. He passed out through the outer protection wall's portal gate and headed toward the stream, which was not all that high for the amount of rain and snow they had this year. He found a narrow crossing point and continued toward the mountainside. He could clearly see the area that had been cleared. He turned his head toward the tree-cutting meadow, and already two of the lift machines had been moved out there. Stopping below the new quarry, he looked to where the new cutting area was and saw Beag already hard at work. Cut stones were being stacked, and some of the wagons were being loaded. He did not want to bother Beag, but he did want to know what he was going to build first.

Walking up to Beag, he asked, "Beag, where are you going to start first?"

"Nuada, I will build the bridge first. Then I want to start some foundations in the village next."

"Yes. Things will move swiftly then."

Nuada nodded in reply, then departed for the village. He passed the outer protection wall portal gate and continued on toward the second valley. He needed to see the new wagon that Mor had been so secretive about. The fresh smell of Spring assaulted his nose as he walked. Trees were regaining their leaves, and the grasses were growing strong. Some of the waterfowl had already returned to the valley, and he watched them fly overhead. He quickly passed the protection wall of the second valley and continued on to the woodworking building. Inside he found Mor and A'Chreag talking next to a massive wagon that shone bright with many brass fixtures. They saw him as he entered and called him over.

"What think you of our new firefighting wagon?"

"So that is what it is. How does it work?"

"We used the idea from some of Amasis's notes and drawings to build it. It pumps water onto a fire. Men stand over here and move this handle up and down, causing water to move through this hose."

Nuada continued to stare at the wagon and finally said, "We have needed of this for a long time. Your work is an art."

Then Mor said, "I have already started to build another. I hope that they will protect us."

They continued to talk about the machine for another hour before Nuada had to return to the village. Stepping outside he could hear that the sawmill was already back to work and that it still fought with the forge for the amount of noise they could make. All three waterwheels were turning against the backdrop of the man-made lake.

Nuada took a deep breath and turned back toward the village. He did not know what to do, as his friends were already busy and would not be waiting at the meeting hall. He took his time returning to the village, following the path by the caves and the crop meadow. He paused below the caves and decided to go down by the lakeside. At the crop meadow, they had already turned the soil for the new crops, and the old waterwheel there that was turned by horsepower stood still. He looked across at the island, and memories of his first home darted through his mind. He shook his head to clear that thought and walked alongside the lake. The air was full of the sounds of birds calling for a mate, and somehow it was relaxing. The sun warmed the air, and Nuada continued on. When he looked up, he found himself just outside of the inner protection wall. He crossed through the portal gate and turned down the street of shops. At the end of the street, the new hospital and storage building stood tall against the ridgeline. He wondered if he should enter and then decided against it. He moved on down the back street near the new foundation under construction there. He paused there to watch some of Beag's men set stone. Then he again moved on to the meeting hall.

He entered the hall, which was almost empty, and drew a beer and found a table to sit at. As he sipped at his beer, he began to feel lonely. His eyes ran around the room and looked for some diversion; there was nothing. He was just about ready to leave when the doctor entered the hall by himself. Nuada called a greeting, and the doctor poured himself some wine and joined Nuada at his table.

They shared some small talk about the people of the village, and then the doctor mentioned that Nuada's son Iolair had brought him a copy of the family history and the story of the valleys. Nuada asked him what he thought of it, and the doctor replied that it was very interesting, but he had some questions about how it came to be.

Nuada answered his questions as best he could, and in the end, the doctor seemed satisfied. Then it was Nuada's turn to ask questions about the doctor. He talked about his adventures as a young man and the places it had taken him. He had fought in two wars in the east and sailed around the whole inland sea, visiting many strange cities. He talked about the people of these lands and their customs. Nuada found it all very interesting and asked many questions. Then soon other village men began to fill into the hall, and they cut their discussion short. Nuada did say that he would like to hear more at a later date, and the doctor agreed.

Then Nuada heard the gruff voice of Beag as he pushed through the door of the hall. He was a bear of a man and made his way to the beer and drew a draft before turning and looking around the room. He saw Nuada and the doctor and walked on over.

"I had almost forgotten how thirsty it makes a man to do my kind of work," he said as he sat down with them.

Both the doctor and Nuada laughed at his words. When Beag was on his third beer, Nuada told him of his walk to the woodworking building and the new fire-fighting wagon that Mor had built.

"So that is what he has been working on all Winter. I will want to see it work."

"I would like to see how it works too," replied Nuada.

Nuada then asked about the new quarry and how the stonecutting was coming. Beag said that the stone was good and that he could probably start the bridge in about five more days. Tomorrow he was going to bring the third lift machine out to the houses in the front of the village for his crew there. Mor was supposed to finish the assembly of the fourth in a day or two, and then it would go to the site of the bridge. He did say that he needed to talk with Mor about the lumber for the scaffolds for the bridge. Nuada then mentioned that he had to prepare for the final tests for his students within the week, and then he would have time to help if necessary.

Just then Mor came through the door and joined his friends. As Nuada needed to refill his mug, he went and got a beer for Mor too. When Nuada returned to the table, Beag was questioning Mor about his fire-fighting machine.

"Well you did not have to keep it a secret. This was something we needed to know about sooner," Beag was saying.

"Then it would not have been a surprise, my friend."

"That is what I am talking about. You go off and do things like this, and we have not any way to plan for it."

"Why? What did it hurt?"

"Now I will have to find a way to build a building for it."

"No, leave that to me."

"But you will still need me to make the foundation and a fireplace to keep it warm too."

"True, but you will find a way. You always do."

Nuada and the doctor watched the action between the two friends and laughed at them. Then Nuada said, "Where do you plan to build this building? It will need to be in the center of the village to do any good."

Mor said, "I have one spot near the wall by the lake."

Nuada tried to see the area in question but failed to find it in his mind. "You will have to show us, Mor."

The rest of that afternoon passed in friendship and good conversation between the friends. Soon it was time for all of them to go home and prepare for the next day.

About a week later Nuada again took a walk out to the front of the village. He passed out through the portal gate and turned toward the open meadow. He followed the stream and came to the site of the bridge construction. He paused about a hundred feet away and watched the lift machine swing cut stone onto the bridge. Both approach ramps had been done, and the arch over the stream was filled with lumber supporting the new stonework going on there. Already stone rubble was down for the street that led to the site from the quarry, and some was started on the side on which Nuada stood. Nuada was again surprised at how quick Beag was working. He figured that at this pace, the bridge would be done in another week. He found a shady spot to sit and continued to watch for another hour. Then a wagon carrying cut stone crossed the stream in a shallow and turned toward the village. Nuada decided to follow and see where it was going.

It went through the portal gates of both walls and followed the street down to the old woodworking building, where it turned and made for the lakeside wall. Nuada was curious. "Was it for the new building for the fire machine?" he wondered.

Then it stopped. Mor was giving directions, and soon it was being unloaded. Nuada walked up to Mor with a question on his lips, but before he could say anything, Mor told him that this was the site of the fire building.

Some of Beag's crew were already setting stone for a foundation, and a large pile of cut lumber sat nearby. Although only a few of Mor's crew were there, it was soon to become a work site. Nuada walked over for a closer look at the site and was surprised at its size. "This is big enough for four of your fire wagons, Mor."

"It is. We will need of that many. And here will be a stable for horses to pull them to where they are needed."

"Do you have any drawings of it?"

"Of course. I will show you later at the meeting hall."

After Mor had returned to work, Nuada walked back toward the school. Tomorrow would be the final test of the year, and he needed to pick up some notes he had left in his classroom.

Outside of the old school building, Pytheas sat on the porch looking over some papers he had. Nuada walked up and joined him. Pytheas looked up and said, "Are you ready for the end of another school year, Nuada?"

They talked for a little while, and then Nuada went to his classroom and retrieved his papers. He went home first and then made his way to the meeting hall.

Mor and Beag had not yet arrived when Nuada walked through the door. He got a beer and sat down to wait for them. About a half hour later when Nuada was finishing his first beer, Mor came through the door. He had rolled-up drawings tucked under his arm and went for a beer first. Then he joined Nuada. "Do you want to look at these now or wait for Beag?"

"I think I will have another beer and wait."

Nuada got up and went for his beer, and as he returned to the table, Beag came through the door. He was muttering, "Stupid idiot."

"What is that all about?"

"Oh one my fools dropped a stone on his foot and broke it."

"What, the stone or his foot?"

That made Beag laugh, and he slapped Nuada on his back and pushed him toward the table. After they settled, Mor pushed the drawings over to Nuada. He unrolled them and began to study the design. Now things began to make sense to Nuada. Besides the stable area in the building, there was a sleeping place for some men too. They would always be prepared for a fire and could respond quickly before it got out of hand.

Nuada slowly put the papers away, and he turned to Beag to ask about his projects. They talked for a couple of hours, and then Nuada had to go home to prepare for school tomorrow.

The day of the testing came, and afterwards he went directly home to grade them, and that took until late in the evening. One more day of school and he would be free for the Summer. Nuada was now looking forward to it.

Around the valleys the crops were planted and the sheep put out to pasture. Construction moved ahead, and the bridge was now complete. Mor had done wonders at the firehouse site, and it was only lacking the roof to be finished. At the stone houses being built out in front of the village, they too had done a lot of the work and were in the finishing stages too although they had made four more foundations for houses out there too.

After Nuada's last class for the school year, he wanted to run out and see all of the changes in the valleys but held himself back and thought that it would be better tomorrow, as he would have the whole day to wander about and see the changes.

That night he slept little and was up long before the Sun had begun to rise. He had let Wolf run, as was his usual thing to do, and waited for his return before setting out to explore the changes.

Nuada knew that today was special, and he made his way to the stable to see if his horse was free or being used elsewhere. Up and down the street in front of the stable, wagons were having horses harnessed to them. Some were already on the move to where they were needed today. It was almost like a parade from the village. Men and animals moved with a purpose. Nuada found that his horse was not being used, so he saddled it and followed the line of wagons out to the front of the valleys.

As he passed the teachers' houses, they were lined up on their porches watching the line go by. Nuada waved as he passed, and soon he was passing through the portal gates of the protection walls and moving toward the bridge. Everywhere there was action as they began to come together for the day's work. Already the lift machines were swinging the large stones onto the site of the foundation wall.

They were massive in size. In the middle of the action, Beag was directing the construction. Beag had started the wall foundation at the ridgeline behind the village. Beyond the construction, the tree cutters were dropping trees as fast as they could. As soon as they were trimmed, they were loaded onto wagons for the trip to the sawmill. Everything moved with the precision of a dance. Nuada was fascinated with how everything fit together, and nothing seemed to get in the way of each other.

He continued to watch for over an hour from his position on the horse. He did glance over toward the new quarry site and saw what seemed like ants pulling down the mountain and carting it off. Finally he turned his horse and followed one of the wagons hauling trees back to the second valley.

He did not rush, as there were so many things going on, and he wanted to see everything. Loads of fresh-cut lumber passed going out to the wall site, and he was surprised by the number of wagons; he did not know that they had that many.

He passed through the portal gate into the second valley, and soon he could hear the noise of the sawmill and the forge working. Like clockwork the wagons unloaded the cut trees and then quickly reloaded with lumber. Nuada did not see either A'Chreag or Mor and turned his horse back to the village. He went through the cut and made his way to the site of the firehouse. Before he got there, he could see the long arm of the lift machine swinging above the houses nearby. When he got there, they were doing the finishing beams for the roof and had started to clad it with lumber for the copper roof. Mor was standing below the work pointing at some detail above him. Piles of lumber were stacked nearby, as were the copper sheets for the roof. Nuada again paused to watch, and time slipped past him.

He finally shook the work from his thoughts and moved out to the sites of the stone houses under construction. Here Beag's small crew was setting stones on the walls of the next four houses and moving quickly with them. He took his time looking around at the work going on there before he decided to return outside of the valleys to the wall construction.

It was nearing midday when he rode out through the portal gates again. Dust from the work greeted him as he rode over the rise to the meadow. Many of the men had stripped their shirts off and continued to work on the wall. All three of the older lift machines were now swinging their loads of cut stones onto the wall foundation. They had moved about a hundred yards further away from the ridgeline now and still kept up the pace of the building. Nuada noticed that some of the men were unloading rubble in between the two inner and outer sections of the wall. Some of Mor's crew were building scaffoldings in this area too. Nuada decided to dismount and sit under a shady tree nearby to watch them work.

Wagons and their loads came and went and each time moved farther along the wall site. Before Nuada's gaze, he watched as more and more of the wall became reality. Beag was still out in front setting the foundation for the wall. Behind him his men worked setting the smaller stones about the foundation.

It was late in the afternoon when the shadows of the mountain behind them started to cast shadows on the work site. Still nobody stopped working.

Nuada remounted his horse and turned for the village again. He went back by the stone houses and then onto the firehouse before returning to the stable. One of the stable hands took his horse, and he crossed the street to the meeting hall to wait on his friends.

Mor was already sitting and enjoying a beer when he walked in. Nuada drew a beer and joined him at their table. He wanted to hear about the work on the firehouse before Beag arrived. Mor told him that the roof was now done, and he only had some minor finishing work to do inside, and then he would go out to the stone houses to do the finishing work there. Nuada asked if he could be of use tomorrow, and Mor welcomed any help he could get.

Soon some of the men began to come into the hall, and finally Beag came through the door with heavy footsteps. You could see how tired he was, and he made his way over for a beer and then sat with Mor and Nuada.

"You look beat," said Mor.

"I am tired, but we made good headway today."

When Beag was on his third beer, he told them of the work that they had done that day. He was at last beginning to relax. Nuada looking around the hall and asked where the rest of his crew was.

"They went to the outdoor cooking area. It was probably a good thing, as many of them smelled."

Mor and Nuada laughed at that remark, and Mor said, "You are no wonder yourself, Beag."

This caused all of them to laugh together, and soon Nuada went over to the cooking area for his evening meal with his family.

For the next week Nuada worked with Mor's crews doing finishing work, and he did not get back out to the wall construction. When the work was done, Mor returned to the woodworking building to work on his other fire wagon, and Nuada took a walk out to the wall construction site.

Nuada crossed the rise and looked down on the wall construction. Now all four of the lift machines were in action, and stones continued to climb upwards at an alarming pace. All of the foundation stonework was done up to the streambed, and they had started on the other side. The opening where the first portal gate was to be built was just an opening in the foundation. Back along the ridgeline, the stones continued to climb and were nearing the height where the top of the wall would be. Still crews added more rubble in between the inner and outer walls. It was packed down as they moved farther along the wall. Wagons never ceased their constant movement of loading and unloading. In a few more weeks, the tree cutters would have to cease cutting as the portal gate was built, and they seemed to know it. Below the wall, the stream was to deep to ford, and there was no other way to move the cut trees. Nuada wondered how long it would take to build the portal gate but remembered how fast everything else was moving and knew that it would not take that long to do.

Nuada stayed until late afternoon watching the work, then walked back toward the village. They had been lucky so far this Spring, as the rain had only come overnight. When Nuada passed through the inner protection wall portal gate, he could not hear the noise anymore of the wagon teams and turned to look back one more time. Then he moved on into the village.

He went to the outdoor cooking area and settled at his table. His mind reached back to all that he had seen that day and how fast everything was coming together. Injuries had been few, and yet they had done so much in the weeks since they had started the work.

His thoughts were broken by some of the village women and their young children on the far side of the cooking area. "I hope when they get older that they realize how hard the men of the village have worked to protect them," he thought.

Nuada stood and stretched. He then turned and walked back toward the school. He stopped across the street from the school, and memories of the past year flooded back. He knew that some of his students would not be back for his classes next Fall, as they had learned all he could teach them. "Perhaps it was time to teach another language to them," he thought. Then he let those thoughts pass.

He turned and walked toward the firehouse. Again he stopped across the street from the building and let his eyes wander over the site. It was a beautiful building, but it was still empty. He wondered when Mor would bring his fire wagon over. Then he remembered that he was waiting until he finished the second wagon.

Nuada then returned to the cooking area to wait on his family and the company of his friends.

The next day Nuada walked to the second valley and looked in on Mor and his project. He found A'Chreag with Mor, and they were installing some mysterious tubes on the second wagon. Nuada asked about them and was told that it was part of the pump system. It was beyond Nuada's knowledge, and he left it at that. Next door at the sawmill they were still loading cut lumber to be moved out to the new protection wall. The supply of trees that were to be cut was down to a small pile, but standing ready to be moved were also the first pair of gates to be hung in the portal gate gap.

Nuada watched the action here for a little while before he decided to go back out to the wall construction. He took his time and enjoyed the walk along the stream. Only three wagons passed him hauling lumber back to the wall. Then as he passed the outer protection wall into the village, he paused to look back toward the lake. He was relaxed and had nothing else to do. Then he again moved over the rise to look down on the wall construction.

The first section of the wall rose up and was nearly complete to the site of the first portal gate opening. The dust hung in the morning air, and men hurried from place to place. One of the lift machines had been moved back to the portal opening and sat still. The other three were still moving stones around the crossing of the steam bed. Nuada watched until he felt that he had to go down there and take a closer look. Load after load of cut stones and their wagons teams moved across the bridge. Nuada dodged around one of the wagons at the bridge and followed the stream to the work area. On the other side, he saw Beag still working with the foundation stones. They had gained another fifty yards for the wall over there. One of the lift machines was on Nuada's side of the stream while the other two were on the side where Beag was working. Already there were lumber forms in place across the stream for the arch that would be built there. Men were setting stones as fast as the machine would lift them into position. Nearby a few men were doing final cutting of the stones to fit into the wall. Nuada noticed that they were using the new iron tools for the stone shaping.

He moved back along the wall to where the portal gate would be hung and watched the men there setting the stones on the wall. Again he looked at the lumber forms that were in place for the construction of the portal opening. The Sun was beginning to get hot, and Nuada moved back to a shady spot near the ridgeline to watch.

All afternoon he watched as progress was made on the wall. At one point, he dozed in the warmth of the day. When he awoke, two wagons with the gates had pulled down near the opening. The lift machine that had been sitting idle came to life and started to lift one of the massive doors up into the air. It was swung around and set on the ground. Then the machine swung back to move the second one. When that operation was done, the machine was again moved down along the wall to move stones for the crew working on the wall.

Late in the afternoon Nuada watched as the shadows from the mountain started to mark the end of another day of work. He got up and started to walk back to the village and to wait for his friends, to hear what they had to say about the construction. He did walk through the stone-house construction site on the way back and found that they had not been idle either. Beag's crew there had most of the walls up on the four new houses.

Nuada moved on to the outdoor cooking area and waited at his table for the crews to start returning for the day. Over the next hour, men drifted into the area, and they talked happily between themselves, telling about their day of work. The women began to prepare the evening meals, and children ran about the whole area. Soon music filled the air, and a long day of work was at end.

The work wagons passed on their way to the stable, and finally the village began to become quiet. At long last, Beag walked into the area and stopped for a minute at Nuada's table to tell him of his day. Nuada got him a beer and listened to his story.

Nuada stayed away from the wall construction for the next four days and spent some time with the teachers. They took Nuada out to the island to show him the grapevines. While he was there, he took a walk to where his old home used to be. He could not recognize the site anymore, as nature had retaken over the whole area. He was disappointed that a part of his past was now lost, but his friends, the teachers, filed him with wine, and after awhile, he did not care about it anymore.

When Nuada did return to the wall construction, he found that the wall was now almost complete to the portal gate site and that the gates themselves had been hung. All of the lumber that had framed the portal gate was removed, and they were moving on down the wall laying stones. However, about fifty yards from the portal gate opening toward the ridgeline, they were still building up. This was to be the site of the first watchtower on the wall. Nuada knew from the drawings that another tower was to be built halfway between the portal gate and the stream.

He walked to the streambed and then crossed the bridge to the other side to see where Beag was on the foundation. He had only gotten about another one hundred yards and was actually working on the crossing over the stream. He was cutting the angled stones that make the arch over the stream when Nuada found him. Sweat poured from his forehead, and with the dust produced, he had a hard time keeping it out of his eyes. Nuada stopped to wet a rag in the stream and walked up to Beag. He thought to wipe his face with it but waited until he had finished with what he was doing. As Beag set his tools down, Nuada said, "Here, wipe your face. It will make you feel better."

Beag scrubbed at his face and head and then said, "Did you bring me a beer too, my friend?"

"I will do that later. How goes the work?"

He looked down the wall and then said, "We are moving along. I wanted to finish this portion of the wall first because if raiders come, we will have some protection. The water on the other side is to deep to ford, and they would have to go downstream about a mile to cross."

"I can see the wisdom of that. If they do attack, then it would give the people time to retreat back to the other wall before they could cross the stream."

"Those were my thoughts too."

"Are the tree cutters back at work too?"

"Yes. They started this morning."

As Beag had to return to his stonecutting, Nuada wandered about the site and then went to the end of the foundation before returning across the bridge to the other side.

It was nearing midday when Nuada turned and went back toward the village. He went through the stone-house site and found some of Mor's crew doing the roofing on the last four houses, and over at the next four houses, the stonecutters were finishing up the walls on those houses. Next to them four more foundations were under way.

Even here on this secondary work project, speed was measured by the job. Nuada shook his head at the way these people worked. Then he moved on to the firehouse again.

Standing in front of the firehouse, Mor was polishing at some of the brass work of A'Chreag's on one of the new fire wagons. Both of the wagons sat in front of the open doors and reflected the sun in their brightness. A whistle escaped from Nuada's lip, as he approached the wagons. Mor turned when he heard Nuada and said, "What think you, my friend?"

"They are an art form, Mor, but do they work?"

"Yes. We tried them at the woodworking shop. They will throw water about fifty yards with two men working the pump."

"Then you have out done yourself. Have you been out to the wall construction site?"

"I was yesterday. How is Beag holding up under the work?"

"He is happy and tired. I also noticed that he has lost some of his belly too."

"When I talked with him, he said that he wanted to give his crews a break in about a week. What do you think?"

"I agree. He has pushed them hard, and the results show it."

"I will talk with the village women about a feast to mark the break then."

As the shadows of the afternoon wore on, Beag finally made an appearance. He was covered head to foot in dust and stone chips. His steps showed a man tired but with purpose. After he had pulled a beer, he said, "I think I can finish the crossing over the stream in about six more days. Then the wall will go up fast after that."

Nuada shook his head in disbelief, and he turned to glance at Mor. He too said nothing, but he had his mouth open in a question.

Nuada spoke first. "You have moved so fast already, and you think you can go faster?"

Beag looked up from his beer and answered, "Oh yes. It was the details that have slowed us down, but once we have passed them, the other work will flow much faster."

Mor spoke up. "I think you are setting too fast a pace as it is. Your crews need of a break, or they will break themselves."

"Do not worry of them. They know what is at stake. Besides I will give them a break soon."

Beag continued to talk about the wall while Nuada and Mor listened in and asked questions from him. Soon the evening meal was under way, and it was a time spent with families.

About six days later Nuada returned to the wall construction site to see how the wall was coming over the stream. Beag was true to his word, and he was in the finishing stages of the portal over the stream. A'Chreag had delivered the gate for the stream crossing, and it had been installed. Nuada walked along the wall looking up at its height. The first watchtower was complete, and they were putting a roof on the top. Sets of stairs were in the construction stages, and they had started the walls for the killing zone by the portal gate there. He understood by the drawings that a second wood gate would also be installed when the trap was completed.

One of the lift machines had already been moved across the stream to where the foundation had stopped before. More of the massive stones were piled nearby and ready to be installed. One of the machines remained at the stream crossing, and the other was still being used to lift stones up on the yet-to-be-completed wall. They had begun the second watchtower, and it added to the massive bulk of the structure. All around the wall wagons moved with a purpose and were nonstop. Outside of the wall, the tree cutters had cleared a large area, giving a clear area of fire for the bowmen, but their purpose was to keep the sawmill working, and they were keeping up with the need.

Nuada knew that the small crew of Beag's that had been working on the stone houses had gone to the second valley to do the foundation work for the other new shop building, and Mor was there with his crews helping. That building would be on the same side of the street as the last two buildings.

The crew of Beag's would return to the stone houses after the break coming up in a few more days. Nuada had been doing finishing work on the last of the completed houses, and it was only today that he had time to see the wall again. He was enjoying his time at the wall and found his old, shady spot near the ridgeline to watch.

The hours passed, and still Nuada sat as the wall grew more complete all the time. Back and forth the lift machines moved at a fast pace, and the men more so. The second watchtower moved skyward as he watched, and the line at the top of the wall became level with those built before.

Nuada started to become stiff from sitting and got up to move about just after midday.

He walked to the first set of stairs that led up to the top of the wall and made his way up. He looked across the vast open area in front of the wall, and then his eyes looked into the distance. There were no signs that anyone was approaching the valleys, and that made him feel good. Next he looked at the detail of the battlements and was pleased in their design. Beag had taken in all the information he could with the design and used it.

Nuada walked over to the first watchtower, and inside he climbed up into it. The view from here was even more impressive than just from the wall itself. It was then that Nuada realized that the wall had a curve to it. The bowmen would have a clear field of fire on any who got that close to the wall. He climbed back down off the wall and made his way to the stream. Beag had left the stream crossing and was back over at the foundation line again. Nuada crossed the bridge and made his way to Beag.

Beag had a table set up there with his drawings spread out on it. He was going over the next section of wall drawings when Nuada walked up to him.

"You are not going to start on the foundation before the break, are you?" Nuada asked.

He turned at Nuada's voice and answered. "No. I just needed to check on some details from the drawings."

"Yes, I heard. We will finish early tomorrow, and then everyone can relax."

"I think you need of it more than anyone else, my friend."

"I am looking forward to it, yes."

Nuada had thought of remaining to watch the construction but made up his mind to return to the village. As he passed through the outer protection wall portal gate, Pytheas was out in the field between the two walls teaching some of the younger children how to use a bow. Nuada watched with interest for a few minutes and then continued on to the street of shops. As he walked along, he glanced at the storefronts but did not stop. He turned at the hospital and followed the street down by the stone houses that were yet to be completed. Here he paused to look at the newest four houses to be built. The walls were part way up, but there remained a lot of work yet to be done.

He went directly home this time and sat on his porch, enjoying the warmth of the afternoon. He began to doze in the comfort of the weather until Wolf came home with the boys and jumped up on him. His tongue washed at Nuada's face until he pushed him away and sat up. Both of Nuada's boys were laughing at Wolf's reaction to their father's shouts. Nuada turned to them and said, "Where is your mother, boys?"

Iolair said, "She has already gone to the cooking area, Father."

"Then gather yourselves, and we will go too."

They set out for the cooking area and their evening meal. Tonight the men of the village seemed unusually quiet, and even the music did nothing to change the mood of the village. Nuada wondered of the reason and realized that it was probably because they were tired. Everyone went home early that night, and the silence of the village huddled over everything.

Early the next morning Nuada could have gone to the second valley to work on the new shop building, but he wanted to return to the wall construction again. He followed the parade of wagons moving out to the wall, and still for some reason the quietness of the village remained.

Two of the lift machines were moving stones onto the wall at the stream crossing, and one was working on the second watchtower. Nuada knew that the fourth machine was at the site of the shop construction in the second valley. The pace of the work continued as before, and Nuada watched as this section of the wall became more complete. Even with the finishing of the wall over the stream, it was not quite one-third done. A lot of work remained for the people of the village to do on the wall.

Beag had turned his attention to finishing the second watchtower, and he motivated his crew every chance he got before they would stop work for the next week. The walls of the tower continued to grow as Nuada watched, and around midday the stonework was completed, and they began to set roof trusses. At the stream crossing, they too had worked hard and were in the final stages of leveling the wall at its completed height.

Already the footprint of the third tower was being built just beyond the stream crossing. Nuada could see Beag moving from place to place, hurrying his men to finish certain work projects. He was not yet ready to quit the work going on, but it showed in the men working that they were ready for the week-long break.

Around mid-afternoon Beag was satisfied with the work and called a halt on the construction. The men were too tired to celebrate, and slowly they made their way back into the village. Nuada waited for Beag, and they walked together to the cooking area as the last of the wagons returned to the stable.

After they had drawn a beer, Nuada noticed the absence of Mor and his crew. He thought that strange, but he probably wanted to do some finishing work on his project too. About an hour later, Mor and his men came into the area, and he settled at the table with Beag and Nuada. Their talk was about simple things, and they had to draw it out of each other as they drank their beer.

Nuada knew that not everyone would get a break from the work, as the sawmill needed the sawdust removed, and the crops needed tending, along with the care of the animals too. He also doubted that A'Chreag's crew would get a break, as their materials would need to be replaced before the next stage of the construction moved on.

A lot of beer was consumed before the meal was ready that afternoon, but it seemed to bring the life back into the village men. Soon the music began to inspire them to talk more, and some actually got up to dance with their mates. Nuada was pleased with this reaction from them.

It was late when Nuada and his family went home. They did not linger but went to bed early. Nuada had dreams about the wall and in hindsight knew that it was the right choice for the village.

- SUMMER AND SATISFACTION -

The needed break brought back life to the village, and they were ready to begin work again. Some of the men had already walked out to the wall site just to look at the wall. Nuada was no exception, as he himself had also walked out to look.

Nuada did take time to walk to the second valley to look at the new shop building there too. He thought that it would probably take another two weeks to finish the building. Then the valleys would have almost all of their industry located in one spot, but the papermaking and the glassmaking would still remain in the village itself. Nuada thought that maybe next year they could do another building for them as well.

The day before the men were to return to work, both Mor and Beag did site inspections and made lists for needed supplies for their projects. Nuada went with Mor, as he would be working on the finishing woodwork in the new shop building for awhile. When Mor had finished his list, they walked over to the sawmill to place the order for supplies. After they stopped at the forge building for some hinges and latches that were needed.

When they had finished, Mor asked Nuada to come with him to the woodworking shop to see his new fire wagon that was under construction. Nuada walked around the new machine and asked questions about the design before they returned to the village.

As it was still early in the day, Nuada walked out to the stone-house site and saw that more stone and lumber had been delivered to the project. Thinking that he may have missed something, he continued on out to the wall construction site. The meadow between the two protection walls in front of the village was empty, and he continued out through the portal gate of the outer wall. He turned left and crossed the rise by the stream. Before him stood the completed section of the new wall, and to the right of it across the stream was the next section to be built.

Nuada looked around and wondered where Beag might be. He decided that he was most likely over where they would be building next and walked down to the bridge and crossed over. Already all three of the lift machines had been spotted for the work that would begin tomorrow. Some of the stones that were already cut were piled nearby, and Nuada knew that tomorrow it would be nonstop for the wagons hauling stone there.

Nuada was still looking for Beag when he spotted him placing marking stakes in the ground a little farther along the line of the foundation. He joined Beag, and they talked about the next phase of the wall. After about an hour, they returned together to the village and the cooking area.

Mor was already there when they arrived, and after drawing a beer each, they sat at the table with him.

Beag said, "I will be glad to return to work, my friends. This had been a boring time for me."

Mor laughed and replied, "But you did get to enjoy more beer this way."

"True, but I could have waited until the work was done."

"What of the stone houses? What are you planning there now?"

"I will keep the small crew working on them so that you will have work to do also, Mor."

Although Nuada was smiling at his friends, he was laughing on the inside at the banter between them. Nuada waited until they had settled into their drinks before he brought up the subject of another shop building next to the new one, for the making of paper and glass next year.

The next morning work resumed on all of the projects, and Nuada went directly to the second valley to do finishing work on the new shop building. Even while he was working on the inside, other men were installing the finishing touches to the roof. Across the street both the sawmill and the forge were humming with noise and kept busy throughout the day. Wagons kept up their pace coming and going. Although Nuada was curious about the other work going on, he was satisfied with doing the woodwork here on this building. Late in the afternoon he had some time to himself and walked across the street to the forge building. Two wagons were loading the copper roof sheets, and A'Chreag was talking with one of the wagon masters. Nuada waited until he pulled out with his load before talking with A'Chreag. They discussed the projects and how they were affecting the work in the forge. A'Chreag seemed pleased that he was keeping busy and had no complaints about the needs of the construction. Nuada asked about his family, and then he had to return to the woodworking at the new shop building.

It was almost dark when Nuada walked back to the outdoor cooking area and joined his friends. They shared some beer together, and Nuada asked about their day. Beag was pleased with the completed work, and Mor said that he could use some more projects. They shared some laughs before the evening meal and then went their own ways.

Time flew by over the next two weeks, and the shop building was complete. Already the weaver and the maker of clothes were moving into the building. Nuada was ready to explore the changes on the wall and at the stone house site. Although his friends had kept him up to date on the work, it was not the same as seeing the work that was done.

Nuada arose early and went directly out to the stone-house construction site. The four houses that were under construction when they took the break were already done, and the next four were well under way. Already the last four housing sites had their foundations built and were awaiting the stonecutters to build their walls. All of Mor's crew that had worked on the shop building were now here at the stone houses doing finishing work.

Nuada spent about an hour looking over the work going on before he walked out to the front of the village and made his way to the wall construction. After topping the rise just outside of the outer protection wall, Nuada looked across the stream and the bridge to where Beag was adding to the wall. Already the wall had moved further down from the stream, and the lift machines were in constant motion. The third tower on the wall was now complete, and the wall was moving farther away from it with every hour that passed.

Nuada crossed the bridge and circled around the construction site to where Beag was setting foundation stones for the wall. Nuada glanced back to where the wall had been before the break and guessed that they had built almost another two hundred yards of wall since then. Then his eyes glanced over toward the quarry site and saw a scar on the face of the mountain where the rock had been torn from it. He noticed that very few of the trees that had once been in this area remained. Everything was now open, and it seemed vast. He also knew that once the wall was complete, houses would soon follow.

Nuada walked back along the wall to the third watchtower and climbed a set of stairs up on the wall. He looked out in front of the wall to where the tree cutters had been working, and again he could not get over the changes in the landscape. The low, rolling land was now open too and would provide a good area of protection once the wall was done.

He looked back along the wall to where some of the scaffolding was being moved again. He found a shady spot to watch and sat down for a while. He was so fascinated by all of the work, he did not notice as the time went by. It was not until the late-afternoon shadows from the mountain dropped over him that Nuada realized that he had spent almost all of the day there. He got up and turned to look out across the wall and glanced toward the horizon. He saw no signs of movement and then climbed back down the stairs and made his way back toward the village.

Once inside the inner protection wall gate portal, he went up the street of shops and looked in on the items the village people had produced for the trader's return. He knew that the trader could return at any time now and was pleased that the shops were fully stocked with trade items.

He then followed the back street back to the stone-house site and saw that even this day that they had made great headway. After pausing for only a short time, Nuada continued on to the outdoor cooking area.

When Nuada entered the area, he saw Iolair and Uilleam sitting at his table, and they were reading some papers that they had brought with them. Nuada went and drew a beer first before he went and sat with his boys. He asked what they were studying, and they told him it was about another people from the Far East that the doctor had provided to them. He asked a few questions about the topic before Wolf came around the table and nudged him for attention.

It was not long after that when the village people began to filter into the area, and it became busy again. Nuada had not seen his fellow teachers in several weeks and was surprised when they came into the area. He went over to talk with them and to see what they had been doing to keep busy. They talked about the caring of the vines on the island and little else. Soon Nuada realized that he was bored with their shallow conversation and made his way back to his own table. Then Mor came into the area. Nuada was going to go talk with him but saw that others needed his attention, and he would wait until later.

Nuada needed to get another beer, and as he was drawing it, Beag walked up behind him and asked if it was for him. Nuada drew a second beer and handed it to Beag and asked him about his day. Beag motioned for them to sit down, and they went back to Nuada's table. He was tired — that Nuada could tell — but he wanted to talk about his work and some of the minor problems that he had that day. When Beag had finished his first beer, Nuada got up to get another. He then began to relax and let the problems of the day pass.

Over the next few weeks, Nuada's help was not needed at the stone houses, and he had a lot of time on his hands. He did keep up his daily walks out to the wall and watched the changes there. On a few these days, both of Nuada's sons went with him, and Nuada enjoyed their company. They were growing so fast now that he had a hard time trying to realize that they were his sons. He felt old around them, and that was hard to accept.

On one of these warm Summer days when Nuada was alone, he did walk out to the wall and made his way out beyond the structure. He wandered beyond the line the tree cutters had made and ventured into the forest beyond. It had been a long time since he had gone hunting, and this reminded him of those days. He listened to the sounds of the forest and what nature had to offer. Although his weapons were never far from him, he felt no need to use them. He was only out for a walk. He was almost out to the old village site of Mor's and then turned back toward the wall.

A lot of this land was open meadow with few trees. It was here that Nuada felt exposed to whatever might be of danger to him or the village. His thoughts were on the need to finish the wall in this direction, to protect the village and its people.

Coming back to the wall construction site from the north, Nuada could see how far the wall had progressed. This took some of the worry from his mind, as Beag had been moving forward quickly with the wall construction. Another tower was almost done, and they were now getting close to the edge of the mountain where it would end.

Nuada paused about a half mile away from the wall and watched the lift machines in motion. The men looked like ants to him from there, but they too were in constant movement. He moved toward the wall again and set his mind on the work being done. He came up to the project from the side closest to the mountain near the quarry site and stopped again. Many of the village wagons were moving with heavy loads back and forth from the construction. Scaffolds lined the wall work, and now they were beginning to build the second portal through the wall. The only shade in the area was from the wall itself, and Nuada felt it would be unwise to get that close to the work. He kept his distance and watched everything going on there. High up on the wall, Beag was giving directions to the other stonemasons. He did not see Nuada, but that did not surprise him because of the work being done.

Nuada circled around the rest of the work and made his way to the stream and a drink of the cold water there. He found a small tree by the stream and settled down to watch some more. Time passed quickly, and finally Nuada decided to return to the village.

On his way back, he went by way of the stone houses to see how they were coming. The last of the houses were nearing their finishing stages, and all of the once-open meadow there was filled with houses. Only the walled area where Jan's crypt and the children who had died in the early years remained untouched. Nuada turned and looked around at the changes there. So much had changed that if he had not been there while everything was built, he would have said that it had been there for a long time. Such was the nature of progress.

His thoughts of what was then and what was now again made him feel old. His steps came slowly as he walked around the area. He made his way back to the main street that led into the village and passed the teachers' houses. Pytheas was sitting on his porch out of the Sun. Nuada decided to seek his wisdom of feeling old that was weighing heavily on his mind as of late.

"Pytheas, my friend. I need to talk with you."

"Come and join me, Nuada. What is on your mind?"

"I have been troubled with the thought of growing old. I have seen the changes in the village, and when I look at my children and see how much they have grown, I feel like I have been here forever."

"I too have seen the changes, although not as long as you, and I do not have children to measure myself by, but I feel the years on me too."

"Then it is not just me?"

"No. All of us feel of that way from time to time."

Nuada nodded in understanding and remained silent. They watched as some wagons passed the house, and then Nuada said, "I must go to the cooking area and wait for my family. Thank you for your understanding, and it has helped me."

As Nuada entered the area, he could hear music coming from the front of the area. Many of Mor's crew were there already, as they had almost finished their projects now. Already they had been gathering firewood for the Fall and had been doing cleanup work around the village just to keep busy.

Mor was sitting at his table when Nuada went and drew a beer for himself. He was looking at some drawings on the table and did not see Nuada at first. Nuada was going to walk on by and settle at his table when Mor looked up.

"Nuada, sit and join me. I have been looking at some drawings for the shop building for the glassmakers and the paper shop. I would like to see what you think about it."

He pushed the drawings across to Nuada, and although Nuada did not feel like thinking about that now, he went over the drawings with Mor. They talked through the layout inside the building and made one small change. Mor was making a note on the drawings before rolling them up and putting them away. When he looked up, he saw that Nuada had other things on his mind.

"Is something troubling you, my friend?"

Nuada told him of his thoughts about getting old and how he had talked with Pytheas about it. "I do not know if it is the changes we have made to the valleys or if it is the sight of my children getting older, but it bothers me."

"We all have those feelings. Perhaps you need to talk again with your creator."

Nuada had not talked with Creatrix in a long time and wondered if this was the reason behind his doubts. He made up his mind to try and seek the wisdom of Creatrix in a dream that night.

Nuada looked across at his table and saw his mate and daughter had arrived. He told Mor that he had to go and would talk with him tomorrow. As Nuada walked across the patio, his two boys also arrived. Nuada joined them and took his daughter so his mate could go and prepare their meal. Nuada asked his boys what they had been up to today, and they told him that they had spent the day by the lake.

After eating they stayed awhile longer before going home for the night. Nuada did not go to bed when the others did but sat by the fireplace and waited for a vision from Creatrix.

At one point he dozed and had a short dream of the construction, but it was disjointed and held no meaning for him. But during the middle hours of the night, he crossed over into the realm of Creatrix. He found himself enveloped in the white fog of Creatrix.

"Awaken, Nuada, and hear of my wisdom."

"I hear of you, but again I have no sight of you."

"As it should be. I have watched and listened to your worries of time passing you by. Fear not. Your time is mine to give, and you are not yet ready to make the changeover."

"Then what is my purpose now?"

"As it has been: to learn and to teach. Your village still pleases me, and your people are as they should be."

"Then I am pleased to do your bidding."

Nuada awoke in the early-morning light, slightly stiff from sleeping where he did, but he felt an energy within himself to do more and this feeling he had to pass onto the others. He changed his clothes and made his way back out to the wall. They were just beginning their day, and already the lift machines were moving more stone onto the wall. Wagonloads of cut stone were lined up nearby and moved through the needed line to where they were unloaded. Nuada saw Beag out ahead of the wall line laying more foundation stones and made his way down to him. Nuada stopped short as a large foundation stone was swung into place beside Beag. He waited until Beag and his small crew with him cleared the supporting lines and let the lift machine swing back out of the way.

"Beag! You still amaze me with your speed and accuracy during this building. How much longer do you think it will take you to finish now?"

"I think I have about eight or nine more weeks of weather to finish, but we may or may not finish this year."

"But the wall itself will be almost done, will it not?"

"Yes. We will have of its protection, but some of the finishing details will be close."

"You mean the last tower, right?"

"Yes. The last tower will be the problem. If we have an extra week, then I will finish this year."

"You are a worker of miracles. I will take no more of your time."

Beag returned to work just as another large stone was swung into place over his head. Nuada turned and walked up the line of scaffolds and beyond. As he walked, he watched the men work with a purpose, and they were hurrying to finish what they could. They had all lived within the valley long enough to understand the way the weather changed as they neared Fall.

Nuada climbed up onto the wall by the third tower and made his way to near the first tower. He looked out across the land in front of him and began to wonder if the trader would come this year or had he had trouble himself.

Nuada found a spot on the south side of the tower in the shade and settled down to watch the land in front of the new protection wall. He also found that A'Chreag had found time to make new bells for warning the village. These were of a different shape than the ones he had made so long ago. He thought that they would also have a different sound too.

The hours passed without incident, and Nuada finally had to stand to shake the stiffness from his body. He walked back and forth also, knowing that the lack of sleep last night added to the feeling. He looked far into the distance again and saw a small dust cloud far to the south. "Could this be the trader?" he thought.

He continued to watch for two more hours as the small cloud of dust kept moving toward the village. He figured that it would take whoever it was until almost dark to reach the new wall. He climbed down from the wall and decided to investigate himself. He could make better time alone, and if it was anyone other than the trader, he would have time to return and warn the village.

He made his way quickly through the portal gate and headed in the direction of the dust cloud. It took him a little over an hour to get within sight of the cause. It was the trader but with four wagons this year. He did not have any people seeking shelter this year with him. Nuada soon joined up with the trader, and they talked. Nuada told him of the new protection wall and said he would go on ahead to warn the others not to worry.

Nuada almost ran back to the protection wall and passed through the portal gate. First he turned left and down to the construction crew and Beag to tell them of the trader's return. Then he made for the outer protection wall of the village to tell them. He told them to send others back into the village to tell of the trader's return. Then he went back to the new protection wall to wait for the trader.

The shadows from the mountain cast a shadow across the meadow in front of the wall when the trader finally came into sight. It seemed to Nuada that it took forever for them to cross the meadow, but he waited patiently for them to pass through the portal gate and killing hole of the wall. He could see some of the drivers looking up at the massive structure and pointing at some point on it. Nuada looked in the direction that they were pointing and saw that many of Beag's crew had armed themselves and were lined upon the wall.

The trader pulled his horse team to a halt just past the outer section of the killing hole, and Nuada climbed up onto the wagon seat, and together they followed the street onto the outer protection wall.

They passed through the portal gate there and pulled all the wagons over near the inner protection wall. The horse teams were shortly unhooked and tethered behind their wagons for the night. Nuada led the trader crew over to the building that was for them to sleep that night and told the trader to come down to the outdoor cooking area after everyone was settled for a meal. Even here armed men lined the inner wall above the meadow between the two walls. Coming back outside of the building, the trader stood with Nuada, and he noticed more of the new construction and commented on its appearance. Nuada took his leave and returned to the village alone.

When Nuada entered the cooking area, he was amazed at the number of the village people there already waiting. Some asked questions of him about what the trader had brought this year, and Nuada's reply was that he had not had a chance to ask about the items yet.

After Nuada had drawn a beer and settled at his table, it took about another half hour before the trader and his crew arrived. He had them settle at his table and went and brought beer back for them to relax with before their meal. Finally Nuada asked about the items he had brought this year and was presented with a list of things. Nuada looked over the list quickly, but the thing that stood out was salt; he had a large supply this year.

When Nuada looked up from the list, he saw that most of the village people had now come into the cooking area, including Beag and Mor. He called his friends over, and they also settled with their beer at the table. Questions followed about the outside world and what was happening there. The biggest news was that the Etruscans had lost badly in their war with the east, and then the people native to their land had revolted and finished their control of that land.

Nuada asked if they had any problems with the raiders from the north, and the trader said no, it had been quiet in that direction. Nuada nodded, deep in thought. His worries about another raid from that direction this year were put to rest.

About that time the village women began to serve the evening meals, and the table became quiet as music began to filter through the area. After eating the trader's crew returned to their sleeping quarters for the night, and Nuada told them that he would see them in the morning.

After they had left, Nuada passed the trader's list around between his fellow consul members to get their comments on what he had brought with him. Notes were made from both Mor and Beag about things that they could use. By the end of the evening, Nuada had a grasp of the items that the village could use and made his way home.

Early the next morning Nuada made his way to the shop buildings by the inner protection wall to wait on the trader. The trader and his crew slept late that morning, and Nuada was becoming bored waiting on them.

Nuada was thinking about going out to the new wall when the trader and some of his crew walked out of the building across the street. Nuada waved to him and walked over to talk with the trader. In the early-morning light, the trader again looked around at the changes the village had gone through.

"You have been busy. Everywhere I look I see new buildings and walls that were not here last year."

"Yes. We are growing. Now here is a list of the things we would like to trade for."

"First show me the items in your shops. Then we will talk trade."

They walked through all of the shop buildings, and the trader made notes and asked questions about the things on hand. Then they walked out to the wagons of the trader and looked through those items. His crew was feeding and watering the horses when they arrived. It took about an hour to arrive at a reasonable deal, and then Nuada had them pull the wagons around to the storage area below the hospital. First they unloaded the traded items and then began to reload the items from the shops. This year there was no gold involved in the trades, and Nuada was pleased with the things that they got in return; all of it were things the village could use.

The trader and his crew would remain in the village for another two days before returning to their own lands. In that time, Nuada gave the trader a tour of the changes in the village. He could not believe the changes in only one year and told Nuada so.

On the day the trader departed the village, Nuada rode with them as far as the new portal gate and wished them a safe journey. He watched them follow the road away from the wall, and when they entered into the forested land beyond the cleared meadow, he turned back and went to look at the wall construction again.

Beag was now building the second portal gate and was making good headway. The new gates for there were already stacked against the wall, ready to be installed. On both sides of the opening, scaffolds reached up high on the wall, and the lift machines were in constant motion. Nuada's eyes followed the foundation and saw that only a short span was left to be finished now. Some of Beag's crew had already cleared the ground and were awaiting the rest of the foundation stones to be laid.

Still wagons were moving throughout the area, and Nuada had to watch his step so as to not get run over. Already the lower portion of the last watch tower was under construction. All of the work crews moved with a purpose.

Nuada walked back across the bridge and made his way toward the village. He stopped on the outer edge of the ridge and turned around to look back at the wall. His eyes took in all of the open ground in front of him and knew that next year they would start to build houses there too. Visions of what was to come swam before his mind's eye. Then he took a deep breath and turned once again to the village.

His footsteps took him past the old outer protection wall and alongside the lake toward the second valley. Many wagons passed going in both directions, either with cut trees going to the sawmill or lumber going back out to the wall. Nuada passed through the second valley's protection wall portal gate and moved on toward the junction of the streets by the workshops.

Nuada noticed that the crew of Beag's that had been working on the stone houses were there building the foundation for the last workshop. Nuada had only brought it up for next year's work, but they had already started it. He watched for a little while and then went to seek out Mor at the woodworking building.

Inside Mor was working on another fire wagon for the village. When Nuada approached him, Mor said, "How did the trades go this year?"

"Very well, Mor. Are you behind the new shop construction across the street?"

"In a way. Both Beag and I decided to go ahead and do as much as we could this year."

"But that was a project for next year."

"I know, but it was needed, and we just went ahead and started it."

Nuada shook his head at the response and decided to let them do what they do. After some small talk, Nuada turned toward the village again, and his steps took him through the cut between the valleys and on past the school. He again paused to look toward the school and was about to go over and look through the classrooms but changed his mind and went on to the outdoor cooking area.

He found the area empty, and he felt that he could not stay there, so he returned outside of the protection walls to watch the construction again. He settled in a shady spot on the ridgeline and continued to watch the work from there. Insects buzzed about his head, but he paid little attention to them.

It was late in the afternoon when the shadows from the mountain again fell across the work area, and Nuada went back to the cooking area to wait on his friends. He drew a beer and settled at his table to wait.

It was not long before men from the crews began to enter the area, and Nuada listened to their talk. Everyone seemed happy and tired. At last both Beag and Mor showed up and got their beer. Nuada waved them over to hear what they had to say about their day. That evening went much the same as many before, and the village slept an exhausted night.

About a week later, Nuada went back out to the wall construction and along the way noticed the golden grasses of the Summer season. He had been so busy watching what the people of the village had been doing that he had failed to notice what nature had been doing. His thought turned to the return of Fall, which was now not that far away. He set his pace and quickly passed outside of the valley and looked down on the wall. He paused to look at it from one end to the other. Then he walked on down and across the bridge to the site of all the work. The final work on the portal gate was being done, and its gates were hung. Beag had again returned to setting the foundation-wall stones and was almost to the end of the line there. They had cut back into the mountain and made it secure for the end of the wall. All four lift machines continued to move with intensity as they moved the cut stones onto the wall. The rubble fill went in almost as fast and was packed between the wall sections. The last tower was almost done but still lacked a roof and some minor details. The walls for the killing zone inside the portal gate were coming along too. Nuada could see no reason why the wall would not be done this year. If the weather held for another week and a half, it would be done.

Nuada then turned and walked to the second valley to see how they were coming along with the new shop building there. Here too Mor's crew was working with an intensity that was not really called for, and they had the walls framed and many of the roof trusses on the building already. There was probably only another week's work on this building.

Nuada returned to the village and stopped at the school. It would soon be time to reopen the school, and the teachers were getting prepared. Nuada was no different, as he had also thought of the school for about a week already himself. The school had already been restocked with its paper and ink supplies. Pytheas had held a teachers meeting, and they went over the coming studies. The number of classes that Nuada would teach was to remain the same this year (six), but he was adding a new language this year, and it would be the Phoenician language.

When Nuada was satisfied with his preparations for the day, he returned to the outdoor cooking area to wait for his friends again. Nuada was going over some of his notes and did not notice the lack of village women in the area.

They had just started to harvest the grains in the second valley, and it would take over a week for them to do that. He did not realize the slight drop in temperature either that marked the coming of Fall. He looked up from his papers when a cloud obscured the light that he had been using. He looked up into the sky and thought that he had not been paying attention to the weather either. It was then that he wondered if they would finish everything needed this year.

They had not held any formal meetings of the village consul for the last three months, as they had all been too busy. It was only through the talks during the evening meals that they really communicated with each other. Tonight they needed to talk about the upcoming Fall feast and an end to the work year.

- FALL AND COMFORT -

In just over a week, all the construction came to a finish. The village women were harvesting the crops from the meadow near the lake and putting them into storage. The village hunters were out for their deer hunt as well. Crews were gathering the last of the needed firewood for the village, and others were hauling the sawdust from the sawmill. The grain mill was making flour now, and at the forge A'Chreag had his crew bringing in the needed ore for the Winter projects. All of the teachers were preparing for the reopening of the school, including Nuada.

The weather was still holding onto the last traces of Summer, and there had been no rain yet. The Fall feast was to be held in about another week to allow the women to finish the harvest. The teachers had also moved their glass-making and papermaking projects to the new building and were happy with their new structure.

Beag had settled into his Winter mode already and could be found every day at the meeting hall drinking his beer. He avoided the crowds by being there instead of at the cooking area. Mor was different; he enjoyed being with people and spent his time in the cooking area.

Nuada did talk to Mor about having a gathering at the new protection wall to celebrate its completion. Mor thought it was a good idea, but Beag did not want any part of it, as he had spent too much time there already this year. So that idea was put on hold until the village had settled into a long rest period.

Two days before the feast Nuada walked back out to the new wall to look around. Outside of the outer protection wall, he followed the ridgeline and then climbed the wall near the first watchtower. He looked into the distance in front of the wall, thinking that there might be something of interest out there but no. Only the empty horizon greeted him. He walked along the wall until he came to the last section to be finished. Here too nothing outside of the wall moved, and he descended the stairs there to begin his return to the village. He turned to look at the quarry site and found it had been shut down for the Winter months also. All four lift machines were parked nearby, and they had their long booms lowered to the ground. The lumber that had been used for the scaffolding was stacked neatly nearby as well. There piles of cut stone were sitting awaiting the Spring housing construction that would begin in this area.

Nuada then made his way back across the bridge and turned up the rise back to the village. The whole area seemed dead, as there was nothing showing any signs of life out there now. They had not even posted any guards out there on the new wall. Nuada passed through the protection walls of the village and turned up the street by the shop buildings.

He walked through the area that held the new stone houses, but they were also empty. He felt alone and made his way to the meeting hall and his friend Beag. He needed someone human to talk with.

Inside of the meeting hall, Beag was sitting and talking with Anoghas; both men were enjoying their beer together. Nuada drew a beer and joined them. Beag's eyes sparkled with laughter, and Nuada wondered of the reason.

"Did I miss a joke?" Nuada asked.

"No, my friend, but Farmer was here awhile ago and asked if I could build him a grain tower in the second valley next Spring."

"It would be useful. So what did you tell him?"

"I told him that I would have so much time on my hands next year that I could build it in my sleep."

Nuada laughed himself at Beag's response and raised his beer in salute to it. "I think everyone will have too much time on their hands next year. Even the number of houses is limited because we do have so many empty ones now."

Beag leaned forward and said, "Then perhaps you should go out and find us more people for the village again."

The thought of seeking more people for the village had not occurred to Nuada until now. It had been a long time since he had ventured out into the wilds. He went quiet and let his mind wander over the lands outside of the valleys.

Later after several more beers with his friends, Nuada began to feel hungry, and he made his way to the outdoor cooking area. His boys were already at their table, and Mor was nearby talking with many of the men he had worked with. He stopped to talk with Mor and told him of Beag's thoughts about finding more people next Spring. Mor thought it was a good idea, but when he asked who he would take with him, Nuada was at a loss for words.

Nuada was still thinking about who to take when he sat at his table with his boys. Iolair asked his father what was bothering him.

"Some of the village consul think I should seek more people for the village next Spring. But the question came up about who would go with me."

"Father? Why not take me? I am ready to see outside of the valleys."

Nuada turned to look at his son, and then he wondered why not. "That is a good idea. It will teach you how to meet others and how to be prepared for trouble too."

Iolair grew excited about the prospect of an adventure with his father, and he too sat quiet for a long time. About an hour later, Nuada's mate arrived with their daughter from the crop meadow. He held her on his lap while she went and prepared their evening meal.

After eating Nuada went back over to Mor and told him that he would go in search of more people in the Spring and that he was going to take his son Iolair with him. Mor thought that it was an excellent idea to take the boy.

The next morning Nuada went to talk with Pytheas about his son's weapon training. After Pytheas had explained to Nuada that he thought Iolair's training was excellent and that he had a natural ability with swords and bows, he asked why he was asking about it. Nuada told him that he planned to take Iolair with him in the Spring in search of more people for the valleys. Therefore, he had to make sure that he would be ready for anything that might happen. Pytheas understood Nuada's concerns and told him not to worry; Iolair could handle anything that would come up and do it well.

Nuada felt better after talking with Pytheas and hearing the praise he had for Iolair. Nuada left the school and walked away deep in thought about the coming adventure. When he looked up again, he found himself out by the inner protection wall. He had not been paying any attention to where he was going or why. He looked out into the open meadow between the walls and saw that Iolair was practicing with his bow alone. He kept out of sight and just watched his son. The boy's shafts were tightly grouped on their targets, and he could fire them very quickly without changing any accuracy of the strikes.

After watching for awhile, Nuada slipped away and returned to the village. He went to the meeting hall and found Beag there already. "Do you not ever stay at home, my friend?"

Beag laughed at the question, as Nuada already knew the answer to it. Then Nuada told him he would go on the quest for more people in the Spring, and he was going to take his son with him. Beag did not know much about the boy, and he asked some questions about him that Nuada answered. Then he said, "I was about his age when I went on my first adventure. It will open his eyes to the real world."

Then Nuada said, "I know he is close to becoming a man, but this will bring a maturity to him that many others lack."

"And what about you? Are you ready to give up your son yet?"

"I do not think that I will be giving him up; rather it should bring us closer together."

Beag nodded and then said, "Then the next thing you know, he will be bringing home a girl for his mate. Then it follows that you will become a grandfather. How does that sit with you?"

"I had not thought of that. You make me feel older than I am."

Beag laughed and then said, "Time does not stand still, my friend. It will happen."

Nuada sat quietly and looked at his own future for a while. Then Beag broke his thoughts by saying, "The day after the feast we are going to hold the first consul meeting of the Fall. Think on any ideas that may come your way."

"I do have one. Do we know how many empty houses we have now? I do not, and perhaps we should make up a census of our people and where they now live."

Beag nodded and said, "It is a good time of year for such a thing, and it will help in our building next year."

"That is what I thought also. It will also help with the school and tell us when we will need to build another school or add teachers."

They continued their talks until mid-afternoon when Mor arrived to have a beer with them. Mor brought up building two more shop buildings near the others for future industry. They discussed that for awhile until others of the village men began to come into the hall. After that all discussion was on hold until the consul meeting.

They sat and listened to the music in the hall and the conversation of the others the rest of the afternoon.

The morning of the feast it broke with a cool taste in the air, and a few clouds were drifting in from the north. Nuada walked to the school and talked with Pytheas for awhile. Then he went and checked on his classroom again. Amasis came in when he was about ready to leave.

"I hear that you may be going on an adventure in the Spring. If you do, I would like to come along."

This took Nuada by surprise, and he asked why.

"I simply want to see more of this land and the people here."

"It will be full of danger, you know."

"I understand, but I think it will be worth the risk."

"Then you are welcome to join me."

They walked out into the hall, and Nuada talked of the dangers involved while they made their way outside of the school. The temperature had risen to a comfortable degree, and the clouds had disappeared. They stood on the steps and talked for a little while before Nuada told him that he had to go back and check on another problem in the second valley.

Nuada walked to the woodworking building in the second valley and was looking for Mor. He found him doing some repair work on one of the wagons and waited until he had finished with his work.

"Mor, I had some thoughts on your fire wagons. If we build more houses in the Spring behind the new protection wall, will we not need a firehouse there too?"

"I had been thinking on that too. Yes, we will need another firehouse there also. But we will need of one here in the second valley also."

Nuada nodded and then said, "Then will you bring it up at the consul meeting?"

"I will. We need of the protection."

They continued to talk, and other things came up that needed to be addressed at the meeting too. It was nearing midday when Nuada returned to the village, and he followed the ridgeline after passing through the cut between the valleys. He stopped at the shop building that held his model map of the valleys and other papers that he had in storage. He looked at the model map and thought that it had been a long time since he had updated it. He considered doing the work but knew that he did not have the time to do so. Along the wall were the two chests that A'Chreag had made for him to store the papers from there. He started to open one but changed his mind.

He then went to the meeting hall and drew a beer. As usual Beag was already there, and they settled down into a long conversation about what Mor and he had discussed that morning. A little later Anoghas and Millert came into the hall and joined the pair at their table. All these two talked about was the upcoming feast that night. Beag was no slouch at eating, and soon they began to get hungry. They finished the beers that they were drinking and made their way to the outdoor cooking area. Wonderful odors drifted through the area, adding to their readiness to eat. Many others were also there, and loud conversations filled the area. The din was added to by the music being played near the front of the patio.

Nuada's family was there, and he went and joined them at his table. Iolair asked about his father's day, and Nuada told him of his conversation with Amasis and his wanting to go with them in the Spring. At that point, Nuada's mate got up to help with the meal preparation and bent over Nuada's shoulder and said quietly, "He is your son. Look out for him."

Nuada turned and kissed her gently on the cheek and said, "I will."

She squeezed his shoulder before turning to go to the fireplaces near the front of the area. He understood her meaning and looked back at his son.

"Iolair, perhaps we should go hunting before the snows come this year."

Iolair was excited at the prospect of going on a hunt with his father, but it was Uilleam who spoke up. "Can I go too?" he asked.

"Not this year, son. Next year will come soon enough, and I will take you then."

"But what about school?" Iolair asked.

"We will go before the school opens, son."

"Then it will happen within a few days?"

"Yes. You can begin your preparations tomorrow. Think of what is needed, and I will go over them with you."

Little more was said that evening about the hunt, and other people dropped by Nuada's table to talk throughout the evening. Nuada's mate remained quiet and said little about the coming adventures. It was late when the family returned home, and Nuada fell asleep quickly that night.

The next morning Nuada awoke before the first light of dawn. He dressed as usual and prepared for another day of dealing with the problems of others. He was sitting at the table going over his notes for the upcoming consul meeting when Iolair came down the stairs to join his father.

"How did you sleep last night, son?" asked Nuada.

"Well enough, but I had dreams of the coming hunt going through my head."

"That is normal. Today I have some important work to do for the consul meeting, so we will leave tomorrow for the hunt if nothing else comes up."

"I will be ready, Father."

Just as the first light came over the ridgeline, Nuada made his way to the school. Pytheas was standing outside of the old school building and greeted Nuada as he approached. Nuada crossed the street and joined Pytheas on the porch of the school. Nuada told Pytheas about his plan to take his son on a hunt and that he should return in two or three days. After they talked for a few minutes, Nuada departed for the second valley and the woodworking building, where he wanted to talk with Mor again.

Inside the woodworking building, Mor had another wagon in for repair and had started to build another fire wagon. He had five of his skilled crew helping, and they were going over some small detail on the new wagon. When Mor was free, Nuada told him of his planned hunting trip, and then they went over some of the topics of discussion for tonight's meeting. When Mor had to return to his work, Nuada walked next door to the forge building to see what was going on there.

Nuada was surprised when he found the building empty, and then he turned back to the village. The weather remained warm although you could now tell that the days were shorter. Nuada slowed his pace as he passed through the cut between the valleys. He thought of going out to the new wall again but changed his mind and continued on to the meeting hall. It was already midday when he stepped onto the porch of the meeting hall and entered. Inside Beag was already enjoying a beer, and Nuada joined him. A few of the village men were also there, but for the most part, the hall was empty.

Late in the afternoon Nuada walked to the outdoor cooking area for his evening meal before the meeting of the consul members. The warmth of the Fall afternoon added to a festive atmosphere, and music added to the feeling. Nuada was enjoying himself, and when the time came for him to leave, he regretted having to go. He made his way back to the hall and the meeting.

It took awhile for all of the consul members to return, and when they finally did, they went about the business quickly. The grain tower was approved, as was the two new shop buildings. They set a plan in motion for ten new houses outside of the outer protection wall on the east side of the stream. A new firehouse was to built in the area of the new houses, but the one for the second valley was on hold for awhile until they could see where the need was. Two new water wells were also approved: one for the second valley and one outside by the new houses.

The plan for a census was also approved, and it was to be done as soon as possible. Farmer put forward a plan to grow more grain crops outside of the new protection wall, and it was also approved for next year. They concluded their meeting with many beers and congratulations for a year of hard work on the completed projects. Beag was the center of attention for his strength of character in getting the work done.

Early in the morning before the sun rose, Nuada and his son Iolair had already packed for their hunting trip. Nuada sent Iolair to the stable for their horses, and he waited patiently for his return. Nuada stood on his porch with the items that they would need and watched as the sun finally rose above the ridgeline.

When Iolair returned, they quickly loaded their packhorse and then mounted the other two and made their way outside of the village. They crossed the bridge and made their way to the second portal gate in the new wall. Once through the gate, they paused and turned to look back at the new wall with its towers.

"We will go north from here and pass Mor's old village. We will do no hunting until the return leg of our adventure, son," Nuada said.

This was Iolair's first time outside of the village, and he looked at every change in the landscape. Nuada had already taught him what to look for as far as dangers involved on this trip. The boy remained alert for any signs of danger, as was Nuada.

By mid-afternoon they came to the old village but did not linger there. They pressed on to the north, and when it came time to camp for the night, they were well to the north of the old village. Their campsite was no more than a clearing in the trees that surrounded them. Iolair tended to the horses while Nuada made a small campfire. They bedded down for the night, and Iolair had a hard time sleeping. The sounds of the forest surrounded them and added comfort to Nuada's sleep.

In the morning they awoke to another warm day, and they quickly packed again. Nuada's thoughts were to continue on in this direction until midday and then turn to the west before turning south again. There were plenty of deer signs, and Nuada knew that they would have success on their hunt.

However, before midday Nuada could smell smoke in the air, and they slowed their pace. They turned in the direction of the smell and moved with caution. About an hour later, they came upon the cause and stopped in a hidden grove of trees. Hiding the horses, they moved forward on foot. They topped a small rise and looked down upon a small village that was on fire, and they watched for the cause. A small band of raiders had the village people surrounded and held in a tight group. Nuada cautiously counted the raiders and found that they numbered about ten. He told Iolair that they would help these people, and they split up and moved down on them from their vantage point.

Nuada was nervous about how Iolair would react to fighting these raiders but knew that Pytheas had great words about his training, and he was his son too. When they came very close in to the raiders, they picked their targets with their bows and, in a very one-sided fight, dispatched them quickly. There was no need for any hand-to-hand fighting, and when they had finished with them, Nuada approached the villagers. He quickly asked if any more of the raiders were around, and when they told him no, he began to relax. Iolair remained alert to the trees around them and the village people too.

While some of the people tried to fight the fire, others had given up and turned their attention back to Nuada. These were poor people with little to show for their village, and Nuada asked if they would like to move to a place of safety and protection. He told them that he would provide food and houses for them too. This caught their attention, and many agreed to move. A few did not wish to give up on their village so quickly though. He then began to tell them of his valleys and the village, and in the end, all of these people agreed to follow him to the valleys.

Iolair had watched and learned how his father had brought so many people into the valleys. He was proud of his father, but it was the wrong time to tell him so.

Nuada had the village people gather all that they wished to take with them, and they moved away from the destroyed village. Iolair returned to their horses and soon rejoined the villagers as they moved south following Nuada. As it neared dark, Nuada had them make camp and prepare for a sleepless night of rest before moving on in the morning.

Both Nuada and Iolair did not get any sleep, as they remained on guard around the villagers.

The next morning they broke camp and continued south toward the valleys. Iolair lingered behind to make sure that they were not being followed. They were making good time, and as they got closer to the valleys, Nuada continued to talk with the village people. They were excited about the prospects of the valleys and all that was offered to them.

It was getting close to dark when they approached the new protection wall. These new people were stunned at the massive size of the structure. Nuada then sent Iolair forward to warn those guards on the outer protection wall of their arrival. Nuada had already passed the new people through the portal gate into the open area behind it when Iolair returned.

Some of the new people began to question Nuada where the village was, as the large, open area confused them. He told them to be patient and led them across the bridge toward the outer protection wall over the sight rise there. When they topped the rise, the other wall came into view, and on top of it were the armed villagers of the valleys.

They almost stopped in their tracks, wondering if this was some trick , but Nuada told them it was only a precaution for their protection. They moved through the portal gate and into the meadow between the walls. Even here more of the village people awaited to greet the newcomers. They helped the new people carry their things, and again they passed the second portal gate and went into the village. Nuada took them up the street of shops and then by the hospital before turning down the street by the ridgeline. Nuada finally stopped in the middle of the new houses and began to assign houses to the people.

They were surprised by the seeming luxury of the houses, and to top it all off, the women of the village brought them food. It took about an hour to settle the new people into the houses, and then Nuada told them that he would return in the morning to show them around the village.

Iolair had gone on ahead to drop off the packs at the house and then return the horses to the stable. When Nuada had finished with the new people, he made his way to the meeting hall and a beer with his friends. He found Iolair inside waiting for him at Beag's table. Nuada drew two beers and sat down at the table. He pushed one across to his son.

"What is this for, Father?"

"You have become a man, and I want you to share in what men experience."

Beag raised his beer in salute and said, "Welcome to a man's world."

They all laughed and drank of their beers together. Mor walked in during the laughter and wondered of the cause. "What is this all about?" he asked.

"We are marking Iolair's manhood," Beag said.

After a few more beers, Nuada and Iolair walked to the cooking area for something to eat. Nuada's mate looked at the bond between the pair and shook her head. She thought, "This is what they needed together."

The next morning Nuada returned to the new houses and the people there. He waited for them all to assemble and then took them around the valleys together.

A small group of the valley's people followed at a distance. They paused outside of the school, and there Nuada told them that it was expected of them to study and learn at the school. This brought a murmur from the group, and then they moved on to the second valley, where he showed them the shop buildings and the mills. They circled the valley and went by the sheep stable and back toward the main village again. He took them up the street by the firehouse, and then they crossed over to the outdoor cooking area where they stopped.

The women of the village had prepared them a light morning meal, and they settled down to relax now. Nuada then gave a speech about what was expected of them and some of the simple rules of the village. After that they were free to go anywhere in the valleys that they wanted.

Nuada then walked to the meeting hall again and sat down at Beag's table. Soon other members of the consul arrived, and they began talking about the new people and the raiders that had attacked them. Nuada gave a simple story about how he had found them, and then the door to the hall opened, and the doctor approached the table.

"I have checked the new people and found them well, but they have suffered from a lack of food for awhile."

Nuada nodded and said, "They are poor farming people and have been on the run from the raiders for over two years. Perhaps now they will find peace."

Farmer spoke up. "Then I will talk to them and find a place for them."

"Yes. Their skills are suited for the fields right now. Perhaps later after some schooling, they will find a better skill," said Mor.

Then Nuada said, "It is late in the year for raiders. I do not know if this means that they will move in our direction, but I think we should provide guards on the new wall until the snows come."

All of the consul members agreed to this, and Mor said he would take care of the guards. Then the discussion turned to other things going on in the valleys. By late afternoon Nuada felt the need to walk and get some fresh air outside of the hall.

His footsteps took him through the outdoor cooking area, which was almost empty, and then on to the school. As he approached the new school building, Amasis came out and stopped to talk to Nuada.

"It seems that I have missed a chance to be on one of your adventures again, my friend."

"It turned out to be different than I had expected, but it worked out well.

"I hear that your son did well too."

"Yes. He had skills that I did not recognize."

"Are you still going to look for more people in the Spring?"

"Yes. I have not changed my mind on that."

After some more small talk, Nuada went on to his classroom and settled at his desk before deciding what he was going to do for the rest of the day. The building remained quiet, and after awhile he decided to walk back out to the new wall.

Nuada took his time on the walk out and listened to the calls of the waterfowl as they prepared for their flight south for the Winter. After he passed the outer protection wall, he paused on the rise that looked out on the open ground behind the new wall. His eyes moved from the area where the lift machines had been stored for Winter to the first portal gate. Mor had been busy and had already posted guards on the wall there. He walked on down to the wall and climbed a set of stairs to look out beyond the wall.

He felt nervous about the new movements of the raiders this year. It was not like them to attack villages this late in the year. They must have some strange reason to do so, but he could not understand of it. He stared at the horizon and found no signs of any movement. He now wished for the snows to come.

Then his thoughts returned to the opening of the school, which was to be within a few days now. He was prepared for his classes, as were his fellow teachers. Then his thoughts drifted back over the past year and everything that had been built. In his mind's eye, he retraced each development and their challenges. Then he turned and made his way back into the village and the meeting hall.

At the hall he drew a beer and joined Beag at his table. Beag himself was lost in thought, and Nuada wanted to ask what was on his mind but held his tongue. Nuada looked around the room and saw that many others there were also lost in their own thoughts. Perhaps it was the new people or the thought of the raiders again, he did not know, but it seemed to affect everyone he saw.

After an hour, Nuada could feel the heaviness in the room and decided that it was time to go to the outdoor cooking area and hopefully a better atmosphere. He cautiously entered the area and again looked around at the people there too. It was better, but it was also subdued. It lacked the smiles and the music that was normal for the area.

Nuada did not feel like another beer, so he just sat down at his table. He continued to watch the village people and tried to understand what was going on in their minds. Finally Mor entered the area, and he looked around at the people too. He joined Nuada and asked, "What is wrong with these people today? I see no joy here, and it makes me nervous."

"I too have seen of this, and I have wondered of the cause. Is it because of the raiders or of the new people?"

"We need to find a way to change their mind-set. Any ideas?"

"A speech would not help, but perhaps some music would take whatever is bothering them away."

Mor nodded and got up to see if he could find some of the musicians to play happy music. Nuada continued to watch the people and waited. Surprisingly Mor talked to some of the new people, and they were the ones who began to play some of their music for the crowd. Nuada could see almost immediately a change in the area's mood. When Mor returned to the table, Nuada turned to him and said, "I would not have thought it possible for them to change so quickly. Why?"

Mor shook his head and said, "They were feeling the sorrows of these people, and now that they see that they are better off here, they are feeling it too."

A little later after Nuada had his evening meal with his family, he began to respond to the joy that these people wanted to share with everyone. Nuada felt better, and after they went home for the night, he slept a long and comfortable sleep.

A few days later it was the opening day of the school. Nuada arrived early and joined Pytheas on the outside of the school. They greeted all of the students before classes and between talked a little about the new people, who seemed to be settling in well. In fact ten of the new students were of the new people: six children and four adults. When Nuada went into the school, the other teachers were standing in the hallways outside of their classrooms also greeting their students.

Nuada went to his classroom and began his day as he had in the past. The time passed quickly, and when he finished his last class of the day, he wondered how it had passed without his feeling it. He lingered in his classroom before deciding to walk to the meeting hall. He gathered his papers and took his time crossing through the streets and the outdoor cooking area on the way to the hall.

Inside he drew a beer and joined Beag and Mor at the table by the fireplace. Nuada looked around the room and saw that the mood had changed much from the other day when it seemed so moody. Mor told him that the guards on the new wall had not reported anything new and that the raiders now seemed to have gone away. Nuada felt relief at those words and then asked how the new fire wagon was coming. Mor gave him a detailed report, at which Beag just snorted at. Nuada laughed out loud at that response and asked him how many beers he had that day. He patted his large belly and said, "Not enough yet."

When Nuada stepped outside to return to the cooking area, he could feel the chill in the air and looked at the sky. A few clouds were developing in the north, and the light wind blew the fallen leaves across the compound in front of him. He knew that it would not be long before they would not be able to gather outside because of the weather.

Nuada's family was waiting for him when he walked toward his table. He kissed his mate and daughter, then turned to his boys and asked about their school day. He had Uilleam in one of his classes, but Iolair was now studying other things besides the language skills. With Uilleam it was history that intrigued him. With Iolair it was mathematics.

After eating, all three of the males had homework to do, so they went home early and sat at the table with papers scattered about, studying. It was late when the last candle was snuffed out for the night and sleep found them.

Within a week the weather changed quickly. It seemed that every day held rain for the valleys, and Nuada would have become bored with it if not for the school.

Because of the weather, Mor had scaled back the number of guards on the new protection wall, but the portal gates were now locked until Spring. The outdoor cooking area remained vacant because of the weather too. In the second valley, all of the new shop buildings remained busy making things that the village needed. Only the mill buildings remained shut down.

One afternoon when Nuada left the school, he looked up at the mountain behind the valleys and was surprised to find snow on the highest parts of it. It was a little early for the snow, so he made his way to the meeting hall and a beer. Inside Beag was drinking his beer as usual, but this time he had rolls of paper spread before him on the table. After Nuada drew his beer, he joined his friend and asked about the papers.

Beag said, "These are the new house drawings for in front of the valleys."

"You changed the design again?"

"Yes. We need some larger houses, and I think these will fill the bill."

Nuada looked at the drawings and agreed with Beag. These were the kind of houses that were needed. They were two stories and held many windows for light. They could hold a family of six with no problem. When Mor arrived, he too saw the need of such houses and asked some questions about the design. In the end, the plans were agreed to, and they became the new standard for the Spring build.

Another week passed, and now light snows were an everyday occurrence. Winter was close, and Mor now had crews assigned to keep the streets clear. The wind remained light, but everyone knew that it would only take one day of high winds to cause major problems. Nuada had returned to wearing his sheepskin belt again, along with his normal Winter clothes, to protect his old wound.

The new people whenever they saw Nuada praised him for bringing them into the village. They had mingled well with the others of the village, and new friends had grown from their presence. Nuada was content with the happiness of his people now and went about teaching as if nothing else mattered.

- WINTER AND FRIENDS -

Another three weeks passed with little change in the weather, but one morning Nuada awoke to the sound of the wind howling through his roof eaves. He got up to investigate and went downstairs. First he stoked the fireplace and then went to the window beneath the stairs. He could feel the draft from the wind around the window before he looked outside to see what was going on. Heavy, wet snow blew past the window, and he had a hard time seeing across the street. He knew that there would be no school today and went back to warm himself by the fireplace.

Soon after his family came down the stairs, and his mate asked about the weather.

"We are in for a hard snow today, and I think that there will be no school for us," Nuada said.

Both of Nuada's sons went to the window to see for themselves. They soon returned and agreed with their father about the weather. After eating a light meal, the family settled down to wait on the weather. Nuada's daughter went back to sleep next to Wolf by the fireplace while the boys read from their school notes. Nuada took some of his old papers from the pantry that Amasis had brought back from Alexandria and was going over the notes about the old machines.

One design caught his eye, and that was for a machine that threw things for a great distance. He thought that if Mor could build these, they would have additional protection at the new wall. He would show the design to him when the weather broke.

Around midday the wind began to ease off, and the snow showed signs of quitting also. Already Mor had crews out cleaning the streets of the village. Teams of horses and wagons were moving through the streets hauling loads of the fresh snow down to the stream, where it would be dumped and floated away. It would take time to remove the drifts away from the buildings, and Nuada began to wonder how the school had fared in this storm.

Although he wanted to go outside and see for himself, he kept caution near because of his old wound and how he had reacted a few years ago. He could wait until the storm actually broke.

Two days later Nuada ventured outside and made his way to the school. Pytheas was there and told him that he would hold off opening the school for two more days. Nuada asked if there had been any damage from the storm and was told no. Nuada decided to make his way to the meeting hall and see who was there. Nuada stopped at his house first and retrieved the old drawings and then moved on to the hall.

Inside many of the consul members were there already and in discussion about the storm. Nuada joined them and listened in on the conversation. Little damage had been done, and what was in need of repairs was brought up. Nuada waited until Mor had some free time and then showed him the notes and drawings of the old war machine.

"We could use these against any raiders or even an army that tried to attack us," Nuada said. "See how they can be turned to change where they throw, and we could use anything for the missiles in them."

Mor was intrigued by the design, and even Beag became interested in the drawings. After spending some time with the drawings, Mor made notes as to where he would change part of the design, and Beag said that he could build a stone platform for them. It was decided to build six of these machines and place them behind the wall.

A little later the snow-removal crews began to arrive at the hall, and it became too noisy to talk anymore. Nuada sat back and listened to the talk from these people and their stories about the storm. He felt comforted with their company.

Two days later the school reopened, and the village returned to its normal ways. When Nuada walked to the school, he was looking at the blanket of white and gray that surrounded the village. Already he was wishing for the warmth of Spring and the things that would bring the village back to life again. He looked up behind the valleys at the mountain, which was wrapped in a blanket of clouds, and wondered if the blue skies would ever return. He shook the thoughts and the chill from his mind as he entered the school. It was time to teach again.

Another week passed, and it was coming up on the time for his midyear test of the students. He let the diversion keep the weather from his thoughts.

Some of his classes would use the old tests he had used before, but the new class of the Phoenician language required a lot of extra work. Then there were the copies that were required for the tests too. It all took any spare time that Nuada had.

When he was finally prepared, he took an afternoon to go to the meeting hall and spent some time with his friends. Nuada was finishing his second beer when Mor entered the hall and joined him and Beag at their usual table.

"Well I just finished the fourth fire wagon. Now I can start on one of those war machines," Mor said.

Nuada's attention perked at those words, and he asked, "Have you figured out how you are going to build it?"

"Yes. The main structure I can build in the shop, but the final assembly will happen on site."

Beag piped up and said, "He has to wait until I build him the rock base for it."

"I want to be there when it is assembled. It should be something to see when it is done," Nuada replied.

"I just hope it works," replied Mor.

Nuada nodded in reply, and they sat back and drank of their beer, thinking about the machine. They all understood how it was supposed to work, but they had never seen one in action.

It was late when Nuada went home for his evening meal, and he found his boys hard at work on their studies at the table. Nuada's mate brought him a venison stew to eat while he asked questions of his boys. Iolair's studies of mathematics were well beyond anything that Nuada had ever experienced, and he was curious about it. Iolair showed him how to work some of the problems and the logic of how it worked. Still Nuada felt confused with the subject.

Iolair was patient with his father and explained that it was no different than the languages that he had taught him.

"Just think of it as a language. Once you understand the rules, the rest will fall into place," Iolair said.

Nuada tried to think of it in that way, and then the numbers started to make sense to him, but he needed more information to really grasp the workings of it. He now felt sleepy, and he hurried his family to bed, knowing that tomorrow was another day of school.

The next week passed quickly, and the day of the tests was at hand. Nuada knew that he would be busy grading the tests for another two days, and then he had to turn the results into Pytheas.

The time passed quickly, and soon it was time for Nuada to begin his testing. His classes seemed long as he waited on his students to go through the testing process. At the end of the day, Nuada felt completely bored and worn out. He had little interaction with his students or even the teachers. He hurried home after his last class and needed a diversion, as he did not feel like grading the tests at this time. He returned to the meeting hall for a break and found of his friends.

While sharing a beer, the conversation was, as usual, about the village and the work projects for the Spring. They too were becoming restless and waiting on the weather to break, but it would be at least another month or two before they could expect the return of the warmer weather. Nuada soon returned home and began the process of going through the tests and grading them. He was up late, and it wasn't until the middle of the night before he found sleep at the table.

Even with the late night, Nuada awoke at his usual hour and finished the grading of the tests. While his family prepared themselves for another day, Nuada's thoughts turned to the weather again. He walked to the front window and looked outside. A light snow drifted across the glass, and the wind was absent. He went back upstairs and changed his clothes, and he washed of himself. Soon it was time to return to the school.

While he was sitting at his desk, Amasis dropped in to talk. They had not talked much since they had discussed the coming adventure to look for more people for the village.

"How went the testing, Nuada?"

"As I had expected. Everyone did well, and I see no problem with their advancing next term."

"I had two students who I found needed additional work, but I too found most were ready to advance."

"Would you like to join me after school for a drink?"

"I would. Perhaps we can talk of the coming adventure too."

Soon students began to enter the classroom, and Amasis had to go to his class as well. Nuada spent the rest of the day going over the results of the tests with his students and forgot about the discussion with Amasis. At the end of the day, Nuada took the results of the tests to Pytheas and waited for Amasis to show.

After he came and gave his test results to Pytheas, Amasis and Nuada walked together to the meeting hall. The snow had stopped, and the sky began to clear. It would be cold tonight.

Inside they both drew a beer and sat at a table. Across the room Beag was downing another beer himself and waved to the pair. Nuada waved back and wondered how many beers Beag had had today. It never showed on him, but he really enjoyed his drink. Amasis asked about the direction they would be traveling on the adventure, as he had little experience in this land outside of when he arrived in the valleys. Nuada told him he thought that they would travel to the west this time, and he himself had little knowledge of the land in that direction. Nuada reminded him of the dangers on such a quest and told him to be prepared for anything.

Toward the end of the afternoon, Amasis had to leave, and Nuada stopped by the table of Beag and Mor before he had to go home for his evening meal. There was nothing new in the village except for three babies who arrived healthy. The mothers were doing well and had no problems although the doctor had been with them for the births. Nuada said his farewells and went home. His thoughts were on the need for the weather to return to the warmth of Spring.

Several more weeks passed, and the routine remained the same day after day for everyone, except for Iolair, who had begun to copy Nuada's dictionary. The weather began to change: Daily rains began to wash away the snow on the ground, and the temperature began to rise. Everyone was now talking about the coming Spring and what they would be doing. Nuada could feel the energy from the village people as they waited on the change.

On one such afternoon while the rains came down, Nuada was at a meeting at the meeting hall. Mor was now talking about moving to the second valley to be closer to the new woodworking building. Farmer was excited about the new grain fields to be planted outside of the new protection wall. Even Beag had his drawings in front of him on a daily basis waiting on the change of seasons so he could begin his work again with the stones.

Even Nuada was not left out of the changes coming. He was ready to make his quest out into the unknown in search of new people for the valleys. His son Iolair was ready too, and they talked daily about what to expect.

One morning Nuada awoke to a quietness in the village. After dressing he went downstairs to look out the window again. There was no rain, but there was a heavy, wet fog that wrapped around everything. Solid objects were now only shadows of what they represented. He could feel the dampness and chill his bones just by looking at it. He turned and went back to his fireplace and poked at the embers before adding more wood to the fire. Soon the house began to warm, and he sat at his table to wait for the rest of his family. He knew that the fog represented the last days of Winter, and that gladdened his heart. He was looking forward to a warm and sunny afternoon. Perhaps he would take a walk again.

His day at school seemed extremely long, as he wanted as much as anyone to get out in the sun again. At last his classes were over, and he hurried out into the sunshine. Several of the other teachers and children were also outside enjoying the sample of the weather to come. After a short pause, Nuada turned and walked toward the cut between the valleys. He passed through and turned left toward the shop buildings. Before he had gone far, much to his surprise, there was Beag setting out stakes in the ground where he was going to build an additional two shop buildings. Nuada slowly approached, and as Beag had his head down looking at his notes, Nuada called out to him. "I see you could not wait any longer. Is this where you are going to start this year?"

He looked up startled and said, "Nuada! Yes, it is one of the first projects, but I will also be building the platforms for the war machines too before I begin on any of the houses."

"I think the weather has changed for us now, and we could begin anytime."

"That is what I believe too. I have started my crews at the quarry already today. I may begin within a few days the work needed."

"Have you seen Mor?"

"Yes. He is at the woodworking building."

"Then I will go bother him and let you get back to work. I will see you at the meeting hall later for a beer."

Nuada walked up the street to the shop buildings to find Mor. Inside Mor was working on a second war machine. To one side sat the first machine in two parts: the base and the swing arm for it. Nuada did not see Mor at first and looked closely at the first machine. It was a true work of art. In every part of it, you could see the craftsmanship of Mor. Nuada hoped it would work as well as it looked. Then just as Nuada turned, Mor came out of the back of the shop.

"Nuada? What brings you here today?"

"The weather and a need to see these machines."

"Those old people knew what they were doing when they designed these. I made only one small change in the design myself."

"I just talked with Beag, and he said that he was going to start the platforms in a few days."

"Yes. That is what he told me too."

After talking about the machine for awhile, Nuada decided it was time to return to the village and the meeting hall. It was such a nice afternoon, he walked back out to the front of the valleys to look down on the wall and the open ground inside it. Already some dust from the quarry marked the place coming back to life. He did not linger but turned and made his way to the meeting hall.

He went inside and found it almost empty, so after drawing a beer, he went back outside to stand in the sunshine and drink his beer. His thoughts turned to the ending of the school year, which he was ready for. He knew that within a matter of weeks he would have to give a final test to his students, and that thought began to dwell on his mind. He had tests to prepare, and this time he wanted to start on them as soon as possible.

Soon Beag returned from the second valley, and he went in to draw a beer as well and then joined Nuada outside. They were having a quiet talk when four of the horse teams and wagons returned from the quarry work. They pulled up alongside the stable across the street, and Beag went over to ask questions of the drivers. He returned shortly with a smile on his face and said, "They made good headway today. They quarried enough rock for two of the platforms. I guess they had enough of this Winter weather too."

It was not long before Mor showed up, and they all returned inside to share more beer together. This was to be the last night for two weeks before Nuada could return and share some time with his friends. He would be tied up with preparing the tests and then giving them to his students. He had no free time now with the ending of the school term.

- SPRING AND THE SEARCH -

School was out, and the crop meadow by the lake had been tilled. Work at the quarry was moving fast as they all began to start the building again. Some of Beag's crews had already started the foundations for the new shop buildings while Beag himself was starting the platforms for the war machines. Nuada wanted to hold off on his search for people until the first war machine had been put together and tested. Mor had finished the second machine and was starting on the third. The sawmill was back at work and competing with the forge to make the most noise. Down at the lake, the waterfowl had returned from the south and were also making a lot of noise, for those who had the time to listen.

Nuada felt relief with the changes in the weather and walked out to the new wall. Beag had laid the foundation stones for the first platform for the war machines. Nuada circled around the work site and watched as the stones were placed higher than he thought they would be. He asked Beag about the work and was told that in order to clear the wall with the projectiles, he had to build them high. Nuada asked how high and was told about twelve feet. He questioned how they were supposed to bring the projectiles up onto the platform, and Beag showed him a drawing of a small lift machine for the rear of the platform. Nuada nodded in understanding, but thought it was not necessary. The test would show if Beag was right about the design.

Nuada wandered about the site for awhile and then made his way back to the second valley and the woodworking shop. Inside Mor was working on the finishing stages of the third machine, and he also had two wagons in for needed repair. They talked for awhile, and Nuada asked him about Beag's design for the platforms.

"I think he is right about raising them up, so as to get enough clearance for the throw of the machines," Mor said.

When Nuada stepped back outside, wagons loaded with cut trees for the sawmill passed in a constant stream and then returned with fresh cut lumber going out to the new housing sites in back of the new wall. He walked across the street and stopped at the new shop sites. The work crews here were making good progress, and Nuada only lingered for a short while. He again crossed the street to where the teachers were now working at making the needed glass for the new houses. He talked shortly with Amasis before returning to the new wall and the work going on out there.

This time Nuada climbed the wall and looked around the open area in front of it. The tree cutters were busy dropping trees, which were then loaded and moved back to the sawmill. The horse teams never stopped, and when Nuada turned to look back into the open area behind the wall, his gaze looked toward the quarry site. It too was busy cutting back into the mountainside and bringing stones out for Beag to use. He looked toward the sites for the new houses and saw piles of stone and lumber being stockpiled nearby. Then his attention was drawn back to the platform site and Beag's crew working there. Nuada walked along the wall and through the towers until he was almost in line with the new platform. He looked back over the wall and tried to see in his mind the workings of the war machine. Finally he sat down and just watched Beag and his crew work. The warmth of the sun felt good, and he almost dozed in its comfort.

Late in the afternoon Nuada climbed back down off the wall and went for a last, close look at the platform. He circled around it and then walked back into the village and a beer at the meeting hall. Inside it was almost empty, as was expected, so he stepped outside to drink of the beer. He looked across the street at the stable and found almost all of the wagons were in use already. It had not taken long for the village to come back to life after the weather had changed. The people were ready to work, and they went at it with a strength of resolve.

Again the old feeling that he was left out of the work tugged at his soul, but he put that feeling aside and remembered that he had another purpose coming up: find more people for the village.

After finishing his beer, Nuada went to the outdoor cooking area and waited for his friends and family to arrive.

When the long shadows of the day were casting down on the valleys, Mor arrived and soon after was followed by Beag. After each of them had drawn a beer, they joined Nuada, and some small talk was shared about their day. Nuada already knew about their progress, but he listened to them talk. They shared much laughter between themselves as they poked fun at each other. Nuada felt lucky to have such friends and knew that much of what drove the people of the valleys was the energy of these two. Too soon Nuada's family arrived, and his friends went to their own tables.

Iolair had given up his childhood ways and was now working in the woodworking building with Mor. He talked with his father about all of the things he was learning there. Uilleam felt left out because he was not old enough yet to keep company with his brother. Nuada understood his second son and told him to enjoy the time he had now because when the time came, he would be looking back and wondering where it had all gone.

Nuada's own thoughts about his childhood in the land of ice and snow came back with a clear freshness. He still missed those days and knew that he would never again revisit them.

When he looked up again, the cooking area was full of laughter, and music filled the air with a freshness of spirit. The people of the valleys were glad that Spring had come at last.

A week later during one of Nuada's trips out to the platform work, he was watching one of the lift machines move stone to the top of the nearly completed platform. Beag had cut a track into the top stones for the war machine, which would enable it to track from side to side. Alongside sat the first of the war machines, still in pieces. A'Chreag had made iron wheels for it to move in this groove. They were small but could hold the weight of the machine. At the rear of the platform, a pivot point, also made of iron, was set deep into the stone work. The small lift machine for the projectiles was now set into place, and a set of stairs giving access to the top of the platform was built. Nuada was impressed at the design of Beag's and told him so. He could not understand of it before, but now it made sense. Within a few days, they would be able to test the machine, and Nuada's nerves were on edge waiting for the completed work.

The crew of Beag who had been working in the second valley on the new shops there were now over at the housing sites and beginning the foundations on the first of the houses. Everywhere horse teams moved needed items to where they were put to use quickly. Nothing was done without purpose.

Nuada made his way back to the second valley to look at the new shop buildings and was surprised at the amount of completed work done already. The stone walls were up on the shops, and a crew of Mor's was beginning the roof framing. Inside others were doing finishing work too. Iolair was among the crew inside, and Nuada had a short time to talk with him before he had to return to work. These buildings would be done within the week ahead, and then the crews would be out at the housing site in front of the valleys.

However, Nuada and his son would be gone by then on the quest for more people. Amasis was also looking forward to the adventure. Nuada stopped at the shop where Amasis was making paper and made sure that he was ready, and although they had talked about what to bring, he had to make sure that he was prepared.

After their talk, Nuada returned to the front of the valleys. This time he walked through the housing site and all of the stacked supplies around them. Beag had staked the sites of each of the houses and the new firehouse too. The site ran from the stream to the base of the mountain behind and was lined with new curbs and sidewalks next to the new street of packed rubble. Although the houses would only line one side of the street, it made a big change in the way things would look when they were completed. This was also the site where Nuada had fought his first raiders long ago, but he did not recognize it any longer.

After looking around, he went down to the wall and climbed back up to look out on the grounds in front of the wall again. His mind wandered out into the distance, and he was thinking about the coming quest. This time he was not going to set a time for his return. He had to find more people, and it could take a long time to do so. He hoped that he would not have to fight raiders on this trip , but he knew that it was a possibility. After a few minutes thinking on the quest, he turned his attention back to the war-machine platform below. Mor had joined Beag, and they were rigging a sling around the base of the war machine from the lift machine. They were about ready to lift it into place and begin the assembly of it. Nuada knew he would be in the way if he went down there, so he stayed and watched from the wall. Slowly the lift machine took up the load and lifted it high into the air before swinging it onto the platform. Next before it was set down, the wheels were put into place, and then it was placed onto its final location. Men had already greased the pivot point and the track for the wheels. Soon the sling was removed, and the lift machine swung back for the long arm of the war machine. Everything was moving quickly, and Nuada was caught up in the process. When they were ready, the lift machine brought the long arm into the air and moved it onto the cradle of the war machine. It was beginning to look like the old drawings, but Nuada also knew that a large-stone counterweight was to be mounted on one end of the swing arm too. Nuada looked around but did not see any such stone on hand. Already the shadows of late afternoon were upon the site, and many were getting ready to quit for the day. Nuada knew that this was the end of the work for today, and it would be probably be tomorrow, when the machine would be completed and ready for testing. He climbed down from the wall and joined his friends, and together they all walked back to the cooking area for some beer and a good evening meal.

The next morning Nuada hurried out to the war machine and got there in time for the lift machine to be moving the counter weight up onto the platform. A cradle of metal on one end of the swing arm would lock it into place while gears inside the base of the machine of A'Chreag's design would keep it from moving. Nuada watched as men fought to set it correctly in the metal sling; its position was critical to the design. Both Mor and Beag were giving directions to the crew, and finally it was done and locked into place.

Beag came down off the platform and was wiping sweat from his face when he saw Nuada. "We are almost done. Mor has some details to adjust, and then we should be able to test this monster."

Already many of the work crews had lined the wall to watch the war machine in action. Several stones, some over a hundred pounds, were up on the platform ready to be thrown over the wall. There was some danger in that they did not know if the stones would clear the wall, so Beag and Nuada walked outside and stood against the wall there to watch.

Soon a shout from the top of the wall called for everyone to stand clear, as they were ready for the first throw. Then it came: A large stone flew high over the wall and landed almost at the rear of the cleared land in front of the wall. That was almost three hundred yards away. After another adjustment, a second stone was launched from the war machine. It landed about halfway across the cleared ground. Then a third stone was launched after changing the direction it was to go. Everything worked perfectly, and they were ready to move on to another platform construction site.

Nuada returned to the village and found his table at the outdoor cooking area. His thoughts were on the war machine, but he was also thinking of the coming adventure. After sitting for awhile, he got up and began to walk toward the second valley and a talk with Amasis again. Inside of the shop building for glass and papermaking, Nuada found Amasis.

"Plan on our quest to begin in two more days. I will have Iolair arrange for the horses," Nuada said.

"I am packed and ready."

They talked a little longer, and then Nuada walked up the street to the new shop buildings, where he found Iolair in the second building.

"When you are done for the day, I want you to arrange for four horses: three to ride and one as a pack horse. We will leave on our adventure in two more days."

Iolair became excited at the prospect of the adventure and wanted to stop working on the building right away, but he knew how his father felt about finishing what was important. Already the new shops had their roofs of copper on, and it was only some minor details inside that needed to be addressed.

Nuada then returned to the village and his usual table in the cooking area, where he drew a beer and waited on his friends to finish their day. About an hour later, he could hear the first of the horse teams and their wagons return to the stable area. He knew that the men would soon arrive too. Mor was the first to arrive, and he drew a beer and joined Nuada at his table.

"That machine is a wonder, Nuada. It is easy to adjust and change where you want the stones to go. I can see little wear on the mechanism, so it should prove to be reliable too."

Nuada listened to him talk about the war machine a little longer before he said, "I am leaving in two more days in search of new people. I will take Iolair and Amasis with me."

"Do you not think that you should take more men with you?"

"No. This way we can move with speed and hide if necessary."

Mor thought for a moment before agreeing with Nuada. His own thoughts on the matter did not mean anything when it came to bringing more people into the village. Nuada had the experience of doing it many times and knew what was needed.

Mor changed the subject to the new houses in front of the village and the design of Beag's for large families. At last Beag entered the area and joined his friends after he too drew a beer to unwind with.

They talked about the new machine some more before turning the subject to the other projects going on. Mor told Beag that he would finish the shop buildings tomorrow, and then he would send his crew out to the new houses. Beag said that he would work on the next platform on the other side of the stream, as it would balance the protection until they had more machines in action.

They continued to talk until the meals were ready that afternoon. The village women had been planting the crops down by the lake all day, and they looked tired. This day would end early for all of the village people.

The next morning Nuada took his time leaving the house, and when he did, he had all of his weapons and other items all ready for the coming adventure. Iolair had done the same, and together they walked back out to the new wall. The night before Iolair had arranged for the horses, and they would be ready and waiting for them the day they were to leave. After Iolair left the stable, he went to the shop where Nuada had stored the map table and for some reason had packed all of the loose items there into the two chests, including his written history of the family and the valleys.

Back out at the wall, they crossed the bridge first and went up to the new-house construction site. Both Beag's and Mor's crews were moving fast on the houses. Walls went up as they watched, and huge timbers marked each floor of the houses. Two of the lift machines were on this site and moving both lumber and stone with equal speed. Father and son circled around the whole area before walking down to the next war machine platform, where Beag was working. They crossed the open ground to stay away from the many wagons moving supplies. Already some of Beag's crews were building another street and the curbs and sidewalks needed for it.

When they got to the site of the platform, Beag was, as usual, in the middle of all the work. Nuada called out a greeting before they moved on to the wall and climbed up to look on the whole area. They were near the last watchtower and could also see the quarry at work too. Here men swarmed across the face of the mountain, cutting stones loose and dropping them down for the final cutting. Nuada turned and looked out to the north before he and his son moved on down the wall to another vantage point.

They stopped again on the portal over the stream and got a different view from there. Then on they moved to where the new war machine sat below them. The work area had been cleaned and now looked totally different from yesterday. Nuada then turned again and looked to the west. His mind was in the far distance, trying to see what lay in store for them out there.

It was just after midday when they returned to the village and sat at their table in the cooking area. Soon after Amasis came in looking for them. He wanted to know what time in the morning he was supposed to meet with them. Nuada told him to be ready before the first light of dawn. Amasis nodded in reply. He then asked about where to leave his pack.

"Bring it to the stable tonight, and we will load everything together in the morning," Nuada said.

The rest of the afternoon was spent talking about the trip together. When the day started to come to a close and the workers were returning to the village, Amasis went to join the other teachers and share of their wine before his part in the adventure began.

After their evening meal, Nuada and his son took their packs to the stable before calling it an early night. Everything was now ready for the next day.

Nuada awoke early and shook his son awake. They went downstairs and ate a light meal before going out the door and making their way to the stable. The only thing that they carried were their bows. Everything else was already at the stable.

Inside the stable, Amasis was sound asleep against the packs, and Nuada woke him. Iolair brought the horses over to the packs and then began to load the packhorse. It was still dark as they moved out of the stable and on out through the village and its protective walls. After passing through the portal gate in the new protection wall, they paused and turned to look back one more time before moving on into the unknown.

After traveling along the ridgeline in a southerly direction for about five miles, Nuada found a game trail into the brush and trees headed toward the west. Throughout the day, the direction remained constant. Toward sundown they found a small meadow in which to camp for the night. They broke the guarding of the camp into three shifts, with Amasis taking the first because of his inexperience in the wilds of a forest. Iolair would take the second shift and Nuada the last before dawn. Nuada warned him that the sounds of a forest at night were different and that his nose was the best at warning of any danger.

"Men stink." he told him. "You will know when they are near."

With the coming of the light of dawn, they broke camp and continued to follow the game trail. The second day was also uneventful, and they made camp deep into the woods. Again they guarded their camp at night in the same manner.

Amasis was becoming familiar to the sounds of the forest creatures and did not fear them. Iolair was learning more every day from his father.

Day three broke, and they continued on. Late in the afternoon Nuada could smell a faint odor of smoke ahead. They found a place to make an early camp, and Nuada moved on ahead to search out the smell. He traveled many miles and had still not found the cause of the smell. As it was close to dark, he turned around and made his way back to the campsite.

"I found nothing ahead, but be more alert tonight. Something had caused the smoke smell," he told the others.

All three slept lightly that night; they were waiting for something to happen. In the morning the smell seemed stronger than last night, and they broke camp and moved forward with caution. Nuada told them to hold back a little while he scouted the land ahead. If he ran into any trouble, he would whistle. That would give them time to prepare for battle or come to his rescue.

Nuada quickly covered the ground he had traveled over yesterday afternoon. He then shifted into a slower pace and was on high alert with all of his senses. The smoke smell still lingered in the air. He pushed his horse over a slight rise, and down below him was a wood-walled village. This was the place where the smell came from; a thin haze of brown smoke drifted around the whole area. He watched from his hiding place in the trees. It had a few guards on the wall and little else to show for its location there. Nuada estimated the population at around fifty, as it had little to show for crops or any animals for food. He thought that they possibly foraged for their food.

He turned and returned to the other two and told them of the small village. "They are not the kind of people we are in search of. We will circle around them and find another way."

They gave the village a wide berth and continued their search. Still they moved toward the west. When they were far from the village in the late afternoon, they made camp again. The tension of the day remained late into the night before all of them could rest comfortably.

The morning of the fourth day broke with some cloud cover. They were ready to move on and find the people that they were searching for. The land was becoming flatter, and they made better time across the thin forest here. At midday they found a stream and began to follow it. It moved in a northwest direction and had only some slight turns in it. Nuada thought that if there were any people in this direction, then they could be found by the water. As dusk formed its shadows on the land, they again made camp.

The sun came up bright and warm the next morning, and they broke camp and moved on along the stream. As before Nuada took the lead and scouted the land in front of the others. Late in the morning Nuada began to feel that something would happen soon, and he slowed his pace. He soon came upon wood-cutters just before the midday and cautiously approached them to ask questions. They had no fear of Nuada and answered his questions fully. Yes, a city was near, and they welcomed traders, which Nuada said he was. He followed their directions and soon saw the city that they had told him of. It was a city with stone walls around it, and it looked prosperous. The main gate was open and welcoming.

Nuada returned to the others, and the trio together rode into the city. They found an open market that was busy, and no one seemed to pay any attention to them. They dismounted and found a place to eat and have a beer together. Nuada's eyes were in constant motion looking over the people of this city and wondered of their lack of fear for outsiders. This was different from any other village that he had visited in this land before. He found some men to talk with, and they shared a few beers together. He needed the information that they provided to him.

Soon he was told of the city elders and where they could be found. Nuada left his son and Amasis to watch over the horses while he went to talk with the city elders. A large building housed the city offices, and Nuada went inside to speak with someone in charge. A man came out of an office and spoke with Nuada, who told him that he was in search of people to move to his city. They also talked of trade between the two cities, and soon an agreement was reached. The man knew of some people who would be willing to move and that they were of many different skills too. This made Nuada's day, and after they agreed to meet the next morning, Nuada returned to the others. They then went in search of a place to sleep for the night and a stable for the horses.

Nuada awoke early again and dressed before the first light of dawn. Iolair awoke, and Nuada told him that he would meet with them at the same place where they had eaten yesterday. He gave his son some of the gold that he had brought with them to pay for the room and the horse stable and then went out into the streets for another look around before his meeting with the city elder.

For a city of its size, it had a clean smell, and that impressed Nuada. He wandered around the city and saw many things that they could do back at home to improve it. He also saw that the city had a standing army on guard at all times. They seemed to fit into the background and were never a threat to the people there. He wondered if it would work back home.

Soon he had to return to the city offices and meet with the city elder. When he got there, the man had not yet arrived, and Nuada was forced to wait on the steps outside. His stomach was telling him about the lack of food this morning, and he wished that the man would soon arrive and take his mind off the food that he needed. About a half hour later, the man arrived and told Nuada that a meeting had been arranged and that he would take him to the people after he checked into his office.

Soon Nuada was following the man down a back street until they came to a large, open area, and there they found the group. Nuada estimated that they numbered about thirty — and that did not include the children who were not present. Nuada and the city official met with the leaders of the group, and after Nuada told of his city, he asked about their skills that could be useful in his city. They were very open to his questions, and he found out that they had been driven from their village by raiders about two months before. They came here for safety and protection and were willing to move on to another city. Soon an agreement was reached, and Nuada told them that he would return early tomorrow morning and that they should be ready to move on then.

Nuada thanked the city official and returned to the eating place and a well-deserved meal with the others.

It was just after midday when Nuada had eaten and told the others of the successful meeting and agreement. Then Nuada had Iolair return to the boarding house and reserve a place for tonight and then over to the stable to make sure that the horses would be taken care of for another night. On his return, the trio walked around the city and observed how it was different from their city.

For Nuada it was learning about how they took care of their sanitation and the disposal of their waste. For Amasis it was learning that they had no schools. But Iolair took in everything about the city and many things that the others missed.

That night Nuada watched as Amasis drew a map of where the city was located, and it included the small village that they had bypassed on the way there. Nuada gave him some information about two other cities that were nearby that the city official had told him of, so that was included on the map as well. That night they all slept well and were ready in the morning for the return trip with the new people.

Another bright Spring day welcomed the trio as they set out for the gathering place of the new people. The leaders of the new group had everyone ready to move when they got to the open area of the city. Nuada led them out of the city through the city gate, and they turned to follow the stream back to the southwest. As most of the people were mounted, they began to make good time. Nuada did ask one of the leaders about the small village that they had encountered before.

"They are more warlike and like to keep to themselves," he responded.

Nuada said, "I thought so. Their village seemed unwelcoming to any who would pass by."

Then he said, "If we cross the stream ahead, there is another village that is more open to outsiders."

"Do you think there would be any there who would like to return with us to my city?"

"It is possible. They have had raiders for years and have suffered greatly."

"Then we will try and see if they are willing."

The group leader brought them to a place where they could ford the stream, and after they had crossed, he pointed the way to the village. It was nearing sunset when they found the village. The group leader and Nuada went on ahead and entered the village while the others made camp for the night. They found the village people had gathered together for an evening meal, and they spoke to their leader. Nuada again described his city of stone and asked if any were willing to move there. The village leader put it before the village people and asked them if they were willing to move. Almost everyone agreed to moving, but there were some who had planted crops that were reluctant to move. Nuada could understand their reasons and wished them well. A plan was then set in motion for the others to join in the morning for the journey to Nuada's city of stone.

The next day the addition of the village slowed the move toward home. They had some livestock, which they called cows, and that added to the slow movement. Also they had a small flock of sheep too. They still continued to follow the stream back toward the mountains.

The village leader had sent out scouts to guard the flanks of the group, and that pleased Nuada with his forethought. They had not seen any raiders this year, but that did not mean that they could not present themselves.

Iolair and Amasis circled in and out of the group all day long, hurrying stragglers. At last they finally made camp for the night. Everyone was tired but had become excited about the move. They were constantly asking questions of Iolair and Amasis about the city, which they answered as best they could.

Nuada could now estimate that it would take about six more days to return home, given the speed at which these people could be moved. Every day the mountains became closer, and that lightened Nuada's heart. One morning Nuada noticed that the stream had turned to become more of an easterly direction for them. That would bring them in north of the valleys. He decided that they would still continue to follow the stream until they came below the mountains and then turn south.

Although Nuada knew that they had a lot of empty houses when he left home, they were bringing more people back than he had planned on. Some would have to wait until more houses were built, but they still had some space in the travelers building, where they could find temporary shelter until the houses were done. Then there was the hospital too. He knew that a simple solution was at hand, but they still would have to wait on permanent houses. He also hoped that his friends Mor and Beag had pushed beyond the plan for houses but knew that the other projects might not make it possible.

Every day now seemed extremely slow for the trio, and they tried to move the people faster, but it was not about to happen. They set their own pace, and that made it difficult for the trio. The only good thing was that there had been no sign of any raiders about.

Then came the day that they had been waiting for. They turned to the south, and it marked a closing of this adventure. Nuada had hoped that it would only take another day to see the new protection wall in the distance but knew that it would probably be another day after that when they could again enter through the wall.

He was tempted to ride on ahead and see the changes in the valleys and talk with his friends but held himself back from doing so. That evening he was talking with Amasis, and he told Nuada that he had marked the new route on the map so as to return to the other city in the future. Nuada was taken by surprise at his being that attentive to the route, as he had not given it much thought. Nuada knew that it was necessary if they were to have trade in the future. Later when they had bedded down for the night, Nuada had a hard time sleeping; his thoughts were on home and his mate.

The next morning they set out as usual, and they persisted in pushing the new people faster. Nuada felt the closeness of home, and his eyes were constantly looking up at the mountains beside them. He wondered how Iolair and Amasis were feeling about being this close to home after their journey.

They did not stop for a midday meal but pushed on toward home. Late in the afternoon the wall started to come into view, and the new people talked among themselves at the sight of it. The tall towers had a shine in the afternoon light and that was what caught their attention. It was about this time that they passed the old village of Mor's, and Nuada kept them away from entering into it. When they had passed it, Nuada sent Iolair on ahead to warn the village and have them prepare for them to enter tomorrow. Nuada expected to be inside the wall before mid-morning, and then he had to find shelter for them before he could relax himself.

They made camp within sight of the protection wall for the night. The setting sun shined off the copper roofs of the towers, adding a golden glow to the wall. Nuada had not seen this from the wall before, and he stood watching it until the sun had fully set. Just when darkness began to surround the encampment, Iolair returned and told Nuada that all was in preparation for them entering tomorrow.

At first light, they broke camp and started the last part of their adventure. Nuada, with the group leaders, headed the following, and soon they passed through the portal gate and on to the open ground behind the wall. Nuada noticed that Beag had finished building two more of the war-machine platforms, and they had already set the machines on the platforms. Everywhere he looked the village men were busy with their building. On the ridge next to the mountain, the new houses looked almost complete, and they lined the skyline.

When they reached the bridge, Mor was waiting. He would take over and settle them into the waiting houses, but for now he wanted them to camp on the far side of the open area behind the wall next to the ridgeline. This would provide an area for their livestock, and he would have a simpler time of sorting them.

Nuada was glad that Mor would take on the responsibility of finding them shelter. They talked for a short time as they moved the people to the campsite and began to settle them out. Nuada told him how many people he had brought back and a little about their skills. Then for Nuada, his son, and Amasis, it was time to return to the village and a little relaxation. Amasis was the first to stop at his house and unload his pack, and then he followed the others over to Nuada's house, where they did the same. Then it was on to the stable and from there the outdoor cooking area and a drink.

It was just coming up on midday when they settled at Nuada's table with a beer. Some of the teachers were there to question Amasis and Nuada about the adventure. Amasis pulled out his map and showed them where they had been.

He was excited about sharing his stories with the others, and they talked together for most of the afternoon. When the sun began to set, Beag and Mor arrived, and they too wanted to know more about the adventure. Although Nuada was tired, he told them the story and answered their questions as best he could. Then Nuada's mate came into the area and sent them on their ways. Then she brought food for Nuada and Iolair. Both were dead on their feet and soon went home and a good night's sleep.

Early the next morning Nuada awoke to a stiffness in his joints and wondered if it was because of sleeping in a comfortable bed for a change. Iolair had also awoke early, and soon both made the walk out to the encampment by the new wall. The streets were filled with wagons coming and going. Everywhere the rush to build was going on. Although they had been gone under two weeks, the changes were everywhere. At the housing site, four more foundations were complete, and new walls were going up. Beag was finishing a fifth war-machine base and platform. Nuada wanted to go and look at the work, but he first had to stop at the encampment and see how things were going with the sorting of the new people. As Nuada entered the camp, Mor had already assigned houses for ten of the new families. They talked for awhile, and then Nuada let Mor continue his work. He now had time to walk around the new construction, and Iolair kept him company.

First they walked down to where Beag was working on the new platform, and they circled it. It was the last one on this side of the stream, and when it was done, only one remained to be built on the other side of the stream. Nuada talked with Beag for a few minutes before crossing the bridge and walking up to the housing site. They walked through one of the completed houses, and the size of it dwarfed even Nuada's house in the village. Inside it had walls that broke up the interior, and Nuada thought that it seemed like a maze. When they went back outside, they walked along the new street and looked at the other houses. Iolair was constantly pointing at some new feature about the houses, and finally they walked back across the bridge and up to the encampment again.

Here Anoghas and Farmer were helping Mor find houses for the people, and when Farmer had a few minutes to spare, he told Nuada that the new grain crops had been planted outside of the wall like they had planned. Nuada thought of climbing the wall to look over the new field but decided that he could do it later. Nuada did talk with the group leaders and asked if they would like a tour of the valleys tomorrow. They jumped at the chance, and it was set up for the next morning.

Before Nuada departed the camp, Mor had another chance to talk, and he told Nuada that he had moved to the last empty house by the shop sites. Nuada knew that he had planned on doing so, but it still came as a complete surprise. One other item also came up: The first two houses that he had built in front of the outdoor cooking area would soon be torn down and the area expanded where the houses stood. Nuada reflected in his mind on how the area would look with the change. He agreed that it was needed, but this was a part of the building of the village that he remembered the most. Mor told him that the families that now lived there would have the first choices of the new, large houses being built behind the new wall, as they had large families.

Nuada walked out of the camp with the changes still going through his mind. He wondered if they were changing too fast. He slowly walked back toward the village, deep in thought. Iolair said nothing but watched his father's thoughts move him on. When they got to the outer protection wall, Nuada continued on by the lake toward the second valley. As they walked, Nuada glanced over to the island and knew that change was a part of living there. Then he stepped up his pace and moved toward the second valley's protection wall. They passed through the portal gate and on down toward the new shops. Nuada again paused at the junction of the streets that led back toward the cut between the valleys.

His eyes took in everything: the mills and all of the shops, the houses nearby, and the still-wild forest behind the shops across the street. "At least they did not change everything while I was gone," he thought.

He turned and looked at the dam and raceway alongside of it. The three waterwheels still turned with the energy needed to run the shops. Nuada nodded, and then they followed the street back toward the cut between the valleys.

Nuada remained silent during the rest of the walk, and when they got to the school, he told Iolair to go on ahead and that he wanted to stop and talk with Pytheas. Iolair said that he would be at the outdoor cooking area waiting.

Inside the old school building, Pytheas was in the office and going over the census that had been done while Nuada was gone. Nuada asked about it and then told Pytheas that he would need to upgrade it for the new people. He nodded and said that Mor was already making a list of the new people, and they would be added when he was done.

Nuada sat heavily in a chair and asked Pytheas what he thought of all of the changes. Pytheas looked at Nuada and then answered slowly, "You are not comfortable with the changes, are you?"

"I know that they are necessary, but when it changes the things that have made this village, it does not feel right."

"You are talking about the tearing down of those houses, right? It is a necessary change, and I think it will make the village better."

Nuada let out a great sigh and nodded his head. "You are right, but I am still uncomfortable with it."

Nuada left shortly and returned to the cooking area and the company of his son. When Nuada arrived, Amasis was talking with Iolair about the adventure. He was filled with an energy that Nuada did not feel, but he listened to him talk and about how great an adventure it had been. Iolair seemed to take on some of the energy that came from Amasis. He thought to himself that they knew nothing about what it took to bring these new people into the village, but they would learn how if they were the ones who had to arrange for their coming. "Perhaps I should have had them with me when the arrangements were made," he thought.

Nuada went and drew a beer and continued to muse on thoughts for the next time that they went in search of people.

Later that afternoon Mor had finished with the new people, and as it was too late to work on any other project that day, he came to the cooking area.

He also drew a beer and joined Nuada at his table. As he sat, he said, "Beag is now planning on building twenty more houses out in front of the valleys, and they will be of the other design that is smaller."

Nuada nodded and turned his head toward the two houses nearby that were to be torn down. Mor turned his head in the same direction and said, "They have served their jobs, but it is now time to change the purpose of this area."

Nuada turned back to Mor and said, "I know, but it will not seem the same anymore."

Mor shrugged his shoulders. "That is progress, my friend."

They both raised their mugs of beer in salute and drank deeply. When the shadows of the late afternoon started to cast their mark on the area, Beag entered and went to draw a beer for himself.

"Well the next war-machine platform is now done," Beag said. "Tomorrow I will start on the last one."

Mor said, "Good. In the morning, I will bring the next machine out and have it mounted. A'Chreag is still working on some of the parts for the last machine, but I hope to have it ready in about five days."

"Good. I will have the next platform ready by then."

Then their talk turned to the people and how they were going to use them. Nuada listened and said nothing. When Nuada's mate arrived with his other children, the pair went to the other table to continue their talk. Nuada held his daughter and looked around the area, as more people began to fill in the empty tables. Soon music filled the air, and it helped Nuada's mood.

Nuada awoke as usual and slowly walked out to the encampment. Wagons passed as he walked, and the team drivers called greetings as they went by. Songbirds filled the air with the sounds of Spring. Nuada happened to look up at his statue as he passed through the portal gate of the inner wall and still wondered at Beag's reason for making it. He moved on and soon was on the rise overlooking the open ground behind the new wall. He turned to look over at the housing site and saw that the construction continued at a fast pace. Soon people would be living there, and that would quickly change the empty feeling of that place. Then his attention was drawn to the last war-machine platform, which Beag was working to finish as quickly as possible. Lift machines continued to move mountains of stone, and it seemed to rise higher by the minute as Nuada watched. Then he turned to the encampment. Even there people were up and moving. Some were tending to the livestock and others just preparing to move to the assigned houses. Nuada knew that Mor would be down there, and he moved on to meet with him and the leaders of both groups of the new people.

Nuada entered the encampment looking for Mor, and he found him with two leaders talking together. Mor had a board with papers on it, and he was checking to make sure that everyone was marked down on his list. As Nuada walked up to the group, they all seemed to see him at the same time and called a greeting as he neared. Nuada waved and smiled back as he joined them. Then he said, "When you are through answering Mor's questions, we will begin the tour of the valleys."

Mor then said, "I am done for now, but we will meet later for the final list of home sites."

As the two group leaders moved to Nuada's side, Mor started to walk off toward the new housing site. Nuada watched him go and then turned back to the two men. "He is one of the finest men you will ever know," he said.

The two leaders looked at each other, and the leader of the first group said, "I think that your valleys have many such men."

Nuada nodded in answer, and then they began the walk around the valleys. They started with the new wall, where Nuada had yet to see the new grain field in front of the wall. They climbed the nearest set of stairs up onto the wall and then walked the distance of it, looking down on all of the work going on. Nuada explained what each project was and even how the war machine worked as they passed. As they approached the last watchtower, they could even see into the quarry site and all of the work being done there. Then they descended the stairs from the wall and moved on across to the housing construction before turning back toward the bridge. As they crossed the bridge, Nuada explained how all of this land had come to be just last year. Both leaders could not believe that all of this had come to be in just one year, but Nuada reassured them that it had.

Then they walked up the rise toward the outer protection wall and continued to follow the stream by the lake toward the second valley. They could see in the distance the main village and asked when they would be going there. Nuada told them that they would be there after seeing the shops and mills in the other valley.

When they approached the wall in front of the second valley, they paused to look at the two towers over the stream and the massive metal gate through which the stream flowed. On their right, the other wall and gate that led by the caves and crop fields also caught their attention. Then Nuada took them on through the portal gate and on down the road to where the other street went back toward the cut between the valleys. From here they could see the shop buildings, and he explained what each was used for and that they still had two that had not yet been occupied.

Then he took them through each of the shop buildings and showed them what they were used for. The woodworking building really caught their attention, and inside Nuada showed them the last war machine being built, and then on over in the back of the shop, he showed them the two fire wagons and explained how they worked. Other projects were around the large shop, and Nuada told them that they would have to ask Mor about them if they were curious. They had also noticed the large collections of wheels and belts that were in constant motion inside of the roof. Nuada explained that they were used to run the machines inside the shops, and he would show them next where the power came from.

They exited the back of the shop and stood near the water raceway, where they could see the three waterwheels in motion. Again Nuada explained how the wheels brought power to the woodworking shop and both the forge building and the grain mill. Then they moved on, still looking at the raceway and the dam that provided the water power for them all. The noise coming from both the forge and sawmill began to drown out all conversation, and they waited until Nuada had finished showing them around the other structures. They then moved on to the houses nearby and continued to follow the back ridgeline street toward the sheep stable and grain fields there. Finally they had circled all around the second valley and were back at the cut between the valleys.

Here Nuada paused again and told them how they had made the cut through the ridgeline between the valleys and that the stone was used for building many of the houses in the village. On the other side of the cut, he took them through the wall there that led to the root crop fields and pointed out that it did feed most of the people of the village and that the women took care of it. They then went back through the portal gate and continued on into the village. They went up the back street to the new firehouse, then turned toward the school.

They stood across the street from the school buildings, and Nuada explained how it was required for everyone to learn here — children and adults alike. Then they followed the back street along the ridgeline to the horse stable and the line of small shops, including the meeting hall. Then it was on to the outdoor cooking area, and here they paused for a beer together. As they were looking around, Nuada told them that it was in the works for the two larger houses nearby to be torn down and the cooking area was to be expanded.

After talking about everything that they had seen, Nuada again took them up the main street toward the inner protection wall. They passed the teachers' houses and then up to the building for travelers. Here they turned down the street of shops for traders and on to the hospital building. After looking through some of the shops, Nuada then took them through the portal gate of the inner wall and into the open area between the walls where some were practicing with their bows. As they were watching, one of them turned and saw the statue up on the wall over the portal gate and asked about it. Nuada told them it was a statue of him that the villagers had done as a surprise and that he thought it was too much of an honor. Then it was on out through the outer protection wall and back toward the encampment.

Nuada was beginning to feel the extent of the tour and needed to get away for some time alone. He let the pair return on their own to the encampment and wandered down to the bridge and across it to where Beag was working. He stood back and just watched as the platform was growing higher by the minute. Soon he became bored just watching and turned up the slope toward the housing sites. Outside of the first of the completed houses, a family was moving in. Mor was standing there talking with the man of the house, and when they were through, Mor turned and saw Nuada.

"Nuada! How went the tour?"

"Very well. They now understand how we work and why."

They walked on down the line of houses, and as they neared the end house, Nuada looked at the new foundations across the street.

"These look like the same large houses as here. I thought that Beag was going to build the smaller houses next?"

"He is. These are for later in the Summer after the others are built."

"Where are those going to be constructed?"

"On the next street over. Follow me, and I will show you."

They passed between two of the new foundation walls and on to the next street. "Here is where the new smaller houses will be built. He will probably start them within a week, if not sooner."

Nuada looked around and saw that Beag had already staked the ground for the new foundations. "Where will the firehouse be?"

"That is over here," he said, pointing toward another set of stakes in the ground.

"But will he have enough time to build all of this? I count thirty houses and the firehouse, and then there is the new well too. That is just here. What of the well in the second valley and the grain tower? I cannot see him finishing all of these projects this year."

"If he can build that great protection wall in one year, he can do all of these this year."

Nuada then understood that they would finish everything. They were driven to do so. Already it was mid-afternoon, and Nuada felt that he should return to the village. He said his farewells to Mor and promised to share a beer with him later. On his way back to the village, Nuada considered that they were only a little over a month into Spring and that Summer held the promise of a long and hard season of work ahead.

While sitting at his table in the cooking area, Nuada also considered the growth of the village, and he thought back to the city where he had picked up the first group of new people and the things he saw there. While they lacked many of the things that the valleys had, they had some things that were not present here. He got up and walked to the meeting hall and retrieved some paper and ink to begin a list of things that needed changing. First, with added growth, they would need to build another school in the new area. Then the question of sanitation reared its head, and he made notes on that subject. He continued to write notes that could be used in the next consul meeting, and it was not until the people of the village began to come into the area that he put his notes aside and watched for his friends.

Mor was the first to enter, and after he drew a beer, he joined Nuada and saw the pile of notes that he had before him.

"What are those?"

"Just some notes about what I saw in the first city that I entered and how they could help us improve."

"Can I see them?"

"They are not yet ready, but at the next consul meeting, I will present them for all to see."

Mor did not seem to mind, as he had so many other things on his mind right now. He would find of Nuada's thoughts soon enough. Soon the area swarmed with people, and finally Beag came in and joined the others. Laughter soon came from throughout the cooking area, and then the music followed. After the evening meal, Mor did drop back by Nuada's table and told him that tomorrow he would start the teardown of the first house nearby. Nuada turned to look at it and then shrugged his shoulders, as if it would stop just because he did not want the change here. Then he quickly made another note on his papers after Mor departed: build another outdoor cooking area in front of the village too. That night after everyone else had gone to bed, he remained awake and continued to make notes; he could not shut off his mind as the ideas came to him.

For the next several days, Nuada remained reclusive and worked at refining his pile of notes. He did not even bother going to the outdoor cooking area for his meals. Both Mor and Beag asked after him from Nuada's mate, but she had no answer for them on the subject, only that he was working on some papers.

Then came the day that Nuada walked out of the house and made his way to the new area in front of the village. He looked refreshed, and when he found Mor at the housing site, he asked how the work was coming. Mor was taken a little by surprise by Nuada's appearance. Then he said, "The new large houses are done, and we have started the smaller houses and the fire hall."

Nuada nodded in answer but did not say anything about his disappearance from his normal routine. The family from the second house that was to be torn down had also moved into their new house there at the construction site too. Nuada had forgotten to look as he passed the houses that morning where Mor had started the teardown of them. To Mor it seemed that Nuada's mind was far away from where he stood, but Nuada was as sharp as ever, and he walked through the new housing site before walking down to the site of the war-machine platform, which was almost done.

Nuada circled around the platform and noticed that Beag was not there. He looked around and then walked back up to Mor and asked about him.

"He went to the second valley to look over the site of the grain storage building that Farmer had picked."

"How are you doing with the new people? How many houses do we still need for them?"

"All of our vacant houses are now filled, and we need five more houses for them."

"That is good. Then they will have shelter within a month. Have you put them to work yet?"

"Most are now working and doing well. A few are still working with their animals, and Farmer has taken care to blend them in with his people."

Mor thought that Nuada was now sounding like himself and still wondered of the reason for his actions earlier. Mor excused himself and told Nuada that he had to get back to work and keep these people motivated. Nuada nodded and turned to walk back to the village. He was looking into the distance and watching everything around him now.

As he walked up to the cooking area, Nuada could now see the destruction of both of the original houses. The first house was now down to the back stone wall and fireplace. The second had much of the roof gone, and they were starting on the stonework too.

Already the area looked too open to Nuada, and he continued to walk on back to the meeting hall instead.

As he entered the hall, he found it empty, and that bothered him. He turned and went back to the cooking area and sat at his table to think. His mind flashed to the work being done outside of the valleys, and he was pleased with what they were doing out there. But as he looked again at the two houses being torn down, he could only shake his head at this change. He thought, "Perhaps I shall feel better when the expansion is under way."

Then he knew that to stay there would only depress him more, so he got up to walk back out to the construction sites and watch the work progress. He walked with his head down and paid little attention to his direction. When he looked up, he found himself down by the lakeside and wondered of the reason why he came there. He looked across at the island, and memories of his first house flashed through his mind. He knew that nature had reclaimed the house, but was it an omen of what was to be there in the village? Perhaps this was what bothered him the most.

He then followed the shore back to the outer protection wall and passed through the portal gate there and moved on to the rise above the new area. He stopped and looked around the whole area before deciding to walk to the wall and a look out on the distant forest.

After climbing the stairs on the wall, Nuada turned to look down on the new grain field in front of the wall. Farmer had done a good job on its layout and had set up a simple fence around it to keep out deer and other animals. Beyond it the tree cutters were still busy dropping trees for the sawmill, and wagons moved their labors through the wall quickly.

A light breeze blew Nuada's hair, and he looked to the north for signs of a late Spring rainstorm. No clouds marked the horizon, and he turned to look back at the war machine below him. These machines had a beauty about them, and Nuada hoped that they would never would be used for their purpose.

He then walked down the wall to where the portal over the stream was. He glanced at the last platform and saw that the crew there was just now cleaning the area around it. He thought that it must be completed and that they were only waiting on the machine itself to be installed.

Over on the left, the wagons hauling stone were now going to the housing construction site. Already he could see that the smaller houses were starting to take shape in only the few hours that he had been gone. All of the lift machines were now up at the site and moving both lumber and stone with quickness in their motions.

He wondered where to build a new schoolhouse and soon thought that it should be near the stream. "But which side should it be on?" he thought. He continued to stare at the area and tried to visualize how everything would look in the future. He gave up trying to look into the future and started back down off the wall. Then he walked to the bridge and almost started across when again he paused to look around.

His eyes darted from the housing construction to the stream again. Then he knew what must be done in the future. They needed to build a low wall alongside the stream, as it would define the area and keep any possible flood from happening. Many of Beag's stonecutters now had a little free time, and it would be a project to keep them busy until they were needed elsewhere.

He wondered if Beag had returned from the second valley as he turned to look for him somewhere in the area. He saw no signs of him and thought about going back up to the housing site, but he knew that Beag would be at the outdoor cooking area soon. So he continued his walk back to the village again.

When Nuada entered the cooking area, he went and drew a beer to wait on Beag. He settled at his table and turned to watch as more of the two houses was torn down. Several wagons were loading the debris and hauling it away. The stone that was removed was being hauled toward the cut between the valleys, and Nuada wondered if it was going to be used for the grain building there.

Soon the shadows of the late afternoon swept over the eating area. A few of the workers were now beginning to enter the area, and Nuada knew that it would only be a short time before Beag arrived.

Soon enough Beag entered and went for his beer first and then looked around the area. He was looking at the houses being torn down, and then he saw Nuada sitting at his table. He walked over and asked, "What do you think of this mess?"

"I do not like it, but I think it is needed."

Beag nodded and took a long drink of his beer. "Well I got the foundation started for the grain storage building. That should make Farmer happy."

Nuada looked at him and said, "Are you ready to take on another project?"

"What do you mean, Nuada?"

"When I was out by the new houses today, I was on the bridge and looking around at the area. Something did not seem right, and I tried to figure it out, and then it came to me. We will need a low wall along the stream there for flood protection and to make the area look complete."

Beag looked at Nuada over the rim of his mug and slowly lowered it and said, "I was thinking about that myself. I have some men that I can spare for awhile, and they could get it done in no time."

"Then let us do the project."

"I will start them tomorrow, my friend."

Soon Mor arrived, and he was told of the new project and agreed with the others that it needed to be done. They talked about the other projects going on, and in the end, it turned out to be a good day for all.

Another week passed, and all of the construction moved ahead quickly. Nuada took one of his morning walks back out to the housing site and looked in on how the wall along the stream was coming. He was happy that they were moving so quickly, and after watching the stonework for awhile, he went up to the housing site to see about the houses. Here too they were moving at a fast pace and now had another four of the smaller houses done and were moving on with the others.

Mor had moved the last of the new people into their houses and had also finished the last of the war machines. Beag was here at the site and was doing more foundations for houses. Nuada saw his son Iolair too, and he was doing finishing work inside one of the houses. All four of them had a few minutes to talk and then it was back to work. Nuada walked back down to the bridge and crossed over. He had to return to the village and go over his notes before the next consul meeting in two days.

On the day that the consul meeting was scheduled, Nuada again walked out to the new housing area, and as he walked down toward the bridge, he noticed how fast the low wall along the stream was coming. The crew there had finished the upper section below the houses and was moving closer to the bridge. It did give the area a finished feeling, and that was what he was looking for.

Nuada crossed the bridge and walked up to the new houses. It seemed that there was not as much dust from the construction as there had been in the village when they were doing the building there. But now Beag and Mor had over two hundred people working on the houses, and the lift machines made everything go that much faster there. In just the two days since he had been there, they had finished another three houses and were moving ahead with six more. It would soon slow down, as Beag would need to take one of the lift machines back to the second valley for the grain building.

Nuada walked up the street and saw that they had also made great headway on the firehouse too. Then he turned back down the hill onto the next street and saw that they had also started digging the new well for there too. He paused, thinking that if he went down this street, he would only get in the way of the wagons hauling supplies and those working too. So he cut across the back of the construction site and made his way below the work. Even there wagons were dropping loads of rubble for another street, and some of the crews were adding more curbs and sidewalks too. Piles of construction materials were everywhere. Nuada then noticed that the noise from there was beginning to hurt his ears, so he moved on quickly.

He went on down to the wall and climbed the stairs near the last watchtower so he could look back on the site above him. A whole new city was rising before his eyes, but as he looked to the right, there was still all of the open ground on the other side of the stream in which to build yet. Nuada had already made up his mind that the new school there would be built near the rise going into the village. In building it there, it would be central to all of the housing sites — but that would not be until next year. The old school would have to do for another year even though it would be crowded this year.

He turned around, still thinking about the work being done and what had yet to come. His eyes looked to the north and took in every detail within sight. Nothing moved, so he walked along the wall to the far end, still looking out over the wall.

He watched some of Farmer's men hoeing weeds from the grain field and then over to the woodcutters, who were still very busy too. The forest in front of the wall was being pushed back farther every day. Piles of branches were stacked for the needed firewood for the Winter all across the back of the open area. He lifted his gaze into the distance, looking for more trouble, but again nothing moved on the horizon. He continued to watch for a short time before climbing back down off the wall and making his way back into the village.

As he passed through the inner protection wall gate portal, he turned right and crossed the street to the shops there. He went into each shop, seeing how they were being restocked for the trader when he arrived again. He was surprised at the amount of items the village people had put together this year. The trader would find a much better assortment to choose from this year.

After seeing everything, Nuada hurried on to the outdoor cooking area and then home to retrieve his notes for the consul meeting tonight. He felt relaxed as he returned to the cooking area and sat at his table to wait on the others.

He was looking through his notes when he decided to get a beer and take his mind off the meeting. Shortly after sitting again, Pytheas and Amasis entered the area, talking about the grapevines on the island, where they had just returned from. Nuada called to them and invited them to join him. After they had drawn some of their wine, they came over to his table. Pytheas spoke first. "What is new this day, Nuada?"

Nuada told them about the speed of the construction and the wall along the stream. Then he told them about his plan for a new school building out in front of the valleys too. This was the first that they had heard of a plan for another school building, and they listened as he told them about where he thought it should be built. They asked about the design, and Nuada told them that nothing had yet been decided on that point. He asked if they had any ideas about a change in how the school would be built for a better usage. Both looked at each other and told him no, the design used before worked well and that they should not change it. Nuada nodded at their response and then told them that it would be going before the consul members tonight for a decision. They continued to talk about the new school for another hour until other people began to enter the area, and the two teachers left Nuada alone at his table.

Soon Nuada's family entered, and Iolair was talking about his day doing finishing work on the new houses when many of the consul members began to arrive. Nuada waved as they passed his table. Then after his evening meal, Nuada arose and went over to the meeting hall for the monthly meeting.

When they called the meeting to order, the first order of business was about what had been done to date and the expected progress of the work. This took about an hour to complete, during which Beag said that the new wall along the stream would be completed within two days, and then he would have his crew there move back to the outdoor cooking area for its expected expansion. All of the planned houses would be done before the next consul meeting too. Also the new grain building would be well-along. Both water wells in the plan would also be done.

Then Mor called for new business. Nuada stood and gave his presentation on what he had found on his adventure in the new city and told how they handled sanitation problems there. When he was done with that, he asked them to consider the building of another school building, and he told them where the teachers had thought to build it and to keep it to the same design as the last building. He explained that they were now overcrowded and needed the new building. A vote was called, and they agreed to build the school and also to consider the sanitation measures used in that other city too.

Beag then took the floor and said because they had done so well this Spring with their building projects, he was considering building an additional twenty of the small houses too. This stunned many of the consul members, as they had no idea that it could be done this year. Shortly after they closed the meeting and enjoyed some beer together.

The next day Nuada went to tell Pytheas that the consul members had approved the new school. This excited Pytheas, and he asked when they would start. Nuada told him that he did not know, but it would be started soon.

After leaving Pytheas, Nuada walked back out to the construction site to watch again. Spring was nearing its end, and the weather was getting warmer every day. Nuada topped the rise outside of the village outer wall and walked on down to the bridge. He paused on the bridge to watch the stonework on the low wall along the stream. They were almost done now, and that added the much needed touch to the whole area. He moved on up the hillside to the housing site and walked through the construction. The large crew here were moving nonstop building the houses. Wagons kept coming and going throughout the whole area. Already they were building another street below the houses now under construction and moving fast. Nuada moved back and forth through the construction, and it was not until almost midday that he realized that it was so late already. He did not really want to leave, as the work mesmerized him, but he knew that other things needed to be done too.

He walked back into the village and stopped at the two house sites that were now completely down, and they were just finishing the cleanup there before starting the new construction of the outdoor cooking area. Nuada knew that within a few days the building would begin, and he looked around at the changes already done. He was starting to feel better about the change, but it still nagged at his sense of what the village was.

Then he walked on down to the school and again stopped to look at what had become so familiar to him. He then wondered if the new school would change this too. He hoped that it would not and then moved on to the cut between the valleys.

After passing through the cut, he turned right and walked around the second valley to the site of the new grain house — actually it was more of a tower than a building. It stood about thirty feet in the air and had round sides. Nuada slowly circled it, and then saw Beag high up on the side of it. He was very close to finishing the stonework there, and that even surprised Nuada. The scaffolds that ringed the tower were a maze of lumber, and it intrigued those who saw it.

Nuada moved on, not bothering Beag, and continued his walk to the mill sites. He could hear the noise coming from the sawmill and the forge before he saw them. Nothing new here — wagons continued to move needed supplies in both directions to the work sites — and Nuada continued on without stopping.

Nuada went back to the village and sat at his table, waiting for the end of the work day. Even here they had started to remove part of the wall that ringed the outdoor cooking area in preparation for the expansion. He looked across the area and could now see the old woodworking building, which was now a food storage building. He wondered how long it would be before they changed that too.

Not long after, Beag was among the first to arrive, and he drew himself a beer and joined Nuada at his table. His eyes were on the work done there as he sat.

"It looks like I will be working here tomorrow," Beag said. "I have just finished the grain building, and they have this area ready for me now."

Nuada nodded and then asked, "I was talking with Pytheas this morning, and he asked when you thought you would begin the new school?"

Beag thought for a moment and then answered, "It will take me about two or three weeks here, and then I will move on to the new school."

"I will let him know then."

Beag took a long drink of his beer and then said, "I will then be able to keep an eye on the work out in front as I work on the school too."

Nuada understood that Beag did not like working in two different areas, as he had a hard time checking on his help. It had been left to Mor to keep the workers moving on the houses, and Beag did not like to divide his control of what should have been his job.

Soon Mor arrived and gave Beag an update on the houses. Nuada listened and did not comment as Beag took in every word. Then the area began to fill with the workers returning for their evening meal. Nuada looked around at their faces and listened to their laughter. They were happy with what they were doing.

Over the next two weeks, Nuada remained close to the cooking area and watched as Beag did the remodeling of the area. Although he retained the same design for the new work, it somehow seemed different to Nuada.

The Summer season was now about a week away, and there had been no letup on the construction work. Nuada returned to the construction area and found vast changes where the houses were being built. The new city area had grown quickly. They had finished the original houses now and had moved on to the next twenty houses. The new firehouse was done, and Mor had brought out one of the fire wagons for it. The building was large enough for three such fire wagons, but it would have to wait until Fall for those.

The whole hillside now began to shine from the copper roofs on the finished houses. Another street was being built too below the houses under construction.

Nuada had also noticed that Beag had found time to come out and stake the foundation lines for the new school on the rise leading into the village. He had left a large area for a playground too. While Nuada stood looking at the school grounds, Farmer passed by on his way to the second valley. He had been out checking on the new grain field. Nuada asked him to think about replanting some trees late in the year around the new houses to give the area a more complete look. He quickly agreed to the idea and said that he would do so after the weather began to change.

Nuada returned to the outdoor cooking area and Beag's company again. He was almost done with the work there now, and soon he would be working on the school. For Beag the best thing about working on the cooking area was that he was close to his beer. He would miss it after he started the work back outside of the valleys. Nuada laughed at Beag's little problem and as a joke told him to ask Mor to build him a mobile beer wagon for his work sites. Beag thought he was serious and said he would ask him to do so. This made Nuada laugh out loud, and he got a serious look from Beag, but they were good friends and understood each other very well.

A few days later while Nuada was doing his walk around the new building site, Mor came to him and asked if he told Beag to ask him to build him a beer wagon. Nuada again laughed at the serious question and replied, "I told him to ask because it was to be taken as a joke. You know how Beag likes his beer, so it was just a natural thing to tease him."

Mor could see how Beag would have reacted to the joke, and he told Nuada that he would carry on the joke too. Nuada then walked back to the bridge and crossed over to the site of the new school building. Beag and his crew were setting the foundation stones and were beginning to set stones for the walls. This building was slightly larger than the last school building, and it would have twenty-six rooms on two floors. Again the thought that they would need more teachers crossed Nuada's mind, but he would leave that up to Pytheas to decide. The lift machine that had been in the second valley for the grain building was now there at the school site. Although it was not needed yet, it was there already.

Beag had started the stockpiling of needed supplies too. Stacks of lumber and stone were placed around the entire structure, and more wagons were dropping the needed items as fast as they could move. Beag had taken about fifty of his crew from the housing site, and now they began the undertaking of this project. Beag had told him that when the school was finished, he would have some of his men do the wall along the stream on this side. Nuada turned and looked around the whole area again and was taken aback at the quick changes there.

As the day wore on, the heat began to build too. Nuada found a shady spot near the ridgeline to watch. Soon he began to strip some of his outer clothing as the heat continued to climb. By mid-afternoon the lift machine was being used to lift in timbers for the first floor of the school. Scaffolding was being raised along the sides of the school, and men hurried about as if lost in what was happening. But everything they did had a purpose.

Toward the end of the afternoon, Nuada did another walk back to the housing site for a final look around. Six more houses were in the finishing stages, and it would only take another few days for the next houses to reach this point too. Mor had started another crew digging another water well below the next line of houses also. At this point, Nuada began his return to the village and the new cooking area.

He sat at his table satisfied with the progress of everything. He let his mind wander back over everything he had seen today. The vision of what was to come began to fill in the empty land outside of the valleys.

As he sat, a breath of the evening wind brushed at his hair, and he looked up as people began to fill in the cooking area. They were talking about the changes and exchanging excited laughter together. They all seemed happy with the work being done. Nuada hoped that this would never change in them. Even he had found himself pleased with the changes here at the cooking area. His doubts about it had gone away. Beag had done wonders with the design, and it served its purpose well. How Mor had found the time to build more tables and benches for there crossed Nuada's thoughts also.

As the shadows of the evening crossed the area, Nuada began to look for his family and his friends. His children were the first to arrive, except for Iolair, who had been working at the housing site. Nuada held his daughter and asked about her day while Nuada's mate retrieved them some supper. Uilleam seemed quiet, as he missed being around his brother, but he had other friends that distracted him.

Then some of the teachers crossed into the area. They had been working at making enough glass for all of the projects. Amasis came in looking tired, and he talked briefly with Nuada before going for a mug of wine with the others.

Next came Beag and Mor. Mor was asking Beag about the design for the beer wagon and laughing as he answered. Beag had yet to understand that it was a joke. They both drew a beer and stopped by Nuada's table for a short talk. Later after the evening meal, Nuada and his family went home for a sound sleep.

In a few days, the longest day of the year marked the beginning of the Summer. So much had already been done, and now they continued to build even more. All of the shops by the inner wall were now fully stocked, and even an overflow of items were in storage below the hospital. While the doctor had little to do, he did treat some minor cuts and scrapes. The people were healthy and happy. It was a perfect end to the Spring season.

- SUMMER AND WAR -

The grasses had already turned a golden brown with the change of the season. The heat did little to slow all of the construction going on. It seemed that every day Nuada went back to the construction sites, more changes were happening.

One morning Nuada walked back to the second valley before going out to the construction sites. It was his intent to talk with A'Chreag, and as he approached the forge building, several wagons of new cut trees were passing for the sawmill. Another wagon was loading the copper roofing sheets that were for the new houses out there from the forge building. A'Chreag was helping to load the sheets, and Nuada hurried across the street to talk with him.

"A'Chreag, my friend. I have not seen of you in many weeks. What is new with you?"

A'Chreag looked up at Nuada's words and replied, "Nuada! Welcome. We have been busy making things for the new houses and the school, but I am expecting another child any day now."

"That is good to hear. Are you going to take some time off to be near your mate?"

"I may take one day, as my crew can handle the work here."

"Have you built any new machines? You were always good at inventing something new."

"I have some ideas, but I have not had the time to make them yet."

They continued to talk about the forge and some ideas that A'Chreag had for his designs. After about a half hour, Nuada left and made his way out to the housing construction site. He passed the new school building and paused to look at the changes from a few days ago. The first floor was now almost done, and they were lifting the timbers for the second floor. Beag was still moving at a great pace and had now pulled a second lift machine there for the higher work on the school. Somehow he had some of his crew install the needed curbs and sidewalks around the front of the new school building. Nuada continued his walk down to the bridge and had to wait as many wagons passed going in both directions across the bridge.

He thought about going on down to the wall and circling the bridge, but he waited up toward the housing site. The whole hillside now looked like it was full of houses, but he knew that it was only because they had designed the streets that way. He could see from there that the two lift machines were being used; they swung needed rock and lumber to the newest houses. Beag had taken many of the men working there over to the school, and this was slowing the building of the houses. But still they were moving along quickly too.

At last there was a break in the wagon traffic, and Nuada quickly crossed the bridge. He walked up the street to the street where they were doing the next set of houses and turned left to get closer to the construction.

Seven houses were now complete on the right side of the street, and the next three were close to being finished. On the left, the foundations for more houses were done, and some of the men were already installing the first layers of stone walls here. This was where he found Mor with his board of notes, talking with some of the finishing crews. After the men hurried off to do the instructions of Mor's, he turned and saw Nuada. They waved at each other, but Nuada did not wish to bother him at this time. Nuada moved on to where they had already finished the second water well, and the stonework around it showed that Beag's stonemasons had done a beautiful job of finishing it.

Nuada turned to his right and followed the street around to the street where they had finished the other houses. Nuada admired the work but thought that all of the houses looked the same there. He went on down the street and circled up to the street that held the larger houses. The houses on the right were complete, but only foundations stood on the left side. Nuada also knew that they were to be finished later in the year. He continued on to the firehouse and then down to the first street that he had walked up.

Already the heat of the day was starting to build too, so Nuada continued on down to the wall and climbed the stairs near the last watchtower. He stood in the shadow of the tower for a few minutes before moving on down the wall. It was a natural thing for him to look out into the distance, to look for trouble. He could see the heat ripple off the open ground out there, but nothing else moved.

As he crossed the portal over the stream, his thoughts were on a light breeze that would make the work more comfortable for everyone. He stopped there for a moment to look back toward the new houses, and then he moved on, still looking out over the wall. He passed several of the men who had guard duty, and they were probably thinking that they were lucky not having to work out in the sun with the others.

On this side of the stream, Nuada could look down on the grain field there and then out to where the tree cutters were working dropping trees. It seemed that every day the tree line moved farther back. As Nuada approached the next portal gate opening, he looked down on the wagons bringing in more trees for the sawmill. He watched for awhile from there, and then as he came to the first watchtower, he climbed back down off the stairs to the open meadow where the cows were still kept. A makeshift fence was now up to keep them from roaming all around the area, and a few of the new men were looking after them. The sheep that the new people had brought with them had been moved back to the second valley with the others.

Nuada crossed the open meadow, looking up the rise toward the new school building as he walked. He had not really looked at the school from this side before, and it dominated the hillside. He turned about halfway across the meadow to the ridgeline and found a shady spot to sit for a while.

It was just after midday when he got up to continue his walk. He got to the area where the school playground would be and stopped again. He was near the back of the school, where one of the lift machines was moving needed rock up onto the wall there. It was there he could see Beag setting stones. He did not see Nuada, and so he continued on to the outer protection wall and a return to the village and a much-needed drink of beer.

He entered into the new open cooking area and went to quickly to draw a beer. He downed it almost as fast and then drew another. There was little shade there, so he walked on over to the meeting hall. He sat outside on the porch and listened to all of the busy sounds of the village.

He was almost asleep while drinking his third beer on the porch when Pytheas happened to walk by.

"Nuada, I was looking for you. Amasis wanted me to give you this map he had made while you were on your adventure this Spring."

Nuada sat up a little straighter in his chair and took the offered map and said, "I had forgotten about it."

Nuada looked closely at the map, remembering the trip back to the valleys. "He did a good job of adding the details to this."

"What was that city really like, Nuada? You never said what it was like there."

"They did a good job of protecting themselves, but I found that they lacked one thing that we have. It is the personal freedom that we share."

"How so?"

"They based everything on wealth, which showed that they were selfish and cared little for each other."

"I think I understand."

"Pytheas, I wrote a speech long ago that explained what our freedom means. I had planned to give it if ever the people here began to question what we are about. I will see if I can find it again, and maybe you can use it in a class in the future."

"I would like to see it and possibly use it, as you say, in the future."

Nuada nodded, and they continued their talks for awhile before Pytheas had to return to the glass shop.

Nuada looked around after he had left and saw that the shadows of the afternoon had begun to close in on the valley. He got up and returned to the outdoor cooking area to find already many of the village people had arrived before him. Mor was already there enjoying his beer with A'Chreag, who seemed in a hurry to leave. When Nuada had drawn another beer and turned around, A'Chreag was leaving the area. He stopped by Mor's table and asked why A'Chreag had left so quickly.

"His newest child is about ready to arrive, and he had to go home."

"Yes. He told me earlier today that it was about to happen."

"Were you out at the housing site today?"

"Yes. I see that it has slowed down a little with the work going on at the school."

"True, but I think that it will be all right, as we now have many empty houses if any more people arrive here."

While they were talking, Beag arrived covered in his usual dust and stone chips. He went directly to the beer and drank one while he was standing there. After he had drawn a second, he came over and sat down, looking exhausted.

"I think you need to slow down, Beag," Mor said.

Beag looked up and shook his head. "Not yet. Soon I will be able to do so but not now."

Mor shook his head and looked across at Nuada, who just shrugged his shoulders. The threesome talked for awhile about the construction and their plans for tomorrow before Nuada had to return to his table and join his family.

During this family time, Iolair seemed lost in thought. Nuada asked him about it, and he replied that he was just tired. Nuada then remembered the map of Amasis and handed it over to his son. "This brought back some memories of that adventure that maybe you would enjoy to think on."

Iolair spread the map on the table and ran his finger over the route that they had traveled. Uilleam looked over his brother's shoulder and asked questions about it. Iolair told the story again to his brother and how they had brought back the peoples to the valleys. Nuada smiled across the table at his two sons. He thought, "They are as close as ever."

During the weeks that followed, Nuada continued to go out to the construction sites and watch the new city grow. The full heat of the Summer was now upon them, and it did little to slow all of the work going on. Mor was moving ahead with the last of the six planned houses, and Beag was moving on with the second floor of the school. Nuada knew that when the smaller houses were done, Mor would move his crews back to the last of the larger houses. Already two more streets were paved with the rubble, and a small crew was installing curbs and sidewalks there below the smaller houses.

Mor had been talking about building another outdoor cooking area down at the bottom of the houses, but that would be a project for next year. Outside of the wall, the tree cutters had moved the forest back another hundred yards, and it opened up more of the land in front of the wall, which Farmer already had plans to expand his grain fields into.

Some were already thinking about the coming Fall and what they had planned to do when the weather changed. Nuada had gone to a meeting of the teachers, in which they talked about the coming classes and the opening of the new school. Three of the teachers were talking about moving out to the new houses to be closer to the new school. Nuada himself would stay at the old school.

The weeks began to blur as Summer wore on. As fast as one thing was done, another was started, and changes were everywhere. Nuada was probably the first to notice the days were getting shorter. Again he began to wonder if the trader was going to come this year. He spent many afternoons looking out over the wall, watching for some sign that the trader was near.

On one of his late Summer walks out to the new city, Nuada again toured the new houses, and many of the workmen were now back working on the larger houses. All of the small houses were now done, and over at the new school, they were just finishing the last of the stonework. There would be many weeks yet of finishing work inside the school. The people could feel the end of the season and looked forward to a time of rest again. Not so, Nuada. Something was bothering him again, and he did not know what it was.

That afternoon while he was sitting at his table in the cooking area, Nuada chanced to see A'Chreag enter the area alone. Nuada waved and called him over. He asked about his new child and the health of his mate. After some small talk, Nuada confided his feelings about an unease that he could not explain. He asked A'Chreag to look after his family if anything were to happen to him and told him of a hidden pathway across the stream that ran from the protection wall of the second valley south behind the mill pond and dam. It was almost the same path that had brought him into the valleys when first he arrived. A'Chreag agreed to do as Nuada wanted, as he too had the same feelings as of late. They shared a beer together before the other village people began to arrive.

One morning while Nuada stood on the wall looking into the distance, he began to see a dust cloud in the distance from the south. He was sure it was the trader, but he had to know for certain. He sent two scouts out to find out, and he waited to hear back from them.

It was late in the afternoon when the two scouts returned. Yes, they had seen the trader, but he had a large group of people with him too. Nuada wanted to know how many and was told that it was a large group. The answer did little to satisfy him, and he made up his mind to go himself the next morning.

The next morning before dawn he dressed in his good clothes, took his weapons, and rode out on his black horse. Around midday he found the trader and his group. He indeed had a large group with him, and as Nuada questioned the trader about them, he asked why they had come. The trader told him that a new group of warriors had come up from the south and had attacked his city. Most of it was destroyed, and they had hardly gotten away from the city before it began to burn. They were seeking a place of refuge, including himself.

Nuada asked if they had been followed, and the trader said that he did not think so. After their talk, Nuada circled around to the rear of the group and waited for the dust to settle. He looked long and hard to the south but saw no other signs of the group being followed. He quickly rode back to the front to meet with the trader and told him that there were no other signs of them being followed, but they had to hurry on to the city before nightfall.

Just as the shadows of night began to close around them, they began to enter through the portal gate of the new wall. Nuada told the trader to have the group camp below the new school and then rode back to the portal gate to lock it for the night.

Many of the village people had come out to help the new people settle in for the night and brought food for them. Mor came out to talk with Nuada, and he quickly doubled the number of guards on the wall. For Nuada it was going to be a sleepless night. He took his horse back to the stable and then walked back out to the protection wall.

He climbed the stairs and went into the first watchtower to wait and see if it was safe. The lanterns within the tower cast an errant glow on the walls. Nuada tried to sleep, but nothing he tried worked. When the first glow of the dawn began to edge the shadows of night away, Nuada walked out onto the wall and looked beyond the forest to see if he could detect any kind of movement. He shifted his sword, which lay across his back, and shook his head. Nothing moved, but he still felt unease. He turned to look at the encampment behind him and found no movement there either.

Then he heard it! A distant drum! He quickly sent a runner back to the village with the message to man the walls. An enemy was near. Within twenty minutes, Mor and Beag joined him on the wall. The men of the village began to fill in the spaces along the wall, and others were getting the war machines ready below them.

Other men of the village went to the quarry, and wagons soon followed them there. They were preparing to bring out more rock to the war machines. Stock piles of arrows were brought from the old woodworking building, and soon they were ready for anything that would come their way.

Iolair found his father and stood close by. The sun was now fully up, and they could see the dust cloud in the distance. Nuada estimated that they were about five miles away. Whoever it was would be here in under an hour. Mor and Beag went about and had many of the men lining the wall get down out of sight. There would be time later to see what it was all about, but everyone knew that a fight was coming.

Then Nuada had a thought. He asked Mor to send thirty men into the forest beyond the open area in front of the wall. They would either cut off a retreat or support an attack against the wall itself by a surprise attack from the rear. If they were chased, they could retreat to the crossing a mile downstream and come back on the other side of the stream.

Mor agreed with Nuada's plan and quickly sent men across the open area and had them hide in the forest. Nuada turned in time to see Pytheas and his mounted horsemen pull up behind the wall by the second war machine. He sent word down to them to go out through the second portal gate and wait by the crossing downstream. Now they were ready.

The drumming got louder as the unseen force approached. As they started to come into view, Nuada thought it was like a parade: very colorful, and they marched in line formation. Banners fluttered in the air as they entered the open area below.

The trader joined Nuada on the wall and said that it was the same people who had attacked his city. He was nervous and quickly returned to his wagons and people. This was not a rabble but an army with a purpose.

Nuada continued to watch as they formed lines in front of the wall. They were in perfect position for the war machines, if they were needed. Then the drums quit. An officer on a horse came forward to talk. Nuada called down to him and asked why they were there.

The man did not understand Nuada's question in the language he used. The officer called back in a language that no one there had heard before, but Nuada quickly understood it, as it was his gift.

Nuada again asked his question, this time in the officer's language. This caught the man off guard, and he quickly asked for the surrender of the city in the name of Pax Roma. Nuada replied that they were a free city and would not surrender.

The officer quickly returned to the other officers, and again the drums boiled, and the army began to move forward. Nuada turned and waved a flag to the war machines below. They let fly from two of the machines, and rock sailed through the air and into the strict formations. Men were instantly crushed from the flying stones of the machines. This caught the army by surprise, and then the men on the wall followed with a volley of arrows into their confusion. Many brought up their shields for protection, but many fell in the first minutes of the action. The arrows continued to fly from the wall, and as fast as the war machines were reloaded, they too added to the fight.

Now the sun was in the eyes of the attackers too. They began to retreat and were greeted with more arrows from the rear. The once-solid formations were now pushed together in more confusion. The attacking army was now half of what had been there a few minutes ago.

They tried to force their way back down the trail that they had come from, but the men in the forest were also taking a toll on them. Just when it looked like they would clear the fighting, Pytheas and his mounted horsemen came charging up the trail. They had nowhere to go.

From the wall Nuada led another group out onto the open field through the portal gate and attacked from that position. The attackers fought well, but they were no match for those who were defending their homes and families.

Within a half hour it was over. None of the attackers lived to tell of the battle. Two of the valleys' men had been killed and several wounded, but it was a very one-sided battle for the valleys because they were prepared for it.

Then it was time to clean up the battlefield. Wagons came outside of the wall and removed the dead and took the weapons left from the battle. Nuada returned inside the wall and was greeted by Mor and Beag as he passed through the killing hole.

"Nuada! You have made another miracle for us. Your plan worked better than I thought it would," said Mor.

Nuada was tired from both the battle and the lack of sleep. Hunger also began to creep into the back of his mind. Dark rings circled his eyes, and he had a few cuts to deal with on one arm. He pushed his way past his friends without a word and made his way back to the cooking area.

He drew a beer before sitting at his table. After taking a sip, he crossed his arms on the table and laid his head down to rest. Soon he was fast asleep. His mind awoke in the realm of Creatrix, and he waited for the creator. "Nuada, hear of me. It is close to the end, and I have a mission for your oldest son. He is to leave of your place and make his way to the west and across the water there to an island that will be rich in ways he will not understand. He will take with him your story of the building of the city and your ways. It must happen quickly. Have no regrets, as I will look after him."

Nuada awoke with a start. He looked around the area and found a few who had also returned to the cooking area. They too were tired from the battle. Then his mind focused on the words of Creatrix. "Where is Iolair?" he wondered. He rubbed the sleep from his eyes and waited for them to clear. He quickly finished his beer and then stood to walk back out to the wall.

Before he had walked across the area, his son entered the area. Nuada took him aside and told him that he had a vision from Creatrix. Then they walked over to the shop building across from the stable where he had stored his things and the map table long ago. Inside Nuada told him what Creatrix had told him, and when the young man began to question the vision, Nuada told him it was not a thing to question. He must prepare himself for the adventure and not tell anyone outside of the family about it. "Am I to go alone?" Iolair asked.

Nuada thought for a moment and then said, "No, I want you to take Amasis with you."

At the back of the shop, Nuada pulled out a chest of bronze, and inside it was lined with cedar.

"In this place the stories of the valleys that you wrote," Nuada said. "When it is time, you will understand what to do with it."

"I do not understand, Father."

"The end of the valleys is near, and Creatrix wants our story to endure. It is your test now. You must leave tomorrow and not look back."

Nuada reached for his oldest son and hugged him tightly. "Now go and prepare yourself, son."

They left the shop and made their way back to the cooking area. Both Mor and Beag were now here, and Nuada went to talk with them. Iolair continued on home to pack for his adventure into the unknown.

Nuada told his friends about a vision from Creatrix and that they must prepare quickly for another battle. He did not give any details about the vision though. His two friends looked at him as though he was mad but did not question him or his visions.

Later in the afternoon Nuada found Amasis and told him that he was to leave with Iolair tomorrow and that they would not be returning to the valleys. Amasis trusted Nuada completely and said that he would be happy to go with Iolair. Nuada did have one word of advice: avoid the cities.

Nuada then returned to his table for the rest of the afternoon and watched the people around him. They were happy and did not realize that an ending was coming. Nuada's only thought was that everything was to be lost. Later when his mate brought him something to eat, he did not even tell her of the vision but looked sadly at his other children, knowing that they would never see of their father again.

Later that night Nuada helped Iolair finish his packing and gave added advice on his travels. Together they spent their last night together and talked about many things. Nuada's mate knew that something was going on but did not question her husband's ways. He would tell her when he was ready to do so.

Early in the morning before dawn, Nuada awoke Iolair and helped him carry his pack to the stable. Amasis was waiting, and they finished loading and collecting the items that they were to take with them from the shop building. At last Nuada gave a final hug to his son and a handshake to his friend. Then he followed them as far as the inner portal gate, where they mounted their horses and rode away.

The light of the morning sun cast a gleam on the statue over the portal gate, which caught Nuada's eye. A tear ran from one eye, and then he turned and walked to the hospital building. Inside he checked on those wounded yesterday, and then he walked back out to the wall outside of the valleys.

Nuada's steps were heavy with the things that had happened and those that were about to happen. He found a place to sit on the wall and let his eyes watch out into the distance again.

It was another beautiful Summer morning that looked over the valleys that day. Then he heard the distant drum again. He quickly rang the warning bell by the watchtower and waited. Soon the men of the valleys again lined the wall and prepared for battle.

Nuada's two close friends joined him, and just as yesterday, they employed the same tactics for their defense. Nuada already knew that the ending would not be the same, but he would not go down without a fight.

He watched as another army of the same people made their parade in front of the wall, but this army was much larger than the other. Its commander seemed to understand the defense of the wall and prepared himself well. This time there was no call for surrender from him, and Nuada watched as he had his men form into tight squares for fighting. Their shields interlocked and protected them from the arrows from the wall.

Then they began to move forward. Nuada called for the war machines below to throw their stones and watched for the results. Some of the groups were hit, and the machines continued to throw down on them. They still held their movements forward and pushed for the portal gate opening. When they were close, stones from the wall began to rain down on them too. Soon arrows from the wall followed. They too shot back at the defenders with arrows from handheld machines. Both sides took heavy losses, and the enemy soon brought up a battering ram for the gate. They hammered at the gate, and then they were through, but they were in the killing box behind the wall. Arrows took their toll on the attackers, but they still pushed forward. Outside of the wall, the enemy brought up ladders and began to scale the wall.

From the forest behind the attackers, arrows found their marks and caused many to turn to face an attack from the rear. Although they could not see who was attacking them from the rear, they fought back with many arrows into the woods. Pytheas held his horse-mounted warriors from the battle. He was waiting until they began to run as yesterday. It did not happen. He was at a loss as to what to do, and they faded back into the forest. The fighting on the wall now began to be hand to hand. Swords clashed between the two peoples in the fight. Still below the attackers were held within the killing zone. They had yet to break through the second portal gate that trapped them. Arrows and rocks took their toll on them until the ram was brought forward to break the gate down, but there were so many bodies in the killing hole that they could not bring it against the second portal gate.

Nuada was splattered with blood from their enemy as he fought hard against their attack. He did not know if he had any wounds, as the blood was everywhere. Then he felt a thump against his back. There was no pain as he continued to swing his blade against the enemy, but there was a wet feeling. The valley people began to lose ground and were forced back along the wall to the portal over the stream. Anoghas, who led the men on the other side of the stream on the wall, pulled about half his men down from the wall, and they hurried across the bridge before stopping and firing their arrows at the attackers on the wall from the open meadow area. It served its purpose, and the attackers began to retreat back along the wall.

Nuada led the charge against the attackers, and they were making good headway until again Nuada felt a thump. This time it was against his chest, and he looked down to see an arrow had pierced his chest. He still felt no pain and pushed forward against those in front of him. Then two more arrows found him. He slumped against the wall and waited for the end to come. His eyes felt heavy, and his arms would not move. All around him men fought hard, and Nuada knew that it was indeed the end of their lives here in the valleys. He closed his eyes and then began to dream.

He awoke in the realm of Creatrix and waited.

"Welcome home, Nuada."

- AN ARCHAEOLOGIST'S DREAM -

P*ersonal note:* My name is James Alistair, and in 1982 I was returning from a dig in central Ireland when I received a call from a friend and fellow colleague, Andrew Donnelly. He was going through a section of his university's storage of Celtic relics. He happened across a case where some items had been discovered in southern Wales from a cave that had been sealed at an early time of the Celtic history there. At first he thought that it was just another common find, but he soon changed his mind because of a chest that had also been re-covered from the cave site. He described the chest as having a relief of bronze characters and a depiction of a wolf on it. It had been sealed with beeswax, and until he had opened it, it had been intact from the early burial date of about two thousand years ago. But what caught his attention was what was inside the chest. It contained maps of eastern France from that early period and showed many of the Celtic cities of the period. Many of them had never been recorded before, and this was the first thing that piqued his excitement over the chest. But then beneath the maps were three separate complete books: one in classic Greek, one in the cuneiform style of the Phoenicians, and the last with some of the classic forms of the Celtic language too, but it was much more extensive than thought. All three books were the same story, and because of the Greek book, all three were easy to decipher. The story itself was about one man who built a city and what happened to it and the inhabitants of it. Now Andrew wanted me to go with him and see if we could find this lost city of the story. I was interested and told him I would fly over to see him as soon a possible; little did I know that it would be a turning point in my life.

About two weeks later after I had settled some unfinished business, I caught a flight to London and met up with Andrew and another fellow colleague, Nigel Edwards. Andrew was excited about his find and wanted to show it to me quickly. We settled into his office, and he produced his copy in English of the story, and I was myself intrigued by the aspect of it being a true account.

Andrew had found some financing for a preliminary dig if we found the site. Soon we were on our way to Paris, and then after acquiring some vehicles and permits, our adventure began three days later.

What was of interest to me was that very few of the early Celtic cities were of stone as the story told. What other items of historical interest would we find after two thousand years? And after countless wars throughout this land, would we find anything at all?

We followed the old map up the Seine River and across countless rivers and streams to the base of the French Alps. The map indicated that our site was to the south of where we were after four days. The land was rugged and, outside of some small villages in the region, void of people.

We did pass one site on the map that had indicated an old village site, and it appeared to be some type of hill fort construction. But this was not our vision of what we would find, so we pushed on.

Another day passed, and we were now in the area indicated for our mysterious city. We were looking for some kind of landmark against the mountainsides. We knew that they had a large quarry site, and its scar should show us the way. Then too there was the stream that should also point the way, if its course had not changed over the years.

Late in the afternoon we did find a stream and decided to camp for the night and wait until daybreak to see if we could see any other markers there. The area was heavily overgrown with trees and underbrush, but that only added to the excitement.

Early the next morning we decided to pack into the base of the mountains and see if we were at the right spot. We left our vehicles and followed the stream. It took us hours to find our way back against the mountain, but we did, and to our surprise, there on the mountainside was an old scar. Now if it was what we were looking for or just an old landslide would be determined within a short time. We also knew that there was supposed to be a wall of stone around the outer limits of the city too. Would it be there?

We climbed an earth berm and stood looking about the whole area. It looked right, but where was all of the stonework? Again trees hid much of what we could see, and we moved slowly forward to investigate. When we dropped down the far side of the berm, Nigel happened to dislodge some loose earth, and there it was: stone that could only have come from a man cutting it and then stacking it. We got out our shovels and began to remove more of the loose earth and found a running line of stones. We had found the outside of the city!

Nigel wanted to stay and uncover more of his discovery, but both Andrew and myself wanted to move on and find the central part of the city that we had read about. Using a copy of the ancient map of the city, we moved on following the stream as a guide. It did indeed climb a small rise, and on the right was a ridgeline as described. We passed over the crest and walked a short distance before finding another wall of stone on the right, which had tumbled down long ago. This was a little harder to climb over, but we did so. Still nothing was easy about our passage here. Underbrush filled in everything around us. Then there was a second wall of stone. It too was as described in the story. We were getting excited about how everything was as in the story, but this wall was more intact, and we even found the old portal gate although the gates themselves had disappeared long ago. We passed through, and to our surprise again, we found some walls of buildings still partially standing. After looking into the ruins of the buildings, I happened to find one old sword with Celtic markings on the hilt. We had hit the jackpot!

Coming back out of the building, I kicked at the ground and found that it hid stonework too. We crossed over to the other side by the wall and found a set of stairs going up. Andrew went first, and I followed close behind. On top of the wall, we looked around as far as we could see, and we then noticed that there was indeed a lake off to the south of the wall. Would it have the island described too? We moved along the wall to where it crossed over the portal gate, and there we found a tumbled statue. Was this the statue of Nuada?

We talked among ourselves and decided that this dig was too big for just the three of us, and we began to make our way back to the vehicles. I did keep the sword that I had found, and we made the encampment just at dark.

By lantern light, all three of us made notes about what we had seen and described it in detail. That night sleep was hard to come by.

Early the next morning we again returned to the city, and this time we followed the stream farther along to the back side of the small valley. Every detail that we had found yesterday was filmed using three cameras: one in color and the others in black and white. The details were amazing. The stonework was dry stacked and without mortar, with very precise fitting of every stone. The labor alone of these stones showed many hours of cutting and polishing. This was not the style of the early Celtic peoples that we had been taught.

They did not build cities of stone in this way; they were barely removed from the hunter-gatherer stages.

We continued on along the raised dike between the stream and the lake. Here the brush was low and did not interfere with our views of the valley. Now we could see the lake clearly, and the island did come into view. As we walked past the island on the lake, we could now see in the distance the continuation of the wall there. From the story, that was where the main village was supposed to be. We would explore that later. Then all at once in front of us stood another high wall, not really ravaged by the years, through which the stream flowed and to the right of it another wall of stone. Our cameras were in constant use.

We continued on through another portal that was filled with debris, and after going on a few hundred feet, we came upon another site that filled us with wonder: the remnants of large stone buildings and behind them a true massive dam structure. Our cameras were clicking like crazy trying to record everything there. This was going to change the way everyone thought about the Celtic peoples. We were constantly talking between ourselves about who could have influenced these people to build like this. We spent about two hours there alone exploring the site.

After eating some of the sandwiches that we had brought with us, we again pulled out the copy of the valleys map and tried to make a decision as to where we would go next. Andrew wanted to see if we could find the cave site, as it was the most likely place that items would have been stored for protection. We finally agreed and moved back through the wall from the dam site.

After crossing through the portal again, we turned left and passed through that portal in the other wall. On this side of the wall here, we found an open meadow that gave us an unrestricted view of the lake and the wall around the main village. We took more pictures and then moved onto where the maps said the cave site was.

It did not take us long to find the entrance to the first cave although it was partially hidden behind a rock wall. We moved into the large opening and at the rear of the cavern found two more openings. According to the story, the one on the left led down to the lake and the one on the right up to another cavern. We could tell that someone in the past had widened the cave leading here. Our flashlights reflected off the dry walls, and as we slowly crossed the floor of the cavern, we caught sight of a pile of objects at the rear.

Andrew was excited and moved forward quickly to examine what we had discovered. Within the pile, he found another chest of bronze, and to his surprise, it had the same markings as the one back at his university, including the wolf head. Alongside of it, he also found a bronze head cap for a walking staff although the wood of the staff had long ago disappeared. We captured more photos of the discovery and then removed it back outside. Already the sun was low, and as much as we wanted to stay and explore the village itself, we knew that we had to return to our campsite.

Again we got back to the campsite just as the sun was about to set. We had brought with us the chest and the staff headpiece. After locking these items in one of the vehicles, we sat down to talk about the events of the day. Already we had discovered more about these people than anyone would have thought possible, and we had just scratched the surface of the valleys. This was possibly the greatest discovery to come out of modern Europe in this century. Already we were talking about a major dig on our hands and started to make plans for a return trip next year with a large contingent of help. There was so much to discover that it would take years to uncover it all, but tomorrow we would enter the main village itself, and we needed to get some sleep.

The next morning after loading our cameras with fresh film, we again set off for the main village in the first valley. We followed the same route as yesterday, as it had little in the way of obstructions. When we passed the cave site, we were on territory that had not been walked on in almost two thousand years. As we came up to the protection wall that surrounded the village site, we stopped and took more pictures of this wall and the surrounding area. Then we passed through another gate portal and into the village site. Row on row of stone houses greeted us. Although their roofs had long ago fallen in on them, they held their distinctive shapes and purpose. More photos followed before we moved on into the village. On our left we could see the indicated cut through the ridgeline that they had done so long ago, but what amazed us was the amount of detail that was on the map we had with us. The whole village was just as it was showing us. We came to the site that was indicated as the school here. It too held its original shape, and we circled it before moving on to where the outdoor cooking area was indicated on the map. We passed what must have been two large houses by the amount of rubble on those sites. Was one of them the home of Nuada? We were quickly using up the film in our cameras as we entered the cooking area. It too was just as described in the story. A low wall surrounded the entire area, and we found what must have been their ovens for their baking. We could feel the people of old around us. We sat on the low wall and talked about the whole discovery. Andrew wanted to move on and see what else was held for our discovery before we had to return to the campsite. We circled throughout the whole area and found little else that day, and I began to wonder if the Romans had used this as a garrison after its sacking. There was little to show for warfare here, so it was possible. We turned with reluctance to leave this place and made our way back to the camp again. This would be our last night here for this year, and I was looking forward to sleeping in a real bed again. The next morning we set out for Paris and the trip home.

Back at Andrew's university, I spent another week with him trying to unlock the secrets of this Celtic village. I was with him when he opened the new chest, and inside it we were in for another surprise. Here were the drawings of the person called Jan and the dictionary of Celtic words and phrases of Nuada. This really opened our eyes into the unknown. Among the other items in the chest were a book of mathematics, some other drawings, and scrolls of other lost civilizations.

It was a jackpot of items of a lost world. Whoever placed these things in the cave, thought they were worth saving, and we were glad they did so.

I have had many thoughts about these people and often wondered if any of them survived the battle with the Romans. They must have; otherwise we would not have the things that we recovered. Then the question arose about why they abandoned their city. Those questions we may never answer.

I returned home the following week still asking questions of myself. Now I am helping Andrew and Nigel find the funding for the next dig in Borg Jan. I know we will be successful, and I look forward to my next visit to this lost city of the Celts.